Richard Laymon wrote over thirty nove[...]
The Travelling Vampire Show won the Br[...]
a prize for which Laymon had previou[...]
A Good, Secret Place (Best Anthology) [...]
Laymon's works include the books of t[...]
The Beast House and *The Midnight Tour*. Some of his recent novels have been
Night In The Lonesome October, *No Sanctuary* and *Amara*.

A native of Chicago, Laymon attended Willamette University in Salem, Oregon, and took an MA in English Literature from Loyola University, Los Angeles. In 2000, he was elected President of the Horror Writers Association. He died in February 2001.

Laymon's fiction is published in the United Kingdom by Headline, and in the United States by Leisure Books and Cemetery Dance Publications. To learn more, visit the Laymon website at: http://rlk.cjb.net

'If you're not already well aquainted with Richard Laymon, get to know him now' *Manchester Evening News*

'A gut-crunching writer' *Time Out*

'In Laymon's books, blood doesn't so much as drip as explode, splatter and coagulate' *Independent*

'This author knows how to sock it to the reader' *The Times*

'No one writes like Laymon and you're going to have a good time with anything he writes' Dean Koontz

'A brilliant writer' *Sunday Express*

'Stephen King without a conscience' Dan Marlowe

'This is an author that does not pull his punches . . . A gripping, and at times genuinely shocking, read' *SFX Magazine*

'Incapable of writing a disappointing book' *New York Review of Science Fiction*

'One of the best, and most underrated, writers working in the genre today' *Cemetery Dance*

Also in the Richard Laymon Collection published by Headline

The Beast House Trilogy:
The Cellar
The Beast House
The Midnight Tour

Beware!
Dark Mountain*
The Woods are Dark
Out are the Lights
Night Show
Allhallow's Eve
Flesh
Resurrection Dreams
Darkness, Tell Us
One Rainy Night
Alarums
Blood Games
Endless Night
Midnight's Lair*
Savage
In the Dark
Island
Quake
Body Rides
Bite
Fiends
After Midnight
Among the Missing
Come Out Tonight
The Travelling Vampire Show
Dreadful Tales
Night In The Lonesome October
No Sanctuary
The Glory Bus
Funland
The Stake

* previously published under the pseudonym of Richard Kelly
Dark Mountain was first published as *Tread Softly*

Amara
and
The Lake

Richard Laymon

headline

Copyright © 2003, 2004, Richard Laymon

The right of Richard Laymon to be identified as the Author of
the Work has been asserted by him in accordance with
the Copyright, Designs and Patents Act 1988.

AMARA first published in Great Britain in 2003 by
HEADLINE PUBLISHING GROUP

THE LAKE first published in Great Britain in 2004 by
HEADLINE PUBLISHING GROUP

First published in this omnibus edition in 2007 by
HEADLINE PUBLISHING GROUP

A HEADLINE paperback

1

Apart from any use permitted under UK copyright law, this publication may
only be reproduced, stored, or transmitted, in any form, or by any means,
with prior permission in writing of the publishers or, in the case of reprographic
production, in accordance with the terms of licences issued by the
Copyright Licensing Agency.

All characters in this publication are fictitious
and any resemblance to real persons, living or dead,
is purely coincidental.

ISBN 978 0 7553 3185 7

Typeset in Janson by Palimpsest Book Production Limited,
Grangemouth, Stirlingshire

Printed and bound in Great Britain by
Mackays of Chatham plc, Chatham, Kent

Headline's policy is to use papers that are natural, renewable and recyclable
products and made from wood grown in sustainable forests. The logging and
manufacturing processes are expected to conform to the environmental regulations
of the country of origin.

HEADLINE PUBLISHING GROUP
A division of Hachette Livre UK Ltd.
338 Euston Road
London NW1 3BH

www.headline.co.uk
www.hodderheadline.com

Amara

*What may this mean
That thou, dead corse,
Revisits thus the glimpses of the moon,
Making night hideous?*

William Shakespeare
Hamlet: Act I, Scene iv

Introduction

By Dean Koontz

As long as I have been on Earth, which is longer than Microsoft Word 5.0 but not longer than the English language, I've been involved in only two traffic accidents. They occurred a little more than a year apart, and the circumstances were eerily the same; I should not have survived either incident, and certainly should not have survived unscathed, but I did.

In the first instance, my wife and I were in a large sedan, stopped at a controlled intersection, on our way to dinner, when a car hit us from behind at (the police estimated) 55 mph, without braking. That day, with spring approaching, I'd had the snow tires taken off the rear wheels and replaced with springtime rubber. The snow tires had been stored temporarily in the trunk of the car until I could tuck them aside in a corner of the garage for use the next winter. When we were hit from behind, the stored tires were two enormous shock absorbers; however, even with the protection they provided, the rear half of the sedan was spectacularly crushed, compacted into about two feet of mangled ruins that were shoved against our headrests. The back doors folded like accordions. The front doors buckled and would not open. The gasoline tank ruptured and sprayed fuel into the passenger's compartment. Incredibly, the engine was still running – and wouldn't shut off. Expecting fire or explosion, I needed perhaps a frantic half-minute to wrench open a buckled door. Our sedan was totaled, but the car that hit us was totaled and *squashed*. We thought the driver of the other vehicle must be dead, but to our amazement, as we hurried to him, he struggled out of his demolished coupe, as unharmed as we were. As it turned out, he was a sixteen-year-old boy who had gotten his driver's license a month previous; he had bought his first car *that morning*. Regarding the wreckage with disgust, he looked at us and said, 'I didn't *need* this,' as though he suspected that we, unlike him, had been driving around with no sane purpose but with the mad hope of being hit from behind and killed. We had just paid off our car loan that day.

Fourteen months later, having moved three thousand miles from Pennsylvania to California, we were stopped at a traffic light, on our way to dinner (going out to a restaurant is seldom viewed as the extremely dangerous undertaking our experience has proved it to be) when a car hit us from behind at (the police estimated) 55 mph, without braking. This time we were in a small sports car, a Mercedes 450 SL, which had no backseat. Because the Mercedes was solidly constructed and brilliantly engineered, the fuel tank didn't rupture and the doors didn't buckle; we got out of the vehicle unscratched. The car that had hit us, a large sedan, looked as if it had been nuked. We were sure the occupant must be dead or seriously injured. We hurried to the driver's door. The window was broken out. The door had buckled. The woman inside was alive – but obviously intoxicated. When we told her to stay calm, that we would get her out, she cursed us and said, 'I didn't *need* this,' putting the emphasis on the word *need*, precisely as the young driver had done fourteen months ago in Pennsylvania. I couldn't get her out of the car, and even the police, who arrived within two minutes, had trouble extracting her, not because she was pinned in the wreckage but because she was determined to stay in there rather than get out and have to face a breathalyzer test. As had happened fourteen months earlier in Pennsylvania, Gerda had made the final payment on our car loan that very morning.

The uncanny similarity of the details of these two accidents suggests to me – as do so many other things in life – a world that operates not always according to the predictable laws of physics and chance, but also and perhaps as often under the influence of a mysterious power with a delightfully Byzantine sense of *story* and with an agenda that is, though perhaps not inscrutable, challenging to analyze and understand. Pondering the significance of these two accidents, Gerda and I posited all sorts of possible meanings and messages to be derived from our experiences. I thought it logical, for example, never to halt at another traffic light or stop sign, but to cruise blithely through the intersection with the expectation that to stop would be to invite an inevitable rear-end collision. Eventually, however, we made only one change in our lives due to these events at opposite ends of the continent: Because we were finally able to afford to do so, we thereafter never took out another car loan but paid cash for each new vehicle we acquired. Granted, on any day that we paid for a new car, we assumed that we were at risk till midnight, but when we made it to that witching hour, the suspense was over!

One evening a few years after the second of these two accidents, Gerda and I went to dinner with Dick and Ann Laymon. In our flivver, we picked them up at their house and buzzed off into the glamorous Angelean night, which glitters with film stars and carjackers, movie moguls and diseased streetwalkers, pop-music divas and babbling urine-soaked hobos (some of whom had no doubt once *been* pop-music divas). We had reservations at a sixteen-star restaurant, outside which even the richest titans of industry wrestle in the street like hooligans over a suddenly available table. We were exuberant at the prospect of superb food, fine wine, and the chance to share dozens of hilarious personal anecdotes about such subjects as the publishing business and dental surgery. Nothing, we thought, could taint this spectacular evening – and then I missed our freeway exit.

As a driver, one of my hallmarks is missing freeway exits, but only when chauffeuring particularly interesting and voluble people. Dick and Ann were so interesting and voluble on this occasion that Gerda was preparing syringes full of Thorazine to calm them down, and I suppose that rolled-up sock in her left hand was meant for my mouth. Anyway, as I regaled Dick and Ann with the story of our two nearly identical accidents, fourteen months apart, I zipped by our freeway exit *and past another one* before any of us realized what I had done. After consultation, we agreed that by switching freeways, we could eventually get back around to where we needed to be, so I switched, and switched again . . . and by some means that was mysterious to all of us, we found ourselves on what seemed to be an unopened section of an uncompleted freeway – and shortly thereafter on a surface street in a neighborhood so grim and forbidding that even the attack-trained pit bulls carried semiautomatic pistols and kept their heads down.

We were familiar with the maze of streets and highways that form an all but infinite Gordian knot binding the limbs and bowels of this great city, yet we were uncertain of our location and flummoxed as to how to find our way out of what seemed about to become a vortex of terror. In a baffling and unconventional move, Gerda consulted a map, as if that would be of any help. Dick and I, on the other hand, voted for the sober and sensible approach: cruising at random into ever meaner streets, in the hope that we would stumble upon a freeway sign and a hasty exit route before we were all shot, stabbed, throttled, dismembered, set on fire, and offered up to the Beast of Beasts on a Satanic altar. Naturally, as we were both writers who had been born with a generous measure of imagination, we saw threats at every turn, which we excitedly pointed out to each other, and we were able to envision – and vividly describe – a virtually endless series of hideous fates that might very well befall us before we found an escape route. Ann, for reasons beyond my comprehension, chose to lean forward from the backseat and consult with Gerda over the stupid map. Anyway, by eventually executing a series of turns that Gerda suggested based on – I suppose – her superior female intuition, we found a freeway and were able to arrive at dinner a tad late but with all of our extremities intact.

After a delicious dinner accompanied by a superb Cabernet, after desserts even more likely than any Barney the Dinosaur performance to trigger a diabetic coma, and after many hilarious anecdotes about the publishing business and dental surgery, the four of us departed the restaurant, stepping between the wrestling titans of industry who thrashed upon the sidewalk, and presented our car check to the valet-parking attendant. Since I had begun the evening talking about our two strangely similar accidents at opposite ends of the country and then had driven the Laymons deep into harm's way, it seemed fitting that the car should be returned with a long, deep scratch/crease on the passenger's side, from front fender to rear – and that the valet-parking attendant should, instead of apologizing, say, 'I didn't *need* this.'

Dick and I exchanged a look, and neither of us needed to say that one of the greatest problems for novelists is that reality is not only stranger than fiction but generally funnier and more deeply disturbing. To get the true flavor of life, it seems to me, a writer has to let his imagination cruise not merely through the precincts of realism where you might find Hemingway but, more important, also into neighborhoods of the fantastic. Dick and I are radically different writers, but what I love about his work is his willingness to drive at high speed into the fantastic – and make it seem, for all its flamboyant qualities, as real as tomorrow's newspaper. *Amara* is one such. Enjoy.

Prologue

Emil Saladat leaped down from the cab of the U-Haul van and rushed to the cover of bushes near the wall. He watched Metar run to join him. The van moved away, its tail-lights disappearing around a bend.

Emil stepped into Metar's cupped hands for a boost. He clutched the top of the brick wall and flung himself onto it.

This was so easy.

This American was a cinch.

No broken bottles embedded in the wall. No electrified wire. No armed guards.

This American, Callahan, was making it so easy that Emil should be ashamed to take money from his people. He would take it, though, just as he had always taken it before, no matter how simple the job. A man must put food into his belly. A man must buy fine gifts for his women.

He reached down. Metar handed him the backpack. He set it on top of the wall, lowered his arms again, and this time pulled the smaller man off the ground.

From his perch on the wall, Emil looked toward the house. He couldn't see it. Too many trees in the way. He knew it was there, however. He and Metar had paid it a visit, just last week.

He leaped from the wall. Metar dropped the pack down to him, then jumped. He held the pack while Metar slipped it on. Turning away from the wall, they started toward the trees.

Out of the darkness sprinted a Dobermann, its feet silent on the summer grass.

This is Callahan's security?

It was laughable.

The dog yelped and tripped over itself as a .22-caliber hollow-point slug crashed through its skull.

Then three more Dobermans raced out of the darkness. Emil fired his silenced automatic, knocking a foreleg from under the lead dog. As it tumbled, the one beside it leaped at him, teeth bared. He stepped toward it, ignoring Metar's cry of pain. The dog snapped, its teeth clattering on the silencer. With quick twitches of his index finger, Emil pumped two bullets into its mouth. He sidestepped away from the lunging, dying animal, swung his pistol from its mouth, and dropped the dog he had previously hit in the leg.

Then he whirled around. Metar, the incompetent fool, was on the ground, fighting for his life as the last surviving dog savaged his arm, trying to get through it to his neck.

Emil fired.

The dog yelped as the bullet tore through its spinal cord.

Then jerked and died.

Metar rolled out from under the heavy body and stood up. He raised his bloody arm for Emil to see, like a child showing a scraped elbow to his mother for sympathy.

Emil turned away in disgust. He hurried through the stand of pine, and saw the Callahan house across fifty yards of neatly groomed lawn. Floodlights illuminated the colonial's pillared veranda. All the windows Emil could see, however, were dark. He ran to the left side of the house, staying far from the lighted front, and leaned against a wall.

Metar, a handkerchief tied around his wounded forearm, ran to join him.

With friction tape, Emil reinforced a panel of the window. His glass-cutter bit into the glass. He cut a rectangle.

A neat job. A good job. That was why his clients paid him well.

Holding the rectangle in place with tape, he pounded it loose and withdrew it. He gave the neatly cut geometric lozenge of glass to Metar, then reached into the gap. Unlatched the window.

It slid upward easily.

Quietly.

Emil climbed through. As planned, he found himself in Callahan's study. He sat on a corner of the teak desk, and watched Metar climb awkwardly through the window.

They crossed the study to the door. Emil eased it open. He peered into the dark hallway, and gestured for Metar to follow.

In the foyer, Metar's rubber-soled shoes made squeaking sounds on the marble. Emil glanced sharply at his young partner. The man shrugged, crouched. Removed his shoes.

Emil flashed the beam of a small flashlight toward the front door. Next to it, on the wall, he found the speaker box and remote-control button.

He pushed the button.

In the U-Haul van parked nearby, Steve Bailey squinted through a haze of cigarette smoke at the iron gate. It began to swing open.

Very good.

In ten minutes, he would be done with this business. He would be away from the house, and on the freeway to the airport. In a couple of hours or so, he'd be with Carla. It was always best with her, right after a job when he knew he was finally safe, and the fear was gone, and he had money . . . good money . . . in his pocket. His cock knew it was time to come out of hiding and celebrate.

Easing his foot off the clutch, he rolled through the open gate. He steered up the driveway, swung left, and drove over the grass to the veranda.

With a hissing sputter, the acetylene torch came alive. Emil watched his partner shoot its flame against the lock panel of the steel door. The metal bubbled and peeled back like the lips of a knife wound.

Raising the goggles to his forehead, Emil stepped silently down the hall to the foyer. He squinted up the stairway.

Perhaps he should go up and put a bullet into Callahan's head? Then he could go about his work untroubled by the man's presence. Murder, however, would increase official interest in the case. That was to be avoided, if possible.

As long as the old man didn't interfere, Emil would allow him to live.

The torch shut off. Sparks winked out.

Emil returned to the door and helped Metar remove the severed lock panel. As he set it aside, Metar loaded the torch into the backpack and slung the straps onto his shoulders.

Slowly, Emil pushed the metal door open.

Robert Callahan, asleep in his upstairs room, heard the quiet drone of his alarm and dreamed of sirens. An ambulance was bearing down on a heap of torn cars. Sarah, lying in the road, raised her bloody head and cried for help.

'There she is,' shouted the ambulance driver.

Robert, for some reason dreaming that he was sitting in the passenger seat, said, 'Thank God she's alive.'

'We'll soon fix that,' said the driver.

The ambulance sped toward her. Lethal as a bullet.

'Stop!'

'It's her due.'

'No!'

She stared with pleading eyes into the headlights. Stared into the face of death.

Robert felt the vehicle jolt as it struck her.

Suddenly wide-awake and panting with fear, he realized the siren was the burglar-alarm amplifier by his bed. Someone had penetrated the collection room.

Emil entered the room, Metar at his side. Walking close to the wall, he shined his light on the statuettes of gold and ivory, on gold necklaces heavy with precious jewels, on scarabs and brooches and glistening rings.

To see so many antiquities in a man's private collection disgusted him. If he had time, he would clean out the entire collection of this grave robber.

But Emil had come only for Amara.

The thin beam of his light found a stone vase, its lid decorated with the jackal head of the god Anubis. Beside it stood a similar container, this with the head of a hawk. His light fell swiftly across two more vases. These were the canopic jars holding the embalmed organs of Amara – heart, lungs, kidneys. Her womb. He must take the jars tonight.

Swinging his flashlight, he found the coffin.

It was the wooden, inner coffin of Amara. The outer coffins and massive stone sarcophagus had never left Egypt. The thieves had taken this only, and the canopic jars. And Amara herself.

Stepping close to the coffin, Emil shined his light onto a golden disk on the edge of its lid. He was thankful to find the sacred seal in place.

Though vermin, Callahan was not a fool.

Leaning across the lid, Emil inspected the second seal. It, too, appeared to be intact.

Reassured, he allowed himself to look down at the carved face of Amara. It was a face of rare beauty, a face that might have shamed Nefertiti herself, had the ladies' paths ever crossed. But their paths were separated by centuries. Amara belonged to the long-dead era of the eleventh dynasty, when Mentuhotep I ruled and gods were young in the memory of the people.

Emil glanced at Metar, who stared as if hypnotized by the beautiful image. With a tap on the arm, he caught his partner's attention. He pointed to the foot of the coffin.

Together, each at one end, they lifted it. They carried the deadweight of it across the room, through the doorway, down the dark hall. Emil's powerful arms strained with the weight. Metar whimpered as wounds from the dog's bite stretched, reopened, bled. At the end of the hall, the carpet ended. He felt the marble of the foyer floor under his feet.

A few more steps, then they could set down the coffin while Metar opened the door.

It was good to accomplish the hardest part first. The canopic jars would be easy after this.

Emil nodded for Metar to stop.

A quick blast shattered the silence. In the muzzle flash, he saw Metar slammed backwards, dropping the end of the coffin. Mist jetted from between the casket and the lid. Dust of the ages. Corpse dust. Even as he looked toward the stairway, a second flash and explosion filled the darkness. He had no time to duck.

Steve Bailey, in the U-Haul van just outside the door, heard the shots.

Holy shit.

They hadn't come from a .22.

They'd come from a high-powered sucker, like maybe a .12 gauge.

Emil and Metar only carried peashooters.

So who had the cannon?

Bailey didn't wait to find out. He dropped the emergency brake lever, rammed the shift to first, floored the gas pedal and popped the clutch.

Callahan lowered the shotgun. His shoulder was numb from the kicking stock. His ears rang as if they'd been slapped.

Stepping down the stairs, he heard an engine just outside the door. It roared, then faded with distance.

Callahan stepped across the dark foyer, careful not to trip over the bodies or the coffin. Near the door, he found the light switch. Flicked it on.

Both the bastards looked dead. One had caught it in the chest. The other had lost most of his forehead.

He turned his eyes to the coffin. It had landed on its side. Bending down, he saw a crack across one of the golden seals.

'Robert!'

He glanced up the stairway. His small, swarthy friend looked confused and frightened.

'Give me a hand with this, Imad.'

'Robert, what happened?'

'These bastards tried to make off with Amara. Same two guys who were here last week wanting to do landscape work.'

As Imad reached the bottom of the stairs, his mouth dropped open. 'The Seal of Osiris,' he muttered.

'I'm not blind. Give me a hand, we'll see how the other one looks.'

Together, they crouched and rolled the coffin off its side. On the marble underneath lay two chunks of gold from the second seal.

Gasping, Imad stepped back.

'Forget it,' Callahan said. 'We'll take care of it later.'

Imad shook his head, his eyes large with fear.

'Let's just get these guys out of here, first. We'll plant them in the garden.'

Still shaking his head, Imad stepped backwards toward the door. He spun around. His trembling hands fumbled with the locks, then he flung the door open, and ran into the night.

Callahan watched him dash across the lawn, white robe fluttering.

'Imad!' The man kept running. 'Better off,' Callahan muttered, and pushed the door shut.

He slept soundly after the hard work of burying the men and cleaning up the mess they'd left in the foyer. Bloodstains were the worst. His snoring was loud in the darkness.

The figure entering the doorway didn't disturb him. He continued to snore peacefully as it crossed the room. He moaned once as it raised the covers on the empty side of the bed.

It climbed in beside him and he knew, vaguely, that he was no longer alone. Sarah must have come back from the bathroom. He was glad to have her back. The bed felt so empty without her.

Rolling toward her, he put a hand out. It would be so good to touch her skin. Sarah had always felt so soft, so smooth. Hungry for her warm, supple body, he reached out, searching for her. His fingers found the figure. Touched. Caressed.

It felt wrong, all wrong. He touched skin that was hard, wrinkled. Cold.

With a nauseating jolt, he remembered that Sarah was dead.

The shock woke him. At that instant, he found himself gazing into eyeless sockets and a leathery, shrunken face.

Something under the sheet touched his bare leg.

Slowly, the mouth opened.

Callahan started to scream.

The head jerked forward, jaws snapping shut, teeth barely missing his throat.

Callahan rolled off the bed. His knees hit the floor. He scrambled, naked, trying to get on his feet. As he started to rise, the mummy pounced upon his back. 'Get off!' he shrieked.

Its dry fingers clutched him by the shoulders.

He heard the clatter of its snapping teeth.

'Get off! No!'

Callahan got to his feet, but the thing kept its grip and stayed on his back as he ran across the room.

Its teeth tore the side of his neck. Its head jerked savagely, ripping.

Callahan dropped to his knees. He reached behind him, hoping to free himself from the creature. He gripped its hair. He jerked. Tresses pulled loose in his hand.

The mouth kept biting and tearing long after he was dead.

Chapter One

Susan Connors, assistant curator of the Charles Ward Museum, was dead. Dead on her feet, that was. She'd been standing all day, directing the two workmen who uncrated the collection, marking her checklist, pointing out where she wished the dozens of ancient artifacts placed for display.

She hadn't been on her feet this long since the day she'd worked a double shift at the Wagon Train restaurant, bussing barbecue ribs and cheeseburgers for conventioneers. Some treat that was. Man, oh man . . . That was – what? – six years ago? She'd been an undergraduate then. A senior.

That seemed like a long time ago.

Aeons.

Almost as long ago as eight o'clock this morning.

One of the workmen, the one called Top, lifted a canopic jar out of its packing case. It was made from alabaster, a stone that looked like fresh, white milk that had been transformed into something hard. Brittle. A sculptured head of a jackal formed the lid. Susan marked her checklist.

'That goes with the others.' She pointed to the stand beside the mummiform coffin where three other stone jars had already been placed. Top carried it across the room. Its weight didn't seem to bother him, though he looked frail and old enough to be the father of the other man. As he set down the jar, he said, 'That about does it, miss. The whole kit 'n' caboodle. Wanta sign here?'

She scribbled her initials on the invoice. Top tore off a copy, gave it to her.

'All set,' he said.

When he and the younger man were gone, Susan sat on a folding chair – the only piece of furniture in the room that was less than two thousand years old, certainly the only piece that hadn't come from the Callahan Collection. Leaning back, she crossed her right foot over her knee and sighed with pleasure. The aches seemed to flow out of her. When that leg felt almost normal, she lowered it and raised the other. The relief!

'Your meditation hour?' a voice asked.

'Tag?' She looked around and saw Taggart Parker standing in the doorway. 'What are . . .?' Then she remembered. Her car had treated her to a flat tire this morning. Tag had given her a lift to work. 'Come on in,' she said, getting up.

Tag unhooked one end of the plush cordon from its post and stepped forward through the doorway.

Into Susan's arms. She kissed him. The day's growth of whiskers was scratchy against her face, but she didn't mind. She pressed herself tightly to him, stroking the soft fabric of his corduroy jacket. She felt a hard shape against her belly.

'Is that a gun?' she asked, trying to sound like Mae West. 'Or are ya glad to see me?'

'Both,' Tag said.

Reaching down, Susan stroked the walnut grips of his Colt Python. 'You've got a hell of a pistol, fella.'

'And I'm good with it.'

'Braggart.' She kissed him again. 'Hey, we'd better knock it off before the boss walks in.' She stepped away, but kept hold of his hand. 'How was your day?'

'Improving.'

'Mine, too.' She swept an arm around to indicate the room. 'Look what I did today. It's the Callahan Collection.'

He scanned the room and his gaze settled on the single coffin. 'What's that, a mummy?'

'Sure is.'

'How about giving me a peek? I've never seen a real live mummy before.'

'Are you sure you want to?'

'I'd love to.'

'She's been dead a while.'

'Is that right?'

'The better part of four thousand years.'

'That long?'

'We don't know much about this gal yet: just what we got from the list Callahan left. Her name is Amara.'

'Amara? That's a beautiful name.' He smiled, teasing.

'And she was a wife of Pharaoh Mentuhotep the First. He ruled Egypt during the eleventh dynasty, about 2,000 BC.'

'Well, let's have a look.'

'Promise not to touch?'

'You don't trust me with strange women?'

'Especially not when you say they have a beautiful name.'

'And so it is . . . Amara, Amara, Amara. A guy can fall in love with a name like that.'

'Okay, promise not to touch. It's extremely fragile.'

'Cross my heart.' He patted Susan's rump. 'Actually, I doubt if I'd want to.'

Together they raised the lid. Susan, who had seen the mummy only for a moment that morning, gave it a closer inspection. The hair was a sweep of shining red, the only part of the once-young woman that had apparently defied time. It must have been elaborately coiffed at the time of entombment. Those who unwrapped her had probably also removed the jeweled hairpins. Her eye sockets were empty. No valuable stones inside, as imitation eyes, as was the ancient funerary practice. No onions to mask the smell of corruption, like they found in Rameses IV. No bags of frankincense and myrrh in the body cavities, either. Robbers had undoubtedly made off with those. Valuable spices were still valuable spices even after they had been drawn from their grisly container. Across the abdomen was a diagonal cut nearly a foot long that had been crudely stitched with twine. The breasts had shriveled into puckered bags. The pubic region had been shaved, probably by the ancient morticians after the young woman died.

Susan realized that Tag was looking away.

They closed the lid, covering that awful face.

'Do mummies all look like that?' Tag asked. His new, pasty complexion worried Susan.

'Are you all right?' she asked.

'I've felt better, on occasion.'

'Ready to leave?'

'I wish we'd left five minutes ago.'

In the subterranean parking area beneath the Marina Towers apartment complex, Tag drove slowly past Susan's Jaguar.

'It's fixed!' she blurted.

'I had a few minutes to kill after I got home from work, so I put on the spare for you.'

'Oh, you're a sweetheart.'

'Somebody isn't. Your tire didn't go flat all by itself. It had help. Somebody with a knife, I'd say.'

'You mean someone intentionally . . .?'

Tag nodded. 'It might've been random, but I doubt it. I think you've made yourself an enemy, Susan.'

She shook her head.

'What about Larry?'

'He wouldn't do that. I mean, that's the last thing he would do. He *paid* for the car, he wouldn't try to damage it.'

'Unless he doesn't appreciate the fact that it now belongs to you.' Tag swung into his own parking space. In spite of his low speed, the tires sighed on the slick concrete.

'I don't think it was Larry.'

'Just a suggestion.'

Their doors banged shut and echoed.

'How about coming in for a drink?' Susan asked.

'Sounds good.'

They took an elevator to the third floor, and walked along the narrow, carpeted hall. At her apartment, Susan opened the door to the warm, rich odors she recognized as enchilada sauce.

'Evening, María,' she greeted the chubby, smiling woman in the kitchen.

María nodded eagerly.

'Everything go all right today?'

'*Sí*. All right.' Her bright eyes turned to Tag. 'Ah, Señor Taggart. Margarita, *sí*?'

'Right.'

Susan left them, and went into the small bedroom that she used for a nursery. Geoffrey, who was busy inspecting his toes, looked up as she entered. He grinned and gurgled.

'Hi there, little guy,' she said. 'Have yourself a good day?' She picked up the baby, kissed his cheek, and pulled out the front of his diapers. They were definitely damp to the touch. She stripped him, dried him, powdered him, and put a new diaper on him. After a brief struggle, she managed to maneuver him into a pair of tiny brown corduroy pants. Then a yellow T-shirt that read: SLIPPERY WHEN WET. 'There you go, my little man.' Hefting him, she carried him into the living room.

Tag came in. He handed Susan a bottle of ProSobee, and a glass of Perrier. 'Cocktails for everyone,' he said. Sitting across from her, he sipped his margarita.

María entered and placed a bowl of taco chips in front of him. '*Gracias*,' he said.

'*De nada*.'

He watched her walk away. 'I sure wish I had one of those,' he said.

'I wish I didn't.'

'What would you want to do, stay home all day?'

'Wouldn't mind. After Geoffrey was born I did it for three months and loved it.'

'What about the museum?'

'It'd still be there when I'm ready for it again. But like they say, the bills won't pay themselves. So I guess I stay with the museum and María stays with Geoffrey.'

'With what Larry makes—'

'I don't want anything more from him. It's bad enough I have to take the child support.' Looking down at the baby, Susan said, 'I'm sure glad Geoffrey doesn't know what a creep his father is.' She smiled at the boy, who stopped sucking long enough to grin. White formula trickled from the corner of his mouth. She dabbed it away with a soft tissue, then looked up at Tag. 'How about staying for dinner?'

'I'd sure like to. I have to get out of here, though. Class tonight. Crowd Management Techniques.'

'You still have to eat.'

'I'll grab something in my apartment.'

When he finished his margarita, he went to Susan and kissed her. 'How about later?' he asked.

'How much later?'

'Ten-thirty, eleven.'

'That's my bedtime,' Susan said.

Tag grinned. 'I know.'

'I didn't get much sleep last night.'

'Me neither.'

'That's for sure.'

'How about it?' Tag asked, smiling.

'How can I refuse?'

He kissed her again. 'See you later, alligator.' He rubbed Geoffrey's head.

Geoffrey belched.

'Excuse yourself, kid.'

As Tag took the elevator to the fifth floor, he considered skipping class and taking up Susan on her dinner invitation. He needed the class, though; with the sergeant's exam scheduled for next month, he needed all the help he could get.

The doors slid open and he stepped into the hallway. He turned left. The corridor stretched out silent and narrow. Though he'd never been in a submarine, he often thought of them when he walked these halls.

A guy could get claustrophobia. A guy could get short of air. So short he finds himself rubbing his throat, his breath coming in short, painful tugs.

As he stepped around the corner, he saw something heaped on

the floor. Something the size of a body, covered by faded, grimy cloth.

In front of his door.

He moved toward it, hand darting to the firearm at his waist.

Chapter Two

The heap in front of Tag's apartment door moved. A head appeared, hair slicked down with filth, face bloated, blotchy and pale.

Tag recognized it at once. He stopped running. Took his hand away from the pistol. 'Mable,' he said.

She smiled by raising her lip. More of a canine snarl than a human smile. From the look of her mouth, her missing teeth were the lucky ones. She rolled until she was sitting up, her back against the door. She straightened the dress over her thick thighs.

'I come to see you, babes,' she murmured.

'How did you find me?'

'Got your name offa your name tag, you know? Got it right offa your tag. That little plastic gadget on your uniform. Then I looked you up.'

'What for?'

''Cause you're my kinda guy. Give a gal a lift, would ya?' She reached out her hand. Tag didn't want to touch the blotchy mitt. Refusing would be awkward, though. Besides, he felt sorry for Mable. She was forty years old and lived with her mother, a slovenly woman who could pass for Mable's old sister, if she stood on the kind side of the street light, that was. Last week, Mable ran into half a dozen members of the Braves, a Pony League team sponsored by a local hardware store. It started with name-calling. Ended with a gang bang.

'When did they let you out of the hospital?' Tag asked. Taking the offered hand, he helped her up.

'Yesterday. First thing I says to myself, I says, "Mable, that nice officer Parker is your kinda guy." So I looked you up and come right over here just to see ya. Ya gonna let a girl in?'

'I have to go out tonight, Mable.'

'I'll go with you, hmmm?'

He opened his door. 'Can't,' he said.

She followed him into his apartment, gave it a quick inspection with dreamy Demerol eyes, and whistled. 'Say, this is some nice place.'

'Thank you.'

'Won't hurt me at all, waiting here. Hmm?'

'Waiting?'

'Sure. You come back, I'll show you a time and a half, babes.'

'I don't think that's a good idea, Mable.' He went into the kitchen. Mable didn't follow, so he quickly took a handful of sliced salami and American cheese from his refrigerator, stuffed it all into a baggie and hurried back to the living room.

Mable's dress lay on the floor.

She was on the couch, naked but for black briefs and a red brassiere that barely cupped all she had to offer. Leering, she slid her tongue over her thick lips. One hand stroked a thick, blotched thigh. Cellulite rippled.

'Aw, Mable.'

'Put it right here,' she said. 'Come on, babes, don't be shy.'

Jeez. Shyness had little to do with it.

'I really shouldn't,' Tag said, trying to look only at her face. 'You're not ready for those kind of games just yet.'

'I'm tougher than I look. Come on, Tag, hold me tight for a little. I won't bite.'

No, maybe not, but I'd wager there's plenty in that tangle of hair that'd bite good and hard.

'Babes,' she cooed. 'I can take you places you've never been before.'

Damned right. The clap clinic. Front of the line. Pants down.

'I'm sorry, Mable.' He picked up her dress and tossed it to her. 'Thanks for your kind offer, but I have an important class tonight. Now get dressed. I'll walk you downstairs.'

'I ain't good enough for you, that it?'

'No, that's not it. I'm in a hurry, that's all.'

'I could have shown you a real good time. Hot and spicy, you dig?'

'I appreciate the offer.'

'Well, I'm staying put till you give me the goodies. Hmm?'

Tag groaned. He couldn't leave, not with Mable still in the apartment. The alternative? Tease those black panties down over her thighs, then . . . oh, man, no. She wasn't a bad person, just more than a little mad.

Mad. Sad. Horny. Hell, what a combination. 'Do you want some money?'

'What do you want me to do for money?'

'Nothing.'

'I'd do anything for you for free, babes.'

'Mable, listen to me, I'll give you money.'

'What for?'

'To leave,' he said. Blunt, okay, and he saw the pain in her eyes. 'I'm sorry, but I have no intention of making out with you. I have an important place I have to be in about five minutes. I'm already going to be late and I can't leave till you're out of here, so please get dressed and go.'

'I ain't good enough for you, that's it. I ain't pretty and cultivated like that whore downstairs.'

He glared, but said nothing.

'Sure . . . sure, I know all about you and her; how you stayed at her place last night, and me waiting for you here all cold and lonesome.'

'You're the one.'

'She's a scrawny nothing, babes. You just climb on here.'

'*You*'re the one who did it.'

'You're not gonna believe what I can do with my tongue.'

'You flattened her tire, didn't you?'

'Me? Not me. No sir, officer.'

'That was a rotten thing to do, Mable. Now get your dress on or I'll run you in.'

'What for?' A brassiere strap slipped, exposing a fat brown nipple.

'Indecent exposure.'

'Oh yeah?'

'That's right,' Tag said. 'Maybe a little trespass, too.'

'Okay, okay.' Mable hoisted up the strap cupping the dollop of breast. 'Hand me up my dress, will you?'

As Tag crouched beside the sofa to pick up the pile of dirty cloth, Mable grabbed him. She tugged his arm. Off balance, he fell onto her. Her arms clutched him tightly. Those hefty breasts felt like twin cushions against him. Sour breath rushed into his face. Her arms clutched him.

'Mable!' he snapped. 'Damn it, you'd better . . .!'

Her mouth pressed against his. Her tongue prodded his tightly sealed lips. Something warm and wet dribbled down his chin.

Trying to push away, his hands sank into those twin mounds of soft flesh beneath the brassiere. She moaned with excitement. 'Oh, that's it, babes . . .'

'Mable . . . let go . . .'

Mable rolled. Both tumbled onto the floor.

'Get—'

Her thick tongue penetrated his mouth. The sour-milk odor made him gag. A hand pushed roughly under his belt, searching . . .

'No!'

He jerked his head back sharply, gasping for clean air. At the same moment, he tugged the roving hand from out of his pants and bent it backward at the wrist until Mable cried out. Using the hand for leverage, he forced her to roll off. He stood up, still keeping the hand bent.

'Okay,' he panted. 'On your feet.'

He helped her by twisting the arm.

'Bastard!' she cried out. 'Cocksucker!'

'Shut up, Mable.'

'Motherfu—' She yelped in pain as he gave the arm a quick turn.

'I said *shut up*.'

Using the twisted arm, he steered her toward the door. 'I don't want any more trouble from you, do you understand? I want you to go home.'

'No, I want—'

'I want you to go home and never pull this kind of stunt again. If you bother Susan or me, know what I'll do?'

'What?'

'I'll tell your mother.'

She jerked her head sideways and glared at him. 'You better not.'

'I will.'

'You better not,' she repeated. This time frightened.

'You be a good girl from now on, or I will.'

'All I wanted was to be nice to you. That's all I wanted. What's wrong with that?'

'The way you went about it. Now, I'll let go of you and I want you to get dressed, then go straight home. Okay?'

'Okay.' Her swollen lips formed a sulky pout.

He let go of her arm. She leaned heavily against the door, arms hanging at her sides, head down, mess of hair dangling across her eyes. Tag turned away. He picked up her dress, handed it to her, and turned his face away as she hauled it over herself. Then he opened the door.

He watched her walk slowly down the hall. Thirty years ago she'd have been a cute kid. Nice. Friendly. Polite in class. At night she'd have heard her mother going down on any guy with a dollar in the next room. It's hard to grow up decent . . . hard to grow up sane . . . after a childhood like that. 'Good-bye, Mable. You take care of yourself, do you hear?'

She looked over her shoulder. He saw tears on her face. Sniffing loudly, she wiped her nose with the back of her hand, turned sadly away.

Tag shut the door. Locked it.

He glanced at his wristwatch.

Too late to bother with the damned class.

Feeling tired and bruised and dirty . . . like something thirty years dead had just crawled over his face . . . he went to the bathroom, turned on the shower. When it was scalding he stood under it, his face up to receive the driving jets.

Chapter Three

April Vallsarra, hands resting on the stone balustrade, enjoyed the cooling breeze playing against her cheek after the heat of the day.

She loved to stand here at night. The air was cool. She took pleasure from the sound of the crickets. The scent of the wildflowers out in the woods reached into her, calming her.

She listened to the music the trees made as air currents ran along the canyon. The surging hiss that would fall away to a whisper. It reminded her of the time she lived in the beach house with her father. The sound of the surf. Especially at night when she lay warm and safe in her bed. Then the waves would surge across the beach.

She stood listening to the sounds in the outside world. The breeze moved across the rooftop terrace, swirled round her bare calves and ankles, tugged at her dress, at her hair.

Often she tried to imagine what those trees looked like. They would move, she decided, like she'd heard how herds of elephants move. She could never know exactly, of course. She'd been born blind. Had to leave home at six years old to attend a school for the blind in San Francisco. That was when her world fell apart. Her parents' marriage broke up. Her mother moved to Canada and she never heard from her again.

She was so miserable at school that at the age of eleven years she tried to take her own life. Tying a noose from panty hose, she knotted it to the shower rail and jumped off the edge of the tub. The rail didn't take her weight; it snapped; she fell to the bathroom floor and broke her wrist.

Her father was the one who saved her.

After a long talk in the hospital, as she waited for her arm to receive the cast, he realized how unhappy she was at the school.

He brought her home.

It wasn't to the beach house, though.

The new home was here in the canyon. In one of the passes that snake between Hollywood and Burbank. Even though you were in the midst of three million people, here was an oasis of calm.

The canyon contained no other houses. Only this one. Her father built the house to his own design. His 'sneakaway', he called it. It was two-storied, built of brick. There was a huge rooftop terrace where her father could barbecue the biggest steaks. Where he could host the coolest parties that were the talk of LA. The guest list would read like the contents of *Rolling Stone* magazine.

By day her father recorded music in his own studio in the basement. And, Jeez, what a studio. John Lennon, dropping by for cocktails, announced, 'Sweet God in heaven, you could put the London Philharmonic Orchestra in here and still have room for the bloody performing elephants.'

The wind sighed in the trees. April tilted her head to one side. The air played on her neck, toying with her hair.

A beautiful place. Peaceful.

Away from everyone. Away from city noise and smog.

She considered what she could have for supper. A salad with shrimp. An ice-cold glass of white wine. Yes, that would be nice.

For a second she thought she heard the scrunch of a foot on the gravel path.

'Dad?'

The word reached her lips before she could stop it.

No.

Couldn't be.

Her father was dead. Shot by a pair of thugs he'd found breaking into his car. He'd been staying in a motel coming back from Nashville. He'd glanced out the window, seen the two morons cracking open his car like a money box. When he'd gone out to challenge them, one had pulled a pistol and . . .

Her hands tightened on the balustrade.

No. Not tonight.

She wouldn't replay the incident. That was ten years ago.

So now I'm here alone. She'd no sooner thought the word *alone* than the sound came again.

Feet on gravel.

But who's there at this time? No one would make the long drive out of town up here to see me in the middle of the night.

'Hello, who's there?'

Her blind eyes moved as if looking down onto the driveway below. She listened.

The wind cried through the trees. Leaves rustled.

'Anyone there?'

No answer. But the sound of a zipper being pulled slowly down.

'There *is* someone there.' Her heart raced. 'What do you want?'

She listened again, heart pounding.

What if it's an intruder?

I'm all alone here.

Lettie came out during the day to bring her groceries, help her clean the house and keep her company for a while. But Lettie was long gone now. Maybe she should phone—

That sound again. Feet on gravel.

Slowly she backed away from the balustrade toward the center of the roof terrace. It was dark. Yet, she knew sighted people still might be able to see her standing on top of the house. Here in the center, though, she'd be out of sight.

But what if they should break in?

Nothing she could do would stop them then. Even if she could reach the phone it would take a while for the police to reach this remote part of the canyon.

She was thirty-three years old. Men had told her how pretty she was. That her shoulder-length hair was glossy. She had a slim figure. Tanned arms and legs.

So whoever broke into the house might not be here for money or the TV.

But her.

A scrunching sound came again. Maybe they were trying to find a window without a steel shutter or an unlocked door.

Her father had been thorough. All the downstairs windows were sealed with steel mesh. After all, she didn't require daylight. Or *any* light, come to that.

The doors were of hardwood. The locks substantial. What was more, each one was covered by a wrought-iron screen.

Maybe they will try and climb up the wall? They'd find me alone on the roof.

Now, in the open, she felt vulnerable. She wished she had a companion to share her home. Someone strong to keep her safe.

She backed into a potted shrub. The leaves prickled her hip through the flimsy material of her dress.

She caught her breath.

Stay calm . . . stay calm. He cannot climb up here. I'm safe.

But was she?

April reached the barbecue and crouched down beside it, her arms clasped around her knees, trying to make herself small as possible.

For a long time she waited, hunched beneath the night sky. For a while the sounds beyond the house haunted her. She imagined a man scaling the outside with a ladder. Or finding an unshuttered window. She imagined the sound of footsteps. She even gasped out loud as she imagined rough hands on her. A fist grabbing her hair, another hand finding her breasts. The sound of the man's hoarse panting.

Shaking, her breath coming in frightened gasps, she waited and waited.

At last, when she heard no more sounds, she felt her way back down to her bedroom.

'Please, God,' she whispered after she climbed into bed. 'Please bring me a companion. Please bring someone to me. I don't want to be lonely anymore.'

Chapter Four

Barney Quinn, night-watchman, didn't care much for the museum. It always seemed too damned stuffy, as if every piece of ancient junk was quietly giving off a stink. Going home in the morning, he smelled the same stink on himself. An old tomb stink. The stink of three-thousand-year-old skulls.

The same stink oozed from those shitty old stone statues in the Greek collection. *Jesus H.* Pretty soon, if he didn't watch out, he'd turn into one himself. And wouldn't that be dandy? Every last one of those buggers had an arm off, or a head, or even a pecker.

They'll open up one fine morning and say, 'Where's old Barney Quinn?' Won't find him till they look in the Greek room and count up the statues. One too many. And here's a statue in a shitty brown uniform. Maybe they'll just leave him standing there, save his family the price of a funeral. Spend that insurance on a new TV. Damn squat for old Barney Quinn. Leave him here in the statue morgue until some clumsy cleaner knocks his pecker clean off. RIP old Barney Quinn.

'Shit,' he muttered.

Need some fresh air. Need some time outta here. Besides, it was about time to visit George.

Crossing the lobby, he went to a metal fire door, shoved it open. The landing was lighted by a bulb over the door. He started down the stairs. *Damn*: the light at the next landing was out. He stepped down into the darkness. At the bottom, he pushed open the outer door. He stepped outside and leaned against the door, propping it open with his back.

The employees' parking lot was empty except for his old Grand Prix. Used to be a good car. Used to be his pride and joy back when he bought it. Everything was good in those days. Before the brass got wind of the Fun House and kicked his ass off the force.

Well, shit, can't win 'em all, can ya?

He lit a cigarette. As he dragged on it, filling his lungs with sweet blue tobacco smoke that went a-tingling and a-singing to his fingertips, he saw the dog near the edge of the lot. Old George, right on time. Pinching the cigarette between his lips, he crouched and clapped his hands. 'Here, boy,' he called. 'Come on. Come to Barney.'

The dog loped toward him, its collar tags jangling.

'Yeah, there's a good guy.'

George ran into his arms, licking his face, damn near knocking the cigarette out of his mouth. 'Yeah, that's my good boy. Sure you are. Bet you're hungry, huh?'

The thick, brown tail swished.

'Come on, then. See what Barney's got fer yer.' After propping the museum door open, Barney walked to his car. The dog kept ahead of him, glancing back impatiently, brown eyes twinkling in the meager street light.

'Hold your horses, boy.'

Barney unlocked his car. Reaching into the glove compartment, he took out a cellophane bag containing a ball of raw hamburger. 'Isn't much, fella,' he apologized. 'You like it, though, don't you? Sure. You keep coming back for more. A satisfied customer.'

He opened the bag. The hamburger was still partly frozen, but it was soft enough to break up. He twisted off chunks and gave them to George. Some he tossed for the dog to catch, enjoying the quick snap that snatched the pieces out of the air. Others he held in his hand. George took these like a gentleman, lifting them delicately away with his front teeth before swallowing.

'That's all, pal,' Barney said, smiling.

George looked up, eyes wide, hopeful.

'All she wrote, fella.'

Kneeling, Barney let the dog lick his fingers. 'Yep. All gone. You come back tomorrow night, though. I'll have some more tasty bits and pieces for you.'

He walked back to the open door of the museum, George prancing beside him.

'Gotta say goodnight, George old pal.'

He patted the brown fur of the dog's back and pulled the door shut. Then he turned on his flashlight and climbed the stairs. Would have to leave maintenance a note about the bulb down there. A guy could break his back there in the dark. Only took one little slip.

At the first landing, he pushed open the metal door and stepped into the lobby. It was dimly lighted. Switching off the flashlight, he hung it back on his belt, then headed for the front doors. Better be certain they're still secure before making the tour of the main floor.

As he turned away from them he heard the *thump*.

Like something wooden falling to the floor. He listened for more sounds, but the museum was silent.

He thought: *That's grave silence, Barney*: a silence to be *felt*.

It had probably been nothing, that thump: a shelf giving way upstairs, or a wire snapping so a piece of that ancient junk fell to the floor. On the other hand . . .

Damn it – he should have kept an eye on the door while he was out feeding George. Some kids might have sneaked in. Or some bum looking for a place to sleep. Or even a damn cat.

Silently, he walked to the main stairway. As he climbed, he scanned the second-floor balcony through the rods of its railing. The area looked clear.

He wished he had his piece, just in case. Damned museum wouldn't let him carry a gun; said they didn't want anybody hurt. 'If there's trouble, Barney, call the cops.' *Sure. I call the cops, and they find a pussy cat in the Callahan Collection.* That'd confirm to everyone down at the station that old Barney was a washed-up piece of horseshit all right. Calling out a SWAT team to save Barney from some liddle puddy cat. *Yeah, right.*

Hell.

Did seem like the noise came from there. He wondered how he got that impression: just because the Callahan Room was closer to the stairway than the others? He stepped to the entrance. Peered in. Dark. Very dark. No light in the room. He could only see vague shapes. Reaching down, he unhooked the cordon and let it hang. His fingers found the switches. *Snick.* A dozen bulbs, concealed above tinted ceiling panels, filled the room with soft light.

Well, how'd that happen?

The lid of the mummy's coffin lay on the floor.

Barney, standing motionless, scanned the room: the display case full of jewelry that was a mass of golds and sky blues, the chariot wheel, the dozens of statuettes, the stone jars, the coffin.

No one there.

Unless some intruder was crouched at the far end of the display case? *They can see me but I can't see them. Are they watching me standing here? Hoping that I shrug and turn away.* Nothing doing. Time to move on to the next floor.

No. Barney, with all those years on the force, wasn't going to be fooled so easily.

Silently, he walked along the case to its end. It concealed nobody.

Okay, so how did the coffin lid get on the floor?

Disturbed by a cat?

Hardly.

Toppled by kids?

Maybe.

Wish I'd got my piece.

Colt .38. Hollow-nose slugs. *Pop one of those caps and the perp's going down.*

He pushed the coffin lid with his toe. Heavy sucker. Stepping over it, he looked into the coffin. He stared at the mummy, feeling a tightness of nausea in his throat.

Hell . . . she looked like *hell*.

Once, when Barney was still a rookie cop, he helped a fireman drag a charred body from the debris of a burned apartment house. A crispy critter, the fireman called it.

This gal wasn't a crispy critter, but she didn't look any better than one. Looked worse, for that matter. Like someone had let the air out of her tits.

He didn't like seeing that red hair on her head, either – how glossy, even how beautiful it looked – not when the rest of her body was such a wreck.

Glancing down her naked body, he saw that she had no pubic hair. Well, damned if he was going to dwell on it. Best put it out of sight.

He crouched. Lifted the coffin lid. Heavy as a door. *Christ*. But he managed to get it onto the coffin.

Turning away, Barney swept his gaze around the room. Everything appeared fine. He walked to the doorway, turned off the lights; darkness swooped back into the room . . . and he jumped at the crash of wood behind him.

Barney whirled round. In the gloom he could make out that the coffin lid was on the floor again.

'Holy shit,' he muttered.

He stared at the lid. Felt sick and chilled . . . and for some reason his balls seemed to shrivel up into the pit of his stomach. A prickling sensation ran up his forearms as the hairs stood on end, feeling for all the world like a hideous spider had dropped from the darkness onto his bare arm and was scurrying up toward his head, determined to climb into his mouth. He rubbed his face. It felt cold. It felt numb, too, as if his nerve endings were in retreat from that awful darkness.

He wanted out; he wanted out fast. But he was afraid to turn his back on the coffin. Afraid, if he turned away . . .

It happened.

The thing he dreaded in the pit of bones that was his skeleton.

It happened like deep down he knew it would.

Swift as someone startled from sleep, the mummy sat up.

Chapter Five

'Hey, A-rab . . . move your ass.'

Imad sipped his neat gin; didn't acknowledge the man.

'You hear me? Move your ass. My lady friend wants that stool.'

'Sir,' Imad intoned, 'your lady friend *is* that stool.'

'Yeah, what's that supposed to mean?'

Imad looked at the girl. She wore tight, faded jeans and a dirty T-shirt. The T-shirt only half there; cut off just below the breasts. The breasts were tiny with points like nails.

Her eyes, with half-shut lids, had a lazy and insolent look.

Imad sipped his drink. 'Does my meaning evade you, sir?'

'Huh.'

'Your lady friend is shit . . . and you're a fly.'

The fist slammed the side of Imad's head, knocking him off the barstool. His back hit the floor. Shouts filled the bar.

The man had him by the wrists, was dragging him across the floor, was pumped up with fury. The girl in jeans hopped alongside him. Imad could see up her shirt. Saw the two small mounds of breast had no jiggle. A shame. He liked a little jiggle. These were made of stone; hardly arousing at all.

The man flung open a side door. 'Gimme a hand,' he snapped.

'Sure, Blaze.'

Blaze? A cute name. A name for a horse.

The girl bent down and helped lift Imad. He staggered between them. Raising his head, he saw that they had brought him into a deserted alley. The walls of the building pressed close. Far down the narrow passageway, cars passed on the street. The alley smelled ripe with garbage.

'Now we'll see who's a fly on shit, camel-fucker.'

Blaze jerked Imad away from the girl. Shoved him against a garbage can. The ripe, fetid smell leaped into his sensitive nostrils with every breath.

The girl giggled. 'Blaze on him!'

As Blaze gripped the back of his collar, Imad reached deep into the sweating garbage. He found a beer bottle. As Blaze jerked him round he swung the bottle and broke it against Blaze's head.

The girl went silent. Now the lazy eyes snapped suddenly wide. Wondering what was coming next.

Blaze dropped to his knees, then fell forward, his face hitting the ground with a *slap*.

Imad turned to the girl.

She laughed once through her nose. One side of her mouth smiled. 'Guess you fixed *him*.' She tried the door of the bar. It was locked.

Softly he spoke. 'Come here.'

'You better not try nuthin'.'

'Come here.'

She took a hesitant step toward him, then stopped. 'Say, mister . . . you wouldn't hurt a girl, would you?'

'Come here.'

She glanced up the alley. Laughed quietly. ''Bout time somebody fixed Blaze,' she said, stepping toward him. 'He's such a prick.'

She flinched as Imad touched her cheek.

'You are a beautiful woman,' Imad told her.

'Me? Hell, you called me shit – I've got ears.'

He slid a hand under her T-shirt. Her small breasts felt firm, but not like concrete. Not at all. The turgid nipples were pliant under his fingers.

Her smile trembled.

'You are a flower,' Imad murmured. 'A lovely, fragile flower.'

'Yeah?' She shook her head.

'Come with me.'

She looked down at Blaze who was still motionless in the ripe goo that dripped from the trashcan. 'Just a sec,' she whispered. Crouching, she shoved a hand into a front pocket of Blaze's jeans. It returned with a pack of bills fastened into a thick, square mat with paper clips.

'Two hundred bucks,' she said. 'We'll split it even-steven, okay?'

'Is it yours?'

'Is now.'

'Did this man take it from you?'

'Hell, no. It's what's left of his pay from Market King.'

'Market King?'

'You know? The grocery store? He's a checker. That's how we met.'

'Let Mr Blaze keep his money,' Imad told her.

'No.'

'I do not countenance theft.'

'Huh?'

'I won't allow it. Return the money.'

'Aw, shit.'

'At once.'

'Please, mister?'

'At once,' he commanded.

With a frown over her shoulder at Imad, she tucked the pack of bills back into Blaze's pocket.

Imad held out his hand. She went to it. Took it.

'Where we going?' she asked, walking with him down the alley.

'To my home.'

'Yeah? Where's that?'

'In Greenside.'

'Greenside *Estates*? In Burlingdale?'

He nodded.

'Sure. I'll believe that when I see it.'

When they reached his gray Mercedes, she looked at him with suspicion. 'This yours?'

'Certainly.' He opened the door for her and she climbed in.

Imad went to the other side to slip into the driver's seat. As he started the car the girl said, 'You must be one of them Arab-oil bastards, huh?'

'Wrong. My parents were Egyptian. I have nothing to do with oil. In addition, my birth was entirely legitimate.'

'Yeah? How you come to live in a ritzy place like Greenside?'

'How come you don't?'

She laughed. 'Shit, who's got that kind of money?'

'I do.'

'You're so loaded, how come you were over at a dump like Shannon's?'

'One meets an interesting set,' he told her.

'Set, huh?' She leaned against him. 'How's mine?'

'Just fine,' he said. Putting an arm behind her, he slipped his hand under her T-shirt. He stroked the smooth skin of her side. Stretching, he reached the breast.

He'd had many women in the months since Callahan's death. He'd met them at parties, in bars, at a university class in anthropology that he took only for that purpose, at church. Whenever possible, he brought them home for the night. He didn't like being alone in the house he'd inherited.

Not at all. It held too much pain for him.

His shame at running away.

His confusion at Callahan staying to be killed.

The memories of the terrible morning when he returned to the house. Finding Callahan naked on the bedroom floor, his skin tattered, chunks torn from him and scattered about as if a beast had tried to devour him but found his flesh unsavory and spit out mouthfuls on the carpet.

The hunt for the mummy. Finding it, at last, wedged behind the refrigerator. Glossy red hair hanging down. Eyeless sockets in the face: twin pits of darkness. Shriveled lips. White teeth.

Nailing it into its coffin.

Then the grim business of the dogs. Carrying them, one at a time, upstairs to Callahan's bedroom. Using their teeth on the grotesque body, tearing the dead flesh until all traces of human teeth were obliterated. The police interrogation. Always back to the gun. Where's the gun, the .22 Callahan used on the attacking dogs? Imad only shrugged. The cops knew it was all wrong: no gun, not nearly enough blood in the room. They suspected Imad. Guessed he'd had a hand in all this. After all, he would inherit the estate. Without evidence, though, they never arrested him.

Alone in the house, he felt haunted by what had happened there. With a woman he had little trouble keeping the memories away.

This one looked at him, half grinning, as the iron gate swung open.

'I got it,' she said. 'You're the chauffeur.'

He began, as usual, with a tour of the house. Though the girl was obviously awestruck by the lavishly furnished rooms, she kept grinning wryly, shaking her head, making sarcastic remarks.

Until they reached the master bedroom.

That was when Imad turned her to face him. He pulled the T-shirt over her head, enjoying the way her small breasts moved as she raised her arms. He unfastened the waist of her jeans. The open zipper revealed a deep V of pale skin, curls of pubic hair, no panties. He peeled the jeans down her legs. She kicked off her sandals and stepped out of the jeans.

She moved back, fixing him with a crooked smile. 'Find what you're looking for?' she asked.

'I believe so, yes.'

'Know what to do with it?'

'The bathtub's that way.' He pointed to a door behind him. 'You may have half an hour.'

'What for?'

'To bathe.'

She laughed. 'Afraid you'll get your pretty hands dirty?'

'I do not intend to wallow in the residue left by my predecessors.'

'Huh?' The heavy-lidded stare again. Insolent. Ignorant somehow.

'Take your bath. I'll shower in the other room and prepare drinks for us. What do you prefer?'

'Rum and Coke.'

Imad grinned. 'Certainly.'

Wrapped in a towel, she entered the bedroom. Her wet hair clung to her head; her skin was rosy.

'You look delightful,' Imad told her. He handed her the drink.

'Here's how,' she said.

They drank. Imad's neat gin tasted fine. He put down his glass and reached for the girl.

'Not so fast,' she said. 'We've got a little matter to settle first.'

'Ah.' Imad smiled, hoping to hide his disappointment. 'A financial matter, I assume.'

'You're quick on your feet.'

'Would a hundred dollars be appropriate?'

'Two hundred.'

Imad laughed. 'In that case, you'd best get dressed. I'll call you a cab.' He turned toward the door.

'Hundred-fifty,' she offered.

'I'll make the call.'

'One-thirty.'

'One hundred . . . with a bonus if you deserve it.'

'Who decides *that*?'

'I do, of course.'

'How much bonus?'

'Whatever I think suitable. Agreed?'

'But a hundred for sure?'

'One hundred for sure.'

'Why not?' She plucked a corner of the towel. It dropped away.

Imad stepped close to her. She slipped open his cloth belt. Parted the bathrobe. Her eyes widened. 'God Almighty, where'd you get a thing like that?'

'I inherited it from my father.'

She took it in her hands and it grew mightily. 'Who was your father? Babe Ruth?' She laughed at her joke. 'Bet you've hit a lot of homers with this.'

He nodded. 'Yes, indeed, I have frequently scored.' He arched his back, trembling with pleasure, as she drew her tongue up the underside of his erect shaft.

Chapter Six

Susan was watching the TV news when her doorbell rang. 'Who is it?' she asked.

'Tag.'

She let him in. 'So how was your class?'

'I didn't go.' They sat down together on the couch. 'Turned out there's this girl who finds me irresistible.'

'It's your aftershave,' Susan said.

'I don't know what it is, but she showed up in front of my door.'

'Who? I thought you meant me.' Susan felt a knot of anxiety. Here it comes . . . so long . . . thanks for everything . . . stay just good friends, huh?

He shook his head. 'Mable Rudge. Took me a while to get rid of her.'

'Three hours?'

'Ten, fifteen minutes. Seemed like hours, though. Then I had a shower.'

'Together?'

'Jeez, no. She was the other side of a locked door by then. But I didn't feel much like facing anyone, you know?'

'Pretty bad, huh?'

'Awful.'

'Recovered?'

'Better all the time.'

'Maybe this will help.' She kissed him on the lips.

'It's a start,' Tag admitted, taking her into his arms. 'It's most definitely a start.'

In the morning, during breakfast, Tag offered to drive her to work.

'I don't have another flat, do I?'

'Not that I know of. I'd just like to drive you to work. It's my day off. Besides, it'll give me an excuse to pick you up this afternoon.'

'Sounds good to me.'

'How does dinner sound?'

'Great.'

Later, in the parking lot, Tag didn't head directly for the exit. Instead, he circled and drove past Susan's car. 'See?' he said. 'No flat.'

'You expected one, didn't you?'

'Let's say it wouldn't have surprised me much. My charming friend Mable is a very jealous lady.'

'Is she the one who did it yesterday?'

Tag nodded. 'With any luck, we've seen the last of her. She knows she'll be in big trouble if she pulls any more stunts.'

'Hope so.'

The drive from Susan's apartment to the museum usually took just over fifteen minutes on the Santa Monica Freeway. Tag made it in twelve.

'You've got a heavy foot there, bud,' Susan said.

'Force of habit.'

'Do you drive that way in your patrol car?'

'Faster, when I can. Nothing better than a Code Three. Really let her rip.'

He turned onto the road leading to the museum. Ahead of them, several police cars were parked near the entrance. Tag pulled alongside one of them. Like the other cars, it was empty. Tag and Susan got out. He took her hand and they hurried up the concrete steps toward the museum's main door.

A white-haired woman reached the top before them.

'I'm sorry, ma'am,' said the patrolman guarding the doors. 'You won't be able to go in, just now.'

'Of course I will.'

'It's a crime scene. Unless you're an employee of the museum, I'll have to ask you to leave. If you want to come back in an hour or so . . .'

'I'm here now, young man. I have no intention of going away.'

'I'm afraid I can't let you in.'

'You most certainly can. What's more, you *will*. This is a public museum. I am a member of the public. I have every right to visit the museum.'

'It's a crime scene, ma'am.'

'That's no concern of mine. Did I commit the crime? No, I should say not. So you just step aside, like a good fellow.'

He didn't step aside.

'Out of my way.'

'Ma'am,' the patrolman said, 'we think that the perpetrator might still be inside.'

'Oh? *Oh!*' The old woman hurried away with fearful backward glances at the building.

'Nice touch, Henderson,' Tag said.

Henderson grinned.

Tag turned to Susan. 'Susan, this smooth-tongued devil is Manny Henderson. Manny, Susan.'

'Nice to meet you,' she said, offering her hand. As Henderson shook it, his eyes dropped briefly to her breasts.

'What happened here?' Tag asked.

'Huh?'

'You told the gal it's a crime scene.'

'Oh. Right. The night watchman turned up dead. Looks like he took a header down the stairs, broke his neck. Homicide's checking it out. They seem to think he walked into a burglary. Either he tripped over himself trying to get away, or they grabbed him and gave him the heave-ho.'

'Who was the watchman?' Susan asked.

'Quinn. Barney Quinn.'

Susan nodded, relieved that she didn't know the dead man. 'Was anything stolen?' she asked.

'Looks like they made off with a mummy.'

Amara

'Amara?'

'A mummy,' Henderson repeated.

'Amara,' Tag said. 'That's its name.'

'What?'

'The mummy's name is Amara.'

'Hell, you mean they give 'em names?'

'They're dead people, Henderson.'

'I know that. Hey, do you want to go in or something?'

'Trying to get rid of us?' Tag asked.

'Just you.' He turned to Susan. 'You should stay away from this guy, you know. He'll get you in all kinds of jams.'

'I'll be careful,' Susan assured him. 'See you later.'

They entered the museum. Across the lobby, the body of the night watchman lay at the foot of the main stairway. Susan saw how his left leg hung sideways below the knee, and how his head had a crooked tilt. How the eyes stared. A horrible sight. A flash unit blinked. The photographer stepped over one of the outstretched arms, and crouched for a shot from a different angle.

Beyond where the body lay, she saw Blumgard, the museum director, talking to a man in a brown suit. A detective, probably. Blumgard looked pale. Jumpy. Even from this distance, she could see the stem of his pipe shaking as he raised it to his lips.

Tag led her toward the body. 'Morning, Farley,' he greeted the photographer.

'Hi, Parker. Isn't this your day off?'

'I'm ever-vigilant. All right if we go upstairs?'

'Help yourselves.'

They climbed the stairway. As they entered the Callahan Room, a small, pale man glanced at them from where he crouched by the coffin lid. He lowered his eyes again and finished pressing a strip of cellophane to an index card.

'Getting some good latents off there?' Tag asked.

'Quite a bunch.'

'A few belong to me and the lady here.'

'That so? You're Porter?'

'Parker.'

39

He wrote the name down. 'And?'

'Susan Connors,' Tag told him. 'She works here.'

'What department?'

'I'm an assistant curator,' she explained. 'This room's my responsibility.'

'Then you must know the missing mummy. Have you talked to Vasquez?'

She shook her head.

Tag turned to her. 'Why don't you have a look round and see if anything else is missing?'

'I have a checklist in my office.'

'Let's get it.'

'Whoa. Before you take off for parts unknown, I want your prints. It'll speed things up for me. You first, Potter. Give me your hand.'

Farley climbed to the second floor. He took a downward shot of the stairs; the body sprawled at the bottom. From his angle, framed by the camera, the stairs looked damned steep. The poor guy must've had quite a time of it. Probably headfirst.

Farley was having quite a time of it himself. Those three glazed doughnuts on his way over had nearly run their course. If he didn't get to the Men's room pretty soon . . . somewhere up here, there had to be one. He walked to the right, checking each door as he approached it. Near the end of the hall, he found one marked WOMEN.

A good omen.

Sure enough, the next door was the one he wanted. He shoved it open, hurried across the tile floor. This one was a three-stall job. He rushed to the first, started to push its door. He met unexpected resistance. Surprised, he took his hand away. The door bumped shut.

'Ooops, sorry.'

He waited for someone to reply.

No one did.

'Y'ought to latch the door, you know, buddy. Hey, you all right in there? Huh?' He waited. 'Anyone in there? Hello?' Squatting, he ducked his head low enough to see under the door. Instead of

Florsheims, he found a pair of brown withered feet. Brown shriveled toenails. Brown bone-thin shins.

He shoved the door open, flinging the mummy backwards. Its head thumped the tile wall behind the toilet, and it slid down, bare feet skidding towards Farley like a mannequin trying to sit down.

Tag jumped aside as the bathroom door shot open and Farley ran out. The photographer stopped short. His face had a sick, gray look.

'What's wrong?' Tag asked.

'I found the missing mummy. In there.'

'I'll go tell Susan.'

They walked up the hallway. Tag noticed how Farley's hand trembled. 'That mummy's a real charmer, isn't she?'

'You've seen her?' Farley asked.

'All of her.'

Farley ran a hand over the sleek top of his head. 'Jeepers creepers. I've photographed all kinds . . . you name it. Gunshot victims, slice and dice, torched corpses, gals with their guts stuffed in their mouths, guys who've been buried in all kinds of shit for years on end . . . but that one?'

'She has that effect on people, doesn't she?'

'Seen prettier.'

'You okay?'

'Sure, just caught me by surprise.' He ran his hand over his head again like he was trying to wipe the image from his brain. 'Aren't mummies supposed to be wrapped? Those ones in the movies, they're always bandaged up nice, you know?'

'This one's a stripper.'

'She looks like crap.'

'The years haven't been kind to her,' Tag admitted, grinning.

He found Susan in the Callahan Room, checking exhibits against the inventory list on her clipboard.

'How goes it?' he asked.

'Looks like everything is here but Amara.'

'She's not far,' Tag said.

'You found her?'

'Farley did.'

'She's all right?'

Farley shook his head. 'She looked like . . . looked terrible. All that red hair. That looks great, but it's how it seems to grow out of the skull . . . makes your stomach . . .' Gulping, he clutched his belly, turned away and wished to God he'd passed on those doughnuts.

Susan hurried down the hall ahead of them. When she reached the restroom door, however, she stopped. She turned to wait for Tag. 'Maybe you should go in first. I mean . . . make sure the coast is clear.'

Farley groaned. 'Miss, the coast won't be clear till she's outta there and I'm afraid I can't wait all day.'

'There's a toilet on the ground floor,' Susan told him. 'Just to the left as you come in.'

'Thanks. Enjoy yourselves.' He hurried to the stairway.

'I'll have a look,' Tag said. He pushed open the door, stepped inside. Nobody at the sinks. Nobody at the urinals. One body in the first stall, its feet visible just below the door. 'Okay,' Tag called. 'You can come in now.'

Susan entered, looking slightly embarrassed. She glanced from the sinks to the urinals.

'Don't believe me, huh?'

'Just checking.'

She walked ahead of Tag to the stall. He watched her crouch and peer under the door, the fabric of her blouse pulling taut across her back, coming untucked from the skirt, showing a band of smooth skin.

'That's Amara, all right,' she said. Standing, she eased open the door.

Tag, just behind her, looked in. The mummy lay straight as a slab of wood with her head against the pipes, her back on the toilet seat, her legs stretched toward the open door, her red hair tumbling down onto the tiles.

'What'll we do with her?' Tag asked.

'Pick her up.'

'Us? Don't you have maintenance men or something?'

'We're the something. Ready?'

'Well . . .'

Amara

'Scared?'

'Who, me?'

'We should wear gloves, so our skin moisture won't . . .'

'Great! Good idea! I'm all for gloves!'

'Back in a flash.' Susan smiled a knowing smile. 'You stay here and keep an eye on her.'

He followed Susan to the door, but stayed inside when she left. Turning, he looked at the stall. He could see the mummy's dark feet and ankles. They were brown. A shiny glossy brown that reminded him of chocolate bars. *Great. Won't want to eat another Hershey bar for a long time coming. Every time I bite into chocolate I'll imagine I'm running my tongue over that four-thousand-year-old foot with its evil-looking toenails. Hell, won't eat almond flakes, come to that.*

He glanced at his wristwatch, hoping Susan would hurry. This was his day off, after all, and standing watch over a withered corpse with brown paper tits wasn't his idea of a good time. He could do that at work; often had.

In fact, this reminded him a lot of his first dead body. It had been in a john, too. Houston, his partner, laughed himself sick at how they found the fat old gal, butt to the wind, head jammed in the waste basket. Said she must be an acrobat. As it turned out, she'd had a heart attack while she was taking a leak and tumbled forward until her head stuck in the waste basket. Tag never could see the humor in it, but Houston wouldn't let it go. Recently, he'd started tying it in with a Polack joke about burying stiffs with their butts up, for parking bikes.

The bathroom door shot open, missing Tag by inches. He stepped out of the way as Maurice Henderson hurried in. 'Parker,' Henderson said, barely giving him a glance as he hurried by.

'How's it going out front?'

'A pain.' At the first urinal, he unzipped his fly.

'You sure you want to do that?' Tag asked.

'Huh?'

'We've got a visitor.' Tag pointed at the stall.

Henderson looked. His face wrinkled as if he smelled something foul. Quickly, he zipped up.

'Meet Amara.'

'Holy Jesus.' Henderson stepped cautiously toward the stall and pushed open its door. For a long time, he stared. 'What the hell's she doing here?'

'Apparently she can't read.'

'Funny. Ha ha. Good God, did you get a look at those tits? Look like flapjacks.'

Someone knocked on the door. 'Come on in, we're all decent,' Tag called.

Susan entered and smiled a greeting at Henderson. 'Glad you're here, Maurice. You wouldn't mind giving us a hand, would you?'

'A hand with what?'

'Amara. We have to move her back to her own room.'

'You mean, *touch* her?'

'That shouldn't bother a couple of tough cops like you.' She held out a pair of gloves to each of them. 'I'll supervise.' Smiling, she stepped to the stall door, pushed it open, and held it in place. 'Once you've snapped on the latex, one of you take her shoulders, one her feet, and we'll just ease her out of here nice and steady.'

'We'd better call in the Homicide boys first.' Tag grinned, glad he'd found a delaying tactic.

'Yeah, Christ. If we screw around with this gal before they've got their pictures and shit . . .' Henderson shook his head.

The homicide team spent less than half an hour in the Men's room. They took statements and photographs, made sketches, lifted fingerprints, vacuumed the tiles under the stall, then left.

'Your turn,' Susan said.

Tag gripped the mummy's thin ankles; Henderson took the shoulders.

'You sure she won't break in half?' Tag asked.

'Maybe you should get her higher on the legs. At the knees?'

'All set,' Tag said.

'All set.' Henderson nodded.

They both lifted.

'She's sure light,' Henderson said, surprised.

'She's been dehydrated,' Susan explained. 'Hollowed out, too.'

'How do you mean?' Henderson asked.

Susan opened the bathroom door and they carried the mummy into the hall. 'They start by removing the brain,' she said. 'They run a probe through the nose, and break through the ethmoid bone into the cranial cavity. Then they use a little hooking device to bring out the brain through the nostrils, piece by piece.'

'Who *is* this woman?' Henderson asked Tag.

'My sweetheart.'

'Lucky you.'

She grinned. 'Once the cranial cavity was cleaned out, they cut into the torso and removed all the organs except the heart. During some dynasties the heart went, too. That's what you'll find in those stone canopic jars beside her coffin: her stomach, liver, kidneys, intes—'

'Susan.'

'You wanted to know why she's light.'

'Now we know,' Tag said.

'How come she isn't wrapped in bandages?' Henderson asked, unable to take his eyes from the shriveled torso. 'I thought they were supposed to wrap these things.'

'They did.' Susan walked ahead of them into the Callahan Room. 'Somewhere along the line, someone removed them from this one.'

'For God's sake, why?'

'We don't know,' Susan replied. 'Okay, you can lower her now. Nice and gently does it. Good. Fine.'

Tag was glad to be rid of the body. He stepped away from the coffin to peel off his gloves.

'Grave robbers might have unwrapped her for her jewelry,' Susan said. 'Or the bandages might have been used to make paper or even medicine.'

'She's making this up,' Tag warned.

Henderson shook his head. 'The sweet nothings she must whisper into your ear at nights, old buddy. It'd give me the heebie-jeebies.'

Susan smiled. 'The paper bit isn't likely. It used to happen, though. In fact, there was an American who got involved in that. A guy named Stanwood, who had a paper mill in Maine. He used mummy wrappings in the nineteenth century for the rag content of his paper. He couldn't get it white, so he sold it to some local butchers for meat wrapping . . . it started a cholera epidemic.'

'A storehouse of knowledge,' Tag said. He turned to the fingerprint man, who was now gaping into the coffin. 'Can we put the lid on now? I guess the old gal could use her privacy.'

The fingerprint man nodded. 'Sure. I'll give you a hand.'

The three men lifted it. As they set it into place on the coffin, Tag saw Susan crouch and pick up a bright chunk of metal. It looked like gold.

'What's that?'

'Part of a seal.' She showed how it fit, like a bit of a jigsaw puzzle into a broken disk of gold on the lid. 'See?'

'It looks like gold.'

'I'm sure it is gold,' she said.

'Right out in the open?'

'This section'll be closed to the public, at least for the time being. We're having a special display case made up for the coffin – with temperature and humidity controls, and a burglar alarm.'

'When will that be ready?'

'In about a week.'

'Hope you still have something to put in it.'

Chapter Seven

Imad woke the girl with his tongue. He licked her breasts, leaving the nipples slick and erect. He licked a trail down her belly. He probed her navel, then the moist cleft between her legs. She stroked his hair as his tongue darted. Soon, her chest was heaving. Her fingers twisted his hair. Her knees lifted and she writhed, rubbing herself against his mouth.

Without stopping, Imad pulled her by the legs. He knelt on the floor at the foot of the bed. He kept pulling. Her buttocks came off the mattress and she slid down, crying out as his stout penis impaled her.

They fell and tumbled. On top of her, Imad finished with quick, hard thrusts that jolted her whole body beneath him.

She hugged him tightly, panting.

'You've earned the bonus,' Imad said.

'Have I?' she gasped.

He pulled slowly out of her, stood up, slipped on his robe.

The girl sat up, her hand against her tingling groin. 'Does that mean we're done?'

He answered with a nod.

'I can stay, if you want.'

'Stay?'

'Sure. One night, maybe, if you want?'

'You can cook?'

'Sure. Want me to make breakfast? I can fix that.'

'All right,' Imad said. 'For the time being, I'll allow you to stay.'

They went downstairs. Imad showed the girl through the kitchen. The vast refrigerator that contained nothing but a bag of salad and a dozen eggs. While she made omelets, Imad went outside and down the long driveway for the newspaper.

The girl turned down the burner under the skillet. She stepped quickly across the kitchen to a telephone. She dialed. Listened to the quiet ringing. The ringing went on for a long time and all the time she listened for the return of the Egyptian who moved like some damned spook.

Hurry up, answer . . . answer . . . he'll be back any moment. If he catches me, he'll—

'Yeah?'

'Blaze, honey, it's me.'

'Hydra? Where the fuck are you?'

'I went home with the camel-jumper.'

'*You what?*'

'Listen. He's got a regular mansion out here in Greenside. I mean, you wouldn't believe it. All these rooms, marble bathrooms, huge TVs. This guy's got so much money it's running out his poop chute. You better haul over.'

'All right!'

'His place is at 285 Greenside Lane. It's got this big wall around it, so you better park outside and climb over.'

'Got it. I'll be over tonight.'

'Why wait?'

'It'll be dark, shithead.'

Hydra heard him laugh. 'What's so funny?'

'What I'm gonna do to that fucking A-rab, that's what. Hope he ain't got claustrophobia, 'cause I'm gonna shove his stinking grease-ball head up his ass for him. By the time I've finished with him, he's—'

'Blaze. Gotta go. I can hear him coming back. See ya tonight.'

Chapter Eight

Shortly before noon, Blumgard called a meeting of the museum staff. Susan took a seat at the long, mahogany table in the conference room. Her stomach rumbled. She glanced sideways at Esther Plum. The prim, silver-haired archivist showed no sign of hearing the noise. If she had heard it, she was the type to pretend she hadn't.

It growled again. More loudly this time. Esther stared at her folded hands.

'Excuse me,' Susan said.

'It's quite all right, my dear.'

'I haven't eaten since seven.'

'I'm sure I couldn't eat a bite, myself, after what happened to that poor man.'

Blumgard entered, shut the door. He stepped to the head of the table.

Susan liked the man. Though he conducted himself with strict formality, he was never quite able to conceal his shyness or his enthusiasm. He loved his work. He cared for those who worked with him, as if they were all partners in a wonderful, shining quest. His eyes were red-rimmed behind his glasses. His hand trembled as he lit his pipe.

'I'm certain,' he began, 'that we're all aware of the tragedy that struck here last night. Barney Quinn was a fine man, a loyal and trusted member of our staff. Many of you never had the pleasure of meeting Barney, since he worked the graveyard shift.' Blumgard's eyes showed that he regretted his choice of words. 'Those of us who did know Barney will miss him.'

He cleared his throat, relieved to be done with that part of the business.

'The police tell me that Barney apparently died of injuries sustained by falling down the central stairway. Whether he fell accidentally or was pushed, they won't say. Or they don't know. Neither do they know how the burglars entered our facility. They found no evidence of forced entry. Therefore, we may assume one of two possibilities: either the robber used a key to gain entry, or they entered with the public and secreted themselves before closing time. I, personally, think the latter possibility the more likely.' He cleared his throat again. 'I also think it likely they will return.'

Esther murmured, 'Oh dear.' Several others at the table frowned and muttered.

'The police suspect youthful vandals may have been responsible. Who else, they said, would attempt to steal a mummy? While their position seems reasonable, in some respects, I have made known my reservations.'

His forefinger curled over the bowl of his pipe and tamped down the loose ashes. 'As many of you know, there has been a recent increase worldwide in thefts of Egyptian antiquities. Some, no doubt, were committed by the same breed who plundered tombs down through the ages in search of personal wealth. This is not the majority, however. It has become increasingly apparent that a great number of these robberies were committed by professionals – Egyptian patriots. Many priceless objects stolen from museums and private collections have been reappearing in Egypt. It's quite possible that those responsible for last night's tragedy had such a destination in mind for our collection . . . a misguided effort to return the mummy, Amara, to her homeland.'

Susan raised a finger, catching Blumgard's attention. 'Yes, Mrs Connors?'

'I think it odd that men like that would remove the mummy from its coffin. From what I've heard of their operations, they'd be more likely to take the coffin – and the whole collection, for that matter.'

'I certainly agree with you. I have no idea why they should see fit to take only the mummy. Nor do I understand why they left so abruptly, taking nothing. Perhaps the police are right in suspecting vandals. I would like us all to assume, however, that this was the work of professional thieves who may return to finish the job they began last night.

'All of us must be on our guard. A word to the docents would certainly be in order. We must keep our eyes open for suspicious behavior, especially as we approach closing time. If you see anything out of the ordinary report it at once to Hank.'

Hank, the daytime security guard, nodded confidently. He looked as if he wanted to grin, but knew it would be out of place at that particular time, with his nighttime counterpart lying cold on the mortuary slab.

'I have contacted the Haymer Security Agency. They will be sending us two armed guards tonight. Hopefully, their presence will discourage any further robbery attempts.'

Blumgard tapped the bit of his pipe against his front teeth. 'Are there any questions or comments regarding this matter?'

Nobody spoke up.

'All right, then. We'll reopen our doors at one p.m.'

Susan bit into her sandwich. The tangy egg-salad filling tasted marvelous. Just enough mustard, just enough ground pepper. Turning the sandwich, she licked the edge where a dollop had squeezed out.

A sound of footsteps made her look up. *Damn.*

She quickly looked away, pretended to concentrate on her sandwich.

Just make eye contact with one of these people and you've had it. They'll hit you up for a quarter, or start jabbering nonsense, or God knows what.

It was the only drawback to eating lunch in the museum park: you had to contend with an assortment of beggars and crazies.

She studied chunks of egg white and pepper in her sandwich as the footsteps came closer. The steps, slow, uneven. In front of her, they stopped.

She didn't look up. Bit into her sandwich. Stared at the woman's black shoes. Broken laces, knotted in a few places. Toes scuffed. Dog turd crusting one heel. Green socks hung limply around her ankles. The ankles looked thick and gray; crimson blotches . . . *Great, my sandwich . . . once it had tasted delicious, but now . . . uh . . .*

Is that ulcer on her shin leaking yellow pus?

'That's it,' snapped a woman's voice. 'Look me over, why don't you?'

Susan raised her eyes to the woman's glowering face. 'I wasn't . . .'

'You're a real petunia, you know that?'

Susan chewed her mouthful, but had a hard time swallowing.

'Think you're prime stuff, don't you?'

'I just want to eat my lunch, thank—'

'Look at you. Look at them clothes. You're a real petunia. Think you're special, don't you? A real princess?'

Susan shook her head, wishing the woman would disappear. 'I don't think anything. I just want to finish my lunch, okay?'

'Where do you get off?'

'Right here,' Susan retorted. Angry, helpless, she stuffed the remaining half of her sandwich into her bag and stood up.

'You ain't going nowhere.'

'I sure am, lady. There's no law I have to sit here and take abuse. So, if you'll—'

She clutched Susan's arm with her big gray paw.

'Damn it! You let go of me!'

The woman's hand shot out, slapping Susan's cheek. 'How's that, huh?' She slapped again. 'How's that? How's a taste of knuckle sandwich for a change?'

Susan's sleeve ripped as she wrenched her arm free. She pushed. The heavy woman stumbled backwards, arms windmilling, a strange growl in her throat. Susan saw the pain on her face as her rump hit the path.

Made her hesitate.

'You okay?' she asked.

The woman kept growling. Lip rising like a canine snarl, exposing gaps where teeth should be, and lousy chunks of enamel and decay where teeth were still rooted into the unhealthy-looking gums.

Susan looked around, feeling guilty, wondering if anyone had witnessed the struggle. Nobody was nearby. She turned again to the woman. 'I'm sorry,' she said, 'but you shouldn't have—'

'Ain't you something?' The woman muttered. 'Knock a person down.' Rolling over, she got to her hands and knees. She stood, brushing leaves from her shabby dress. 'What'd I ever do to you, huh?'

'You hit me for starters. Tore my blouse . . . You ought to be locked up.'

Susan started to leave. Hearing rapid footsteps behind her, she looked back and saw the woman charging. She tried to run, but a hand gripped her collar. It tugged backwards, pulling her off balance. She felt herself hit the concrete. It didn't hurt much, but then the big woman was on her – sitting on her, the big buttocks crushing down on her stomach; the woman pinned down her arms.

'Get off!' Susan twisted, trying to throw the woman off.

'Lay still.'

She began to yell for help, but the woman let go of one arm long enough to smash her in the face.

'Listen here, princess.'

Susan stared at the pale, bloated face, with its cluster of pimples around her mouth, like spotty lipstick. The face broke into an ugly smile, revealing more of those brown teeth stubs.

'You just keep your dirty whore hands off my guy, you hear? You got no right. Keep off. You don't, I'm gonna do a job on you . . . a real thorough job, you understand?'

'You're Mable.'

'That's me, honey.'

'Tag's going to hear about this.'

'He does and you're fer it. You and your runt.' With a smile, she started working her mouth.

Susan knew what was coming. Couldn't believe it. The last person to try such a thing was her older brother when they were little kids, and he'd missed on purpose. Just planning to gross her out a little.

Mable, she realized, didn't plan to miss.

She bucked and twisted as a stream of drool spilled from Mable's mouth. Pressing her lips shut, she turned her head away and closed her eyes. The sticky wetness dropped onto her cheek and rolled toward her ear. She felt its crawling path across her skin.

With a harsh laugh, Mable climbed off.

Susan used her sleeve to wipe away the gelatinous mass. Sitting up, she watched Mable limp away, heavy arms swinging.

Susan got to her feet. Her wet sleeve clung to her arm. Some hair close to her ear was matted. As she bent down to pick up her lunch bag, she caught the sour-milk stench of the woman's spit.

Gagging, she rushed into the bushes.

Chapter Nine

Tag climbed the stairs, careful not to touch the railing. If he could have stopped breathing the moment he entered the building, he would have preferred it; the place smelled like a garbage can. His foot slid as it mashed something on the step. He didn't look down to see what it was. When he reached the second floor, he headed down a hallway to apartment 202.

He couldn't knock on the door without touching it, so he thumped it with the toe of his shoe.

'What you want?'

'Mrs Rudge? This is Officer Parker from the police. I'd like to speak to you.'

'Hang on.'

He waited. The door opened.

Mable's obese mother stood blocking the entry, a cigarette hanging out of her mouth, fists on hips. Her T-shirt and boxer shorts revealed more than Tag ever wanted to see.

'What's your story?' she asked, squinting through the smoke.

'May I come in?'

'Suit yourself. Got nothing to hide.' She stepped backwards, the motion rippling her flesh.

'Is Mable here?'

'See for yourself.'

'I asked you: is she here?'

'I don't see her, do you?'

'Are you aware of her recent activities, Mrs Rudge?'

'You mean do I know you been pronging her? Sure. She's my girl. She don't keep secrets.'

'I haven't been "pronging" her.'

'That ain't what I hear. What I hear, you can't get enough of her.'

'That's not true.'

'That you beg her to do it without no protection.'

'I wouldn't—'

'You should wear protection, you know? Sheaths don't cost the earth.'

'Listen to me—'

'And that you force her to do things that aren't nat-chral for a girl.'

'I've done nothing.'

'From what she says you prong her like some guys prong a farmyard animal.'

'*Listen to me.*'

'Gettin' bloodstains out of underpants ain't no picnic, I can tell you.'

'Listen. I've never had intimate relations with your daughter.'

'Inta-which?'

'I've never pronged her.'

'That a fact?'

'It's a fact.' Tag said, his skin crawling at the thought of it. Him and Mable . . . *hell*.

'Horseshit. Can't trick me. You been layin' it to her, sure as you're standing here. Made her bleed time and again, too, and not jus' from her womanly parts.' A column of ash dropped from the cigarette in Mrs Rudge's mouth. It crumbled to powder on a huge hill of breast, adding a patch of gray to her grimy T-shirt. She batted the ashes off, setting the breast in motion. 'Don't bother me where you stick it. You can stick Mable from now till your dick curls up and drops off, don't offend me. But wear a sheath. I don't want her knocking up. We don't want us a brat around here, crapping the place up.'

'Mrs Rudge, do you want Mable busted?'

She blew smoke out of her nose. Least, she tried. One nostril must have been blocked. Smoke jetted thinly from her left nostril only.

'Mrs Rudge, in the past two days Mable has flattened a tire, assaulted a lady friend of mine, and assaulted me.'

'You?' She grinned.

'That's right.'

'You like the rough stuff? Mable's the girl to dish it.'

'I don't want to arrest her, Mrs Rudge. That's why I came over. I want you to talk to her, explain I'm not interested in having a relationship with her, and let her know she'll be thrown in jail if she pulls one more stunt.'

'How'd you mean that you don't want a relationship with her?'

'I don't want to prong her, screw her, poke her, pork her, touch her. I want her to leave me alone.'

'Yeah?'

'Yes.'

'So you're dumping her?'

'I've never had a relationship with her in the first place.'

'What the matter with you? You queer?'

'I already have a lady friend.'

'No law you can't have two.'

'Thanks, but no, thanks.'

Her eyes narrowed through the billowing smoke that began to burn Tag's throat. 'You telling me you don't like my Mable?'

'Not as a lover.'

'That so?'

'That *is* so.'

'I can see you never done her, then, or you'd be whistling a different tune. You go on and let her show you a time before you start badmouthing her.'

'I'd rather not.'

'Social services guy who had her case couldn't get enough of her. Bought her chocolates for her fifteenth.'

'Mrs Rudge, I'm not interested. Understand that.'

'My Mable, she wants you.'

'Well . . .'

'I like to see her get what she wants.'

'She won't get me,' Tag said.

'Don't go counting on that.' She laughed. 'Shoot, maybe we'll both get you. Good-looking hunk like you. Young and strong. We could make ourselves a cop sandwich, with you in the middle . . . yeah.' She gave him a long look-over. 'I bet you could make us both plenty happy.'

'Give her my message, please.'

'I guess she'll get back any minute now. How about you wait, tell her yourself? Beer in the cooler?'

'No, thanks.'

A mean look turned her eyes to slits. 'Don't, then. Who wants you, anyhow?' She flicked her cigarette butt at his face.

Tag flinched away. The burning stub nicked his ear.

'Good-bye, Mrs Rudge,' he said. 'Please remember to pass on what I've told you to Mable.'

On his way out he noticed the cigarette smoldering a black hole in the carpet. He mashed it dead with his heel, then walked away without looking back.

Chapter Ten

'How did it go?' Susan asked.

'Not so good. Old Mother Rudge thinks Mable and I would make a handsome couple.'

Susan grinned. The bruised side of her face felt stiff, but didn't hurt much.

'You could simplify things by pressing charges,' Tag said.

'I know, I know.' She bounced Geoffrey on her knee. He grinned and giggled.

'You shouldn't feel sorry for Mable.'

'I can't help it.'

María came into the room, beaming and carrying a margarita. She handed it to Tag. 'You make the best in the world,' he told her.

'The best! *Sí. Gracias*, Señor Tag.'

When she left, Susan said. 'Can you imagine what it must be like being Mable?'

'I'd rather not.'

'What does a woman like that have to look forward to?'

'Prison, more than likely.'

'I mean it. She hasn't got a thing going for her. I had a friend like that in college. She wasn't mean like Mable, but she looked exactly like her. We were roommates my first year at Weston and I got a pretty good idea what it must be like. Everybody stared at her all the time. She was the butt of a thousand awful jokes, mostly behind her back, but she knew what was going on. When it came time to rush, she gave it a try, but none of the sororities would touch her. That's the main reason I didn't pledge. If they could be that cruel, I wanted nothing to do with them.

'She never had a boyfriend. Guys dated her, sometimes.' Susan shook her head. Anger and sadness. 'It was just like a big joke to them, though. None of them gave a damn about her. They just knew she was an easy screw. They didn't care how ugly she was, as long as she put out. They treated her horribly. One night, some guys got her drunk and passed her round. When she came back to the room she could hardly walk. She was bleeding. She couldn't stop crying. I stayed up with her, the whole night, because I was afraid she might do something. You know, slash her wrists or something?

'The next day, I helped take her things to the railroad station. She got on the train and she never came back.'

Tag frowned, staring at the drink. 'What happened to her?'

'I don't know. I never heard from her again. But Mable makes me think of her, you know? I figure her life is tough enough without me trying to get her locked up.'

'Know something, Susan?'

'What?'

'You're a pretty nice lady.'

'Am I?'

'I want to take the nice lady out to dinner.'

'Sounds good.'

'I'll go upstairs and get into a suit.'

'Ah, a *dinner* dinner.'

'Right. Complete with necktie.'

'A necktie party! How exciting. I'd better make myself spiffy, then.'

'I'll give you fifteen minutes.'

'Half an hour.'

'Twenty minutes.'

'You're driving a hard bargain, Parker.'

A red-coated teenager was waiting in the restaurant's driveway. 'He's not gonna get his hands on *my* car,' Tag said and kept driving. He found an empty stretch of curb a block away.

In the restaurant, the maitre d' led them to a corner table.

'A libation?' Tag asked. 'Pepsi, Perrier, Mountain Dew?'

'I think I'll break down and have a real drink.'

'Don't break down at my table.'

A waiter came. Susan ordered a vodka gimlet, Tag a margarita. The waiter returned quickly with the drinks.

'To the most beautiful mummy in town,' Tag said.

'Amara?'

'You.'

They sipped their drinks. It was a good gimlet: strong, and easy on the Roses lime. 'Hmmm, this's my first in over a year,' Susan admitted.

'See what you've missed.'

'It'll probably go straight to my head, and I'll get giggly.'

'I've never seen you giggly.'

'Not a pretty sight.'

'I can't believe that.'

'Shameless flatterer.'

'I don't want this going to your head, but I think you're the most beautiful, charming, intelligent and sensitive woman I've known since my childhood sweetheart, Gretchen Stump.'

'Gretchen, huh? You always keep throwing her in my face.'

'She's hard to forget. You run a close second, though. Really. And you do have an advantage over her.'

'I'm honored you should think so.'

'She had one flaw.'

'You never let on.'

'Yes. Gretchen had a backwards eye. Looked in, not out. She was always fond of it, said it helped her see what was on her mind. Hideous to look at, though. Looked like a peeled tomato with a piece of spaghetti dangling down.'

'That's disgusting.'

'You should see what we had to do to keep it moist.'

'That's *really* disgusting.'

'I would've married her, except for the eye. Yours look fine, though.'

'Thanks.'

'So . . .' He shook his head. Even though he was still smiling the glint of mischief left his eyes.

'So?' Susan asked.

'Have you decided what to order?'

'What were you about to say?'

'Well, it would've been tacky under the circumstances. I mean . . . I shouldn't have brought Gretchen into it.'

'Into what?'

'Susan, how would you like to marry me?'

She sat back, stunned. She stared at him. 'You mean, you want . . .'

Tag nodded. 'Since you don't have a backwards eye . . .'

She laughed, but the laughter sounded strange and far away in her ears, and then Tag was blurry and she realized she was crying.

He started to talk. 'Of course, we'll have to wait for your divorce to become final, but that shouldn't be more than a few weeks. What do you think?'

'I . . . I . . . well, it's such a . . . Are you sure?'

'I'm sure I want to spend my life with you.'

'Oh Tag.' She grabbed her napkin. 'I'm sorry. I . . . here I am, falling apart . . . and you . . . you told me not to break down at your table.'

'I'll forgive you this time.'

'What . . . what about Geoffrey?'

'I'll be the best father I can.'

'Tag, Jeez . . .'

'How about it?'

'Are you sure? I mean you . . . do you know what you're getting into?'

'Does that mean your answer is yes?'

'I suppose it does, huh? Yes. My God! I can't . . . Wow! I don't know what to say.'

'I think you've already said it.' He picked up his margarita. 'To us.'

'Mr and Mrs Taggart Parker.'

They drank. Then Susan set down her gimlet and wiped her eyes. 'I must look a fright.'

'You look fine. Ready to order?'

'Not till I've . . . sheesh, my hands won't stop shaking. Why don't you get us another round of drinks? I'll go freshen up.'

During dinner they made plans. Both wanted a simple wedding. Both wanted only a family and a few close friends attending. They decided to move into Susan's apartment, since it was larger than Tag's. They would keep his bed; it was larger. Her chest of drawers; his was decrepit. His stereo system; her CD player skipped tracks all of its own accord. Both TV sets, both VCRs, both cars; neither microwave oven (both were glitchy as hell). They pretended to argue about Tag's favorite chair, a maroon monster that dropped stuffing from its tattered cushion.

'I won't let it inside till it's housebroken,' she said.

'We can put newspapers under it.'

'You have to promise to clean up after it.'

Susan finished her last bite of prime rib and excused herself.

'Going to freshen up again?' Tag asked.

She nodded. Instead of freshening up, however, she went to the cashier. Through the glass of the display case, she studied an array of cigars. She decided on an Antony and Cleopatra because of its romantic name.

Back at the table, she presented it to Tag. 'To go with your coffee,' she said.

He turned the cigar slowly in his fingers, smelt it appreciatively, then looked at Susan and beamed. 'I think we'll get along just fine,' he said.

They took the elevator to the third floor of the Marina Towers. Holding hands, they walked down the narrow corridor to Susan's room.

A dead cat was hanging from her doorknob by a hind leg. Blood still trickled from its neck. It had no head.

Crooked words on the door dripped like wet paint:

> *THIS PUSSY STANK*
> *YOU DO TOO*
> *SEE YOU DED PITUNYA*

Chapter Eleven

Such a bitch! And what a bitch. A Grade A bitch. A gold-medal bitch. An Oscar-winning bitch . . . he couldn't believe what he was hearing.

'Wait a minute, Janey. Let me get this straight.'
'There's nothing to get straight, Ed!'
'But—'
'No buts, no excuses.'
'Janey, I never even touched her, never mind—'
'Screwed her?'
'Yes.'
'So you admit it?'
'No, of course not.'
'Liar.'
'Listen, Janey, someone's been *lying* to you. I love you. I—'
'Yeah, some way to show it.'
'It's true.'
'The moment my back's turned . . .'
'Janey.'
'. . . You screw my best friend.'
'She's making it up.'
'Yeah, as if.'
'She is. Listen, Janey, she's been trying to break us up.'
'Why would she do a thing like that?'
'Because she's jealous.'
'Oh, right.'

'She was always hanging out with you. Now we are together, she's been pushed out. At least, that's what she thinks.'

'The phrase is *"were together"*, Ed.'

'So you are dumping me?'

'See, you are smarter than you look.'

'But out here?'

'Yep.'

'Aw, come on, Janey. We're miles out of town.'

'Should have thought of that before you got all sticky-dicky with Pamela.'

'Jesus, I've told you. I never.'

'Like she made up that mole on your inner thigh?'

'Hell, Janey. She could have seen that in the pool.'

'Yeah, like she'd stare at your legs through binoculars when you go swimming.'

'Might've done.'

'Might've nothing, you two-timing rat.'

'Janey?'

'Enjoy the walk, rat boy.'

'Janey, this is insane – you can't just dump me out here. Janey! *Janey!*'

Ed Lake was conversing with dust. Janey slammed down on the gas in her open-top 4X4; she was gone. Dust showed as a white billowing cloud in the moonlight and all Ed could see of the car were its lights traveling like a fireball down the canyon.

Great, oh great. Not only does she dump me, she dumps me here.

And 'here' was a barren hillside road ten miles from home.

Got to do some walking, Eddie boy.

'Don't call me Eddie,' Ed grunted under his breath. 'Whatever you do, don't call me Eddie.'

The moon lit the blacktop in front of him. At least he could see.

His sense of direction should get him home before sunup.

But, hell, there was some walking to do.

No time like the present, Eddie boy.

He set off. With the time close to midnight it was silent. There were no cars. No houses that he could make out. Just road, dusty hillside, stars, a moon. And Eddie Lake. Just been dumped by the girl he loved.

Ouch. Just thinking that made him hurt inside.

Don't it sting, Eddie boy? Rejection? Being dumped?

'Don't call me Eddie,' he grunted to himself.

And walked.

Walked fast. Angry. Angry at being dumped. Angry at Pamela, Janey's so-called best friend, who'd been spoon-feeding the lies. Those damn lies that Janey had swallowed so easily.

Damn.

Ouch – being dumped hurt. And so unfair. He couldn't believe it.

Janey had been nice earlier, so sexily nice. Whispering into his ear that they should drive out here where it was quiet. She'd suggested that before. They'd made out in her open-topped car, her long legs wrapped around his back. Her soft lips finding his in the dark and pressing passionately, her tongue working, while he stroked her bare breasts, running his fingertips over her nipples, feeling her body encircle his . . .

No, don't think that now. Concentrate on following the road home. He walked angrily again. She'd lured him out here just to dump him out in the wilds.

Ed Lake had just finished his sophomore year at Riverside High. He was sixteen. The proud owner of a VW Bug that he was carefully resurrecting nut by bolt in his parents' garage. And yes: deeply in love for the first time. Now the bitch had gone and . . . hell, the bitch had dumped him right there in the . . .

Uh, hello. What's that?

He stopped. Stared.

That didn't make sense. The hillside was strewn with big boulders. Now two of the boulders were moving.

He strained his eyes at the pale bumps and shaded hollows. He tried to make the most of the moonlight, but apart from the straight man-made lines of the road everything at either side of it was a random jumble of shapes.

But he'd swear to it. Two of those boulders were moving. They weren't rolling either like in a landslide, but sliding along . . . almost creeping.

Boulders? Boulders didn't creep.

People crept. Murderers crept.

Eddie, don't let your imagination fool with you.

'Don't call me Eddie.' He tried to sound flippant enough to stop the shivers but it didn't work.

The shivers came. His stomach felt as if it shriveled in on itself.

Janey didn't seem that important anymore.

All of a sudden he realized it was more than just annoying to be dumped out in the wilderness.

Heck, it might be dangerous, too. He wore expensive clothes. The watch on his wrist flashed in the moonlight.

A mugger might just want to check out whether or not it was a Rolex.

Ed walked.

The hunched boulder-shapes moved, too. Now he convinced himself that they were a pair of muggers.

But muggers don't hang around out on barren mountainsides, do they? They lurk in city alleyways or haunt movie-theater parking lots where there are people to prey on.

Here, there was nothing to mug apart from rabbits.

He walked faster . . . worked hard to stop running. Once you run they know they've spooked you. That's when they start running, too. Running to pounce on their victim.

And you're the victim, Eddie boy. That was the voice inside his head reinforcing the obvious.

The hill road angled downward now. Ahead the barren hillside gave way to lower-lying land filled with scrub. Beyond that were trees; the makings of a wood.

He walked, feeling perspiration roll across his skin beneath his shirt. He loosened a couple of buttons. But the night was too hot to cool him.

Hell, I'm gonna give Janey a piece of my mind. Pamela's not going to get away scot-free, either. I'm gonna get my own back for this one.

If I ever get the opportunity.

He glanced to his right up the hill as the two hunched figures moved toward him. They moved faster now, aiming to cut him off.

Probably gonna cut you up, too.

Now he did start to run, his feet slapping down against the blacktop, his arms flailing. Breath came in spurts through his throat.

He looked up at the jumble of shadows. He couldn't make out details, but the two shapes sped down at him. They were too fast. He couldn't outrun them. Jesus, he couldn't even scream to anyone nearby for help. He'd be at their mercy.

Jesus H. I'm only sixteen. Sixteen! I only lost my cherry three months ago. They're gonna bury my bones in the dirt at the side of the road, I'm never gonna—

'Leave me alone!' he yelled as the figures broke out from the shadows.

He stopped as the pair ran in front of him, cutting off his escape route.

He stared.

Rubbed his eyes.

Then laughed out loud.

A pair of goats ran across the road, hooves clattering, their horns glinting in the moonlight.

Christ, he really was out in the wilderness. Wild goats! They were as scared as he was. They ran, kicking their back legs, stirring up puffs of dust as they vanished under the bushes.

Now, when you're sixteen there are certain things you don't want people to see. One is what you do in the bath. Another is blushing when a girl speaks to you. Another is the diary you keep hidden under the bed. And then there's this one. Running in terror from a couple of runty little goats.

Jeez. He could just imagine his friends falling around laughing if they ever heard about this.

Not that they would.

This is just between me and you two goats, he thought to himself, grinning. *I won't tell if you don't. Scaring each other in the middle of the night, huh? What a trio of saps.*

Easier in his mind now, Ed carried on walking, this time with a hand casually in his pocket and sometimes whistling a few notes from a song. The air was still. There wasn't a sound, and the moon still burned with a bright cold witch-fire in the sky.

The road leveled out. Soon the boulders were gone, then it was scrubby bushes. Half a mile after that came the trees that crept closer to the road, shutting it in until only a split full of stars showed overhead.

He glanced at his watch. One a.m. His parents might have woken up and realized he wasn't at home. But they treated him like a mature adult. They trusted he wouldn't do anything stupid. So maybe they wouldn't worry yet. He hoped not.

His feet whispered across the road surface. He was maybe averaging four miles an hour. He guessed eight miles separated him from home. If he kept up this speed then two hours from now would see him slipping his key into the front door.

That didn't seem so bad.

Ed Lake heard the whisper of leaves.

Then he heard another whispery sound.

This was someone breathing.

Someone close by.

He sensed a presence right behind him.

Turning, he saw a shadow there.

The shadow swung an object.

One that hurt far more than the pain of being dumped by Janey.

He just had time to clutch the side of his head before the shadows swamped him.

Ed Lake opened his eyes. There were bars. Bars going up and down with thinner bars running from left to right. It looked like a fisherman's net made out of steel.

The first phrase that went through his mind was *Holy shit!*

He reached out to touch the bars. Bad move. Any kind of movement made his head hurt like hell. He touched his temple. Felt crisped stuff there. It matted his hair.

Dried blood. He figured that much.

This time he kept his head still and allowed his eyes to do all the moving.

Still hurt his head, though.

But he persisted.

Through the bars he saw white-painted walls. Light came from fluorescent strips in the ceiling. So he was in a room.

In a cage.

Holy shit! I've been knocked unconscious and dumped in a freaking cage. Now what?

His mouth tasted like a hog had crapped in it. His watch had gone from his wrist . . . mugged . . . *But why put me in a cage?*

Fresh meat for the tiger.

This thought made Ed sit up. His mind spiraled. He wanted to vomit. The pain rocketed through his skull . . . but he had to check.

See that there weren't any hungry tigers in the cage with him.

Already he could feel their teeth in him. Chomping down. Tearing. Ripping. The pain . . .

'Yeee-ow! Take it easy.'

'What?'

'You got yourself a nice whacko on the skull there, buddy. You should lie down for a while.'

'W-what'd y . . . ya do that for?' Ed's words came stuttering out as his head spun.

'I ain't done nothing, buddy. I'm just your roomie.'

'Where . . .'

'Here. Next pen to yours.'

Ed took a deep breath. The room slowed its spinning. His eyes focused and he found himself looking through the bars of the cage at another cage identical to his. Eight by four, while maybe six feet high. Steel bars. Objects dangled by cords from the roof bars. His eyes located its occupant.

A guy of around twenty with blue eyes and blond dreadlocks grinned back at him. The guy lay on his side, one elbow propping him up. There was a match gripped between his teeth.

The blond guy lay grinning at Ed for a while. Then he said, 'Well, buddy . . . welcome to the beast house.'

'Beast house?'

'We're the beasts.'

'I don't understand.' His head ached so much he wanted to vomit. 'Beast house?'

Amara

The blond guy leisurely slapped the bars of his cage. 'We're in the pens, buddy, so we must be the beasts.'

'Shit.'

'Head sore?'

'Like you wouldn't believe.' Groaning, Ed sat up.

'It'll pass.'

'Yeah?'

'Did for me.' The other prisoner used his fist to mimic a clubbing motion against his blond head. 'I got double whacko. Here and here.' He pointed. 'They had to stitch my scalp. You got off lightly, pal.'

'Yeah, feels like it.' Ed retched.

'Clean it up with toilet tissue and dump it in the bowl.'

'Huh?'

'The plastic bowl there in the corner of your penthouse suite, sir. That's the bathroom facility.'

'You said, "They had to stitch my scalp." Who are *they*?'

The blond guy didn't answer. 'Speak a little lower. Sleeping beauty gets grumpy if you wake her.'

Still dazed, Ed looked round. Another cage around three feet from the end of the one he occupied was separated from it by a walkway of sorts. Angling his head, he saw a mound beneath a red blanket. A hand attached to a slender wrist protruded. From one end coils of heavy red hair spilled over the foam mattress and onto the floor. Ed looked at the contours of the blanket, guessed there was a curving hip under there that shaped it.

Girl, he told himself. A girl with exotic red hair.

I wonder what she looks like . . .

He pulled back from his own curiosity.

Inappropriate or what, Eddie? You're in a cage. It's not the time to think woman, *it's time to think* out!

'Don't call me Eddie,' he murmured to himself.

'What's that you say, buddy?'

Ed looked at the blond dreadlocks. They reached down the guy's back to his rump. Dazed, Ed shook his head.

'Nothing.'

The guy gave an easy wave. 'The name's Marco. You?'

'Ed Lake.'

'Yo, Eddie. Welcome aboard.'

With a groan Ed lay down on the foam mattress. His head ached.

'You best get some rest while you can, Eddie boy,' Marco told him.

'Why? We going somewhere?'

'Nope.' The guy grinned. 'But you're sure to get a visitor soon.'

'What kind of visitor?' Ed didn't like the sound of that.

'You'll see.'

'Yeah.'

'So rest. Get your strength back.' The grin widened. 'Believe me, you're gonna need it. You're gonna need every drop.' The last sentence amused the guy and he began to chuckle.

He was still chuckling when the lights went out, plunging the room into darkness.

Chapter Twelve

The dog howled at the moon. Every night the old man had come to the parking lot, called softly, 'George . . . where are you, boy? Here, George. See what I've got for you.' The dog would speed out of the shadows across the lot, past the single car that still carried the odor of the old man, and to the foot of the fire-escape steps.

There the old man would open up a bag. Inside would be chop bones, the remains of cold cuts or even raw hamburger. This had gone on longer than the dog could remember.

Night after night. The old man smelling of strange odors like ancient bones. The man would feed him there at the back of the museum, make a fuss of him. But he wasn't there tonight. There were more lights in the building than usual. The dog's keen ears picked up voices where there were usually none. Even though the big brown dog could clearly make out the voices of the strangers, he couldn't understand the words.

Certainly none of the all-important words in his vocabulary.
George. Food. Walk. Play. Here, boy. Good boy. Roll over.
Instead:
'They're paying us to do what?'
'See that no one makes off with some old dame in the coffin.'
'Jesus H . . . Amara? That her name?'
'Search me.'
'This place is like a tomb anyway.'
'Say that again. Those stone statues are creeping me out.'

'Did you know the guy?'

'Who?'

'Guy who took a dive down the stairs.'

'Uh-huh – Barney Quinn.'

'Wasn't he on the force?'

'Sure, but they kicked his sorry butt out.'

'So, what'd he do?'

'Got careless.'

'What? Poked the Police Chief's wife?'

'Nah, not even the Chief'd do a thing like that.'

'That ugly?'

'Hell, yes.'

'What this Quinn do, then?'

'Accepted a little cash here and there in return for turning a blind eye to some whorehouses.'

'Hard darts.'

'Could happen to anyone.'

'Whoa, Beckerman, sounds close to home.'

'None of your business. Go check on the Greek room again.'

'I was only—'

'Yeah, only poking your great schnozzola in deep where it doesn't belong.'

Tilting his head to one side, the dog out in the lot heard the voices recede with the footsteps. Two men walking in the building. One small and thin. One thickset and limping.

The dog padded up to the rear doors, put his nose to the crack between door and jamb and sniffed hard, pulling the cool air from inside the big stone pile into his sensitive nostrils. George smelled the musty odors again. Ancient bones. Stone and wood artifacts from faraway places. Faraway times. Handled by many different hands.

George smelled the two strangers patrolling the museum in place of his old friend who'd appear every night with food. The strangers smelled of the tortillas they'd wolfed down before the start of the shift. The dog even smelled the scent of woman on the fingers of one of them where he'd rolled his wife's sister during a little afternoon delight.

George's sense of smell was keen, picking up the scent of three-thousand-year-old goatskin on which was inscribed verses from the Egyptian *Book of the Dead*. His hearing was phenomenal. Heard the tick of the clock in Blumgard's office. Heard the two guards' footsteps on the upper floor. His eyesight was good too, far better than humans allowed. He could see the flutter of tiny moths against lighted windows three stories above his own shaggy brown head.

But there was more.

Much more.

A sense humans could only guess at.

Not identify. Not prove.

George possessed a sixth sense. Inside the building he sensed something stir. Something dark. Something terrible. Something vengeful. Something with the capacity to terrify, maim. Kill.

He sensed it stir again. Sensed dark purpose. He sensed it ready to move again soon.

The dog threw back his head and howled at the cold moon.

Chapter Thirteen

'Don't waste your time. They're set in concrete.'

Ed Lake glanced up at Marco as the blond-haired man shook his head.

'They're set in tight. The doors are double-padlocked. All the bars are welded together . . .'

Ed heaved at a bar.

'. . . So you won't be able to even bend one.'

Damn. The man was right. But it wouldn't stop Ed from trying. After a while Marco shook his head. 'You should listen to me.'

'Why? I want out, don't you?'

'You should save your strength like I told you, buddy. You're going to need it.'

Ed tried kicking at the bars but whoever had dumped him here had removed his shoes. All he did was hurt his toes. The bars didn't budge.

'Save your strength,' Marco repeated. Then he sat down, with his back to Ed.

In frustration Ed slammed the cage door with his hand. It made a ringing sound. Fuming, he stood for a moment, but could only straighten so far because of the height of the cage ceiling. He had to stoop. His back began to ache. The pain started in his head again, too, where he'd been struck.

Ed took stock.

I was walking along the woodland road. Someone sockoed me. Out cold, I was brought to the building, dumped in the cage. When I came to, I talked to my roomie who looks a little kooky to me. Then the lights went out. I slept. I woke hours later when the lights came back on. How many hours I don't know.

So, I'm looking at the cage again. It's around eight feet by four. Six high. Welded steel bars set in concrete. Sawdust bowl for a toilet. Foam mattress is a bed. Otherwise bare as a rhino's butt. Hanging from cords tied to the cage roof bars are your fundamental toilet items: hairbrush, toothbrush, mirror (the kid's kind, made from harmfree plastic); then there's a water bottle (also plastic), mouthwash, deodorant, talcum powder, facecloth and Bible.

The cage's appearance with all those items tied to the cords made Ed think of fruit hanging on vines.

When he crossed the cage he had to push them aside so he left a path of toiletries and the Holy Bible swinging backwards and forwards.

He looked up. A narrow walkway with a handrail ran around the wall some six feet off the ground. That would allow a person to simply step from the walkway onto the roof of the cage.

The cage ceiling's strange as well.

Half of it, where there were no bars, was clear Perspex. Very thick. *Certainly couldn't put my fist through it. Probably bulletproof.*

'Wasting your time, Eddie . . . no way out.'

'At least I'm trying, Marco.'

'Your funeral, bud.'

'Yeah?'

'Should save your strength.'

'Why?'

''S gonna be put to the test soon.'

'How?'

Marco shrugged and went back to examining the end of the match he was chewing.

'What's going to happen, Marco?'

'You don't listen to my advice, bud, so why should I waste my breath?'

Restless, Ed examined the cage again. He'd not noticed earlier but there was a section of false Perspex ceiling. This lay just a few inches beneath the roof proper of the cage. This chunk of Perspex was maybe two inches thick, seven feet long and just over two wide. It was suspended from the cage roof by what looked like a substantial bolt in each corner. Looking at them more closely he saw something like windlasses connected to each bolt. The windlass mechanism sat on top of the cage roof. He recalled the windlasses he'd seen on his uncle's sailboat. You turned the handle to raise and lower the main sail.

'Hey . . . hey, Marco, can this section of Perspex be raised and lowered by turning the handles?'

'That's what you figure?'

'Yes.'

'You figure right, Eddie.'

'And what's this aperture in the roof of the cage?'

'Figure it out.'

'I'm asking you, Marco.'

Marco said nothing but sat with his back to Ed, his spine up against the cage bars.

'Marco . . . Marco?'

Marco didn't reply.

Just kept that broad back of his turned to Ed.

'Marco, why won't you answer? Marco?'

'He won't answer because he's saving his strength. He might be next.'

Ed turned to see who spoke. He saw that in the next cage a figure had partly emerged from beneath the red blanket. He found himself looking at a high-cheekboned face. Green eyes gleamed at him, while tumbling down over shoulders – *bare shoulders* – was thick red hair.

Ed caught his breath. Sheesh, the woman was beautiful.

Around twenty-five years of age, he guessed. There was something about the firm shape of her lips that suggested experience. The directness of her gaze reinforced that line of thought.

She stared back at him. 'You ask questions. You rattle the bars of the cage. You don't give anyone a chance to get some shut-eye, do you?'

'Who are you?'

'More questions.'

'You'd be the same . . . I – I mean what are we doing here? Who brought us here? What—?'

She touched her lips. 'Shh. You should listen to Marco. Get some rest.'

'But why? What's—?'

'Why, what, when? There you go again.'

'But what is—?'

'Listen to me. It could be your turn next. You'll need your strength.'

She lay there raised up on one elbow, the blanket covering her.

Ed walked to the end of the cage that was nearest to hers, squatted down. The eyes burned back into his; beads of green ice. 'But how long have you been here?' he asked.

'Hard to tell. We've no way of telling the time. Can't tell night from day.'

'But you've seen who's holding you here?'

'Sort of.'

'Jesus.' He ran his fingers through his hair. 'This is kidnap. They can't do this.'

'I know.' She spoke casually, almost disdainfully. 'The cops would arrest, the courts would convict. But until they're caught what're we gonna do?'

Marco spoke up. 'What we gonna do? I'll tell you what we *have* to do. Play their game the way they want it played, otherwise we're dead.' He lay down on the mattress and covered himself with a blanket.

'Marco's right,' she said. 'Play along.'

She moved on the mattress to get comfortable. The blanket slipped down, exposing the top of her breast. Ed saw the smooth, milk-white mound. Found himself trying to catch a glimpse of nipple. She looked *great*. Even in this deepest of deep crocks of shit he saw that. She saw Ed's interest. He blushed, looked back up into her face. Her gaze searched his face, appraising him.

'You ever acted in a play?' she asked.

Strange thing to ask in a situation like this.

'Ever been in a play?'

He nodded. '*Dracula*. We staged it in school last year.'

'Good. If you can act you've got a chance to survive when it's your turn.'

'Chance to survive. Why? What's going to happen?'

'Questions again. We're not here as schoolteachers. We're victims. Do you understand that? We're—'

'Please tell me,' he said. 'If I'm going to get through whatever this is, I need your help.'

She sighed. 'It doesn't happen every day but from time to time, we—'

'Hey!'

The suddenness of the lights going out again caught Ed by surprise. In the darkness he heard the woman catch her breath. From behind him Marco spoke. 'Whatever's going to happen's going to happen now, buddy. Prepare yourself.'

Ed Lake shivered as he crouched there. The darkness suddenly seemed cold against his skin. Drafts stirred through his hair. He looked round with wide eyes.

Saw nothing.

The darkness was total.

Air played over his skin again. Shivers ran down his back. His whole body seemed to shrivel inside.

What was happening?

More importantly, what would happen to him?

Not to be able to see. Hell, he didn't like this.

There could be anyone out there in the room. Guys with guns. Guys with knives. Or maybe a noose to slip round his neck.

The drafts came again. A sense of movement from above. Door opening. But still no light.

Door closing.

Footsteps.

Footsteps descending stairs.

His own breathing grew loud. Jerky. Frightened gasps. His heart hammered loud in his chest.

Holy Christ. What's gonna happen? What they gonna do to me?

Rustling sounds. The sound of clothes?

He didn't know. But it seemed close.

Maybe they'd open the door of his cage. Could he strike out, then run?

But where? This darkness. He couldn't see a thing. But how could the person who entered the room see where they were going? Nightscope goggles, maybe.

They'd see Ed crouching there, looking right and left, up and down, his eyes gleaming silver disks in the infrared light, his lips a black slash across his face. Using nightscope goggles they'd see him, all right. But he couldn't see them.

He hugged his knees close into his chest. His muscles ached with the tension. His teeth chattered.

Then he heard a whispering voice. He was sure it wasn't the girl or Marco. No . . . wait . . . he tried to make out if . . . no, he couldn't even tell if it were male or female.

The whisper continued. It seemed to be giving instructions to someone.

Maybe to him.

But he couldn't make out the words. The whisperer was very low, hoarse-sounding.

Wait. He heard the girl speak.

'Yes.' At least, that was what he thought he heard her say, but her voice was low, too. There was something intimate about the conversation between the two. They talked as if to keep it private from Marco and himself.

Maybe he should speak up?

No.

Don't do that.

Keep out of it, otherwise it might bring the whisperer to you. And there was something about the whisperer that made his skin crawl.

This was bad. Baaa-aaad.

The whispering voice was terrifying. It whispered instructions. Orders. Commands.

Something had to be obeyed.

The . . .

Silence.

All Ed could hear was his own respiration.

In.

Out.

In.
Out . . .
And his heartbeat. Pounding.
He struggled to slow his breathing. Struggled to listen.
Had the whisperer gone? There was no movement. No sounds.
Certainly no more whispered commands.
Maybe he should speak now? Ask the other two what had happened. The whisperer had vanished. They were alone now.
The sudden shriek rocked him backwards.
It came again. He covered his ears. Tried to shut it out.
Silence.
Then another scream. A sighing one that started high then descended into a low moan.
He turned to the source of the sound. But there was only velvet darkness pressing against his eyes.
Jesus, sweet Jesus, what's happening?
A cry. Then three more in quick succession. *Ah! Ah! Ah!*
That was the green-eyed girl. Had to be. He recognized the voice.
Then: *'Please!'*
Sure, it had to be her.
'Please!'
Then another cry.
Was she in pain?
Or was someone screwing her?
Because he heard her breathy moans. Heard a loud intake of breath, then another cry followed by a quivering, *'Oh, God, please . . . please!'*
He sat in the darkness, listening. But not sure what it was that he was hearing. OK, it could be pain.
But it sounded like sex. He remembered Janey's panting cries when he thrust into her. Those moans of pleasure when he worked his tongue around her nipples; her breathless *'Please'* when she begged for more. She'd pull his head to her breasts, panting, *'Please . . . suck harder.'*
'Oh . . . oh . . . I – I. *Please!*'
This *'Please'* came, he imagined, through gritted teeth. A *Please* pushed out as sensation overwhelmed her.

God, yes, this sounded like sex.

His heart beat faster. For a different reason now.

A warm flush spread through him. He felt himself hardening.

He couldn't believe his reaction. Felt betrayed by it. Embarrassed.

But the beautiful woman with the erotic green eyes had aroused him when her blanket had slid down to expose part of her bare breast.

Now that he heard her experiencing a white-knuckle ride of sex in the raw . . . this was something else. With her every pant, every cry, he felt himself harden to the point where he needed to do something about it.

He imagined her full white breast quivering. Her hair lashing as her head whipped from side to side in the throes of ecstasy.

Jesus . . .

Oh, Jesus.

Sweet, sweet Jesus.

If she didn't stop making those sounds soon he'd explode.

Panting, moaning, gasping cries, shrill squeals. It made him tingle all over. He wanted—

Christ, he wanted—

Then it was suddenly over.

Silence.

For moments nothing, but the sound of his heart seemed to come right back at him from the walls.

A moment after that the lights came on.

Ed blinked.

Straightaway, his eyes went to the cage that contained the woman.

And there she was.

He looked, unable to stop his gaze darting all over her, taking in every tiny detail. He leaned forward until his face pressed against the bars, staring at her, trying to process and understand what he now saw in front of him.

His gaze traveled down her from head to toe. Her back was to him. She knelt on the floor, her face to the bars.

She was naked apart from a pair of denim cut-offs. These were cut high, revealing the swelling mounds of her buttocks. The back pocket had been torn almost off and dangled down, reaching the back of her leg. Her legs were long and shapely. Even from this angle he could tell that. With white skin. Milk-white.

He found his gaze traveling up from the bare soles of her feet, the toes resting against the floor, up her thighs, up over the smooth curve of her buttocks, tightly clad by pale denim. Then to her bare back. The toned skin that looked so smooth and flawless. A little further up it disappeared beneath a swathe of copper hair.

She did not move. She didn't make a sound; she just knelt there, her face pressed against the bars of the cage. Her two slender arms were raised above her head. Her fingers curled about the rounded shaft of the bars. There was something erotic about the grip. Gently encircling. He shivered with pleasure.

Unable to take his eyes from her, he watched.

This went on for whole moments.

Then she moved.

Turning, she faced him, still in that kneeling position. She looked exhausted.

His gaze traveled up from her cut-off jeans. The fastening button was gone. The zipper had slipped down a little in a V of soft blue material, exposing creamy skin. His gaze caressed her flat stomach. Then he was seeing her breasts.

No!

He looked at her in shock . . . for a moment he didn't believe what he saw.

But then he did see.

And only too clearly.

They'd cut her breasts. Thin slits radiated from the nipples. It was like a child's picture of the sun done in blood. The roundness of the nipple. Then the sunburst effect of cuts from a sharp blade.

As he watched in horror he saw blood swell proud of the cuts, bead, then trickle downward. A drip from the tip of a puckered nipple.

She folded her arms in such a way that they cradled her breasts from beneath, supporting.

She looked up at him. Her green eyes were rimmed red. Her lips were full and moist. She was breathing deeply. She gazed into his eyes.

For a while she stayed like that, allowing her heavy breathing to settle and quieten.

He didn't know what to say . . . What could he say that would be of help? Even though the cuts in the skin looked superficial her breasts must have been excruciatingly painful.

As he watched, she licked the tip of her middle finger, then tenderly wiped the blood from a cut. She did this again and again. Licking her finger. Stroking a cut in the skin. Soon her lips were slicked red with blood.

From time to time she glanced up at Ed as she worked. Her eyes large now.

When she'd done, she said in a calm, strong voice, 'Don't worry yourself on my account.' Her lips twitched to form a ghost of a smile. 'You see, I'm tougher than I look.'

With that she lay down on the foam mattress and covered herself with the blanket.

Chapter Fourteen

Imad pushed the button on the control box on his dashboard, and watched the gate swing open. He drove through slowly, one hand caressing Hydra's bare shoulder.

She leaned against him.

He parked, and walked her to the front door. In the moonlight her evening gown looked as sleek as the surface of a lake. It was a low-cut, backless dress. He'd bought it for her that afternoon at La Mers.

'I'll take you out for a wonderful dinner tonight,' he'd said earlier.

'In my T-shirt?'

'No, of course not. We'll go to Beverly Hills and buy you something appropriate – an evening gown fit for a princess.'

'Princess, huh?' She smirked and shook her head.

She looked marvelous in the dress. During dinner at Henri's, he'd hardly been able to keep his hands off her. Now there was no longer any need to.

He opened the door. Led her into the foyer, locked the door, pulled her into his arms.

'You're so gorgeous,' he murmured.

He kissed her, tongue pushing into the moist warmth of her mouth. She sucked it down more deeply into her. His hands slid down the curves of her back. They glided over her buttocks, feeling their small, firm mounds through the expensive fabric of the dress. She had no underwear on; he had bought her none. He found the dress's slit that had kept him breathless all evening with glimpses of bare flesh.

Inserting a hand, he caressed the back of her leg, the slope of her rump. He slipped his hand to the front and stroked upwards, pressed the crisp thatch of hair, the wetness between her legs. She writhed, moaning, as his fingers went into her. Sliding, moving, caressing, rubbing.

He was hard and aching.

She rubbed the front of his pants. Opened them. Freed his engorged organ. Slid her hand along the thick shaft.

Lowering herself to the marble floor, she pulled him down on her. With one hand, Imad managed to untie the strap behind her neck. He swept the filmy bodice away from her breasts. He gnawed the turgid nipples. Clutching her shoulder, he held her in place while he rammed.

He suddenly jumped in pain. Reaching back, he touched his stinging buttock and winced.

Blaze crouched behind him. A cigarette in one hand. A .22-caliber pistol in the other.

'Hurt?' Blaze asked with a leer. He sucked on his cigarette, tapped off the ash, and jabbed the red tip into Imad's other buttock. Again, it burned like a hornet sting. 'Get up, camel-humper.'

Imad stood. Pulled up his pants. As he zipped them he looked at Hydra. She lay on her back, knees up, crotch slick. Her eyes were shut. 'Bitch,' he said.

Her lips curled in a smile.

'Take me to your safe,' Blaze ordered.

'Safe? I have no safe.'

'Don't shit me, man. Just take me to it, and open it up. The sooner I've got what I want, the sooner I'll get out of here.'

'But I cannot take you to a safe if there is none, can I?'

'A house like this *always* has a safe. I can find it myself if I have to.'

'It's in the bedroom closet,' Hydra said. Imad looked at her, stunned. She grinned and sat up. 'So I'm a snoop,' she said. 'Sue the pants off me, why don't you?'

'There's nothing in it,' Imad protested.

'Sure,' Blaze breathed.

'I speak the truth.'

'Sure you do.'

'It is the truth.'

'Let's go up and see.'

'Hang on.' Hydra tied the dress behind her neck. The beautiful dress Imad had bought for her. He wanted to tear it from the ungrateful bitch, rip it to pieces; let her wear the soiled rags that matched her filthy soul.

'Okay,' she said. 'Let's roll.'

They followed Imad up the stairway and into the master bedroom.

'Right in there,' Hydra intoned, pointing at the closet.

Imad opened the door. Turned on the closet light and pushed aside his hanging clothes, revealing the face of the wall safe.

'Open it,' Blaze hissed, eyes gleaming.

'I assure you . . .'

'Shut the fuck up! Open the safe! Now!'

He spun the dial. It whirred quietly under the touch of his trembling fingers. When he'd finished the combination, he turned the handle and pulled open the door.

'Step back, asshole.'

Imad backed out of the closet. Blaze stepped in. Greedy face eager.

'Damn!'

'I told you . . .'

Blaze came out, shaking a thin notebook. He flipped it open. 'A fuckin' diary.' He flung it to the floor. He aimed the pistol at Imad's face. 'Okay. You've got five seconds. Where's your money?'

'In the bank.'

'Don't shit me, A-rab.' He cocked the pistol.

'Don't, please. I will tell you.'

'Spit it out.'

'There's a secret compartment in the safe. I keep my valuables there. It's at the back. You simply push the upper left-hand corner of the rear panel.'

'Okay, that's more like it.' Blaze stepped into the closet. He turned to the safe.

Lunging forward, Imad swung the closet door shut.

Hydra reached for it, trying to tug it open. He jabbed his elbow into her stomach, grabbed her, flung her backward against the door. He pressed her against it.

The door jerked, but held.

'Open up!' Blaze yelled. 'Okay. Okay, you asked for it, asshole!'

Hydra called out in panic. 'Blaze, no. Don't shoot. He's holding me against the—'

Three gunshots made quick flat *bangs*. Hydra screamed in pain, her body twitching with each shot; her face twisted, flushed bright red then drained to a waxy white color.

'Shit!' Blaze cried out.

The door jumped, but Imad held it shut, pressing himself against Hydra's convulsing body. He glanced to the side. Four feet away stood a straight-backed chair. If he could get to it . . .

Another shot cracked out. Hydra's head dropped forward onto Imad's shoulder. Behind her, the door was punctured by a tiny, splintered hole.

'See what you've done?' Imad yelled.

Clutching Hydra with one arm, he pulled her aside. He threw open the door, shoved her at the startled man, and slammed the door. Spinning away, he grabbed the chair. Thrust its back under the knob.

With a crash the door shook but held.

'Let me outta here, shit face!'

The gun popped two new holes through the wood; bullets whined through the air near Imad's head.

From its place behind the bedroom door he took Callahan's .12-gauge Browning shotgun. He pumped a cartridge into the breech, stepped toward the closet. Aimed.

Fired. The gun jumped, slamming pain through his shoulder. It knocked a four-inch hole in the closet door. He pumped, and fired again.

Through the gaping hole in the door, he saw Blaze and Hydra on the floor. Blaze's chest was a sheet of flowing blood. The left side of Hydra's face was gone – as if a beast had bitten it off, bones and all.

Chapter Fifteen

April Vallsarra moved through the house easily. She didn't bump into furniture or knock against walls. She knew every inch of the building. Anyone who didn't know her would have sworn that she wasn't blind.

She glided from the kitchen to the lounge with a glass of milk in her hand. With an unerring sense of direction she made for the armchair in the center of the room, sat down, and lightly touched a remote control. Music filled the room.

This was her father's music. She listened to it often. On good days, it was as reassuring as him actually being there. Bad days it made her cry. She'd think about the thugs that took his life away.

Tonight the music helped comfort her. She'd been so lonely today she'd felt a physical ache in her bones. Thirty-three years old and living alone in a big house out in this remote canyon.

Her home was her entire world. There was no world beyond this one. Two floors, five bedrooms, three bathrooms, a kitchen, a lounge, a dining room, a roof terrace, a vast studio basement.

That was it. April Vallsarra's universe.

She wished she could find someone to love to share it with her.

Someone who loved her.

Thirty-three years old. Single.

Alone.

Aching for a loving companion.

Why had life dealt her this blow?

She wished she had a lover tonight.

Amara

She sipped the milk as she listened to the music that her father had created single-handed. Years ago he'd worked alone in the basement studio. First he'd recorded the bass guitar line. A rhythm that was solid enough to anchor the other instruments. Then, painstakingly, he had overdubbed the electric guitar and keyboard parts. Track by track. Layer by layer. Then he'd mixed the sound on the vast mixing desk there.

Months later he had the finished music. A huge symphony played by an orchestra of electric guitars, computers and synthesized percussion. At times he'd replayed it so loudly that she'd had to clamp her hands over her ears and leave the studio.

But the studio underground was so perfectly soundproofed that she couldn't hear the music once the series of three doors had been closed in the corridor that led to the stairwell that, in turn, led to the ground floor.

Her father would invite his friends across to listen to the music. Sometimes he'd debut a piece on the rooftop patio. Many times April had joined them there, sipping drinks on comfortable loungers, enjoying the cooling breeze after the heat of the day. And from the sophisticated sound system installed there they'd listen in awe to the music as it swooped and soared, filling the night air with the shimmering tones of guitars.

Afterwards, her father's friends would congratulate him. Although she could never see their faces of course she recognized the voices. There'd be a sprinkling of Hollywood actors, a band member or two from The Grateful Dead, Jefferson Starship, The Eagles, Talking Heads. Later years would find representatives from newer bands such as REM, Grandaddy and Krakow.

She listened to the pitter-patter of guitar notes. Keyboards swirled like restless spirits, whooshing round the room from speaker to speaker.

That hollowness came to her again. That sense of loneliness that was so great it felt as if a cavern had formed inside her. Empty. A vacuum.

Her hand rested on the cool silk of her dress. She felt her thigh beneath.

She imagined that it was a lover's hand squeezing her leg before gently gliding upwards, up over her stomach, up to her throat where it would slide round the side of her neck, then pull her gently toward her lover's lips.

But who could love a girl like me? I'm blind. Most men wouldn't be interested.

Oh, yes, they'd be interested in the sex. In years past she'd had many lovers who'd stayed a few weeks before dumping her.

But was there anyone out beyond those walls who would commit to loving her forever? To make her a wife?

She had money. Royalties from her father's albums saw to that. She could hire more help around the house. Even a nanny if children came along.

But how could she reach out there into the city and make a man notice her? How could she make him fall in love with her and care for her?

She finished the milk and set the glass down on the table beside the chair. Music filled the room. But it was no longer a comfort.

She needed a companion now. Right now. But she knew that she couldn't conjure a lover out of thin air. Equally, that craving for companionship was near-overwhelming. She wanted to cry out. Wanted to beat the walls with her fists. Wanted to push her fists into that empty ache in her stomach.

Even pain would be preferable to that gnawing emptiness.

This was the time of night when desperation grew intense.

A desperation that often led to shameful thoughts. Even more shameful deeds. But what could she do?

If only a knock on the door would sound right now. And she could open that door and welcome in a stranger who would take away this ache of loneliness.

Chapter Sixteen

Beckerman watched the flashlight beam shoot through the dimly lighted room and sweep up a pair of pale legs. The gal had a hand over her crotch. She had a knocker missing, like someone might have hacked it off with a cleaver before doing the same to her nose. Maybe took them home for souvenirs.

'Turn you on, Gonzalez?' he asked.

'Up yours, man.' The younger watchman swung his beam to another statue: a nude, armless male.

'Look at that, will you? Damned Greeks don't show diddly on the gals, but they've got the guys hanging out all over the place. That seem fair to you? Huh, Gonzalez?'

Gonzalez didn't answer. He turned his flashlight to another statue, then another.

Beckerman suddenly understood. 'Christ, Gonzalez, you take a prize.'

'Hey, man, you can't be too careful in this line of work.'

'Careful, right. You gotta be real careful you don't die of boredom. You're new, you'll see.'

Gonzalez checked another statue. 'You're the soul of respect. Quinn died here last night.'

'Proves my point. The guy died of boredom. Fell asleep on the stairs.'

'You think that's funny, Beckerman?'

'It ain't as funny as a shit attack in a whorehouse, but it'll do.'

'I don't think that's fu—'

'Holy shit!' Beckerman grabbed Gonzalez's arm. 'That one moved!'

'Huh? Which?'

The pale beam jerked from statue to statue.

'There! See?'

'Where?'

'Yeek! Here it comes!'

Gonzalez wrenched his arm away. He shoved Beckerman. 'You think that's funny, man?'

'I *theeenk* so,' Beckerman said, mimicking him.

'I'm gonna break your face.' He shoved Beckerman again.

'Hey, lay off. Can't you take a joke?'

'That ain't no joke.' He raised his flashlight like a club. 'This is a joke?'

'Calm down, hombre. For Christ's sake. You want to—'

The sound of a thud interrupted him. 'What the hell was *that*?'

Gonzalez was already running for the doorway.

'Wait up, damn it!' Beckerman called, keeping his voice a loud, hoarse whisper. He rushed into the hallway and found Gonzalez standing motionless, gaze searching the poorly lighted area ahead, revolver out.

'Don't be so eager, kid. Let's stay cool, and take it slow and easy . . . and stay alive. If we've got bandits we'll contain 'em and call the cops. No fancy shit, right?'

Gonzalez nodded.

'Okay, let's have a look.'

They stepped forward silently. As they approached the entrance to the Callahan Room, Beckerman saw that the cordon was hanging loose. He could remember hooking it into place himself, after an earlier inspection of the room. He pointed at it. Gonzalez nodded.

Crouching by the entry, Beckerman looked inside. Nobody in view. But the lid of the mummy's coffin lay on the floor.

It hadn't been there earlier.

He straightened up. 'I'll stay here,' he whispered. 'Go phone the cops.'

'Forget it, man. We can take 'em.'

'Do what I said, okay?'

'*Su madre,*' Gonzalez muttered, then rushed in.

Beckerman pulled his revolver. Followed. Their light beams crisscrossed the room. Strange shadows lurched on the walls, jumped, writhed; phantom shapes. Beckerman kept his finger off the trigger to stop himself from snapping off shots at them.

Then the overhead lights came on, killing the shadows. Beckerman took in every corner. He found no one. Gonzalez, hand on the light switch, grinned nervously at him.

They went to the coffin and looked in. It was empty.

'Oh shit,' Beckerman muttered.

'Hey, man, maybe they moved it?'

'Someone did.'

'I mean, the museum people put it someplace else, you know?'

'You're an optimist, kid. Face it, we've been ripped off. Let's get it in gear.' He was already running as fast as his limp would allow. 'You secure the front door, I'll check the rear.'

They split up. Beckerman ran down the hall to a fire door at the far end. He pushed the metal door open gently, trying not to make a sound. For a few moments, he listened. He heard nothing. Stepping onto the landing, he eased the door shut.

A single dim bulb above the door provided the only light. Sidestepping, he looked up the stairwell toward the third floor. The light didn't carry far. As he stared at the dark upper stairs, his tense excitement changed.

Changed to fear.

He raised his flashlight. His thumb poised on the switch, ready to send a beam into the darkness above him, but he didn't dare; couldn't bear to push the switch.

Hadn't felt like this since he was a kid. A kid lying in bed, rigid with terror, staring across the room at the black opening of the closet. That yawning maw. Nothing inside the closet. Nothing harmful. Nothing to hurt a kid. Okay? He could prove it by turning on a light. To turn on the light, though, he would have to get out of bed. If he moved, *IT* would leap out, grab him, gnaw the life out of him.

Lowering the flashlight, he turned away. He took two steps across the landing, wanted to look back over his shoulder – just to make sure – but didn't because it would be too much like gazing into that closet once again.

He started slowly downward. The bulb from the landing threw his huge shadow on the wall ahead. He felt nervous, looking at it. What if a second shadow suddenly appeared beside it?

You're going nuts, he told himself.

He was glad when he turned at the next landing. No more shadow. Below him, the light of the first floor looked like an old friend.

He hurried down to it.

Yeah, and you know you're following Quinn's footsteps; just don't go tripping over your own feet, okay?

He opened the door, looked out. No sign of anyone. Careful to avoid turning his gaze toward the upper stairs, he crossed the landing and stared down toward the basement.

He had a new shadow. He watched his feet to keep from seeing it. At the next landing it disappeared. But there was no friendly light shining below. Only hostile darkness. That same hostile darkness that once occupied his open closet.

Where was that light? Why was it no longer shining? The damn thing must have burned out. Shit.

Or did someone take care of it?

He turned his flashlight on. No hesitation. He was beginning to feel some of his old confidence.

That all changed, halfway down the steps, when he heard a sound behind him. Scraping sounds like a dead, windblown leaf skidding across concrete. A dry sound.

He whirled around.

He stared.

The thing was standing half a dozen steps above him. In the bright beam of his flashlight, he saw more than he wanted to: arms and legs like sticks, bulging joints, red hair falling in glossy swathes; a gaunt and eyeless face.

Its mouth opened wide.

He screamed as it leaped down at him, red hair billowing.

* * *

Gonzalez heard the scream. He ran across the lobby, flung open the metal door of the fire exit.

'Beckerman!'

From below, he heard faint sounds. Splashing sounds like water spattering concrete. He rushed down the stairs. At the landing, he shone his light into the darkness. Something was on Beckerman, hunched over his sprawled body, head jerking like a dog tearing meat from a carcass, only he couldn't see clearly because of the mane of hair that blazed fiery red in the beam of the flashlight.

It wasn't a dog.

It had red hair like a woman.

It was working on Beckerman's neck. Blood flew, raining against the walls and floor. Crimson. Liquid. Rivulets of gore.

With alarming speed, the creature scurried off the bloody body and turned. The light beam hit its face.

Gonzalez went numb. He wet himself. Warm liquid ran down his leg. As it drenched his socks and pooled in his boots it helped bring him back to reality.

'Freeze!' he shouted.

The creature attacked, arms reaching out, mouth gaping, eyes twin pits of darkness that seemed to plunge into eternity.

Those teeth.

Those god-awful white teeth.

Framed by black, dead lips.

Gonzalez reacted. Dropped the flashlight. Clutched his right wrist. Aimed. Snapped off four shots, the blasts coming so fast they sounded like one continuous, terrible explosion.

He knew the bullets hit the target. They had to. The range was nothing. An arm's length. But did they stop the thing?

Did they hell.

It rushed against him. Red hair, a billowing mass around the shriveled face. Good God, it looked as if the creature's head had burst into flame. Swirling reds, golds; the hair seemed to double the size of the body.

At that moment it struck. He jammed the muzzle to its chest, fired his last two rounds.

Their impact hardly made the thing twitch. Like shooting a cardboard box. Cordite smoke billowed.

Fingers clutched his face and hair. Claw fingers. Fingers with curling, misshapen fingernails. Gonzalez stumbled backwards, fell onto the landing, lost the revolver; it went skittering across the floor, sending out sparks as gunmetal collided with marble.

The face pressed toward him, mouth snapping; its eyeless sockets eager somehow. Those voids filled with something more than darkness. Something unseen, hungry, evil, murderous.

He tried to shove the snapping mouth away. The dry stick tongue worked behind the teeth. Raising his hands, he pushed at the shriveled head, trying to force it back. The head twisted quickly, shaking the mass of hair that tumbled over his own face; ancient tresses fell into his mouth; dusty curls reached the back of his throat. He convulsed, gagging at the mouthful of hair.

He lost his grip on the twisting head. Its teeth caught two of his fingers. He felt the bite, heard the crunch of bone, saw his hand come back with finger stubs dripping.

The thing clawed his face. He cried out as it pierced his left eye.

He heard teeth snapping.

He heard flesh rip as they found his throat.

He heard . . .

. . . Nothing . . .

Chapter Seventeen

The girl with red hair and green eyes was watching Ed when he woke up. She lay on her side, gazing through the bars of the cage.

Ed Lake waited for her to speak.

She didn't.

Didn't move either.

Merely watched his face.

Ed remembered how he'd heard her being tortured in the dark just a few hours ago. He burned inside, outraged that someone could do such a terrible thing and . . .

. . . And he burned because he remembered something else. He remembered how the cries she made had turned him on.

Christ, he thought she'd been having sex. That she was enjoying. Not hurting.

But that didn't make it all right, did it? He remembered how he couldn't take his eyes off her naked back when the light came on. It was only when she turned that he'd seen how the skin around her nipples had been sliced in a sunburst effect of radiating cuts.

Now . . .

Well, now she just stared at him with those green eyes.

So what do you say in a situation like this? When you're in a cage? When the stranger in the next cage has just had her breasts sliced?

Hi ho, honey. You're looking chipper.

Hardly.

Those nipples of hers must be aflame with pain.

Not that she showed the hurt, though. Her gaze was steady.

At last he had to say something, even if totally lame-brain: 'Are you okay?'

She didn't answer. Just kept on staring.

'I'm sorry what they did to you. It was terrible. I mean it must have . . .'

Her eyes looked into his.

He clenched his fists. 'The motherfucker should have his heart ripped out . . . ripped right out, the bastard.'

She gazed at him. Then: 'Don't become too involved with what happened.'

'But . . . hell, it was barbaric . . . the way you bled.'

'I can take it.'

'Take that mutilation, but—'

'Listen, do you know what the alternative is?'

'The alternative?'

'The alternative is far worse. Ask Marco.'

'That's right.' Marco's voice came from behind. Ed glanced back at the blond guy in the next cage. 'The alternative is . . . *grrch*.' As he made the noise, he drew his finger across his throat.

'They've killed people?'

'Then where you goes nobody knows.'

'But you people talk like this is normal. That this is how the entire world is.' Ed couldn't believe how the pair accepted the situation. 'Remember who you are. You've been kidnapped by crazies, put in cages and now you're being tortured.'

Marco said. 'You learn to adapt.'

'It's out of our hands,' she said.

'If you don't accept that this is your life now you'll crack up.'

She nodded. 'Then you're as good as dead.'

'Jesus H. Christ,' breathed Ed. 'I'm not going to surrender to this. I'm not.'

'Your funeral, bud.' Marco lay back down on his mattress. 'Wonder when they'll bring breakfast today?'

'Soon,' she said.

'Hope it's not hard-boiled eggs. They lock me up tight.'

She shrugged. 'Might be bacon sandwiches. We haven't had those for a while.'

'I hope the coffee's hot. It's been tepid the last couple of days. Boy oh boy, that's one thing I hate. Tepid coffee.'

Jesus H. Get this! They're talking like a couple of people staying in a cheap hotel. Not a godforsaken torture chamber. Ed wanted out. This was madness. Maybe these two were mad?

Hell, maybe *he* was mad?

Imagining this.

Maybe he was in a psychiatric ward somewhere.

The shock of being dumped by Janey was too much.

Now he was in a rubber room; he was shot full of lithium, drooling, kacking his diaper, whining for Mom. But not here. Not in this beast house. Where bad things happened to decent people. Where invisible torturers came in the dark.

'Hello . . . hell . . . owe.'

He snapped out of it. Looked across at the girl.

She held her hand out through the bars. The blanket was pulled up over her breasts, preserving her modesty.

'Hello,' she repeated. 'Anyone home?'

She smiled, straightened her fingers. They were just inches from his cage. 'Guess we haven't been properly introduced. My name is Virginia.' Her eyes were solemn. 'Don't laugh. My parents told me I was conceived there.'

Marco chuckled. 'Count yourself lucky your mother wasn't screwed in Nantucket.'

She sneered, 'Thank you, Marco Polo.'

'It's not Marco Polo, it's Marco *Paulo*.'

'Like who cares?' She looked at Ed. 'So? What do you want me to call you? Mister?'

He reached out. Took her hand in his. He felt her fingers squeeze his fingers. It seemed like a gesture of affection. An electric thrill ran through him.

Hell, what a way to shake hands. What a situation!

But she was beautiful to look at.

Beautiful to touch.

Before he could stop himself, he pictured himself embracing her, burying his face in that thick, copper hair. *Jeez, what's wrong with me?*

Those thoughts zipped through his head in a flash. He found himself saying, 'I'm Ed Lake.' She still held his hand so he found himself adding lamely, 'I go to school at Riverside High.'

'You don't say.' She smiled. 'I went there, too. A few years before you, though.'

'Great,' Marco said. 'The perfect place for a high-school reunion. In a cage.'

At last she withdrew her hand.

Don't do that, he thought. *Don't. I like touching your skin.*

But she lay back down on the mattress on her side with the blanket pulled up over her breasts. Her shoulders were bare, though. The skin was smooth, flawless. And despite her injury, and the strain she must be under, she looked good. Sort of glowed. An erotic power shone in her eyes.

'I'd lay off chumming up together across there, Eddie boy.'

'I'm not chumming up.' Ed was annoyed by Marco's tone. The guy sounded jealous.

'Looks pretty chummy from the deluxe suite over here.'

'Knock it off, Marco,' Virginia told him. 'He's just being nice.'

'Just being stoopid.'

'Hey!'

'Like I said, Eddie.'

'Don't call me Eddie.'

'Like I said, *Eddie*, you've gotta save your strength.'

'There you go again, why do I have to save my strength?'

He gloated now. 'You'll find out. So save your strength. Save every drop.'

A kind of sullen silence settled over the room. No one spoke. Virginia and Marco retreated under their blankets. Ed didn't know if they were sleeping or not. He glared at the humped mound where Marco lay. Why did he keep talking about 'saving your strength'? What was all this? The guy wouldn't elaborate. Neither would Virginia, come to that. So, Jesus H. Christ, why? What kind of test would he face? The thoughts were still running hot through his skull when the lights went out.

Oh, God. Here we go again. This time it's my turn. His belly shriveled. The strength bled out of him.

He turned his head left and right.

Too dark.

Saw nothing.

Heard nothing.

Just like last time.

Then he'd realized someone had entered the room. Then had come cries from Virginia as the sadist ran a card-cutter along her tit.

Bastards. If he could get his hands on them.

Wait . . . it's happening. He sensed movement. Heard a rustle. Felt a whisper of a draft across his bare arms. The hairs stood upright on the back of his neck. Shivers spiked his back. He clenched his fists.

Coming for you, Eddie boy.

Gonna get you good and hard. Maybe do a little blade work on your face in the dark.

No, they won't. I'm going to punch out.

Fists clenched, he waited.

Waited.

He pictured the sadist in the night-vision goggles.

He can see you. You can't see him. He has power over you. You see nothing in the dark.

But, yeah, Eddie boy, he sees all right. He sees victims.

Maybe they're going to work on Virginia. Maybe cut her again. She'll start crying out. Start panting.

You'd like that, wouldn't you, Eddie?

Don't call me Eddie.

Wanna hear her squeal? Wanna hear her say 'Please' again in that way that makes you throb between your legs?

Christ, why did the mind chatter always run away with him? He couldn't stop those tormenting thoughts. Devil thoughts. He pictured Virginia near-naked beneath the blanket. Maybe stuff was happening to her again . . . maybe she felt the cold—

Uh.

He blinked as the lights flickered on. He looked round. This time, he expected to see their captor. But the room was empty again. Empty apart from the three cages with their three occupants.

Virginia sat up blinking. She held the blanket high up her chest.

Marco made a hoot. 'All right! Breakfast time!'

Ed's eyes swiveled. A tray had been left outside the bars of his cage. It was one of those molded ones they give you on airlines. In one hollow was an English muffin, in another scrambled egg. In the third strips of bacon. Beside the tray, a cup of black coffee.

'Ed. Eat everything,' she told him.

'My appetite isn't what it was.' He gave a grim smile.

'Eat everything. Force yourself. Keep your strength, Ed. For Godsakes, keep your strength.'

Why?

What's going to happen to me?

He nearly asked the questions but something reined them back in. Anyway, he had a suspicion that he'd find out real soon.

Over in his cage Marco had slid the tray through the gap in the bars and had begun to eat. 'Not hot, but good,' he sang. 'Hmm, smoked bacon.'

Now Ed saw the reason for the airline-style trays. They were narrow enough to pass through the bars. The English muffin was surprisingly good. Someone had been generous with a splash of melted butter. The scrambled eggs were mixed with ground black pepper the way he liked it. Spicy. Gave a little heat, too, to the otherwise lukewarm egg. The bacon had cooled during the journey from the kitchen to the cages. But it was okay. The coffee was tepid but strong. With no forks he followed his two roomies, eating with his fingers and using the English muffin to mop the tray. He noticed the other two ate hungrily, enjoying the simple meal. He glanced at Virginia. She ate, sitting with her back to him.

Her back was bare. With a free hand she flicked back the long copper hair so it wouldn't trail into the food. That bare back. It was beautiful. When she reached for her coffee he saw the pale orb of her breast jiggle a bit.

Just a little bit. But it was sexy enough to warm his loins.

Marco sang out again, 'Eat up, eat up, Eddie, old buddy. Food equals energy, you know. You're gonna need it soon.'

Chapter Eighteen

The rear door of the museum opened.

Amara stepped out into the warm night. She stood motionless, head tilted back as if taking in the beauty of the pale moon.

Then she started across the asphalt of the parking lot.

From the edge of the field, George watched. His ears heard the dry skin of the creature's feet whisper against the blacktop. His sensitive nose picked up odors, too. Sweet spicy odors that didn't quite mask the smell of ancient bone and flesh. The scent of the tomb still clung to the mass of hair that seemed to possess a life of its own. One moment it hung in heavy swathes down the hard glossy skin of the back, the next a warm up-current of air caught it, lifted it, bore it upward so individual hairs separated and floated around the skull-like head.

A red mist.

A mist like airborne droplets of blood.

The dog watched.

Never seen anything like this before.

Never encountered such a figure.

Yet deep down sensed its nature. A dead thing walking. He sensed its dark and terrible power.

Amara paused. Turned her dark, rounded head; hair floating around it. Each strand swimming in the night air.

The dog sensed life in the strands of hair that reached down beyond the crust of the corpse's buttocks, down to the back of its legs. He watched the hairs writhe and dance in the moonlight. Although the dog could not put into words what he witnessed, the image that came into his canine brain was of snakes.

As if each red hair was a blood-red snake, only as thin as a fiber. Each one malevolent. Each one possessing eyes. Each one of the thousands of hairs seeing the brown dog shivering at the edge of the parking lot.

Amara saw, too.

She walked in the direction of the frightened dog.

So frightened he stood as still as one of the statues in the museum. So frightened he could hardly breathe.

The creature moved toward him. Its naked body gleamed like hard black resin in the moonlight. Black tarry lips parted. White teeth glinted.

The dog wanted to run. Wanted to turn tail. Wanted to kick up dust with his paws. Gone. History. Back across town where this dreadful thing could never find him.

But he couldn't move. He could only stand, panting hard until his lungs hurt inside his ribs.

He watched the creature quicken its pace toward him. Although it had no eyes he knew it saw him perfectly. A brown dog shivering with fear. Vulnerable. Unable to save itself. A small life soon snuffed out. Dog bones broken. Brown fur scattered to the winds.

A whimper reached the dog's throat. Nothing more.

It could do nothing. Move nowhere.

His eyes rolled upward to see the figure loom over him. With the moon behind, it stood in silhouette. A hard outline revealing bone-thin limbs; a hard rounded head covered with hard skin. And, surrounding the head, a vast halo of floating hair through which the moonlight burned in a bloody flame.

It extended its arms, hands hooking, fingers turning to claws.

The bat flew into Amara's hair. Leathery wings beat the curls, bat claws became entangled in red tresses as it struggled to free itself. As Amara's hands went to tear the tiny struggling creature from her hair, the spell was broken.

George barked once at the strange creature, then dashed away.

Chapter Nineteen

Imad wrapped the bodies in plastic garbage bags and maneuvered them downstairs. Hydra was easy to carry. Blaze, however, weighed far too much and had to be dragged.

He left them on the rear sundeck. In the tool shed he found a shovel. He walked across the moonlit lawn to the flower garden. Began to dig. Dig deep.

Perhaps he was digging near the very spot where Callahan had buried the other intruders so many weeks ago?

The thought unsettled him.

Callahan had killed with the same shotgun. He'd no doubt used the same shovel, dug in the same vicinity, the metal blade chopping in the soil with the same awful crunching sound like an ax through firm flesh.

Callahan had died that night.

Perhaps . . .

Imad shivered, wiped the sweat from his face, kept on digging.

He kept on digging until a hand swung up from the soil to slap the shovel. With a scream he leaped back. The hand dropped out of sight into the darkened pit.

He stepped cautiously to the edge of the hole, and peered in. An arm was exposed from the shoulder to the fingertips. The edge of his shovel, he realized, had probably caught it in the elbow joint, making it jump like that. *And slap the shovel like that!*

Nevertheless, he couldn't bring himself to dig anymore.

He filled the hole.

Hiding the rotting corpse once more.

The smell . . .

Imad retched.

With great effort, he dragged the bodies through the house and out the front door. One by one, he swung them into the trunk of his Mercedes.

Then he drove for miles.

In the darkness of a wooded road, he unloaded them. He returned the plastic bags to his trunk, fearing that they had his fingerprints. Then he climbed into his car. As he backed away, his headlights shone on the green of Hydra's dress.

Someone might remember the dress. Expensive. Exclusive. Not many of them about. They might remember the couple who bought it: the dark little man with the girl young enough to be his daughter, but obviously not his daughter because she was light-skinned. No. They had a different relationship; even the dumbest could guess what that relationship was.

He climbed from the car. He removed her dress, being careful not to look at the awful gap where part of her face had been.

He backed away. In the harsh beams of the headlights, her skin looked like raw dough.

Imad remembered the pleasure he had taken from her body. How she had moaned and writhed beneath him. Her pointed nipples. How they'd hardened beneath his probing tongue.

Such a waste.

But she had been greedy and stupid . . . and careless about her friends. She had done this to herself. If it had not ended now, it could only have ended at the side of a different deserted road, on a different midnight, with a different set of wounds.

He backed the car away.

The headlights retreated, leaving her in darkness.

Chapter Twenty

Tag woke up in a sunny bedroom, a sheet keeping him warm against the fresh morning breeze. He lay on his side, his back to Susan. Her hand was on his upthrust hip.

'Morning,' he said.

'Hi.'

She moved, fitting herself against him, breasts pushing against his back, lap warm against his rump, thighs against the backs of his legs. He felt her lips on the nape of his neck.

'Sleep well?' she asked.

'Mmmm.'

He rolled over and held her. She was incredibly smooth and warm. He kissed the curve of her neck, the hollow of her throat. He lingered over her nipples, taking each in his mouth, rolling them with his tongue. His hand slipped between her legs. The telephone rang.

'Damn,' she muttered. She turned away, picked up. 'Hello?'

She listened.

'Oh my God! I see . . . sure . . . yes, okay . . . I'll be right over.' She hung up.

'What happened?'

'The guards. They were killed last night. Two of them.' Her face looked as though she smelled something bad. 'Their throats were ripped out.'

'Their throats? That's how Callahan died. These guards, did they have dogs with them?'

'I don't think so.'

'Let's get over there and see what's up.'

'That's why they called. They want me to inventory the Callahan Collection again to see if anything's missing but the mummy.'

'It's gone again?'

She nodded. 'They've already searched the museum.'

'Did they check the men's john?'

'First, probably.'

She sat up. Tag watched, warmed by the sight of Susan's body as she swung her legs off the bed and stood up. She disappeared into the bathroom.

Tag dressed, thinking. This was Saturday, the only time this week in which his day off coincided with hers. He'd planned, vaguely, on taking Susan and Geoffrey to the beach. Since she had to go to the museum, though, he would go along. The inventory shouldn't take long. Besides, this would give him a chance to check out the killings. He picked up his Colt Python, clipped its holster to his belt.

As he was tying his shoelaces, Susan came out of the bathroom, still naked.

'All finished,' she said.

Tag knew he should wash his face, shave, brush his teeth, comb his hair. Instead, he took pleasure watching Susan step into her brief black panties. He moved in behind her. Reaching around, he cupped her breasts in his hands.

'Aren't you going to shave or something?' she asked.

'Can't tear myself away.'

She turned to him. They kissed. He slid his hands down the smoothness of her back, pushed them under the slick sheath of her panties, caressed her buttocks. Skin silky, oh-so-smooth . . . hell, oh-so-desirable. He wanted to ease them down then—

'We have to go,' she whispered against his mouth.

'I know, I know.'

Reluctantly, he took his hands away. He went to the bathroom. By the time he'd chased the heat of sheer lust away, he found Susan dressed in slacks and a loose-fitting white blouse.

On the way out, she looked into Geoffrey's room.

'He's sleeping,' she said.

They told María goodbye, explaining they had to go out in a hurry and, no, they'd have to skip breakfast. Tag eyed the fresh pancakes and syrup regretfully. All his appetites were keen this morning.

Susan stepped back as Tag opened the front door. Stains still showed on the hall carpet, though Tag had scrubbed it last night after men from the Department of Animal Regulation had taken away the cat's body. The door was stained, too, but the words were no longer legible.

'Hallway's clear,' he said.

He took her hand; they walked to the elevator.

'You'll be coming in?' Susan asked.

Tag nodded.

'Might as well park out back, then. We can use my regular space.' She directed him to turn left near the museum entrance where three police cars were parked. At the corner, the road curved to the right. 'Follow it to the rear,' she said.

In the back of the museum, they came to a sign that read: EMPLOYEES PARKING ONLY. She pointed out her reserved space. At its head, S. CONNORS was painted on a low concrete curb.

'They'll have to change that to "S. Parker",' she said.

'Soon, I hope.'

'Can't till the divorce is final. That'd be bigamy.'

'Also bad form,' Tag added.

He parked and they got out. The sun was a heavy, pleasant pressure on Tag's face. He took a deep breath of air rich with the scent of flowers. At the sound of yelling, whooping kids, he turned his eyes to the field beyond the parking lot.

A boy in the weeds took a combat stance, aimed his pistol at a running suspect, and yelled, 'Blam!'

'The kid's good,' Tag commented.

'Maybe you should go over and recruit him.'

'I'd rather play along.'

'No fair. You'd use real bullets.'

'Sure, but I'd only shoot to wound.'

Susan took hold of his arm, laughing. It was a tense laugh. Tag looked into her eyes; saw fear. 'What's wrong?' he asked.

She smiled, shrugged, and shook her head sharply. 'Nothing.'

'You're really upset.'

'I'm okay. Just a little scared, that's all. Anything wrong with that?'

'No, it's—'

'I mean, I'm trying to handle all this. Right? I'm okay . . . haven't broken down yet. Kept my head, so far. I'm keeping it all together, aren't I, Tag?'

'Sure.'

'I shrugged it off when that first watchman got killed, didn't make a fuss about messing with that damned mummy in the john, didn't crack when that disgusting Mable beat me up or killed that poor little kitten and hung it outside my home.' She swallowed. Her face was fixed rigidly, but her eyes filled with tears. 'And now there are two dead men in there and I don't even know them, and I've got to go in . . . *must* go in . . . only the last thing I want is to go in there. *I don't want to.*'

All her control broke. She flung herself against Tag, hugging him tightly, crying like a lost child.

He held her. 'It'll be all right, Susan,' he said, soothingly. 'Please don't cry. It'll be all right. It'll be all right, believe me.'

Chapter Twenty-one

'So, how long have you been here?'

'Doesn't the guy ever stop asking questions?' Marco complained.

Ed Lake sat on the foam mattress in the center of the cage. He'd been talking to Virginia but Marco lobbed in comments. Virginia sat with the blanket round her, facing Ed. Marco lay on his back, feet crossed, and resting them on one of the horizontal bars of the cage so that they were higher than his body.

'How long?' Virginia shrugged. 'Hard to tell.'

'Days? Weeks?'

'Weeks, I guess.'

'And you, Marco?'

'Always. I've been here always.'

'Always?'

'That's what it feels like.'

Virginia nodded. 'You can't tell night from day in here. We guess the lights go on for around six hours, then off for four. It's a completely artificial day-night cycle.'

Marco laughed. 'If we weren't tough cookies it could screw us up.'

Ed rubbed his jaw. 'How did you get here?'

'Don't remember,' Marco said.

'You must remember something.'

'Not me. You might say I'm of no fixed abode. I moved from place to place. I'd been staying with a girl over near the beach until she threw me out. Then I took to sleeping on a bench outside a shopping mall.'

'Can't have been easy?'

'I made it easy, brother. I took the girl's stash of weed. I got mellow every night. Hours just seemed to float away on a summer breeze.'

'Then what?'

'I went to sleep on my bench one night. When I woke up, here I was in the beast house. Someone had whammoed me as I slept. Easy-peasy.'

Ed looked at Virginia. 'You?'

'It seems so stupid.' She looked embarrassed.

'No more stupid than I felt.' Ed smiled. He remembered being dumped in the wilds by Janey.

'I'd been to a party,' she said. 'Drank too much, then I walked home.'

'Now that was stupid.'

'Tell me about it. But I lived just down the street. A three-minute walk at most. So, there I am alone in the middle of the night in a quiet neighborhood when all of a sudden – wham.'

'Knock on the head.' Ed touched his still-matted hair.

'No, a stun gun, I figured. Didn't see anyone, just felt a jolt like someone had kicked me in the small of the back.' She shrugged. 'Woke up here with Marco as my neighborino.'

'And we've been inseparable ever since.'

'Yeah, inseparable.' She didn't smile.

Ed looked round. 'And you've never heard any noises from outside? Anything to tell you where you might be?'

'Look at the white panels on the walls.' Marco pointed with his bare toe.

'Soundproofing,' Virginia added.

'Yeah,' Marco chuckled. 'In this place no one can hear you scream.'

'That's not funny.'

'Sure is. Remember George? That guy who split his sides laughing?'

Ed lifted his head. 'George?'

'An ex-roomie,' Marco said.

Ed looked at Virginia. 'There have been others here?'

'Some.'

'What happened to them?'

Marco wriggled his bare toes. 'They come . . . they go.'
'Jeez.'
'So it's best to play the game to their rules,' Virginia said meaningfully. 'They ask, you *do*. Got that?'

Ed still couldn't believe they took this lying down. They sounded so damn passive, so damn *accepting*. Like the fight had gone out of them.

'But surely the cops are out searching for us?'

Even Virginia laughed at that one.

Marco knelt up. 'Now that kind of doofus talk makes me need to take a leak.' He pulled down his zipper. 'Watch out, you folks in the front row. *You will get wet.*'

He knelt up and pointed himself in the direction of the bowl full of sawdust. His aim, Ed saw, wasn't all that it should be.

Jesus Christ. It can't get any worse than this.
Wrong, Eddie.
It's just about to do exactly that.

The lights got killed. That same instantaneous plunge into darkness. Maybe this was the lights-out phase for sleep. But Ed doubted it. Surely the period of light had been too short.

He heard Marco murmur. 'Ladies and gentlemen. Fun in the beast house is just about to begin.'

Ed's scalp tingled. Suddenly it felt cooler in the room. He looked round but as before he couldn't see a thing in that total darkness.

Here it comes, he told himself.
Here it comes, Eddie boy.
Did you keep your strength like Marco said? Or did you drizzle it all away asking questions?
But what will they make me do? What kind of challenge am I going to face?
Maybe it won't be me.
Maybe Virginia? Might be Marco?
It doesn't have to be me this time. They might not be interested in me and—

'Lake.'

Holy shit, they're talking to me.
'Lake.'
But how do they know my name?
Marco told.
Hey, maybe Marco's in on this. When the lights go out how do I know that Marco doesn't simply unlatch the cage door and come out to do his funky stuff? He might have sliced Virginia's breasts. He's got the night-vision goggles hidden somewhere.
He walks round. Seeing us. We don't see him.

The thoughts blasted through Ed's brain. They were paranoid thoughts but, hell . . . Maybe they were *both* in on this. Both Marco and Virginia could be his captors. This could be their game.

Pretend to be captives in cages. Pretend they were just like him.
But why?

To get inside his head, of course. Enjoy his fear close up. Watch his face when he reacted.

Marco went on and on about keeping his strength up. Working on him. Working on the scare centers of his brain. Maybe that was it.
But what about Virginia's injuries?
Self-inflicted.
But, hell, that must hurt.
Maybe moviemakers' fake blood?

'Lake.' The voice came again. It was a man's deep voice. Eerily slow, too. Inhuman-sounding.

It sent ice down his spine.

'*Lake. In a moment. I will give you instructions. You will follow those instructions to the letter. Otherwise you will be punished. Do you understand?*'

He remained in the same frozen crouch position, not moving so much as a finger.

'*Nod if you understand, Lake.*'
So they do see me? Jesus H. Christ. He'd never been so scared.
'*Nod if you understand, Lake.*'
He nodded.

'*When the lights are switched on again, go immediately to the panel that is suspended beneath the roof of the cage. Lie flat on your back on it. Then present your penis.*'

'What!'

'*Present your penis. Present it in such a way that it will pass through the aperture in the top of the cage.*'

'No way. I'm not sticking my cock through no goddamn hole!'

Virginia hissed: 'You've got to, Ed. Remember, play by their rules.'

'But, shit . . . I can't. I mean I really—'

The deep bass voice continued calmly. '*Lie on the panel. Present your penis. This is a matter that requires no further discussion.*'

The light flickered on. He glanced at Virginia. Solemn, she nodded. *Do it, Ed.* Marco had retreated under the blanket as if he didn't want to witness what happened next.

Holy shit.

What were they going to do?

To take his dick out of his pants and push it through a hole in that Perspex. Jesus.

What's wrong, Eddie? Afraid of runaway lawn mowers?

The thought escaped before he could rein it in. Lawn mowers and penises. They were three words that didn't belong in the same sentence. No way.

But what choice did he have?

Skin crawling like a jug full of ants had been poured onto him, he made his way across the cage. In front of him the transparent panel was at eye level as he crouched there. Maybe ten inches or so separated it from the transparent roof of the cage. It would be like lying on a bunk bed that nearly touched the bedroom ceiling.

Virginia whispered. 'Use the bars at the side to climb up, then slide onto it on your back . . . that's it. Now push your feet against the bars to move yourself along.'

It wasn't easy. He yanked his back muscles working his way onto the panel. His forehead butted the Perspex top of the cage. He couldn't raise his knees to use his feet so he had to worm his way further along, pressing his palms against the panel.

Jesus H. He felt like he'd become a sandwich filling now, with the glass panels forming the two slices of bread.

Present your penis.

That's what the deep voice had told him. *Present? What a way to phrase it.*

But, good God, what would they do to his dick once it was poking up in the fresh air? You couldn't feel any more vulnerable than this. That's why guys outdoors took a leak facing a wall or a tree. You felt uncomfortable exposing your cock to the wilderness. It felt so unnatural.

A passing eagle might mistake it for a tasty snake.

It wasn't easy in that confined space but at last he took his dick from his pants and . . . yes . . . *presented* it. Gritting his teeth, he poked the head up through the hole in the Perspex. Fortunately, the hole was smooth round the edges, so there should be no nasty cuts. He tried to lift his head to see how much of itself it did *present*. Only he couldn't lift his head on account of the sheet of Perspex above his face.

Was Virginia watching?

Was *Marco*?

He didn't know whether to feel terrified or embarrassed. Mortally embarrassed.

Terminally embarrassed.

Shoot.

Then the worst thing happened.

The worst he could imagine.

The thing he didn't want to happen just went and happened anyway.

The damn lights . . . they went out. It was dark again.

And here I am lying with my dick pushed through a hole in the Perspex.
He swallowed, gritted his teeth, waited for the next installment.

OK, buddy. You can pause the tape now. I've seen enough . . . The mind chatter didn't help. Especially when it began talking about runaway lawn mowers.

Swirling blades. A soft column of flesh. *Who's gonna win that wrestling bout, Eddie boy?* He closed his eyes. Not that it mattered. He wouldn't see what happened next in the dark anyway.

He waited.

Waited.

Minutes sneaked by in no particular hurry.

Maybe this was the test . . . to lie there with his dick poking up above the Perspex. This could be a psychological challenge. Not physical.

A rustle sounded close by.

The drafts came again. Cool air played over the end of his manhood. A manhood that wanted to shrivel back into his body where it would be safe from whatever lay out there.

He pressed his lips together. A cry tried its darnedest to escape.

He wanted to yell: NO! NO! NO!

But he must keep quiet.

Revealing his fear might only excite his captor into . . . no, he didn't want to speculate any further than that.

The sensation came that somebody was moving above him. He heard a whispering sound. Feet moving across the floor.

Holy shit!

The Perspex floor flexed above him. Had someone stepped from the elevated catwalk onto the cage roof?

Moments later came a faint squeaking sound.

Oiling the lawn-mower blades . . .

No. Someone was tightening the bolt arrangement that supported the panel that held him. Slowly he was being raised up toward the underside of the cage.

This went on for several minutes.

Inch by inch he felt himself being winched up tight to the roof of the cage. He felt his entire body pressed hard against it. His hips were crushed full against it; his skin burned with the pressure.

Was the intention merely to crush the life out of him?

But just as the pressure against his ribs made it difficult to breathe it stopped.

Then came the next shock.

Something touched his penis.

He could see nothing in the darkness. And right now he didn't want to. What if it was a blade? *Remember the cuts on Virginia's breasts?*

Was it his turn?

But this was light. A feathering motion. Faster.

It was a tongue!

Someone's tongue flickered lightly against the end of his cock.

He remembered the man's deep voice . . . *Oh, holy Christ, not that!*

His reflex action was to recoil but the panel he lay on held him firmly against the underside of the roof. He couldn't move even a fraction of an inch. He was wedged tight against the Perspex. Only his cock was free and that was being . . . well, he couldn't believe it but it was being licked with a rapidly flickering tongue. First the very tip. Then down the shaft.

Now fingers . . . encircling. Gentle, tentative.

But then firmly. Holding his cock upright so the whole mouth could slip over it, gorging, swallowing.

Teeth next. Leastways, that's what his runaway imagination anticipated. Teeth clamping hard. Biting. Rending. Ripping.

He could hardly keep from screaming. But somehow he held the scream inside his body. He sensed his survival depended on it.

And then came something even more shocking.

The ultimate betrayal.

In utter disbelief he realized his body was responding to that sucking mouth. Felt himself stiffen, felt himself rise, growing big in the mouth.

The Perspex flexed above him.

Whoever was above him was getting excited. They were moving, getting in a better position to suck at him.

What had happened to him? Why was his body becoming excited by the attentions his penis was receiving?

He felt disgust . . .

Worse, he felt turned on. With involuntary movements he tried to thrust his hips forward into the face of his abuser. His heart hammered. He wanted to writhe in pleasure, only he was constricted by the two sheets of Perspex that held him sandwiched so tightly.

Then the mouth was gone.

Relief.

Disappointment.

He didn't know which emotion was the strongest. Saliva cooled on the end of his penis. It throbbed as it stood erect above the Perspex.

Then it happened so fast.

He gasped with disbelief. Understanding only too well what was happening to him now.

More importantly, what was happening to his cock.

He clenched his hands. Gritted his teeth. Curled his toes so tightly that his feet ached.

Someone had slid onto him. The sensation was different. He knew that someone now knelt on the Perspex above him. Taking his cock into them. Inside.

But inside what?

He felt a slick encircling.

Felt the motion, too, as they lowered themselves, then raised a little before sliding slowly . . . slowly down his erect shaft.

Please – he wanted his cock to shrivel back.

But the perfidious hank of meat wouldn't. It became so swollen that it felt as if it would burst. He'd never been as hard as this. Or as thick. He felt himself penetrate deep into this captor's body.

But what was he penetrating?

He could feel the moist lips, the clenching muscles.

It reminded him of when Janey sat on him and impaled herself on his cock.

But there was that man's deep voice . . . *Dear God* – and here he was enjoying this . . . no, *loving* this sensation.

It didn't take long before he felt himself ready to ejaculate.

But he remembered Marco's talk of saving his strength. He knew he must hold back until his captor had been satisfied.

Still the motion continued. The rising, falling. The tightly encircling collar of flesh about his flesh.

He must delay. He couldn't permit himself release.

They were insatiable. His captor rose and fell above him for hours. He heard them panting. But they said nothing.

They were inexhaustible. A squeaking sound came to him and he realized it must have been their perspiring hands taking the weight against the Perspex and slipping backwards and forwards.

He centered himself on the pain as the Perspex squeezed his ribs. The pain distracted him from coming to orgasm.

His captor must be satisfied first.

Punishment would follow if he disappointed.

The Perspex flexed above him. In the darkness he saw nothing. Heard nothing but the squeak of moist palms against Perspex and muffled panting. No words.

This won't end . . . this will never end.

On and on. The perpetual motion of flesh against his flesh.

But then it changed. Louder panting, convulsive movement from above. Spasms.

Then the body was gone from his. He heard the bolts turn and the panel lowered. In a moment he'd slithered off, soaked in perspiration. He thought he'd have orgasmed with his captor but sheer willpower on his part had prevented his release.

Still hard and still slick from his encounter he crawled on his hands and knees across his cage. Found his mattress in the dark. Curled up tight on it. Kept his eyes shut. Waited for the hours to pass.

Chapter Twenty-two

Imad woke up late in the morning, still tired. Bone weary. He had not fallen asleep until dawn and feverish dreams had made the sleep a broken, frightening business. Flashes of dream returned to him. A woman weeping brokenhearted in the closet. A grimy hand slapping lifelessly at his windowpane. The green dress, torn and bloody, whirling around his bedroom; falling on his face, smothering . . .

Dreams.

They can't hurt.

But they can torment. They can haunt.

Tonight, he would find himself a woman for comfort.

He thought of Hydra spiked on his erection, writhing on it, head thrown back, small breasts thrust out. Hydra twitching as the small bullets pierced her back through the closed door as Blaze had fired from within the closet. Hydra, half her face gone, a dark cavity where there ought to be a cheek and a cynical eye and a glossy forehead . . . and a hole where part of her brain should have been, and . . . He clenched his fist, perspiring.

She was like Amara, that way.

Amara.

That fiend had caused all this – filled him with fear and guilt, started him searching the low parts of town for women. Certainly, there had been women before. Many of them. But there had never been the desperation. There had never been a Hydra.

She was Amara's fault.

He should go to the museum and defecate at Amara's feet. Throw hog fat onto the wizened corpse. For ancient Egyptians, like Jews and Moslems, pigs were unclean animals. Long ago in Egypt criminals were sometimes sewn into pigskins and buried alive. It killed their spirit and deprived the man of his afterlife with the gods.

He was tempted to take Callahan's memoir along, too. It would be a relief to be rid of it.

No.

Callahan had said to keep it in the safe unless Amara walked. So far, all seemed well.

So far.

Perhaps she had only walked that night to avenge herself on Callahan. Perhaps.

In any case, he would return the memoir to the safe and go to the museum without it to defecate at Amara's feet. A ripe offering of turd for her late Egyptian majesty.

Laughing sourly, Imad climbed out of bed. He would not defecate at Amara's feet today. Nor tomorrow. The farther he remained from the hideous thing the better.

He put on his robe and slippers, then went downstairs. Outside, the morning was sunny and hot. A wonderful day for the beach. Perhaps he would go there later. Perhaps he would find a lovely young woman, ripe and golden in a bikini. And willing. She must be willing, of course. If Imad's good looks and charm and mammoth bulge at the crotch were insufficient to woo her, his wealth would likely accomplish the task.

He picked up the morning paper. As he walked back to the house between beds of sweetly scented flowers he slipped off its string and opened it. On the front page, he saw no mention of bodies being found in remote woodland. He waited until he was inside before studying the paper more thoroughly. He checked each page. As he progressed he began to realize that there would be no mention of the bodies of Blaze and Hydra. After all, didn't the paper go to press late in the night? At perhaps two or three a.m.?

Nothing would appear, he realized, until tomorrow morning's edition. Assuming the bodies would be found by then.

He was about to fold the paper shut when an article caught his eye. Merely a single column beneath a blurry photograph of a middle-aged man in a uniform.

WARD WATCHMAN KILLED IN FALL
The night watchman at the Charles Ward Museum fell to his death late Thursday night, police officials stated. According to a police spokesman, the watchman, Barney Quinn, 53, sustained severe neck injuries in his plunge down the main staircase to the museum's lobby. The cause of death is under investigation.

Quinn, a former police officer with the . . .

Imad skipped the biographical details, but returned to read the first paragraph again and again. *The Charles Ward Museum . . . severe neck injuries . . .* It told him little. Even so, it frightened him. There was more meaning in that dark print for Imad than he dared to imagine.

Amara . . .

Chapter Twenty-three

'Blam, blam!' Toby yelled.

Byron kept running. If he could just get to the clump of bushes, he'd circle around and ambush Toby.

'Hey! I gotcha!'

'Did not,' Byron shouted over his shoulder.

'No fair! I gotcha right in the heart!'

'I've got a bulletproof vest!'

'Do not!'

'Do so!' Byron ducked behind the bushes. Looking back, he saw Toby walking slowly toward him through the high, brown weeds. The boy's lips were sticking out.

'I *got* you!' Toby called. 'No bulletproof vests. We agreed.'

'Okay, I'll take it off.' Byron sneaked sideways, staying low behind the bushes. Then sprang out. '*Ker-plam! Plam, plam!*'

Toby turned to him, startled.

'Three shots right in the heart.'

'Ha, ha. I'm wearing a bulletproof vest, too.'

'Yeah, but I've got armor-piercing bullets!'

'Do not!' Toby raised his plastic pistol. 'Blam! Right in the puss!'

Byron grabbed his face, spun around, flopped to the ground. When he opened his eyes he found himself staring into a leathery, eyeless face. He scrambled to his knees and peered at it. Then at the rest of the body. All that hair . . . red like the red foil you sometimes get on chocolates . . . and skin. Dry. Hard. A glossy look. For some reason it reminded him of the skin of a melon, only dark brown. He could even smell it. A spicy smell. Like a deli store. One that needed airing out badly. The spicy odors settled thickly in the back of his throat.

'Wow,' he whispered. 'Toby . . . hey, Toby!'

'You're dead.'

'Toby . . .'

'At least you're supposed to be.'

'No. Come here.'

'Gotcha right in the puss.'

'Come here and take a look!'

'I know that trick, so no can do.'

'Toby. Take a look! This is really cool! Quick!'

Toby, holstering the made-in-Hong Kong weapon, ran through the weeds to join Byron.

As they both stared at the dark face, a spider crawled out of its left eye socket, scurried down its ruined cheek that was as ridged and wrinkled as a 3D relief of the Rockies.

At last Toby managed to ask, 'What is it?'

'A body.'

'I saw my Uncle Frank's body. Looked nothing like this critter.'

'Maybe this one's older?' Byron suggested.

'Maybe it isn't even a body. Maybe it's a dummy. Somebody put it here to scare us.'

'Looks like a body to me, a naked body,' Byron said. 'A real old one. Like maybe an Indian that got killed a hundred years ago.'

'What are those?' Toby asked, pointing.

'Her tits, stupid.'

'Yuck.'

'See that? She's a girl.'

'You sure?'

'Jeez, Toby, don't you know nothing? If it hasn't got a whang, it's a girl. That's how you tell.'

'I knew that.'

'Sure you did. *Sure*.'

'I *did*.'

'The only way it isn't a girl is if a guy gets his whang cut off with a knife. Then he turns into a girl, anyway. They call 'em trans-sectionals.'

'Sure. I knew that. Everyone knows that.'

'Yeah.' Reaching out, Byron touched the brown skin of the body's shoulder. It felt dry and wrinkled, like beef jerky, before smoothing out across the chest to that melon skin effect, then rising to hollow breasts that looked like . . . well, they just looked gross. 'Oooh, you oughtta feel it.'

Toby nodded. He looked pale, but he knelt in the weeds, poked a finger into the mass of red hair. It scrunched dry as the weeds themselves that were under his knees. The hair felt springy at first but his finger got entangled with it the deeper he pushed. For some irrational reason he thought something would be in the hair. Something that'd *bite*. He withdrew his finger and touched the same shoulder as Byron now pawed. 'I don't think it's real.'

'Sure it is.'

'We better tell our folks.'

'Are you kidding? They'd take it away from us.'

'It isn't ours anyway.'

'Is now. Finders keepers.'

'What do you want it for?'

Byron shrugged. 'Come on, let's take it over to my house.'

'This way,' Byron said, leading the group of children across his backyard. There were five of them: Barbara and Tina, who'd been skipping rope in Tina's driveway; Hank Greenberg, found shooting baskets alone; and the Watson twins, picked up on their return from the A&W. He could have dug up half a dozen more neighborhood kids, but Barbara was getting impatient and she was a big mouth. Big, *loud* mouth. After the group was finished, he'd have Barbara out of his hair. He could take his time and round up a bigger bunch. Guaranteed no big mouths.

'It better be good,' Barbara said, 'or you've gotta give us our money back.'

'Oh-ho no,' Byron told her. 'It's fifty cents a look and you can't have your money back, no matter what.'

'I'm not gonna look, then.'
'Okay. Get outta here.'
'No.'
'Want to get pounded?'
'Give him his money,' Tina said. 'If it ain't any good, I'll get my brother on him.'

At the corner of the garage Byron halted the group and took the admission fees. The Watson twins paid with a fresh, stiff dollar bill. The others paid in quarters. He counted the take: $2.50.

Pretty good.
But that's only the start.
This's gonna make me rich.
'Okay,' he told them. 'Follow me.'
He led them behind the garage where Toby was waiting.

'Feast your eyes,' Byron announced, trying to sound like a ringmaster. He swept his hand toward a long shape propped against the garage wall. A white sheet shrouded it from top to bottom.

'Bet it's Tommy Jones,' Barbara said, sarcastic, and reached for the sheet.

Byron shoved her away.
'Hey!' she snapped.
'Don't you touch it.'
'It's just Tommy Jones. And this is just a rip-off. Come out, Tommy.'
'If it is,' Tina said, 'I'm going to fetch my brother and there's gonna be some busted noses round here.'

'It isn't Tommy, it's . . .' Byron paused for dramatic effect. 'It's the body of an ancient Apache squaw.'

'Oh, sure.'
'Everyone stand back,' Byron advised. 'You don't want to be standing too close.'

Barbara stepped away. She folded her arms across her T-shirt. Her face wore a smirk.

'Ready?' Toby asked.
'Wait.' Byron turned to his audience. 'You've gotta promise to keep it a secret and never tell a soul.'

'It's something dirty,' Barbara muttered.

Tina giggled. 'Tommy's probably in his birthday suit.'

'Cross your hearts and hope to die,' Byron said.

They all crossed their hearts except Barbara. 'I'm not gonna hope to die. It's against my religion.'

'Okay. But you've got to promise. If you tell anyone, we'll pound you.'

'You and who else, doofus?'

'Jeez, Barbara,' Tina said. 'Let's see what it is.'

'I know what it is. It's Tommy Jones with his peter out.'

The Watson twins giggled.

'Tommy's in Yosemite,' said Hank Greenberg. 'His uncle's gotta place up there. They go fishing in the—'

'Hey! You guys want to see this or don't you?' Byron sounded short of patience now.

'Sure,' Barbara said, arms still crossed, still belligerent. 'Let's see what the big deal is.'

Byron nodded to Toby.

Toby tugged the sheet. As the sheet pulled loose, revealing the dried body, the figure tipped forward. The girls screamed. They leaped out of the way as it fell into their midst, hair flaring out, sightless eyes staring into their faces. Still screaming, they ran. Didn't stop running. Piercing screams faded into the distance.

Hank, pale and shaking his head, backed away. 'You guys are nuts,' he muttered. Then he ran, too. Made it as far as the driveway, tossed his cookies, then carried on running.

'They're gonna tell,' Toby said.

'Let 'em . . . just let 'em. We'll just say they lied.' He felt the money in his pocket. $2.50. This was just a start. He was gonna be the richest kid in town.

'But what about *her*?' Toby pointed at the mummy lying face down, its hair covering its back in a swathe of tumbling curls.

Byron stared at her, frowning. This was his cash cow. He wasn't losing it for nothing. 'I've got it! We'll hide her someplace. In my bedroom. Under my bed. They'll never think of looking there.'

'Is anybody home?' Toby asked.

Byron shook his head. 'Mom took the baby with her when she went shopping. Come on. Take the head.'

Chapter Twenty-four

'I feel so grubby,' Susan said as they left the museum later that morning. Tag held her hand. They walked down the broad, concrete stairs. 'Like I've been touched by something really disgusting.'

'Not my hand, is it? I swear I washed it this morning.'

She laughed softly. 'No, it's not your hand. I'm sure your hand is immaculate.'

'It's not *that* clean.'

'No, but don't you ever feel that way? Like you're contaminated from just being close to where such awful things have happened?'

'I feel that way a lot. You know what takes care of it? A long hot shower, strong soap, a couple of drinks, a good meal, clever conversation – preferably not alone. A little siesta.'

'Preferably not alone,' Susan repeated, the smile still playing on her lips. 'Sounds like it might do the trick. I really have to spend more time with Geoffrey today, though. We don't see enough of each other as it is.'

'We've got the whole day ahead of us,' Tag said.

'I'm feeling less grubby by the second.'

'Just doing my job, ma'am.'

They went to Tag's apartment. The siesta came first, but they didn't sleep. Then they took a long hot shower, soaping each other, growing excited by the feel of slippery skin, and making love awkwardly in the tub with water pelting them like hot rain. When they were dry and dressed, they took the elevator down to Susan's apartment.

She made Tag a Bloody Mary. She drank Perrier and played with the baby while María made tacos for lunch.

'This has turned into a pretty decent day,' Tag said.

'Not half bad,' Susan agreed. She felt good. Her skin tingled. She felt warm inside, pleasantly satisfied. The horrors at the museum, the threat of Mable, seemed far away.

After lunch, they took Geoffrey outside for a stroll in the sun. Tag looked happy pushing the baby carriage. They walked for blocks, finally arriving at a municipal park where they sat in the bleachers and watched kids playing softball.

'Geoffrey's going to be a real slugger,' Tag told her.

'What makes you think so?'

'I'm gonna teach him.'

Geoffrey turned his wide eyes on Tag and grinned as if he understood.

When a foul ball shot toward his face, he blinked, kept grinning. Susan gasped with fright. Tag flung out a hand, caught the ball, tossed it back to the kids with a good-natured, 'Here you are.'

'I think it's time to leave,' Susan said quickly.

They were watching television later that afternoon when the telephone rang. Susan picked it up. 'Hello?'

'Hello? Miss Connors? Is Taggart Parker in?'

'Yes, he is. Just a moment, I'll see if I can tear him away from the game.' She waved the phone at him. 'For you.'

'Marty Benson?'

She shrugged.

Tag took the phone. 'Hello . . . ah, Marty. What've you come up with?' He listened for a long time, nodding at first, then frowning. Finally, he said, 'Okay, thanks a lot.' Hanging up, he turned to Susan. 'Marty's with the Medical Examiner's Office. I asked him to call me when they finished with Becker and Gonzalez.'

'That was quick.'

'They put a rush on.' He sat down and stared at the television. The crowd went wild but he didn't react. He was lost in thought, frowning.

'Well?' Susan asked.

'The wounds on both men match. They weren't made by dog teeth.'

'Then by what?'

'By a human.'

'*Jesus.*'

'Gonzalez got off some shots before he was killed. He hit something and knocked out plenty of tissue and bone. They analyzed it . . . and it was old, real old. Dead tissue. Traces of natron, some chemical they used to . . .'

'I know. Part of the mummification process. They used it to speed up the dehydration which in turn halted decay of the flesh.'

'The upshot is, they're pretty sure the tissue came from the mummy.'

'He was shooting at Amara?'

Tag sighed into his folded hands. 'It sure looks that way. And get this: they found scrapings of the same flesh under Beckerman's fingernails. Also long red hairs on the body that matched those found in Amara's coffin.'

'What does that mean?'

'If I threw you down on the floor right now and ripped off your clothes . . .'

'You wouldn't dare.'

'And you tried to fight me off . . .'

'Which I would, since María's in the kitchen.'

Tag grinned, but he looked tired. 'You might scratch me. You'd likely end up with some of my skin under your nails. Maybe some of my hair lying around.'

'And they found Amara's skin under Beckerman's nails, and some of her hair on his clothes, which means he was fighting with her?'

'That's how it looks. It's impossible, of course.'

'Ever heard of a guy by the name of Lazarus?' Susan asked.

'Sure. I've also heard of little green men from Mars.' He shook his head. 'Maybe Beckerman and Gonzalez ran into robbers in the stairwell, and one used the mummy as a shield. That could explain how she got shot. Then the guy flung her at Beckerman and he scratched.'

'Okay, but they were killed by human teeth.'

'The robbers could have done it.'

'Oh? How?'

'They subdued Beckerman and Gonzalez and used the mummy's teeth to finish the job.'

Susan's eyes widened. '*Manually?*'

'Like this.' One hand holding his forehead, he used his other hand to work the jaw.

'That's pretty far-fetched,' Susan told him.

'Considerably less far-fetched than a living mummy.'

'Suppose Amara did kill them?'

'That's pretty hard to suppose.'

'It would explain a lot, though, wouldn't it?'

Tag grinned, shaking his head. 'Sure. It would explain everything. Only problem is, dead people don't walk. Dead people don't bite.'

Chapter Twenty-five

'You'll never make it into pictures.'
 'Says who?'
 'You've gotta have an agent.'
 'I'll get one.'
 'How?'
 'They'll be listed in the phone book. I'll call them up.'
 'Yeah, right. As if that doesn't happen a hundred times a day.'
 'I've got experience; they'll see me.'
 'Showing your jugs on a hardware poster isn't much experience.'
 'I've done TV ads.'
 'When you were fifteen.'
 'I'm only seventeen now.'
 'TV ads for a burger joint that no one's ever heard of outta North Carolina.'
 'And corporates . . . I've done corporate video.'
 'That's not the movies, is it? Charlottesville ain't Hollywood and you know it, Grace.'
 'No one asked you to come.'
 'I'm not staying to get boned by old Joe now you've gone.'
 'Pix! You said you wouldn't bring that up again. *You promised.*'
 Cody slammed the steering wheel with his palm. 'Pix. You keep quiet about that now.'
 'It's the truth,' Pix protested.
 'I don't care if it is the truth. We agreed that's history. We wouldn't talk about Joe again. Okay?'
 Pix was sixteen years old. She chewed a strand of her long blonde

hair; face sullen, she stared out the window at passing traffic.

He slammed the steering wheel again.

'*Okay?*'

By way of reply: 'I'm hungry, Cody.'

'We'll eat soon,' Grace said. 'We'll be in LA in a couple of hours.'

'I want something now. I'll start feeling sick if I don't eat soon.'

'Want an apple?' Grace sounded tired. This journey was taking it out of her.

'I don't like apples.'

'You ate one this morning, Pix.'

'That's 'cos there was nothing else.'

Cody aimed to be diplomatic. He couldn't stand another row after driving near-nonstop for the last three days. 'I'll find a diner.'

Grace shook her head. 'No diners. The police'll be looking for the truck.'

'Don't worry,' he told her. 'I'll park up then walk. No one will recognize me.'

'Yah,' Pix sneered. 'You're hardly America's most wanted, Cody.'

'You lay off that.'

'The FBI are sure going to put every man they've got on the case,' Pix said, then held her nose so when she talked it sounded like a police radio. 'Attention. Attention. Be on the lookout for Cody Wilde, eighteen years of age, gas-station jockey from Going-Nowheresville, suspected of stealing fifteen-year-old Ford pick-up, worth approximately one hundred and three dollars, eighteen cents. Shoot on sight. I repeat. Shoot on sight.'

'Pix, will you quit it?' Cody fumed. *Would you believe it? Who runs away from home with their girlfriend only to take the kid sister along? A kid sister from hell who's whined, who's kvetched, who's complained for the last two thousand miles straight.* Still, better that she came along than being left home with Joe.

He glanced at Grace sitting beside him. She was beautiful. Dark Latino eyes. She had a great body. The body of a dancer. He knew he was in love with her, and he knew they were doing the right thing, escaping that hell-hole where she lived with her indolent mother and Joe who was . . . hell, who was no great shakes as a human being, never mind a stepfather.

Amara

The plan was to shoot for Hollywood. They both knew she could make it into movies if she got the right breaks. She *could* dance. She *could* act. A couple of years ago she'd starred in a whole string of TV ads for Chucky Burger in their hometown. She'd made good money, which she'd set aside for college.

Wise kid.

But she hadn't banked on Old Joe moving in.

Huh, the college fund?

Joe found it, took it, spent it.

Grace's mother never even roused herself from in front of the TV. Never accused Joe. Most she whined was: 'Grace. I'm sure he had his reasons . . .'

Pix sang out. 'There's a diner. Hey, stupid. A diner!'

'I see it.'

'You've gone right past it.'

'I know. I'm going to park up, then walk back.'

Grace looked uneasy. 'The road's awful busy. What if there's a cop—'

'Don't worry.' He pulled off along a dirt track that led into the desert. 'We can't be seen from the road here.' Parking the truck behind a mound of tires that some litter-louse had dumped, he switched off the motor. The relief of silence after hours of hearing the roar of the engine. Boy, Cody loved the sweet silence.

Not that it would last.

'I'm so hungry I could choke,' Pix said, winding down the window. 'Gee, it's so hot I could choke.'

Grace gritted her teeth. 'You want to choke? Be my guest.'

'Some sister you are.'

'Some sister *you* are, Pix. You begged to come with us, now you bug us nonstop.'

'Well, Hollywood's a stupid choice. You'll never get into pictures.'

'So what do you suggest, Pix?'

'New York.'

'New York?'

'We could've got work there!'

'Pix!' Cody slammed the steering wheel with his hand again. Sweat burned his eyes. His back ached from driving clean across the country.

137

He felt dirty. Needed a shower. Needed a drink; a cold, cold beer. This endless arguing he *didn't* need. He took a deep breath to steady his temper. 'Pix. What can I get you to eat?'

When he took the orders he told them to stay put until he came back. 'I'll be twenty minutes, tops,' he told them.

'Ice cream . . . bring some ice cream.' Pix leaned out the window.

'It'll melt,' he told her, then walked away.

Grace watched Cody go. He walked like a Wild West hero along the desert track back to the highway. His brown cowboy boots raised dust with that nice even stride of his. She watched the way his lean body in the denim jeans and jacket moved. There was a confident rhythm there. He glanced back at her and smiled that easy smile that she loved so much.

In her ear Pix humphed. 'I bet he takes ages. And I bet he forgets the mayonnaise.'

Grace hoped this was for the best. Maybe she should have stuck it out back home a little longer?

I could have married Cody. Found a place of our own. Being a teen runaway sounded glamorous. But these long hours on the road in a stolen truck were taking their toll.

Sure the truck was stolen from Mom's boyfriend.

And, for sure, the truck had been bought using *her* money for the TV work she'd done.

But she was certain that Joe would have reported it as stolen. And stolen by his girlfriend's daughter and lover. And maybe he would claim that they'd kidnapped Pix, too. Just to add a little more seasoning to the charge sheet. Cody could get time for this. Even though everyone knew that Cody was the gentlest, kindest guy you could ever meet. Okay, so he didn't shine bright at school where she'd first met him more than five years ago. But he was the last man on Earth to pull a mean stunt or bad-mouth anyone behind their back.

She didn't want to see him in trouble with the cops.

Maybe she could have stayed?

Maybe.

Maybe gone to her own private hell, too.

It all went crazy last week.

Joe had leered at her plenty. He even took to fingering her underwear in the laundry basket and making cheap comments. 'Bet Cody likes you in this. You dance for him like they do down at the Snake Pit? Dance with your back to him and rub your butt in his crotch, huh?'

Then last week she'd been woken by hands touching her under the sheet. She'd smelled beery breath panting into her face. Heard grunting. 'Your mom's sick. I haven't nailed her in a week. Looks like your lucky night, Grace.'

'Joe?'

'Old Joe, friendly old Joe,' he slurred. 'Now pull up that nightie . . . up over your hips . . . there's a good girl.'

'Get off me . . .'

'C'mon, Joe ain't gonna hurt you.'

'No.'

'Nothing you ain't done before plenty, I bet.'

She reached out, yanked the light cord.

In the blaze of light she looked up to see Joe kneeling on the bed, pawing the sheet from her, his chin slick with saliva. With his other hand he was working himself hard. Panting. Face nearer crimson than red. Watery-eyed stare fixed excitedly on her body.

'Nice tits. Nice and firm. Big, too,' he muttered in surprise. 'Bigger than I thought . . . never would have guessed.'

'No, please, Joe.'

'Joe won't hurt yer.'

'*Get off—*'

'Might even enjoy it. Might want more in a day or so.'

'Don't touch me. Ow!'

Joe had clamped his thick fingers on her breast. Squeezed hard.

'Gonna get those nipples all pert and erect. Little nip'll do the trick.'

She took a deep breath, ready to scream the walls down.

'You do, you little bitch, and I'll bang your little sister, so you be nice to me and your sis stays virgo intacto. You follow?'

Grace had frozen then. She knew that he would. Mom wouldn't do anything. Maybe she could hear now as she lay there in her own bed, shutting out the sounds, thinking about the lives of the soap stars who she cared about so much more than her real family.

'That's it. You lay nice and still, Grace. Oooh-ay, have you ever seen a boner as big as that?'

'Joe,' she whispered. 'Please don't do this to me.'

'Once this baby goes inside, 's gonna stir your brains some.'

'Don't . . . please.'

She looked down as his hand went to her throat. He squeezed. A message: *Don't mess with me, or else.*

Then his hand went down.

Down.

Down to her breasts again. They formed hard mounds in the cool air.

He kneaded them. Squeezed. Pinched nipples between nicotine-stained finger and thumb. Pinched hard until it brought a cry to the back of her throat. But she clamped her lips to stop the cry escaping with the ferocity it demanded.

'Good girl. You know when to keep your mouth shut.' He pinched her nipple until it turned black and congested. 'Although I like it when a girl knows to open her mouth when the time's right. Know what I mean?'

In terror she looked up at his beer-sodden face. His jaw stubbled with gray.

He's going to rape me.

He's going to rape me and I can't stop it. He'll do the same to Pix if I resist. Oh, Mom, how could you?

She'd lain there. Looked up at the ceiling. Those rough hands squeezing, stroking, probing. She looked at the posters of pop groups on the walls. Tried to concentrate on them. Block it out. She focused on the picture of James Dean tacked to the back of the door.

Joe's fingers reached down to the cleft between her legs. Fingers pushed hard.

'*Stop it.*' Her arm swung up and she scratched the side of his face. She couldn't take this anymore.

Joe looked down at her in fury. Bloodshot eyes grew to the size of eggs in his face.

'I was tryin' to be nice . . . if you don't want nice you can have rough.' He slapped her.

Her head whipped back against the pillow. Her face felt numb; her mind swam, dazed.

'Now I'm gonna flip you over . . . I'm gonna nail you in the ass . . . teach you a little respect.'

Grace felt his hands on her body, turning her over. A second later she lay on her stomach, her bare bottom upward. Then he was on her. The weight of him pushing so hard in the small of her back she felt her spine would snap.

Agony.

Unbearable agony.

Got to shout. Got to scream.

But he pushed her face into the pillow. Now she couldn't even breathe.

'Gonna show you. Once this baby goes in, 's gonna split you like a melon.'

She felt him pushing at her. Trying to force his penis into her, but she was too dry. He couldn't slip inside.

'Got a little trick of my own,' he panted in triumph. 'This does the trick.'

He shifted his weight off her but still pushed with one hand in the middle of her shoulder blades, holding her down. She lifted her head, turned it.

In the mirror of the dressing table she saw what he did next.

Her stomach turned in disgust.

He hawked wetly before spitting a great mouthful of sputum into his cupped hand. Then he rubbed it onto the bulbous swelling on the end of his penis.

'Lubrication.' He grinned. 'Good ol' slippery lube.'

She felt him lower himself back . . .

No . . . can't . . . won't . . .

With his weight shifted from her top half she pushed herself up onto her left elbow while with her right hand she reached back. Grabbed his balls in her fist.

'Don't you dare,' he snarled. 'I'll beat you—'

With all her strength she squeezed . . . twisted . . . pulled.
His scream set all the dogs in the neighborhood barking.

Now a week later, here by the pile of tires in the desert, Joe was thousands of miles away.

Pix was safe.

Although that didn't stop her complaints. Complaints about the long journey. Complaints about sleeping in the truck. Complaints about an uncomfortable this . . . an irritating that . . .

After Grace had cooled Joe's ardor she'd grabbed what she could, including Pix, then fled the house in Joe's truck. There came a confused whirl of telling Cody everything. Then the crazy dash out of town at the dead of night.

Now here.

'Here' was a desert.

With the sun going down. And with stumpy trees that looked like zombies from some bloodthirsty horror film.

She'd switched on the radio for a while. Surfed the stations. One carried a news report of two guys being killed at a museum; the theft of a mummy . . .

She found a music channel. Flamenco music . . . she liked that . . . made her think of faraway places. Mexico . . . beautiful dancers whirling in brightly colored skirts beneath starry skies.

'I hate that music,' Pix said. 'Find some rock.'

Thud.

At that moment a hand struck the windshield. Grace started. In the back Pix gave a yelp of fright.

She looked out to see three guys. They weren't old. Could have been high-school dropouts. They chewed gum and smoked black stumps of cigars. The one who'd thumped the glass looked at her through mean eyes. Grinned.

'It's Christmas, guys,' he told his buddies. 'Christmas come early.'

Chapter Twenty-six

While his parents were off in their bedroom getting dressed for a party, Byron ate his hamburger in the den. He watched a rerun of *Superman*. Then the news came on.

He was stuffing the final chunk of toasted bun into his mouth when the blonde newswoman said, 'Closer to home, our own Charles Ward Museum was the scene last night of a brutal double killing. Two security guards from the Haymer Agency, Arnulfo Gonzalez and Ernest Beckerman, were found slain in the museum when it opened this morning – this, on the heels of the death of guard Barney Quinn on the previous night. Lenny Farrel was on the scene this morning with our live-action mini-cam to give us this report.'

The picture changed to a curly-haired man holding a microphone. Byron recognized the museum's main entrance behind the man. 'With me is Lieutenant Carlos Vasquez, the officer in charge of the investigation.' He turned to the broad-faced man. 'Lieutenant, there's been a great deal of rumor afloat regarding the manner in which the two guards met their deaths. Can you shed some light in that direction?'

'Until the medical examiner has completed his investigation, Lenny, I'd prefer not to speculate.'

'We have information that they appeared to have been mauled by an animal.'

'I'd prefer not to speculate on the cause of death.'

'According to an earlier police statement, Lieutenant, the men were killed while trying to foil a robbery attempt. Was anything, in fact, stolen?'

Vasquez nodded. 'A portion of the Egyptian collection does appear to be missing. We assume it was taken by the perpetrators.'

'By "missing portion", are you referring to the mummy?'

'Yes. A mummy does appear to have gone.'

'A mummy?' Byron muttered. He stared at the television.

'Are other items missing?'

'Not to our knowledge.'

'Thank you, Lieutenant.' The reporter gestured to someone off at the side. The camera turned, showing a young woman who looked awfully pretty – even prettier than Byron's favorite teacher, Miss Bloom. She had soft hair, bright blue eyes. The neck of her blouse was open. Her skin looked like gold. One side of her face was bruised. Maybe someone had tried to punch her out. But who'd do something like that to such a pretty woman?

'Susan Connors is assistant curator here at the museum, and in charge of the Egyptian collection. Miss Connors, can you speculate as to the motive for the robbery? The missing mummy? Was it worth killing for?'

'I suppose it must be in some eyes. Three men are dead.'

'How much intrinsic value does a mummy have?'

'Normally, not more than a few thousand dollars. Their chief value – the reason they've been the targets of robbers through the centuries – is the objects buried along with them, either in the coffin or wrapped inside the linen bandages. This one had already been plundered . . . unwrapped. If she was buried with jewelry and precious artifacts it was stolen long ago. She's really nothing more than a pile of skin and bones.'

The reporter nodded. 'So you see little reason for stealing her?'

'She's a significant piece of historical heritage. That alone gives her a certain value. Some collectors would go to great lengths to have her.'

'Her? You will know her name, then?'

'Yes, hieroglyphs on the mummy case tell us her name was Amara.'

'And so people have gone to murderous lengths to steal Amara.' The reporter's face filled the television screen. 'Two men dead of causes the police refuse to disclose. Another killed in a mysterious fall, Thursday night. Amara, the missing mummy. The police appear to be baffled. This is Lenny Farrel, reporting to you from the Charles Ward Museum. Back to you, Bonnie.'

Nervously, Byron looked out the den window at the street. An hour had gone by since the newscast. Any second, the cops were sure to show up, blue lights flashing, sirens whooping. Cops with guns drawn. A bullhorn crackling. *'Come on out, kid, we know you're in there . . .'*

But maybe none of the other kids had seen the news. Maybe he was safe from arrest.

'You okay?' Karen asked, looking up from Jane as she peeled off soiled diapers.

He smiled for her. 'Sure.'

'You look kind of sick.'

'I'm okay.'

'Sure?'

'Yeah.'

He wished he could tell Karen about the mummy. It would make him feel better, talking to someone. She was nice. She was his favorite baby-sitter. Sometimes she let him stay up late to watch some creature feature. If he showed her the mummy, though, she'd probably tell on him.

The cops would take him away.

There I am in the cuffs. The cop's hand pressing down on my head as I climb into the back of the cruiser with its flashing blue lights. And there would be Barbara, ringside, grinning. *Hell.*

The cops might bust him for killing those guards. They'd be sure to think he did it. His prints would be all over the mummy. Maybe he'd get the gas chamber. In his mind's eye he saw Barbara, in the ringside seat again, right at the front where she could look through the glass panel of the chamber. Grinning all over her face. Grinning as he choked. Blue lips . . . bulging eyes. And the last thing he'd see would be Barbara's grin. *Hell.*

A black and white patrol car appeared on the street. Byron's stomach knotted.

They're here.
Come for me.

No messing.
Maybe one of the dead guards was a buddy of the cop?
'Don't bother with the arrest on this one, Bill . . . this one's personal . . . this kid killed my best friend . . . Just blow the little freak away the second he shows his face . . .'

Oh, Holy Christ on a motorcycle. Byron's chest turned slick with sweat under his shirt. He craved the john . . . fear did that to people . . . he'd crave the john in the gas chamber. Barbara would scream with laughter when he peed himself . . .

Holy Jesus.

The car kept moving. The cops seemed more interested in chatting to each other. Hadn't even looked in his direction. As he breathed a sigh of relief as the black and white car cruised out of sight, a bicycle turned up along the driveway. A girl climbed off.

Barbara!

She tipped the bike onto its side, leaving the back wheel turning, then came up the driveway with long, self-important strides.

'Karen, can I go out for a second?'

'Your mother said to stay inside.'

'Just on the porch, okay? Somebody's here. I've gotta talk to her.'

'*Her*, huh?' She gave a knowing smile. 'Okay, but don't leave the porch, do you hear, Bryon?'

'I won't.'

Byron opened the door as Barbara was reaching toward the bell. He stepped out quickly, let the screen bang behind him.

'What do you want?' he asked.

Folding her arms, she grinned in her stuck-up way. 'I know.'

'Know what?'

'Whatcha think?'

'Search me.'

'I know your secret?'

'Yeah?' His mouth went dry.

'I know all about you and that mummy.'

'You don't know nothing.'

'Oh, yeah? I watch *Eyewitness News* every night. A young lady has to keep herself informed.'

'So?'

'I know all about it.'

'Like what?'

'Like it was stolen from the museum.' Barbara's eyes gleamed. This was pure candy for her. 'Like the guards were slaughtered like sheep.'

'So what?'

'I'm going to tell.'

'Tell who?'

'Who else? The cops.'

'You better not,' Byron warned. He took a threatening step toward her, but she held her ground.

'You don't scare me,' she told him.

'You'd better not tell.'

'I won't. But only if you let me see it again.'

'I haven't got it.'

'I bet.'

'I haven't. We took it back where we found it and left it there. Honest.'

'Then you won't mind the cops searching the house?'

'No. Why should I? I haven't got it.'

'Sure.' She scratched her thigh, then turned away. 'See you tomorrow, Byron. On *Eyewitness News*.'

He watched her walk toward her bike. With her short hair and T-shirt and shorts, she didn't look much like a girl. She didn't act like one, either. But she *was* a girl. Byron had a policy not to beat them up. You might threaten to pound them, but that was only talk.

It's chickenshit to beat up girls.

Guys didn't do that.

Not real guys, anyway.

He wished Barbara was a boy. He'd knock the daylights out of her.

'Okay,' he said. 'I've got it.'

She turned round, grinning. Came back to him. 'Let's see.'

'You can't come in.'

'Then bring it out.'

'Yeah, I can just walk through the house with it.'

'So?'

'The baby-sitter will see it, brain-box. How about tomorrow?'

'No dice. Show me, or I'll blow the whistle.'

'Whistle?' Startled, he looked at her hands.

'That's just an expression . . . a figure of speech. Don't you know *anything*, Byron? Now let's go in and have a look.'

'Okay. Come on. But keep your mouth shut. I'll do all the talking. Got that?'

'Just get on with it, Byron.'

Feeling humiliated, manipulated, he led her into the living room. 'Karen, this is my friend Barbara. I have to show her something in my room.'

Karen smiled strangely. Knowingly. 'In your bedroom?'

Byron nodded.

'This is a new one. What do you want to show her?'

'Nothing much.'

'Oh, you're just being modest,' Karen said, the smile broadening.

'Huh?'

'Okay, go ahead. But leave your door open.'

'Sure.'

They went down the long hallway to Byron's bedroom. The room was dim in the light of the evening sun, but Byron didn't bother with a lamp. Kneeling, he reached under his bed. Grunted. Started to pull. 'Help me, will you?'

'I should say not. Imagine the germs.'

He managed to slide the mummy out by himself. 'There,' he panted. Barbara peered at it. Her nose wrinkled. 'That's disgusting.'

'Sort of.'

'She's naked.'

'Whatcha want me to do? Put her in panties and a bra?'

'You've probably been playing with her, haven't you?'

'Have not.'

'I'll bet.'

'You can see her front bottom.'

'I haven't touched her. Not *those* places. Who'd want to?'

'Only a creepy pervert like you.'

'Oh yeah?'

'Yeah, you can see your finger marks on her butt.'
'Cannot.'
'Pervert.'
'Am not.'
'If you're not a creepy pervert, what're you keeping her for?'
'Finders keepers.'
'Are you going to give her back?'
'Why should I?'
'She belongs to the museum, that's why. She was stolen. Finders keepers doesn't work when it's stolen. You still go to jail.'

Byron shrugged. 'Well, I might give her back. I'm keeping her tonight, though. Toby's gonna bring his Polaroid over tomorrow. We're gonna take pictures of her.'

'That is gross.'

'It'll be neat. You can get in a picture with it, too, if you want.'

'Who'd want to?' Contorting her face, she touched the chocolate-brown mummy with the toe of her sneaker. The empty eyes seemed to stare into hers while the red hair formed a shining red halo around the skull-like head. And as for those teeth . . . 'Do I get to keep the picture?'

'Sure.'

'Okay, then. You can keep it till tomorrow. I'll let you. But then you've got to take it back.'

Byron nodded. He had no intention of returning the mummy, but it seemed a good idea to let Barbara think he would. That'd keep her quiet for tonight, anyway. Keep her from telling her parents who'd then tell the cops. By tomorrow, maybe he'd think of something else. He pushed the mummy under his bed, its hair crackling with static as it dragged across the nylon carpet. He'd best open a window wide, too. Disperse the stale deli smell. The thing seemed to sweat garlic and onion odors.

'What time tomorrow?' Barbara asked.

'Ten. In the back of my garage.'

'And I get a picture free?' She was calculating the value of such a picture. That center-of-attention kind of value it would bring at school. 'It won't cost me anything?'

'It's free to you. But only you.'
'Byron, one more thing.'
'What?'
'Give me a buck.'
'Hey!'
'If you don't, I'll tell. Tonight.'
'You wouldn't.'
'The cops will be all over you like a rash.'
'That ain't fair!'
'It is, too. You made me pay to see it. Now you have to pay me to keep quiet.'
'You only gave me fifty cents.'
'So what? A buck or these lips start flapping.'
'Good thing you're not a guy, Barbara. I'd flatten you.'
'You and who else?' She held out her hand for the money. Grinned. 'Give.'
'You'll be sorry,' Byron muttered. He reached into a front pocket of his jeans, pulled out a crumpled bill.
'Thanks. See you tomorrow.'
He stayed in his room while she walked away. A few seconds passed. Then he heard footsteps approaching. Karen appeared in the doorway.
'Did you two fight?' she asked. 'Or . . .'
'Oh, Barbara's a creep.'
'I thought you said she's your friend.'
'Well, she isn't. She's a creeping crud. I'm going to bed.'
'All right.'
Karen paused at the doorway. 'You haven't left anything under your bed?'
He flinched. 'Like what?'
'Left something there you shouldn't?'
'Like what?'
'An old piece of pizza or garlic sausage?'
She's going to look under the bed. She'll see the mummy.
He stood by the bed with his calves hard against the bedframe side. 'Nothing's under there, my mom made me clear everything out yesterday.' *Liar-liar-pants-on-fire.*

'It just smells a bit . . . well, spicy in here.'

'I ate a hamburger earlier. I'll brush my teeth.' He didn't know why he said that, but it sounded fairly convincing. Well, kind of.

'Best do that. And open the window wide for some fresh air.'

Karen left. Byron flopped backwards onto his bed and lay there, trying to figure a way to get his dollar back.

He dozed off.

When he woke his room was dark. He got up. On his way to the bathroom, he heard quiet voices. Karen must've had Eric come over. They were probably on the couch like the other time, kissing; other stuff, too, that made Karen pant: *Oh-oh-oh-oh-oh* . . . like she'd trapped her finger in the door.

Byron wasn't interested. In the bathroom, he washed his face, brushed his teeth, peed. He returned to his bedroom. Shut the door, and stripped. The night was hot. Instead of wearing his pajamas, he put on a clean pair of jockey shorts. He climbed into bed. The sheet felt cool. A delicious ice-cream feel. He liked that. Rested the palms of his hands down on it. A second later he began to heat up again, so he tossed the top covers aside, and lay on his back, staring at the dark ceiling.

Tomorrow, maybe he and Toby could round up a whole bunch of kids. With ten kids they'd make five bucks. Ten bucks with twenty kids. That'd give them five each. For eight-fifty he could buy one of those Super Whack Slingshots. How many kids would that take? Let's see, fifty cents times . . . times . . .

He was asleep.

A night breeze disturbed the shade. A scratching sound filled the room.

Chapter Twenty-seven

Grace stared out the windshield. The three men looked in at her. Dirty, unshaven. The T-shirts they wore were ragged-looking. Oil-stained. Maybe even a little bloodstained, too. The setting sun turned their skin red. The one who'd swatted the windshield made a rotating motion with his finger.

Wind the window down.
No way.
Lock the doors.

She flicked the catches on the inside of the old truck.

The guy slapped the windshield again.

'Don't you know the meaning of the phrase "antisocial"?' He grinned. 'We only want to talk.'

She shook her head. Behind her, in the rear seat, Pix whimpered, scared.

'Hell-owe . . . hell-owe in there. Speak English?'

The guy grinned. His teeth looked as if he'd spent the day sipping road tar.

'Can you spare us all a cigarette, miss?' He grinned back at the others.

Grace caught her breath, forced herself to speak. 'Sorry. I haven't got any. I don't smoke.'

'Miss?' With exaggerated politeness, he pointed through the windshield at a pack of cigarettes on the dashboard. They'd have belonged to Joe. He called them 'Steppin' stones to heaven'.

'Miss? Aren't those cigarettes?'

The guy flicked the cigar butt at the window. It bounced. Sparking.

Nodding, frightened, she fumbled the cigarette pack from the dashboard, opened the window a crack, just wide enough to slip them through.

'Why, thank you, miss.'

'Keep them. Please.'

Now go away. Go away. The plea hammered inside her head but they didn't go away.

They sidled up to the passenger window. All three pressed forward to look through the glass at her. She was wearing shorts. Her brown legs stretched out long and enticingly into the well beneath the dash.

They grinned at each other.

Coming to a secret agreement.

'Grace?' Pix sounded strained. 'Let's get away from these men.'

'How?'

'Drive away.'

'Can't.'

'You gotta.'

'Can't. Cody took the key.'

'Sis, these guys are gonna hurt us. I know it.'

'They can't get in. The doors are locked. They'll—'

'Hey!' *Thump.* The big guy, the one who seemed to be in charge, swung his fist against the door. 'What you talking about in there?'

'Nothing.'

'Seemed like somethin'.'

'No—'

'You talkin' about us?'

'No.'

'Not nice talking about people behind their backs.' And to the others: 'Is it, fellers?'

'No, it ain't. Damn rude.'

The three laughed. One slapped the roof of the pickup, sending a thunderous clamoring round its interior. They laughed even more when they saw the frightened reaction from inside.

Where's Cody? Dear God.

Grace glanced back through the windows. The only things she saw were desert. Dry bushes. The pile of tires that was nearly the size of a house. And, dear Lord, it was getting dark. The sun sinks fast in a desert, she knew that. Plunges toward the horizon like a stone. Soon it would be dark. Soon the men would get impatient. They were horny now. They wouldn't wait.

Not when they could see the curve of her breasts through her shirt.

Didn't have time to put on a brassiere when she left home.

Didn't have time to grab much.

Only the clothes she stood up in. Truth of the matter: she wouldn't be wearing those soon if these three roughnecks had their way. And as for Pix in the back. They leered at her, angled their heads to see up her tiny skirt. For a sixteen-year-old she had a full, woman's body. They could see her nipples through her T-shirt.

'C'mon, open the door.'

Thump.

'We're not going to eat you, are we?'

Grace gave a scared shake of her head.

'Aw!' They were enjoying the situation. One, in a greasy bandanna, hooted: 'Come out, come out or we'll blow your house in.'

This led to a chorus of *little piggies, little piggies* and then hog snorting.

These guys weren't just boisterous. They were buzzing on something. Maybe some of that cactus juice. The sort that gets you high . . . and dangerous.

'Now we *are* gettin' impatient,' the big one said, speaking so close to the window his breath fogged it. 'Open up.'

'No.'

'Open up or we're coming in after you.'

'Make 'em squeal like pigs,' shouted the one in the bandanna. 'Man, I love to hear 'em squeal . . . just like this . . . *heee-yeee-heee-yeee.*'

They laughed again, louder. Their leers got hornier. They were cooking now. They wanted in; they wanted body contact and heat and dirty things Grace had only heard about.

'Open the door, bitch.'

'Go away!' she yelled.

'Open the door or I start shooting.' The big guy bunched a rag round his pocket where he'd carried it through a belt loop. Poking from the rag, Grace saw a black barrel.

'Grace, he's got a gun,' Pix cried. 'You gotta open the door.'

'No.'

'They're gonna kill us if you don't.'

'They're gonna kill us if we do. When they've finished with us.'

Pix groaned. 'Oh shit. Stop them, Grace. Please . . .'

She slammed her hand onto the horn. Didn't make a sound.

Damned old truck. Did anything work?

Outside the three guys fell about.

'What a heap of junk,' laughed one. 'Bet even the door locks don't hold.'

The tall one tugged at the passenger door handle. With a sick-sounding click the lock gave out, worn to shit by use. Grace watched in horror as the door opened.

'Oh boys—' the gang leader smiled '—it's show time.'

Grace looked up into his face as the smile turned into a grin. 'Me firsties, boys.'

The guy in the bandanna scowled. 'Hey . . . why do I always get sloppy joes?'

'You complainin'?'

'No, but—'

'Keep your mouth shut, then.' He spoke to Grace. 'Your call, girl. Make it easy on yourself or make it hard. Doesn't matter a damn either way to me.'

The third one hooted with excitement. 'Make her squeal, Joe. Just like a little pig. *Hee-yeeee! Heee-yeeee . . . uck.*'

Grace thought a big black bird had swooped down on the guy.

A tire?

A big truck tire came out of nowhere. It sailed down out of the sky and struck the guy tread first on the shoulder. The pig squealer went down like a chunk of the moon had fallen on him.

The other two looked round in confusion. Grace leaned forward and looked at the top of the tire mound. A figure appeared in silhouette. A second later, Cody ran down the slope of black rubber. Tires spilled from the mound. Cascaded down. A dark avalanche. Tires bounced. Struck the side of the truck. Bounced over it, the two guys fending them off as best they could.

Cody appeared by the side of the truck, steadying his balance. 'Okay,' he told the two guys. 'It's finished. We're moving on.'

'What about our buddy? Look what you've done to him.'

The pig squealer had managed to pull himself up onto one elbow in the dust. His head sagged. The guy was only semiconscious.

Joe, the gang leader, squared up. 'You say it's finished. We say otherwise.'

'Yeah.' The bandanna wearer backed him. 'We say when it's finished.'

'Look.' Cody held up his hands. 'Don't let this get out of control. We don't want any trouble.'

'Says you.'

'Look what you done to our buddy. Bust his shoulder, then say you're moving on.'

'Payback time.'

'Careful,' Pix warned. 'He's gotta gun.'

'Yeah.' Joe smirked. 'So you get out of here, pretty guy. We've got something that needs attending.' He winked at Grace. 'Say, you've got a nice soft mouth.'

'Sucks like a Hoover, I shouldn't wonder.' The guy with the bandanna chuckled.

The guy on the floor mumbled, 'Shit, my shoulder.'

Cody advanced across the sea of spilt tires. 'I'm not backing off. Quit this before someone really gets hurt.'

'Yeah, my gun can do some hurtin' if you don't do some vanishing into the desert over there.'

Grace leaned forward, looking at the bunch of rag with the black tube in Joe's fist. 'Cody?'

'You okay, Grace?'

'Cody. It's not a gun.'

'Shut your face, bitch,' Joe growled.

'It's a—'

'Bitch, shut—'

'A pen.'

Joe scowled in fury. 'So who needs a gun, Cody? Come and take the pair of us.' The guy flung the rag and pen away.

'I don't want any trouble,' Cody said. 'We'll just be on our way. Forget that—'

'No way. You're going to have to fight your way out. Or are you yellow?'

'We're leaving.' Cody made to get into the truck but the tall, mean-looking guy was on him. Dealt him punches to the side of his head. Cody tottered backwards. Steadied himself.

The guy in the bandanna grinned. 'Guy's chicken, Joe.'

'Time to deck the bastard,' Joe said as if it was a dull chore, but one that had to be done. He stepped forward, fists swinging.

Cody blocked them.

Moved forward lightning-fast.

Fists flashing in the setting sun.

Cody didn't aim for the face. Instead, landed half a dozen crunching body blows into Joe's lean frame.

Joe rolled back against the pickup, straightened, then walked forward, fists raised. Then he paused as if forgetting what he was supposed to be doing. Took another two steps before dropping into the dirt, sending up a billow of dust.

The guy in the bandanna had come round the truck, maybe figuring to do some kicking once Cody was on the ground. Only it was Joe on the ground. When he saw Cody turn to him with that look in his eye . . . that look that told you someone *meant* business, he backed off. 'It's cool, man, it's cool. I don't want no trouble.' He ran back around the truck, tripped over the guy with the bust shoulder, then loped away along the track. Seconds later Joe and the other guy followed, one holding his side, the other holding his shoulder.

Five minutes later Cody sat with Grace and Pix in the pickup. He handed Pix the brown paper bag with the sandwiches. For a long time she stared into the bag. Above them the stars came out.

'I knew it.' Pix looked up. 'Cody. You've forgotten the mayonnaise.'

Chapter Twenty-eight

Neither Virginia nor Marco asked what had happened to Ed when the lights went out. He was thankful for that. Explaining any aspect of his experience would have been difficult. Explaining his fierce arousal would have been impossible.

Maybe that was how it was in the beast house, as Marco called this room full of cages. They did whatever their captor required of them, then went on with their day-to-day lives in captivity.

Certainly they wouldn't discuss it with each other. He remembered how evasive Virginia had been when he'd asked her about her injured breasts.

Now he lay on the mattress.

Tried to forget.

Failed to forget.

That sex had been so shameful. He didn't even know who he'd been screwing. Man or woman?

Trouble was: the sex was good.

No, it wasn't.

It was the best.

Best ever.

Overwhelming animal sex that had just about blown his mind.

Later the lights went out. He found himself trembling with either fear or excitement, he couldn't decide which. When they came back on again he realized there'd be no repeat of the bizarre sexual act. Instead, lunch appeared.

Same airline trays.

Same tepid coffee.

Only this time there was a sandwich and two bright red apples. His two fellow captors ate theirs immediately. As if still ashamed of what he'd done he waited under his blanket until they'd done before he ate. The sandwich was chunky turkey on wholewheat. It tasted pretty good, considering.

He realized as soon as he'd eaten that he would have to make use of the sawdust tray.

Oh, man. Just when he thought he couldn't suffer any more embarrassment it was turned up another notch.

No one watched. He found himself wiping himself with the toilet paper in such a way that the action would be as quiet as possible.

But no one commented. No one looked his way.

Later Marco spoke. He sounded pleased. 'Who's a pretty boy, then?'

'Not you, Marco,' Virginia said.

'Must be. I got a chocolate-chip cookie with my lunch. Home-baked.'

'So?'

'You two guys didn't.'

'So what does that make you?' Ed was irritated by Marco's smug attitude.

'It makes me the favorite with the big guy upstairs.'

Ed looked across to see Marco beaming through the bars of the cage. He glanced back at Virginia. She shook her head.

'Leave him, Ed. He's only trying to mess with your head.'

'Says who?'

'Says me, Marco.'

Ed looked at Marco's mouth. His lips were full and red for a man's. Even as he watched the tongue darted out to take a crumb that lodged in the corner of his mouth.

Could it be . . . ?

No. Ed's flesh crawled.

But *could* it be Marco that had abused him a few hours ago? Maybe Marco *was* his captor? He could have an accomplice who turned out the lights and operated the mechanism, raising the panel to the roof of the cage. Then all Marco had to do was unlatch the door, climb onto the cage roof and then . . . and then . . .

Ed swallowed. No, he didn't like the way those thoughts led him. That Marco was in on this . . . even the instigator.

But it could be the truth. Marco might be playing some sick game.

He glanced at Virginia. She looked back at him, green eyes cool as ice. Was she in on it, too? Two kooky kids who'd built their own fun house where they brought kidnapped men and women.

The more he thought about it the more likely it seemed. But was he just being paranoid?

'What are you thinking about, Ed?'

He colored. 'Nothing.'

'Nothing?' Virginia angled her head. 'Seemed an intense nothing.'

'Uh?'

'You were scowling at me.'

'Sorry.'

'Thought I'd done something wrong.'

'No.'

'That I'd offended you.'

'Not at all.'

She looked him in the eye. 'You'll let me know if I step on your toes, won't you?'

Right then she looked so vulnerable. He wished he could reach out through the bars of the cage to embrace her.

'Because,' she said, 'if you think bad things about me I'll wish you dead.'

For the next hour or so, Ed Lake felt like the odd man out. A little while ago Virginia and Marco had been bickering. Now they were chatting to each other. About nothing much in particular. About vacations they'd had as kids. Seemed they'd both been to Lake Placid. Both had fathers who had fished. Both had kept hamsters. Both shared the same birth sign. Taurus. They'd swapped reminiscences. Suddenly they had *so* much in common.

They're trying to exclude me. Make me feel lonely, Ed told himself. *Mind games.*

Two people buddy up. Shut the other out.

She toyed with her hair as she spoke to Marco. Once she'd let the blanket slip as if to deliberately show her breast to him. He smiled a lot, tilting his head as they spoke. Because Ed's cage was in the middle they had to look through the bars and through *him* as they talked.

The conversation was cut short.

Even though the killing of the lights usually brought a frisson of fear for Ed, this time he welcomed it. Because normally with the darkness came silence. Everyone stopped talking.

Again it was the same. Rustling sounds. Drafts, as if the door to the room had been opened, then closed.

A voice came. For a moment Ed thought he was being addressed and obeyed before he realized it was a different name.

'*Paulo. Move to your right. Keep moving until you reach the cage bars . . . now turn round.*'

They used Marco's surname, just as they had used Ed's.

Ed heard movement from Marco's cage. He was obeying the commands.

'*Let the bars of the cage take your weight. Splay your feet. Lower your body. Keep your back to the cage bars . . . now . . . bring your head back.*'

It was the same deep voice. It was loud, too, and seemed to come from no single direction.

Odd.

Then: 'Please . . . I'll do anything—'

That was Marco's voice.

'I'll do anything . . . please!'

Then the light flickered. It didn't come on completely but the fluorescent strips were strobing on-off. Ed saw a figure briefly. It was outside the cage. It was doing something to Marco. Marco's arms were outstretched, crucifixion style. His hands seemed to flutter, fingers spasming.

Then darkness.

Ed waited a long time, until he was sure their captor had left, then said, 'Marco?'

Silence.

'Marco?'

There was no reply.

Ed lay on the foam mattress. There was no other sound. Virginia didn't speak. He felt cold inside.

He tried to sleep. Couldn't. His side ached where he lay in the same position, but for some reason he couldn't bring himself to change it.

The lights went on.

Outside the cage bars there was a tray containing slices of melon and a cupcake. A carton of milk beside that.

He looked into Marco's cage.

Marco leaned against the bars, his arms straight out, wrists tied by wire to the uprights. His eyes were open. His throat had been cut. A great grinning crimson wound.

Blood pooled on the floor around him.

For a time Ed stared at the dead man. Virginia stared, too. Said nothing.

Then Ed pulled the tray through the gap in the bars and started to eat.

Chapter Twenty-nine

Karen, astride Eric's lap, rocked gently back and forth, making his thick organ move slightly inside her, rubbing just a bit in a delicious way that would make it last. It was in her deeper than seemed possible. As she rocked, eyes shut, she felt his hands inside her open blouse, stroking her back, squeezing her breasts, teasing her nipples.

The baby, in the nursery at the end of the hall, started to cry.

Karen felt like crying herself.

Just when she'd wanted to start screaming with pleasure.

'Oh, shit, shit, shit,' Eric muttered.

She kissed him. 'It's all right, honey. I'll just be a minute.'

'Come on, don't go. She'll stop pretty soon.'

'No, she won't. Not till she gets her bottle. Besides, she'll wake up Byron. Would you like him to walk in about now?'

Eric could only groan with despair.

In so deep.
In so good.
Didn't get better than that.

He helped lift Karen as she raised herself off his lap. She felt him slide out. It left her feeling empty; hollow now. 'I'll be right back,' she said. Straightening her skirt, she looked down at his erection. It stood like a wet, shiny post of flesh. Kneeling, she kissed its swollen head. 'Don't go away,' she whispered.

Buttoning her blouse, she hurried into the kitchen, took a pink bottle of formula from the refrigerator. Then went down the dark hallway. A night-light was on in the nursery. Jane was on her back inside the crib. Wailing.

'It's okay,' Karen soothed. 'Everything's okay.' She slipped the latex nipple into Jane's mouth. Tiny, eager hands clutched the bottle. 'Nighty-night,' Karen said. 'Sleep tight.' She waved to Jane and left.

Even as she hurried back to the den, she felt a tremor of anticipation. Her fingers trembled as she opened the buttons of her blouse.

The baby's crying had disturbed Byron's sleep. He rolled onto his back. The sheet under him felt hot and wet, so he edged sideways to find a fresh place. His foot dropped over the side of the bed. He let it hang there.

He was almost asleep when something brushed the bottom of his foot, tickling. He wondered, vaguely, what it was.

A bug, maybe.

A moth fluttering near his foot.

Suddenly the smell of spices and garlic seemed strong in the room. The blind rustled in a dead breath of night air.

Foot tickled again.

Damn bug.

Byron began to raise his foot.

Something clutched it in a tight, dry grip. He gasped with fright. Tried to kick free. Tried to pull away. The grip only tightened.

He sprang out of bed. A single dark hand had him by the ankle. A single dark hand connected to a stick-thin forearm that vanished into the darkness beneath his bed. Crying out, he lunged toward the shut door, dragging the creature from under the bed. Its hair crackled against the carpet. Flickers of blue static shimmered across its head.

A second hand grabbed his ankle. Looking down, he saw the mummy pulling itself toward the ankle like you'd pull yourself up a tree with a branch. Its elbows bending. A flash of face – eyeless sockets, teeth glinting white. It bit.

Byron cried out in pain.

Twisting, reaching for the door, he fell backwards. The thing scuttled up his body. Its fingernails cut into the flesh of his legs, tore at his genitals through his shorts, slashed gashes in his chest. Gouged furrows across his shoulders. The mouth, hideously wrinkled, came down on his face. The eye sockets were huge empty craters. He turned away, but the teeth sank into his cheek. Ripped. Ripped again. Looking up, Byron screamed at the sight of his own flesh hanging from its mouth, dripping red.

'What the hell was *that*?'

Karen shook her head. The baby started to cry again. 'I'd better go see.' She climbed off Eric, chilled with concern, and reached down for her blouse.

He clutched her arm. 'You stay here.' Fastening his pants, he rushed into the dark hallway.

Karen put on her blouse. She bent down to pick up her panties and heard Eric yell as if startled. She froze, gazing toward the hallway. Something slammed heavily against a wall or the floor. She listened for the sounds of a struggle but the cry of the baby hid any other noises.

'Eric!' she called.

Quickly, she stepped into her panties and pulled them up beneath her skirt. She took a step toward the hallway. Stopped.

Didn't want to go there.

Couldn't.

'Eric! Are you all right? Eric! If you're playing a trick on me, it's not funny.'

She took a step backward, eyes on the hallway entrance.

'Damn it, Eric!'

Out of the darkness stepped a wrinkled brown figure, clutching Jane to its chest. Its hair tumbled down in copper swathes from a skull-like head. The baby cried with wild terror.

Screaming, Karen spun around and ran to the front door. Threw it open. Dashed across the lawn to the sidewalk. With a glance over her shoulder, she saw the thing appear in the doorway with Janey. Her foot passed through an empty space as she went off the curb. Staggering forward, balance gone, she looked into dazzling headlights and felt the car break her apart.

Chapter Thirty

Cody downshifted as the traffic thickened. The pickup lumbered up the incline, the big motor taking the strain.

'You sure you two are okay?' he asked.

'Yeah, no problem,' Pix said as if the subject bored her.

'That was a close one.' Grace rested her hand on his thigh. 'Thanks, Cody.'

'What matters is we're away from them now.'

'The creeps. They must hang around out in the desert, waiting for people to come by. It makes you wonder how many women they've—'

'Hey, hey,' he said softly. 'Put it behind you. It's over . . . they're just losers.'

'Dangerous losers.'

The familiar whine came from the back. 'This is Hollywood. Where are the damn movie studios?'

'Pix, they're all over the place – behind those big walls.'

'But I can't see nuthin'.'

'You will.' Grace sounded determined. 'We're going to make it here.'

'Yeah. *Right.*'

'Hey, Pix.' Cody stopped at a red. 'Give your sister a break, can't you?'

'But it's dumb to haul out here. We should have gone to New York.'

'Pix—'

'There'd be work there . . . even for a lummox like you.'

For a moment Cody sat fuming.

Put little sister on a Greyhound bus. Send her back East. She was doing her best to break Grace's will to succeed. *Huh, talk about sibling rivalry. Come on lights, change.*
They stayed fixed.
Red.
No go.
Don't move.
Even though it was way late he saw lights in the houses that clung to the sides of the Hollywood Hills. Along the road in front of him were restaurants, hotels, all-night stores. Lights blazed. *Here we are*, they seemed to say to him, *this is LA. The city of dreams. If you're lucky.*
A figure lurched from the shadows.
Pix screamed. 'Grace! Look out!'
The dark shape leaned forward, laid a brown hand on the part-open window where Grace sat.
Cody watched her twist round as the mummy leaned right into the car.
The light was red. Cars lined up in front of him. He couldn't move. But gunned the engine just the same.
Looked in horror as the mummy reached out a hand.
'Cody!' Grace cried.
He reached out his arm around his girlfriend's shoulders and scooped her close.
The mummy extended its brown paw toward them both.
Pix shouted, 'It's going to get Grace!'
The mummy loomed in.
Closer.
Reaching.
'Here,' it said. 'Take.'
Cody felt Grace's slender body quiver with fear against him.
'Take,' the mummy repeated. In its hand was a green card not much bigger than a cinema ticket.
The mummy pushed the bandage up where it had slid down over one eye. 'Present this at the Pyramid Diner down the road to your left. You get a free side salad.'
'Sweet Jesus,' Grace cried. 'You scared me half to death.'

'Special promotion,' monotoned the guy in the mummy costume. 'Free side salad. Set midnight feast for five ninety-nine. They got genuine Egyptian beer, too. And apple pie just like mummy used to make.'

Dazed, Grace took the card from the bandaged figure. The card bore the drawing of a mummy. *Pyramid Diner: 24/7: Why eat like a king when you can feast like a pharaoh? Entitles bearer to one free side salad.*

Cody shook his head. 'Los Angeles. City of Angels. What a place!'

Pix added, 'Los Angeles. City of the dead, more like.' She looked out the rear window to watch the man in the mummy costume shuffling along the line of waiting cars, handing out more of the cards.

Horns sounded.

'*Green*, Cody, you big lummox.'

As they pulled away, Grace said, 'Cody, we best find somewhere to spend the night.'

'Motel,' Pix said hopefully.

'No can do.' Cody shook his head.

'We'll have to find a parking lot,' Grace added. 'Or a quiet side street.'

'What? No motel?'

'We can't.'

'Shit.'

Grace looked back at her sister. Her arms were folded. With her mouth sulky she stared out.

'We don't have enough money for a motel, Pix.'

'How much we got? They can't be that expensive.'

Cody spoke. 'Eight dollars, thirty-three cents.'

'Oh great.' Pix shook her head in disbelief. 'We're thousands of miles from home, in Los Angeles, and we haven't even got ten lousy bucks between us.' She lay down on the back seat, glaring up at the pickup's grubby roof. 'How we gonna survive here. D' ya hear me, you two? How we gonna survive?'

Chapter Thirty-one

Ed Lake was making use of the sawdust bowl when the lights went out. Taking a leak in the dark wasn't easy. Felt weird, too.

Also, he knew what might be coming his way.

Maybe I'm next?

Is this where I get my throat slit just like Marco?

Poor kid. How would that knife blade have felt as it was dragged through his throat? Just the thought of that sawing motion of cold metal on his Adam's apple shut off the flow.

Ed shook himself. Then zipped up as fast as he could.

What now?

He waited in the dark.

Waiting for orders.

They came.

'*Virginia . . . Virginia . . .*'

So Virginia's favored with first-name treatment.

'*Virginia. Stand up.*'

Ed made his way back to his mattress by touch alone in the darkness, feeling across the concrete floor until he found the hunk of foam. He sat. Waited. Listened. His heart beating faster.

Would Virginia be killed this time? The thought of seeing her lying there with her beautiful throat gashed open made him shrivel inside.

There in the dark he could see nothing. But he heard all right. He heard Virginia's frightened breathing.

And did that panting sound loud!

He tried to block the thought, but it sounded as if she was sexually aroused. He thought about her copper hair tumbling over bare shoulders. A glimpse of her cleavage as she tried to keep the blanket high with trembling hands.

Jesus, what they gonna do to her? Please don't kill her. Please, she's so young and beautiful. She's got a whole life in front of her.

'Virginia, stand up.'

So their captor would be in the room now. Looking at Virginia through nightscope goggles. Seeing her skin gleam, and her eyes shine like lamps in the infrared.

Ed looked in the direction of where he imagined Virginia stood in the center of her cage. She'd be so frightened. She wouldn't know what was going to happen next. She must have been thinking about Marco, too. How he'd hung there with his throat cut. And how later the lights had been killed and they'd heard a dragging sound as his murderer dragged the body away. Following on from that were wet slicking sounds as someone worked at the bloodstained floor with sponges.

'Virginia. Drop the blanket.'

The voice was deep, masculine. But there was something strange about it. Ed listened hard. Again, it came from no single direction. It didn't even sound completely natural.

'Remove your clothes . . . now stand facing the bars . . . slip your hands through the loops.'

Ed's eyes widened in the darkness. *Loops? Some kind of restraint?*

Virginia made little gasping sounds. Whispered words that he couldn't make out. Then he heard something that made the shivers pour down his spine.

She spoke . . . a long-drawn-out 'Oooooh . . .'

He tilted his head, listening hard, trying to interpret the sound. Was it hurting? Was it pleasuring?

He sat with his knees hugged to his chest.

There was a rustling sound. Clothes? Paper?

Like the voice, the sound seemed to have no single source. It came from every direction.

Virginia's breathing quickened. She made soft 'Hmm' and 'Uh' sounds. Ed's heart thudded.

Then: 'Please . . .'

He remembered the last time when he'd heard her pant like this. They'd cut her breasts.

If only I could get out of this cage and get my hands round the bastard's throat. I'd fucking squeeze the life right out—

But then everything changed.

Virginia gasped. 'Please . . . yes, yes . . . deeper. Put your fingers inside . . . that's it . . . deeper. Please, deeper . . . ah . . .'

Ed couldn't believe it. She wasn't in pain . . . this was pleasure for her. Overwhelming pleasure.

She was having sex with her captor. Virginia was horny. She was enjoying whatever was being done to her. How could she? Was she some kind of slut to surrender to her captor so completely, then enjoy their attentions so *completely*?

So what makes you so squeaky clean, Eddie old buddy? You surrendered too. You enjoyed your captor's proclivities.

He hugged his knees to his chest, hearing sounds of rapture.

Virginia's gasping for breath, her murmurs of pleasure were turning him on. He felt so horny. He sensed himself growing large, his cock straining against the fabric of his pants.

I want to join in, he thought, unable to hold back the thoughts any longer. *I want to be nailing Virginia and I want her to make those hot sounds in my ear. Sweet Jesus listen to her. She's having great sex. She's so turned on. She's so hot. She loves what's happening to her.*

In his mind's eye he saw her. She'd be standing facing the bars, her hands held high by loops that restrained her, that held her there, her nakedness pressed hard against the bars.

But what is happening to her?

Couldn't tell.

No way of knowing.

But, sheesh, it sounds good.

So good it makes my cock ache. I want to explode.

But can't get that kind of one-handed relief here in the dark.

My captor's wearing funky night-vision goggles. They'd see me jerking off. They'd have something to say about that. Might be against the rules. I might wind up with my throat cut. But listen to Virginia panting.

Just picture her. She's naked. She's shackled to the cage bars. Her head's rolling, swishing hair down her curving back, as the captor does something to her. But what a helluva something!

Finger?

Tongue?

Dildo?

'Virginia. Slide your feet further apart.'

That weird voice again. It—

Holy shit.

Suddenly he knew why it sounded strange. He knew what it reminded him of. It was the same as a recorded voice played back at a slower speed. The voice was low, manlike, but distorted. And it came from different directions because it was being broadcast over speakers placed around the room.

So maybe the guy isn't a guy after all?

Maybe it's a gal?

And you know what that means, Eddie?

The sounds of rapture you're hearing now are a lesbian love-fest.

Wow.

Right on!

He found himself smiling. Now this was hot. Gal on gal.

Maybe he could suggest a threesome?

Not that he got a chance.

The deep voice commanded him to lie on the platform again.

And again the same commands as he was winched up hard against the Perspex ceiling. To unzip himself. To 'present' himself. This time, he didn't hesitate.

Lying flat on his back there he unzipped, then guided his penis through the hole in the Perspex. Already he was hot and erect. In fact, he felt the muscles straining against the confining skin. Wanted to explode.

Wanted to explode there and then.

For moments cool air played around the head of his cock.

This waiting's driving me insane. I can't bear it. I want to feel that soft mouth again with its busy tongue.

Movement from above. Although he saw nothing in the darkness he felt the Perspex flex slightly as someone stepped onto it. More movement as they positioned themselves. He imagined a woman . . . a beautiful, mad woman who captured victims and kept them as sex slaves.

Right now he imagined her naked, positioning herself over him, ready to sit on his swollen, throbbing member.

And, good God, was he right!

He felt soft flesh touch the tip of his penis. Soft lips that were hot. A downward movement. A sense of parting. Slickness. An eager downward thrust, followed by a slow return upward, the lips encircling his shaft, the exquisite dragging sensation, before the next thrust down.

He moaned.

This was beautiful.

This he loved.

He was entering the body of his captor and nothing could be nicer. No way.

She must be kneeling above him on the Perspex ceiling. She straddled his cock. Impaled herself on the hard shaft. Now rose and fell, no doubt her head twisting with pleasure, a look of bliss on her face.

He felt the tight encircling flesh travelling the length of his shaft . . . Down, down, down. All the way. Then back up, up, up, until the lips nearly parted from the tip.

Only not quite.

Then down again, encircling, squeezing, stroking.

It happened.

With a yell he came fast and furious into the body, expending every drop into that moist softness. His hips bucked, pressing hard against the Perspex as he tried to gain just another quarter of an inch of penetration.

Then . . .

Over . . .

Spent . . .

Sagging . . .

'*You did not wait.*' The deep voice held cold anger. '*You should have held back, Lake. For that you will be punished.*'

Chapter Thirty-two

Ed Lake didn't have long to wait.

The lights had flickered on and he'd wormed his way from the platform with the words still ringing in his ears: *'You should have held back, Lake. You will be punished.'*

He saw Virginia standing there. She was wearing the denim cut-offs. Her arms were crossed in front of her so that they hid her naked breasts.

She was watching Ed. Her green eyes were sympathetic, her demeanor serious.

'I'm so sorry, Ed,' she whispered.

'But all I did . . .' It wasn't easy to admit. 'All I did was come too soon.'

'That's a crime . . . at least it is in their eyes.'

'But who are *they*?'

She shook her head, her eyes downcast; unhappy with the situation but powerless. 'I don't know.'

'Listen, we've got to do something to get out of here.'

'We can't.'

'But we've got to try.'

'No, Ed.'

'We can't stay locked in these cages all our lives.'

'I know. But you saw what happened to Marco.'

'We've got to fight back.'

'Don't say that, Ed.'

'Why not?'

'They might be listening.'

He looked round, then said loudly, 'I don't give a damn if they are listening. They can come and suck my big one for all I care.'

'Ed,' she warned.

'But we can't just give in and be treated like animals. We're human beings.'

'We're also caged, Ed. They call the shots.'

'You going to let them do whatever they want with your body, Virginia?'

'Oh, Ed.' She sounded pained. 'We've got to play by their rules, otherwise—'

'They kill us?'

'Yes.'

He looked at her. 'Is that what's going to happen to me now?'

'I don't know.'

'They've threatened me with punishment.'

'It might not be as bad as you think, or—'

'Or . . . *chkkk*.' He ran his finger across his throat, imitating a blade.

'It might,' she agreed.

'Then I'm going to go down fighting,' he boomed. 'D' ya hear that, whoever you are, you little creeps? I'm gonna go down fighting!'

The lights went out.

Oh, shit.

Deep, deep shit.

The moment the darkness swamped them was when Ed knew they were coming for him. He, she or they . . . what did it matter now? They'd used him up. Now he was going the same way as Marco.

Throat sliced open. Then dragged somewhere. Dumped in a shallow grave, or even fed piece by piece into a furnace, for all he knew.

Leastways, this is how it ends.

After a moment or so of darkness he felt the draft as a door opened somewhere. Then the whisper of feet on concrete.

Here they came. His captor.

Or captors.

He should fight. He really should. They shouldn't be able to just stroll up and carve his trachea like that. They'd have to fight to take him.

But his insides shriveled, leaving an empty space in his gut. The strength had gone from him.

What if he was to plead for his life?

The thought of begging revolted him. But if it gave him a chance? They might leave him with a warning. *That's it. Don't do it again, Eddie boy. Beg . . . plead . . .*

If only.

Or should he offer up his throat? If they cut cleanly and fast then it would be over quick. No pain.

At least no more pain than need be.

The first cut is the deepest. Yeah, an old song. But there was a truth in the line. And didn't condemned criminals use to tip the executioner, way back? So they'd kill in a way that was merciful. No agony. No screaming.

'Jeez. Okay, okay. Get it over quick.'

'Lake, remove your clothes.'

He did as he was told, moving by touch in the darkness.

'Now move forward to the cage bars . . . Closer, Lake. Closer . . . move your feet until you're hard up to the bars.'

Did as he was told. Kept his eyes tight shut. Clenched his fists.

Come on, get it over with.

Do it.

Use that blade.

Then came a surprise. A terrible surprise.

'Oh, God, no.'

His heart lurched. His stomach plunged.

A hand closed round his testicles.

'Oh, please, God, no.'

He waited for the hand to grip tight. Squeeze ferociously. Then for the tingling edge of a blade against his soft scrotum.

Gonna whip off your balls, Eddie boy.

Then let's hear how you scream.

His eyes opened with shock, staring into the darkness. They'd never opened as wide as this before. He felt they'd simply pop out with the pressure inside his skull. And just for a second he did see. There was a faint reddish light coming from somewhere. He thought he saw a cowled figure – almost like a monk. And goggles of some sort.

They *were* wearing goggles. Round ones. Welder's goggles?

Then the dim red light died. Once more there was darkness.

Suddenly the grip on his balls changed. *Here comes the knife.*

Wait for it . . . wait for it. They were positioning the blade nice and close to his groin.

Suddenly the hand was gone. Maybe his captor was gone, too. That was it! Mind games again. Inflict psychological pain rather than physical. If that was the—

Then he felt a cold pressure against his foot. To be precise, against his little toe.

That was strange. *Why should—*

He didn't have any more thinking time than that. He heard a loud metallic tap – metal on metal. Then a crunch. A loud one.

After that there was no time for rational contemplation. That was out of the window, along with standing still.

A wave of agony flashed up his leg. It set his brain alight.

The next thing he knew he was rolling on the floor, screaming, holding his foot.

Only his foot no longer seemed the same.

The lights had been on for a whole hour. He lay on his side. The concrete floor must have been hard and uncomfortable but he didn't notice.

'I'm sorry what they did to you. Listen, Ed, I'm sorry.' Virginia must have repeated the words many times but when he didn't respond she let him alone.

He lay there without moving for what seemed an age. He lay looking through the bars of the cage at something that lay on the floor.

It was a small object. Almost insignificant.

It lay in a pool of blood on the concrete. A little island in a sea of blood.

'I don't believe they did that,' he said to himself at last. 'They cut it off . . . they cut off my little toe.'

Chapter Thirty-three

When Ed Lake woke his severed little toe was gone. The blood had gone, too. All that remained was a wet area of concrete.

So, like a goofy kind of Tooth Fairy, they'd come in the middle of the night.

Taken the toe. Left him nothing in return. Some Toe Fairy . . .

He laughed.

'Now that does surprise me,' Virginia said from the next cage.

'What does?'

'They cut your toe off and you find it funny.'

'Considering Marco, and what the alternative might have been, I'm damn lucky.'

'I guess you're right. Go ahead and have yourself a belly laugh.'

'Maybe it's not *that* funny.'

'Hurt?'

'Like hell.' He rubbed his head. 'Maybe it's the blood loss. I feel drunk.'

'Probably that and shock, too. Drink plenty of water.'

'Good idea.' He reached for a water bottle that hung from one of the roof bars.

She looked at his foot. 'Still bleeding?'

'Nope. I clamped a mountain of toilet tissue to it. Stopped eventually.'

'I guess it's a good sign.'

'I'll say,' he said. 'If it hadn't stopped I'd have bled out.'

'No, it's a good sign they did what they did.'

'You mean they just wanted to teach me a lesson?' He chuckled at his bloody foot. 'To toe the line?'

She nodded, her copper hair sweeping down over a bare shoulder. 'They must value you being alive.'

'Maybe I can demand better accommodation.'

She smiled. 'Wouldn't push it, buster.'

'And how's the . . .' He indicated his chest, then blushed, suddenly awkward. 'I mean have—'

'The cuts on my breasts? They're healing, Ed.'

'Was that punishment, too?'

'Nah, they did that for fun.' She flicked back her hair. 'They do all kinds of freaky things for fun.'

'Like when they made you put your hands through the loops?'

'We decided early on that it would be bad etiquette to ask each other what they did.'

'But I—'

'We decided it was a way to maintain at least some small area of privacy.'

'We?'

She sighed and shook her head. Her eyes took on a sad, downward cast as she remembered. 'There were others when I first got here. I even shared this cage with another girl. One by one they all . . .' She shrugged. 'They were all taken but me.'

'And Marco?'

'He was brought in later.'

'So you decided you wouldn't talk about how they abused you?'

'Our captors call the shots. I've told you.'

'So you go along with it?'

'Have to. If you want to live.'

He moved his foot as he sat on the mattress. It had started to throb again. Where the little toe had once connected with his foot was now a gooey red-black scab.

'They cut off my little toe,' he said.

'I know. You've already told me.'

'When they make me lie up on that shelf they tell me to put my penis through a hole in the Perspex roof of the cage. Then they—'

'Ed.' She looked at him pleadingly. 'What our captors do to us they do in the dark. It's secret.'

'Then whoever it was sucked me. Then stuck my cock inside them.'

She turned away, briefly burying her face in the blanket.

He continued. 'I was forced to have sex . . . but get this, I loved it. They excited me. It was great sex. I was really turned on.'

She sat, resting her elbow on her knee. She gazed at him with those green eyes for a moment, then shook her head. 'I know what you're doing.'

'You do?'

'You're saying we should share the experiences of what they do to us.'

'Keeping it secret doesn't help.'

'So if we share, if we confess, it makes us stronger?'

'Yes. But there's nothing to confess. *We*'ve done nothing wrong. But if we tell each other what happens to us . . . the abuse we suffer . . . then we're not so isolated. We can lend one another emotional support.'

She nodded. 'Guess we might as well. After all, the old way wasn't that effective, was it, now? Remember what happened to Marco?'

He looked at her.

She said, 'So you think I should tell you what they did to me?'

'I can't force you to talk.'

'No . . . well . . . it's . . .' She took a deep breath. Then, making a decision, she spoke in a no-nonsense way. 'The last time they made me their plaything I was ordered to stand facing the bars of the cage. In the dark they must have hooked loops to the bars. They made me put my hands in.'

'You were restrained by the loops?'

She nodded. 'Like lassos. They pulled tight round my wrists. Then they began touching me.'

'Hurting?'

'No. Gentle.'

'Was there anything about the hands?'

'You mean anything distinctive about them? Anything identifiable?'

'It might help us later.'

'You mean when it comes to identifying them for the cops?' She gave a sour laugh. 'Some hope, Ed. Anyway, here comes the confession, Hollywood style. They touched my body. Stroking me up and down. Then they ran their hands up inside my thighs to between my legs. They worked at me with their fingers.' She looked at me defiantly. 'There. Does that supply the picture for you?'

'I have to ask this, Virginia. Have they raped you?'

'Direct kinda guy, huh?'

'It could be important.'

'No,' she said. 'They haven't. Always fingers.'

'Nothing else?'

'No, always fingers. But there's something else.'

'Go on.'

'They were small, slender. I'm sure they were a woman's.'

'Jesus.'

'Yeah, so you heard what you thought you heard.' She looked him in the eye. 'You heard a red-hot lesbian lust-fest.'

Ed blushed.

'Does that turn you on?' Her voice sounded hard. 'Did you get all horny as you listened in the dark?'

'Virginia, I didn't—'

'Course you heard. That's what made you pop your cap too soon. But more fool you – they hacked off your toe for that mistake.'

'Virginia, I'm sorry.'

'Sorry for what? For being a horny teenager?' She pursed her lips as if ready to let fly some insults. Then she let out her pent-up breath. 'No, I'm sorry.' Her gaze softened. 'You see, I don't get out much. Makes me cranky.' Her lips twitched into a faint smile. 'Forgive me, Ed?'

'Nothing to forgive. But we've learned one thing. We need to stick together.'

Then Virginia caught him by surprise. Letting the blanket fall from her she crossed the cage to the bars nearest him. Her heavy breasts swayed. He allowed his eyes to take her in. She was naked apart from the cut-offs. Her hair coiled down; heavy strands slipped over her shoulder to brush her nipples.

Ed imagined the sensation must have been a pleasant tickle.

The cuts were healing fast now.

Boy, she looked good. Despite everything, her face glowed. She looked healthy. Vibrant.

She knelt down against the bars. Slipped her hand through. Reached out to him.

'Ed, will you hold my hand, please?'

'Be my pleasure.'

Avoiding catching the raw wound on his foot, he slid across the floor until he sat near the bars. He stretched out to her. Took her hand. She grasped his tightly. He squeezed back.

Suddenly the pressure of her hand in his became the most beautiful thing in the world.

'Partners?' she asked.

'Partners,' he agreed.

Time passed. Ed Lake's foot healed. During this time the funky games continued in the beast house. The lights would go out. Sometimes it was Virginia who got the attention. Sometimes Ed.

He kept his strength up so he could perform.

And performances went on for hours. He'd lie on his back on the platform.

Either it was the hungry mouth that worked his cock or it was the equally ravenous orifice.

But he was certain it was a woman now.

Of course he never saw. Too dark.

And he never let himself orgasm until his captor had been sated.

Afterward, whatever had been done to them, Ed would talk to Virginia. They shared their experiences. They discussed every detail – what their captor did, how they smelled, how they felt. Whether their captor climaxed. Whether Virginia or Ed climaxed.

Did it feel good?

Did it feel bad?

Sometimes it was so *bad* it was great.

Talking helped. Talking made them stronger.

They began to discuss how they could strike back.

Chapter Thirty-four

It came for him. It staggered, legs moving with awkward stiffness, an arm reaching out.

He backed away, breathless with horror.

Backed into waiting arms.

Crying out, he spun and stared into Hydra's leering half-face. Naked, she fell to her knees. She clutched his erection. She guided it slowly toward her face.

'Fuck my brains out,' she said. Laughing, she eased him into her head. He felt the tissues part around his stiff organ.

Heard the *squish*.

'Hey! Hey!'

Somebody shook Imad.

'You okay?' A woman's voice asked through the darkness.

He sat up, turned on the bedside lamp. The woman beside him swung up an arm to shield her eyes. She lay on top of the sheets. She was older than Imad and bony. Her skin was slick with suntan oil – a coconut oil that smelled rich and inviting. He remembered their encounter at the beach, where he'd offered to rub the oil on her back – and she'd accepted. He remembered bringing her home, drinks, a meal, and taking her to bed where they oiled their bodies and wrestled in an endless slippery contest of lust.

'Louise,' he murmured, at last remembering her name.

She uncovered her face. A handsome face with thin lips and high cheekbones and clear blue eyes. She gave him a tentative smile. 'Are you all right?'

'I dreamed.' He smiled. Shrugged. 'It was nothing.'

'It sounded just awful.'

'We all have our crosses to bear, do we not?'

'That's for sure. Me included.'

'I apologize for waking you. However . . .' He smiled. 'Since we are both awake now and the night is young . . .' He massaged one of her small, soft breasts.

She held his hand as if she wished to keep it there always. 'The night isn't all that young, Imad. I'm afraid I have to be on my way.'

'No.'

'I really hate to go, but I've got a job to get to.'

'At this hour?' he asked. 'It's nearly eleven.'

'Yeah. I go on at twelve. Waitress over at Clyde's. You know, Clyde's? Has this dumb sign out front. "Twenty-four Hour Service Day or Night"?' She laughed softly. 'Anyway, it's been cool.'

Turning onto her side, she kissed him long and hard.

She was gone. Alone in the huge house, Imad went to the wet bar and poured himself a glass of gin. He took it to the couch, sat back, used the remote to turn on the television. He pressed the buttons, watching a few seconds of each broadcast before turning to the next.

He settled for an adventure show in which a lithe brunette was being pursued by a gunman. She wore a T-shirt and shorts. Imad was pleased to notice that she wore no bra. He watched the breasts dance as she ran.

Then she hid and knocked the gunman unconscious with a flowerpot.

Rather silly, but Imad enjoyed the view of the woman, and was disappointed to see the show end.

A frowning, white-haired man came on. 'In just a few minutes, on *Eyewitness News* at eleven, we'll tell you about a miraculous rescue at sea, the President's latest energy proposal, and a bizarre double murder at one of our local museums. This and more from Bonnie, Lenny and me after a brief time-out.'

Imad watched the museum story. The cops behind the crime-scene tape, forensic specialists moving around in their white coveralls. Views of the Callahan Room. A close-up of the empty mummy casket. Then Imad went upstairs to the safe. He opened it. Removed the small black notebook.

He glanced at the title page and shivered.

The Memoirs of Robert Callahan.

THE MEMOIRS OF ROBERT CALLAHAN

The Fearful Descent

Though I wish, for reasons that will shortly be obvious, to prevent my Egyptian activities from coming to the public's attention, I find myself compelled to record the extraordinary events surrounding the discovery of the mummy, Amara. I shall take precautions that these pages remain concealed during my lifetime and the lifetime of my dear wife, Sarah. If eyes other than my own are now reading this manuscript, it may be assumed that we have both met our final fate. Disclosure of my activities cannot harm us now and may serve to prevent further tragedies.

In the year 1926, my father and I traveled to Egypt for the purpose of lending his expert assistance to the famed Howard Carter, who had recently unearthed the tomb of the boy king, Tutankhamun.

In Luxor, we met Mr Carter. He welcomed my father heartily, for they had worked together several years earlier with Theodore Davis at the tomb of Mentuhotep I. He was not so enthusiastic, however, about my presence. He must have felt that my youthful age of eighteen years, no matter how mature my attitude to work, would prove a hindrance. I am pleased to record that his attitude in this matter changed remarkably once he saw how I aided my father in the intricate details of his work. My copious, exact notes soon earned Mr Carter's respect.

It was my bravery, however, that won the respect of the Egyptian youth, Maged. We met on a December night. Suffering from the oppressive heat, I wandered beyond the boundaries of our encampment in hopes of chancing upon a stray, cooling breeze. I longed for the winters of my Wisconsin childhood: to be sledding down a slope, a chill wind battering my face, snowflakes blowing, the night lit by a full moon! I was close to weeping with frustration when suddenly an urgent cry entered my consciousness.

Never one to flee in the face of a crisis, I rushed forward and discovered half a dozen youths engaged in battering a young fellow senseless. I attacked. In the brief affray that followed, I struck several telling blows on the bullies and sent them scurrying for safety.

Maged introduced himself, using passable English. (His father, I learned, had served with the British during the Great War.) He offered me his gratitude and his friendship.

At first, he explained that the boys had fallen upon him for the purpose of committing robbery. After our friendship had grown, however, he finally confided in me. It seems that Maged, no innocent victim, had made vile suggestions to the sister of one of the boys. When she refused him, the young Maged showed his hostility by defecating on the family's doorstep. It was no wonder that her brother and several of his comrades reacted with violence.

Over the weeks, Maged proved to be an invaluable companion. The little Egyptian led me about in the night. We found his enemies. Fought with them. Won battles with our fists. We drank stolen raki. On regular occasions we whiled away the nights in the arms of tawny, lusting women with dark orbs for eyes who showed me delights I had never known.

It was because of Maged, and the wild times we shared, that we made the discovery that has so altered my life.

On a January night, after saying goodnight to Father, I met Maged at our agreed rendezvous point. From there, we traveled a long distance on foot across the desert until we reached a village of mud-brick houses. In one of these, Maged assured me, we would find a pair of twin sisters whose beauty and sexual talents would spoil me for all other women.

I waited outside while Maged entered one of the houses to fetch them. Soon, he reappeared. The two girls following behind him were beautiful indeed, though no older than seventeen. For long moments, I stared at them in the moonlight, struck with awe. I greeted them in Arabic. They smiled lasciviously, but spoke not a word. Maged quickly informed me that they were deaf-mutes. At first, I was troubled by this revelation. I soothed my conscience, however, by reminding myself that the five piasters we intended to pay the girls for their expert services was a handsome amount for such peasants. The fellahin who worked at the tomb, after all, received only three piasters for an entire day's labor.

Taking one girl by the hand, I followed Maged into the dunes beyond the village. There we spread blankets on the sand. The girls disrobed, revealing their beauteous skin to the moonlight. Their eyes were dark, lustful, their breasts small peaks, tipped with velvety dark nipples. My whole body was a mass of scintillating sensation as I anticipated whiling away the night with these desert beauties. I was ready to take mine at once, but Maged restrained me and indicated that he and I should be seated.

The girls stepped away from us, their bare feet leaving dainty prints in the sand. With olive oil cupped in their hands, they caressed one another until their skin had a glossy sheen in the light of the moon. Then they danced. Never have I seen such a dance; never before nor since; and it has always lingered in my mind, to be recalled on balmy nights when my heart is restless. The memory is painful, as exquisite memories so often are.

I see the flow of their bodies moving as if to a wonderfully haunting, erotic melody. But there is no music. The only sound is the distant barking of pariah dogs.

I see the naked girls caressing themselves, hands rubbing pointed breasts, sliding over smooth bellies and thighs, stroking over the darkness between their legs while they turn and writhe as if spitted on great phalluses. I see them move closer to one another. Reaching out, their fingers meet. Then they are drawn together like lovers long apart, lovers starved for the touch of one another, starved for the taste.

The taste of forbidden love.

Prohibited desire.

How long they continued, I don't recall. I wanted them to dance forever, yet I wanted them to stop instantly so that I might sate the appetite that strained my entire being. At last, their bodies slid apart. They stepped toward us, chests heaving, hair wild. They had, no doubt, expended themselves several times in the course of their strange dance, but their half-shut eyes held a promise of boundless delights.

I stood motionless as one of the twins slowly removed my clothing. She smelled of far-blown sand and olive and woman. A moonlit droplet slid to the tip of her nipple, shimmered there, containing all the vibrant colors of the rainbow. I longed to lick it off, that drop of woman-heated oil. When the last of my clothes fell to the sand I leaned forward, my tongue finding that drop of oil, licking, rolling the flavor around my mouth and swallowing.

Had I been cheated out of the next few minutes, I should have counted my life a waste. But whispers of the girls' departure from the mud-brick village were tardy in reaching Kemwese, their father. Before his arrival, I spent myself with each of the girls. I was standing, a twin upside-down in my heated embrace, my head hugged by her slick, golden thighs, my tongue darting into her sweetness, my phallus throbbing within the tight constriction of her mouth, when a sharp blow to the back of my leg toppled me (it was only with rare good fortune that I avoided a tragedy regarding the girl's teeth).

As I rolled in the sand, I glimpsed Maged making a dash for safety. A sandaled foot kicked my breath away. Hearing a struggle behind me, I managed to look around. The naked girls were at their father, clutching his arms and legs, fighting to save me. They proved no match for the enraged monster. He battered them aside and came at me, roaring.

His foot slashed toward my face. Catching it in both hands, I twisted, throwing Kemwese down. At this moment, I might have chosen to run and save myself. This, however, was against my combative nature.

Never one to abandon a fight, I attacked the growling savage. I fell upon him, fists pummeling his face. I heard a satisfying, gristly crunch as my knuckle smashed his nose. No sooner did blood gush from the nostrils than his arm swung up and struck my head with the force of a club. Dazed, I tumbled away.

I was only vaguely aware of the huge man lifting me. He raised me high above him, then tipped my head downward and drove me toward the sand. My neck should have snapped like a rotten twig when I hit the ground. Somehow, it didn't. The blow shocked every inch of my frame, however, and I was powerless to prevent the beast from working his will upon me.

He lifted me again. I knew, in what remained of my conscious mind, that I would soon be dead. Rather than throwing me down again, however, he began to carry me. Where he was taking me, I had no idea. Nor did I care. I only hoped, in a fogged, dreamy way, that if he continued to carry me long enough, some of my strength might return and I might yet save myself.

At length, he reached his destination. He flung me to the ground. Though I hadn't the power to raise my head, I could see that we were near the ruins of the Temple of Mentuhotep. Grunting, Kemwese pushed aside a large block of stone. I immediately recognized his intentions. Horror coursed through me, clearing my mind and giving me new strength. Raising my head, I saw a small black patch in the sand beneath where the rock had rested. A hole. A dark, shadowed hole reaching downward into the belly of the desert.

When Kemwese came for me, I threw a handful of sand into his face. Blinded and coughing, he groped for me. I rolled out of his reach. I got to my hands and knees and crawled, trying to gain my feet, but my body obeyed the commands of my mind in only the slowest fashion and soon he had me by the foot. He dragged me backwards, dragged me toward the awful hole. My fingers clawed at the sand. All sense of manhood broken by the horrible prospect awaiting me, I cried out for forgiveness. I begged him. I offered him money. At the end, I threatened him with terrible vengeance.

It was useless.

He raised me by both feet. I saw the black pit, like a tunnel to Hell, below my face. My hands dug into the sand at its edges, but to no avail.

Then he released me.

I plunged headfirst into the blackness.

Screaming.

The Awful Pit

I fell, petrified by an unreasoning fear that I might plunge forever through the lightless void. I had little time, fortunately, to dwell on the horror of that thought. Abruptly, I hit the bottom of the shaft and lost consciousness.

When my mind returned to me, the aches in every limb of my body quickly reminded me of the gravity of my situation. The darkness was so intense that I blinked several times to be certain that my eyes were indeed open. The lumpy pressure on my back told me that I was lying face upward. I raised my arms. I felt great relief and comfort in touching my still-naked body; my face, my chest and belly, my privates, my thighs. The hands, touching familiar places, gave me a warm feeling that I was not entirely alone in this strange and frightful pit. They also confirmed that I was still whole, at least as far as I could reach. I stirred my legs. They seemed unbroken.

As I lay there continuing to stroke my body and regaining a sense of reality, I began to assess my situation. The devil Kemwese had undoubtedly left me here to die. That being the case, he must have covered the opening of the pit with the enormous block of stone that had originally sealed it. Even should I succeed in climbing to the top, I would be powerless to shift the rock. My best chance of survival, however, seemed to lie in that direction.

Gazing into the black space above me, I tried to determine whether Kemwese had, indeed, rolled back the stone. If he hadn't, I should certainly be able to see the light of stars or the moon. Nothing was visible. Nothing.

I decided I must attempt to climb out, nonetheless. First, however, it would be wise to explore the confines of my prison.

As I stirred myself to sit, the uneven ground beneath me seemed to wobble. Lowering a hand to the lump beneath my bare hip, I touched a pliant surface that I immediately recognized as hide. My fingers explored further. The hide felt wrinkled, sunken. Pressing it, I felt the solid roundness of bone below the surface. With a gasp, I flung my naked body clear of the creature.

There, shivering, I huddled in the darkness and gazed in its direction. I could see nothing, of course. To confirm my fears, I finally ventured forward. My hands again encountered the dead flesh. I explored it briefly before realizing, with an agony of horror and revulsion, that my fall had been cushioned by the desiccated corpse of a man.

He, like myself, was naked. I wondered if he, too, had been caught in debauchery with the daughters of Kemwese. The thought chilled me, in spite of the pit's dreadful heat. Perhaps my end would be the same as his.

'No, damn it,' I said. The sound of my voice was dreadfully loud in the confined chamber. Silly, I know, but I feared for a moment that I had startled my deceased companion awake. I listened, half expecting him to speak. Or, worse, to advance and to lay his dead fingers on my naked body.

To my great relief, he didn't.

All I could hear was my ragged breathing.

A dry, labored sound.

From that point on, I took pains to remain silent.

Starting at the feet of the dead man, I began to inch my way along the boundary of my cell. I crawled on hands and knees across ancient dust. Dry as dead skin on the back of my throat. I let my shoulder brush along the stone wall to keep my orientation. After proceeding in this manner for no longer than a minute, I set my hand down on someone's face. I screamed.

The sound came back at me like a banshee howl.

Jabbing my eardrums so hard that they hurt.

For a long time, I crouched against the wall, panting in the hot air, struggling to regain my composure. Then I ventured forward. With hesitant hands, I familiarized myself with my new neighbor. His flesh felt stiffer than that of the other man, leading me to the assumption that his residence in the pit had been more prolonged. My hand searched along the length of a naked limb. I could not tell whether this was an arm or a leg until my fingers met a bag of shriveled skin and a hard stick of dried flesh as thick as my thumb.

Scrotum; phallus.

Both sucked dry of moisture by the desert air.

Briefly my hand roved over a sunken stomach; a chest; through skin I could feel the ridges of ribs. Then I found the husk of the throat and hard roundness of the head with cotton-candy tufts of hair.

I left him behind. Continued my exploration. My searching hands moving over the dust through the utter darkness. My reaction to the next body was more easily controlled. I did not scream. I merely removed my hand rapidly from his foot.

This man was fully clothed. I checked his pockets. In his shirt pocket, I found a pack of cigarettes and a small box of matches. Carefully sliding open the box, as if it contained the most valuable treasures of Egypt, my fingertips found the matches. Counted them. Eight. Eight precious matches. I struck one.

Nothing.

Duds.

Spent matches.

Was I doomed to sit out the rest of my life in this arid chamber beneath the desert?

To die slowly of thirst?

Madness claiming me first. As this all-engulfing darkness bore down on me.

Would tomorrow find me singing to my dead companions while holding their dry hands for comfort?

No . . . *take care*, I told myself. *Try the matches again.*

This time I felt the box until I found the abrasive strip. I must have run the match head along the smooth-paper side.

I struck again. The match's phosphorus head sparked in the darkness, then burst alight with such brilliance that pain shot through my eyes. In a moment, however, the pain passed, and I found myself gazing upon a horrible scene. I groaned.

For there, gathered around me in the bottom of the shaft that was no larger than a dozen feet in diameter, were the dried corpses of five men. The one in front of me, the clothed one, still held a revolver in his shrunken hand. I saw a hole in his right temple, the stain from the copious outpouring of blood and brains darkening the dust around his head where it lay.

Another corpse, across the floor, had gaping wounds in its thigh. I had little doubt how they got there. The grim thought entered my mind that I, too, might soon be driven by extremities of thirst and hunger to consider partaking of my companions.

One in particular, a bald, lean man clad only in undershorts, looked fresher than the others. I doubted that he had been dead more than a few days. Perhaps his body still retained enough moisture to quench the thirst that would shortly begin to torture me. There might be as much as half a pint in the bladder. No. That would be—

Fire scorched my fingers. I dropped the match. Darkness swallowed me and I stood motionless among the dead, considering my next course of action.

At length, I crouched beside the man who had taken his own life. Groping blindly, I found his pistol. I had the devil's own time getting it out of his hand, and finally resorted to breaking two of the fingers. With the gun free, I carefully released the cylinder catch. The cylinder swung sideways. I tipped the barrel upwards. Six loads dropped into my other palm. By touch alone in the darkness I deduced from the open ends of the cartridges that two were expended shells, while four were still whole, hence live cartridges. From their size and weight, I guessed them to be of .38 caliber. I reloaded and set the pistol aside where I would have no trouble finding it.

For the present, I had no need for the weapon. The fact of its presence, however, was a great comfort. I knew that, should circumstances offer no alternative, I need not be reduced to a groveling, inhuman beast. I would simply take my own life, as my inert companion had, and be done with it.

With that settled, I groped once more in the dark. With a new sense of assurance I stripped the man of his trousers. I found a penknife in one of his pockets. Using that, I cut his pants legs into long, narrow strips. When I had a dozen of them, I struck another precious match. Six left, I told myself. Only six. I applied its flame to the end of the strip and found that I had created a rather satisfactory source of light. Paying out fabric as needed, I made a close inspection of the chamber by the illumination of the burning cotton.

The stone wall, I noticed, sloped gradually inward above me. This ruled out the possibility of climbing to the top of the shaft. Might there be another way out? Certainly, my predecessors hadn't found one. Their failure, however, constituted no certain proof that such an exit did not, in fact, exist.

Here, my knowledge of Egyptian tombs stood me in good stead. The pit, my prison, had obviously been constructed in ancient times. Its proximity to the Temple of Mentuhotep might indicate that it had been built during his reign, possibly as a secret entrance to his tomb. It was not unusual to find such passages, often designed as elaborate mazes complicated with false entries, dead ends, and portals concealed in walls and ceilings for the purpose of foiling tomb robbers.

I exhausted most of my supply of makeshift wicks in a useless search of the walls and floor. While my flame still burned, I quickly fashioned more strips from the dead man's trousers. Then I renewed my search, looking for the slightest clue that a secret passage might lie behind the stone wall of my cell. I found no such clue. Had I a pick, I might have battered my way to freedom. With bare hands, I was powerless.

Allowing my light to die, I sank against one of the walls. I was sweaty, exhausted, coated in dust. My hopes of escape had faded to a dim prayer for a miracle.

As I sat in the blackness, surrounded by my silent companions, an idea began to form. It seemed impractical at first. It seemed less so as I thought about it. Though the top of the shaft was higher than my frail light reached, any object that might take me closer to it seemed worthwhile.

Perhaps, after all, the passage to the tomb had been placed midway up the shaft wall. Such a manner of concealment was not unknown to the wily priests of those ancient times.

Thus, with the project justified in my mind, I set about constructing a platform of the bodies. It was a ghoulish task. In the darkness, I dragged each from its place of rest. Their joints were stiff, their skin tough. I grew to know their flesh by their manner of undress, by the various configurations of their limbs. Some had died prone, others sitting. I made use of these differences in constructing my platform, often sacrificing height for sturdiness.

At last, by clever stacking of four cadavers against the wall, I had a platform as high as my chest. I lifted the last body, the one most recently dead. He seemed less brittle than the others. Also his limbs had stiffened into convenient positions. I stood him upright on top of the others, leaning him slightly backwards against the wall. When he was securely in place, I lit a strip of cloth, the upper end of which I had earlier inserted in his mouth. I adjusted the burning tip at the side of the platform so that it wouldn't hinder my progress.

Then I began the awful climb. The bodies trembled precariously under my feet, but I was careful to place my weight only on the strongest points: a hip here, a shoulder there. At last, I reached the top of my platform. I stood motionless, gripping the wall, gathering my strength for the most strenuous part of the climb.

The flame had inched slowly up the strip of cloth. As I paused, it ignited the hair of one man, blazing briefly, illuminating the chamber with flickering white light, filling my nostrils with a terrible stench. When the fire died, I inspected the end of my taper.

Half the strip yet remained. I intended to use its flame, when I reached the summit, to ignite another makeshift taper, which was wound around my neck. This would save me the use of a precious match. The matchbox was tied at my throat, however, so I wouldn't be at a loss for light should the original taper expire during my climb.

Without further hesitation, I inched sideways. I swung the burning taper away from the knees of my ghastly companion and let it hang beside him out of my way. Pressing my body to his, I began to climb him. It was a horrible business, all the more so because of my nudity.

I was perched upon his bent knees, one hand pressed to the wall, the other gripping his left shoulder, when the light failed. The sudden darkness unnerved me, but I knew that I would soon fall if I didn't continue upward. Sliding a foot up his dry leg, I sought the bony protuberance of his hip. I found it. When I felt secure there, I raised my other foot. It, too, found a hold at his hip. Perched more precariously than ever, I leaned forward, my knees gripping him as if I were a child shinnying up a tree. Carefully, I straightened up, leaning full against him. I felt his face against my belly, then against my privates. I shall not tell of the nightmarish images that passed through my mind as I made my slow way upward.

I was almost onto his shoulders when he moved. My hands sought purchase on the stone wall but found none. The corpse continued to slide out from under me. In an instant I was falling. One foot struck the top body of my grisly platform and punched through it as if it were a plank of rotten wood. From there, I tumbled backwards through the darkness.

The ground struck me a terrible blow. As I lay there, stunned, a body fell on me. Then another. I flung them aside, and scurried out of their way.

Hunched against a wall, I gazed at the darkness. I listened intently. Beyond the drumming of my own heart, beyond the windy gasping of my lungs, I heard other sounds. Muted, incoherent babbling. The papery sounds of dry flesh dragging across the gravel floor.

I knew they were coming for me.

'No!' I shrieked.

I thought I heard their sandy laughter.

With palsied hands, I unlooped the strip of cloth at my neck. I tore open the box of matches. Poised to strike one, I hesitated. Better to die in the darkness, certainly, than to look upon the creatures – the dead creatures – crawling toward me. But I had to see!

I struck a match. In its sudden glare, I saw one reaching for my foot! Another, sitting upright, grinned. The rest, still in a heap, writhed as they tried to untangle their twisted limbs. It took me several agonizing moments to realize their movements were an illusion created by the flickering light of my match.

I lit an end of my taper and watched. Finally, I convinced myself that I was in no danger from my companions – that the danger resided only within my troubled psyche. My eyes turned to the shining nickel plate of the revolver.

Time to end it all, I thought.
Time for the kindness of oblivion.

I got to my feet and realized that I had lost the matchbox. Lowering my gaze, I scanned the floor until I spotted the small box. As I crouched to pick it up, I noticed an usual shadow at the base of the wall. I dropped to my hands and knees. With my free hand I reached into the shadow . . . deeper . . . deeper . . . A hole!

It was more than two feet in diameter. Inserting my arm as far as possible, I found no obstruction. Surely this was the passage I had searched for!

Such a fool I had been! Such a timorous fool! It had never occurred to me, during my careful search, to look *behind the bodies*!

I laughed out loud. Had the others, seeking a way out, made the same mistake? Indeed, had Kemwese placed his first victim over the hole on purpose to conceal the passage from his future prey? I shouldn't have put it past the devil.

For the next few minutes, I cut new strips from what remained of the trousers. I tied them around my neck. Once more, I secured the box of matches at my throat. Then, clutching the revolver in one hand, I slithered into the hole and began my quest for freedom.

The Tomb of Amara

I made my way slowly, laboriously, through the narrow passageway. At times, the stone walls squeezed my shoulders and I feared I might become stuck. Turning back, however, was out of the question. I knew what lay behind me: certain death. Ahead, there was hope.

The rough walls pressed in on me. They scraped the naked flesh of my body. Had I been afflicted with claustrophobia, the blackness and suffocating heat and tight, constricting walls would surely have driven me mad. But I kept my sanity and pressed onward.

Finally, my outstretched arms found open space instead of confining stone. I inched forward as far as I dared. Tucking the revolver into the gap beside my chest, I used both hands to free a strip of cloth from my neck and light its end.

I found myself near the ceiling of a chamber. It appeared to be about twelve feet in length and width. The floor, however, was out of sight. Paying out my makeshift taper, I lowered the burning tip as far as possible. I was still unable to see the floor, so I pulled up the strip and tore off its last few inches. I let it drop. It fluttered downward for some distance before stopping. I watched it burn on the floor no more than twenty feet below me.

With no choice in the matter, I clutched the revolver and writhed forward. As I hung over the lip of the hole, about to fall, I pushed away from the wall with all my strength. I maneuvered myself in midair, much as a diver would, and hit the floor feet foremost. My legs buckled, of course. I tumbled forward. The ground dealt me a terrific blow. I remained conscious, however, and a quick survey of my limbs indicated that the fall had bruised and battered me, but nothing was broken.

Eagerly, I lit a match and ignited one of my cloth strips. I found, to my relief, no unwelcome company in this pit.

I also found the door of a tomb.

A strange golden disk decorated with the scepter of Osiris had been applied as a seal to the stone door and was held in place by hemp cord. My feeble light showed several kinds of hieroglyphics engraved on the door. Under my father's tutelage, I had learned to read the language as if I had been born to it. Unfortunately, someone had chiseled and scratched the glyphs, rendering them indecipherable.

I had seen such work before. This, no doubt, was the tomb of an outcast, or heretic, one whose name was anathema.

The realization made hackles rise on my naked flesh. As a skeptic in matters supernatural, I should not have been unsettled to find myself at the tomb door of one damned by the ancient priests. Unsettled I was, however: I could feel malevolence like vapor rising from ice. It chilled me to the bone.

Stepping away from the door, I began to search the walls for a way out.

There was none.

None that I could find.

This came as no great surprise; my route to this chamber was surely the only manner of entry or exit.

I was glad for the revolver. At least it would give me a speedy end, not the slow and maddening agony of death by dehydration.

I blew out the light and sat in a corner. Not yet time to end myself. There would be plenty of time for that later. I tried to push aside the grim thoughts and consider possible avenues of escape. My mind found no answers.

At last, I decided to try my luck with the tomb. Though I dreaded the thought of the place, I was quite curious about it. Besides, there was only one way to find out, with certainty, what lay beyond the sealed door. Anything was possible, even my salvation.

I moved across the black chamber to the door. Fighting my reluctance to touch it, I lit one of my tapers and set to work.

I started calmly enough. As I progressed, however, my frenzy grew. What if I should be unable to force the door? What if I should succeed, only to find myself no closer to escape? All the while, I fought against my dread of the unholy person entombed within. I wanted only to huddle in the chamber's farthest corner, but my fevered mind told me that my only chance of survival lay in opening the door. I raged as I ripped the hemp loose. I yelled and roared like a lunatic as I strained at the stone slab.

At last it groaned.

Dust fell from the sealed edges of the door.

The door moved.

Swung open.

I cringed away as a foul gust of hot air breathed into my face and extinguished my light. The rank odor made me gag. It had the smell of dead, decaying snakes. In the darkness, I pictured the tomb to be a charnel house where dying vipers waited eagerly to swarm over me. Where hooded cobras swayed. Fangs dripping venom. I knew this was impossible: the nightmare of an overwrought mind. Only renewed light could still my fears, however. With shaking hands, I struck another match. I lit my taper, and peered through the door's opening.

There were, of course, no snakes.

Gazing at the small area revealed by my light, I stepped into the tomb.

At first, I thought it was empty. Surely, robbers had cleared the room of all its treasures: the countless necessities secreted with the corpse to assure its comfort in the afterlife – the utensils, the weapons, the furniture, the effigies of servants. No doubt the sarcophagus and mummy had also been removed.

I looked round at the walls. Normally these would have been covered with paintings, depicting the life of the deceased: hunting fowl, fishing by spear for the fat fish found in the Nile; or there would be representations of the deceased with members of their family. Also there should have been hundreds of hieroglyphics describing the life of the individual entombed here, the victories, the names of their children. There should also have been prayers and verses from the great Egyptian *Book of the Dead*.

Instead, the walls had been covered entirely with some black pigment. It still contained a reddish-brown tinge. This, too, I had seen before. In the tomb of one of the priests of the Pharaoh Akhenaten, the heretic king who banished Egypt's vast family of gods in favor of a single deity, the Aten. I recalled standing in the disgraced priest's tomb and hearing Howard Carter describe how later priests would have erased the name of the evil priest, then painted the walls with the blood of pigs. An animal considered unclean by ancient Egyptians. This and the destruction of the dead priest's identity would have destroyed his soul in the afterlife.

This had happened here, too. The erased name on the tomb door. The painting over of wall paintings and hieroglyphics in the despised blood of swine.

Whoever had been buried here must have been truly hated by later generations, who had set out so thoroughly to seek vengeance on the spirit of the deceased.

I comforted myself with the thought that the evil one had long ago met the same fate as countless other mummies. Even now, perhaps, it was residing in a far-off museum. Or, like so many others, it had been ground into powder by some luckless European, now long dead, as the miracle cure of his day. Or it might have simply been used as kindling for some Bedouin's fire.

As I proceeded across the chamber, however, my light fell upon a canopic jar. Nearby lay the stone lid of the sarcophagus; near that, the mummiform lid of a coffin.

A chill penetrated my body. My bowels cramped, my privates shrank as if trying to retreat into my groin. For a long time, I simply gazed at the open sarcophagus, afraid to move.

My taper grew short. I realized that if I didn't act quickly, I would be plunged into darkness. That thought quickened me to action. I unwrapped a length of cloth from my neck – the last such strip – and lit it. The dried-blood walls seemed to feed on the light, making the chamber gloomier and gloomier.

With only the slightest hesitation, I stepped to the side of the sarcophagus and gazed into it.

I wasn't shocked, at first, by the strange sight below me.

Here was a person – a dead person, to be sure – but not so different from myself. He had brown hair. He wore a shirt and trousers, a leather belt, boots with neatly tied laces. Since he was lying face down inside the inner wooden coffin, I was spared the sight of his face.

Only when I looked more closely did I notice the mummy beneath him. A portion of its head was visible. I saw its red hair, lots of red hair that filled the spaces between the body and the coffin wall. Saw its eyeless sockets. I had the impression, for a moment, that it was kissing the dead man's neck.

The odors also. Through the smoke of my burning tapers I caught musty scents of ancient spices. Probably the ones that had been placed into the body cavity of the mummy to mask the smell of post-mortem decay.

I raised the man's head. The mummy's head also lifted and I realized its teeth were buried in his throat.

Stepping away from the coffin, I put the revolver to my temple.

Pulled the trigger.

Salvation

Had the revolver discharged and ended my life at that moment in the tomb of Amara, many would have been saved from the miseries later visited upon them. But if there are gods they are wily devils, tricksters that toy with our fates. They saw fit to let the hammer drop on an empty chamber.

I drew back the hammer for a second try.

As my finger began to press the trigger, I heard the distant, echoing call of my name. It was the voice of my companion, Maged.

Backing my way out of the tomb, I turned my eyes toward the tunnel high on the chamber wall. There I saw the shaky, dancing beam of a flashlight.

'Maged?' I called.

'Robert!' The delight in his voice made me smile.

My desperation, my madness, my suicidal helplessness, fell away, vanishing as the morning mist on the Nile vanishes before the dawn sun. I felt the sudden joy of a man who, chased by nightmare demons, awakens to a golden dawn.

Finally, the light beam fell upon my face.

'Ah, my friend!' Maged called. 'Always the explorer. I thought I should never find you.'

'You certainly took your time about it.'

'I went for a rope.' It dropped from the tunnel's mouth. 'Coming up?' he asked.

'Are you alone?'

'Most surely.'

'Secure the rope, then, and come down. I've found something you ought to see.'

A few moments later, I saw my young friend sliding down the rope. He hurried to my side. His joy was such that he embraced me.

'I ought to bash your head,' I told him, grinning.

'Were not the sisters everything I promised?'

'They were marvelous, marvelous. Only you neglected to mention their father.'

'A tyrant, that man.'

'Tyrant? He's a murderous lunatic! But enough of that. Let me show you what I've found.'

I showed him the door of the tomb, with its defaced hieroglyphics. His mood turned somber. He was reluctant to enter the tomb, but I persuaded him at length. I took his flashlight and led the way. Even with his olive skin his face paled visibly when he saw what gory blacks and rust browns painted the walls.

'Truly this is the tomb of a despised one,' he said. 'Never have I seen every inch of a tomb wall painted with hog's blood before.' He made sure his body made no contact with the unclean blood of the swine.

'Come along,' I said. He joined me beside the sarcophagus. I shone the light inside and lifted the man's head so that Maged might see the mummy's teeth embedded in the throat.

He backed quickly away. 'We must go.'

'What's the hurry?' I asked, rather enjoying his fright.

'The Bride of Set,' he muttered.

'What?'

He was gone. In spite of my refreshed humor, I was not eager to remain alone with the ghastly pair. I hurried after Maged. I was no sooner outside the tomb than he began to push its door shut.

'Don't bother,' I said, stopping him. 'We'll only have to open it again.'

'Please! It must be sealed.'

'Must it?'

'She will arise from the dead to seek after the blood of her slayers.'

'Nonsense.'

'It is true, Robert.' He pointed to the defaced glyphs on the door. 'Much has been destroyed, but this was once her name. *Amara!*'

I peered at it. True, the little that remained legible may have been part of the name 'Amara'.

'We must leave at once,' Maged told me, 'and find a holy man to reseal the entrance.'

'What we *will* do, Maged,' I said firmly, 'is figure out how to take her and her coffin out of here.'

His eyes widened with fright. 'We must not. You don't understand, Robert. You have broken the seal of Osiris guarding the doorway. Its magic is destroyed. Without it, Amara will walk the night.'

'She's dead, fool.'

'She is of the dead who lives.' Maged pushed the tomb door shut and leaned his back against it. Perspiration glistened on his face. His eyes were large . . . frightened. I'd never seen him like this before. 'Please listen, my friend. I will explain.'

'Speak your piece,' I told him rather impatiently.

'The banished god Set, slayer of Osiris, is the one recognized by both Jew and Christian alike as the one you call Satan.' He took a breath and continued. 'Set came in the night to Amara who was the favorite wife of Pharaoh Mentuhotep. He gave her the seed of his loins, that she might bear him a son. In return for her favors, he promised Amara the gift of eternal life.'

'Bunkum,' I said in contempt.

Maged ignored my remark. 'The god Set, the evil one, he wished his son to be Pharaoh after Mentuhotep, and lead the people of Egypt to their doom. When Amara gave birth, Mentuhotep suspected treachery, for the son had wicked eyes . . . snake eyes. He put Amara to death.'

'What about the baby?'

'It too was executed, and entombed with Amara.'

'I didn't see it.'

Maged gave an elaborate shrug. 'Robbers, perhaps . . .'

'Well, your story is charming, but it's utter bunk.'

'It's true, Robert. Believe me.'

'Where'd you pick it up? I've never run across the story before.'

'When I was a child, my grandmother whispered it to me in the night. She said, if I was bad, Amara would come for me and eat my throat.'

'We wouldn't want that, would we, Maged?' I said and laughed. 'Come along, let's be off.'

Vengeance

My first order of business, after recovering from the ordeal of the pit, was to deal with the villain Kemwese.

I stayed away from the Tutankhamun diggings all day so the bastard wouldn't suspect that I had escaped from his death-hole. When night came, I dined with my father. He enquired about my battered appearance and I satisfied his curiosity by explaining that I'd taken a nasty fall down the hotel stairway. The subject was dismissed.

After we separated, I went to my room. I waited there, trembling somewhat with anticipation. Shortly after dark, I heard a knocking at my door. I opened it and Carmen entered, wearing a glittering cocktail gown that revealed her milk-white shoulders. Her cleavage was breathtaking.

Carmen was her stage name – or rather bed name, if you prefer, for she was a whore. She was a fabulous whore, renowned throughout Luxor. She stood nearly six feet tall, with hair the color of wheat and breasts like the silos of her Iowa hometown. All her orifices were portals to unspeakable pleasure. But they were costly to enter, and only those of us with considerable wealth could afford to journey there.

I had been with Carmen many times. I was one of her favorites, as she told me time and again. When I spoke to her that afternoon she readily agreed to my request.

'For that kind of dough,' she had said, 'I'd blow King Tut himself.'

Naturally, I didn't explain my entire plan.

'Now let me see if I've got it straight,' she said, sitting on my bed, her long legs stretching out. 'I go to this guy's house and I say my friend and me, we got attacked by a gang of cutthroats out by the temple ruins. Right?'

'That's it.'

'And would he come and help, 'cause I think my friend's hurt real bad?'

'Exactly.'

'And I get him out there and get him all worked up and—'

My engorged organ stopped her words. For the next half-hour, I used her with such vigor that we both finished sweaty and exhausted. When we recovered, we dressed and set out for the home of Kemwese.

At his village, I pointed out the mud-brick house. Carmen went to it while I hurried away. I rushed through the darkness. Soon, I reached the stone slab, the entrance to Kemwese's horried prison. I hid myself in the shadows of the nearby temple ruins. There, I waited.

The wait was a lengthy one. I sat on the rough stone, watching the desolate landscape before me with its endless vista of sand. For all the world I must have looked like Ahab searching the waves for his damnable White Whale. No one can know the horrors of the charnel pit; no one can know the rapture I felt as I waited in the moonlight to take my vengeance upon the man who had put me there.

Man?

No! *Human fiend.*

My heart pounded. My hands trembled. Yes, even my teeth chattered, in spite of the night's heat. Several times I laughed, muffling the sound with my hands.

Finally, Carmen appeared. Her golden tresses cascaded down her back. Her hips swayed as she walked.

She was holding Kemwese's hand. His robe gleamed as white as bone.

'I do not see your friend,' Kemwese said.

Carmen swirled away from him, her laughter trilling through the silence.

'Where is the friend who was beaten?'

Her forefinger tapped the side of her head. 'In here, Kemwese. I made him up.'

'And why is that?' he asked. He crossed his arms over his massive chest.

'To drag you away from your village. What we're gonna do, it's got to be a big secret.'

'Kemwese does not pay for his women.'

'Course not. This isn't business, sweetheart. This is just for pleasure. My pleasure.' She went to him, long, slender arms held out, her gold bracelets glinting.

I watched from my hiding place, trembling. They embraced, they kissed. Soon Carmen was naked and standing upright as Kemwese lavished kisses on her shoulders, on the vast twin mounds that were her breasts. He fell to his knees like a worshiper at the temple of her body. As he lapped between her legs, she pulled the djellaba over his head and flung it aside. Now he was naked, his body hairy like a gorilla's. Taking his face away from her womanhood, he crawled behind her to dwell on her rear parts. He forced her down and mounted her. It surprised me not the least to discover his preference.

Once he was firmly implanted, I left my place of concealment. I made my way stealthily toward the pair. Soon, I was standing close behind Kemwese, watching the hairy mounds of his buttocks twitch and jiggle as he rutted. From the frenzy of his exertion and the rhythm of his beastly grunts, I guessed that he was on the verge of expending himself. I wanted to cheat him of that moment, so I stepped forward quickly and brought down the revolver. Its butt cracked against the bastard's skull. To my chagrin, the impact triggered a bowel movement.

I pulled the unconscious body off Carmen and saw that I hadn't prevented his climax after all.

'Damn,' Carmen muttered, getting up. 'Damn, look what he did!'

One of her calves bore a glistening dark smudge. She used Kemwese's djellaba to clean herself.

For the next few minutes I busied myself with binding the hands and feet of my quarry. I knew the hemp would not restrain him for long after his return to consciousness. I didn't intend that it should.

'All done?' Carmen asked when I finished tying him.

'Nearly.'

'Nay, now, sweetheart, you said we'd just truss him up and leave him bare-ass. If you've got any other tricks up your sleeve, you can count me out.'

'There's nothing to worry about, Carmen.'
'Not for you. You ain't the one went in his house, honey.'
'Who saw you?'
'He had these two gals with him. A couple of twins.'
'They won't tell.'
'I'll just bet.'
'They're his daughters. They hate him more than I do. Besides, they're both deaf-mutes.'
'You sure about that?'
'I'm positive. Were you seen by anyone else?'
She shook her head. 'I don't think so, but that don't change the picture. If you want to pull some nasty business here, I'll take a walk, thank you very much.'
'It won't take long,' I told her. 'If you prefer not to watch, go on ahead. I'll catch you up in a few minutes.'
'What're you gonna do to him? Some homosexualist thing?'
'No.'
'What, then?'
'I thought you didn't want to know.'
'I guess I don't.'
'Like I say, take a little stroll. I'll catch you up when I'm done.'
She agreed to that.
When she walked off, hips swaying, I dragged the unconscious body of Kemwese to the side of the stone slab. I pushed it away from the hole. I turned to Kemwese and slid him forward until his legs as far as the knees dropped out of sight.
I slapped his sweaty face until the eyes blinked open.
'Remember me?' I asked.
He scowled, his gaze burning into me.
'Time for a dose of your own medicine, my friend.'
I was delighted to see the terror that suddenly twisted his face as he understood what I meant, and realized that the lower half of his body had already been swallowed by the pit.
Down he went.
Down, down, down.
He cried out in pain as he hit the bottom.

'Nasty fall,' I called down.

I crouched at the edge of the pit, grinning. He cursed me and my ancestors; my sons and their sons. He threatened me. That he would peel the skin from my body; that my male member would be worn as a trophy on his belt. Finally, however, much to my satisfaction, he began to cry and plead for mercy.

I pushed the stone into place and left him there.

With great restraint, I allowed a full week to pass before returning to the pit. Maged and I went there in the dead of night. I had told my friend nothing of Kemwese. The purpose of our excursion, I'd made clear, was to determine the best way of removing the mummy and its coffin from the tomb.

Maged was against the whole affair, at first. He reminded me, at endless and tedious length, of Amara's nasty reputation – indeed, her demon-like nature. In my turn, I reminded him that dead is *dead*.

He was unconvinced. Those fright stories of his grandmother's had embedded themselves deeply into his heart and soul. Then I told him of my plans for the mummy – as well as my plans for myself. I described my family's private collection of Egyptian antiquities. I told him that we possessed no mummies, as yet, and how my heart was now set upon adding such an infamous lady as Amara to our collection.

He argued that it was silly and dangerous and impossible. Aside from the hazards of Amara herself there were laws. I was surprised by his familiarity with Egypt's restrictions on the removal of artifacts, and even more surprised by his knowledge of problems we would face with the United States authorities, who look upon mummies as little more than germ-infected corpses.

'I know ways,' I said, 'of getting around all that rubbish.'

I explained about my father's friend, the smuggler.

Maged was adamant; he wanted no part in such dealings. Then I explained that, of course, I would not only have Amara smuggled into the US, but Maged as well. He would live with my father and me, as just one of the family.

'Is this true?' he asked, dumbfounded.

'You have my word on it.'

From that moment forward, Maged was as brash and energetic about the project as if he had originated it himself.

I watched him climb down the knotted rope. He disappeared into the pit and I was glad I had not mentioned Kemwese. His surprise at meeting our old friend would be marvelous to see.

Quickly, I followed him into the darkness.

When I reached bottom, I shone my flashlight over the grim collection of corpses. Kemwese was not among them. This troubled me somewhat, in spite of my certainty that we would find his body nearby: in the tunnel, or the adjoining chamber, or Amara's tomb.

After all, no man could survive a week without water in this climate. And there was no other exit; I was reasonably certain of that.

Because of my lingering apprehension about Kemwese, I insisted on being the first to enter the connecting tunnel. In my restored condition, the narrow tunnel had little effect on my nerves. True, it was often a tight squeeze. Overall, however, the tunnel seemed less confining, less threatening, than previously. My only concern was Kemwese. What if he should squirm towards me out of the darkness? I knew this was rubbish. Nevertheless, the idea of it would not leave me.

I was greatly relieved to reach the opening at the tunnel's end. Eagerly, I searched the area below with my light.

My dread increased, however, for there was no Kemwese in the room below.

I debated whether to broach the subject to Maged and decided against it; what useful purpose could it serve? It would give him a warning to be cautious, true enough. On the other hand, it might be enough to frighten him into abandoning the project. I couldn't take a chance on that, so I kept my silence.

I secured a length of rope to a corner of the masonry, as Maged had done on the night he saved me. Then I squirmed out of the tunnel. With my legs wrapped in hemp, I lowered myself head foremost to the floor of the room. Then I helped Maged down.

The door of Amara's tomb was shut, just as we had left it.

Could Kemwese have entered and pulled it closed after him?

I drew the revolver from my pocket. I didn't fail to notice a faint smile on Maged's face.

Amara

'Dead is dead,' he whispered.

Together, we pulled open the door of Amara's tomb. We swung the beams of our lights inside.

In my memory, the next instant seems endless. And yet I know it lasted no longer than a blink or two of the eye.

I saw Kemwese on his back, gazing at us with dead eyes. The flesh of his naked body had been savagely torn.

Facing us, seated on his chest, arms resting casually on her upthrust knees, was the mummy, Amara.

As if sitting on a cushion.

Relaxing.

Patiently waiting for us.

The Living Dead

With shocking suddenness, Amara leaped from the body.

Maged hurled the flashlight at the monstrosity. It struck her head, distracting her for a moment as it entangled itself in her voluminous red hair. We leaped through the entrance. Flinging ourselves against the heavy door, we somehow managed to force it shut before the awful creature could reach us.

Despite the pressure on the other side of the door, our combined efforts were sufficient to hold it shut. The strength of Amara was such that neither of us alone could have held it closed. As we pressed our shoulders to the rough stone, I searched my mind for a method of escape.

If we simply made a dash for the rope, Amara would certainly fall upon us before we could climb to safety. If one of us stayed behind to hold the door as long as possible, the other might be able to climb to freedom. The one remaining, however, would be compelled to face the mummy alone.

At the time, I knew only that she was dead . . . and yet alive.

I had no desire to exchange blows with such a creature.

Unworthy thoughts entered my mind, thoughts of making a sudden dash for the rope, leaving Maged to face the hideous creature by himself. Ashamed, I reminded myself that he was my best friend, nay, my only friend, and that he had saved my life. I could not leave him at the mercy of the awful hag.

And yet, I knew we could not hold the door shut forever. At a loss, I asked Maged's advice.

'It is simple enough, Robert. The god Set gave Amara power only to walk the night. At dawn, she will again be as one who is dead.'

'Are you sure?'

'This is what my grandmother told me.'

'Then I hope your grandmother was right.'

Neither of us knew precisely what time dawn would arrive that morning. Shortly after five o'clock, however, the pressure on the other side of the door ceased. As a precaution, we waited until six o'clock by my watch. Then we opened the door.

Amara had returned to her seat on Kemwese's chest.

As we entered her tomb, she remained motionless.

The ghastly thought came to me that Maged was wrong, that we were being lured into the tomb by trickery. I found my gaze locked onto that terrible figure. Its eyeless sockets, mere twin pits in the ruined face, seemed to look right into my own two living eyes. Her naked body was brown; wrinkled hideously in parts, elsewhere, as smooth as melon skin. While tumbling in a copper cascade from the skull-like head, down around her shoulder, covering one breast that hung as empty as a poor man's leather purse, was that lustrous hair. How hair could still look lovely and alive attached to that ancient husk of a corpse was beyond me.

A movement beside me roused me from my near-trance. I was tempted to hurry away, but Maged walked forward to shove the thing with his foot. It fell sideways.

'You see, Robert?' he whispered.

I breathed a sigh of relief. 'And you say that it won't . . . get up . . . before sunset?'

'That is what my grandmother told me.'

'Excellent.' With trembling hands, I lit a cigarette. I paced the tomb, smoking it, and thinking. Blue smoke rolled across the walls painted with pig's blood. At last, I said, 'Let's box her up.'

'What?'

'We'll put her back in her coffin and see if we can get it – and her – out of here before dark.'

'Now?'

'No time like the present, my friend. Especially for a nasty job.'

A nasty job it proved to be, indeed. With Amara inside, the coffin was too heavy for us to handle with ease. After carrying it from the tomb, we removed her. I climbed the rope to the tunnel overhead. Below, Maged tied the lidless coffin to the rope. He lifted and guided it while I pulled. Though the coffin was not unmanageably heavy, I had great difficulty hoisting it to my perch and pulling it in after me. It plugged the tunnel's end. I tried, squirming backwards, to pull it along after me. Soon, however, it began scraping along nicely. I realized that Maged was at its other end, pushing. It was a tight fit. Had the tunnel not been perfectly straight, we would never have succeeded.

The going became extremely hard during the final yards when the tunnel slanted upward to the floor of the first pit. I pulled as best I could, and Maged pushed with superhuman effort.

At last, we finished. We fell, exhausted, to the floor as if joining the five old corpses in their rest. When I had recovered my breath, I lit a cigarette.

'The rest of the job will be a snap,' I said.

I was almost correct.

The coffin lid gave no trouble at all. Nor did the four canopic jars. The final stage of the task, however, required us to deal with Amara herself. This was a singularly grim bit of business that set our nerves on edge. As we maneuvered her through the tunnel, we both worried that she might suddenly come alive in our hands. Neither of us spoke of it, at the time. Much later, however, in the safety of my California home, we shared our memories of that day.

Maged, who had been in the lead, confided, 'I was certain her head moved. I couldn't see a thing, of course, but somehow I *knew* that she had turned her head and intended to nip my arm.'

It was with considerable relief that we placed Amara inside her coffin and covered her horrible, naked body with the lid.

We couldn't raise her out of the pit that day. It was not a job for daylight. And yet, we were both loath to deal with Amara at night.

Maged had a solution. We climbed out of the pit, seeing nobody in the vicinity, and pushed the stone into place to conceal the opening.

Maged's solution took the form of a gnarled old man named Ramo who lived not far from Kemwese's hut.

We found him sitting alone in his dark hut. He wore a gray, tattered djellaba and a gold-cloth turban that had seen far better days. I saw at once that something was amiss about his face. The mouth seemed out of kilter, long and stretching across the side of his face. This was due, I later discovered, to an old knife wound that had laid open his right cheek and never healed correctly.

Maged spoke to the man in Arabic, explaining that we had blundered into the tomb of Amara, destroying its sacred seal and so destroying the magic bonds that had contained the creature. Amara had walked. We wished Ramo to use his powers, as a priest of Osiris, to seal the coffin.

He asked to see the broken seal of Osiris. Maged, with commendable foresight, had pocketed the golden disk. He removed its pieces from his pocket and presented them to Ramo. The old man fondled them, grinning. His grin was a hideous sight indeed, as it drew back not only his lips but also the ragged edges of his cheek, exposing what remained of his molars.

He explained that his father had fashioned this very seal, many years ago – a dozen years before Ramo himself had been born. At the time, robbers had plundered Amara's tomb. They had stripped off her winding clothes, stolen her jewelry, and taken her mummified infant from its resting place at its mother's side.

Amara had remained still until the child was taken. Then she had abruptly clutched the nearest robber and killed him. The two survivors, fearing Amara's vengeance, escaped from the tomb, then came to Ramo's father. They paid him well and he fashioned the seal of gold to prevent Amara's escape from the tomb.

We offered to pay Ramo twice the amount his father had received, and he agreed to work the gold into a pair of seals, one for each long side of the coffin's lid. He would bless the seals, according to ancient rite, and their magic would prevent Amara from rising.

They were finished two days later. Just at sunrise, Maged and I dropped a rope into the pit and descended. We expected this. We flashed our lights among the sprawled corpses and found Amara lying beneath one of the naked men.

The sight of it made my flesh crawl. I envisioned all of the bodies stirring in the blackness of the pit, lurching toward the new female in their midst who summoned them with her open legs.

We tumbled the man aside.

I carefully averted my eyes from his privates, afraid of confirming my fears.

We lifted Amara, and put her inside the coffin. We put the lid in place. Then we affixed the twin seals of Osiris at the seams of the lid, hammering small nails through holes made in the gold for this purpose by Ramo.

The job finished, we left the pit and covered its entry with the rock. We would not return until arrangements had been completed to smuggle Amara home.

Conclusion

Many years have gone by since my activities in Egypt. My father died long ago, though not before I was able to delight him with the addition of Amara to our Egyptian collection.

Maged married shortly after coming to live with us. We employed him and his wife as servants until their untimely deaths. Their offspring, Imad, lives with us still.

In 1929, I married the beautiful Sarah Guthrie. Though we wished for children, Sarah was unable to conceive. We bestowed much of our love on Imad, especially after the tragedy that robbed him of his true parents.

That incident took place in 1936 when a house guest named Clive Hargrove opened Amara's coffin. I had spoken to him over dinner about the strange legend surrounding the mummy. As was my policy, I never spoke of what I had witnessed myself. Maged and I had agreed to carry the secrets of our discovery to our respective graves.

In the dead of night, Hargrove entered the Collection Room, and carefully removed the nails holding the seals in place.

Sarah and I slept peacefully through the night. In the morning, we discovered Maged and his wife in their bedroom, mutilated and dead. Their baby, Imad, was missing from his nursery.

I hurried downstairs to the Collection Room, and found Hargrove dead at the foot of Amara's coffin.

The lid was resting upright against a wall, where he had apparently left it.

I found Amara inside the coffin. In the embrace of her withered arms was the unconscious form of the baby, Imad.

The tragedy affected us deeply. Determined to prevent a reoccurrence, I ordered a steel door be installed to make the Collection Room as secure as a bank vault.

That was not enough. Vaults could be entered, nails pulled, seals broken. Only with her infant at her side, however, would Amara's vengeful spirit be still. If I could return the stolen child to her, she would, hopefully, rest in peace forever.

I knew that the child had been taken a dozen years before the birth of the old priest, Ramo. Guessing his age to be near seventy, I calculated that the robbery had taken place during the 1840s.

With luck, the mummy might have found its way into a museum. Otherwise, it had likely disappeared into a private collection, or been destroyed.

My search led me to London, where I spent weeks in the British Museum, searching for references to infant mummies. There I became overly familiar with the work of one Dr Thomas Pettigrew.

'Mummy' Pettigrew, as he was called, astonished London theater audiences with public unwrappings of mummies. He was all the rage. His act went on for twenty years, during which he cut, hacked, and ripped his way through the winding clothes of hundreds of mummies. The morbid business delighted his audiences, for one never knew what treasure or oddity might lurk beneath the crusted bandages.

Among his subjects were several mummified babies.

The London *Times* of 16 March 1843 reported that Pettigrew's audience had been stunned the previous night by the 'strange movements' of an infant he was attempting to unwrap. While many suspected Pettigrew of trickery, he claimed that the child 'stirred as if alive'. Before his claim could be investigated, he 'committed the child to the flames'.

The child, I am reasonably certain, was the missing son of Amara and the god Set.

My search was over. I returned home, disappointed. In the years since then, I have taken exceptional care to avoid a repetition of the tragedy that took Imad's parents. To this date, all has been well.

Amara

Sarah and I grow old, however. One day, we shall be gone. I have willed my Egyptian collection to the Charles Ward Museum, which has agreed to house it in a special 'Callahan Room'.

I cannot, however, forget my experience with Amara. Though I intend to leave specific instructions that the seals of the coffin remain intact, I fear that, one day, the hideous crone will walk the night in search of her stolen child.

If Amara should stir from her coffin, Imad (or his descendants) are obligated by the terms of my will to present this memoir to the museum administration. It is my hope that such parties, familiar with the strange ways of the ancients, will believe what I have written, and that my words will help them to understand the nature of the hag.

Robert A. Callahan
Greenside Estates
Burlingdale, California

16 April 1968

Chapter Thirty-five

The Memoirs of Robert Callahan.
Memoirs? Or nightmares?
Imad closed the small black notebook that was testament to so much horror and anguish.
This was the first time he'd read the book even though he'd known of its existence. It told him much of the father he'd never had time to know and of Robert Callahan, the kindly man who had adopted him.
He set the book down on a table. Right now, the urge came upon him to shower in water that was near-boiling; to scrub his skin until he bled. Because not only did the memoirs reveal the manner of his parents' death, it told of how he'd been taken by the mummy to its coffin, and how Robert Callahan had discovered the infant Imad asleep in the dead arms of Amara.
He closed his eyes and moaned, the muscles in his face twitching. Flashbacks.
Memories long repressed . . . of the creature bending over his crib in the dead of night. The withered face, the empty sockets where its eyes should have been; the wash of red hair tumbling onto him like a gush of blood, falling across his face, smothering him.
He rocked on the bed, perspiring, nausea rising in the back of his throat. That smell. Pungent spices. And, worse, the grim odors of the tomb.
Amara had reached out and picked him out of his crib. She'd cradled the infant Imad against her dead skin, pressing the baby's face to her

withered breasts. He remembered now. He'd seen the blood of his parents still fresh on the monster's teeth. It even glued the hair together into thick gore-covered strings that had brushed against Imad's face.

The mummy had then taken him to the coffin before daylight had broken.

Right then, Imad wanted nothing more than to take a full bottle of gin and retire to bed where he might be able to drown the memories under a torrent of alcohol.

No. There is important work to be done, he told himself. He must obey Robert Callahan's instructions to the letter.

Chapter Thirty-six

In the dark, Ed Lake heard the order.

'*Present yourself.*'

As he lay there on the panel, pressed tight to the Perspex, he maneuvered his erect penis up through the hole into the receiving orifice. It felt warm and snug. Muscles contracted tight around his organ. That delicious friction again . . . up, down, up, down. There, in the darkness above him, his captor moved, pleasuring herself, filling herself with his manhood.

Don't know how long I can keep this up . . .

Pun intended, Eddie?

Ed was being forced to perform every few hours. And – hell – each performance could last hours. All that friction was taking its toll.

What happens when my strength goes? When I can't pull an erection anymore? They're gonna gash my neck. I'm gonna die in a rush of blood. Just like Marco.

Hell . . .

The body rocked above him in ecstasy. The Perspex flexed. *Gotta be strong.* If it broke . . .

Freedom.

But that stuff was tough. It was made to protect bank cashiers from bullets. Might flex a little. It'd never break. He'd never have it so easy. *Might as well accept it, Eddie boy, you're going to remain a sex slave for as long as you can keep it up. You're going to need to poke to survive. Fuck to live. Otherwise . . .*

Otherwise your nice, soft throat's for the chop.

But he couldn't perform like this forever. One day he'd have an attack of the floppy Joes. *Then it's the big sleep for you, Eddie.*

Don't call me Eddie.

The mind chatter gave way to exhausted rambling. Random thoughts flitted through his head as he pushed his loins upward into the receiving body above.

Didn't a Turkish princess once keep a baboon for this purpose? She was a nympho. Couldn't get enough, so she visited a wise woman who advised her to procure a big buck baboon. Baboons have their own harems to service. Baboons could fuck tirelessly from sunup to sundown.

Nice story.

But where do I buy a baboon at this time of night?

Ed, keep your mind on the job. Nearly slipped out then.

Jeepers creepers, am I losing the erection? I'm bending inside her.

Think sexy thoughts, think sexy thoughts . . .

Panic ripped through him. That didn't help. Didn't help one bit. If he couldn't perform. If he disappointed his captor he was sure he'd lose more than a toe this time.

He pictured Virginia. Pictured her naked and panting hotly over him. In his mind's eye she rubbed her breasts in his face. There were thin, white scars around the nipples. That didn't matter. He imagined they were having great sex. She was moaning. She was crying out his name. Crying louder . . .

Then he realized a cry had escaped his captor. This had never happened before. His captor's orgasms had been confined to a juddering, a breathlessness.

This was a full-blooded shout.

The voice came in a deep booming roar that filled the room.

'Oh, Jesus . . . Yes!'

So loud it sounded like the voice of God. Ed felt as if his skull would burst beneath the avalanche of sound.

Then it cut dead.

Silence.

The body slipped from his cock with a lubricious sucking sound. Then – gone.

Later the lights came on. When Ed at last managed to squirm from between the platform and cage roof he collapsed exhausted to the foam mattress. The hairbrushes, toothbrushes, electric razor and water bottles hanging from the strings tied to the cage roof swung crazily, making him feel even more light-headed. Unscrewing one of the bottles he drank deeply. Man, that was good.

Virginia stared at him through the bars of their respective cages, her eyes wide with astonishment.

'That sound she made . . .' She shook her head, incredulous. 'What do you make of that?'

Ed drank more from the water bottle. The cool liquid felt wonderful. He only wished he could soak his overheated genitals in an ice bath. The relentless friction had left his flesh fiery and sensitive. Exquisitely sensitive. To touch himself could be hell one moment, heaven the next. His nerve endings must be raw.

Taking the water bottle, he sat cross-legged on the mattress.

'You heard the voice?' Virginia's green-eyed stare fixed on his face.

'I heard.' He gave a tired shrug. 'Couldn't miss.'

'Well, what does that tell us?'

He took a mouthful of water. Rolled it. Swallowed. 'Tells us that she's wearing a mike.'

'Can't be wired, so it must be a radio mike.'

'And when she speaks to us the voice is electronically altered. Made deeper.'

'Then instantly relayed back through hidden speakers in the room.'

'I guess.' He let his shoulders sag. 'Sweet Jesus. I need to rest for a year and a day.'

'Lie down,' she told him.

As he did so he glanced across at her. She lay on her side. Not bothering now to cover herself; the blanket had slipped down, exposing one full breast. Copper hair tumbled deliciously over it. A fine sight. Very fine indeed.

Virginia, you saved my life today.

He was going to say the words. Nearly did. Nearly told her that when he'd started to soften during sex he'd thought about her.

Let's say she stiffened my resolve, he thought.

But they needed to filter the facts.

Virginia spoke. 'Let's recap, then.'

'From the beginning.'

'Okay, from the beginning. We know we're being held in cages in a building that's well out of town, in the boondocks.'

'Or is soundproofed.'

'Or both.' She looked round. 'The more I look at this place the more I can believe we're locked up in an old TV studio.'

'The back lot that MGM forgot.'

She gave a wan smile. 'Not a movie studio. Not big enough.'

'So a redundant TV studio?'

'A studio of some kind. Maybe even a recording studio.'

'So, fill in the picture, Virginia. What's our situation?'

This was an old routine now. Using clues and guesswork to figure where they were and what was happening to them.

Virginia continued. 'We're held in some secret location, in a soundproofed room. We're well fed. We're kept in relatively comfortable conditions.'

'A two-star beast house at least.'

She smiled at the little joke. A beautiful smile. A winning smile that warmed his fatigued body. 'A beast house with en-suite bathroom.' She nodded at the sawdust bowl.

'And we can pitch as good a theory as any – that we're kept here as sex slaves.'

'Sounds raunchy, doesn't it?'

'Yeah, but like any day-job it becomes a dull grind sometimes.'

'Say that again.'

'It becomes a dull—'

'Whoa – figure of speech, Ed.'

He grinned. 'I wish I was in that cage with you.'

She grinned back. 'I wish you were in this cage with me.'

'We could keep each other warm.'

'We'd be stimulating company for each other.' She gave a suddenly shy smile. 'What do you think?'

'I think so too.'

She wagged her finger in a mock-scolding way. 'Back to business, Mr Ed Lake. What's our current position?'

'Lying on concrete in a cage.'

'You know what I mean . . . our situation.'

'Our situation. We know that when the lights go out our captors visit us. They move around unseen in complete darkness.'

'How?'

'Because they are wearing some kind of hi-tech head gear. Nightscope goggles.'

'So they see us.'

'But we don't see them.'

'How many?'

He rubbed his jaw. 'How many captors? Let's figure not more than two. Maybe only one.'

'Hmmm . . .' She looked thoughtful. 'I guess two.'

'Oh?'

'It's a lot of work for just one. Supplying food, taking away waste.'

'But not an impossible workload.'

'No, but then there were Marco and the others.'

'I see.' He nodded.

'They were carried here unconscious. Also the corpses had to be manhandled out of the cages and disposed of.'

'That would take one mightily powerful individual.'

'Or two people.'

He nodded again. 'I agree on that point, Virginia. At least two captors, then. But . . .' He shrugged. 'How many do we have sex with?'

'I think I know.' Her shoulders made a little hopping motion. 'Strange what you think about under these blankets, huh?'

'We've got plenty of thinking time, hon.'

She smiled at the endearment. Then: 'I believe there are two captors. We only have sexual contact with one.'

'How can you tell?'

She touched the tip of her nose with her finger. 'Scent.'

'Huh?'

'Sometimes after the lights have gone out and you sense one of them close by you catch a little of how they smell.'

'Go on.'

'The one who moves the sawdust bowls and brings in the meals has a slightly sour odor.'

'You *do* have a good sense of smell.'

'The "warder", as we'll call her, gives off the sour odor. It's like the smell of milk on someone's breath.'

'And the one who . . .' He lifted a shoulder. 'Who pleasures herself at our expense?'

'Smells sweet. She bathes regularly. She uses good-quality beauty products – oils, powders, that kind of thing.'

'Anything else?'

'Yes, it might sound odd, but she smells young.'

'You can tell by her body odor?'

'Yes, I think so. Don't you think people in different age groups smell differently?'

'Well . . . I don't know. I guess you're right. But . . .' He shrugged.

'Trust me on that one, Ed: *I know*.' She smiled. 'I was a dental hygienist. It brings you into close contact with people of all ages, all walks of life.'

'Oh . . .' He took a breath. 'Okay, but we refer to our captors as "she". Now, I'm sure the one who fucks around with our bodies is female. How do you know the sex of our warder?'

'Brace yourself for this one, Ed, it doesn't sound pretty.'

'Shoot anyway.'

'I've been here long enough to know she has cycles.'

'Huh?'

'She has periods and, like I say, she doesn't exactly devote much time to the bathroom.'

'You mean you can smell her period? Jeez.'

'Like I said. Not pretty. But, yes, I can smell menstrual blood.'

'Wow, I'm impressed, Virginia.'

'Thanks.'

'And that paints a fuller picture. We know our captives are two women below menopausal age. One's our warder.'

'The other our Sex Queen.'

Ed drummed his fingers on his knee. 'But this can't go on, can it?'

'No. But what can we do? We're in the pen, remember?'

'There's got to be some way of hitting them. Some way of doing so much damage that we can escape.'

'How?'

'Wait till they get close, then grab them through the bars.'

'You can't see them. It's completely dark when they come in.'

'But when she fools around with us through the bars. She's close then. You can *feel* her closeness to you.'

Virginia shook her head. 'They always order you to put your hands through restraining loops. What about when you lie on the platform? There's no way of reaching her then?'

'No, there's bulletproof glass between her and me, even though it's only around an inch thick.'

'You couldn't smash it with your fist?'

'Not a hope.'

'And you can't reach round the outside of it?'

'Nope.'

'The hole?'

'What about the hole?'

'The hole you . . . *present* yourself through.'

'Oh.'

'Think about it. She sits on that with her pussy pressed to it. Imagine how vulnerable she is then.'

'You mean that instead of pushing my dick through I should push my hand up and somehow grab her from the inside?'

'Yes.'

'Wouldn't work.'

'Why?'

'The hole's big enough for my dick. Not for my hand.'

'Damn.' Her gaze became downcast.

'Virginia . . . Virginia, look at me. Believe it. We'll find a way out of here. And we're going to hurt these bitches so badly they'll curse the day they were born.'

Ed was jolted awake. Blinking, he opened his eyes. Darkness again. Inky darkness that revealed nothing. But he heard shouting. A male voice: indignant, a throaty anger, demanding to be let out.

'I'll rip your heads off . . . d'ya goddamn hear me? I'll tear you apart!'

Thumping sounds. Someone was hammering cage bars.

'You can't do this to me! D' ya know who I am? I run this neighborhood. When I tells people to do, they *do*! Ya hear me? I said, *ya hear me*?' There was more furious rattling.

'Take it easy.' Ed spoke softly. 'You'll hurt yourself.'

'Hey, who's that?' The voice had a New York accent with a splash of Italian.

'Ed Lake.'

'You let me outta here, Lake, or I'm gonna break every bone in your goddamn body.'

'I can't, I—'

'What ya mean, you can't? Let me out of this freakin' cage. Now!'

The voice had power. People would tremble when they heard that voice.

Ed hissed. 'Ssh.'

'Don't shush me, you asshole.'

'Listen, you've got—'

'No, *you* listen.' The voice raged in the darkness. 'You listen to Romero Cardinali. You open the cage now and you and your children and their children escape with their lives. Got that, asshole?'

'Mr Cardinali, I can't let you out, I'm—'

'You working for the Jamaican Yardie boys?'

'No. I'm—'

'Then it's got to be Ratzioni . . . I tell ya, Fat Ratz is gonna nourish coyotes after this. In fact, I'm going to feed his balls to the coyotes one at a time and he can watch, the double-crossing—'

'Mr Cardinali.' Ed's voice grew to a shout. 'I've nothing to do with Jamaicans or anyone else, I'm trying to tell you that . . .' The lights came on. Ed paused, his face burning as if he'd made a fool of himself, shouting like that. Then he spoke in a near-whisper. 'I'm trying to tell you that I'm in a cage like you.'

A plump, balding man stood in the cage once occupied by Marco. He wore black pants, white shirt, no shoes and could have passed for a wine waiter or even a funeral director. He looked around fifty and was sweating profusely. He also looked very, very angry.

'You sure you're locked in there, kid? You're not puttin' me on?'

Virginia spoke. 'He's not. We're both prisoners here.' Then she added, 'Like you.'

He shrugged his shoulders and adjusted his shirt collar as if composing himself. 'So what's the deal?'

'Deal?'

'Yeah, deal. You stoopid, kid? Deal! What's going down? Why're we here?'

'You should save your strength, Mr Cardinali.' Ed realized he sounded just like Marco the first time he spoke to him. 'Sit down. Save your strength. You're going to need it.'

'Hey, no little schmuck gives Romero Cardinali no orders.'

Ed sighed. 'Suit yourself.' He lay down and covered himself with the blanket.

'Hey, you schmuck. Don't you go to sleep on me. Hey, you . . .'

I tried, Ed told himself. *I tried to help him.*

The man raged on. 'Hey, what's going on here? Where is this place? I'm gonna have my people tear it down brick by brick. I'm gonna find who's responsible for this. They don't know the kind of guy they're jerking around here. Keeping me in a cage, for God's sake. They're dead. D' ya hear? Dee-Ee-Ay-Dee . . . dead! D' ya hear that, ya jerks!'

Ed groaned. He wanted to sleep. But sure as eggs were eggs sleep wouldn't come easy now with Mr Cardinali. *Our new roomie.*

Chapter Thirty-seven

Ed Lake sat in the dark with his back to the cage bars. He listened to the argument. He knew Virginia was listening too.

Shoot, listen to the guy.

Mr Romero Cardinali was saying no dice. 'What kind of freaking guy do you take me for, you jerk? I'm no whore. You—'

The bass voice boomed. *'Lie on the panel. Present yourself as instructed.'*

'You can go preeee-zent yourself, you weird little fuck. When I get my hands on you you're gonna wish—'

The voice thundered over his: *'Cardinali. Do as you are instructed.'*

'So, you know my name, you pervert. You went through my wallet when you knocked me cold. You'll wish *you* were out cold when I start work on you. I'm gonna cook your dick in a microwave. I'm gonna drill through your kneecaps.'

The guy's got balls, Ed reflected. *For now, anyway.*

'Cardinali, present yourself. Otherwise you will be punished.'

'Punished? Ha! Come and face me like a man. Stop skulking away in the shadows, you little freak.'

The electronically altered voice had fooled Cardinali like it had fooled Ed at first. But the more he heard the deep, velvet voice the more he could hear a woman's inflections.

Cardinali raged on.

Once Ed had hissed across at him. 'You've got to do as they say.'

'Sez who, cheeseball?'

'It's me, Ed Lake. Do as they say. They'll hurt you if—'

'Like I'd take orders from you, kid.'

'Listen, I'm trying to save your life. If you don't—'

'Shut it, kid. Romero Cardinali's gonna headline this particular gig, d' ya hear me?'

'Okay, okay.' Sighing, Ed closed his eyes.

Ed heard Virginia whisper to him. 'You tried, Ed. Whatever happens next, your conscience will be clear.'

The deep voice persisted. Maybe the thickset bull of a man interested their sex mistress? Did she have a thing about gangsters? Only he wasn't interested. He wasn't going to play their erotic games and no, he wasn't going to 'preeee-zent' himself through the hole in the Perspex roof of the cage. 'Ya think I'm gonna wave my whang in the air for your appreciation, then ya got another think coming . . . Now do yourself a favor and unlock the damn cage otherwise I'm going to slice you from ass to eyebrow!'

More insults came out to fill the dark void. The guy was in good form. Knew words that Ed didn't, and Ed thought he was a pretty streetwise guy.

The guy was laying it down how he was going to dismantle the owner of the deep voice piece by piece when he gave a sudden, surprised '*Hey!* What did ya prick me with?' His voice grew louder. 'Why don't ya put on the light and try pricking me when I can see ya? You pile of shit. I'm gonna be your own personal hairdresser, do you hear me? I'm gonna shampoo your hair in gasoline. Then I'm going to drop a match. You're gonna get the blow-dry of your life, believe me, you little . . . liffle sh-shit. Hey, wass iss? Wass zisss . . . what ya shot into me? Injected sumfin?'

Ed sat up straight, heart beating. The man's speech was slurred. The volume became lower. The bars clanged as if someone had fallen against them.

'Bash . . . bass . . . bastards. Cowards . . . bast—' Then a deep thump.

Down and out. Someone had KO'd the guy with a hypodermic.

For a little while all Ed heard was the sound of snores.

Then there were other sounds . . . Scraping. Clicks. The sound of panting.

Jesus. Ed strained his ears in the dark. He opened his eyes wide.

Wide as they could go, only he could still see nothing in that inky soup. The breathing got louder. Bumps. Scrapes. A grunt. Someone exerting themselves. *Holy shit.* Was someone having sex with the gangster as he lay there unconscious? Maybe this time with his bare butt 'preeee-zented'?

Ed didn't want to allow his mind to roam too far in that direction. His front body parts were sore enough. He didn't want to receive any attention from the rear as well.

The sounds went on. *My God, what're they doing to Cardinali?*

Ed didn't like the sounds. He didn't like them at all.

The lights took a while to come back on. For a long time Ed had sat in the darkness listening to the snoring grunts coming from the man. Something had happened. Something shitty. Only Ed couldn't begin to guess what.

After a while: 'At least he's not dead.' That was Virginia's voice.

'But they've done something to him.'

'Given him a shot of some drug. He's out cold.'

'Done something else, too. Heard them working on him.'

'Dear God.'

He heard her breathe deeply. 'Best brace yourself when the lights come on. It's bound to be something bad.'

'I was just thinking the same. Poor guy.'

'He was his own worst enemy, Ed. He should have done what they told him.'

'Maybe he had a stronger sense of self-respect.'

'What's that supposed to mean?' She sounded hurt.

'Nothing,' he replied.

'We're survivors, Ed. We've got to remember that.'

'Sure. I'll remember.'

'Woss . . . 's wrong?'

'Heads up,' Virginia hissed. 'Sleeping beauty's waking.'

'Hey, woss 'appenin'? What gives?'

Ed listened to the man's groggy exclamations. He could talk, anyway. Maybe their jailers hadn't punished him harshly after all. Just a shot of some drug to show him who was boss.

A moment later, the lights flickered on. Ed blinked against the brilliance. He looked in the direction of Cardinali. He saw him through the bars.

Holy shit. What have they done to him?
The bastards . . . the sadists . . . trussed him like a dead deer.
Almost.
Not quite.

There were differences. Ed looked at the man in the next cage. He was standing on a three-legged stool; one of those old-fashioned milking stools. Around his neck was a noose. The other end was tied to the roof beam of the cage. It had become a gallows.

'Hey, what they done to me?' squealed the guy. 'What's the game?'
No game.
They were serious . . . dead serious.
'Mr Cardinali,' Virginia called in alarm as the stool wobbled. 'Stand still. Perfectly still.'

'What they done?' The guy still had a dumbstruck expression on his fleshy face. He couldn't work out what had happened.

But Ed saw.
Saw clear as day.

Their captors had drugged the man. Then, as he'd lain unconscious, they'd somehow winched him upright, stood him on a stool with a noose round his neck and his hands either tied or cuffed behind his back. Ed couldn't tell which because the man was standing facing him on the rickety stool.

But why hadn't he strangled as he'd hung there unconscious? Then Ed saw. They'd supported his body weight with a harness that had been buckled to the roof crossbar. The guy couldn't fall and choke anyway. Even if you kicked the stool from under him.

So what's the deal?

The guy couldn't be comfortable.
But it wasn't as if he was in mortal danger, was he?
Then the light went out again. Moments later, more cursing. A whispering voice. Then a moan in the darkness. *Cardinali?* 'Please . . . listen, I apologize. From now on I'll be good. *Please* . . .' The note of defiance was well and truly history now. Instead: pleading.

'Please. I'll do anything. But don't do that. Please, don't do that! *Don't!*'

Ed heard rustling. Chinks, something like chain links. A frightened gasp.

Then murmuring. Fast, too fast to hear properly.

Virginia said, 'Listen to the guy. He's praying.'

'Oh, hail-Mary-Mother-of-God . . .' Cardinali's voice was low and rapid. 'Please-have-mercy-on-me. Mary-Mother-of-God, I'm-a-sinner. I-ask-for-your-forgiveness-in-this-my-hour-of-darkness . . .'

The light flickered. Brilliance filled the room once more.

Ed looked across at Cardinali.

His heart lurched.

He heard a cry of shock in his own throat.

Bad.

This was bad.

The poor guy didn't deserve this.

'Oh, my God,' Virginia breathed behind Ed.

Ed looked up at the guy through the bars of his cage. They were sadists. They *really* should have their fucking hearts torn out.

Romero Cardinali still stood on the rickety three-legged milking stool. Still had his hands cuffed or tied behind his back. Still had the noose round his neck. But now something was missing.

The harness.

Now he'd recovered consciousness they'd snuck down here in the dark and unbuckled it. They'd done it from the top where it had looped over the crossbar, not risking entering the cage with the conscious gangster. His feet were free – he could have delivered a killer of a kick.

The web of the harness dangled down by the side of his waist now like a strappy hula skirt. But it was Cardinali himself who drew Ed's gaze.

He stood there trembling. You could see his knees shaking. In turn, that made the stool wobble.

'Take it easy. Take it real easy.' Ed spoke in a soothing voice. 'You're okay . . . just don't make any sudden movement.'

'Please help me.' Cardinali whispered as if fearing that talking would unbalance him. 'Please. I don't know how much longer I can stand still.' The stool wobbled.

Ed looked up at the man's face. It was a mask of terror. Terror turned his eyes into shining spheres in his head. Perspiration rolled from the crown of his bald head over his face and on down his neck to slick the rope around his neck. The hemp itself was stained dark with sweat.

Ed glanced back at Virginia. She stared in horror at the man.

'What can we do?' he whispered to her.

'What *can* we do?' She echoed the words in a helpless tone. 'We're here; he's there.'

'Hey . . . hey. I know ya talking about me . . . what're ya saying?'

Ed turned. 'You've got to stay as calm as possible. Keep still.'

'Ha.' The sound came as a squeal. 'Keep still? Easy for you to say, kid. But look at me, kid. Look at me!'

The moment his voice got louder his legs wobbled more, making the stool rock.

'Keep as still as possible,' Virginia told him. 'We're working on it.'

Ed shot her a questioning look.

She gave a little shrug. *What can we do?* she seemed to be saying.

Ed turned to the guy. 'Just breathe nice and slow. Keep as still as possible.'

'I think I'm getting the cramp.'

'You're not. Try to untense your muscles.'

'Aw, Jesus, ya gotta be kidding me.' The man sounded close to weeping. His face turned a tomato red.

Ed saw him try to move his feet just a little further apart. Just a little. To distribute his weight that bit more evenly. In fascinated horror Ed's gaze traveled up the sweat-soaked body to the noose around the thick neck. The guy was doing his best to balance there. But he was tiring. That stool was rickety. He'd swear one of the wooden legs was loose. *Oh, shit.* Watching the guy was unbearable.

What if he sneezed?

Coughed?

Even developed an unbearable itch in the small of his back?

Maybe the noose line was slack enough for him to step down onto the floor. No, not a hope. There was hardly any slack at all. If the guy even tilted too much left or right the rope pulled taut. That in turn tightened the noose around the guy's neck. Already it had started to dig a little into the soft flesh of his throat.

How long could he balance like that on a small stool? Especially with his hands bound behind his back?

Maybe that was it?

'Sir,' Ed said. 'Can you loosen your hands?'

'They're tied . . . with wire.'

The stool wobbled.

The man gave a sharp cry.

Recovered his balance.

Nearly, that time.

Nearly . . .

Virginia spoke up. 'It's the only way, sir. Can you work your hands free from the wire? Once you do that you can just reach up and pull the noose off over your head.'

'Okay, okay . . . I'm trying.' His lips pressed together in concentration, Cardinali worked his shoulders as he tried to slip his bound wrists free of the wire.

'How's it going?' she asked.

The guy sweated hard. 'Purgatory. Freaking purgatory.'

'Keep trying.'

'I *am* trying.'

'Breathe slowly. Deeply. Don't panic.'

'Hey, who's panicking, lady?' Cardinali sounded more like his usual, cocksure self. 'I'm doing it. The loops are slipping down my hands.'

Ed looked at the man's dripping face. Triumph sparked in the eyes. Cardinali raised his face, concentrating hard on those loops of wire that held his hands.

'They're coming loose. Once I get them over my knuckles I'll be off this damn perch, I can tell you. Assholes.'

'Careful.'

'Nearly there. Nearly—'

Jerked his elbows. Trying to pull free.

Ed shouted, 'Watch out!'

'Nearly there. Nearly – Ahh!'

Cardinali fell.

The stool shot from under his feet to slam against the bars of the cage. The force of the impact shattered it.

Cardinali didn't fall far. The rope snapped tight. Tongue sticking out. Eyes poking hard from the sockets as he swung backwards and forwards. His legs ran in thin air like a cartoon character who'd run off a cliff.

Then the guy's body started jerking. It didn't last long. After twenty seconds he hung limp at the end of the line. His neck had stretched thin, maybe as much as twice as long as it had been before.

Looks like we're back to two again, Ed told himself as the lights went out.

What now?

When the lights came on what must have been a couple of hours later Cardinali was gone. So was the rope that had hanged him. So was the wreckage of the stool that his death throes had kicked against the cage.

Ed shook his head. 'He didn't last long.'

Virginia shrugged. 'Like I say, you must obey them.'

'But how long can we last?'

'We're doing fine so far, aren't we?'

'Sure.' Ed looked down at the scabbed foot. 'My little toe's made it to freedom. Now I only have to get the other ninety-nine percent of me out.'

'Take it easy, Ed, save your—'

'Yeah, yeah, I know. Save my strength.' He gave a sour laugh.

'Then save it.'

He walked across the cage to look through the bars at the empty cell next door.

Ouch.

The area of flesh from which his little toe had once sprouted burned furiously. He'd stubbed it on something.

He glanced down.

Hey.

Now that might be interesting.

Quickly he bent down, scooped up the object and returned to his mattress. He sat cradling it on his knee.

'What've you got there, Ed?'

'Ssh,' he hushed.

She whispered back. 'What is it?'

'One of the legs from the stool.' He gave her a quick glimpse. *Can't be too careful.* Lights might go out, then his prize would quickly vanish. 'They must have missed it when they cleaned up.'

'What are you thinking, Ed?'

'See? It's more than a foot long. Look how it's broken at that end. It's as sharp as a spear.'

'Oh, my God.'

'"Oh, my God" indeed. It's miracle time.'

'Don't let *them* see it.'

'Don't you worry. I'm keeping this baby safely wrapped up in my blanket.'

'But what are you going to do with it?'

'Cast your mind back to when we were talking earlier.'

'Go on.'

'Remember we discussed the hole in the cage ceiling?'

'Yes.'

'And how you wondered if I could somehow reach through it?'

'Sweet Jesus. You think you can?'

'Going to try.' He took a peek at the wooden stake cradled in his arms. 'This needs some work first. By the way—' he shot her a wild grin '—have you ever seen anyone harpoon a fish?'

Chapter Thirty-eight

The telephone rang. Susan lowered the paperback she'd been reading and glanced at the clock. Almost midnight. She got up from the couch. 'Expecting a call?' she asked Tag. He shook his head and returned his gaze to the *National Review*. Susan picked up the phone.

'Hello?'

'Am I speaking to Miss Connors from the museum?'

The man pronounced each word with precision; someone educated the expensive way.

'Yes, this is Susan Connors.'

'I must speak to you at once about Amara.'

'Who is this, please?'

'My name is of no importance.'

'I would like to know whom I'm speaking to. This isn't—'

'I saw you on the television news.'

'But you can't—'

'Listen to me, please. This is vital.'

'Do you know where Amara is?' Susan asked.

'I must see you. Then I will explain.'

'Maybe you should call the police?'

'The police? They would scorn me or accuse me. They would not believe. Perhaps *you* will believe. I saw in your face the look of one who understands.'

'What am I supposed to understand?'

'About Amara. May I see you?'

'Well . . .'
'Please, Miss Connors. This is of great importance.'
She sighed. 'Okay, when?'
'At once. You are at 2102 Coral Reef Road?'
'Yes. It's the Marina Towers. Apartment 325. But how did you—'
'I will be there soon,' he said quickly and hung up.
'Who was that?' Tag asked.
'Wouldn't say.'
'Mysterious?'
'Whoever he is, he's coming by.'
'Now?'
'He wants to tell me something about Amara.'
'At midnight?'
'He sounded serious.'
'Could be he's only serious about getting alone with you.'
'I doubt it.'
'That sort of thing happens when you get on TV.'
'We'll see.'

Imad, outside the Marina Towers, heard the buzz of the lock. He rushed to the door and thrust it open before the buzzing could stop. The lobby was plush, with thick carpets, soft lighting, paneled walls. It smelled of pine-scented air freshener.

A little artificial, Imad thought. *Not bad, however, if one must live in the confines of an apartment.*

He slipped Callahan's memoir under his arm and pressed the elevator button. He was surprised that the elevator didn't open immediately. Considering the hour, one would hardly expect to find it in use. After a short wait, a bell rang quietly and the doors slid open.

He was prepared for the possibility of finding a person inside. He was not, however, prepared for a person like this. She simply didn't belong in a clean and ostentatious building such as the Marina Towers: she belonged in a dark, shabby tenement that reeked of stale cigars and urine.

'Going up?' she asked.
Reluctantly, Imad stepped into the elevator. The doors rolled

silently shut. Politely, he smiled at the filthy woman. She smiled back.

The smell of her filled the cubicle. A horrid stench like sour milk, sweat and something eminently suggestive of . . . well . . . Imad swallowed to keep himself from gagging. Until the elevator stopped, he breathed only through his mouth. Even then something of her odor secreted itself on his tongue.

The doors rolled back.

He stepped out.

The woman stayed.

Thank heaven.

Relieved, Imad breathed deeply.

A small sign on the wall indicated that apartments 301–335 could be found by following the corridor to the right. As he turned that way, he glanced back at the elevator. Its doors were still open.

The woman must have one of her stumpy thumbs on the 'door open' button.

Was she waiting for him?

Did she have an accomplice hiding nearby?

Feeling uneasy, he quickened his stride. The hallway was narrow and dimly lit. It turned. He followed it, watching the door numbers. He was passing 319 when he heard a sniffing sound behind him. He looked back.

The woman stepped around the corner. She waved at him, wiggling the thick fingers of one hand. The other hand, he noticed, was behind her back.

He hurried forward. Past 321, 323. At 325, he quickly knocked.

The woman was getting closer. She had a peculiar way of walking, head forward and tipped slightly to one side, legs wide apart.

He knocked again. Still the door didn't open. He plucked a scrap of paper from his shirt pocket. He held it at arm's length to catch the poor light. Read it again. Yes, 325 was correct.

He smiled nervously at the woman. She was close enough now to smell.

Her eyes fixed on him. They were dull, filmy, yet he saw some powerful emotion there.

But what?
He knocked again.
Open the door.
Please.
The woman licked her lips. A squishing sound that turned his stomach.

'Who ya want?' she asked.

'The occupant of this apartment,' he replied.

'Me, too.' The woman balled her fist. Then she pounded on the door.

Chapter Thirty-nine

Grace Bucklan looked out through the windshield. The bright lights of Hollywood. They burned in front of her but they might as well have been on the dark side of the moon. As the man said: *So close, yet so far.*

Okay, so tomorrow we start knocking on doors, she told herself. Agents, production offices. Hey, at a pinch maybe even some movie-extra work. That should bring in cash until they could . . .

'I can't sleep,' Pix complained from the backseat.

'Try,' Grace said.

'It's gone midnight,' Cody said, looking at the clock on the dash. 'We should all try and get some rest.'

'Any more salami left, Grace?'

'No, just crackers.'

'There was one piece left. You said that was mine.' Pix's voice got all whiny. 'You promised, you greedy hog.'

'You ate it twenty minutes ago.' Cody made an effort to sound calm. But the kid sister was really starting to eat him up. 'Do you want a drink of water?'

'No, I want some proper food. I'm hungry.'

Grace snapped. 'We've got crackers and that's it.'

'We're gonna starve.'

'We're not going to starve. I'll find some work tomorrow.'

Pix snorted. 'Yeah, Grace. You're gonna be a movie star by the end of the week.'

'I will find work.'

'All you're gonna find is some guy who'll pay you fifty bucks a throw to video you with your jugs out.'

'*Pix.*' Cody's patience was all gone. 'Just cool it, this isn't easy for—'

'I want to go home!' Pix slammed the back of the seat with her palm. 'We can't live like this . . . sleeping in a parking lot? Jeez!'

'We can't go home.'

'Can.'

'You *know* we can't go home.'

'Yeah, because you say Mom's boyfriend took a shine to you.'

'He tried to rape me.'

'Drama queen.'

'Pix—'

'He thought you were giving him the come-on.'

'It wasn't like that. He—'

'If you hadn't flirted with him—'

'He'd have raped you, too. Don't you understand, Pix? We were both in danger.'

'Danger, huh?'

'Yes, in danger. The moment he got you alone he'd have—'

'Danger. We're in more danger here. Sleeping in a beat-up truck in a deserted parking lot. We're gonna get mugged; we're gonna get raped; we're—'

'Pix!' Cody slammed both hands against the steering wheel. 'We're not happy about sleeping rough. But this is the best we can do until we can earn some money. Then we'll book into a hotel.'

'Wuppy-do.'

Grace rounded on her sister. 'That's your problem. You're never satisfied. You just want more and more. Nothing's good enough for you. Why don't you take your things and just—'

'Hey, ssh . . . *Cops.*'

Cody pointed.

A black and white cruiser pulled into the parking lot. Without any fuss or hurry it glided across the blacktop toward them.

'Oh, shit.' Grace groaned. 'They've seen us.'

Pix said, 'So we took a crappy old truck without permission. It's hardly crime of the century. They're not gonna throw us in—'

'*Pix.*' Cody pointed at the sleeping bags. 'Hide under there; don't let them see you.'

'I'll do no such thing.'

Grace pleaded, 'Do it, Pix. Otherwise they'll send us back home. You know what Joe will do to us.'

'Drama queen,' Pix grumbled. Nevertheless, she lay down on the backseat and pulled the sleeping bags over her.

The cruiser slowed down. A brilliant light filled the pickup as the cop shone his flashlight at them. Cody glanced back to see Pix's foot showing from beneath the sleeping bag. Reaching back he thwacked it.

'Hey!' Pix squeaked.

But she withdrew her foot from the edge of the seat. Cody reached back and adjusted the sleeping bag so no part of the sixteen-year-old girl could be seen.

The police car pulled up alongside so they were side window to side window. The cop twirled a finger, signaling Cody to wind down his window.

Immediately a blast of light struck Cody in the eyes. He tried to shield them with his hand but he could see nothing. But he knew what was happening well enough. The cop would be giving Grace and him a close look-over, probably taking a good gander inside the pickup too.

If Pix should move . . .

Maybe the cop would think Cody had kidnapped her?

He'd certainly realize something was amiss when he ran a check on their license plate and found that the vehicle was stolen.

The cop switched off his flashlight. Cody blinked. Looked into the face of a gum-chewing cop of around fifty.

'Okay,' he said. 'Which one of you two is going to confess?'

Cody fixed a polite smile to his face but his insides felt as if they'd just melted and run into his boots.

'Confess, officer?'

'Yeah, confess to criminal insanity . . . or is it pathological stupidity?'

Grace spoke as pleasantly as she could. 'I'm sorry. I don't understand. We—'

'Yeah, yeah,' the cop growled. 'Don't take me for the stupid one. I've seen your plates. You're from North Carolina. How long does it take me to figure out what two kids from North Carolina are doing in Hollywood?'

'We were just—'

'Yeah, taking a nice vacation.'

'We thought—'

'And now you've booked yourself into the luxurious Rodeo Drive Parking Lot.'

'We were just taking a break, we—'

'Kid.' He fixed Cody with a steel-eyed look. 'Do I seem that stupid?'

'But—'

'No, listen to me, kid. I've seen this happen a hundred – a *thousand* times before. A couple of kids from the boondocks decide to make it in the movies, become big stars with a million in the bank and a house on the beach, so they ship out from Wyoming, or Illinois or—' he nodded in the direction of the license plate '—or North Carolina. They come to Hollywood. They spend all their cash. They live in their car or sleep on a park bench. Before you know it they're into prostitution; into drugs. Guys like me are pulling them off the streets and throwing them in jail. Not long after that the paramedics are pulling them out of some ditch where they've been dumped after being shot or beaten to death. Now, you tell me, am I just stupid and you really have driven thousands of miles to make out in a parking lot, or am I somewhere close to the truth?'

Grace didn't take this lying down. 'But I'm not like the rest. I've got acting experience. I worked on TV.'

He shook his head. 'Sorry to bust your dream, miss. But most of the kids that come here *are* like all the rest. They've all got good reviews when they starred in the school play or they've earned a few bucks appearing in some TV commercial for Mighty Joe's Cattle Feed or whatever. They all come here so full of optimism you think they'd crack open from head to toe.' He wagged a finger. 'But give them twelve months and they wind up blowing some guy with the pox for twenty bucks . . . and guys like you—' he nodded at Cody '—have to learn to take it up the butt or go hungry. Now, am I painting a clear enough picture for you?'

Grace was about to protest, but Cody clasped her hand. Nodded. 'We get the picture, sir.'

'Good. Now, you look nice kids. So do yourself a favor: *go home*. If you haven't enough money for gas, call your folks, you can reverse the charges: get them to wire the gas money out to you. Whatever heat you're gonna take from your parents for running away isn't going to be one percent of the heat you're going to take out here.' He paused. 'And just if I haven't concentrated your minds on the issue, check out the press. Some fine young people just like yourselves have been going missing from hereabouts over the last couple of years.'

'Murdered?'

The cop shook his head again. 'Who knows? Never been found.' He gave them a relaxed wave. 'Now, remember what I said. You point that truck back east. Don't stop until you've reached your front door. Now you take care of yourselves. Good night.'

With that he drove slowly away.

A moment later Pix sat up primly in the backseat. 'See? What did I tell you?' She folded her arms. 'Now can we go home?'

Chapter Forty

Claire Thompson, propped in her bed, watched *Casablanca* on television for the umpteenth time. She knew most of the movie by heart and often mumbled the words in unison with Rick and Ilsa and Victor Lazlo. It was the saddest movie she knew.

She'd first seen it in the old Palace Theater in Charleston, Illinois. The year was 1944. She was seventeen and in love with Junior Clyde. He took her to the movie, to King's Drug Store afterwards for a cherry phosphate, then to the Harrison house. The Harrisons were on vacation. They sat on the porch swing of the deserted house. Kissed. Petted. She let Junior go further than usual that night. He wanted to go all the way, but she refused. She never did let him. Not that night or the next night. And then he was inducted. He became one of Uncle Sam's infantry . . . the poor bloody infantry, they called it. But Junior was proud to be fighting. On the troop ship he enjoyed the camaraderie and used to lead the singing in the mess with his buddies. Even on the ship they trained hard. Physical exercise. Weapon skills: rifle practice, marksmanship, bringing down the seagulls that trailed the ship; learning how to strip a Thompson submachine gun blindfold then reassemble it so it was ready to fire when the sergeant gave the command. And the endless boot-polishing, of course.

In one of his letters to Claire, Junior said he'd been to North Africa. To Casablanca. There really *is* a Rick's Café Américain, he'd written. But where were the Germans? They were pulling back faster than the

Americans could advance. At this rate he'd be marching into Berlin still with desert sand in his boots.

But then the Germans did make a stand in a narrow mountain pass in the middle of nowhere. Their 88-millimeter guns lit up the night sky. Stukas screamed down, dropping bombs, strafing with machine guns. Two weeks later, Junior Clyde was killed in action.

On the screen, Rick said, 'We'll always have Paris.'

Claire gasped, a loud sob that made Herb groan and roll over.

She wiped her eyes. Felt her heart give as if this time it would break. Stay broken forever. She thought about the photograph of Junior that she still kept hidden in a drawer.

Then a long, wailing cry came through the open window. The eerie sound made goose bumps rise on her flesh. She pulled the sheet up to her throat. The cry continued. A cat. It had to be a cat.

It sounded so much like a baby, though. Like a baby crying in pain and terror.

Must be in the backyard. Must be close. Just outside her window. Close as that.

Tossing back the sheet, she climbed from the bed. She walked to the window and looked out. Her eyes scanned the moonlit concrete, the lounge chairs, the shimmering surface of the pool. At first, she didn't see the dark figure standing motionless near the diving board. Then it slowly turned toward her. She gasped at the sight of the baby in its arms.

She stared. Shivers in her spine. The dark figure seemed to notice her and stare back. Claire suddenly felt frightened and vulnerable. She wanted to step away from the window, but she was afraid to move – as if the least motion might trigger a horrible attack.

The thing didn't move. Claire felt its cold hatred. In the poor light, it looked like a strange, starving woman. But all that red hair. Pouring in glossy tresses down her back. Down over her shoulders. Such beautiful hair. Yet the legs? Horribly withered. Like dark sticks.

The crying baby couldn't possibly belong to such a creature. It must have been stolen from its mother.

Claire's breath became a quiet, trembling whine.

The baby kept crying.

Kept pulling at her heartstrings.

The thing continued to stand there, staring at her. Hating her.

Claire trembled, clutched the sill for support. Her knees were so weak she sagged.

'For Christ's sake, what's all that racket?'

Herb's voice startled her. She flinched and turned to him. Quickly, she sidestepped away from the window. Then she leaned weakly against the wall, shaking.

'Claire? What's wrong?' He rolled out of bed and rushed to her.

'The window,' she gasped.

He looked out. 'Jesus H. Christ!'

'It's got a little baby!'

'I can see that. Quick, call the cops.'

He hurried to the nightstand.

'No, Herb!'

He took out his pistol. Checked it. Six rounds. Man-stoppers.

'Please! Don't go out there!'

'I'll take care of it – you call the cops.'

'No!'

He ran to the bedroom door.

'Herb, please!'

He didn't answer. She heard his bare feet thumping as he ran down the hall.

She grabbed the bedside phone and dialed 911. Then listened to the ringing. Once, twice. Far off in the house a door bumped open. Footsteps sounded. On the sixth ring, her call was answered.

'Operator. How may I help you?'

'I need the police. It's an emergency.'

'Where are you calling from?'

'Westing Vale.'

'Just a moment, please.'

'Hurry!'

She listened to more ringing.

This time no one was going to answer.

The phone would keep ringing. *Herb's all alone out there.*

257

The police are never going to come in time to—

'LAPD. Officer Kerry, how might I help you?'

'We need help! Quick!' Craning her neck, Claire tried to see Herb through the window. She could see only concrete and a corner of the pool. The wrong corner.

'What's your address?'

'Eight-two-five Ash Road.'

'Name?'

'Thompson. Claire Thompson.'

Herb shouted, 'Stop!'

Dropping the phone, Claire rushed to the window. Her heart beat so wildly against her ribs that it hurt.

'Put it down!' Herb commanded. He was on the far side of the pool, close to its edge, a dozen feet from the thing. 'Put down the baby,' he repeated. His voice had a shrill, hysterical sound that Claire had never heard in it before. His arm was straight out, the gun aimed high. 'Put the baby—'

The creature raised the infant overhead.

Herb fired. The flash lit up the pool area, while the report of the gun snapped as sharply as a firecracker.

The baby shrieked as it was thrown. Claire watched it fly at her husband, its legs kicking as it tumbled through the air. He dropped the gun. Tried to catch the tumbling child, but the force of the impact knocked him backwards. The baby splashed into the pool.

The creature rushed Herb, its long hair flying out.

Claire ran. She ran to the bedroom door, down the hall, into the living room. The poker. She needed the poker. Rushing to the fireplace, she bumped a corner of the coffee table and cried out in pain. But she didn't stop. She clutched at the stand of fireplace tools, knocking it over with a metallic clattering . . . and grabbed the poker. It was heavy – wrought iron – with a hook near the end. She ran through the open glass door to the yard.

Across the pool, the creature was on top of Herb. His arms were up, hands shoving its chest and shoulders. His harsh breathing had a panicked sound, the way it did sometimes during his worst nightmares.

The thing bore down on Herb. Its stick arms reaching out for him, while it tilted its head from side to side. In the meager light the hair gleamed dull copper.

As Claire ran along the pool's edge, she glanced at the water. The baby was floating facedown.

In a corner of her mind, she knew that she might be able to save it. The decision was simple: the baby wasn't hers. Herb was.

The thing's claw fingers tore Herb's face. His arms gave way. Its head darted down.

'No!' Claire cried.

Raising the poker as she ran, she thought she saw the thing kiss Herb. Its head jerked savagely, though. It came up, flesh hanging from its mouth. Droplets of blood spotted the poolside tiles.

Screaming, Claire swung the poker down. It whacked across the creature's back with a resonant thump, as if she'd drummed a hollow log. The thing paid no attention. It thrust its head against Herb's throat. Claire turned the poker hook downward and struck again. She watched the curved spike pierce the back. She noticed other holes already in the dark flesh. Awful, gaping holes. In the moonlight, they looked deep and empty. As if there was nothing inside. Nothing.

She started to bring the poker down again, this time on the head. But suddenly the creature twisted. A hand grabbed the poker. Off balance, Claire staggered forward, almost falling onto the thing. Its other hand clutched her nightgown. It pulled her. Tossed back its head, flicking the red hair from its face. In horror, she gazed into eye sockets as empty as the holes in its back.

Letting go of the poker, she strained to free herself from the claws. The claws were pulling her down to a gaping mouth, its teeth stained red with Herb's blood.

She realized she was only caught by her nightgown. Quickly, she tore the bodice free of the shoulder straps. The gown skimmed down her body. She threw herself sideways, splashed into the pool, kicked away from the wall.

Coming to the surface near the pool's center, her bare shoulder brushed against the baby. She stood in the waist-high water and lifted the child. It was silent. Motionless. Its mouth hung open. Water trickled out. Claire pressed her lips to its mouth and blew in gently, keeping her eyes on the creature.

The thing seemed to be watching. Herb, beneath it, lay motionless. Legs sprawled out wide. In the moonlight the thing had become a silhouette again. Hunched. Predatory.

Slowly, Claire began stepping backwards. She continued to blow into the baby's mouth and ease the air out by lightly pressing its chest. The body felt warm against her bare breasts. She could feel its small chest inflate as she blew, but that was the baby's only movement.

Finally, her back touched the wall. The entire width of the pool now separated her from the creature. It was on its hands and knees, facing her, its mouth hanging open.

Could she beat it in a race to the house? Unless it was incredibly fast her chances looked good. Her main obstacle would be climbing from the pool. Once she was out, she could reach the open back door in seconds.

Keeping her eyes on the creature, Claire turned just enough to set the baby on the pool's edge. In one fluid movement, the thing leaped to its feet and began to run. Its feet made a hard clicking sound against the tiles, as if it were dry bones striking the floor, not flesh and blood. The hair flew up around its head as it moved, a copper-colored halo in the moonlight.

Claire spun around. She flung herself forward, sprawling with a great spray of water onto the concrete. Getting to her knees, she picked up the baby. She looked back.

The thing was already past the diving board, arms out as if reaching for her; its hair flying behind it in the slipstream.

She scrambled to her feet. She ran flat out, the baby clutched to her breast, eyes on the open, sliding door. She felt clumsy and slow. The strength drained from her legs. She didn't think she could take more than a dozen steps before she collapsed exhausted.

If only she'd stayed in the pool!

Her feet slapped the pavement. Behind her, she heard the strange, dry sounds of her pursuer's feet. *Click! Click! Click!* The sound of bones striking the hard surface of the ground. *So close!* And closing all the time.

She even heard the crackle of static in the thing's hair. The rustle of dry skin.

From inside the house came the ring of the doorbell, followed by harsh, rapid knocks.

'Police!' a voice snapped.

She lunged through the doorway and spun round. The creature wasn't far behind.

But far enough.

Claire's left hand grabbed the door handle and jerked. The door rolled shut: a heavy glass partition that would give her time to reach the front door and let in the police.

The outstretched arms of the creature dropped, but it kept coming. Full speed. Those pitlike eyes glaring at Claire. Hating. She watched, amazed.

Its head smashed into the door. The glass exploded. It burst through, that mass of red hair erupting inward into the house like burning napalm. Its bone-thin arms reached for her.

With a yelp of surprise, Claire lurched away.

It caught her by the hair.

'Help!' she cried.

It tugged her off balance. She stumbled backwards. Felt the slice of glass shards underfoot. The piercing of fragments through soft flesh.

A sharp crash. The front door shot open. Just before she went down, she saw a pair of policemen rush in, guns drawn.

They'll save me, she thought as she fell. *They'll save me*. And then something like ice chopped into her back.

Chapter Forty-one

Jason Brown crouched in a combat stance and aimed into the moonlit room. He saw a naked white woman falling backwards – no, *jerked* backwards – by a weird-looking woman behind her. The falling woman had a baby in her arms. As she hit the floor, her body spasmed stiffly as if jolted by an electric shock.

The weird one bent over her, its long hair cascading forward to hang down over the naked woman. The dark figure pulled the baby from her arms.

'Freeze!' Brown yelled.

The weirdo spun away.

Kraus, Brown's partner, fired a warning shot into the ceiling. The weird gal leaped through the broken door and ran. She looked to be naked, too. But horribly bony. Horribly thin. Some disease, maybe.

'Get her!' Brown snapped.

As Kraus ran out, Brown holstered his revolver and crouched beside the fallen woman. She was lying across the broken door, back arched. Her mouth and eyes were wide, her body quaking with convulsions. Brown tried to lift her. No dice. She seemed to be stuck. Bracing himself, he clutched the sides of her rib cage and lifted her straight upward. There was momentary resistance before she came unstuck. He carried her away from the door, set her down on the carpet, and looked back. A broad glass blade remained where she had been. Still upright at the bottom of the door's aluminum frame.

He searched her neck for a pulse.

Found none.

No sign of respiration, either.

With a single shake of his head, he sprang away from her and rushed through the break in the door, barely clearing the dark shard of glass that had ended the woman's life.

Outside, he saw a body across the pool.

'Oh, motherfucker,' he groaned. He started forward, feeling sick, thinking it was Kraus. Then he realized it wasn't in uniform. Relief surged through him. 'Kraus!' he called. 'Kraus?'

'Over here. Quick.'

The voice came from the right, from beyond a high wood fence. Brown ran to it, holstering his revolver. He jumped, caught the top, scrambled over it. Dropping to the other side, he found himself in an alley.

Kraus was standing close to a telephone pole, looking into the darkness of a carport across the alley. There were two cars inside the shelter.

'She's in there, behind the Pontiac,' Kraus whispered.

'Put your piece away. We'll go in with batons.'

'Christ Almighty, Jase, did you see the dead guy by the pool? This gal's a brain case.'

'We don't know she did that. We don't know anything about her, 'cept she's got a baby with her. She still got the baby?'

'Yeah. I'm not so sure it's alive, though. It's been awful quiet.'

'She armed?'

Kraus shook his head.

'We drop an unarmed lady, pal, they'll roast our asses. We hit the kid, they'll fry us in Mazola.'

Kraus holstered his service revolver.

They both slipped batons from the loops on their belts.

'I'll go in, flush her out,' Brown said. He stepped briskly across the alley, eyes searching the darkness in front of the Pontiac. 'Come on out, ma'am,' he said in his best persuasive voice. 'No call to be alarmed. We won't harm you. We just want to talk.'

He reached the rear of the car. Ahead, he still saw no sign of the woman. He walked along the car's side, past its back door.

'Ma'am?'

He stopped beside the front tire, gazing toward a two-foot gap between the bumper and the wall. If she was there, she had to be crouching awfully low, or lying down. He leaned over the hood. Not there.

Not in front of the other car, either.

Could she have crawled under one of them?

Perhaps. From what he saw, she was as skinny as they come.

He got down on his hands and knees, and looked.

Nothing.

He climbed to his feet, dusting his pants with his hands as he did so. Then walked quickly past the front of the Pontiac, angry, daring the woman to show herself. She didn't. Nothing. Not so much as a hair. He glanced down the space between the cars. He stepped past the front of the other car, dropped to his knees, and peered under it. Then he hurried toward his partner.

'She ain't there, Kraus,' he snapped.

'She has to be.'

'You see her run out?'

'No.'

'You see her run *in*?'

'What're you driving at?'

'You fucking well know.'

'I *saw* her go in there, damn it.'

'Which way did she *really* go?'

'I told you.'

'What happened? You figure it ain't healthy, tangling with a brain case? Figure she might do you like she done them?'

'I tell you, I—'

'You've pulled this shit before, Kraus. *Accidentally* losing suspects.'

Kraus backed away, shaking his head.

'This time the sergeant's gonna hear about it.'

'For Christ's sake, Jase . . .'

'Yeah, for Christ's sake,' he said, mimicking Kraus's whine. 'That babe killed two people, looks like. Snatched a kid, maybe killed *it*, too. And she's gonna be walking free and easy because you haven't got a pennyworth of balls in your bag. Now you tell me which way she went, man, or your name's going down engraved in shit. You hear?'

'Jase, you don't under—' Kraus's face twisted. 'I saw her, Jase. Saw her up close. I chased her, okay. I saw her go over the fence. She . . . she had to use both hands on the fence, and she had the baby, so she bit into one of its arms and carried it in her mouth. Christ, man, it was like a dog carrying a bone. The kid didn't . . . didn't cry or nothing. I'm sure it's dead, Jase, or it would've—'

'Get on with it.'

'See, I went after the gal and went over the fence . . . she was standing right there. Like she'd been waiting for me. Close to me as you are.'

'And you let her get away.'

'Jase, it's not a *her*. It's an *it*. I don't know . . . maybe it was a woman once. Not anymore.'

'Just what have you been sniffing, man?'

'It hasn't got eyes, Jase. Just a couple of holes. And its skin isn't like skin . . . parts of it are smooth and like . . . I don't know . . . like shoe leather. Other parts are all dark and shriveled and hard. 'Cause I touched it. See, I didn't know what the hell was going on, maybe it's a guy in a mask, or something. So I told it to put down the baby and turn around . . . I was gonna cuff it, see? But it just stood there, like it was watching me, daring me to go for it. And the head's just like a skull, only there's all this shiny red hair still stuck to it . . . the hair even moved like it was . . . I don't know . . . just weird. Completely weird . . .'

'Then what?'

'Then I took out my cuffs and grabbed one of its hands. I never felt nothing like it. Like a dried-up old corpse, you know? Then the thing . . . it opened up its mouth and I saw all these teeth and I . . . I just backed off. I just backed off, Jase. You would've, too. The thing's not human, Jase. Or if it is, it's been dead a long time, like years and years. I think it's that mummy, the one that disappeared from the museum.'

'Bullshit. Which way did it go?'

'You going after it?'

'Fucking right.'

'Don't, Jase. I'm telling you, it's a goddamn mummy.'

'It's a perpetrator, asshole.'

'Okay, okay. Fine. A perpetrator. Good luck. It went that way.' He pointed south down the alley. 'I'll go to the car, call in for backup.'

'You do that.'

Brown started down the alley at a trot, gaze searching. No sign of it ahead. *It? Her! Kraus is out of his fucking mind. Seen too many horror shows. Either that, or he made up all that shit to get himself off the hook.*

Only thing, the asshole hasn't got enough imagination to invent stuff like that.

The gal *did* look pretty weird, what he saw of her in the house.

At the end of the alley, he slowed down and scanned the crossstreet, the shadows of trees along it, the lawns and houses.

That thing – that gal – could be anywhere.

Hiding in the shadows.

Waiting.

Then he noticed the street sign to his left. He ran closer to make sure.

The sign read: MAPLE.

Holy shit! Some bad action had gone down on Maple while they'd been in the Burger Palace. He didn't know what. They'd got this call to see the woman on Ash as soon as they'd returned to their unit and checked in. Dispatcher was sending all kinds of units over to Maple, though. Sounded like a massacre.

Brown rushed across the street and entered the alley. Ahead of him, nothing seemed to move. He might as well keep going, though. This was the last block before the field. If it – she – headed that way, headed into the field, she might be easier to spot. Long as she didn't hide in the bushes or something.

He walked swiftly, looking into the darkness of the carports, of gaps between garages, of shrubbery along fenced backyards. He was halfway down the alley when a gate swung open. He whirled around.

A dark, gawky figure. Something in its arms. A pale bundle? Or maybe . . .

His hand jumped for his pistol, drew it, aimed. Drew the hammer back with his thumb.

'Freeze, mother!'

'Don't you "mother" me, nigger.'

A black woman. In a dark nightie. And the object in her arms was no baby, just a plastic bag.

Brown holstered his pistol. 'I'm sorry, ma'am.'

'Lady can't take out her trash without she gets jumped by a jive cop.'

'Here, let me get that.' He took the bag from her.

'Why, *thank* you.' Her voice sang with sarcasm. 'What you doing out here in the middle of the night, if I might inquire?'

'Police business.'

'I didn't *think* it was doggy business. But something sure smells not so sweet round here . . . like onions. Or a deli that should be requiring some spring cleaning.'

Smiling politely, Brown dropped the sack of garbage into the can and shut the lid. 'I'm not aiming to alarm you, ma'am, but there's a murder suspect in the area.'

'It ain't me, so I'll haul my pretty tail right on out of here, thank you very much.' She spun away.

He watched her pass through the gate, and didn't like the feel of being alone again. No one to watch his back. Now that's not a good situation to be in for a cop.

He continued down the alley.

He was near its end when he noticed the pale shape on top of a garbage can. He squinted, trying to make out its features. Looked like a kid. A baby. Sitting naked on the lid of the can, arms hanging at its sides, legs straight out, head drooping.

Brown shook his head, grinning with relief.

Just an old plastic doll someone was tossing out.

Hell, Reba might like a doll like this if it was in good condition. No point in letting it go to waste.

As he reached for it, he saw its light, wispy hair stir in the breeze.

'Oh, Jesus,' he muttered. 'Oh, Jesus Christ!'

He drew back his hand quickly before he could touch it.

'Jesus.'

He staggered forward as a sudden weight struck his back. Pain lanced his head. He fell against the garbage can, toppling the baby. It tumbled. Its skull made a hollow cracking sound on the concrete apron of the garage.

Brown went down on top of it.

Chapter Forty-two

It was going to be another of those nights. Loneliness worked at her bones. It became an ache inside of her that could no longer be endured. April Vallsarra turned on the bed, twisting the sheet in her hands.

Yes, there were tricks she used to while away the often sleepless nights. But they were only tricks. Made her feel cheap. Ate at her self-worth.

She'd wake in the morning and rush to the shower where she'd try and scrub away the sense of shame.

Never quite scrubbed herself clean of those particular memories. No matter how hard she worked with the soap.

Now here it was again. The hallway clock downstairs chimed away the early hours. April was lying wide-awake in that desolate, lonesome place between late night and early morning. Those seemingly endless hours when the rest of the world slept soundly and she, April Vallsarra, lay wide-awake and craving.

She craved companionship. A friendly voice. Sometimes she could hug a pillow and make believe that she hugged a lover.

Didn't work tonight.

She shifted position in bed endlessly, trying to get comfortable. No result. The bed was hard right now. Even when she could lie still for more than a moment she sensed that silence pressing down on her. Sensed, too, loneliness haunting the house.

Being blind was no bar to moving around the house at night in the dark. She did this now, walking from room to room, her negligée flowing. Even though she could not see them she knew her father's gold and platinum disks hung in their frames in his den. She couldn't bear to be in the room. She caught the faint scent of him there. It brought back too many painful memories.

She retreated to the kitchen. It seemed vast, an echoing desolate place.

Moments later she found herself climbing the stair. Blind from birth, she moved with confidence, never missing a step or blundering against the stair rail. She climbed quickly to the roof terrace.

The stars there would burn brightly above her. For a while she'd imagine what stars would look like, never having seen them. But she'd heard they were magical lights in the sky.

Wish upon a star.

She'd heard that phrase before.

She stood in the warm night air. A gentle breath of wind tugged at her negligée. Air whispered around her naked calves. The floor tiles were cool beneath her feet. That coolness felt nice. *What if I were to slip out of my negligée and lie on the floor? That cool hardness would press along the length of my body. It would feel wonderful.*

The breeze came again. She heard the rustling of trees out in the canyon. They were whispering busily.

'What have you heard?' she found herself asking them. 'What's going to happen tonight?'

Angry, she clenched her fists.

Now that was the curse of loneliness.

Lonely people talked to themselves. They talked to pets. They talked to their TV. They even talked to the trees.

But who is there to talk to? I'm a blind girl. I live alone. I have no friends.

So what else is there for me to do?

'You could wish upon a star.'

She felt the grim smile on her face as soon as she made the flippant remark. Yes, she could. It wouldn't do any harm. Wouldn't do any good, either. Nothing she did made any difference to her life.

Once, when she couldn't make anything good happen, she'd decided she must make something bad happen. Anything to break the monotony.

She'd pulled a knife from the block in the kitchen and cut her finger. Cut so deep that she'd heard the blade scrape across bone.

So she had a choice now. Cut her body again.

Or: wish upon a star.

She moved forward to the wall that ran around the roof terrace and raised her face. Tried to feel the starlight falling on it.

There was cool air, nothing else.

The stars would be up there, though. For a moment she allowed herself to believe in the fairy tale.

Wish upon a star. Then dreams will come true.

'I wish . . . I wish someone would come tonight. Someone who will change my life forever.'

The breeze blew harder. Trees rustled, branches creaked. The air moving down the canyon gave such a moan that she turned her head, startled. The moan sounded human.

No sooner had she composed herself than she experienced a moment of certainty.

Someone will come tonight. They will change my life.

The force of the premonition caught her by surprise.

Yes.

Someone would come.

When they did come nothing would ever be the same again.

'Please,' she whispered to the breeze. 'Come soon.'

Chapter Forty-three

They only come out at night . . .

That's what Grace told herself as the visitors to their pickup in the parking lot became a steady stream.

First had been the German hooker that tapped on the window.

From a hundred yards away she'd looked great. Slim body. Long legs. Big, blonde hair. Short skirt.

Close up?

Yeuhhh-uckkk.

She looked as if she'd been pulled from a coffin.

Her teeth were as yellow as the whites of her eyes. She'd tried to cover blistering cold sores on her lips with lip gloss that was a ghastly pink. Her throat was as wrinkled as a scrotum.

'You vonna do some business?'

'Pardon?' Cody had said.

'Vont business?'

'I don't think—'

'Mebbe a threesome with your girlfriend there. We can make with the suckling pig, ya?'

'I'm sorry . . . no, we're just staying here overnight.'

'Sleeping here in der lot?'

'Yes.'

'Good luck, honey.' She gave a dismissive shake of her head. 'You're gonna need it.'

Then she walked away, swaying her hips. The backs of her legs were a mass of bruises.

Next up, a laid-back Mexican.

'Okay, bro.' He pulled on a cigarette. 'What's it to be? Smoke, blow or mainline?'

'We don't want anything, thanks.' Again Cody, always the polite one. Never one to cause offence.

'Suit yourself, buddy.' The Mexican shrugged. 'Enjoy the view.'

As the time approached one a.m., the people came and went. Hookers, rent boys, drug dealers.

This was *Vice-R-Us*.

'We're never gonna get any sleep here,' Pix complained.

'It'll quieten down soon,' Cody said. 'Once they realize we don't want anything from them.'

'For once I'm going to have to agree with Pix.' Grace nodded through the window where two tall black women walked toward them accompanying a six-year-old child in stilettos. 'We're not going to get any rest tonight.'

The child turned out to be a dwarf. Aged probably around forty, dressed in black spandex, hair in pigtails. The three turned aggressive when they realized they weren't going to be hired to turn some tricks.

The dwarf kicked the pickup's door.

'This some kinda peep show?'

'Yeah, you got cameras? Is this TV?' The one in the Carmen Miranda fruit hat was clearly a man; stubble bristled through face powder. 'If we're gonna be on TV we want five hundred bucks apiece.'

'We're not a TV crew. We only want to—'

'Come out here and I'll scratch your eyes out, mister.'

'That pussy cat next to you, too.'

The dwarf sneered. 'These people from the 'burbs, they drive up here and watch people like us. Then they grope each other and get all horny.'

'Yeah,' said the she-male. 'If you do that, we should get paid.'

'Sex ain't free round here, y' know.'

Cody held out his hands, placating. 'We're just spending the night here. We've got nowhere to stay.'

The dwarf looked at them shrewdly. 'I know a place. Got entertainment, too, if you know what I mean?'

'Here's fine,' Grace said.

'Here's not fine,' Pix muttered from the back.

The dwarf looked them over. 'Hundred bucks a night. You three can watch while we—'

Grace said. 'Please, we just want to sleep.'

'Sleep here ain't cheap either.' The transvestite curled a crimson lip.

'Yeah,' the dwarf said. 'Hand over twenty bucks and we'll leave you to get all warm and snuggled up. How's that sound?'

Cody held out his hands through the car window, a gesture of helplessness. 'We don't have any money. We can't— Hey . . . hey! *My watch!*'

'Cody. *Cody!* Stay in the truck. No . . . don't follow them.'

'But they . . . ah, *shoot.*'

'Great, oh great,' Pix sang out. 'You let a midget and two guys dressed as girls steal your watch.'

'They just grabbed it. I—'

'What's for an encore, Cody, you big lummox, you gonna let someone steal your pants, too?'

Grace rounded on her sister. 'Just shut up, can't you?'

'Why should I shut up? We're thousands of miles from home. We're out on the streets. We're broke. Would anyone shut up when they're up to their ears in this kind of crap?'

'It's only temporary, Pix.' Cody tried to keep his cool.

'Temporary, my butt.'

'I'll find work tomorrow as an extra,' Grace said. 'They pay by the day.'

'"I'll find work",' Pix mimicked. 'The only work we're gonna find is the same as what these people coming up to the truck do.'

Grace fumed. 'Pix, stop causing trouble. Lie down . . . go to sleep.'

'Fat chance.'

'Try.'

'Yeah?'

'Please try, Pix.'

'I don't see it myself.'

'Why not?'

'We've got more visitors.'

Cody sighed. 'Oh, shoot.'

Two men walked up. One black, one white. Both big. Big as pro wrestlers. They wore T-shirts with the sleeves cut off to reveal their bulging biceps. Even though it was the middle of the night and dark they wore sunglasses.

Pix slid down in the backseat. Just before she covered herself with the sleeping bag she murmured, 'These guys don't look friendly.'

'Shhh,' Grace hissed.

'Betcha they've got guns. Betcha they start shooting at us.'

'For crying out loud, Pix,' Cody whispered.

'Just keep quiet, Pix. Please.' Grace turned to see the two men come up to the side window.

Just like the cop earlier they made a turning motion with their fingers.

Wind your window down.

No way. Grace didn't like the look of these men at all.

Muggers?

Rapists?

Or maybe they just shot people for fun.

They made the turning motion again. Grace saw the chunky gold rings on their fingers.

'Best wind the window down,' Cody said.

'Cody? No.'

'Just a little,' he said. 'If they have got guns the glass isn't going to stop any bullets.'

'Oh, Jesus, Cody.' A sob caught in the back of her throat.

This pair oozed pure menace.

She opened the window a crack. One of the men leaned closer until his lips almost touched the glass.

The man slipped his sunglasses down so that his penetrating stare could lock onto Grace's eyes.

'Yes?' she said in a small voice.

'Lady. Do you believe Jesus Christ died in order to save your immortal soul?'

* * *

'Jeepers creepers!' Pix exclaimed when the two heavies had gone. 'You can't escape Jehovah's Witnesses. Even out in a parking lot in the middle of the night.'

Cody pulled a smile. 'At least they weren't peddling sex or pushing drugs.'

'No, only religion.' Pix folded her arms again, lips pouting sulkily. 'Are we ever gonna sleep tonight?'

Grace sighed wearily. 'Maybe we should move on, Cody?'

'But where?'

'There must be somewhere peaceful in Hollywood.'

'Yeah,' Pix sneered. 'The graveyard.'

'Pix, how many times have I told you not to . . .'

Christ on a motorcycle, Cody thought sourly. *Here we go again.* The two sisters had been at each other's jugulars ever since they'd started this journey . . . this crazy journey . . . yeah, the future wasn't so rosy now. Gloomily he watched prostitutes strutting their stuff on the road by the lot. Johns came . . . then they *came* . . . then they went.

If I have to spend another night in this truck with those two I'll go nuts. Grace is beautiful. She's the one I want to stay with . . . but with that kid sister tied to us like a ball and chain? Oh brother.

Something clunked against the side of the car. Startled, Cody looked sidewards to see a brown face looking in at him. He recoiled from the eyes.

Hell.

He'd never seen eyes like that.

Not natural eyes, anyway.

They set his heart racing.

He heard Pix and Grace react in fear, too, giving squeals of fright.

A finger tapped on the glass. A hard clicking sound as the nail struck. Cody looked into the eyes. They shone pure silver. They were alien eyes that made him think of some creature from a monster movie. The voice that came from the mouth wasn't at all extraterrestrial.

'Hey, you guys,' came a drawl. 'It's time we had a talk.'

Cody rolled down the window.

'You've been sitting out here some time,' said the guy with the silver eyes. 'What ya doin'?'

Sighing, Cody repeated their story. 'We're just trying to get some sleep.'
'Sleep?'
'Yes, we don't have anywhere to go.'
'Motels are plentiful, y' know?'
'I know.'
'So rent a room.'
'We don't have any money.'
'That a fact?'
'We only got in today.'

The man with the silver eyes nodded. Cody could see now that the eyes were silver only because of silver contacts. So no close encounter of the third kind tonight.

Not that.

Worse. Far worse.

A close encounter of the Colt .38 kind.

Cody saw the man pull aside the bottom of his jacket to reveal the black butt of the firearm jutting from the waistband of his pants.

'I think maybe you're sussing out Andre's territory.'
'We're not cops,' Cody said quickly.
'Who said you were?'
'But you suggested—'
'I suggested nothing about the police force, man. What I am suggesting is that you might be thinking of moving into my territory.' He pronounced 'territory' in an easy drawl, each syllable clear and precise: 'Terry . . . tory.'
'No. We're only staying here for tonight.'
'But figuring to do some dealing, huh?'
'No.'
'What? Coke? Grass? Speed?'
'No.' Cody sounded annoyed now. He bunched his fist on the steering wheel. 'Now go away and leave us alone.'
'Oh, big guy.'
'Listen, we've just about had enough tonight.'
'Listen, baby, you haven't had nearly enough.' The man grinned, the silver contacts catching the moonlight. 'If you've come looking for trouble you've come to the right place.'

'Leave us alone.'

'Or?'

'Leave us. I'm warning you.'

'*You*'re doing the warning?' The man's hand went to his pistol.

Pix shrieked. 'He's going to shoot us.'

'He's not,' Cody said, angry.

The guy grinned again. 'So which of you two is right?' He looked at Grace. 'And you, pretty lady, what do you say?'

Cody opened the door, looking as if he was about to take on the guy with the silver eyes.

The guy stepped back, nodding. 'So you *do* want to muscle in on my territory?'

'No, we've just had a hell of a day. We want to be left alone.' Cody growled now.

Grace reached across and grabbed Cody's arm. He was polite, he was slow to anger, but once his fuse was burning . . . well, watch out.

'Leave it,' Grace pleaded.

'But we've been pushed around by every jerk in LA.' Cody quivered with rage. 'I'm not taking it anymore.'

'But he's got a gun,' Pix cried. 'He'll shoot you, Cody.'

'She's right, Cody,' Grace said. 'Get back in. We'll drive away. Find somewhere quiet.'

The man rested his hand on the gun and gave a shrug. *Okay, so what's it going to be?*

'All right.' Cody closed the door. 'We're leaving.'

'You think I'm going to let you just go after you've insulted me? Tried to walk into my territory?'

'I did no such thing.'

'You sure did, baby.'

'Look. We don't want any trouble. We just want to find somewhere quiet—'

'But you've *got* trouble. You're in Andre's territory now. You insult me to my face: "jerk", you called me. I want reparations, you hear? Reparations.'

'We're truly sorry,' Grace said in an effort to placate the man. 'We really are. We're tired. We've driven—'

'Not good enough.'

'Well, what *is* good enough?' Cody clenched his fist again, his face burning with anger.

All that shit today.

Now this.

A jerk.

A jerk with a gun, though. How dangerous is that?

'Tell you what, baby.' The man's eyes glinted silver. 'I'm a reasonable guy. The girl in the back. She gives me a good blow job and I'll consider that full and good reparation.'

Pix cried out. 'No, I'm not doing that.'

'That's the price, babes.' He eased the gun from his pants.

'No way,' Cody said. 'You'll have to put a bullet in me first.'

'Suits me.'

Pix grabbed Cody by the shirt collar, shook hard. 'Cody, you can't let him make me!'

'She's only sixteen, she's just a kid,' Cody said.

'Kids younger than her working these streets.'

'*Cody?*'

'Now I'm gonna unzip my fly.'

'Cody!'

'Moisten those lips for me, baby.'

'No.' Pix bunched herself into the corner of the seat, arms tightly around her knees. Eyes wide and scared, she shook her head, muttering, 'No, no, no . . .'

Andre pointed the gun into Cody's face.

'Listen up, babes. That's the price of you driving away from here. The girl in the back with the tight little mouth's gonna give me the best blow job in town.'

'No, she won't,' Grace said.

'Oh, won't she?'

'No,' Grace said firmly. 'I will.'

Chapter Forty-four

Through the peephole, Susan saw a swarthy, black-haired man with a grim face. She opened the door.

He lunged into her. She stumbled backwards, and the man fell to his hands and knees. Susan landed on her back.

In the doorway stood Mable Rudge, hunched slightly, grinning and panting. She held a butcher knife.

'Hi, petunia,' she said and pushed the door shut with the heel of her foot.

Susan climbed to her feet. She stood motionless. 'What do you want?'

The man started to get up. Mable kneed him over. 'Stay down, fella, or I'll slit your gizzard.'

'I'll happily leave,' he said.

'Lay on your back and shut up.'

He obeyed.

Mable stepped past his feet. She held the knife out in front of her, waving its point in small circles.

Susan backed away.

'Know what's gonna happen to you, whore? I'm gonna cut your face – gonna cut your nose off, that's what.'

Susan glanced at the bathroom door. It was open a crack.

'That's for starters. I'm gonna make you look so bad that Tag Parker'll puke when he sees you.'

'Tag!'

Mable charged.

Susan dodged and flung a lamp in her path. Mable kicked it aside. Snarled like a dog. Raised the blade.

'Freeze!' Tag shouted. He stood in the bathroom doorway, pistol aimed.

'Gonna fix her!' Mable yelled. She ran at Susan.

'Stop!'

'*Shoot her!*'

He didn't fire. His attention wasn't on Mable now but on the dark man dashing across the room.

The man sprang onto Mable's back. She plunged forward, arms swinging, blade flashing. Susan leaped out of the way and the big woman plowed into the sofa with an 'Umph!' The man, still on her back, grabbed her right arm. He twisted it. Mable growled and dropped the knife.

Susan rushed forward. She grabbed the knife and backed away.

Mable, no longer struggling, lay motionless beneath the man. She was half on the couch, her face pressed to its rear cushion, her knees on the floor. The seat of her grimy dress was torn, exposing a strip of doughy buttock. It dimpled. Susan looked away.

Tag came forward, holstering his revolver.

'Why didn't you shoot?'

'I might've hit our friend here.'

The small man looked over his shoulder and smiled. 'Imad Samdall.'

'Taggart Parker. This is Susan Connors.'

'Ah, yes. Miss Connors. And this is . . .?' Reaching back, he patted her soft rump. It quivered.

'Hands off,' she muttered.

He smacked the back of her head. 'Shut up. You threatened my life. Because of that I need not be civil to you.' He climbed off Mable's back. 'Sit on the couch and be silent.'

'You fuckin'—'

He slapped her. This time her whole face quivered with the force of the blow.

Mable's eyes narrowed. Her mouth shut. She turned around and flumped down onto the couch. This time she sat there. Said nothing.

Her cheek began to burn bright red from the slap.

'You've really done it this time, Mable,' Tag told her. 'Assault with a deadly weapon.'

'I just wanted to throw a scare into her.'

'Yeah.' He stepped toward the phone.

'Oh, you ain't gonna arrest me, Tag?'

'You'll go to jail for this one.'

'I didn't hurt nobody. I just did it for you.'

'I warned you not to interfere.' He reached for the phone and flinched as it rang the second he touched the handset. He picked it up. 'Hello? Yes, she is. Just a moment, please.' He nodded at Susan.

She took the phone. 'Hello?'

'Susan? This is James Blumgard. I'm sorry to disturb you, but I've received a most disturbing call from the police department. I'm sure there's some mistake. They're bewildered themselves. They seem to think, however, that our mummy has been involved in several killings that occurred tonight.'

'*Involved?*'

'They apparently believe Amara *committed* them. I know that sounds ridiculous. I don't know how they could even suggest such a thing. It appears, however, that one of the officers actually confronted the killer. He's sure it was a mummy. What's more, he's *convinced* it was Amara. Now maybe this was someone in disguise. I can hardly believe otherwise, though the officer insists that isn't the case. At any rate, the police would like a representative of the museum to be on hand as a consultant and so forth. I thought you would be the logical choice, since the Callahan Collection falls within your bailiwick.'

'What would I be doing?'

'They'd like you on the scene. I realize this may be an imposition . . .'

'No. You were right to call. I do have a problem, though. Maria's off for the night, and I don't have anyone to leave Geoffrey with.'

'Perhaps you could take him along. I'm sure there's no danger. The police simply want you to interview the officer involved; to establish whether his description does, in fact, fit Amara. They may ask for suggestions and so forth. I doubt it will take more than an hour.'

'Well . . .'

'I would go myself, but you're far more conversant with the subject.'

'I'll go,' she said.

'I appreciate this very much, Susan. Let me give you the address.' Blumgard told it to her and she copied it down. 'Keep me informed.'

'I will.'

'Goodnight, now.'

'Goodnight.' She hung up, turned to Tag. 'That was Blumgard. There've been some killings and get this – the police think Amara's involved.'

'As the perpetrator?'

She nodded.

Imad frowned and walked toward the door.

Susan said, 'I have to go over and talk to the police. Will you come?'

'Of course.'

Imad knelt near the door and picked up a black notebook.

'We'll have to take Geoffrey.'

'Before you leave,' Imad said, 'it would be wise for you to read this.'

'Now? I don't think there's time for—'

'Please. It is important.'

'What is it?'

'The journal of Robert Callahan. I was his ward and companion, you see, before his demise. He left instructions that this must be placed in responsible hands, should Amara walk. Unless I am mistaken, that situation has developed.'

'It's walked before?' Tag asked.

'Indeed.'

Imad gave the journal to Susan. She flipped through it, glancing at the handwritten pages. 'It's awfully long.'

'It tells you many things that you have to know.'

'Why don't you come along and fill us in along the way?'

'I'm sorry, no. I wish to have no further dealings in the matter. If you would permit me, however, I'll assume responsibility for Mable.'

'Can you handle her?' Tag asked.

'Most certainly. We could telephone the police from here if you like. If not, I'll be pleased to escort her elsewhere.'

Susan glanced at Tag.

Tag nodded.

'You're welcome to stay.'

Chapter Forty-five

Cody looked through the windshield. The pickup's headlights revealed the road as it twisted ahead. On either side the rocky walls of a canyon rose up into the night sky. He drove without speaking. Beside him, Grace sat gazing out the side window. Behind them Pix, flat on her back, stared at the underside of the truck's grimy roof.

He downshifted as the road in front ran downhill. The canyon widened a little. Here there were only rocky outcrops and occasional trees and bushes. No houses. No gas stations. This was a dark slice of wilderness tucked away in a corner of LA.

At last Pix asked, 'Grace . . . how could you do that?'

'Pix,' Cody warned.

'Shit . . . you sucked the guy's dick.'

Grace said nothing. Just stared at passing trees, which were becoming more numerous along this stretch of road.

'You didn't even know him. And you let him put his dick in your mouth.'

Grace still said nothing. Jerkily, she grabbed the water bottle and drank from it, her pink lips tight round the end of the wide neck of the bottle; her mouth forming a perfect seal. Cody found himself looking at her mouth, unable to shake the memory of what had happened half an hour ago.

'Afterwards, why didn't you spit?'

'Pix,' Cody said. 'Your sister did what she had to do, okay?'

'I think I'd have chosen the shooting.' Pix shook her head. 'Oh, man . . . he'd even pierced the end of it . . . a gold stud.'

Cody glanced back. 'Don't talk about it. Your sister doesn't need reminding.'

'But to suck a stranger's dick like that. Jeez, Grace, I thought he was gonna choke you, it went in so—'

'*Pix, enough now.*'

Cody glanced at Grace. Still she hadn't spoken. Hadn't spoken since the guy . . . since she'd . . . *Oh, shit.* He didn't want to activate the mental playback.

'Couldn't you have jumped him, Cody? You yellow or something?'

'He had a gun, Pix.'

'Yeah, but he was distracted, you dork.'

'And you think I could have grabbed the gun off him while—'

'Yeah, if you'd got your ass in gear.'

'Hell, you try pulling a stunt with a gun in your face.'

'While he had his dick in my sister's mouth you could have done something.'

'Yeah, slugged him with the cracker box, maybe.'

'But then maybe you enjoyed watching him unload himself into Grace's mouth. I saw you getting all hot and sweaty and—'

'*STOP!*'

Cody's head spun as Grace shouted.

'Stop the truck!'

'Don't worry about Pix. She'll be quiet from now on, won't—'

'No! It's not that. Look!'

'What?'

'Don't you see?'

'See what?'

'Stop the damn truck, and look!'

He braked.

'What've you seen, Grace?'

'There, through the trees . . . no, further to the right.'

Pix sounded worried. 'What is it? What's wrong?'

Cody looked.

Saw nothing.

Nothing except trees and boulders and the rock walls of the canyon.

There were no houses, no buildings, no cars – zilch.

Cody began, 'Grace, I still don't see—'

'I saw a woman in the trees.'

Pix snorted. 'Forget it. We've had enough stranger danger for one night.'

'No, it was a woman. She was holding a baby.' Grace stared into the darkness. 'She was hurrying.'

'But what would a woman be doing out here in the middle of nowhere, carrying a baby?'

'She must be in trouble,' Grace said. 'I'm going to help.'

With that she swung open the door, jumped out of the truck and ran away into the trees.

'Don't let her go, you big lummox. You don't know what's out there.'

'Okay, okay.' Cody grabbed the flashlight from under the dash.

'She might get herself killed.'

'I know that, too,' he said grimly.

He climbed out, began to follow Grace. He caught a glimpse of her through the trees as she ran through a shaft of moonlight. He also glimpsed another figure further on. For some reason, it seemed to move strangely. Moonlight glinted on it and he thought he saw long red hair cascading down the figure's back. And was it clutching something pale to its chest?

Too far away to see properly.

But for some reason just that glimpse of the hurrying figure, hunched over the pale bundle, sent a chill down his spine.

Something not right about it, Cody.

Something dangerous.

'Grace,' he called. 'Grace . . . wait!'

But Grace ran after the figure.

He switched on the flashlight and ran through the trees after her.

Behind him he heard cracking twigs.

Looking back, he saw Pix following him.

'Wait in the pickup,' he told her.

'Yeah, as if.'

'It might not be safe out here.'

'It's gonna be safer out here even with a big lummox like you than alone in that heap of junk.'

'Pix—'
'I'm coming with you.'
'Okay . . . but stay close.'
Together they ran up the slope.

Chapter Forty-six

Knife in hand, Imad watched the door swing shut. He turned to Mable. She sat motionless on the couch, glowering at him.

'Now, Mable, tell me. What is so special about this man whose name is like a game played by children?'

She shrugged.

Her thick lips pouted, sulky-looking.

'What is so special that you would risk prison, even death, to mutilate or kill his girlfriend?'

Her eyes narrowed. She said nothing. Her plump fingers knotted together on her lap.

'Tell me.' He reached for the telephone.

'I like him,' Mable said.

'You like him. Isn't it evident that he doesn't like you?'

'Huh?'

'And he certainly wouldn't like you any better if you harmed Susan.'

'He was nice to me.'

'To protect Susan, he was prepared to empty his revolver into you. He'd have done exactly that if I hadn't intervened, Mable.'

'So?'

'I saved your life, did I not?'

'So what?'

'Isn't that a rather special gift?'

'What do you mean?'

'I gave you back your life when it could have been so easily taken.'

'What do you want from me, you filthy A-rab?'

'Tsk, tsk, so impolite.'

'I don't owe you nuthin', A-rab.'

'And incorrect, too. By parentage I am Egyptian. But legally I am as American as . . . how would you put it? Momma's apple pie.'

'You American? You're putting me on.'

'Oh, indeed I am telling the truth.'

She frowned. 'So what do you want from me?'

'Want?'

'Must want something.'

'Now, let me see.' He rested his fingertips together. 'Mable, it's now in my power to grant you another favor. I needn't call the police, you realize.'

She stared at him. Her glower softened. 'Will ya let me go, then?'

'Oh, Mable, my dear, I can hardly do that. I told Susan that I would assume responsibility for you. To let you go would be the height of *ir*responsibility. You might simply attack her again.'

'I won't. I promise.'

'Words. Mere words. As long as you're infatuated with Tag, you'll continue to be a threat. No, I cannot let you go. I can, however, take you with me.'

She rubbed her hands on her soiled dress. She licked her lips.

'You will be in my custody, much as you would be in police custody should I decide to call them. The difference is this: there will be no handcuffs, no jail, no trial. I'll give you a comfortable room and good food. There will be a TV for you to watch. And books if you should wish to read . . . ah, no books, perhaps. Reading might not be to your taste. But magazines and a radio.'

'What's the catch?'

'Isn't there always a catch?' He smiled. 'This is the catch. You will not be allowed to leave the house alone until I'm satisfied—'

'A house?' she asked, suddenly beaming.

'Indeed. I live in a rather elaborate house. One might call it a mansion.'

'Shoot . . . you want me to live there?'

'For the time being.'

She slapped her knee. Her calf quivered. 'I get it! You're wantin' to screw me. Gee, I've never been screwed by an A-rab before.'

'Screw?'

'Sure. Whyn't you just come out and say it?' Bouncing off the couch, Mable lifted her dress. Her pasty white thighs were mottled with bruises. Her knees were scabbed. There was a fresh scratch from the recent tussle running the length of one meaty thigh.

Imad saw she wore no panties, but her groin was hidden below the roll of her stomach. Her huge breasts quivered as she struggled to pull the dress over her head. Tufts of black hair hung from her armpits.

She talked excitedly. 'No, sir. Never been poked by an A-rab. I've been done by a Mexican and a whole bunch of Cubans. And there was this guy from Austria – or was it Australia? – he tied me up with a clothesline and nailed me good and hard. Couldn't sit down for a week, I can tell you. Here, just help me get this dress off, then we can screw.'

'No!' Imad snapped.

'I know it's what you want, hon. Mable don't mind what you do, or how you do it.' She stretched out her arms to him. 'Come here, hon. Enjoy.'

'No! I insist you lower your dress immediately. Cover yourself, for God's sake. Or I will phone the police. Believe me, I will do that unless you behave with correct modesty.'

'Correct modesty,' she grunted as she pulled the dress down. She scowled at him. 'You queer?'

'Hardly.'

'Wish I was a boy?'

'Mable—'

''Cos if you are that way inclined I can take it like a man.'

'Mable. This is neither the time nor the place for—'

'Good a time as any.'

'It is not.'

'Might as well mess up someone else's couch as your own.'

'You are filthy and you smell like a garbage truck.'

'Can't get it up?'

'I dirtied myself enough when I was forced to subdue you. I certainly don't relish further contact at such close quarters.'

'Fuck you, Charlie.' She dropped to the couch.

'So there'll be no further contact until you've bathed and brushed your teeth. Which you will do immediately after we arrive at my home. Understand?'

One side of Mable's mouth curled upward. 'You *do* want to prong me.'

'No,' he said. 'Not until you are clean.'

'Oh, baby. I get the picture.'

'So what shall it be, the police or me?'

Licking her lips, she slumped on the couch and lifted her dress again. 'Do me now,' she said. 'Show me how you do it A-rab style.'

'You're wasting your time with these antics.'

'Aw.'

'Come along, Mable.'

'What's your name again?'

'Imad.'

'Imad.' She stroked her hands down her hips and raised a knee. 'I like you, Imad. Don't you want to put it right in here?'

He set the knife on a lamp table and went to her. She smiled up at him.

Smiled as, moaning, she used her fingers to massage and probe herself. Fingernails became slick.

'Oh . . . Imad. Right here, right here,' she whispered.

Imad slapped her cheek so hard her face wobbled.

'Hey!'

He slapped her again. A loud *thwack* filled the room. 'Get up.'

She got to her feet. Her face was red. Imad saw tears in her eyes.

'Whatcha gonna do? Beat up on me before you screw me?'

'Mable—'

''Cos that's happened to me before when I got gang-banged. They beat the crap out of me, then . . . then one after another they screwed me.' Tears ran down her face. The cheek with the burning red handprint grew slick with them. She used both plump paws to rub her eyes.

'Mable—'

'I thought ya liked me,' she sobbed.

'You must learn to obey, Mable. Once you understand that you will find inner contentment. Understand?'

'But I . . . I—'

'Mable. Learn to obey. Now, follow me.'

Imad led the way across the room. As they passed the lamp table, Mable grabbed the knife.

'No!'

Chapter Forty-seven

Amara held the baby to her dry chest. Her red hair had spilled forward, partially covering the infant. She walked through darkness, her shins whispering against the dry grass.

She'd been walking for a long time now. At first there'd been dwellings. Lights had shone from windows as if they'd been lit by burning torches. But after walking for some time the houses had ended. She'd walked away from the town and into a range of barren hills.

As if by accident rather than purpose she moved down one of the hills and into a canyon. She held the baby tight, her talon-like hands pressing it against her withered breasts.

Amara continued walking through the darkness. She entered an area where trees grew and passed among them, weaving in and out, never pausing.

Never tiring.

Driven by ancient purpose.

It was as she walked some distance from a road yet parallel to it that the truck stopped. Its headlights lit a shining path in front of it.

Then a figure left the truck at a run.

A man's voice sounded on the night air. 'Grace . . . Grace. Wait!'

The figure of a woman ran into the trees. A moment later two more figures left the truck. A man and a second, younger woman. They ran after the first who'd already disappeared.

Amara walked on. She knew the first woman followed her. But that

was of no importance. The ancient purpose drove her on. Nothing would distract Amara.
Nothing would get in Amara's way.
Nothing.
No one.
Death came on swift wings to anyone who interfered.

Chapter Forty-eight

'Ed, what're you doing?'

He glanced up through the bars at Virginia. 'I've already told you. I'm making a barb. When this baby goes in it's going to *stay* in.'

'You're making too much noise . . . and the sawdust on the floor . . . they'll see it.'

He groaned with frustration. 'Look, Virginia. The point of the stake is sharp enough, but it needs a barb to stop her escaping.'

'But they'll hear you. And they'll see the sawdust when they bring in the food.'

'Virginia—'

'And when they see it they'll know what's happening.'

'I'll think of something.'

'And you'll wind up like Marco and Cardinali.'

'Okay. Lemme think.'

'Ed. The lights could go out any minute, then—'

'Whammo. I know.'

'Move the sawdust bowl so it catches the sawdust.'

His face burned. Seemed so obvious. Catch the sawdust in the wee-wee bowl. *Why didn't I think of that?*

Because you're busy planning on doing some hunting with that harpoon of yours, Eddie, old buddy.

Yeah, gonna harpoon me some fresh meat.

'What's so funny?' she asked.

'I'm just imagining the bitch's surprise when she sits on this instead of on my pecker.'

'Don't get overly optimistic.'

He ran his finger over the wickedly sharp stake. 'Oh, I just know this is going to work like a dream.'

'You've got to avoid being caught with it first. Okay, Ed?'

'Okay, Virginia.'

'We've solved the sawdust mess, so what do you figure to drown the noise?'

He gazed at the edge of the cage bar that he'd been using as a file. It worked surprisingly well.

But noisy as hell.

Squeaked like a chorus of mice every time he ran the wooden stool leg backwards and forwards across it.

'Could you use less pressure?' she suggested.

'Tried. It doesn't scrape away any of the wood when I do that.'

'How much further to go before you've made the barb?'

He looked at the wooden shaft. About four inches back from the point he'd managed to file a cleft. A 'V' shape, it went maybe a quarter of the way through the stool leg.

'Another half an inch. Then I have to work on making the point of the barb sharp, too. When I've driven it into her I need to pull back quick.' He demonstrated, thrusting the chair leg up then tugging back hard. 'So the barb, here, digs into her flesh. Then I've got her like a hooked fish.'

Virginia looked suddenly uncomfortable and crossed her legs. 'I get the picture.'

'Barbaric. But needs must.'

'Yeah, needs must.'

'Let's see if this works.' He licked his finger and ran it along the edge of the bar he used as a file, moistening the metal. This time when he worked on the barb it didn't squeak. He nodded. 'Slippery when wet.'

'It's stopped squeaking now but is it cutting?'

'Yeah, it's cutting. I just need to keep wetting it.'

He worked for a while. Then . . .

He ran his finger along the eighteen inches of hard wood to touch the point lightly. A thought occurred to him. An interesting one at that.

'A bit like staking a vampire,' he told her. 'Only I'm not going through the ribs.' He stabbed upward with the wood. 'I'm going up through the crotch instead.'

'Oh, Jesus . . . You don't have to state the obvious.' She scrunched up her face, imagining the pain. 'You're going to inflict one hell of an injury, you know?'

'I *do* know. But after what she's done to us? Couldn't happen to a nicer person.'

'Well, I'd stuff some tissue in your ears – she's going to scream the place down after you push that thing . . .' She grimaced. 'You know where.'

His grin became wider. 'You know something . . . it's going to be music to my ears.'

Lights out.

All right!

Ed was in a state of readiness.

Ready, Eddie?

He stifled the grin in the dark. They'd see with their nightscope goggles. They'd know he planned some surprise.

He sat on the blanket. He'd slipped the sharpened wooden chair leg that formed the lethally sharp stake down the leg of his pants.

Is that a harpoon in your pocket or are you just pleased to see me?

It was all he could do to stop himself laughing out loud. He'd waited for this. Payback time. Once the bitch had this rammed up inside of her as far as her spleen she'd be going nowhere fast.

She'd scream like a stuck pig, though. Which as analogies went was pretty accurate. He rested his fingers on the harpoon, feeling the thick, hard roundness of the shaft through the material of his trousers.

This is a stickup, honey.

A stickup you're never gonna forget.

He sat there in the dark, waiting for the command to climb up onto the platform and 'present himself' through the hole in the Perspex.

Drafts slipped into the room. A door had opened somewhere. He heard rustling. A whisper of feet moving lightly across the concrete floor.

Nearly here.
Not long now.
Ready, Eddie?
I'm ready.
He stroked the thick shaft inside the leg of his pants.
Then he heard whispering.
'Okay.' This was from Virginia.
Shit.
Oh, shit, shit!
Their sex mistress had chosen Virginia, not him, for this session's entertainment. Maybe he could still stake their captor as she worked on his neighbor. But it was dark. Dark as hell. He couldn't see squat in the darkness. There wasn't a hope of skewering her by sheer chance.
No. Must be patient. Must wait.
He covered himself with the blanket, just in case his captor should glimpse the rod-shaped protuberance in his pants. There was little chance that they'd mistake *that* for his dick.
He heard murmuring from the next cage. Virginia began to breathe heavier. The breathing became panting. Then she moaned.
Oh, that moaning.
Erotic moans.
Sexy moans.
It always fired him up inside. He imagined Virginia standing facing his cage, feet apart. Naked. Her hair spilling down the long curve of her back to her gorgeous butt. Her long thighs. Shapely calves.
And there was a shadowy figure doing great things to her.
Working at her between her legs with slick fingers.
Stroking, parting, entering.
She gave a little cry.
Oh, Eddie. That was the sound she made when being entered. Those fingers were inside now. Finding her clit. Toying, pressing gently, probing. Teasing.
Shit. His heart hammered.
The sounds of pleasure were making him horny.
Horny enough to distract him from what he planned to do with the sharp stake when he got a chance.

He listened hard, his eyes straining into the darkness. Hearing moans, little gasps, muttered 'pleases', 'yessses'.

Then it went wrong.

The note of the whispering altered.

He heard Virginia give a frightened gasp. 'I'm sorry . . . I didn't mean to . . . I'll try harder.'

More whispers. They sounded as if they could be instructions but Ed couldn't be certain.

Their captor's voice boomed. That same deep timbre that made the bars of the cage quiver. *'Stand with your back to the bars. Slip your hands through the loops. Quickly.'*

'Please . . . I'm sorry. I—'

'Do it.'

Sounds of movement. Then silence.

Ed listened. All he could hear was his blood thumping in his ears.

What was going to happen to Virginia? What had she done wrong? He thought of Marco with the grinning slit in his throat. The blood. The image came blasting, too, of Cardinali toppling off the stool to hang by his neck, jerking, choking.

Had their captor grown bored with Virginia?

Then he heard a sound. It was the swish of an object moving fast through the air.

Thwack.

A stick or a belt.

Swish.

Thwack!

'Uh! Please!'

Virginia pleaded with the invisible sadist. But still the beating went on. *Swish. Thwack.* Then came Virginia's sharp gasps. She panted. Moaned. Cried. Still the blows fell. The blistering snap of a weapon against soft flesh.

Later, when the lights came on, Ed saw Virginia lying face down on the foam mattress. She was completely naked. Her hair fanned out across the floor where she'd thrown herself down.

Ed blinked.

Saw the injuries.

Saw a dozen or more cruel red lines that seemed to burn bright across the soft rising mounds of her bare buttocks.

She winced as she moved.

Gingerly raising her head, she looked at Ed. Her eyes brimmed. 'When you get your chance don't hold back. You've got to hurt the bitch. Hurt her. Do you hear me?'

He nodded.

All he had to do now was wait.

It would happen soon. He knew that. Felt it in his bones. *Endgame*.

Chapter Forty-nine

Cody thought: *This is crazy. Who on earth is Grace following out there?* He paused as he ran up the wooded incline. Maybe that's it. Maybe Grace *is* crazy. The incident with the guy with the gun back in the parking lot might have sent her over the edge.

'Slow down, you big lummox,' Pix panted. 'I can't keep up with you.'

'You should have stayed in the pickup.'

'Yeah, and waited for the next oral-fixated weirdo to come ambling by? Think again, Cody, you simpleton.'

'Pix, shush.' He held his finger to his lips.

'What you mean, shushing—'

'Ssh. Pix, I'm trying to listen for your sister.'

He stood for a moment, shining the flashlight ahead through the trees. Listening for the sound of footsteps. Where was Grace? She'd taken off after the strange-looking gal like a missile. Now she was out in the dark alone. *Hell . . . who knows what might happen to her out there?*

This canyon was such an out-of-the-way place.

Might there be bears?

Or Hell's Angels ready for some fun?

Or backwoods boys who were bored with making pigs squeal?

Hell.

Might just get killed out there.

'Cody?'

'What?'

'I don't like it out here. I wanna go back.'
'You should've stayed in the pickup.'
'I wanna stay with you.'
'Make your mind up, Pix.'
'I wanna stay in the pickup with you.'
'We've got to find your sister.' He scanned the forest. All he saw were boulders, tree trunks and a glimpse of stars through the branches.
'Cody?'
'What is it now?'
'Will you hold my hand?'
'*No.*' He looked at her, startled by her suggestion.
'Please.' Suddenly shy-looking, almost demure, she held out her hand.

He shook his head. 'Pix, just stick close behind. I think she went this way.' Without waiting for a reply, he struck off through the trees, shining the light in front of him. He was sure Grace had headed along the path. He walked quickly, not looking back.

He knew Pix was following.

Was positive about it.

Heard her whispering, 'Please, Cody. Hold my hand . . . please . . . *please . . .*'

Grace hurried along the woodland path. It zigzagged down the hillside. She followed the figure that was moving downhill in front of her. The figure had long red hair. It clutched something pale to its chest. Its arms and legs were very thin.

It was difficult to see clearly in this mixture of moonlight and shadow, but Grace was sure it was a woman. What was more, the woman seemed to be clutching a baby.

But the stick-thin woman looked odd. Seemed to move strangely. There was something about the gait. Something stiff-jointed.

And what would a woman be doing out here in a godforsaken canyon at two in the morning? She had to be in trouble. She might be on the run from a bullying, abusive boyfriend.

After what had happened tonight to Grace – how she had been forced into oral sex with the armed stranger – she was determined not to sit back and let innocent people suffer. The world couldn't be such a cruel place. There had to be times when good people did the right thing – they had to help people in need.

She moved down the sharp incline at something like a run, catching hold of tree trunks to steady herself. Her feet raised puffs of dust that showed as white clouds in the moonlight. Sometimes branches caught at her clothes, her hair, but she struggled on, breaking free.

If she could break free of the memories of the past few hours.

Break free of that salt taste that still clung to her lips.

If she dedicated herself fully to helping the poor woman with the child then maybe that would be enough to make her forget. Once she thought she heard Cody calling her name. Only there wasn't time to stop. Once she'd caught up with the woman she could go back.

Grace saw herself in her mind's eye leading the dazed (maybe even battered) woman and babe back to the pickup truck. Then they could drive her to a women's refuge where she'd be safe from the abusive rat who'd made her flee in the middle of the night.

Grace was sure her imagined scenario about the woman was right.

Yet, the woman did look strange. There was something about the round shape of the front of her head. It was almost skull-shaped.

Of course it has to be skull-shaped – you're seeing her head, stupid.

But it's more like a skull bereft of flesh . . .

No . . . that's your imagination, she told herself, panting as she ran down the hill. *Imagination and a trick of the moonlight.*

There goes a woman in trouble.

Your mission? To help.

You're gonna do this. By saving her you're gonna save yourself from those memories. Those dirty, corrosive memories of the . . . of the way he filled your mouth . . . how he pushed in so deep you thought you'd choke on his—

No.

She snapped off the thought.

Save the woman and her baby.

She ran harder through the near-darkness.

And ran straight into the arms of a phantom. They closed round her. A leering face with a twisted nose pressed hard against hers.

The phantom held her tight. Bony fingers pressed into her shoulders, seeking her throat.

Struggling, panting, she fought to free herself.

As she pushed herself away a shaft of moonlight fell through the branches.

Her attacking phantom was a tree. Nothing more. The phantom's arms were branches; its face marks in the bark where a branch had sheered off.

Stupid runaway imagination, she scolded herself. *Stay focused.*

Taking a deep breath, she found the path again. Scuff marks in the dirt revealed that the woman had passed this way. But that was odd . . . Grace squatted down to look closer at the dry dirt. She saw something that made the hairs on her head stand on end. There was a footprint. But it was a bare footprint.

Could the woman have walked all this way along the canyon without some kind of footwear?

Or perhaps she'd lost a shoe walking down the steep slope, only was too exhausted or too frightened to stop and put it back on?

This was getting stranger by the minute.

Grace hurried along the path. Soon she reached a break in the trees that afforded her a better view of the canyon. Up ahead she saw a lone house.

In the distance, she also glimpsed the slight figure of the woman. She seemed to be making for the house.

Okay . . . me, too, Grace told herself.

Chapter Fifty

'It's not gonna work.'

'It is.'

'Not.'

Ed wished she'd shut up. They'd been on this subject for a long time. *Too damn long. Damn pessimist.*

He glared at Virginia.

'Don't look at me like that, Ed Lake.'

'I'll look at you how I damn well please.'

'Look,' she began. 'It's because we're getting tense about the whole situation.'

'I'll say we're tense.'

'Eddie—'

'We're locked up here in cages. We're used as sex toys. We're probably gonna be murdered.'

'Eddie—'

'We're probably gonna wind up in a shallow grave out in the woods.'

'Eddie, you haven't thought it through, you're missing—'

'I haven't. I've got the harpoon.' He brandished the stool leg. 'I'm going to use it.' His face burned. 'And another thing, don't call me Eddie.'

'I thought you might like it.'

'I don't. "Eddie" reminds me of some dog from a comedy show.'

'Okay, Edward . . .'

'Ed. Please.'

'Okay, Ed.'

'That's better.'

'Sheesh.' She touched her forehead as if she'd lost her train of thought. 'You've told me the plan. You impale the woman. The barb holds her in place. You have her trapped, right?'

'Right.'

'But that doesn't get us out of these cages, does it?'

'But she'll be no longer a threat.'

'And you've forgotten something else.'

'What?'

'We think there's two of them.'

'Shit.' He slapped his forehead. *Holy Christ, I'm an idiot. A gold-plated idiot.*

'The one we've nicknamed The Warder. What's she going to do when she sees her partner squirming on top of that pole?' She fixed her green eyes on the stake in Ed's hands. 'She'll probably get hold of a gun and . . . well, for you and me: *Los Endos*.'

'Holy Christ. I just didn't think . . . Virginia, I'm an idiot. But I was so sure about this. I thought I saw a way out.'

Virginia looked him in the eye. 'Ed. I'm not saying *don't* do it. I'm just stressing that the end result might not be what you expect. But . . .'

'But?'

'But if you want to go ahead and do it, do it. Okay?'

'You mean at least nail one of the bitches?'

Virginia nodded. 'And you never know, you might hurt the Sex Queen so bad that her friend panics and runs for it.'

'So then we sit here and starve.'

Virginia gave one of those little jerks of her shoulder. 'Can't say that everything will turn out rosy for us. But you never know. We might get lucky. Sex Queen might have the keys to these padlocks. Then we're free as birds.'

'So you're with me on this?' Lightly he pressed the lethal point of the stake with his thumb. 'Even though it might not work out one hundred percent?'

'Go for it, Ed. It's getting so we've nothing left to lose.'

Chapter Fifty-one

There is someone out there, April told herself with a growing sense of wonder. Someone's coming through the trees toward the house.

Her years of blindness had developed in her an acute sense of hearing. She listened.

Heard the nighttime breeze running in hissing swirls along the canyon to play among the trees. Depending on her mood, it could be such a lonesome sound. Now it had become strangely thrilling.

It seemed to be whispering to April: *'They're here, they're here, they're here.'*

Here is my savior.

Someone to banish loneliness.

She tilted her head to one side, feeling the breeze fingering her long hair. It stroked her neck, tugged lightly at the hem of her negligée, sending a delicious shiver up her thighs.

Concentrating now, she filtered the sounds.

The cry of a bird.

The breeze in the branches. The groan of a tree trunk. Rustling grass.

A whispering through the potted shrubs on the roof terrace where she stood with her hands on the wall that separated her from the twenty-foot drop to the driveway below.

She heard another sound, too. Faint but distinct to her sensitive ears. A rhythmic *scrunch, scrunch*.

That was a pair of feet advancing along the gravel drive to the house. Even though the footsteps sounded very light, there was something purposeful about the stride. She lifted her hand to push back her hair from the side of her head. Turned it slightly, so she could hear more.

Sometimes she could even hear the breathing of a visitor. Occasionally she could even catch their scent, too. But not tonight. The breeze was too strong. It would carry the visitor's scent away down the canyon before it could reach April's delicate nostrils.

April imagined what her caller would be like. From the lightness of their step she pictured someone young and slightly built.

Even though she couldn't imagine their looks she knew one thing. Her visitor would be beautiful. A divine spirit had brought them here to put an end to her loneliness.

The *scrunch-scrunch* of feet on gravel grew louder as they neared the house.

April Vallsarra waited. Almost here. Almost . . .

Then, a moment later, the footsteps stopped. There was no sound but the breeze in the trees, whispering, sighing.

Her caller – her *savior* – would be standing there below her in that magical radiance that sighted people called 'moonlight'.

April waited. She was patient now. She sensed that her caller might be nervous or even afraid. She didn't want to say anything that would frighten them away. Perhaps they'd spent days trying to pluck up courage to make this trip to the remote house in the middle of the night.

So, nice and easy does it.
Take your time.
Don't rush.
Make them feel comfortable.

She smiled down in the direction of the figure, even though she could only guess at where they stood. But it must be close. She heard a slithering of stones beneath their feet when they shifted their balance.

Even so, they must be standing still. Gazing up at her. Perhaps tongue-tied.

A young man?
Shy, but quite beautiful.

Was he as lonely as she had been? Spending solitary nights praying for a companion? Another person to love and to be loved by?

Softly, April spoke. 'Don't worry. I can't see you but I know you're there.' She paused. 'My name is April Vallsarra. Have you come here to see me?'

There was no reply. Her visitor was indeed so shy as to be tongue-tied. She hoped they wouldn't flee in a fit of nerves.

So she spoke reassuringly. 'It's a lovely night. I wish I could see the stars, but I guess you've already noticed. I'm blind. Can you describe the stars to me?'

No reply.

'Don't worry. I can imagine them. I imagine them as little round cushions that are soft and warm to touch, if only one *could* touch them.' Her laugh came as a light trill. 'That sounds absurd, I know. But I've never seen them, never seen anything, come to that, so when people try and describe what objects *look* like I have to translate it in the only way I can. The sun I think of as being pointed to the touch and quite hard. The moon for me is soft and cool. Stars are soft and warm and if one could touch them they'd tingle against your fingertips.' She smiled downward. 'And I imagined as a girl that if you listened hard enough you could hear them singing . . . small, light voices that sang sweet rising harmonies. See?' She shrugged. 'If something as profound as sight is missing from one's life it's hard to replace it with a substitute.' She paused, thinking. 'The same goes for love. If you don't have someone to love in your life you try to find substitutes. But they're only clumsy facsimiles of the real thing, because there is no genuine substitute for real love . . .' She paused, suddenly feeling awkward. 'See, there I go. You can tell when someone lives alone, they start talking too much. What about you? Tell me about yourself.'

No reply.

'You can't live that close. The nearest houses are three miles away. And I didn't hear the sound of a car . . .'

Silence.

'Did you walk?'

Nothing.

'Then I guess it must be a nice night for a walk. Nice and cool now.'

Again a faint sound as if her caller had shifted their center of balance on the gravel drive.

'It doesn't matter,' she said gently. 'You don't have to talk. I understand.' She smiled. 'It's nice to have someone here. Believe me, incredibly nice.'

She felt the breeze stroke her bare shoulders. It pressed her negligée against her body. It felt like cool hands, gliding down her back.

Lovely sensations.

April shivered. A kind of thrilling shiver that made her tingle all over. Her breasts prickled with goose bumps and her nipples rose.

'We'll talk here as long as you want,' she said. 'Or, if you wish, you can come inside.'

Grace could see what was happening but couldn't get through. Between her and the driveway to the house was a thicket of thorn bushes. She'd be torn to shreds if she tried to force a way.

Instead, she would have to walk along the path for a further two hundred yards into the trees, then, she figured, double back somehow in order to bring herself to the entrance gates.

But she saw. What she did see didn't make a hatful of sense. Leastways, there was something strange about the scene.

In the moonlight, a good hundred yards or more away, stood the figure she'd been following.

The figure stood at the base of a flat-roofed house. Grace looked up at a second figure. A woman with shoulder-length dark hair.

They seemed to be having a conversation. But it was way too far away for Grace to hear what was being said. She looked hard at the first figure. The moon wasn't all that bright and now some cloud was scudding in front of it, so that the scene went from silvery radiance to deep shadow.

The figure Grace had followed through the wood was a woman. She had a head of long copper-colored hair. When the moon shone at its brightest Grace saw metallic red tints. Awesome hair.

Only the body looked so thin as to be emaciated.

Legs like sticks, Grace told herself. *Thin arms too*. They held the still-silent baby to her chest.

There was some quality about the woman on the driveway that made Grace's skin want to crawl off her bones. Something was wrong about it.

Once, when the moon flickered through the cloud, the figure turned briefly as if to look at Grace.

She recoiled.

That's not a woman . . . that's a dead body. She has no eyes, only empty sockets.

But a dead woman walking?

Surely a trick of the meager light?

And that baby. It never moved once. Never made a sound.

Grace shivered.

She didn't like what she was seeing . . . leastways, she didn't like what her imagination was *telling* her she was seeing.

Corpse of a woman carries dead baby to house in the middle of night.

Snap out of it, Grace Bucklan. You've gone through hell. You're a teenage runaway. You've driven thousands of miles. You've been attacked. You've been forced to go down on a stranger at gunpoint. Now you're out in some god-forsaken canyon alone. You haven't slept properly in days.

No wonder your mind is playing weird stunts on you.

That isn't a dead woman – a dead, naked *woman – you see. It's a woman in distress. Now somehow she's reached this house. The homeowner is talking to her from the roof.*

Telling her to go away?

Driven by the sense of injustice in the world, and an overpowering desire to help someone in need tonight, Grace walked along the woodland path.

She'd do the right thing.

She'd help the half-starved woman and the infant.

Then her conscience would be clear.

April spoke softly to her caller. She knew they were still there below her on the drive.

'It's late . . . I guess it must still be dark. Are you hungry? Thirsty?'

No reply.

'Surely you must be ready to rest after your walk all the way up here?'

April heard the shifting of gravel as her caller moved a foot. She interpreted that as them being tired.

'Why don't you come in for a while? You can rest. Have a cold drink.' She fingered the soft fabric of her negligée. 'There's no hurry to leave, is there?'

Again a movement of small stones beneath feet. She interpreted this in the affirmative. She'd bring her caller into the house. They'd like her home. They'd like *her*. They'd want to stay. She was sure of it.

Her heart surged with happiness.

For a split second she could hear her father's admonishment: 'Now, now, April, you simply don't invite strangers into the house just like that . . .'

You're not as lonely as I am. You don't know what it's like. Lonely people don't even feel the touch of another's hand for so long that they fear they will go mad. Isolation is cancer. Loneliness, the death of spirit.

She patted the top of the wall in excitement. Anxiety, too. She didn't want her caller to retreat into the woods. Clearly they were incredibly shy.

'Just stay there. Please be patient. It will take me a little time to find my way downstairs and open the door. But please stay a while.'

Lifting the front of her negligée with one hand so she didn't trip, she hurried for the doorway that led to the stairs.

In her heart April was certain. After tonight nothing would be the same ever again.

Cody glanced back at Pix. 'What's wrong?'

She stared at him. Her eyes were bright in the moonlight. Her expression looked . . . it looked . . . well, odd. Cody shifted uncomfortably. He'd just climbed onto the fallen trunk of a tree to see if he could get a better view. Perhaps spot the AWOL Grace.

His girlfriend had acted so weird. But then, she'd suffered stress and a half over the last twenty-four hours.

Only now it was little sister's turn.

She stood with her feet apart so the little skirt was stretched tight. Her arms hung down by her sides. Her shoulders were high, though, as if she was tense.

And worse?

It was that stare of hers. She stared right at him.

The moonlight's falling on her . . . she's turning into a werewolf . . .

Nope.

Worse than that.

'Cody?'

'What's wrong? Do you feel ill?'

'I've been thinking . . . I'd like it if you kissed me.'

'*What?*'

'I can't get it out of my head . . . I want you to kiss me.'

'Pix, stop fooling around.' He forced a grin . . . a leg-pull of hers. She'd done plenty of those in the past. 'We're looking for your sister. She might be in trouble.' He jumped down from the log.

'She's just using you, Cody. She wanted you to bring her here just so she could be in the movies. She doesn't really love you. Not the way—'

'Pix.'

'I love you.'

'Pix. Stop fooling.'

But she didn't seem to be fooling.

Not by a long way. She lunged forward, grabbed his head in both hands and yanked it down so her lips slammed against his.

'Pix. No. Stop it.' The words came out in a garble. Her tongue was already straining through his lips into his mouth. ''S not right, Pix. Grace . . .'

'Grace isn't here. Hold me tight, Cody.'

'Nn – ghhh.' Her tongue shot into his mouth again, working with a muscular ferocity against his. Her hands went everywhere. *Everywhere*. Cody couldn't believe it.

Was there madness in the Bucklan family? First Grace, now Pix?

'Pix, you mustn't do that, it's . . . *Pix!*'

She pushed herself forward against him. He felt her small, firm breasts against his midriff. She kissed like a demon. As much fury as passion.

He retreated.

Caught the heel of his cowboy boot on a branch. Fell heavily on his rear.

She pounced.

Trying to unbuckle his belt.

Trying to tug down his zipper.

All the time her mouth clamped on his.

'Pix . . . Pix, stop it!'

He reached up, grabbed her by the shoulders and swung her down so that she slammed back against the forest floor.

Even though he heard the 'Uph!' of her breath knocked from her, still she didn't let up.

He rolled on top of her, gripped her wrists.

That was when she melted beneath him. 'Okay,' she whispered. 'You be on top. It'll be nicer.'

'No, Pix. Listen, I don't want you. I love your sister.'

'But I love *you*, Cody.' A little of the old whiny note returned.

'No, you only think you do.'

'But I can't stop thinking about you. I keep imagining you kissing me. I imagine you—'

'Pix, no. It's wrong.'

'Is not.'

'It is.'

'But I can't get you out of my mind,' she whispered.

'When did all this start?' he asked.

'When we left the pickup.'

He looked at her, astounded. 'You mean you've only started having . . .' He searched for the word. 'Having feelings for me in the last few minutes?'

'Yes.' She nodded, solemn. 'Now I can't stop thinking about you.'

'Oh, for Pete's sake, Pix. You don't fall in love as quickly as that.'

'Love at first sight.'

'You've seen me plenty.'

'Cupid's arrow.'

'Lack of sleep, more like.' Still holding her wrists he knelt up. 'Now, I'm going to let you go. But no weird stuff. Okay?'

She looked up at him with big, gooey eyes. 'Whatever you say, Cody.'

'All right.' Releasing her, he stood up, dusting off his pants as he did so. 'Now you get up onto your feet. Then you're going to follow me as we go look for Grace.'

'Whatever you say, Cody.'

Her meek voice made him uneasy, but at least she was no longer trying to suck the lips off his face.

She held up her hands.

'Help?'

'But no more wrestling me, all right?' He switched on the flashlight. 'Now stick close, d' you hear?'

'I will.' She gave him a shy, girlish smile.

Dear God. This I don't need.

They walked on. In a little while they reached a clearing that revealed a house.

'Sheesh,' Pix breathed. 'If ever there was a haunted house, that's the one.'

In the moonlight Cody could see a figure move cautiously through the open gates and along the driveway. He shook his head, puzzled. 'There's Grace. But what on earth is she doing?'

Pix slipped her hand into his. 'Looks to me as if she's paying a visit to the spook house.'

Grace reached the gates to the drive. They were old and rusted and didn't look as if they were even capable of closing any more. She moved quickly along the driveway in the direction of the house that stood perhaps fifty yards away.

The curve of the driveway meant she lost sight of the front of the house for a few seconds. She walked in deep shadow. The trees reached over her in a way that was nothing less than nightmarish.

What was she getting herself into?

This was trespass now.

Might just get myself shot by a jittery householder.

The half-starved woman with the baby might already be inside. This could be her home.

But it had just looked so odd. How she'd stood there clutching the silent baby to her while the woman on the roof, dressed in nothing but a negligée, had talked.

Had to be something peculiar going on here. Mighty peculiar.

Grace glimpsed the roof of the house above the bushes. It was empty now. Whoever the occupant was had gone down into the main body of the house.

She rounded a bend in the drive, gravel crunching beneath her feet. Her heart was thumping: she was close to finding out exactly what was going on here. The urge to answer the mystery was more powerful than the urge to turn back and find Cody.

She needed closure on this. She had to know that the woman and baby would be safe.

But what if this was her home, and the home of her abuser? Grace might land herself in hot water. If she caught the woman's husband, boyfriend or whatever beating up on her what would the man do to Grace to keep her silent?

Heart pounding, she paused behind the last bush before open ground. There was the lawn in front of her. The house. It seemed to tower above her now. A forbidding structure.

More like a castle than a home.

A castle with ghosts. She shivered.

Do it, Grace. Solve the mystery. If you're satisfied the woman and baby are safe, leave. If not, call the cops.

She peeped over the bush.

Nothing was happening. There was the woman and baby. The woman's copper hair cascaded down her back to below her buttocks.

Those thin dark legs. So stick-like.

Like bones without flesh.

As Grace tried to decide whether to approach the woman or wait there came movement from the bottom story of the house.

A door opened. A large one. It could have led to a basement garage. That was all.

No one appeared to welcome the woman. The door opened and that was that.

For a second the woman with copper hair stood still. She faced the dark opening where the door had been.

Maybe she's afraid to enter?
Wondering who's in there?

The pause didn't last long. The woman with copper hair moved forward to be swallowed by the doorway.

Now Grace was alone in the dark. And she was still none the wiser about what had happened to the woman with the baby in her arms.

What would become of them?

There was no movement, but something *was* happening. Grace heard a thin squeaking. A mechanism, maybe.

Metallic clanking. Not loud but definitely coming from the house. Then a rattle as if a shutter was being lowered.

But still the mystery.

What's happening to the woman and her baby?

Now Grace knew she couldn't turn and walk away.

She was involved now. That meant she must act decisively. A life might have to be saved.

Without hesitating, she ran lightly across the lawn, avoiding the noisy gravel. Her feet whispered on grass.

She was at the doorway.

Then she was inside.

Darkness. She could see nothing but the pale opening of the doorway behind her. Finding a wall, she followed it, running her fingers across its hardness, into the depths of the house.

Chapter Fifty-two

'What did Grace go into the spook house for?'

Cody glanced across at Pix. She stood there in the moonlight. Her arms were folded and a mystified expression creased her face.

'I don't know. She had to have had a reason, I guess.'

'Reason, huh? She's gone crazy, that's reason enough.'

'Come on,' he told her. 'We've got to get her out of there.'

'Somehow.' Her expression showed she didn't like this.

'We've got to do it, Pix. She might be in danger.'

'Yeah, that's what I was thinking.' She shook her head. 'I guess that means *we*'ll be in danger, too.'

'*Pix, come on.*'

'Better not be another guy who wants to put his dick in my mouth. That's really gonna send me over the edge this time.'

He gave her a reassuring smile and held out his hand. 'Don't worry, I'll look after you.'

She looked delighted that he'd offered her his hand. Taking it, she walked with him, keeping up with his brisk pace toward the house.

Spook house. The girl's words came back to him as he looked down on the lonesome place. Yeah, Pix might not be far from the mark at that.

Grace tripped on some object in the dark. Why hadn't the owner of the house turned on any damn lights?

She hit her knee on the floor. Bare concrete. *Ouch. That stuff's pretty unyielding.*

Keeping her lips pressed together she got to her feet. Now she kept her back to the wall as she moved on. This was smooth and slippery, almost a wood texture, but her fingertips felt a myriad of small holes, too.

Just what was this place? It seemed way too big for an underground garage. She heard clanks of metal on metal. The sound didn't echo back as she'd expect in a garage. It died instantly as if something had swallowed the echo.

This smooth material under her fingers, perhaps.

Even as she slid along it she felt the surface turn to fabric. It yielded slightly as if there were a layer of stuffing under it.

Smooth hard walls. Now walls that yielded under fabric to her touch. Who'd fix padding to the inside of their garage? She frowned. If only someone would switch on the lights.

This wasn't just weird.

It was frightening.

All she wanted was to see if the emaciated woman and her baby were safe. Now this had taken a whole more sinister turn.

She was in a strange underground room.

A bunker?

There was total darkness. Yet sounds of activity. Clanks, rattles, scraping sounds. The squeal of a mechanism in need of some lube. And the sounds were swallowed up somehow as soon as they were made.

Her hip knocked against an obstruction. Racks of some kind? Her hands reached out. Touched objects. Files? Books?

Grace realized the racks and the wall made a kind of gully. Quickly she slotted herself in. Crouched down. If the lights came on she might not be seen.

Not straightaway, anyway.

And suddenly it seemed safer to be out of sight.

Chapter Fifty-three

The deep masculine voice boomed out through the darkness. '*Lake . . . Lake. Move up onto the platform. Present yourself. Do it quickly.*' A breathless panting filled the room. It sounded amplified. '*Obey, Lake. You will be punished if you do not hurry.*'

Grace hunkered down between the racks and the wall.

Holy Christ. What kind of place was this? What was that voice?

Whose was that voice!

It thundered from every direction. She looked round. But could see nothing in that absolute dark.

And where were the woman and child?

Shit. She wanted out. Wanted out now. Before—

Before what?

Before something BAD happens.

She didn't even like the smell of this place. Disinfectant odors hung in the air. Those were mingled with something like the smell of stale herbs and onions. A musty unpleasant smell that worked its way into her nostrils. The kind of smell that made you want to go shower.

'*Lake, onto the platform. Present yourself. Hurry!*'

Who's Lake? That bass voice was commanding him to go to a certain place. *A platform?*

And to do what?

Present himself. That's what it sounded like. Present himself for what?

Grace scrunched herself down even further between the shelving and the wall.

Didn't want the lights on now.
Didn't want to be seen.
Because this was a bad place.
A mad place, too.
Something terrible happened here.
Right then she knew: something terrible was going to happen again. Soon . . . real soon.

'Lake . . . Lake, move up onto the platform. Present yourself. Do it quickly.'

The moment Ed Lake heard the words he thought: *All right. Let's roll!*

Knowing that his captor – his Sex Queen – could see him through the nightscope goggles she must wear he moved across the cage in a hunched walk, feeling the sharpened stake beneath the leg of his pants. Its cold, hard shaft pressed against his bare thigh.

Here goes, buddy. No retreat now.

He squirmed onto the platform. He lay flat on his back, hearing it squeak as it began to raise him to the Perspex roof of the cage. Toward the hole that he'd slipped himself through so many times before.

He had to go through with this.

Even though it had been different tonight. He'd heard a lot of movement. Clanking sounds. Rattling. The squeal of a mechanism. A door to the outside had opened nearby. Even though it had been dark he'd fancied he'd caught sight of some dim radiance. He'd felt fresh air come blowing through the bars of his cage.

He'd heard Virginia catch her breath before whispering, 'They're bringing someone new in.'

'But they've never done it like this before?'

'No,' she'd confirmed. 'Must be someone special.'

Then there'd been the smell of onions and spices. A musty smell. Stale. Unpleasant.

'Lake! Present yourself! Hurry . . . Hurry!'
Okay, here goes nothing.
If it works . . . payback time!

If not, he'd be joining the late Marco and Cardinali before you could say, 'RIP.'

He slipped the wooden stool leg from the waistband of his pants. Quickly, he pressed his thumb against the point.

Just checking.

Gotta make sure it goes in sharp end first. And, my God, it's sharp, all right. The barb, too. Wickedly sharp.

Please, Jesus, bless this weapon of vengeance.

For vengeance shall be mine, sayeth the Lord. Vengeance shall be mine.

Ed exulted.

I'm in!

April Vallsarra's body burned with exultation. Tonight, she'd done it all by herself. She hadn't needed Lettie to help her.

Tell the world blindness isn't a handicap!

Tell the sighted they're not all-powerful!

Because I've done it. I've caught one all by myself.

Exultation melded with excitement. Excitement generated lust. White-hot lust that flamed and burned and seared.

Got to have release. Got to let it out!

As she fastened the belt that held the radio-mike transmitter around her slender waist she recapped the stages of her near-miraculous feat. First, she'd moved unerringly downstairs after telling her visitor to wait.

She'd switched off the lights in her father's basement studio, then moved swiftly down the steps with the confidence of a sighted person in brilliant daylight. There, she'd unlocked the padlocks that held the empty transfer cage in place. This she'd wheeled single-handed to the steel roller-door.

If you could have seen me, Lettie. The times we hauled that together. Today I did it by myself. I don't need you anymore.

I'm self-contained.

I need no one to nursemaid me.

After that it had been surprisingly easy. With the open-ended transfer cage close to the roller door she'd pressed the switch to open it. It had scrolled up.

In the darkness her visitor had unwittingly walked forward. Not knowing they were entering the cage.

Not realizing they were entering the trap. Then it had been simplicity itself. She'd pressed the quick-release lever. The cage door had clanged shut, trapping her visitor. By touch, using her bare feet, she'd located the loops on the floor and had quickly snapped the padlocks in place, locking the cage in position so its occupant couldn't tip it up and escape.

Then she'd returned to the roller-door controls and pressed the button. Seconds later, clanking, it had rolled back, into place, sealing the basement studio from the outside world.

Now she had a third prisoner.

She'd done it all by herself.

April wanted to laugh and to spin round and round with her arms out, reveling in the moment.

Relishing her victory over the world of sight.

Instead, she knew she had to keep silent until the microphone was in place. In a second she'd slipped on the headset. Now whenever she spoke the radio mike would carry her voice to the electronic synthesizer that her father had once used to compose his music. Its circuits would transform her voice into one of those deep male movie-trailer voices.

Her captives would believe they were dealing with some thundering giant of a man. Not a slightly built blind girl.

Now she was so horny she could burst.

She would have loved to pleasure herself using her new guest but that would have to wait, until all the formalities had been gone through, when the new guest would be transferred to the third, static cage and conditioned to obey her orders.

No . . . it would have to be Lake tonight. She would make good use of his body.

She switched on the radio mike, issued the order: '*Lake . . . Lake, move up onto the platform . . .*'

She would enjoy his body tonight. She'd make good use of him, as she had before.

She thrilled at the recollection of his male hardness entering her.

Amara

How she'd knelt on the cool Perspex and felt his hot erection jutting proud of the hole in the cage roof to work inside her. Exciting her. Making her shudder with pleasure, until she—

No, don't hurry.
Don't rush this.
Take your time.

Virginia and the new guest – the oh-so-silent one – would hear the sounds of love tonight. *Now isn't that an exciting concept? They hear. Only they do not see.*

Tantalizing, isn't it?
Teasing.
Might make them want to touch themselves.

And what of her new guest? April Vallsarra didn't even know its sex. Not that it mattered. Like many an adventurer before her she'd drunk deeply of many different springs.

By sense of touch alone she moved from the elevated walkway that ran around the basement studio and onto the Perspex roof of the cage. Her body throbbed with anticipation. She hungered for Lake's hard member to push deeply into her.

She felt the hole with its smooth edges in the Perspex. There would be Lake lying just below her now. He'd be anticipating, too. She knew he loved this now as much as she did. She'd felt his tremors of excitement through his cock as he entered her. And felt many times his passionate eruption that flooded her with his liquid warmth.

Oh yes . . . yessss. She couldn't bear to wait another minute.

Kneeling down on the cool roof of the cage, April reached down, clasped the hem of her negligée and raised it up to her hips.

When she spoke, her voice came back to her in a boom: '*Lake, present yourself.*'

She went down.

Ed Lake heard the command.

'*Lake, present yourself.*'

Above him a weight settled, slightly flexing the Perspex.

What if she reached down to touch his cock with her fingers first? Then she'd feel the wooden stool leg. She'd know what he planned.

His heart hammered in his chest as he lay there, gripping the pointed shaft in his hand.

Because it was too long to push straight up and his own body was still partly in the way he'd have to push at an angle. He clenched his fists around the wooden shaft, ready to force every ounce of his strength into the upward thrust, through the hole in the Perspex and on into the most intimate part of her body.

'Lake. Present yourself. That is an order.'

I hear and obey, oh mighty one!

He drove the point up through the hole. Thrust as hard as he could.

Then flinched at the sound of the deafening scream.

Chapter Fifty-four

Jesus H. Christ! What's that?

Grace smacked her palms to her ears. That screaming . . . hell, it sounded like sheet metal being torn in two.

Her eyes opened wide. But she could see nothing in this darkness. It was black as damnation down here. Not a glimmer of light.

And the place shook with screams.

Deep male ones.

Only they were weird.

There was no single direction to them. Like being in a cinema with surround-sound. The yells came from everywhere at once . . . they were distorted, too, with a kind of electronic overdrive that powered them to a nerve-stripping intensity.

Madhouse.

Freaking madhouse.

Now Grace really did want out.

Had a burning need to bug out of the house. A burning need to run outside and hide in the cool silence until her ears stopped ringing.

'*Aaaaa – hhh – gugh.*' Skull-cracking decibels. '*Lake . . . why? Why?! Uhhhgh!*'

Now Grace heard rushing sounds. The same you get when someone breathes into a microphone. Snapping and deep *umph* sounds, too. A mike being knocked.

Then came the sound of amplified weeping. Someone was in pain. In real pain that Grace couldn't even begin to imagine.

Another voice rang out in the darkness. 'You deserved that, you bitch!'

'*Lake. I loved you.*'

'Yeah, loved me enough to keep me in this stinking cage. Loved me enough to put me in fear for my life every single minute of the damn day . . . that's what I call tough love.'

A third voice; this one female: 'Ed. Can you reach her? Can you find a key?'

'I've got her hooked, Virginia. Got her damn well hooked. All I have to do is twist the shaft a little.'

'*Lake, no. Please!*'

'What's it like to be on the receiving end, huh?'

'*Lake, pleee—*'

Grace cringed as the voice rose into a scream.

The one called Lake must have twisted the shaft and caused hurt. Whatever that involved.

'*Uu . . . ugh!*'

'You took us for a pair of saps,' Lake said. He sounded triumphant. 'We know that you're a woman. We know that you altered your voice with some gizmo.'

Grace had to get away from the madhouse. She started crawling along the floor on her hands and knees.

'*Lake, please! I'm hurt real bad . . .*'

The female voice pitched in: 'And serves you right. Suffer, you bitch!'

Grace wanted to curl into a ball until the screaming stopped. Only by now she thought it never would.

Gotta get out . . .

Gotta get away . . .

Must be a door somewhere near.

She felt along the wall, fingers hunting for an exit . . . a door . . . even a window . . .

What's that?

Her fingers found something.

Hard. Oblong. Fixed to the wall. Size of a peppermint. Her mind swam dizzily.

It's a . . .

. . . Light switch . . .

Not being able to see in the darkness, Ed Lake could still feel.

He lay on his back on the platform and hung on to the harpoon he'd made from the stool leg.

Fish wriggled.

Fish squirmed.

But let go?

Never!

No, sirree.

He'd caught her. He'd felt the point of the stake punch through skin deep into flesh. In his mind's eye he saw how it was. He was lying flat on the platform, she was directly above him, just inches away on the other side of the Perspex roof panel. The two people were connected by the stake passing through the hole into her— Well . . . go figure.

What made it difficult now was the blood. It ran hot down the wooden shaft.

Blood's slippery stuff, Ed thought, surprised. It made it hard to grip onto the shaft. What was more, his Sex Queen was writhing and screaming. One hard tug and she could pull the slippery thing from his hands.

Then what?

She'd order her accomplice to slit his and Virginia's throats.

Or maybe she'd just abandon them there. Leave the two of them to die of thirst in the dark.

And where was the accomplice?

Maybe she'd panicked when she saw the Sex Queen suddenly convulse in agony.

Ed Lake knew he must hang on to this bloody pole, slippery as it was. Sex Queen could have the keys to the cage. They could bargain. Her life for their freedom.

'Hang on in there, Ed!' That was Virginia shouting encouragement. 'And while you're at it, hurt the bitch!'

* * *

Even in darkness, Amara saw.
Amara waited . . .

April Vallsarra writhed in agony. The pain was overwhelming. She could hardly form two words in a row before the sheer *hurt* overwhelmed her thought process. Then she howled in pain.

At first, the synthesizer returned her screams to her in a deep bass roar.

Then the microphone headset was thrown clear of her by the convulsions. Instantly, her cries of pain became a high shriek.

But down through the blazing red inferno that was her agony, one word roared through her head.

Revenge.

Damned if you do, damned if you don't.

Grace wrestled with the problem. If she switched on the lights she'd be able to see. But then the people doing the shouting and the terrifying screaming would be able to see *her*.

Then maybe it would be the turn for one Grace Bucklan to do all the screaming.

Shit to that, she thought.

But if I switch on the lights, then run for the door, maybe they'll never catch me? Besides, they sound to be too busy doing stuff, freaky stuff, *to one another. Just listen to that woman howl. Sounds as if she's making out with a branding iron.*

And if I stay hiding in the dark here they're going to find me sooner or later.

What about the woman and her baby?

Uh . . . solve that one when you get to it.

Still keeping her finger on the light switch, she levered herself to her feet. When that light came on she wanted to be running hard.

Away from this madhouse. Back to Cody.

She took a deep breath. *Here goes.*

Grace flicked the light switch.

Still lying on the platform, still gripping the slippery shaft, still praying for a miracle, Ed Lake blinked in surprise as the light came on.

He looked at his hands.

Somehow he was wearing crimson gloves.

Ugh . . . only they weren't gloves.

Contorted with agony, April Vallsarra gulped down lungfuls of air, trying to suppress the pain.

Blind, she didn't see the light.

Grace raised her hands to shield her eyes. The strip lights were dazzling.

She'd meant to run.

Run like lubed lightning for the door.

But she didn't.

Couldn't.

What she saw fixed her rigidly to that square yard of concrete.

She looked at the scene that could have come from a carnival for the damned. In the harsh light were four cages. Three were the size of pickup trucks. One was a smaller wheeled cage.

But Grace's gaze was drawn to the cage nearest her.

Now that was weird.

That was a tableau as bizarre as it was terrible.

A young guy dressed in pants, shirt and with no shoes lay on a platform just below the underside of the cage roof. On the cage roof knelt a beautiful woman dressed in nothing but a flimsy negligée – the same woman Grace had seen on the roof of the house.

She was kneeling with her face down, almost touching the roof that was made out of glass. She was writhing, her two hands gripping a dark stick that protruded from the guy's hands below into her throat.

A splash of ice shivers crashed over Grace's body.

Dear God . . .

She saw what was happening now.

The guy had stabbed the woman in the neck with some kind of spike. The woman couldn't drag herself off the point. She was caught. Bleeding profusely.

Blood ran down the spike, over the guy's hands, dripped down onto the cage floor.

Gross-out . . . she must have been in agony.

Must be dying, too.

Holy shit!

Ed Lake stared up at what he'd done.

Now, in that brilliant electric light, he could see the damage. And what exactly had been damaged.

It wasn't as he'd thought.

She hadn't sat on the hole this time to receive his cock into her. No. Instead, she'd been going down on him when he'd stabbed upward in the dark with his homemade harpoon. The point had gone into her throat just below her jaw.

Gone in deep enough for the barb to hook.

She was going nowhere now.

No escape.

But, Jesus, look at all that blood.

The red stuff gushed from her.

Wet his hands, slicked his chest, pooled on the raised platform. For the first time he got a good close look at his Sex Queen as she knelt above him on the Perspex. He was looking through a rose-tinted smear of blood on the transparent material. But he saw enough.

She was around thirty. Shoulder-length dark hair. Slim. Wore a negligée. Its transparency permitted him a glimpse of curved orbs of breasts tipped by dark nipples . . .

But no nightscope goggles?

'Ed . . . Ed . . .' Virginia called to him. 'Ed. She can't see you . . . she's blind!'

Blind?

Holy moly. So that's how she moved through the darkness.

The Sex Queen was weakening. The microphone headset that piped her voice through the synthesizer had slipped off to lie on the glass roof of the cage. She still cried out but the noise was softening to a moan.

So when the next scream came, Ed was startled by its power.

It also came from another part of the room.
Virginia?
No.
Not from her.
Still holding on to the wooden shaft, he twisted his head. There, outside the cage, was a girl in her late teens.
Who the hell was she?
But there was no time to worry about identities. The girl screamed again. The scream was pure terror. She was pointing, too.
But not at the skewered blind woman.
At something else entirely.

Chapter Fifty-five

Just when it seemed as if it couldn't get any worse, it did just that.

Grace had watched the guy holding the blind woman down in a kneeling position. The spike he held driven deep into the woman's throat. Harpooned.

Sickened by the scene, Grace wrenched her gaze from it.

Only to see something else.

Something far worse.

For a second she'd stared uncomprehending at the figure in the smaller cage, the one nearest the steel roller-door. It was the woman she'd followed through the woods.

Now she stood there in the center of the cage. A dark emaciated body. Long copper hair.

She stood almost casually, as if her surroundings didn't faze her.

Then Grace realized why.

She's dead.

Grace stared at the corpse standing there, motionless. Her gaze swept over the cadaver. It was naked. Ancient-looking. Its breasts had shriveled. Round the neck the flesh was wrinkled, then further down the chest it became smooth. For some reason it reminded Grace of melon skin.

A melon-skin torso; a beef-jerky neck? *Gross.*

Then, framed by beautiful copper hair that glinted in the light, was the most hideous face . . .

Little more than a skull, its lips had shrunk to expose the teeth.

There were no eyes in the head. Where they should have been were empty sockets that plunged twin pits of darkness deep into the head. Across the corpse's stomach was a long gash that had been crudely stitched.

Grace's own skin suddenly felt as if it wanted to crawl off her back. Her stomach heaved. Her knees went weak.

Hanging from one claw hand was a dead baby. Held by one leg, it swung gently. Apart from that motion the figure didn't move.

Grace had seen things like this in museums. In history books. On TV.

She was looking at a mummy.

An ancient Egyptian mummy that had been stripped of its bandages.

But why the baby?
Why here?
Why now?
In this madhouse.

She realized the guy lying on the platform and the girl in the adjoining cage were staring at the mummy too. Trying to work out in their heads what was happening.

They seemed to guess. Both wore expressions of disgust mingled with horror.

I wanna go now.
I wanna run from this place. Never look back.
This is a place that should be burned to the ground and the earth sown with salt. That's what you do with haunted houses, isn't it? That's the Biblical way to deal with evil places.

Silence settled onto the big room.

All Grace could hear were soft moans from the wounded woman on top of the cage who'd grown feeble now from the blood loss.

It was the thing in the third cage that had gotten everyone's attention.

It was during this pregnant silence that *it* moved.

The mummy slowly raised its face, as if those eyeless sockets could gaze up at the lights in the ceiling.

Slowly the head lowered. Rotated left. Rotated right.

Looking at its surroundings.

It uncurled its fingers. The baby fell with a thud to the concrete floor.

In no hurry, it moved.

Dear God. The mummy *walked*.

It crossed the cage, long tresses curling down its back, bouncing softly as if they moved with a life of their own. It stopped. Reached out slowly. Fingertips brushed the bars of the cage. The mouth parted slightly as if it said something to itself.

Grace moved with her back pressed to the wall. She'd get past the caged mummy, then race for the roller-door. She'd heard it clank as it rolled down. She knew she could find the control that opened it.

Then she'd be away from here.

She wouldn't stop running until—

'Please help us.'

Grace's head jerked back. The girl in the second cage was speaking to her.

'We've been held here . . . we've been prisoners. Find a key to unlock the cages.'

The man nodded furiously. 'Please help. We're dead if we don't get out of here.'

'But . . .' Grace pointed at the mummy that was running a claw finger down the bar of the cage.

'Don't worry about that.' The woman talked quickly. 'It's in a cage – it can't hurt you.'

'But it's dead . . . *it's dead.*'

Only she saw the dead thing move. Saw the copper hair hanging lustrously down from the skull and on down its back. She saw dead, hard flesh that was beef-jerky brown.

Saw holes in the torso.

Bullet holes?

'Please help us!' The guy let go of the spike. Bloodstained, he slithered from where he'd been sandwiched between the platform and the glass roof of the cage and let himself down to the concrete floor. The blind woman flopped down onto the cage roof. Lay still.

The guy reached out a bloody hand through the bars of the cage toward Grace. She looked in horror at the slick fingers, the drips of crimson forming on his fingertips.

'Help us.' His eyes were huge in his head. 'Help us . . . Hey! Where are you going? Don't leave us here. *Please don't leave us . . .*'

Chapter Fifty-six

Grace ran past the cages. She gave the one containing the mummy as wide a berth as possible.

The bloodstained man shouted, 'Where are you going? You can't leave us here . . . we're dead if you go.'

'Come back,' called the woman in the second cage. 'Please!'

Grace ran to a shelf on which stood a metal box. 'I'm not leaving,' she panted. 'I'm looking for tools. I'll need something to break open the cages.'

The woman in the second cage reached through the bars to grip one of the pair of padlocks that sealed the doors. 'These are tungsten. You'd need dynamite to smash them. See if you can find a key.'

'A key? Where?'

The guy pitched in. 'There's gotta be keys somewhere nearby. Look for them.'

'But they could be anywhere in the house.' Grace shrugged. 'It'd be like looking for a needle in a—'

The woman jerked her head at the mummy. 'The padlocks on that one were unlocked sometime in the last half-hour . . . the keys must be close by.'

Grace ran round the room, looking at the walls for a hook. Those elusive keys might be dangling nearby. Or were they slipped into a drawer in the desk that was just around the corner? Did the harpooned woman still have them?

Unlikely. *Sure as hell don't have pockets in a flimsy negligée.*

Even so, Grace craned her head to look at the blind woman. She wasn't moving. Her lips had turned blue and her whole body was a glistening mass of blood.

She turned again, searching through shelves. Dozens of shelves. In seconds she was dizzy with the exertion. Blundering past the cage that held the guy she decided to start her search again at the entrance to this chamber of horrors.

The guy gripped the bars of the cage, shouting encouragement.

Breathless, her head spinning, Grace ran down the other side of the cages, thinking only about the key that must be somewhere nearby.

Then something appeared to block her path.

She stopped, blinked. Then screamed.

It was a thin, dark arm.

Hell and damnation!

The mummy had lunged out at her. She'd been focused on finding the key; she'd almost forgotten the monstrosity in the cage. Only now it had suddenly got mobile. Its fingers slashed through the air, reaching out, flexing, trying to grasp her.

Grace screamed again, stumbled back as the fingers swiped down, catching the material of her T-shirt. She looked down – the thing's sharp nails had slashed four vents in the cotton. She glimpsed her own skin.

And, God, that hurts. The monster has scratched me.

Don't let it come close again. Don't!

As the mummy lashed out at her once more, Grace flung herself back against the wall.

'Keep your distance from it,' called the woman in the second cage. 'It can't reach you if you keep away from it.'

Damn right.

I'm not going near that thing again.

Grace stumbled to the far end of the room, her heart thumping hard in her chest. Dazed, she found herself hitting the steel roller-door. The crash reverberated in her head. Taking a deep breath, she looked for what must be there.

And there it is.

Come to momma.

Set in an oblong panel beside the door were buttons marked *Up* and *Down*. With her balled fist she pounded *Up*. Immediately, she heard the hum of an electric motor. With a rattling sound the roller-door began to scroll upward. But it was slow . . . too slow.

She willed it to move faster.

Inch by inch it rose.

But at last moonlight spilled between the bottom slat of the door and the concrete floor. A cool breeze stroked her ankles.

I could leave, she told herself in surprise. *I don't have to help these people. I don't have to stay in this place with the dead creature with copper hair and its dead baby. I could slip through the gap between the door and floor now. Then I could run.*

I could leave this chamber of horrors. Never look back.

But . . .

Conscience. She knew she'd have the fates of the two people lying heavily on her for the rest of her life if she ran out now.

Had to help.

Had to.

She backed away from the door, her gaze searching the wall as she did so.

Got 'em!

There by the door was something like a coat hook. Hanging from it was a large steel ring that held a dozen or more keys.

She glanced back at the guy and the girl in the cages. They weren't saying anything. But they were staring hard at her. Perhaps fearing that she would simply run out through the now-open doorway and into the night, never to be seen again.

Instead, she grabbed the key ring.

This time she moved past the mummy's cage with caution, walking with her back to the wall and facing the emaciated creature behind the bars.

Uh, but now that's bad . . . that's really bad.

As Grace walked the mummy rotated its head. It had no eyes, but Grace knew the thing was tracking her. Watching.

In case she got too close again. Got within striking distance of those raking fingernails. The mummy's upper lip curled back. The thing was snarling at her.

'Virginia,' the guy cried, 'she's got the keys.'

'Great,' the one he'd called Virginia breathed. 'But get us out of here real quick, huh? Something tells me time might be running out.'

Grace advanced on the guy's cage. He gave her a winning smile. 'Thank you. You are an angel.' He moved to the cage door as if ready to run the moment she released the padlocks. 'My name's Ed, by the way. My roomie's called Virginia . . . oh, thank you, thank you . . .'

He beamed with such gratitude that Grace felt herself blushing.

'My name's Grace,' she said, studying the keys. 'It looks as if you've got yourself into a situation here?'

'A situation and a half . . .' He nodded at the key ring. 'It's probably one of the smaller ones. Something like a Yale.'

'Make it quick.' Virginia pulled the blanket round her, looking suddenly cold. 'I don't think our new neighbor's gonna be patient for long.'

But which key?

Now that she had them in her hands there looked to be nearer two dozen. The key for the padlocks might not even be in this bunch.

'Try one at random,' Ed suggested. He flashed her a grin. 'Process of elimination.'

Grace tried one with a green fob.

'No go,' she said. 'Doesn't even go in.'

'Okay, go to the next.'

Her hands were shaking. She'd grip a key. Then the thing would slip from her fingers, clinking around the ring.

Got a grip, then tried it in the lock.

'It goes in. But I can't turn it.'

'Must be getting close,' Ed encouraged.

'Hurry it up, guys.' Virginia sounded worried. 'The new girl's making a move.'

Grace started back.

'Don't worry,' Ed told her. 'Whatever the damn thing is it's staying put. It can't bust out of the cage. It's—'

Clang!

The noise was terrific. The sound of a hard object slamming into metal.

All three whirled round. The mummy had moved across its cage. With the flat of its hand it struck the cage door as if to knock it open. The whole cage shook with each blow.

'Don't worry,' Ed shouted. 'It'll hold . . . it'll hold.'

Grace saw him turn back to her. Fix her with his stare. In a calm voice he said. 'Just work through the keys, Grace. It'll be there, trust me.'

Her hands shook so much that when she tried the next key the entire bunch slipped from her perspiring fingers to the floor.

Take your time, she told herself. *Concentrate. Don't panic. You can do this. You can really do this.*

She selected a key with a yellow plastic grip.

Now, nice and easy does it. Slip the key into the padlock.

'This is it!' The words burst from her lips. The key turned easily.

She pulled open the padlock hasp and slipped it from the steel loops that secured the cage door.

'Well done,' Ed told her. 'One down, one to go.' He smiled. 'Knew you could do it, Grace.'

Grace smiled, encouraged. 'Piece of cake.'

Then she did the wrong thing.

She glanced across at the mummy. Her insides turned to water as she watched the creature extend one of its beef-jerky paws through the cage bars. Then, without any hurry, without any fuss the fingers crept around one of the pair of padlocks.

The hand tightened into a balled fist around the tungsten padlock. For a second the hand quivered as the monster applied pressure, then—

Crack!

The padlock snapped like it was made from pastry.

Slowly the creature uncurled its fingers, allowing the destroyed padlock to fall to the concrete floor.

Then it paused.

Grace looked into the twin pits of darkness in the thing's face.

And she knew.

That monster's watching me. It's thinking, 'I'm coming for you now . . . I'm going to finish what I started . . .' Grace felt the tingle on the skin of her stomach where the monster had slashed her with its razor nails. *Gonna be more of the same soon. Slashing, scratching, ripping.*

'Grace.' Ed spoke firmly. 'Snap out of it.'

'Uh?'

'You've got to unlock the padlocks.'

As if awakening from a dream she shook her head. Then she selected another key. Tried it.

'Not the right one,' she said.

'You can do this, Grace. We trust you.'

She tried another.

And another.

No luck . . . no goddamn luck.

Her heart began to hammer again. Her breathing quickened.

Beads of perspiration slid down the small of her back.

Next up. A key with a white plastic grip.

She tried it.

Then stood there, blinking. Not believing what had happened.

'Way to go, girl!' Ed was jubilant. 'You've done it.'

He reached through the bars, worked out the hasp, then flung the padlock to one side. He pushed open the cage door. Free at last.

He breathed deeply as if the air outside the cage was so much sweeter.

'Hey, guys . . .' Virginia sounded nervous. 'You won't forget me, will you?'

Grace turned to see the mummy reach through the cage door again. It snapped off the second – and final – padlock that kept it prisoner.

Slowly it pushed open the door.

'What the hell's going on here?'

Grace turned sharply when she heard the familiar voice.

'Pix?'

'What's with the cages?'

'Pix, get out of here . . . run!'

Grace waved her sister back as she walked through the doorway. She saw Cody at the girl's side.

'Both of you . . . run! Get away from here!'

Cody started to walk toward her. 'What's the matter, Grace? What's going on here? You—'

Then the thing leaped. Its copper hair flared out behind it as if the monster had somehow caught fire.

Then it was on Cody. Pix screamed.

Grace ran to help. Horror-struck, she saw the thing knock him flat to the ground. Then it was crouching on his chest, its bare, shrivelled rump pressing on his stomach as it gnawed at him.

'Leave him . . . let go!' Grace shouted at the creature.

For all the good *that* did.

Grace saw its teeth gnawing.

Cody screamed. His arms flew out to either side, spasming.

Then came a fountain of blood from his throat.

His body convulsed, twitched, then lay still. Eyes staring at the ceiling.

'Cody!' Pix screamed. She hurled herself onto the mummy, punching, clawing.

The creature sprang to its feet, turning as it did so. The savage movement threw Pix clear across the concrete floor. Dazed, she went sprawling.

'Bitch! Murdering bitch!' Grace yelled.

'Grace,' Virginia warned. 'Don't go near it! Keep away!'

Ed moved so the cage was between him and the mummy. 'Grace, come this way round . . . don't let it spring at you.'

'I've got to help my sister.'

By this time, Pix had managed to sit up. She looked groggy from the blow.

'Hey, don't forget *me*, guys,' Virginia pleaded.

Grace remembered the keys in her hand. She threw them through the bars of the cage. Virginia picked them up.

Ed jerked his head toward the mummy. 'I wouldn't be in a hurry to get out just yet, Virginia.'

'Don't worry . . . I'm going to bide my time.'

Grace cast a despairing look at Cody. He lay in a growing pool of blood.

He was my first love . . . he was the first man I'd slept with . . . now this . . .

Pix groaned. 'Oh, my head hurts.'

The mummy turned. It must have noticed Pix move.

In a weird way . . . almost gliding . . . it crossed the concrete toward her. Even as it moved it altered its posture. Tipping its top half-forward, hand coming up . . . this was attack mode . . . it was going in for the next kill.

'Pix! Run!'

'Run? Can't even stand . . . my head.'

With a yell Ed charged. Intercepting the mummy, he grabbed it by the waist, lifted it from the floor with it facing him.

Grace watched in disbelief. It looked almost as if he was dancing with the creature. The mummy opened its mouth . . . its teeth dripped crimson. Then it plunged its head downward so fast that its copper hair rippled in the air behind it.

In a few gnawing bites, it had torn most of Ed's face off.

But even with nothing remaining of his visage but a bloody mass, he still moved with the mummy. Waltzing it across the floor toward a cage with an open door.

Grace saw Virginia move fast. With lightning dexterity, she worked through the keys on the ring. In ten seconds she had both padlocks open.

Then the cage door crashed open.

Not stopping to look back, she ran.

Grace glimpsed her face, wild with terror, looming close to her own. Then she was gone through the doorway and out into the night.

'Help me, Grace . . . my legs don't feel right.'

But Grace had to see what happened to Ed. He'd sacrificed himself to save them.

Ed had managed to carry the mummy as far as the cage but didn't have the strength to push it in. He pressed it as hard as he could against the bars. They could have been a pair of lovers necking against a wall. He pressed the creature back hard. The thing held Ed's head in both its hands while pushing its face against what was left of his in a grotesque parody of kissing.

But this was gnawing not smooching. Teeth ripped. Crushed. Tore.

Grace heard the ripping of muscles and the cracking of facial bone.

Blood pattered down to the concrete, pooling in a slick mass that reflected the lights above.

Then Ed's legs lost their strength. A moment later his arms dropped by his sides.

Still gnawing at his face, the mummy didn't let him go as he slowly folded down to the floor.

'Come on!' Grace pulled Pix to her feet. Then, gripping her hand so hard that the girl cried out in pain, she dragged her outside.

Then she ran.

She didn't stop running until they were both back at the pickup.

When she started the motor Pix managed to rouse herself groggily. 'Where now . . .'

'Home,' Grace panted. 'We're damn well going home.'

Chapter Fifty-seven

While Tag drove, Susan sat beside him. Geoffrey lay snug and asleep in his baby seat in the back of the car. The journal rested lightly on her lap. Susan skimmed it by flashlight, looking for the first mention of Amara.

She was halfway through the journal before she noticed the words 'sarcophagus' and 'mummiform'.

'Here we go,' she said. And began to read: '"...The mummy beneath him. A portion of its head was visible. I saw its red hair, its eyeless sockets; I had the impression, for a moment, that it was kissing the dead man's neck."'

'Charming,' Tag said.

'"I raised the man's head. The mummy's head also lifted and I realized its teeth were buried in his throat."'

'Same m.o.,' Tag commented.

Susan read silently for a while. '"The bride of Set,"' she said finally. And then: '"She will arise from the dead to seek after the blood of her slayers."' She read more in silence. 'Callahan wants to take her out of the tomb.'

'That was his first mistake.'

'"You have broken the seal of Osiris guarding the doorway. Its magic is destroyed. Without it, Amara will walk the night." The seal. Remember the gold disks on the coffin? Same idea. We had written instructions left by Callahan. They said that on no account should we tamper with them, but they were already broken when the coffin was delivered. Without the seals, she walks the night.'

'Pretty damned hard to swallow, Susan.'

'Your own police officers claim she killed these people.'

'I just can't believe that someone who's been dead for almost four thousand years – or for four seconds, come to that – can be walking around murdering everyone in sight. I mean, can you?'

'I don't know.'

Tag flicked his turn signal. Its quiet clicking was the only sound in the car as he steered up a long, curving off-ramp.

'On the other hand,' he said. 'Damn. On the other hand, there wasn't any evidence at all of any human presence. And plenty to support the idea that Gonzalez and Beckerman were attacked by the goddamn mummy. Gonzalez obviously shot it. His fingernail scrapings . . . I mean, there are certainly a few ways to explain all that. We've been through them. But everything falls neatly into place if you accept the mummy as perpetrator.'

'Callahan's death, too.'

Tag nodded. 'The business about the dogs always did sound suspicious. Where was the .22 he used to shoot them? I think the Burlingdale boys just jumped to the obvious conclusion, and didn't worry about the discrepancies when they closed the case.'

'But Callahan *knew* about Amara.'

'Maybe he didn't know the seals were broken. Or maybe he broke them himself for some reason.'

'A form of suicide?'

'Could be. He was old, his health failing, his wife recently killed. Maybe he just wanted to end it all.' Tag shrugged. 'Or maybe he had a different reason for breaking the seals. Could've done it, I suppose, to stick Amara on the robbers.'

'That could be it. Something sure made them leave in a hurry – and empty-handed.'

She shone the flashlight onto the journal and flipped through a few more pages. Then the car turned a corner. Spinning red and blue lights flashed on her face, and she saw four police cars on the road ahead. They were double-parked, blocking half the street. A coroner's van sat in the driveway of a house on the left, its rear doors open. Another van, this one marked EYEWITNESS NEWS, blocked a driveway across the street.

Susan saw people everywhere: in clusters on the sidewalk; a couple strolling directly in front of the house, glancing toward it as if only casually interested; others peering out of windows and doorways of nearby houses.

At this time of night, she told herself. It was the early hours of the morning but the lure of a crime story had drawn enough people out of their houses to fill the sidewalks like it was the middle of the afternoon.

On a lawn, somebody was being interviewed by a TV newsman. The camera lights lit the scene vividly.

'Looks like Vasquez,' Tag said. He drove slowly past the patrol cars and parked.

They climbed from the car. Geoffrey stirred in Susan's arms as she eased him from his baby seat. The lights flashed against his shut eyes. She pulled the comforter so it hung over his face.

They were halfway up the driveway when a voice called, 'Miss Connors! Susan Connors!'

'Oh damn,' she muttered.

Tag grinned. 'You're already a celebrity.'

A short, curly-haired man hurried toward her, followed by a man with a minicam on his shoulder, another with a glaring light.

'Lenny Farrel, *Eyewitness News*.'

'Yes, I remember.'

'Miss Connors, are tonight's killings related to the recent disappearance of the mummy from the Charles Ward Museum?'

'There appears to be a connection. That's why I'm here.'

'Did the police request your presence?'

'Yes.'

'What would be the nature of the connection?'

'No comment.'

'We've heard speculation that tonight's killings were committed by someone resembling the missing mummy, Amara. Do you give credence to such speculation?'

'Do you?'

'According to a reliable source, a patrolman reported over the air from his radio car that he confronted a suspect near the crime scene and that said suspect conformed to descriptions of the mummy.'

'I wouldn't know about that. Now, if you'll excuse me.'

'Before you go, Miss Connors, would you care to elaborate on your role with—'

'Excuse us,' Tag said, stepping between the newsman and Susan. With an arm around her shoulders, he led her away.

They entered the house. Vasquez followed them inside and shut the door. Susan glimpsed several men near a woman's body. She looked away.

'What'd you tell that s.o.b.?' Vasquez asked.

'Nothing. He seemed to know plenty, though.'

'Kraus spilled his guts over the radio. Every bastard in town with a police scanner thinks we've got a homicidal mummy on the loose. The mayor's gonna go crazy.'

'What do you think?' Susan asked.

'I think we'd better get our hands on a suspect fast and it better not be a goddamn zombie.' He looked around. 'Kraus, haul it over here.'

A thin, gray-faced policeman hoisted himself from a sofa. He came across the room, squinting through the smoke of a cigarette pinched between his lips. As he reached the group, he took the cigarette from his mouth. 'Yessir.'

'Kraus, this is Susan Connors from the museum. You want to tell her what you saw?'

'I don't know what I saw.'

Vasquez's eyes narrowed. 'Give it your best shot.'

Kraus dragged on his cigarette. 'I think it was the mummy.'

'We'll be the judge of that,' Vasquez said. 'Describe it.'

'Well . . .' He sighed, blowing smoke out his nose. The skin round his eyes was red, sore-looking. 'I pursued the suspect into the alley. I'd say it was a female, five foot four, red-haired. Long, right down her back. Reached her legs. Very thin, like a . . . like a pile of bones.' His shaking hand poked the cigarette back between his lips. He stared at the bundle in Susan's arms. His right cheek began to twitch.

'Tell her about the eyes.'

'Didn't have any. Just . . . empty sockets. I saw right into her head. Like the head was empty . . . just a shell, you know?'

'What else?'

'Well, there were these holes. In her chest and back. But no blood or anything. They looked like bullet holes. Some of them did. She looked as if she'd been stitched up across here.' He ran his finger across his belly. 'Clumsy-looking job of it someone'd done, too.'

'What was she wearing?'

'Nothing.'

'Nothing at all?'

'She was naked.'

'What else?'

Kraus shrugged. His stare was still fixed on Geoffrey. 'Is . . . is that a baby you've got there?'

Susan nodded.

'Christ, that isn't . . . Not the one *she* had?'

Susan frowned, confused.

'The suspect was carrying a baby,' Vasquez explained. 'The McLeash child. We had three fatalities at their place. Baby-sitter, her boyfriend, and a kid. The baby's missing. Apparently, our suspect grabbed her.'

'Killed her,' Kraus said.

Susan felt sick. She took deep breaths, trying to control her sudden dizziness and nausea.

'Okay, Kraus. Tell her what happened after you confronted the suspect.'

He tapped a length of ash into his open palm. The palm was shiny with sweat. 'Well . . . it ran up the alley. South. With the dead baby. Brown went in pursuit, and I returned to the car to call for backup.'

'And made a fine botch of it.'

'Yessir,' he said. The ash turned muddy in his wet hand.

'Where's this Brown?' Susan asked.

'Someone knocked him cold. Probably the perp. The doc says we won't be able to talk to him until the morning.'

'And there's no sign of the mummy now?'

'We've given the alley a search. Our men came up with zip. Right now my men are combing the field by the museum. The alley led right to it. Maybe they'll come up with something.'

Chapter Fifty-eight

Amara held the baby by one arm, dangling it at her side, its feet swinging so close to the ground that they caught the dirt every now and again, raising a puff of dust. Moonlight cascaded down.

Once Amara stopped in one of the silver beams to gaze up at the moon. Her shining hair fell back from her head, cascading down her back. Her eyeless sockets admitted the lunar radiance to her empty skull. Her lips peeled back from the teeth in a silent snarl.

A wild dog howled somewhere in the distance.

Amara stayed, allowing the moonlight to bathe her face. Then she walked on.

After a little while the canyon ended. It opened out into fields. Beyond the fields lights burned in streets. She walked faster; sometimes during her progress through the undergrowth, bushes tugged at the baby. Each time, she kept walking. The baby pulled free.

She joined a trackway that ran through the fields.

She wasn't far away now. She could sense it.

Felt its pull.

Amara walked faster.

Soon.

Chapter Fifty-nine

'Momma's gonna kill me,' Mable said from the backseat. They were her first words in nearly fifteen minutes.

'She doesn't have to know,' Imad told her.

'She's gonna know. That was her best knife. She's gonna kill me.'

'I'll buy her a new one.'

'Ain't the same.'

'A knife is a knife.'

'This knife ain't.'

'Oh?'

'John Wayne gave it her.'

Imad glanced at her in the rearview mirror. 'John Wayne? Really?'

'Back in 1958. She won it as a prize and John Wayne presented it.'

'That's what she told you?'

'Sure – don't you believe it?'

'It's not for me to believe or disbelieve.'

'So she's gonna kill me. It was a genuine Bowie knife like cowboys use.'

'Mable, whatever kind of knife it was, I was not about to let you bring it along.'

'Think I'd stab you?'

'It did, indeed, cross my mind.'

'You're my friend, Imad.'

'Well, thank you.'

'Even if you do call me names and say I stink and won't let me sit in front with you *and* hit me.'

'I'm sorry about that.'

'I don't call you names.'

'I'm aware of that.'

'Or say you stink.'

'I do not stink. I've always been particularly fastidious about personal hygiene. I expect others to be equally fastidious.'

'Huh?'

'I'll teach you, Mable.'

For a few moments there was silence. Imad took his foot off the gas, slowing as they approached the gate. The car's lights shone against the tall ironwork.

'Imad?'

'Yes.'

'How come you're being nice to me?'

'So you'll allow me . . . now, how do you put it? Allow me to prong you.'

She snorted. 'That ain't the reason. How come? Nobody's ever nice to me. How come you are?'

He shrugged. 'To atone for my sins, perhaps.'

'You're a sinner?'

'Indeed I am.'

'You a Catholic?'

'No.'

'Good thing. My momma, she's against 'em.' Mable leaned forward in the rear seat. 'You won't be Jewish, then?'

'No, I am not.'

'Mohammedan?'

'No.'

'Must be something, Imad.'

'My mother's family formed part of Egypt's Coptic Christian community.'

'Coptic Christian?'

'That's right.'

'Good,' she said, satisfied. 'Momma never said nuthin' against Coptic Christians.'

'I'm pleased to hear that.'

Imad pressed the remote button. The gates swung open. He drove through and the gates swung silently shut behind them. Ahead, the house was brightly lit.

'What's that?' Mable asked.

'That, Mable, is home.'

'Whose home?'

'Mine.'

'No shit.'

'It most certainly is.'

'No, it's not.'

'It's not?'

'Is it?'

'It is.'

'Well, I'll just squat.'

Chapter Sixty

For more than an hour, Grace Bucklan drove the pickup through the darkness. Its nose pointed east.

You shouldn't run from monsters, she told herself. *You should confront them. I'm going home. I'm taking my sister home. I'm going to kick Mom's boyfriend out the house. If Mom or the molesting skunk protest then they can just try explaining it all away to the cops.*

Grace's head was in a whirl. Images of the last couple of hours fired through her brain like machine-gun bullets.

Pix sat beside her in a daze, eyes staring into space. She had a bump on her forehead where she'd collided with the concrete floor in the chamber of horrors. But she didn't seem badly hurt.

But maybe Grace wasn't thinking straight.

Maybe she should tell the cops about what had happened? About Ed and Cody. They'd been eaten alive back there. Now both of them were dead.

She might tell one day. She could even write the whole thing down in a book.

But not now.

Now all she wanted to do – longed to do – was to drive fast.

They were going home. Leaving the madness behind.

Grace heard Pix give a horrified gasp.

'What's wrong . . . Pix?'

Pix said nothing. Instead, she stared with horror at her hand as it lay open in her lap. Grace glanced down.

She saw strands of copper there, shining in the light from the dashboard.

It was hair from the creature's head. The hank of hair was close on three feet long. Pix must have yanked it from the mummy when she'd launched herself on its back as it attacked Cody.

Hell, there were even shreds of black matter at the ends of the hair where the godforsaken stuff had rooted into the scalp.

Grace wound the window down, snatched the copper hair from Pix's hand and tossed it out. For a second it stayed with them, pulled by the slipstream of the truck.

It's following . . .

Grace floored the accelerator. In the mirror she glimpsed the hair writhing in the moonlight before slowly spinning down to lie on the road.

With the last trace of the thing gone from their lives, Grace eased off the gas. She glanced at Pix. Her sister sat with her eyes closed, a tear rolling down her cheek.

Grace's own eyes pricked. When she touched one with her knuckle it came away glistening wet.

There'd be a lot more tears ahead, she knew that for nothing. But they'd make it. They truly would.

Chapter Sixty-one

It had been a long walk back from the canyon to the edge of town where her destination lay. Amara walked on, untiring, indefatigable. The baby hung by one arm, its feet sometimes catching the grass with a whispery sound.

All the time the moon shone down, sending a silvery light through Amara's empty eye sockets. When she turned her head in that predatory way the copper hair swished in waves down her back.

Once a feral cat attracted by the smell of the baby padded up close behind her as she walked. It closed in, attracted by the faint odor of milk still clinging to the infant.

The cat slinked in closer, its eyes on the silhouette of the figure with the moon shining behind it.

The cat moved noiselessly, confident that its presence was undetected.

Closer, closer. Its nose almost brushed the head of the baby as it swung backwards and forwards.

The silhouette of the human moved quickly, yet with a smooth rhythmic walk. The cat's sensitive nostrils picked up strange scents from the human. It didn't have the same odors that it was accustomed to.

Its nose touched the head of the baby; it risked an appraising lick.

At that moment the figure turned on the cat, the hair flaring out; an explosion of blazing copper. The human head lunged at the cat, lips curling back, baring teeth that smelled of congealing blood.

The cat screeched. Turned. Bolted into the undergrowth.

Presently, the mummy neared the brilliant lights of buildings. Before the track ended it turned and walked through a broken section of fence into an overgrown field. She walked smoothly, unhindered by the vegetation.

The field ended.

She walked across the asphalt of the deserted parking lot to the building.

Once there, she scraped at the museum's rear door. Her fingernails left score marks. She found the knob, as if by accident, and pulled. The door stayed shut.

In the distance dogs began to howl. Every animal in the neighborhood raised its snout to the moon. Soon the howling of dogs filled the air in eerie chorus.

Amara pulled at the door again. Then, staggering away from it, she wandered in circles. Now her movements were aimless. Weak.

She pushed her way into a thick border of geraniums. There she lay down on the dirt.

She hugged the baby to her breasts.

Chapter Sixty-two

Virginia returned to the basement where she'd been held all those weeks. Light burned brightly. The cages were empty now. She stood for a moment, breathing the scent of the place. That same smell was in her skin now. She'd smelled it as she'd bolted from the house and into the canyon, trying to find her way back to the city.

For some reason she'd found herself sitting on a rocky bluff, gazing at the city lights for a long time. Then she'd turned round.

Returned to her place of torture.

Now she stood in the void of the basement. Two torn corpses lay on the floor. Streams of crimson congealed on concrete.

Without even thinking it through . . . without thinking *what* she was doing or *why* she was doing it she entered the cage that had once imprisoned her.

She sat down cross-legged on the foam mattress. She gazed up at the hairbrush, toothbrush and water bottles hanging from cords tied to the cage's roof crossbars. This was a horrible place. But somehow the outside – and freedom – seemed even more horrible. Here – inside – there were strict rules and order. Outside in the city there was lawlessness and disorder.

She closed her eyes. That was how she stayed until she heard a faint moan.

The woman looked dead. She ought to have been dead.

The stake was a bitch to remove as well. Ed Lake should have been proud of the barb he'd carved into the stool leg. It had worked a treat. The harpoon had gone in deep. It had lodged tight. Virginia had to work hard to loosen it from the woman's throat.

An inch either way and it would have gone either through the windpipe or through the major arteries. As it was, it had lodged in soft muscle tissue.

After a great deal of work the blind woman lay on the bed, her throat wadded and bandaged. A little blood had seeped into the white crepe.

Virginia watched the blind woman sleeping on the bed. Her breathing wasn't at all deep but at least it was regular. The woman's eyelids were black, her lips blue and her skin white as porcelain because of blood loss. But with rest, along with plenty of fluids, she'd make up the lost blood in a few days. The wound would heal.

Virginia walked round the house. She soon saw that the woman lived alone. The one she and Ed had referred to as 'The Warder' was nowhere to be seen. Maybe she just dropped in occasionally to help out.

Letters on a bureau soon gave Virginia her one-time captor's name: April Vallsarra.

Knowing the name was important to Virginia. She rolled it round her mouth, repeating it as she climbed the stairs back to the bedroom. 'April Vallsarra . . . April Vallsarra . . .'

When she reached April's bedroom she went to the woman's bed and sat down on it.

April was beautiful. Her complexion flawless.

Then some thoughts that were startling came to her.

Virginia had never experienced such an intense relationship before as the one with April Vallsarra. What was more, Virginia realized she didn't care for her old home, or her day-job.

'Hell, I might live to regret this,' she told herself as she gazed down at April. 'But I've reached a decision.'

Virginia leaned forward to kiss the sleeping woman on the lips and whispered, 'I'm staying with you.'

Chapter Sixty-three

The large brown dog named George pushed through the weeds to the edge of the parking lot. He stopped on the asphalt, and sniffed the air.

Then he trotted to the rear door of the museum. He sniffed the seam at its bottom, his tail swishing.

Backing off, he sat down. He stared at the door. He barked impatiently.

A sound in the bushes caught his attention. He cocked an ear toward it, still watching the door. When the sound came again, he got up to explore.

He walked along, nose to the asphalt, sides heaving as he sniffed. Sometimes a snorting sound escaped his mouth as the scent grew stronger.

Near the geranium border, he began to growl. A thick strip of fur bristled upright on the nape of his neck. The growl rumbling deep in his throat, he sprang into the bushes.

For a few seconds, the night's quiet was broken by the clamor of the dog: his barks, snarls, his yelps of pain. The flowers swished, petals flew.

Then he backed out of the bushes, tail down. He swung round and ran across the parking lot, favoring his left foreleg. Halfway across the lot, he stopped and looked back as if to check he wasn't being followed.

Then he broke into a run again, dragging the baby by its leg.

Chapter Sixty-four

'What do you make of it, Mrs Connors?'

Susan shook her head, frowning at Vasquez. 'I don't know what to think. Officer Kraus's description does seem to fit the mummy. Apparently, there's also some evidence that Amara was involved in the museum deaths.'

'Do you honestly believe— no, I can't even ask. It's too . . .' He fished for the appropriate word. 'Outlandish. The fact is, though, that unless Kraus has completely lost his marbles, our suspect has a physical appearance similar to your missing . . . artifact. Do you have photos of the thing?'

'At the museum.'

'All right. I'd like you to go over there and get them. We'll run them by Kraus and see what he has to say. If he gives us a positive make, we'll want to run off duplicates for my men.' He glanced at his wristwatch. 'We'll be here another half-hour or so, wrapping things up. Can you get back here by then?'

'No problem. We can make it in ten, fifteen minutes.'

'Excellent.'

As they left the house, Lenny Farrel of *Eyewitness News* rushed across the yard. 'Miss Connors! A few questions, Miss Connors!'

'We're in a hurry,' she called back.

He kept coming. Tag pointed at his face. Farrel stopped and stood motionless as if frozen in place. Only when Tag lowered his arm did the newsman move. He turned away, muttering to his cameraman.

'Persistent bastard,' Tag said.

'It's his job.'

'He can have it.'

Tag opened the car door for Susan and she climbed in. He pushed it gently until it latched. At his own side, he took the same care to make as little noise as possible. He leaned across the seat to look at Geoffrey. Susan uncovered the baby's face.

'Still asleep,' she said.

'That kid'll sleep through anything.'

'Pretty near. Once he's zonked out, he's out for the night. Till daybreak at least.'

Tag started the car.

'Nothing wakes him up but his stomach.'

'I'm the same way,' Tag said, pulling away from the curb.

With the night still warm they drove with the convertible's top locked back. Tag took it nice and steady so as not to disturb the baby despite what Susan had told him about the way the baby slept. The warm slipstream feathered their hair.

Susan reached under her seat and picked up the Callahan journal. 'Wish I had time to read all this.'

'Plenty of time later.'

'Later might be *too* late.' She opened the journal to the page where she had left off and used Tag's flashlight to continue reading above the gentle rush of air through the open-top car. '"She is of the dead who lives,"' she read aloud.

'Great.'

'"The banished god Set, slayer of Osiris, came in the night to Amara . . . gave her the seed of his loins, that she might bear him a son. In return for her favors, he promised Amara the gift of eternal life."'

Tag shook his head. Concentrated on the road in front of him.

Susan read on in silence.

Then they reached the museum driveway. The car's lights shone on the pair of mock-Egyptian columns that flanked it.

'Go on to the back. We'll take the rear stairs. It'll be quicker.'

'What about the guards?'

'Aren't any. Blumgard decided against it, after what happened last night. I think he feels responsible for those poor guys. Doesn't want any more killings on his conscience.'

Tag drove around the side of the building to the deserted parking lot in the rear. He pulled up to the back door of the museum and shut off the engine.

They climbed from the car into the moonlit lot.

'Look,' Tag said.

In the field beyond them were the distant, sweeping beams of half a dozen flashlights. Far across it, Susan saw the spinning lights of patrol cars.

'Hang on a second,' Tag muttered. He opened the trunk of his car. 'Somewhere in all this junk . . . in case Amara's returned to her lair . . .'

Standing beside Tag, Susan watched him push aside a sleeping bag, a coil of rope, a pack of road flares, a first-aid box, tools, hiking boots, odds and ends of clothing. He pulled out a hatchet. 'Bullets might not stop her, but I bet this will. This was my grandfather's; he'd keep it as sharp as a surgeon's scalpel.' He touched the keen edge. 'I try my best to keep it as old Grandpa would have wanted.' Shooting her a smile, he tossed the hatchet's leather sheath into the trunk, then closed the lid.

'Want me to get your keys?' he asked.

She nodded. Tag opened the purse that hung from her shoulder as she held Geoffrey in her arms. The kid didn't peep. He slept the sleep of the innocent.

Tag looked in the purse. 'Phew. A lot of junk in here.'

'Not as bad as your trunk.'

'Ah.' He pulled out the key ring and held it in front of her eyes. 'Third from the left . . . no, your left.'

'Got it.'

He pinched it away from the others and led the way to the door.

He turned the key in the lock and pulled. The door opened noiselessly, releasing a wave of cooler air from within.

He held the door open for Susan.

She entered, the baby held securely in her arms. Her gaze

immediately lowered to the concrete floor where the guard named Beckerman had been found. In the light of the new bulb overhead, she saw that the area had been cleaned. A shaded area remained on the concrete, though – it would probably always be there.

She climbed the stairs behind Tag. They reached the first landing. Where Gonzalez had died. His blood was no longer visible on the green paint of the wall, but it lent a rust tint to the porous concrete at her feet.

Turning, she followed Tag up the next flight of stairs. Hatchet in hand, shirttail half untucked, he might have been a maniac in a horror film. Even the shadow he cast became a menacing doppelgänger.

Nicholson in The Shining, *she thought.*
Come and take your punishment, Susan.
Gonna crack your head good and hard, girl.
Gonna feel your entrails tonight . . .
Damn imagination. Slippery as I don't know what.

Every shadow seemed to harbor some waiting demon.

Now she couldn't look at her lover without seeing him as some homicidal maniac with his grandpa's hatchet.

Why isn't Tag saying anything?
What's gotten into him?
The spirit of a dead murderer. Redrum, Susan, Redrum . . .

She hugged Geoffrey more tightly to her chest, ready to take the hatchet blows to her own back rather than allow them to fall on her son's unprotected head.

No.

Just her stupid imagination.

Tag's probably nervous, too.
Not like him to be so quiet.

'Tag?'
'Huh?'
'You okay?'
'Just hoping the goddamn thing doesn't come charging down at us.'
'Lovely thought.'
'Isn't it, though.'
'Just give the gal forty whacks.'

'Sure.'

'I don't think she can be in here. She hasn't got keys.'

'If a four-thousand-year-old mummy can walk around biting people, maybe she doesn't need keys.'

'Walks through walls?'

'Why not?'

'Yeah.'

'Wish we hadn't brought Geoffrey,' he told her.

'Wish you hadn't said that.'

'If . . .'

'What?'

'If something *does* happen, take him and run. Don't look back. Don't stick around to see how things turn out. Okay?'

She clutched her baby more tightly. Just hearing the words made her skin crawl. 'Okay.'

He reached the upstairs door, opened it.

Peered out.

'Looks all right.'

Susan was glad to get out of the stairwell. Just for a moment back there the walls seemed to be closing in on her. Her heartbeat was so loud she thought the noise would wake Geoffrey as he snuggled against her breast.

She hurried along the corridor, staying close to Tag's side. At the door to her office, she pointed out the correct key. Tag slid it into the lock. Opened the door. He turned on the lights and they entered.

Tag held the baby, supporting its head in the crook of his elbow, while Susan went through the file cabinet. She flipped through the folders, found one bearing Amara's name, and slid it out. She checked it. The photographs of the mummy were inside. 'Okay. Let's go.'

She took back her sleeping baby. Switching off the lights, they left the office.

'Wait here a second,' Tag said. 'I want to take another look at the coffin.'

'What for?'

'See if she's there.'

'Oh, Tag.'

'The old bird might have come home to roost.'

'The museum door was locked. She couldn't—'

'Susan, it's worth just a peek.'

'I'll go with you, then.'

They walked further up the corridor. Tag shone his flashlight into the Callahan Room. 'Wait here,' he said and stepped over the roped cordon.

She watched him cross the room, the beam of his light sweeping its corners, illuminating faces of statues – animals, men, gods . . . demons – the painted eyes stared back. Finally he aimed the beam down into the open coffin.

Suddenly feeling a chill on her back, Susan whirled around. She gazed down the dark hall, but saw nothing.

Nothing but shadows. Nothing but gloomy doorways. Moonlight glinted through window glass.

Faraway, just on the edge of her hearing, she heard a dog howl.

Stepping to the rail, she looked down at the gallery below. There were figures down there, but they were all carved from stone. Nothing moved.

Tag climbed over the cordon.

'Nobody's home,' he told her. 'Coffin's empty.'

'Now can we go?' Susan asked.

'Sure.'

'Let's take the front way. I don't think my nerves can handle the stairwell again.'

'Fine.' He shot her a reassuring smile.

They walked silently down the carpeted corridor, and down the sweeping main stairs. She chose a key for Tag once again and soon they were exiting through one of the big glass doors. Susan breathed deeply of the warm night air. 'Feels good to get out here,' she murmured.

'It'll feel even better, getting home.'

They walked down the concrete steps. She missed one, tumbled forward. Tag reached out for her.

Missed her.

She turned in midair, determined not to fall on Geoffrey. Going down, the walkway pounded her shoulder, her hip. Her neck muscles took a savage yank. She rolled onto her back. Geoffrey squalled.

'You okay?' Tag asked, concerned. He crouched over her, helping her.

'I think so. Christ, what a klutz.'

He helped her to her feet.

She cradled Geoffrey, patted his back. 'It's all right, honey,' she whispered. 'It's all right. There, there . . .' To Tag she said, 'Scared the hell out of the little guy.'

'The big guy, too. You sure you're okay?'

'I'll probably have some dandy bruises.'

Geoffrey continued to wail as they hurried toward the rear of the museum. The sound carried way across the field.

'I've got a bottle in the car,' Susan said. 'That'll calm him.' She kissed the baby's wet face. 'Yeah, you had a nasty shock, didn't you? Didn't know your mom has two left feet.'

'Hope he didn't inherit them. It'd make it tough, buying shoes.'

'Yeah, you want your bottle, don't you? That'll do you just fine, won't it?'

They reached the car. Tag pulled open the door for her. She climbed in. As Tag hurried to the other side, she slipped a plastic bottle out of her diaper bag. She thumbed its cap off, then slipped the teat into Geoffrey's wide, pink mouth. The crying stopped. He sucked on the nipple, the bottle glugging as he drew out its creamy contents. Susan watched the drizzle of bubbles running up through the transparent plastic.

This night journey had made her son hungry.

'There,' Susan soothed.

'Fantastic,' Tag whispered. 'All praise the magic bottle.'

She smiled. 'He'll be asleep in no time.'

Steering out of the parking lot, the convertible's lights blazing, he put his arm around Susan's shoulders. 'It's been a rough night.'

'I wish we could just go home. Go to sleep. Forget everything.'

'We'll just drop off the pictures of old mummy gal and let them worry about the rest of it.'

The long, straight road led through the museum park. It was lined with cherry trees. Beyond the trees, the grounds looked peaceful and deserted in the moonlight.

'This whole business . . . I don't know . . . My life has always been nice. Basically nice, I guess.' She shrugged, sleepy. 'And now all this.' She stroked Geoffrey's head. 'There are horrors all around us. You know? Hell, you're a cop; you know that better than me.'

'Life's like a stroll through the park,' Tag said. 'Enjoy, but beware of the dog piles.'

She laughed wearily.

Tag grinned.

Then he shrieked.

The car swerved wildly. Twisting, Susan saw the head of the mummy behind the seat. The copper hair bloomed around the head, the eyeless face loomed forward, its lips curled back baring the teeth. The jaw clamped onto Tag's shoulder. It began ripping shirt and flesh.

Geoffrey started to howl.

'Hatchet!' Tag cried.

It had been on the seat between them. Now it was gone.

Chapter Sixty-five

A car horn blared. Headlights flooded the scene of the creature grabbing at Tag's face and hair with its shriveled hands. Its teeth snapped, trying to rip his face.

Susan jerked the steering wheel. The car swung right. The onrushing car sped past, kept going.

Careful not to crush Geoffrey, she dropped sideways; her head pressed Tag's lap. She clawed the floor, found nothing.

The hatchet must have slid under the seat when it fell.

Damn.

The monster was going to rip Tag to shreds.

She glanced up to see blood already smearing his cheek. His eyes blazed as he fought to control the car.

And as he fought the attacking mummy, too.

Brakes screamed and the car spun out, throwing Susan against the dash. Head twisted toward Tag, she saw Amara above him, teeth tearing his hair as he tried to bat it away.

And with no roof on the convertible the creature could reach freely over him to attack his unprotected head.

She saw all this. Saw the emaciated cadaver of the mummy now supple and swift, invested with an uncanny life force. Its long hair billowed out behind in the slipstream. Once, twice, three times it ducked its head, snapping at Tag's face. A gash opened above his left eyebrow where the teeth struck.

Then she saw the pistol at his waist.

The car stopped with a harsh jolt. Geoffrey slammed against her breast, the impact making the baby squeal. Her back hit the dash again. Tag was flung forward against the steering wheel, bringing Amara halfway over the top of the seat.

Susan, wedged into the space between the seat and the dashboard, realized she was stuck.

She struggled to free herself. Above her, the withered arms of the mummy flapped, hands savagely pulling at Tag as its jaws worked, snapping teeth shut like a steel trap. It lunged forward again and again. The withered breasts crinkling against Tag's head.

He punched upward, trying to keep the lethal jaws at bay.

Pushing Geoffrey along the seat, she clutched Tag's belt. Got her hand on the pistol.

Tugged.

The pistol was stuck.

'Hatchet!' Tag yelled.

Her fingers worked a strap off the pistol's hammer. She jerked the pistol free. Aimed at the ravaged face with the dark shadowed pits for eyes.

Christ, it's right by Tag's head, biting his shoulder, trying to get at his neck. If I miss . . .

Susan writhed sideways. Knees on the floor, hips against the seat front, she thrust the muzzle toward the mummy's forehead.

Fired.

The gunblast resounded, deafening her. A big, empty hole appeared just below the hairline. A patch of hair blew off the top of Amara's head as the bullet exited. The bullet, still so hot that it glowed, sped into the night sky as a spark of silver.

The mummy, apparently undisturbed, tore off Tag's collar.

Tag's eyes were closed.

Unconscious?

Dead?

Susan lunged forward. Snarling, she rammed the muzzle against Amara's shut mouth, shattering the front teeth. She shoved hard, forcing the head backwards. Her forefinger jerked the trigger. Explosions thundered in the air, one after another, following each other so fast that they sounded like a single roar. Bone and skin sprayed from the exit wounds.

Hanks of hair flew, filling the air with glittering red strands.

Susan fired the last round. The head jerked, wrenching the pistol from Susan's hand.

Now the thing moved for a different target.

The mummy's hands reached for Geoffrey.

'No!' Susan shouted.

Scooping the baby off the seat, Susan hugged him tightly. She lunged sideways.

With her free hand she levered the handle. Threw herself against the door.

It shot open. She tumbled to the road, knocking the breath from her body. Geoffrey whimpered. Not pausing, she scrambled to her feet, then looked back at the car. With the roof folded back she could plainly see Tag in the moonlight. He was motionless, slumped over the steering wheel.

A shadow within the car moved, rising, falling, then rising again. Something that moved in an uncanny, unnatural way.

A second later – *thump*.

The mummy flopped to the road. Its ruined face appeared under the open door. Susan even heard the rustle of the heavy tresses of hair.

Geoffrey's crying was like the scream of a siren in Susan's ears as she started to run.

She ran up the middle of the unlit road, Geoffrey clutched to her breasts, her long legs pumping, her sneakers almost silent as her feet flew. Soon her breathing came in noisy spurts, her heart hammered.

Looking over her shoulder, she saw Amara in the headlights.

On its feet. Running.

Running strangely, arms flapping in the air, long hair fluttering.

Running like a blind lunatic.

Running with awful speed.

Running with dreadful purpose.

Running.

Susan felt a scream in her chest. As she ran, she heard it: her own piercing scream mingling with Geoffrey's howls. The hysteria of the noise added to her fright.

She clenched her teeth, cutting off the scream.

With a glance back, she saw the ghastly creature gaining on her. 'Jesus!' she gasped. 'Oh, sweet Jesus . . .'

She tried to run faster. Her legs felt like stone. They seemed to be cramping, cutting the length of her stride.

Feet now . . .

Growing heavier.

Felt as if the soles of her sneakers were stuck against the asphalt. Each step became a physical effort. Pains ran up her calf and thigh muscles. Her heart pounded. She wanted to scream again, but there was no air left in her lungs.

From behind, she heard the mummy's approach. No gasping from it. No breathing at all. The only sounds, the quick, papery scrape of its feet on the pavement and the faint crackle of its hair as sparks of static ran through it like witch fire.

Pain suddenly seared her shoulder. She heard the rasp of tearing cloth. Felt a tug. Twisting, she whipped her arm across the swatch of fabric torn from her back. The mummy held on tight, but the cloth gave.

Suddenly free, Susan stumbled sideways.

Amara stood motionless, piece of cloth in hand, as if confused.

Scrambling to the side of the road, Susan set Geoffrey down on the dirt shoulder. She stepped back, looking down at him briefly; his eyes were bright in the darkness. Then she turned to face Amara.

The strip of cloth dropped from the mummy's blackened paw. A breeze caught it, tumbling it against her bony leg before blowing it down the road.

With her forearm Susan wiped sweat out of her eyes. She was panting heavily, her heart racing.

The mummy staggered sideways as if to go round her. Its hair swayed.

Susan sidestepped to block the creature. She backhanded sweat from her upper lip.

The mummy sidestepped.

So did Susan.

Its mouth opened slowly, lips pulling back like a dog snarling, baring bullet-shattered stumps of teeth.

With a snarl of rage, Susan attacked. She threw herself low against the creature, driving into its belly, throwing it backwards. Like tackling a mannequin of papier-mâché. It doubled over her. Its nails raked her back.

Then its head slammed against the asphalt.

Susan clutched the thing's throat, panting in rage. Through the gaping mouth, she saw asphalt where her bullets had taken out the back of its head.

Her thumbs punched through the brittle windpipe; it felt like breaking dry spaghetti in her fingers.

No effect. *Why should it? The thing hasn't even got lungs.*

No lungs, no brains, no heart, no blood.

Yet she was trying to kill it.

She *had* to kill it. It wanted Geoffrey.

Its flailing hands clawed the side of her face, tore off a front panel of her blouse, scratched gouges in her breasts and down her ribs.

If she could just keep the head down, just keep the shattered teeth away... but the pain was numbing. Her strength ebbed with the flow of blood.

And the thing was so strong.

A crooked hand darted at her face. She turned quickly. The fingers missed her eye, but dug into her cheek. The other hand clubbed the side of her head, stunning her.

Susan saw herself falling sideways. Felt the creature move.

This time it seemed to make no effort – as if the earlier battle had just been a simple exercise in toying with her. One-handed, the creature reached round, gripped the collar of her blouse and lifted her from the ground as easily as she could lift a puppy by the scruff of its neck.

The road, trees, moon swung crazily.

Then she was lying winded in the grass at the side of the road.

The mummy had just thrown her ten feet or more.

From her face-down sprawl she lifted her head just enough to see the mummy climb to its feet. Then it lurched across the road, closing in on Geoffrey who lay kicking his legs on the curb.

'No!' she shrieked.

Susan scrambled to her feet.

Swayed.

Moon and trees whirled round her as she tried to keep her balance.

'No!'

The creature kept walking, heedless of Susan's staggering approach.

The copper hair hung down strangely behind the mummy, clumps of it gone. A huge empty hole gaped where the back of the head should have been.

With both hands, Susan grabbed the hanging hair and yanked. The mummy stumbled backwards against her.

She hooked an arm around its head, another across its chest. The skin felt hard and scratchy. The touch of it made her retch – her own skin felt as if it would crawl from her body – but she didn't let go.

She stumbled back, dragging the writhing creature farther away from the roadside where Geoffrey lay sobbing.

A hand reached backwards. Fingernails dug into Susan's belly.

In pain and rage, she cried out. Wrenched the head with all her strength. She heard ripping, crackling sounds – a loud snap – before she fell back to the ground.

Amara stood above her. Slowly turned away. Walked with awkward, staggering steps back toward the baby.

Susan still clutched the mummy's head to her breasts. Shaking violently, she flung it aside. As it rolled from her, she got to her hands and knees. She fell as she tried to stand.

Raising her face from the road, she watched the thing.

Headless.

A deep cleft showed where the neck had been torn out. Vertebrae poked up from desiccated skin.

Susan tried to stand.

Couldn't.

She wanted to weep in frustration.

Her baby . . .

A roar filled her ears.

Amara

She didn't know what it was. Didn't care.

Then the headlights blazed across the mummy. Tag's car slammed into it, knocking it high off the road. It cartwheeled over the car, bouncing off the trunk. An arm broke off.

Susan watched the torso hit the road. The arm fell nearby, hand first as if trying to break its fall.

The brakes squealed. The car swung into a tight U-turn. Blue smoke from the spinning tires filled the air.

Susan saw Amara stand.

The car started forward.

The mummy staggered toward it.

The car hit more slowly this time, knocking Amara backward onto the road. The convertible turned and its rear tire bumped over the legs.

The car stopped. Tag looked back from its side window.

Susan gazed at the mummy. Its legs were crushed flat, but it used its remaining arm to raise its torso off the road.

Tag backed up slowly.

Susan heard the awful *crunch* as the tire rolled onto Amara's chest.

The car door opened. The hatchet flew out, its head clanking on the pavement. A moment later, Tag hauled himself out. At the end of a bloody arm, he held his pistol. He fed cartridges into its cylinder.

Susan climbed to her feet and went to him. A wry grin reached the corners of his mouth. She kissed him gently, then hurried to the roadside. She picked up Geoffrey. His small hand clutched a hanging strand of her hair and tugged.

'Over here,' Tag said.

She crossed the road.

'Stand back,' he told her. 'Well behind me.'

She stepped farther back from the car.

Two quick shots split the stillness. Through the ringing in her ears, Susan heard a heavy, liquid spatter. A dark puddle began to form beneath the car. The stench of gasoline stung her nostrils.

Amara's remaining hand reached toward Tag, fingers hooking into claws. Clutching.

He lit a match.

Tossed it.

The burning match rose in an arc, then fell toward the pool of gasoline.

With a soft *whup*, like a flutter of a bedsheet on a line, flame engulfed the open-top car.

And Amara's body.

Tag stepped back, moving a safe distance from the car. A few moments passed and the gas tank exploded, sending a ball of fire into the night sky.

In the red light, Tag looked to Susan like a strange, avenging phantom as he picked up the mummy's severed arm and tossed it into the flames.

The hungry fire consumed the dry stick of a limb, blue sparks popping from the crackling bone.

Tag limped across to her. He smiled at Geoffrey, stroked the baby's cheek, then put his hand across her back. She leaned against him, relishing the strength of his encircling arm.

'Awful thing to do to your car,' she said in a small voice.

'After that passenger, it'd have never been the same again anyway,' he told her. Then he laughed wearily.

Susan jerked. Gasped with pain. Looking down, she screamed.

The head of Amara was clamped to her ankle, gnawing, its copper hair stretching out behind it like the body of a snake.

'Christ!' Tag yelled.

Susan shook her leg. The teeth worked, biting deeper. Grinding. Embedding.

'My God! Get her off! Get her off me!'

Tag ran for the hatchet.

'Hurry!' Pain burned her leg like fire. She couldn't shake free. She couldn't use her hand to try to pry the head loose – not without putting down Geoffrey. She clung to him tightly. '*Tag!*'

He ran to her. The hatchet chopped into Amara's head. Split it. But the teeth didn't loose their hold. He chopped again . . . again. Each blow knocking off clumps of the head, each blow jarring the teeth so that they ripped more flesh from Susan's ankle.

'Shoot it!'

'The bullet'd hit your foot,' he panted.

With a final blow, he broke one of the jaw hinges. He worked the wedge of the hatchet head between the bones.

Then pried them apart.

The teeth opened. Loosened. Susan felt them leave her skin.

Though only one hinge of the jaw was still connected, the teeth gripped Tag's hatchet relentlessly. He tried to shake them off.

Couldn't.

Without leaving Susan's side, Tag hurled away the hatchet and the biting remains of Amara's head. They disappeared into his flaming car.

The long hair caught fire. It crackled fiercely.

Red sparks swirled high into the night sky where they faded and – at last – died.

The Lake

Chapter One

Tuesday, April 29, 1986

Verna Lavette clapped her hands.

'My *favorites*!' she squealed.

Almond marzipan, walnut whirls and those *scrummy* caramel creams . . .

'Oh, *thank* you,' she said, her chubby face wreathed in smiles.

'No problem, sugar,' the man said. 'My pleasure – as always.'

Verna looked sheepish. 'Can I have one now? Before . . .'

'Sure. Have one, two or three. Makes no odds, but . . .' He glanced at his wristwatch. 'Best make it snappy. No time to lose.'

Sucking on a caramel cream, Verna looked at her benefactor. Well, she pondered, he ain't *really* my benefactor. *I* give *him* plenty, in return for his dough – ooh, yes, and the candy. Don't forget the candy.

She made a face.

Sure, she did her bit.

Got the scars to prove it, too.

Yessir. All things considered, the Candyman got pretty much what he wanted.

He must like what I do – and how I do it, she told herself. Keeps a-comin' back for more.

Like now.

The room was dark, except for the Anglepoise spotlight by Verna's bed. He was telling her to take off her slip, all slow and sexy, like Marilyn Monroe.

It always began like this.

Then, the action moved on to . . . other things . . .

Some guys had weird ideas, and her Mr Candyman was no exception. At times she wondered if it was worth her while. The things he made her do, an' all.

Verna sighed. In *her* job – never mind the way she *looked* these days – she needed every goddamn cent she got. While she could still get it.

And, no question, the Candyman paid her good.

She watched him adjust the spotlight, so that it lit up her left side. Feeling around in his holdall, he brought out a Polaroid camera.

He put it to his eye, squinted into the viewfinder and ran off a couple of shots. Testing for light conditions. Verna knew the score inside out.

He waited a moment. The mechanism whirred and spewed out the prints.

He peeled off a picture and watched it color up.

Frowned, muttered 'Shit!' and tossed it on the bed.

The result was not to his liking.

The second one turned out okay.

Mr Candyman grinned approval. His teeth gleamed briefly in the lamplight.

That's my baby.

Now. Down to business.

Sweat broke out. Speckling his upper lip.

Placing the Polaroid camera on Verna's nightstand, he brought up a small silver one from out of his holdall.

Verna smiled. *One a' them classy Japanese jobs – nothin' cheap about this guy.*

Dollar signs danced before her eyes.

The Candyman was naked.

Verna stared at his erection. Tilting slightly, stiff and strong, poking out from all that dark curly hair.

I wish, she thought, hungrily, the familiar tingly rush teasing her center like crazy.

Do things right first time – and maybe, just *maybe*, Verna gets to taste some a' that.

She sighed. The Candyman wasn't into sex; he was only interested in his goddamn pictures. God knew she'd *tried* to play it for sex, but

The Lake

he just got angry. He'd slugged her in the kisser a coupla times.

If he weren't so good-lookin', he'd be just your average creep, she decided. But a mighty good-lookin' creep, I'll say that for him. The quiet type, too; don't say much.

Bastard sure knows what he's doin' with a camera, though.

Verna shivered. A gal could go off the boil, time it takes . . . She studied the Candyman's face. It was set. Engrossed. Maybe he's one a' them porno guys, she thought, making heaps a' dough selling dirty pictures. She'd done a few porno flicks in her time, so she knew the score. Hell, there were plenty big bucks in that game.

On the other hand, maybe the shit jacks off on 'em, all on his lonesome in a dark little room someplace . . .

Who cares? I do the job 'n' I gets my fee . . .

Tossing back her blonde hair, Verna swung into action.

Ready for my close-up now, Mr de Mille.

She posed. Puckered her lips. Lifted her shoulder, looked at the camera, and smiled coyly. She crossed an arm over her breasts and slipped off a shoulder strap.

Candyman focused the lens.

'Let it fall, slowly. Hold your breasts, sugar. Play around with them . . . Like you're making sweet love to yourself . . . That's it. Now for the next shot . . .'

Verna had done it all before. Many times. She'd lie on the bed; spread out, like one a' them sacrificial virgins you read about in history books.

Oh, yeah?

She almost laughed out loud.

One thing's for sure. Verna ain't no fuckin' virgin!

Candyman took a few shots. Then he straightened up, and replaced his camera on the nightstand. He opened up his holdall. Put the Polaroid job inside it. His pants and T-shirt were already in there.

Neatly folded.

Out of the way.

He came up with a knife.

Verna shuddered. One false move with that baby, an' I can kiss my candy goodbye.

385

He leaned over the bed, blocking the light from the lamp.

Her heart beat faster.

She looked at the blade. Felt a sharp, stinging thrill between her legs. Got her juices going, all right, but it sure was scary.

Too goddamn scary. Not really knowing what the fuck he was gonna do next . . .

With a forefinger, he traced a line from her throat, right down to her pubic bone. For a big man he had a soft touch. Light as a feather.

She wriggled, and shivered.

'Ooh, that tickles . . .'

'Ssshhh. Not a sound, sugar. Mr Candyman's about to create a masterpiece here.'

Verna closed her eyes.

Let him have his kicks.

Any which way he wanted. After all, he was the guy with the dough . . .

'*Heyyyyyyy, whaddya . . .? Aaaahhhggg . . .*'

Blood sprayed the Candyman's face.

He grunted, opened his mouth and licked his lips.

The knife slicked down Verna's torso, jerking a little, going past her breastbone. The Candyman slowed down, then dug in deep, opening her guts like she was a sheep in a slaughterhouse.

Verna's red mouth sagged a little in surprise.

Her baby blues snapped open wide, then quickly glazed over.

Fascinated, the Candyman stared into them. He liked the way Verna fixed her eyes. All that black eyeliner. And those long black lashes. Way back, she'd told him that she'd been a singer at some club in downtown 'Frisco. Yeah, it figured. Gals in Verna's line a' business knew all about make-up.

He stood back, tilting his head.

An artist surveying his masterpiece.

He liked what he saw. Verna was a work of art.

Picasso's 'red period'.

He stared at his creation.

Opening her up had made her breasts flop over, each pointing

The Lake

outwards, either side of the bloody ravine down her middle. Her breasts were big and white and splashed with red.

How 'bout that?

Candyman's 'red period'.

His lips curved in a tight smile.

All that blood . . .

He dug the way it flowered beneath her, like some exotic jungle orchid.

A strand of black hair peeked out from beneath the blonde wig. He removed the wig. Watching the way her head wagged; all loose like a rag doll. Her lids drooped. She coulda still been alive. Asleep.

He tossed the wig to the floor.

Carefully, he stroked her long black hair, smoothing it into place over her shoulders.

He rearranged her arms, so that they stretched out from her body. Engrossed in his work, his mouth opened slightly.

Verna's legs gaped apart; blood oozed from her orifice.

It was still pumping from her belly.

Should be slowing down about now . . .

Mmmm. She looked like a five-pointed star.

Interesting.

'Doing the bitch a favor,' he murmured, 'rearranging her like this. Only way *she*'ll ever get t'be a ìstarî!'

Neat, huh?

Grinning, he stabbed the knife deep into Verna's middle. Her body shook; her breasts wobbled precariously. Spats of blood sprayed up from her guts. Landed on his belly.

Glistening gobs of it clung to his pubic hair.

His head buzzed inside. Like it was full of swarming bees.

He got angry. Couldn't stop stabbing . . .

'*You fuckin' bastard, evil bitch! Rot in HELL! You hear ME?*'

Sweat beaded his brow, droplets stung his eyes. His breath came out in harsh, wheezy grunts.

Seconds later, he'd calmed down.

Wiping his hands on Verna's bedsheet, he picked up his camera and clicked away.

Chapter Two

Wednesday, June 25, 1986

The footsteps got closer.
 He, *it*, was almost *on* her now.
 Her legs pumped hard. Her lungs gagged for air.
 The thing followed with superhuman speed.
 Christ. I can't go fast enough – or far enough!
 Heaving, panting, she drew to a halt . . .
 A bony hand clawed her shoulder.
 Hooked her throat.
 NO. My God. NO . . . PLEASE!!!

Deana jerked awake, heart pounding, nightgown twisted up above her waist, clinging like a live thing to her sweat-soaked skin.
 Her breathing evened out a little.
 Puffing out a gusty sigh, she relaxed.
 It was only a dream.
 Dream?
 Try a fucking *nightmare*!
 She sighed again – in relief this time. Turning her head on the sodden pillow, she saw familiar shapes in the weird half-light. She relaxed some more.
 Then . . .
 What was that?
 Her heart began racing again.
 She could hear *something*.

The Lake

Footfalls.

Soft, scrunching sounds on the gravel outside.

Her eyes darted to the window. The filmy curtains stirred in the breeze . . . Moonlight filtered pale gray beams across her bed.

She scanned the window. Saw a tall, hunched shape move across it. Shaggy hair sticking out from beneath a long floppy hat.

This is for real.

I'm not dreaming now.

The shadow paused, stiffened and turned, looking over its shoulder like it was scared of being followed.

Then the big hook nose pointed forward again.

Like a giant bird of prey . . .

It carried a hatchet on its shoulder.

Oh my God!

Can this really be happening?

It's my nightmare come true!

Deana clamped a hand over her mouth, stifling the scream rising in her throat. Her breath huffed out in ragged, hurting gasps.

'Ah'm a-comin' to getcha, baby . . .'

A harsh, breathy voice. She couldn't believe it!

If this really IS a nightmare, I gotta wake up fast.

Sliding a hand under the bedsheet, she found her thigh. She pinched it, hard.

Ouch! *Shit!* Okay, so I'm not dreaming. I'm awake.

Jesus. If I *am* awake . . . who is *that* outside my window?

A burglar?

Carrying a hatchet?

Killers carry hatchets . . .

Mad ax murderers!

But why pick on me?

Who'd want to kill *me*?

Nobody I can think of would want me dead.

Except maybe that bitch Nancy Guildenschwarz – she *hates* me like hell after Allan ditched her and dated me instead . . . Even so, Deana reminded herself, Nancy's short, plumpish – *and* she's a girl.

Not a tall, thin *man*.

Unless Nancy's people put out a contract on me.

There's a thought.

Wouldn't put anything past that bitch. Always boasting that her dad had connections . . .

Name like Guildenschwarz, he sure *needed* connections.

Like a mouse in a maze, Deana's mind scurried through her past, searching for a tall scarecrow man who hated her enough to sneak around her house in the dead of night.

With a hatchet for company . . .

Nah. Nobody hates me *that* much. Do they?

Jeez, I hope not.

If she yelled for Mom, he might smash through the window and hack her to death before Mom could get to her.

Best stay quiet, Deana thought. Pretend I'm not here.

Deana shut her eyes tight, held her breath, slid down under the bedsheet, pulled it over her head and lay there, heart racing, till she almost suffocated.

Then, peeking from under the bedsheet, she scanned the window again.

Nobody there. Only the moon, casting ghostly rays onto her bed.

Perhaps the thing with the hatchet never happened?

Oh yeah?

Deana wiped her face with a corner of the sheet.

It was awfully hot.

Hot, shitty, oppressive and muggy.

Another summer night in Marin County.

'Cept it wasn't just 'another summer night'.

A mad axman's out there, sneaking past my window.

Stalking me.

Looking for me. Wanting to hack me to death.

Deana listened, willing her heart to slow down.

A warm mistral rose up from nowhere, whispering into the night, tossing the leaves of the citrus tree outside her window. The rustling

The Lake

sounds should have been familiar and friendly.
Tonight, they didn't seem that way.

In the past, she'd loved that big old tree.

At age ten, when she and Mom first came to live in this house, she'd imagined small furry creatures hiding away up there; birds nesting in its branches. Mornings, she'd lie in bed watching it. At night, she went to sleep listening to its quiet, scurrying sounds.

Now it shivered and rustled like something in a horror movie.

It was so scary.

Her gaze switched to where she'd last seen the intruder.

Hoping she wouldn't see him again.

Trying to convince herself that the shadowy shape didn't exist. Hadn't really happened at all.

She waited . . .

But there was no Mr Hatchet Man. Just her tree. Its leaves stirring softly in the night breeze . . .

Making long black shadows on her ceiling.

Raising her head off the pillow, Deana squinted at the clock on the nightstand.

00:10.

Gone midnight.

A good time for nightmares.

And weird dreams.

She stretched; letting her tense, coiled-up limbs ease out, running her tongue over bone-dry lips.

Her eyes darted nervously to the window.

Just checking.

Fearful that the same spooky sequence would start over again.

Wide-eyed, waiting, she counted to thirty . . . forty . . . fifty . . . sixty.

No sign of the Hatchet Man.

Swinging out of bed, she peeled off her nightgown. It was soaked with sweat. She spread it over the bedrail, grabbed her robe and shrugged into it.

It felt soft and comforting to her damp, chilled skin.

She tied the sash tight.

Wouldn't do for Mr Hatchet Man to catch her naked.

Mr *who*?

That was a nightmare, dummy, and don't you forget it.

Still her breath came hard and fast.

Calm down, she told herself.

You're safe.

The doors are locked.

Mom's in the next room . . .

Everthing's okay. Honest.

In the busy flickering shadows, familiar things greeted her like old friends.

She made for the kitchen.

Opening the fridge door, she reached inside and took out a jug of lemonade.

It felt good and cold.

Mom had made it only yesterday. From fresh lemons. It was her own special brew and Deana knew it'd taste bittersweet, tart, with just a dash of honey.

The way I like it.

The glass jug clouded up on its outer surface. It felt deliciously cold in her hands. Licking her lips, she watched the pale liquid swish around inside it – almost *tasting* that first almighty swig as it hit her throat.

First, she set the jug on the table and went over to the sink. Turning on the cold faucet, she cupped her hands and splashed water over her face.

Then grabbed a hand towel, patted herself dry.

Feeling better, safer, all the time.

It was only a nightmare, she told herself again.

Deana downed two glassfuls of juice, knowing that she'd probably spend the rest of the night going to and from the bathroom.

Who cares? I'm awake, I'm alive and I'm all in one piece!

Back in her bedroom, she caught that same weird figure slink past the window.

Again?

The Lake

NO!
Frowning, she stared hard. But saw nothing.
Just the curtain, stirring softly.
And her tree, murmuring in the breeze.
Wonderful. I'm going crazy. My mind's playing tricks . . .
She set her refilled glass on the nightstand, took off her robe and climbed into bed.
She yawned, glad that the nightmare was over.
She felt safe again.
And sleepy.
Her lips curved in a smile.
As her lids closed, she thought about the party tomorrow night . . .
Tomorrow night?
Tonight, she reminded herself.
Deana yawned again, going through the scenario of telling Mom how she and Allan would be going to the movies after dinner. Mom'd be furious, but she'd soon simmer down. Hey. Mom knew how it was; she'd been there herself, hadn't she?
Once upon a time.
So she keeps reminding me.
Deana smiled sleepily. It felt good, touching her naked body beneath the sheet, the soft breeze wafting through the window.
Thinking about the dinner party – and afterwards, when she and Allan would slip off together.
'Mmm . . .' she whispered. 'Tonight, we're gonna have the time of our lives!'

Chapter Three

'If I were the suspicious type,' Deana said, 'I might think that car is following us.'

'But you're not,' Allan said.

'A little bit, maybe.' She looked over her shoulder. The other car was still beyond the last curve, its headlight beams dim and barely visible through the narrow rear window of Allan's Mustang. Seconds later, the headlights appeared. One was out of alignment, throwing its beam crooked and high. Deana didn't like the cross-eyed look. It made the car behind them seem a bit demented.

'How about turning around?' Allan suggested. 'You're making me nervous.'

'It's making *me* nervous.'

'Probably just some guy on his way to Stinson Beach. Once you're on this road, you're on it for keeps.'

Deana faced the front. Her hands were sweaty. She wiped them on her kilt. 'Maybe you should slow down and let him pass.'

'You've seen too many *Friday the 13th* movies.'

'*You* dragged me to some of them.'

'I love the way you squeal and cover your eyes . . . and peek through your fingers.'

'Maybe we should have gone to a movie,' Deana said.

'Losing your nerve?'

'It's awfully dark out here.'

'It's supposed to be.'

The Lake

'How soon's the turnoff?' Deana asked.

'It's coming up.'

'Well, if he makes the turn, too, I say we forget it.'

Allan turned his head toward her. She couldn't see his expression in the darkness, but he obviously wasn't thrilled by the idea of forgetting it. She couldn't blame him. He had suffered through the dinner with Deana's mother and grandparents, which must've been quite a drag for him, probably able to keep his spirits up only by reminding himself of what was planned for afterward.

'One more thing,' she had told him on the telephone before the party.

He had responded with an 'Uh-oh.'

'This isn't an "uh-oh", pal, this is an "ah-ha". Once dinner's over, you and I will be free to amscray. I was thinking of somewhere very dark and very secluded, perhaps in the vicinity of Mount Tamalpais. You might want to bring a blanket.'

Maybe dinner hadn't been such a drag for Allan, after all, Deana thought. If the nervous, excited looks he'd given her were any indication, he'd been too busy imagining sex in the woods to be bored with the family gathering. She'd had a difficult time herself keeping her mind on the festivities. By the time they were clearing away the dishes, she'd been such a wreck that Mom had asked whether she was upset about something.

Well, see Mom, it's like this. Allan and I aren't actually going to a double feature. We thought we'd find a place over by Mount Tam where we'll have a little privacy; we've only done this kind of thing once before, and we were both a little loaded then, so this will almost be like the first time and I'm a little tense.

Just a little tense, that's all.

The clicking sound of Allan's turn signal brought her back to the present. She realized that she was gripping her thighs and trembling. Calm down, she told herself. This is nothing to be scared about.

'It went right on by,' Allan said after making the turn. For a moment, Deana didn't know what he was talking about. Then she remembered – the car that had been behind them.

'Well,' she said in a shaky voice, 'I guess we're in luck.'

Allan downshifted, the car growling like a determined animal as it started to climb the steep road, headlight beams pushing into the darkness. Deana felt herself sink deeper into the bucket seat.

'Wouldn't a breakdown be fun about now?' Allan asked.

'A laugh riot.'

Maybe this area is a little too secluded, she thought. And too dark – and scary. She found herself thinking about last night. *Nightmare on Del Mar*, starring, ta dah . . . Mr Hatchet Man. Uhhh . . .

She turned her eyes to the safe, familiar green glow of the dashboard instruments.

'We should've gone to a Holiday Inn,' she muttered.

'I thought you were against motels.'

'Yeah, well, I might be changing my mind.'

'Man, I wish you'd changed your mind half an hour ago. Want me to turn around?'

'No, that's okay. We're already here.'

'I don't mind. A bed. A shower. Heyyy.'

'Maybe some other time.'

'Is that a promise?'

'It's a thought. We'll think about it, okay? It still seems kind of . . . I don't know . . . tawdry.'

'Tawdry?'

'Look it up.'

'You're definitely weird, you know that? It's all right to fool around in a car or in the woods someplace, but you do the same thing in a motel room and it's tawdry. Does that make sense?'

'It must,' Deana said, 'or why would I feel that way?'

'Because you're nuts?' Allan suggested.

At the top of a rise, the road leveled out. Ahead was a wide, moonlit clearing – the parking area for the outdoor theater. When they'd been here last month for a production of *Othello*, the lot had been packed with cars.

Now it was deserted.

'Looks like we've got the place to ourselves,' Allan said.

'I figured we might.'

Allan drove to the far end of the lot. He stopped at its edge near

The Lake

the start of the footpath leading through the trees to the theater. He turned off the engine. 'Well, here we are,' he said, sounding a little nervous himself. He killed the headlights. Darkness closed over the car. He took the key from the ignition, pushed the key case into a front pocket of his corduroy pants, and rubbed his hands on his legs. Twisting around, he reached between the seat backs and brought the blanket through the gap.

Outside, the night breeze chilled Deana's legs and seeped like cool water through her sweater. Shivering, she gritted her teeth. She wrapped her arms across her chest. Allan joined her in front of the car. 'Cold?' he asked.

'A little.'

He fluttered open the blanket and draped it over her shoulders like a cape.

'There's room for two,' she said, holding out one side.

He huddled in close against her, drawing the blanket across his back and slipping an arm around her. They walked slowly toward the path. The blanket felt warm and good. So did his hand stroking her side. They were just a few steps along the path before his hand found its way beneath her sweater. She moaned as it moved over her bare skin. It roamed higher.

'Hmmm?' A surprised, questioning sound.

'Fooled you,' she said.

'You were wearing one at dinner.'

'My last stop in the john before we left. It went in the hamper.'

With a sigh, he reached and caressed her breast.

'God,' he whispered. He drew her around to face him. She lost her end of the blanket, but let it fall as Allan hugged her tightly, both hands now under her sweater and rubbing her back, his mouth open and urgent against hers. Breathless, Deana tugged out his shirttails. She sucked his tongue. She stroked his bare back. His hardness was a stiff bulge against her belly, the feel of it stirring a warm, moist tremor deep inside her.

Allan eased Deana away and lifted her sweater. Her skin, bare to the night breeze, crawled with goose bumps. Her nipples, already erect, grew so hard that they ached and then his hands were on them. Warm.

Enclosing her breasts. Squeezing. The heat in her breasts was almost like pain and she threw back her head, squirming.

His hands loosened as if he feared he might be hurting her.

'Toss anything else in the hamper?' he asked in a husky voice.

'Could be.'

He reached for Deana's hips but she danced backward, out of range. She pulled her sweater down. 'Not here,' she said.

'Where?'

She shrugged. 'We're too close to the parking lot.' She waved a hand in that direction. She could see moonlight reflecting on the windshield of Allan's Mustang. 'Let's go in farther.'

'Over by the theater?'

'Yeah.'

'How about on the stage?'

She flung out her arms. 'All the world's a stage, and all the men and women merely—'

'Props,' Allan put in.

'The bard you're not.'

'Can you see it? There we are, right in the middle of the theater, surrounded on every side . . .'

'You're being redundant.'

'Surrounded by all those high rows of seats, empty seats, while we . . .'

'Make the beast with two backs.'

'Screw our heads off,' he said, curling a hand over the back of Deana's neck.

'Yeah,' she sighed.

'And as we lie there,' he whispered, 'our naked bodies sweaty and tangled . . .'

'Gleaming in the moonlight . . .'

'. . . From off in the distance, high up in the seats, comes . . .' He took his hand off Deana's neck, and slowly clapped.

She stared through the darkness at him. He kept on clapping. 'Christ,' she muttered.

He clapped again and again.

'Cut it out, you're scaring me.'

The Lake

He stopped. He laughed softly.

'Let's go back to the car,' Deana said.

'You're kidding.'

'No, I'm not.'

'Deana, it was a joke.'

She turned away. He caught her from behind and wrapped his arms around her belly. She settled back against his warmth.

'I want to get out of here, Allan. It was a rotten idea in the first place.'

'Man, that's the last time I'll tell *you* a story.'

'Yeah, well, somebody *could* be around here. How do we know?'

'We don't.' His hands moved up to her breasts.

She stroked the backs of his hands as they caressed her through the sweater. 'We'll go someplace else, okay?'

'Like where?'

'Someplace that isn't . . .' Allan gently pinched her nipples and she caught a ragged breath. 'Isn't so dark,' she said in a shaky voice. 'A street near home.'

'In the back seat?' She nodded.

'Wouldn't it be better . . .' His voice stopped. His fingers spread out, hands still holding her breasts but motionless.

'Allan?'

'Shhh.'

'What?'

Then Deana heard it, too. 'It's just the wind,' she whispered.

'It's a car.'

Deana's insides went soft and loose. She tightened herself.

If it was a car, where were its headlights? Allan took a hand off her breast. The warmth went away. He pointed. At first, Deana saw only strips of moonlit parking lot in the spaces between the trees. Then a dark shape crossed one of the strips. More like a chunk of shadow than a car.

'It's probably someone like us,' Allan whispered.

'What do you mean?'

'A couple. You know. Looking for a good place to mess around.'

'God, I hope so.'

'Let's get back to the car.' He picked up the blanket. Deana stayed close to his side as he walked along the path. She still heard the car, but she couldn't see it. Just before the end of the path, Allan crossed to a tree. She followed. Ducking behind its trunk, they looked out at the parking area.

The Mustang was only a few yards away. The other car was directly behind it, motionless near the middle of the lot. Its headlights were off. Its engine idled. The glare of the moonlight on the windshield prevented Deana from seeing inside.

'What do you think?' she whispered.

'I don't like the way it's just sitting here.'

'Do you think he can see us?'

'I doubt it.'

For a while, they watched the car in silence.

'This is crazy,' Deana finally said. 'Why doesn't he go away?'

'Maybe it *is* somebody making out.'

'With the engine going?'

'It's like he's waiting,' Allan said.

'Yeah. For us.'

'Don't worry. Nothing can happen as long as he stays in the car and we stay here.'

'What if he gets out?'

'Comes looking for us?'

'Yeah.'

'It'd be easy to hide from him. He wouldn't know where to start looking. Maybe we could even double back to my car.'

'Maybe we should just go to your car. Right now.'

'You think so?' Allan asked.

Her heart pounded so hard that it made her chest ache.

'At least we'd get it over with. We can't wait around all night. And we don't really know what he's doing in there.'

'Maybe just enjoying the scenery,' Allan suggested in a nervous whisper. 'You want to give it a try?'

'I don't know.'

'It was your idea.'

'Yeah, well, I'm not so sure about it.'

'It's either that, or we try to wait him out.' Allan looked over his shoulder at Deana. 'Maybe we should go ahead with our original plan.'

'I'm glad you haven't lost your sense of humor.'

'He might be gone by the time we get back.'

'And if he isn't and he nails us,' Deana said, 'at least we'll have shared a few moments of bliss.'

'Bliss?'

'*Shit*,' she muttered.

'Ditto.'

'We're going to feel like a couple of prize idiots after we stroll out to the car and drive off and he's still sitting there.'

'Does that mean you want to do it?' Allan asked.

'No, I don't want to do it, goddamn it, I'm scared shitless, but what sort of choice do we have?'

'We'd only be out in the open for a few seconds.'

'Yeah. What's he going to do, spray us with lead?'

Allan pushed himself away from the tree trunk and stood up straight. He took a deep, loud breath and blew it out. He had the wadded blanket under his left arm. He dug his right hand into the pocket of his cords, took out his keys, and picked through them until he found the car key.

'Did you lock your side?' he whispered.

'Yeah. I always do.'

'Okay, you take the keys. Once you're in, reach across and unlock my door.'

'Don't give me this ìladies firstî stuff. You're quicker than me.'

'Deana.' He sounded ready to argue, but paused. He was silent for a few seconds. 'I know what we'll do,' he said. 'You wait here. I'll go out to the car and bring it right up to here. Sideways, so it'll shield you. Then you just jump in, and off we go.'

'Don't be a . . .' She shook her head. That's right, she thought, snap at him for offering to take all the risk. Leaning closer, she kissed him softly on the mouth. 'You're all right,' she whispered.

'You, too.'

She stroked his cheek. She almost said that she loved him, but decided it would sound too sappy and melodramatic. This is it. End of the road. I love you. Violins. Hand in hand, the lovers stride toward their rendezvous with death.

An hour from now we'll be laughing about this.

Sure. Maybe in a week.

'We go out together,' she said.

'I really think . . .'

'You and me, pardner. Butch and Sundance.'

'Please. *Not* Butch and Sundance.'

'Let's get it over with.' She took the blanket from him. He didn't put up a fuss, apparently realizing that they would have to rely on his speed if something went wrong. She held his hand. It felt wet and cold.

They stepped out from behind the tree and walked through the high grass straight toward the front of his Mustang.

The headlights of the other car came on. Deana's stomach gave a cold lurch. One of the beams was high. It crossed the other. She moaned.

'Just act normal,' Allan said.

A foot in front of the bumper, they let go each other's hand and split up, Deana walking to the passenger door while Allan stepped to the driver's door. She gripped the handle, thumb on the latch button, ready. Forcing her gaze away from the other car, she looked across the Mustang's low roof and watched Allan bend over. She heard the rasp of his key entering the lock, the quiet thump of the button popping up. Allan swung his door open.

The other car sprang forward, roaring. Allan's head snapped toward it. He was bright in the glare of its headlights, hunched over, mouth wide.

'Get in!' Deana yelled. Dropping the blanket, she ducked and peered through the door window. The ceiling light was on. Allan dived at the driver's seat. The other car hit his legs, yanked him out. Deana lurched back, numb, as the speeding car ripped off the driver's door.

It was slow motion.

It was impossible.

It was the door flipping upward, twisting, skidding across the hood

The Lake

of the Mustang with a trail of sparks and the car rushing past with Allan in front, hooked over the bumper, out of sight from his waist down, the rest of him draped across the side of the car, arms flapping loosely above his head.

Brakes screaming, the car had too much speed to stop before the edge of the lot. It bumped over the grass and smashed into a tree. The tree caught Allan in the rump. He was thrown backward from the waist, hair flying, arms flinging out.

The back-up lights came on. The car shot backward. Allan rolled loose, hung in the air for a moment in front of the one working headlight, then dropped and tumbled.

Deana was numb, frozen. But there was a lucid corner of her mind that somehow took control. She peered through the window of the passenger door as the other car raced backward. Allan's keys lay on the seat where they must've fallen when he was hit. Though she knew that her door was locked, she thumbed the latch button anyway and jerked. The door stayed shut. The other car had stopped slightly ahead of the Mustang. Its door opened.

Deana ran.

She ran for the woods, not looking back.

Chapter Four

Dad sat at the kitchen table, drinking coffee and puffing on a cigar, while Mom helped Leigh with the dinner dishes. Most of the dishes, after being rinsed, went into the dishwasher. The crystal glasses, however, Leigh didn't trust to the machine. Those were done by hand, Mom washing them while Leigh dried.

It didn't take long because there were no cooking utensils to contend with; the food had been prepared by the chef at the Bayview, delivered and served by two of Leigh's best waiters, who had since returned to the restaurant.

When the last crystal wine goblet was dry, Leigh suggested after-dinner drinks. Dad, stubbing out his cigar, asked for Scotch and water. Mom wanted Baileys. Leigh stayed in the kitchen to prepare the drinks while her parents headed for the living room.

The evening had gone quite well, she thought. Dad and Mom both seemed to be in excellent spirits, as if oblivious of the rather scary fact that Dad was now only a year short of sixty.

Hell, they're young. Damn young to have a thirty-six-year-old daughter and a granddaughter who will be starting college in the fall. They're both in good health. They've got plenty to be happy about.

Me, too.

Leigh took her time pouring the drinks.

I've got two great parents, a beautiful, intelligent daughter, a thriving restaurant considered the finest place to dine in Tiburon. Not to mention the house. Fabulous house.

The Lake

So what's this jittery feeling in my stomach like something's wrong? Nothing is wrong. Probably just that Deana's out. It's impossible to relax completely when she's gone at night. So much could happen. A breakdown . . .

Allan seems reliable, though. He'll take care of her.

That amused Leigh.

Other way around: Deana would be the one to take charge if a problem came up. Nothing *will* come up. She'll waltz through the door around one o'clock – after the movies are over.

If they went to the movies at all.

Leigh set the glasses on a silver serving tray. She knew she was a bit tipsy, so she concentrated on holding the tray steady as she carried it past the dining area and down the single step to the living room. Mom was in the stuffed chair, Dad standing by the glass wall staring out at the view. He turned around as Leigh set the tray on a low table in front of the sofa.

'I can't get over your view,' he said.

'Me neither.' Leigh had lived in this house for eight years, and still found herself staring out at the vista daily.

'That was a lovely dinner,' Mom said.

Leigh handed her a snifter of Irish Cream. 'Beef Willington is Nelson's specialty.'

'It's such a shame that Deana had to leave early.'

Leigh smiled, and fought an urge to roll her eyes upward. Mom had to start on that. Well, she could be counted upon to start on something, especially after a few drinks. 'Mom, she and Allan cancelled a dinner reservation so she could be here.'

'Why would she have a dinner reservation for *tonight*? Didn't you tell her . . .?'

'We originally asked you over for last night, remember? But you and Dad had the club banquet.'

'It still wouldn't have killed her to stay.'

'She has a life of her own,' Dad said. He took his Scotch and water from the tray, and sat on the sofa. Leigh lifted her glass of Chablis off the tray. Holding it carefully, she lowered herself onto the sofa beside Dad. 'I'm sure she has better things to do,' he continued, 'than spend Friday night was a bunch of old fogeys.'

'We're hardly old fogeys,' Mom pointed out. 'It wouldn't have killed her to spend one evening with her family.'

'She sees you all the time,' Leigh said. 'It's not as if you live in Timbuctoo.'

'Wherever the hell *that* is,' Dad said. Smiling, he took a drink.

'What do you know about this Allan?' Mom asked.

'She's been going with him for a couple of months. She met him in drama class.'

'He's an *actor*?'

'I think he intends to be an attorney.'

'Great,' Dad said. 'We could use a lawyer in the family. You know what they say – every family needs a lawyer, a doctor, and a plumber.' He grinned. 'And a restaurateur, of course.'

'He's hardly part of the family.'

'I don't know, Helen, they looked pretty serious to me.'

'Don't be silly.'

'And it is probably no coincidence,' he added, 'that they both plan to attend Berkeley in the fall.'

'Berkeley,' Mom muttered. She rolled her eyes upward. 'Don't talk to me about Berkeley.'

'I don't think it's the same as when I was there,' Leigh told her.

'Well, thank God for that.'

Dad settled back against the cushion and crossed his legs. He looked at Leigh. 'You turned out pretty well for a radical hippie chick.'

'Let's drop *this* subject,' Mom said. 'Uhhh. The absolute *hell* you put us through. Do you have any idea of the *hell* you put us through?'

Leigh sighed. She didn't need this. 'It was a long time ago,' she said.

'Your senior year in high school. That's when it all started. You were just Deana's age. She's such a fine young lady. You don't know how lucky you are.'

'We're all pretty lucky,' Dad said. He patted Leigh's knee, and gave her one of those looks that said, 'Sorry about this. You know how Mom gets.'

'How do you think you'd feel if Deana came home one fine day, dressed up like one of those "punks" you see on the street corners in

The Lake

the city? How would that make you feel if her lovely hair was all chopped off and spiky like a bed of nails, and *green*? Or orange! Or maybe she comes home with a Mohawk, looking like Mr T!'

Leigh couldn't hold back her smile.

'You'd be smiling out of the other side of your face, young lady. Suppose she had a safety pin in her cheek?'

'I never did any of that,' Leigh told her.

'Only because it didn't happen to be iinî at the time.'

'What movies did they go to?' Dad asked.

'I'm not sure. A double feature in San Anselmo, I think.'

'We went to see—'

'You should've seen yourself,' Mom interrupted. 'You looked like one of those Manson girls.'

'Mom.'

'Helen.'

'God only knows what might've become of you if we hadn't shipped you off to Uncle Mike's.' A pause. 'And then look what happened.'

Leigh felt as if an icicle had been thrust into her belly.

'Damn it, Helen!' Dad snapped.

'Well, it's the truth. You *know* it's the truth.' Her eyes watered up. Her lower lip began to tremble. 'Don't raise your voice at me,' she said with a tremor.

'You push it and push it. We're supposed to be here for a good time. The *last* thing Leigh needs is to have that summer thrown into her face.'

Mom took a drink of Baileys. She stared into the snifter, weeping quietly. 'I was . . . just trying to make a point.'

Leigh got up from the sofa. Crouching next to her mother, she said, 'Hey, it's all right.' She had a lump in her throat, tears in her own eyes. She stroked her mother's hair. 'That was so long ago. Everything's fine now, isn't it?'

'You put us through such hell.'

'I was pretty much of a creep there for a while. But now is what counts. The present. I'm not so bad now, am I?'

'Oh, honey,' Mom sobbed. 'I love you.' She pulled Leigh's head down and kissed her. Leigh stayed at her side while she took out a

Kleenex and wiped her eyes and nose. Her mascara was smeared, making her look a little weird, somehow reminding Leigh of Bette Davis in *Hush . . . Hush, Sweet Charlotte*, though Mom didn't look nearly as old or weird as Charlotte. 'The Beef Willington was absolutely delicious,' she finally said, signaling her recovery.

'It's Nelson's specialty,' Leigh said. Hadn't they been through this before? She didn't mind. 'You two really should come to the Bayview more often,' she said, returning to the sofa and picking up her wine.

'We don't like to take advantage,' Dad said, looking vastly relieved. His eyes were red. He, too, must've been weeping.

'You're not taking enough advantage,' Leigh told him.

'You'd see us there more often if you'd let us pay for our meals occasionally.'

'If that's what it takes,' she said.

Some of the tension remained, and Leigh's parents soon got up to leave.

'I wish we could stick around till Deana gets back,' Dad said, 'but that might be a while and I've got eighteen holes waiting for me in the morning.'

They walked toward the door.

'Why don't you and Deana come over next week?' Mom suggested. 'We'll barbecue and the pool's nice and warm with all this hot weather we've been having.'

'That sounds nice.'

'And tell Deana to bring her friend.'

'All right.'

'We really didn't get much of a chance to visit with her tonight.'

'I know. I'm sorry about that.'

'You should bring a friend, too.'

Let's not start on that, Leigh thought. The one touchy subject that had fortunately been avoided until now.

'Really, darling, you're thirty-six and—'

'We'd better be on our way,' Dad interrupted. He hugged Leigh and kissed her cheek. 'I had a wonderful time, sweety. Thanks so much for the dinner and presents. And give our love to Deana.'

'I will. Happy birthday, Dad.'

The Lake

He patted her rump and turned away to open the door.

'Next Saturday, all right?' Mom asked.

'You're on.'

They hugged and kissed.

Leigh followed them out to the driveway, waited there while they climbed into the Mercedes, and waved as Dad backed the car up the steep driveway.

Inside, she shut the door, leaned back against it, and sighed.

Over.

At least Deana hadn't been around to witness Mom's tantrum.

She gathered up the glasses, took them into the kitchen, and rinsed out the milky residue of Mom's Irish Cream. She would wash them properly in the morning.

She had the house to herself. It felt good. If only she could get rid of that nervous feeling about Deana. From several years of experience, however, she knew that wouldn't go away until Deana returned.

She looked at the clock. Not even ten-thirty. The first movie was probably just ending. Deana probably wouldn't be home till one. A long wait.

So make the most of it.

Out on the deck, shivering as the breeze found its way through her gown, Leigh twisted a knob to heat the water in her redwood hot tub. She hurried back inside and walked down the long hallway to her bedroom at the far end of the house. There she slipped out of her clothes and put on a soft, bulky bathrobe.

There was a greasy stain on the breast of her gown from a glob of hollandaise that had dripped off an asparagus spear. She took the garment into the bathroom and scrubbed at the spot with hot water. She threw the gown over a bedroom chair. It would have to go to the cleaners. She tossed her undergarments into the hamper. She lined up her shoes on the closet floor. No hurry. She wanted the water in the redwood tub to be good and hot before she ventured out again.

Dropping onto her bed, she checked *T.V. Guide*. One of the local channels would be showing a repeat of an old *Saturday Night Live* show at eleven. She remembered watching one of the current *SNL*s with Deana a couple of weeks ago. Deana had found humor in strange places.

Generation gap.

She thought about her mother.

Mom's right. I'm damn lucky Deana hasn't gone freaky the way I went when I was her age.

Pretty harmless stuff, though.

Except for that sit-in. That's what got to them, the idea that their wonderful daughter almost got herself thrown in the slammer. That's what did it. That's why they sent you to Uncle Mike's . . .

Her stomach knotted cold.

Quickly, she rolled off the bed and took a towel from the closet. She hurried down the hall.

Don't think about it.

Do not.

I'll watch the TV when I come in. Or read a book. Anything that takes my mind off what Deana is up to right now.

Leigh left the foyer light on, then made a circuit of the kitchen, dining area and living room, turning off all the lights. Stepping outside, she slid the glass door shut behind her. She flicked a switch to start the bubbles, climbed the three stairs beside her tub, and dropped her towel onto the platform. She took off her robe. Gritted her teeth at the chill of the breeze.

Quickly, she stepped over the side of the tub. The warm water came up her leg to the knee. Not bad, but it would get better as the heat increased. She lifted her other foot over the edge, stood on the submerged seat, then stepped off and crouched, covering herself to the shoulders, sighing with relief as the water eased the chill. For a while, she didn't move. The water swirled, its warm currents caressing her like gentle, exploring hands.

Then she glided forward, stretching her hands to the front rim and peering over the top, higher than the deck railing so she had an unobstructed view.

Below, most of the houses at the foot of the hill were lit. A lone car circled the cul-de-sac and pulled into the Stevensons' driveway. Off to the left, a car crept up Avenida Mira Flores, turned toward her, and dipped down the slope. Much too early to be Allan's car. Over the tops of the hills, Leigh could see a piece of Belvedere Island rising out of the bay, dark except for a few specks of light from street lamps, house windows, and cars.

Beyond Belvedere, far off in the distance, the northern end of the Golden Gate Bridge was visible – red lights on top of its tower, cables sloping down. The bridge was often shrouded in fog, but not tonight. Nor was there fog sneaking over the tops of the hills beyond Sausalito. Too bad. The fog was always so lovely in the moonlight, glowing like a thick mat of snow and always moving, always changing. She watched the headlights of cars on Waldo Grade, then lowered her gaze to the lights of Sausalito.

Leigh rarely went to Sausalito anymore. It was no longer a town, it was a traffic jam. She shook her head, remembering how she used to love that place. Back in her high-school days. A century ago. God, the hours she used to spend there, wandering around. It had street people then, not just tourists. It had the Charles Van Damm: the ancient, beached stern-wheeler had been a coffee house in those days, and she used to sit in the smoky darkness far into the night, listening to the singers. The guy with the twelve-string who did 'The Wheel of Necessity'. Leigh sighed. She hadn't heard that song in about twenty years.

Staring out at the swath of Sausalito lights, she could hear it in her head – the pounding thrum of guitar chords, the raspy, plaintive voice of the singer. What had become of him? What was his name – Ron? He was the best. 'The Wheel of Necessity.' She'd forgotten all about that song. It must have been Mom's talk about the early days that had helped stir her memory.

Ah, the water felt good. Releasing the tub's edge, Leigh eased backward to the far side. The bench rubbed her rump. She sat low, stretched out her legs and let the roiling water lift them. She held on to the edge of the seat to keep herself from drifting up. The water was very hot now, wisps of steam rising off its surface.

She closed her eyes.

'The House of the Rising Sun', that was another one the guy used to sing. Sometimes, she hadn't been able to force herself to leave. On a couple of occasions, she didn't get home until almost two o'clock. No wonder she drove her parents crazy. If Deana ever stayed out that late . . .

She wondered what Deana and Allan were up to. If they had really stayed for both shows, they would have to drive straight back here to arrive by one o'clock. Deana had said she would be back by one, and she was reliable that way.

What they probably did, they split before the second feature so that they'd have some time to make out. Deana was usually straight with Leigh; on matters like this, however, she might bend the truth a bit. Only natural, Leigh thought. The girl wouldn't want to announce that she was fooling around.

Just be careful, honey.

Yeah, like I was.

Pregnant at eighteen. Not exactly a picnic. It worked out, though. It worked out fine.

Charlie.

No.

Her eyes sprang open. Her heart raced. She took deep breaths.

No. That's one little trip down memory lane you don't want to take.

You filthy whore! shrieked in her face.

Leigh groaned. She stood up fast.

I'm not going to remember, she told herself.

Her warm wet skin, hit by the breeze, turned achingly cold from shoulders to waist. She started to shake. Gritted her teeth. Crossed her arms over her breasts. Drops of water rolled down her back and sides.

The shock treatment did its trick, forcing her mind into the present.

The memories of that time didn't come often, but when they did they could tear her apart if she let them. Fortunately, there were the tricks. She had taught herself plenty of ways to stop the assault before it went too far. This was a new one, and hurt less than punching the nearest wall or digging her fingernails into her leg.

If she relaxed into the warmth again, however, the memories would start once more. Once that terrible door in her mind was open, it stayed that way for a while. The thoughts had to keep busy with other matters.

She started to sing 'Waltzing Matilda'. She sang it quietly in a shaky voice as she climbed from the tub, towelled herself dry, and put on her robe. She kept on singing it while she turned off the bubbles and heater.

In the kitchen, she looked at the clock.

11:15.

She wished Deana were here.

Probably parked somewhere – maybe nearby. If they'd left the movies early, though, they'd be careful not to return too soon and blow their cover.

Leigh smiled.

The kid was no dummy.

Hope she's smart enough to use something. If she had taken care of that little matter, though, she had kept it to herself.

Don't depend on the guy, for God's sake.

Maybe I should have another talk with her.

Hell, if she hasn't gotten the message by now, it's probably too late.

In her bedroom, Leigh took off her robe. She put on a light silken nightgown.

From the way that Deana and Allan acted around each other, Leigh was pretty sure they had already made love. The idea of that, shocking at first, no longer bothered her. Hell, the girl was eighteen. What kind of girl *hasn't* done it by eighteen? And Allan seemed like a good kid.

Just don't knock her up, that's all I ask.

Save the bambinos for after college.

In the den, she inserted a tape of *The Way We Were* into her VCR. Before turning it on, she got herself a glass of wine from the kitchen. Then she switched on the television and sat on the sofa.

When her glass was empty, Leigh stretched out. A pillow propping up her head, she watched the movie. She had seen it many times. The hot tub, followed by the wine, had left her feeling languorous. After a while, she let her eyelids drift shut.

The jangle of the telephone startled her awake. Thrusting herself up, she grabbed the phone off the lamp table. 'Hello?'

Deana.

It wasn't Deana.

'Leigh. It's Dad. 'Fraid we'll have to call off that date next Saturday, hon. Had a message to say your Aunt Abby had a heart attack. She's in intensive care. So Mom and I are catching a flight to Boulder just as soon as we can.'

'Oh, Dad . . .'

'It's okay, Leigh. Don't you worry none about your Aunt Abby. She's in safe hands and we'll be looking after her when she comes out of hospital. Sorry to spring this on you, honey – after such a wonderful evening an' all. We both enjoyed it so much. Now this. Matter of fact, your Mom's packing as we speak, so . . .'

'Sure, Dad. Have a safe flight. And tell Aunt Abby she has our love.'

'Speaking of which – young Deana, has she . . . ?'

'Deana's okay, Dad. Tucked up in bed right now . . .'

A white lie; reasonable at a time like this. Can't have Mom and Dad worried about Deana. 'Sides, she's gonna show up any minute, now . . .

'She shouldn't worry you like this, Leigh. Get to grips with the situation before—'

'Before she ends up like I did at her age?'

'You know what I mean, young lady. Now, sounds like my presence is required elsewhere . . .'

'Okay, Dad. Safe journey. Love to Mom.'

'Sure. Catch up with you later, honey.'

Leigh's stomach began to churn. Something was not quite *right* about tonight; she was sure of it. And it wasn't only the news about Aunt Abby, either. Put it down to Deana, she told herself.

For God's sake, Deana. *Where are you?*

The phone jangled again. Leigh caught a ragged breath.

Deana. Something's wrong . . .

She snatched up the phone again.

A man's voice said, 'I'd like to speak to Leigh West.'

'This is Leigh West.' Her heart pumped hard. She felt dizzy.

'This is Detective Harrison of the Mill Valley Police Department. I'm calling about your daughter . . .'

Chapter Five

Glancing over her shoulder as she made her break for the woods, Deana saw a figure leap from the car. He was tall and cadaverous, with strangely long arms. He loped after her, waving a meat cleaver overhead. He was dressed all in white and wore a chef's cap that wobbled and flopped as he ran.

Whirling away from him, Deana dashed onto the path. She had a good head start. She was in good shape from running every day before school. If he wasn't fast enough to overtake her quickly, she might get away.

I *will* get away, she thought. I have to.

If he catches up, he'll kill me.

She couldn't hear him. He must have been far behind, but she didn't dare slow down.

She pumped her arms, threw her legs forward in long, fast strides, felt the breeze in her face.

I'm really moving. He'll never get me.

She looked back.

He was three strides behind her, a white silent phantom grinning in the moonlight.

No!

Deana lunged to the right, leaving the path, her only hope to lose him in the trees. The underbrush tried to snare her feet. But it'll slow him down, too, she told herself. She jumped over a dead branch, hurled herself through a narrow gap between two tree trunks, made a quick turn, and scurried up a slope. Near the top, the slope became very steep. She clawed at weeds for handholds. Her feet slipped on the dewy ground.

A quick tug at her waist. Clutching the weeds, she twisted her head around. He was beneath her, a hand clenched on the hem of her skirt.

'Ho ho ho,' he said, and yanked.

Deana clung to the weeds. With a raspy tearing sound, the skirt released her. It whipped down her legs, and the waistband jerked her toes from the ground as it slid under them. The man cried out. Skirt in his hand like a dark banner, he flew backwards and tumbled to the bottom of the slope.

Deana scampered to the top. Panting for air, she leaned over the edge and saw him start to climb again. She stepped back. The forest floor was dappled with moonlight. She found a fallen limb and picked it up. Raising it over her shoulder, she crouched near the edge.

Seconds passed. She listened to the rustling sounds of his climbing. Then his head appeared. He had lost his chef's cap in the fall.

He had the cleaver clamped between his teeth.

Deana brought the limb down with all her strength. It cracked against the top of his head. Losing his hold on the weeds, he dropped backwards. His arms waved. His back hit the slope and his legs kicked up at the darkness.

He somersaulted back down the slope.

He was still falling when Deana threw aside her branch and rushed away. As she ran, she wondered if she should have followed him to the bottom and hit him until he couldn't get up again – until he was dead. Too late for that. But maybe the single blow had been enough.

She couldn't count on that.

At least she had given herself some time. If she could just find a hiding place . . .

Climb a tree, she thought.

Slowing down, she glanced at the nearby trees. One had a fork in the trunk that looked low enough to reach. She rushed over to it. Leaping, she grabbed the thick branch and pulled herself up. She wrapped her bare legs round the trunk. Writhing, she hugged the branch. She twisted, kicked, hooked a foot over the crotch of the trunk,

The Lake

and finally managed to squirm onto the branch. Straddling it, she let her legs hang down while she scanned the woods.

Her pursuer was nowhere in sight. Maybe he still lay at the bottom of the hill, unconscious or dead. If the blow with the stick hadn't done it, maybe he had broken his neck in the fall or struck his head on a rock.

Tipping back her head, Deana looked at the branches above her. If she got high enough, she would be safe. He would never be able to spot—

Cold fingers wrapped her ankles.

Her breath burst out from her.

He was beneath her, grinning up.

'Now I gotcha,' he said in a low voice.

Impossible! Where had he come from?

'No! Please!' she gasped.

He pulled, forcing her down hard against the branch between her legs. Deana shoved at the branch with both hands, trying to ease the hurt.

He swung on her ankles, his weight a torture, his momentum scraping her against the bark. Blood spilled from her, splattering his face. Gazing down, she saw a split crawl out of her pubic hair, widening as it climbed to her navel. Her sweater was gone. She was naked and the fissure was moving toward her chest. She felt the thickness of the branch tearing her insides, driving into her like a wedge. Her rib cage broke open. And still he swung beneath her . . .

In horror, she saw her breasts on each side of the branch. *When it reaches my neck, my head will pop off.* 'Please stop!' she shrieked – and woke up gasping.

Deana was in bed, in her own room. Wiping sweat from her eyes, she looked at the alarm clock. Almost three o'clock in the morning. She was tangled in sweaty sheets.

She unwrapped herself and sat up. Her sodden nightgown clung to her body. She peeled it off and tossed it to the floor. The air felt good on her hot skin.

Crossing her legs, she held on to her knees and took deep breaths.

Her heart began to slow down. She remembered the nightmare vividly. A strange nightmare – such a horrible, distorted version of what had happened that night.

If only the reality, too, had turned out to be a nightmare.

Allan.

In her mind, she saw the car carrying him through the night, smashing him against the tree. She shivered at the memory, and wrapped her arms across her chest.

According to the police, Allan had died almost immediately from the massive injuries. But Deana hadn't known that until later, while she was waiting in the police station.

Fleeing through the woods, she had ached to return to Allan, get him into the car and rush him to a hospital. But *he* was back there, pursuing her. So she raced on, then hid for a long time high in a tree, and later made her way down to a road where a teenaged couple on their way back from Stinson Beach gave her a lift to Mill Valley. She didn't even ask them to take her back to the theater parking area.

For all she knew, then, Allan might still be alive. But the man might be there, waiting, and Deana couldn't ask these strangers to risk their lives. She was afraid for herself, too. She had escaped, and the thought of returning filled her with terror.

It wouldn't have done any good, going back. She knew that now, but the guilt remained and would probably be with her for a long time. The fear, too.

Sleep had been a refuge. She'd slept through most of the day after getting home, and had gone to bed early last night. She wished she could go back to sleep now, but she felt wide awake and she was afraid of the dream. What if it came back?

What if it returned every night?

And maybe that *other* nightmare she'd had, maybe that had been a portent of things to come. It was too spooky to think about.

Swinging her legs off the bed, Deana reached up and turned on a lamp. She crossed her room to the dresser, took out a jersey nightgown, and put it on. The clinging fabric felt good against her chilled skin. She left her room and made her way down the dark hallway to the bathroom. After using the toilet, she returned.

The Lake

With pillows behind her back, she sat in bed and opened a book. As she started to read, a quiet sound from the hallway made her stiffen. Her gaze darted to the door. A moment later, her mother appeared.

'How are you doing?' Mom asked.

Deana shrugged.

'Want to talk?'

'Sure.'

Mom sat near the end of the bed, turning sideways to face Deana, a leg drawn up beneath her nightgown. 'Trouble sleeping?' she asked.

'I had this lousy rotten nightmare.'

'Rough, huh?'

'It wasn't fun. He caught me. Split me right up the middle.' Trying to smile, she drew a finger up the front of her nightshirt. 'The mind plays funny tricks.'

'Hilarious tricks,' Mom said.

'Does it get any better?'

Mom shrugged.

'How did you . . . cope with it when my father was killed?'

'I guess you helped pull me out of it. When I found out I was pregnant, it gave me something new to worry about, so I stopped dwelling on the past.'

'Maybe I should run out and get pregnant.'

'I don't recommend it.' Lowering her eyes, Mom frowned. 'There was something else, too. Your father . . . it's hard to think of him as your father . . . the young man who got me pregnant . . .'

'Charlie Payne,' Deana said.

'I didn't know him very well. I didn't actually love him. That must've made a difference. I took Charlie's death pretty hard. I mean, I was there and it was partly my fault, so I had plenty of guilt to deal with, but I know it would've been a lot worse if I'd actually loved him.'

'What is there, a family curse or something? Look at us. Both of us lost boyfriends – lovers. You were eighteen, I'm eighteen. It's kind of weird, don't you think?'

'There isn't any curse.' Something about the tone of Mom's voice made Deana wonder.

'Just bad luck?'

'We were both taking chances, honey. Going where maybe we shouldn't have been. It doesn't take a curse.' Mom patted Deana's leg through the blankets, and stood up. 'The important thing is not to blame yourself for what happened.'

'Not so easy.'

'I know. Don't I know.' Bending over, she kissed Deana. 'See you in the morning, honey.'

As she headed for the door, Deana said, 'You'll come with me to the funeral, won't you?'

'Of course. We'll go out tomorrow and buy you something appropriate.'

Chapter Six

The mother's face was hidden behind a black veil, but she felt the eyes focused on her, watching her, hating her. The preacher, standing beside the grave, spoke calmly of the sure and certain hope of resurrection. The mother, voiceless, damned her.

It's not my fault. *Please*.

'And so,' the preacher said, 'as the coffin sinks slowly into the ground, we bid a fond farewell . . .'

The mother started to move. She walked around the end of the grave, slowly.

Stay back.

No, don't point at me. Oh, my God!

She took a step backward as the mother approached but bumped into someone behind her.

'You! You did this to him. You filthy whore!' The pointing hand opened and darted forward, smacking her face. 'You murdered him with your lust, you whore! Monster!' To the others, she shouted, 'Look at her! Look at the monster! *This* is what murdered my boy!' The hands clawed at her, ripped her blouse open, tore it from her shoulders, grabbed her naked breasts.

Crying out in agony, she squirmed and tried to pry the fingers loose.

'*You* should be dead, not him! Not my boy!'

'No! Let go!'

'You killed him, whore!'

She was dragged forward by her breasts, whimpering. Then the mother twisted and flung her down. She hit the edge of the grave with her knees. Wildly flailing her arms, she caught her balance. But a shove from behind sent her tumbling.

'*That*'s where you belong!'

She fell and fell.

She wanted to scream out her terror, but she couldn't get a breath.

Why is it so deep?

It always is.

She'd been here before. She realized that now. Familiar territory, this bottomless grave.

Only it's not bottomless.

She knew that. And she remembered what was below. Choking out a whimper, she flapped her arms and kicked, desperate to stop, to take flight, to get the hell out of here.

Pitch dark. Grave dark.

But she could see in the dark.

The coffin didn't have a lid. There had been a lid when it was lowered, but not anymore. He wore a necktie and brown suit. His feet were bare. His face, as pale as chalk, glowed beneath her.

Okay now, don't, she thought as she fell closer. Please don't.

Oh, but he will.

Oh shit he will he always does but they were dreams before and this is real and he's really dead so he won't open his eyes this time, not this time, or reach up like a goddamn zombie to grab me, not this time.

The holes where his eyes had been opened wide.

He reached up.

'*NO!*'

Leigh heard her voice and opened her eyes as she thrust herself away from him. Below was her powder-blue pillow. She was on her hands and knees, gasping.

It *was* a dream. Of course.

Thank God.

And thank God morning was here.

Still braced on stiff arms, Leigh lowered her head.

Scratch one nightgown, she thought.

It used to happen a lot. But the last time, Deana was about four.

The Lake

Talk about Allan's funeral, that's what did it. The last thing before sleep.

Leigh rolled off the bed. When she stood, the nightgown slipped the rest of the way down. She stepped out of it, picked it up, and inspected the damage. The gauzy fabric was split down the middle, breast to belly, and one of the straps had been wrenched from its seam. One for the ragbag.

No, better get rid of it. You don't want Deana seeing it. Deana didn't know about the dreams. Or about the funeral of Charlie Payne. And finding out wouldn't do her any good.

Leigh looked down at herself.

She groaned.

Edith Payne didn't grab her for real in nightmare-land and do this. Leigh had done it to herself.

But this was a new twist.

Not even in the old days when the dream came regularly did she ever wake up to find fingernail marks on her breasts.

Tiny little crescent moons.

They looked a lot like the ones Edith Payne had given her the day of the funeral.

Chapter Seven

When Deana woke up, she heard bathwater running. It was unusual for Mom to take a bath first thing in the morning.

She remembered the shopping trip. To buy a black dress. For tomorrow's funeral.

Her fresh morning eagerness collapsed. Her stomach went jittery and she knew that she had to get up fast or she would lie here immobilized, sinking.

She swung her legs down, sat on the edge of the bed, and wondered if she could force herself to go running. She always went running as soon as she got up. She loved it – the peacefulness of the quiet streets, the smell and feel of the morning air, the way it felt when she was pushing to make it up a slope and especially when she reached the top and there was level road ahead and she would really go all out.

Night. The woods.

Deana went numb.

She saw herself racing through the darkness, dodging trees. She felt the terror.

You weren't going to think about that.

It was the running that saved me.

She rubbed her thighs, trying to make the goose bumps go down. As she rubbed, she stayed away from the bruises and scrapes she had got shinnying up the tree.

I *will* go running, she decided. She had to do something, and maybe it would wipe her mind clean, at least for a while.

The Lake

Pulling the nightshirt over her head, she stepped to the dresser. She put the nightshirt away, and opened the drawer where she kept her running clothes. The faded red shorts, neatly folded on top, were Allan's. His gym shorts from Redwood High. Deana lifted them from the drawer and held them up by the waistband.

He had worn them that day on the Dipsey Trail. They were too small for him, and the seat had ripped when he'd squatted to catch his breath. It had happened at the top of those endless stairs. They weren't even out of Mill Valley by then, and still had miles to go before reaching Stinson Beach – including a stretch through Muir Woods which was certain to be crowded with tourists. When the ripping sound came, he reached back and felt around. 'Uh-oh,' he said. 'We'd better go back.'

'We can't.' She reminded him that Sally and Murray would be waiting at the beach that afternoon, to give them a lift back to Tiburon.

'We can *drive* over and meet them.'

'Oh, come on. We can't let a little rip stop us.'

'It's not so little.'

'Let me see.'

'Are you kidding?'

'It can't be that bad.'

'I haven't got any . . . uh . . . just a supporter.'

'How tacky.'

'Ha ha ha.'

'Take off your shirt. You can tuck it in back there – eclipse the moon, so to speak.'

'I've got very fair skin,' he said. 'I'd sunburn. How about if I use your shirt instead?'

'Normally, I'd be glad to give you the shirt off my back.' Mimicking him, she added, 'I haven't got any . . . uh . . .'

'I know, I know.'

Allan finally took off his T-shirt and wore it like a tail the rest of the day. Later, he gave the shorts to Deana, gift-wrapped but still torn, as a memento of the journey.

Elbows on the dresser top, the shorts pressed to her face, Deana tried to stop the weeping that had begun when she started to remember. She wiped her eyes dry, but they filled again.

The seam in the rear looked almost as good as new where she had stitched it with the sewing machine.

Maybe best, she thought, to put the shorts away. Hide them in the bottom of a drawer, or something, so they wouldn't be around to remind her of Allan.

Hell, I don't want to forget him. If the memories hurt, it's only because they're *good* memories. I'll wear these shorts till they fall apart, and then I'll still keep them.

Sniffing, Deana stepped into the shorts and pulled them up. The tear-wet seat clung to her skin.

She put on a bra. God knows, *that* hadn't come from Allan. It was an elastic harness made for running – the female equivalent of a jockstrap He'd liked the flimsy, transparent kind that unhooked in front. Or none at all. The look on his face. That first time she hadn't had one on and he hadn't known it until he'd reached under her sweatshirt and touched her breast instead of fabric.

In the mirror, she saw herself smile. Just a bit. She looked like hell with her eyes all red and puffy.

Allan hadn't said anything. He'd moaned.

Deana pulled a T-shirt over her head, took socks from the drawer, and sat on the edge of her bed to put them on.

After that night, she'd started making a game of it. Sometimes she wore a bra, sometimes she didn't. It drove Allan nuts, each time they were together, until he found out one way or another. He never came right out and asked. He observed. He pulled little maneuvers such as running his hand down her back. If he determined that she was wearing a bra, he relaxed. If she wasn't, he spent the rest of the evening watching her chest at every opportunity – apparently eager to catch a jiggle of breast or evidence of nipples pushing against her clothes. If she wore a loose top, he kept trying for glimpses down the front. And Deana would help him by bending over a lot. Obsessed, that's what he'd been.

Been.

Oh shit oh shit.

Deana sprang from her bed. It's okay to think about him, she told herself. Just not all the time.

She took her shoes from the closet. She put them on quickly, grabbed

The Lake

the front door key off her dresser, and hurried down the hall, slipping the long key chain over her head. She dropped the key down the front of her shirt. It felt cold for a second against her skin.

'Back in a while,' she called out through the silence.

'Hey!' came her mother's voice. 'I want to talk to you.'

'*Mom.*'

'Come here.'

Deana backtracked to the master bedroom. She crossed to the bathroom door. It was open a crack. 'Yes?'

'You're not going out to run, are you?'

'That was the plan.'

'I wish you wouldn't.'

Keep it light. 'Gotta stay fit, Ma.'

'Not today, all right?'

'Why not?' She knew why not.

'Because.'

'Mom.'

'I just don't think it's a good idea.'

'You want to turn me into a hermit?'

'You know what Mace said.'

'Mace? You mean Detective Harrison?'

'Yes, Detective Harrison.'

'I know what he said. He said to be careful. I'll be careful.'

'I don't want you going out alone. Not for a few days, anyway.'

'I *need* to run, Mom.'

She heard some quiet splashing sounds from behind the door. Then Mom said, 'Okay, but I'll go with you.'

Deana didn't want to wait. She didn't want company. It wouldn't be the same. 'You'd never be able to keep up with me.'

'You're talking about the gal who wipes you off the tennis courts.'

'You don't want to get sweaty after your bath.'

'I'm not kidding about this. I don't want you going out alone. I mean it.'

Deana sighed. 'Is it all right if I wait for you out front?'

'Where out front?'

'On the driveway. I'll just warm up while I wait.'

'Where on the driveway?'

'At the bottom.'

'All right. But keep your eyes open.'

'Yes, ma'am.'

'I'll be right out.'

Deana started away. Christ, Mom thinks the guy's out there. Ready to pounce on me. Or run me down.

What if she's right?

That is just what I need on top of everything, a good case of paranoia.

'I don't want to frighten you,' Harrison had said. *Mace*. 'You and the Powers boy might very well have been random victims. On the other hand, it's possible that the assailant knew precisely who he was after. If he was after *you*, Deana, then he might make another attempt. You and your mother need to face that possibility and take precautions. Do you understand?'

'He wasn't after me. I mean, it had to be random like you said.'

'Not necessarily.'

'I already told you: I haven't dumped any boyfriends, I don't have any enemies, I—'

'This could be a guy who spotted you at the supermarket and followed you home. It could be a guy who stopped beside you at a traffic light, or sat behind you one night at the movies. And seeing you triggered something. Maybe you wear your hair the same way as a girlfriend who jilted him. Maybe you've got his mother's blue eyes, and she used to abuse him. It could be a hundred things. Do you understand? There's a good chance it *was* random, but you have to act as if you were the intended target. At least until we nail this guy. I don't want you to end up . . . hurt.'

Detective Harrison had sounded as if he really meant it, as if he cared. And somehow as if his lecture, even though addressed to Deana, was actually spoken for Mom's benefit. Something going on there. A subtle undercurrent.

It must have made an impression on Mom. Calling him Mace.

Deana opened the front door, pulled it shut behind her, and stepped over the *San Francisco Sunday Examiner and Chronicle*. She looked back

The Lake

at the paper. Part of her routine was to bring it down from the top of the driveway each morning when she finished her run. She always found it near the top of the driveway – sometimes hidden in the geraniums. This was strange. No matter how good his arm, the paper man couldn't possibly have winged the *Chronicle* all the way to the front stoop. You couldn't even *see* the stoop from the road. He had either driven or walked down the steep driveway to get it here. Really going for Brownie points. Maybe it's somebody new.

Maybe *he* did it.

Deana felt a chill crawl up the back of her neck.

Paranoia must be contagious. Like the flu.

She scanned the ice plant-covered slope across the yard, the hedge at the top, and the weed-choked stretch of hillside behind the Matson house. It all looked normal. The hedge up there was a bit too skimpy to conceal anyone.

At least this is taking your mind off Allan.

She walked past the kitchen windows, and stopped on the broad concrete apron in front of the garage.

The paper man got ambitious, that's all.

One steep mother of a driveway. Narrow, too.

She shook her head.

The geraniums along the sides of the driveway were not skimpy.

Get off it.

Deana stepped closer to the garage. Facing the driveway, she took a deep breath. The morning air smelled sweet and clean. She did a few jumping jacks. When she started the toe-touching exercises, her rump brushed the garage door.

Thatta way, back to the wall. Nobody's gonna sneak up on *you*. No, sirree.

Chicken shit.

She took five steps forward, count 'em, five.

That's better.

That wasn't better. She felt exposed.

What's keeping Mom?

You wanted to go running alone, remember?

She sat down. The concrete, still in shadow, was cold through her shorts and worse against the backs of her legs. She leaned forward, stretching, grabbing her shoes.

I would have been just fine except for Mom's little talk. And she had to remind me of what Harrison said.

The way you wear your hair.

Bull.

She bobbed her forehead between her knees.

Saw a madman in a chef's cap bounding down the driveway, waving a meat cleaver, and looked up fast and saw no one.

Where'd you get this chef's cap nonsense?

Oh yeah, the dream.

Lovely little dream – and all that weird shit the night before.

Legs spread wide, Deana leaned forward, touched her right hand to her left toe, left hand to right toe. The stretching muscles felt good.

She flinched at a sudden bumping sound, then realized that it was only the front door shutting. Mom. That was pretty quick, actually. She got to her feet and hitched up the shorts that had been inching down her rump during the exercises.

'What took you so long?' Deana asked.

'Are you kidding? I'm still wet.'

Deana stared. Mom looked so normal. So *good*. As if this were just any other fabulous Marin County morning. Except for the blue baseball cap covering her pinned-up hair, she was dressed in white – knit shirt, shorts, socks and shoes, all white. Which made her fair skin look almost bronze.

Deana had rarely seen her with her hair up.

'My gosh, Mom, you've got ears.'

'Anything wrong with them?'

'They're rather large, is all.'

Mom grinned. 'Have you looked in a mirror lately?'

Deana's own smile slipped.

Sure have, Mom.

She remembered it well. A red-eyed girl clutching gym shorts.

'Not to change the subject or anything, I thought you promised to stay down here.'

'I did.'

The Lake

Mom raised an eyebrow. Then she swept down from the waist, touched her toes, and made a quick catch as her baseball cap dropped.

'Oh, you mean the newspaper.'

'That's right, Watson. Here, hold this.'

Deana took the hat.

Mom resumed touching her toes. She had a few drops of water on the backs of her legs. No cellulite. She *was* in terrific shape. Always had been. Maybe that was one reason why Deana had started running last year. She'd been getting a bit pudgy, and it was damned embarrassing to have a mother who looked better than you in a bikini. Some of her boyfriends, take Herb Klein, for instance, spent more time ogling Mom than—

'At least you didn't *leave* without me,' Mom said.

'I didn't bring down the newspaper. I didn't touch it.'

'How did it get there?'

'I suppose the delivery guy was feeling energetic.'

'Jeez,' Mom said, 'and Christmas isn't for six months.'

'Maybe he's angling for a Fourth of July tip.'

'Weird.' Mom swung her arms around, then took the hat from Deana and flopped it onto her head with the bill high. She squinted up the driveway. Looked at Deana. Raised one side of her upper lip to show her distaste for the chore ahead. 'Well, I'm ready when you are.'

'I'll make it easy on you.'

'Oh, thanks. You're so thoughtful.'

Deana started up the driveway, leaning into its slope, not pushing. Mom stayed at her side.

It was like climbing a stairway. Taking the stairs two at a time.

She thought of the stairs at the start of the Dipsey Trail. They sure nailed Allan. Let's try not to think about Allan for a while. Let's just think about running, the good feel of working muscles. And getting closer to the top.

Halfway there.

Three-quarters. No sweat. She glanced at Mom. Mom smiled.

The mailbox at the top came into view.

Then the car.

Mom said, 'That's a great place . . . to leave a car.'

It didn't block the driveway. It was parked on the other side of the street. But nobody ever parked there because of the blind curves.

Deana didn't see anyone inside.

She stopped at the edge of the street.

'What's the matter? Pooped?'

'Mom.'

The tone of Deana's voice turned her mother's face strange.

Deana's gaze swept the street and hillside as she walked on numb legs toward the old red Pontiac Firebird. She stepped in front of it. The grille and headlight on its right side were smashed in. 'My God,' she muttered.

Mom grabbed her arm, pulled her. 'Quick. Back to the house.'

They ran.

Chapter Eight

'It needs something.'

'*You* need something,' she said. 'A frontal lobotomy.'

'That's no way to talk to the man who's going to immortalize you.'

'My foot,' she said.

'Precisely.'

'You'd better hurry. If I fall in, I'll tear your face off.'

'Behave.' Still squatting on the bank of the stream, Mace Harrison raised the Nikon to his eye and studied the situation again. 'Nah, no good.'

'Kee-rist.'

He stood up. 'I've got it. Come on back.'

Mattie reached out her hand. He grabbed it and pulled as she leaped across the running water. Her bare feet landed on twigs and she winced.

'Right back.'

'Where are you going?' she asked.

'My first-aid kit's in the car.'

'Good idea, Charlie. You may need it.'

'Buck up. We'll be done shortly.'

Mattie rolled her eyes upward and planted her fists on her hips. 'You know,' she called at his back, 'real models get big beans for this kind of shitski.'

'Don't think I'm unappreciative.'

'No, not you.'

He made the top of the wooded embankment, jogged past a deserted picnic table to the parking area, and opened the trunk of his Trans Am. He glanced around to be sure nobody was nearby, then lifted his twelve-gauge Ithaca shotgun, raised a corner of the blanket on which it had been resting, and took out his first-aid kit.

He hurried back to Mattie.

'What's the big plan?' she asked.

'A Band-Aid on your toe.'

'You jest.'

'Not me. Mark my words, it's just the touch that's needed. An air of vulnerability for an otherwise perfect foot.' He opened the plastic case, took out a bandage, and offered it to her.

'You'd better apply it. You're the *artiste* around here.'

'Fine. Sit.'

'Where?'

'On the ground.'

'It's *wet*.' She wrinkled her nose. Then, with a heavy sigh she sat. 'You owe me for this, Charlie.'

'You'll sing a different tune when your foot's hanging in the De Young.' Tearing off the wrapper, he crouched at Mattie's feet and picked the paper away from the adhesive strip.

'Why can't you be normal and shoot nudes?' she asked.

'Leaves nothing to the imagination, my dear.'

She wiggled her toes. 'That turn you on?'

He nodded. The bandage on the big toe might be a little too obvious. The third toe seemed best, though the Band-Aid was really too large for it.

Mattie leaned back, bracing herself up on stiff arms.

Yes, the third toe. He reached for it.

Mattie raised the knee of her other leg and swung it far to the side. 'Does *this* turn you on?'

He looked. The cut-off jeans were very cut-off – no more than a frayed seam remained between the legs. 'How inelegant,' he said.

Mattie chuckled. She kept her left foot fairly steady while the bandage was being applied, but waved her bent right leg from side to side, whispering, 'Now you see it, now you don't . . . *Now* you see it, now you don't.'

The Lake

'All set.' He patted the bottom of her foot. 'Assume the position.'

'Bet you can't stand up straight.'

'Matter of fact, I already am.'

He pulled her hand, and they both stood up. Mattie bent over to check him out. 'Well, shitski, hon, you could knock me over with a feather. Want me to take care of that for you?' She didn't wait for an answer. 'I know, I know.' Turning away, she stretched out her leg until her foot found one of the small flat-topped rocks a yard from the bank. Arms out for balance, she pushed away from shore with her other foot. Once she was perched on the rock, she pivoted carefully until she was facing him. Then she swept out her right foot, planted it on a nearby rock, and took a deep breath. 'Fire away.'

Crouching, he framed the foot, the water shimmering around the rock. 'Beautiful,' he muttered. He snapped the shot. The camera's automatic advance buzzed. He clicked, straightened up a bit for a new angle, took another shot, sidestepped to the left and took more, stood up straight, took more, then waded out with the cool water filling his sneakers, bent down and snapped a few extreme close-ups.

'What dedication,' Mattie said.

He waded ashore, changed the lens setting for six feet, picked up a stone and tossed it underhand at Mattie's midsection.

'Hey!' she yelped.

She caught the stone. But her quick movement was enough to upset her precarious balance. She flapped her arms as she fell backwards.

He got it all on film – Mattie's stunned expression as she snatched the stone, her flapping arms, her splash when she hit the stream back first, feet flying into the air. Then her furious drenched face as she sat there scowling at him. He kept clicking away as she staggered to her feet and waded toward him. 'I suppose you think you're cute.'

He lowered the camera so that it hung by the strap, and protected it between his arm and side. 'Don't do anything foolish,' he warned as she approached. Mattie had a brown belt in judo. She could throw him ass over head into the stream, and he had no defense short of decking her with a punch. He wouldn't do that.

He didn't like the way she was grinning. 'Mattie, my camera.'

'Pity.'

'My beeper.'

'Oh, your precious beeper.'

'My revolver.'

'A little water won't hurt that.'

'It'll *ruin* my holster.'

'Not to mention your ego, big man.' She grabbed the front of his shirt. Instead of dropping backward, planting a foot in his gut and sending him on a trip, Mattie pulled him against her. The wetness soaked through his shirt.

'I'm going to wait,' she murmured against his mouth. 'When you least expect it, wham.'

'Fair enough.'

'Now, how about tooling me over to my place so I can get out of these duds?'

'You may feel free to get out of them at my place.'

'*Haw.*'

'We'll give them a spin in the dryer, they'll be good as new. Which isn't saying much.'

She swatted his rump. 'Let's move it then, Charlie.' She stepped into her sandals.

They climbed the slope. They were nearly at the top when his beeper sounded.

'I don't believe it,' Mattie muttered. 'There goes our Sunday.'

When they reached the car, he opened the trunk and pulled the blanket out from under the shotgun. Mattie wrapped the blanket around herself, then sat in the passenger seat. 'Maybe it's a wrong number.'

'Most likely.' He called headquarters on his cellular phone. 'Harrison,' he said.

'Mace, you just got a call from a Leigh West. She said it concerned the Powers case.'

Mace took the number, broke the connection with headquarters, and put the call through.

'Hello?' The woman's voice sounded taut.

'Miss West, this is Mace Harrison.'

'I'm sorry to bother you; but you said we should call if anything

The Lake

suspicious happened and the car's out on the street right in front of our house.'

He didn't need to ask what car. 'Any sign of the driver?'

'We didn't see anyone.'

'Is your house locked up?'

'Yes.'

'You're in Del Mar on Mark Terrace, right?'

'That's right.' She gave him the address.

'I'll be there in ten minutes.'

'We're not absolutely sure it's the same car, but—'

'I'll be right over.' He put down the phone. 'The Powers case,' he told Mattie as he swung his Trans Am around. 'That was the mother of the girl. There's a car in front of her house. She thinks it's the one that ran down the boy. Want to come?'

'Like this?' She plucked the wet shirt away from her breasts.

'I can drop you off.'

'Hell, I don't want to miss anything.'

'Didn't think so.'

She bent over, lifted the hanging blanket, and brought her shoulder bag up from beneath her seat. She took out a comb and brush. Then she twisted the rear-view mirror in her direction. Mace's rear visibility was gone, but he didn't protest.

'Guess I shouldn't have stoned you,' he said.

'Those photos just better not show up at roll call.'

'On my honor.' He accelerated to make it through an amber light on Throckmorton. There wasn't much traffic in downtown Mill Valley. He knew he would make good time.

'Should we notify Tiburon PD?' Mattie asked.

'We'll check it out first.'

'You think *he*'s up there?'

'If he is, he hasn't made his move yet. They're secure in the house.'

'Unless he's inside with them.'

It was a disturbing possibility, one that Mace had already considered.

* * *

Leigh hung up the phone and turned around in time to see Deana slide a butcher knife out of its walnut holder. 'What're you—?'

The girl pressed a finger to her lips. She walked quietly across the kitchen to where Leigh was standing. 'Follow me,' she whispered.

'What is it?'

'Shh. Come on.'

Confused and growing alarmed, Leigh followed her past the dining area. What was happening? Had Deana seen something, heard a noise? My God, does she think the killer's in the house? He couldn't be. The doors . . . don't kid yourself, anybody who wanted to get in . . . maybe the guest-room windows.

She scanned the living room. Deana was several strides ahead of her, shoes squeaking on the foyer tile. Leigh rushed to catch up. Beyond the girl's shoulder, she saw the narrow shadowed hallway stretching ahead of them.

Deana *wasn't* planning to search the place?

Leigh almost reached out to grab her, but Deana made a quick lunge into the bathroom, caught Leigh by the hand and yanked her through the doorway. She swung the door shut behind them, locked it, then hurried to the tub and checked behind its frosted-glass shower panels. Turning to Leigh, she let out a loud breath. 'Just being careful.'

'Do you think he's in the *house*?'

'He might be. I mean, I don't really think so, but who's to say he isn't? I just think this'd be a good place to wait until your policeman gets here.'

'He's not *my* policeman.'

'Then how come you called him instead of the Tiburon police?'

'Because this is his case. He knows what's going on.'

'Uh-huh.'

Leigh shook her head. Deana boosted herself up and sat on the counter beside the sink. 'You know what some people have,' the girl said, 'is a safe room. Some actress has one. Victoria Principal? It's the bathroom. You have a reinforced metal door put in, with special locks. You have a telephone put in. That way, you've got someplace to go if there's trouble. You can call the cops, and nobody can get to you. The lock on *this* door wouldn't keep out a four-year-old.'

The Lake

'I wouldn't want to live like that,' Leigh said.

'You don't have to *live* in the john. It's just so you have a place to go . . .'

'No pun intended?'

Deana grinned. Lowering her head, she scraped the knife over her thigh. 'This thing isn't very sharp.'

'It isn't supposed to be a razor.'

She lifted the knife away, and ran her hand up from her knee to her shorts. 'I'm gonna start looking like a werewolf. You're lucky you're a blonde.'

'You've got lovely hair,' Leigh said, stepping past her.

'Yeah, everywhere. What did my father look like, King Kong or something?'

Leigh felt a cold ripple in her stomach. She took off her baseball cap and started to unpin her hair.

'You don't talk about him much,' Deana said after a while.

'There's not much to say.' Crouching, Leigh took Deana's blow-dryer from the cabinet under the sink. 'Mind if I use this?'

'Help yourself.' Deana reached down beside her knee, slid open a drawer, and took out her hairbrush. 'Here.'

'Thanks.'

'Gotta fix yourself up for your policeman.'

Leigh plugged in the dryer, turned it on, and started to brush her hair as the hot air blew through it.

'You never told me how he died,' Deana said in a loud voice.

'Yes, I did.'

'I mean, not *how* it happened.'

'It's a long story.'

'Okay, so?'

'Mace'll be here in a minute.'

'Well, that's . . .' Deana stopped. Frowning, she leaned forward and peered at the bathroom door. 'Turn it off, Mom.'

Leigh silenced the dryer. 'Did you hear something?' she whispered.

'I don't know. That thing's so loud.'

Leigh stood motionless, holding her breath. She flinched at the sudden sound of a thud.

A car door shutting.

'It's probably Mace,' she said.

Deana hopped to the floor, cranked open the bathroom window, and looked out. Leigh gave her hair a few final strokes with the brush. She heard footsteps on the walkway leading to the stoop.

'It's him,' Deana said. 'He's got a gal with him.' She stepped away from the window. 'You think it's his wife?'

'I wouldn't know.'

'Don't worry about your hair. Hers is wetter than yours.'

The doorbell rang.

'Just a second,' Deana called out. She picked up the knife.

'Why don't you leave that here?'

Deana raised an eyebrow, kept the knife, and held it at her side, blade forward, as she stepped to the bathroom door. She turned the knob slowly, keeping the lock button depressed so it wouldn't ping out. She jerked the door open fast. Nobody there. Leaning out, she looked both ways. 'The coast is clear,' she said.

The *ghost* is clear, Leigh thought, following her out. That's what Deana used to say when she was about four and didn't know any better. It didn't seem like very long ago. Now she's eighteen, and looking after *me*.

Deana led the way to the front door and opened it.

'Come in,' she said, lowering the knife.

Mace stepped in, followed by the woman. The woman's short brown hair was slicked down. Her blouse and cut-off jeans looked wet. 'Any trouble?' Mace asked.

'We haven't seen anyone,' Leigh said. 'We were worried he might've gotten into the house, though, so we waited in the bathroom.'

'It's about the only door with a lock,' Deana added.

'Good place to wait,' Mace said. 'Ladies, this is Sergeant Blaylock. Sergeant, Leigh and Deana West.'

They nodded greetings.

'I'll take a look around,' he said. He turned away. As he walked up the hallway, he lifted his shirttail and pulled a small revolver from a holster at the back of his belt.

Sergeant Blaylock stayed.

The Lake

'You got one, too?' Deana asked.

She patted her shoulder bag. Her head moved slightly as she scanned the living room. 'I heard you own the Bayview,' she said, glancing at Leigh before returning her gaze to the room beyond. 'That's a fabulous place.'

'Thank you.'

'Anytime some guy wants to impress me, that's where he takes me. Works, too. Maybe I could hit you up for the veal scalopini recipe. Or is that classified information?'

'I'll get it for you,' Leigh assured her. The recipe *was* supposed to be kept secret, but she liked Sergeant Blaylock. She felt a bond with this slim, attractive woman who looked as if she'd just lost a sorority tug-of-war. She didn't know why she felt this bond. Maybe it had to do with the sergeant coming to her home on a Sunday morning, ready to put it on the line for her. 'For your eyes only,' she added.

'Fair enough.'

'Are you Harrison's partner?' Deana asked.

'Used to be. When we were in radio cars.' She frowned toward the corridor. 'Mace!' she yelled.

'Yo!' he called back.

'He might take all morning,' she said, 'but when he's done you can bet your patooties you won't have anyone creeping out at you.'

'Are you two on duty?' Deana asked.

Leigh wished she would quit.

'We are now,' the sergeant said.

'How come you're all wet?'

'Sorry about that.' She looked down, apparently to see whether she was dripping. 'You know the Old Mill Stream in Mill Valley?' She fluttered the front of her blouse. 'This is it, Charlie.'

Charlie.

What *is* this, Leigh wondered, a conspiracy to keep dredging up Charlie Payne?

'We came right over, so I didn't have time to change.'

'If you'd be more comfortable in dry clothes,' Leigh said, 'you're welcome to something of mine.'

'No. Thanks anyway, Ms West.'

'Leigh.'
'Leigh it is. I'm Mattie.'
'I'm Deana.'
'I caught that.'
'You called me Charlie.'
'Yeah, I do that.'
'My father's name was Charlie.'
Here we go again, Leigh thought.

But it didn't go any further because Mace came striding down the corridor. He held his short-barreled revolver close to his shoulder, pointed at the ceiling. 'It's all right back there,' he said. Before reaching them, he stepped down into the den and disappeared behind the fireplace area that separated the den from the living room.

A little while later, he walked past the rear of the fireplace and made a circuit of the living room, checking the sliding glass doors and looking behind furniture. At the far side of the living room, he unlocked the door, slid it open, and stepped outside. He vanished, then reappeared, walking the deck that stretched along the entire rear of the house.

When he came back, he headed for the kitchen. Leigh heard his footsteps on the floor, then the squeak of the door opening into the garage.

Finally, he returned. 'The place is secure,' he said, and put his revolver away. 'That's to say, nobody's here but us. There's no indication of forced entry. You've got drop pins on your sliding doors, which is good. You should do something about the windows, though. Pick up some quarter-inch dowel rods to drop in the runners, that's the easiest way. Cut them off in lengths that'll let you open the windows a few inches for fresh air, but no farther.'

'We'll have to take care of that,' Leigh said.

'You might want to invest in an alarm system that'll tie into a private security patrol. Oh, and the gravel strip under the windows is a good idea. Announces the presence of intruders in that area. As and when, of course.'

Leigh nodded.

The Lake

'Let's take a look at the car.' He opened the front door. 'Do you have your keys?' he asked.

'I do,' Deana said, pulling a chain out of her T-shirt. A house key dangled at its end.

They stepped outside. Mattie shut the door.

'That's another thing,' Deana said, pointing at the newspaper on the stoop. 'It's always up at the top of the driveway. When I came out this morning, it was right here.'

'Okay. We may want to have the lab check it.' They crossed to the driveway. A shiny black Trans Am was parked in front of the garage. 'What time did you first notice the car?' Mace asked as they started up the sloping pavement.

'Around eight-thirty,' Leigh said. 'Just before we phoned.'

'We were supposed to go running,' Deana added.

'What did you do when you saw it?'

'Hauled ass back to the house.'

'Deana.'

'Sorry.'

'Did you hear any unusual sounds? Last night or this morning?'

'No.'

'Nothing.'

Just before they reached the top of the driveway, Leigh saw the old red Pontiac. Even in the bright sunlight, it looked ominous. It reminded her of that movie *Christine*. The car in that movie was red, too, but not a Pontiac. It had a life of its own, and she imagined this one starting up with no one inside. It won't, she told herself. It damn well *better* not.

They crossed the road. Squatting, Mace touched the exhaust pipe. Then he peered through the open driver's window. Mattie, beside him, looked into the back seat. She opened her shoulder bag and followed Mace to the front, where he bent down and inspected the smashed-in areas.

Mattie took out a notepad. She started writing.

'The damage appears consistent with the facts of the hit,' Mace said. He dug a pocketknife out of his pocket, pried out a blade, and scraped at the bent metal grille. His knife point came away with a tiny pile of powder that looked like rust. He picked it off, rubbed the dust with his thumb, sniffed and tasted it.

Deana looked at Leigh and wrinkled her nose.

'We'd better have a crime-scene unit come out,' he said.

'Then this *is* the one?' Leigh asked.

'I can't say for sure. It's a strong possibility, though.' He looked over his shoulder at Mattie. 'We'll notify the Tiburon PD. They'll need to be in on this, but they'll probably be agreeable to letting our people handle the detail work.'

'Save a lot of back and forth,' she agreed. She hurried across the road and started down the driveway.

'Doesn't she need my key?' Deana asked.

'She can call from the car.' Mace put away his knife. Getting down on his hands and knees, he lowered his head almost to the pavement and looked under the car. Then he stood up. He brushed gravel off his palms.

'What now?' Leigh asked.

'We wait for the lab people to do their work. It won't take long to find out whether the blood down here matches up with the Powers boy.'

'Shouldn't somebody search Del Mar?' Leigh asked.

'This car has been here for hours. He's long gone. But he left the car behind, and that was a big mistake. It'll help us nail him.'

'It's probably stolen,' Deana said.

'Undoubtedly. But we'll get some physical evidence from it. Maybe fingerprints, maybe hair samples, maybe fabric particles. When we run down the car's owner, we might find out if he witnessed the theft – if that's what it was. All this will take time, though. I don't want you two staying in the house.'

Leigh felt her stomach flip as if the street had suddenly dropped from under her feet.

Mace looked from Leigh to Deana. His gaze settled on Leigh's eyes. 'I don't want to alarm you, but . . .'

'You're going to do it anyway.'

He smiled slightly. 'Afraid so. You know what it means, of course, the car being here.'

'Exactly what *does* it mean?' Leigh heard a tremor in her voice.

The Lake

'It means that (a) the killer knows where Deana lives, and (b) he paid her a visit.'

'Why?'

'Unfinished business.'

'*Jesus*,' Deana muttered.

'He was here,' Leigh said, 'so why didn't he *do* something?'

'We don't know what he did or didn't do.'

'I can think of a couple of things he *didn't* do,' Deana said, and tried for a smile. The corner of her mouth trembled for an instant. She licked her lips, wiped them with the back of her hand.

'He might have left the car here as a message,' Mace suggested. 'A warning that he can get to you if he wants. Or maybe he's toying with you.'

'Toying?'

'This guy is not a normal person. He's probably totally different from anyone in your experience.'

'You mean like a psycho?' Deana asked.

'That's what I mean.'

'Move over, Norman Bates.'

'So there's no telling what he might do.'

'You think he left it here just to scare us?' Leigh asked.

'Anything's possible. But—'

'They're on the way,' Mattie said, striding across the street.

'What were you about to say?' Leigh asked Mace.

'I think you should check into a motel, unless you have friends or relatives who wouldn't mind putting you up for a while.'

'That isn't what you were going to say,' Leigh challenged him. 'It was something about the car and why it's here. To scare us or *what*?'

'It would just be a guess.'

'I want to hear it.'

'All right.' Mace looked uncomfortable. He lowered his eyes for a moment, then met Leigh's gaze. 'That unfinished business I mentioned earlier? I think he came here intending to finish it. Last night. But something went wrong. The car's still here. I suspect the reason it's here is because it quit on him. He realized that he couldn't count on it for his getaway. That's why he didn't go through with his plan.'

Chapter Nine

'Do you have a plastic bag large enough for this?' Mace asked, looking down at the thick edition of the Sunday newspaper that lay flat on the stoop, tied with string.

'A waste-basket liner?' Leigh asked.

'That'd be perfect.'

'You want to get one for us?' she asked her daughter. The girl went to the door.

'Why do you need the paper?' Leigh asked.

'There's a good chance that your visitor put it here.' He stepped onto the grass, and Leigh followed him along the front of the house. 'Maybe he was good enough to leave us some prints.'

'Can you get fingerprints off newspapers?'

'These days, you can get them off almost anything. Our lab people have chemicals that interact with the body oils left by . . . Look here.' Stopping, Mace pointed down at the flower bed. The soft soil had been mashed down by shoes.

A glance at Leigh's feet convinced him that she hadn't made these impressions. Her feet were too small. And the daughter, who was only a bit taller than Leigh, probably didn't have feet this large either.

The footprints led through the flower bed to the guest-room window.

Mace looked at Leigh. She was standing rigid, gazing at the ground, the fingertips of one hand stroking her lower lip.

He felt sorry for her. He could imagine what she must be feeling – scared and vulnerable. The bastard had actually crept right up to

The Lake

her house last night while she and her daughter were inside, maybe fast asleep. Perhaps he'd even seen them.

From where Mace stood, he couldn't spot any damage to the window or frame. 'It doesn't look as if he tried to break in.'

'But he could've,' Leigh said, 'couldn't he?'

'It wouldn't have been too difficult.'

Leigh shook her head slowly. 'It's just getting worse. What do you . . . do you think he wants to kill her?'

'Either that or take her. I think I mentioned Friday night that he might have some kind of obsession. Maybe he wants her.'

'God,' Leigh muttered.

'Don't worry. We'll see that he doesn't get another chance.'

They both turned toward Deana as the girl approached with a white plastic bag. 'What's up?' she asked. 'Did you find something?'

'He was here,' Leigh said. She pointed to the ground.

Deana looked at the footprints. 'Oh, wonderful,' she muttered.

'We should be able to get a good estimate of his height and weight from these,' Mace said.

'Not to mention his shoe size,' Deana added in a quiet voice. She didn't like the way things were turning out.

Mace led the way to the stoop. Taking the bag from Deana, he crouched over the newspaper and carefully slipped his fingers under one of its strings without touching the *Blondie* comic strip beneath. When he raised it, the paper tilted.

Out of its folds slipped a small white knob, maybe a bone or a polished rock. It hung at the edge of the newspaper, held in place by a rawhide strip that ran through its center and stayed trapped inside the paper.

With a ballpoint from his shirt pocket, Mace hooked the rawhide and eased it out.

The thong was knotted at its ends. It swung from the tip of his pen like a strange, primitive necklace.

'Mom!'

Mace looked, saw Leigh with her eyes rolled upward, her knees folding. He sprang at her, thrust his hands under her armpits and slowed her fall as she sank to the stoop, unconscious.

Chapter Ten

Tuesday, June 25, 1968

When she got home late that afternoon, she had a story ready: a purse-snatcher had grabbed her shoulder bag when she came out of the movie theater on Market Street, she had fought him off, and that was how the sleeve of her granny dress got torn.

One look at her parents, and Leigh knew that the story wouldn't wash. They were standing in the living room like a couple of mannequins left behind in a hurry – Dad sideways near the window, head down and turned her way, one hand on the back of his neck – Mom in front of the fireplace, facing her, the fingers of both hands mashing her lower face. Mom's eyes were red, accusing. Dad's eyes were haggard, blank.

Obviously, they both knew.

Leigh forced a smile. It felt crooked. 'I guess I'm in for it now,' she said.

Dad's eyes stopped looking blank. 'If you see an amusing side to this situation,' he said in an icy voice, 'I would appreciate your filling us in. We fail to see the humor.'

'Do you have any idea what you've put us through?' Mom asked, lowering her hands and clutching them in front of her waist.

'I'm sorry,' she mumbled.

'*You*'re sorry?' Dad said. 'Well, so are we.'

'How . . . how did you find out?'

'They interrupted the Giants game,' Dad said.

'My God, how could you do such a thing?' Mom blurted.

'And there you were.'

'It made your father physically ill.'

'I'm sorry I lied. But you wouldn't have let me go if I'd told you about the demonstration.'

'You're goddamn right about that.'

Leigh cringed. She'd rarely heard her father use profanity.

'Kids are over there dying, for God's sake, and here you are in a get-up like some kind of hippie freak, holding hands with a bunch of long-haired creeps who want nothing better than to destroy a way of life . . .'

'Nobody wants to destroy anything.'

'Bull*shit*!'

'We just want the war to stop.'

'I'm not going to debate the war with you. That isn't the issue.'

'It is, too.'

'How do you think Colonel Randolph would feel,' Mom asked, 'if he saw how you—'

'He'd still *have* his son,' Leigh snapped, 'if it weren't for that murdering bastard in the White House.'

Dad turned white. He crossed the floor so fast that Leigh didn't have time to move, and slapped her hard across the face.

She was stunned. Dad had never slapped her before.

Whirling around, she ran to her room, slammed the door, and threw herself down on her bed.

She had stopped crying by the time Dad came in. He sat on the edge of the bed. He had been crying, too. He stroked Leigh's forehead, lightly brushing the hair aside. 'I'm sorry,' he said.

'I know. Me, too.'

'Your mother and I . . . we try to understand. If we didn't love you so much, do you think we'd care one way or the other if you were out there? . . . You could've been hurt . . .'

'Maybe I was. Did you ask?'

'No. *Were* you hurt?'

She shook her head.

'Well, that's lucky. How did your dress get torn?'

'One of the—' She almost said 'pigs', but she didn't want to start him up again. 'A cop grabbed me. But I got away from him. Then I took off. I was supposed to *let* them bust me, that was the idea, but I figured you and Mom would really hit the ceiling if you had to come and bail me out.'

'You're right.'

'I guess you hit the ceiling anyway.'

'I spent four years of my life fighting for this country, honey. I can't help it, but my blood just starts to boil when I see a bunch of pampered kids who never worked a day in their lives spitting on everything that—'

'Don't get started, okay?'

'Burning the American flag.'

'Dad.'

'Mouthing off about "the establishment". My God, it's the dreaded "establishment" that puts the food in the bellies of these people . . . *I*'m the establishment. Me and all the other people who worked our butts off so that our kids could maybe have it a little better than we did. And *we*'re the enemy? Am I a warmonger? Is Colonel Randolph? Do you think he *likes* this war? My God, the man's been devastated by it.'

'Then he should be out there marching against it.'

Dad shook his head, sighed. 'I would never wish anything bad on you, honey. I certainly hope you don't have to learn this the hard way. You're all idealistic right now and you're sure that peace and love will rule the world if you just march around and sing a few songs about it. But I'm afraid you're in for a rude awakening. There are bad people in this world.'

'Tell me about it,' she muttered.

'I intend to, whether you like it or not. There are people out there – and governments – that would be more than happy to wipe out you and me and your mother, our whole country if they're given half a chance. Guys like your pals Castro and Ho Chi Minh.'

'They aren't my pals. Neither is LBJ.'

He ignored that, and went on. 'Guys like Charles Starkweather and Richard Speck.'

She'd heard of Speck, but didn't know who Charles Starkweather was.

The Lake

'Do you think your pacifism would work on them? Turn the other cheek to them, and they'll cut it off for you.'

'I get the message.'

'Do you? I doubt it. I think your mind's been so twisted around by all your long-haired friends that you don't know which end is up anymore. We've been pretty lenient with your weird outfits and anti-everything buttons and staying out till all hours at that place in Sausalito. But we trusted you to have more sense than to get involved in something like this today. We brought you up to know better.'

'You brought me up to do what I think is right,' Leigh said. 'And I think it's right to protest against the war.'

'Well, you're mistaken. And it's high time for a crackdown.'

'Let me guess, I'm grounded.'

'At the very least, young lady.'

'What ever happened to freedom of speech?'

'You can feel free to *speak* whatever you like, but I will not allow you to march with the Great Unwashed and get yourself thrown in jail.'

'I didn't get thrown in jail.'

'Not this time. And, believe you me, you won't get another chance at it. Not while you're living under this roof.'

Leigh pulled the pillow down over her face. 'Are you done?'

'We just want what's best for you, honey.'

'Yeah, sure.'

'You'll understand someday when you have kids of your own. Now, why don't you get cleaned up for supper? We'll try to start out on a new foot, okay?'

'All right,' she muttered.

When her father had gone, she took her robe into the bathroom. She pulled her dress over her head, turned it around, and looked at the buttons pinned to the front. A peace button. One with Uncle Sam pointing, not his finger but a revolver. One read, 'Make Luv Not War'. Another, 'The Great Society: Bombs, Bullets, Bullshit'. Another, 'War is Unhealthy for Children and Other Living Things'. Dad had called them 'anti-everything buttons'. He was so blind. Couldn't he see that they were pro-peace and love?

Leigh let the dress fall to the floor. She moaned from her aches as she bent down and untied the leather thong around her left ankle. The bell strung through it jingled softly. She set it on the counter.

Reaching behind her neck, she untied the other thong. She held it up and stared at the dangling ornament. She had found the thing in the sand near Point Reyes Station a few months ago. She didn't know what it was. Maybe that was why she had kept it. The small, rounded thing with one side curled inward seemed too light to be a stone. It looked and felt like ivory. She suspected that it might be some kind of shell or fish bone, though its shape was so peculiar that she couldn't imagine what kind of creature it might have once belonged to.

It came with a hole through the middle, so she had strung it on a rawhide lace from one of her old hiking boots and made herself a necklace.

She thought of it as her 'sea-thing' necklace. Sometimes as her lucky necklace.

It hadn't brought her much luck today.

She set it down carefully beside the ankle bell, and looked down at herself. Pressing in on her left breast, she flattened it enough to let her see the reddish-blue mark across the ribs just beneath it. A police nightstick had done that. The same nightstick, wielded by the same pig, had left a bruise the size of a quarter on the jut of her hip bone.

That fucking Gestapo pig.

Leigh had seen lust in his eyes when he went at her, ramming low with the end of his stick. He was aiming between her legs. But she'd moved fast enough so that it had pounded her hip instead.

Leigh turned around. She looked over her shoulder at the mirror, and saw three strips of bruises across her back. The seat of her panties was shredded and speckled with blood from when they had dragged her by the feet. She pulled the panties down and wrinkled her nose at the sight of her scraped buttocks.

Yeah, Dad, she thought, tell me about the bad guys.

Three days later, Leigh was on a TWA flight to Milwaukee.

From her parents' point of view, the Bay Area was a hotbed of radicalism. A month with her Uncle Mike and Aunt Jenny, two thousand miles away from it all, would keep her safe from such influences and give her a chance to learn how people looked at things in solid, down-to-earth Middle America.

She didn't *have* to go, of course. Mom and Dad wouldn't force her. If she refused, however, she would be restricted to the house for the entire summer.

Leigh decided to take her chances with the boondocks.

Once she agreed to go, her parents changed. They seemed a little giddy. The Prodigal Daughter had returned. Instead of slaying the fatted calf, they took her out to dinner at the White Whale on Ghirardelli Square. Leigh let herself slide back, at least for the time being, into the role of the well-bred daughter. She didn't want to spoil their mood. Besides, acting rebellious would have been difficult; she enjoyed fine restaurants too much. The dim lights, the quiet sounds of people dining, the pleasant aromas and delicious food. She could never walk into one without starting, right away, to feel good.

Her parents seemed to forget that the trip to Wisconsin was a ploy to remove Leigh from harmful influences. It was a special vacation for her. She would love it – the woods and the lake, the swimming and boating and fishing. They wished they could go with her, but of course Dad's job made that impossible. On second thought, maybe they could arrange to come up for a week later on. It would be terrific.

Mom took Leigh shopping the next day. At Macy's on Union Square, they bought a conservative dress and shoes for the flight, two sundresses, an orange blouse, a pair of white shorts, a modest one-piece bathing suit, and an assortment of undergarments. Leigh went along with her mother's suggestions, though she fully intended to spend most of her time in T-shirts and cut-offs.

At Dunhill's, they bought a soft leather tobacco pouch and a tin of Royal Yachtsman tobacco for Uncle Mike, a pipe smoker. At Blum's, they bought a box of candy for Aunt Jenny. They ate lunch there, and finished with a dessert of Blum's fabulous lemon crunch cake.

Leigh expected to be taken home when they returned to the car after lunch. Instead, Mom drove her to North Beach. 'You'll need some reading material, I think.' They went to the City Lights, then to a second-hand bookstore across the alley. Mom waited while Leigh loaded up with paperback editions of *Franny and Zooey*, *Soldier in the Rain*, *Boys and Girls Together*, *The Ginger Man*, *In Cold Blood*, *Love Poems of Kenneth Patchen*, *Just You and Me*, and *The Strange Case of Charles Dexter Ward*. Mom raised an eyebrow at the selection, but kept her opinions to herself and paid for all the books.

Leigh woke up on Tuesday morning feeling excited. The trip, to be sure, was a form of banishment. But she found herself looking forward to it anyway. The trip would be an adventure. She'd be on her own during the flight and, if her aunt and uncle would stay out of her hair enough during the visit, she might even be able to enjoy herself. At least they weren't her parents – maybe they wouldn't try to control her life while she was there.

At the boarding gate, Mom wept. Dad gave her a fierce hug.

'Be on your best behavior,' Mom said.

'Save some fish for us, honey,' Dad told her.

'You're definitely coming out, then?'

'We wouldn't miss it.'

Leaving them, Leigh hurried along the boarding ramp with light, quick steps. She almost started skipping. She felt free and wonderful.

When she reached her seat, she opened her purse and took out her peace button. She pinned it to the top of her crisp, proper Macy's dress. Then she tied the rawhide thong behind her neck, opened her top button, and slipped the sea-thing in. It was smooth and cool on the skin between her breasts.

The pin and necklace let Leigh feel more like herself.

They can change where I go and who I see, she thought, but they can't change who I am.

Chapter Eleven

Leigh hadn't seen her aunt and uncle since their trip to California when she was twelve, but she recognized them immediately when she stepped through the gate.

Uncle Mike looked a lot like Dad, especially his eyes. He was bigger, though – built like a football player. And, unlike Dad, he sported sideburns and a bushy mustache. His hair was considerably longer, too. Dad wouldn't have approved of his brother's appearance. Leigh felt relieved. She gave him a hug. His corduroy jacket smelled of pipe smoke.

She kissed Aunt Jenny on the cheek. The woman was surprisingly short. She had once been the same height as Leigh. Now the top of her head came only to Leigh's chin. She was still as slim, however, and she still had a humongous bosom. She no longer wore the weird harlequin glasses she'd had six years ago. Now she wore round lenses with wire rims. Granny glasses. A very good sign.

'You sure have sprouted up,' Aunt Jenny told her. 'I considered it myself, but chose not to. I enjoy conversing with belly-buttons.'

Uncle Mike reached for Leigh's carry-on. 'Let me take that for you.' They started walking. 'So how was your flight?'

'Just fine.'

'They feed you?' Jenny asked. 'We've got a pretty long haul ahead of us.'

'We've got snacks. Or we can stop along the way.' Mike smiled around at Leigh. 'Are you still crazy about McDonald's?'

'Not quite like I used to be.'

'God, I remember you hogged my fries.'

This might not be so bad, Leigh thought as she walked with them toward the baggage-claim area. Then she thought, don't kid yourself. Maybe they're not as uptight as Mom and Dad, but they're the same generation. They'll have a lot of the same hang-ups, even if they do seem pretty cool for people their age. So you'd better watch out.

Their car was a battered old station wagon. Mike loaded Leigh's luggage into the rear, tossed in his corduroy jacket which must've been smothering him in this hot, muggy weather, and came around to the passenger side. 'Don't see why we can't all pile into the front,' he said.

Leigh sat between them.

'So,' Mike said as he started to drive, 'we hear you've been dabbling in hippiedom.'

Here we go. 'A bit,' she admitted.

'I don't see that the movement's produced any worthwhile literature.'

'I wouldn't say that,' Jenny told him. '"Hey, hey, LBJ, how many kids did you kill today?"'

'Ah, but where are the Ginsbergs, the Ferlinghettis, the Kerouacs, the Gary Sniders?'

'Mike misses the beatniks,' Jenny explained.

'I was in Ferlinghetti's bookstore just yesterday,' Leigh said.

'City Lights? No kidding. We stopped in there when we were out visiting you folks. We sandwiched it in between the McDonaldses, so to speak. Do you remember that?'

'I don't think so.'

'It was the high point of the trip for Mike,' Jenny said.

'Who've the hippies got? Kesey? He's all right. *Cuckoo's Nest* is all right. But who else?'

'Ginsberg's still writing,' Leigh said.

'Yeah, but he's not a true hippie. He's an over-the-hill beatnik. There's a difference.'

'Not a whole lot,' Jenny said.

The Lake

'Do hippies wear berets? Do hippies play bongos? Do hippies recite poetry in coffee houses?'

'Mike's a closet beatnik.'

He started to declaim *Howl* in a deep, thundering voice.

'Oh, Jeez, spare us.'

Leigh started to laugh.

After a few stanzas, Mike quit his recitation. He and Jenny started asking the kind of questions that Leigh expected from relatives she hadn't seen in years. How were her parents? How was school? Did she have a boyfriend? What did she like to do in her spare time? What did she plan to major in at the university? Did she have a career in mind?

They talked about themselves: the high school where Mike taught English and Jenny taught music; their cabin on Lake Wahconda; the new Chris-Craft they'd bought two weeks ago; a drowning the previous summer when a fisherman's boat had capsized in a sudden storm; a legendary muskie named Old Duke that was said to inhabit the lake.

By the time they'd been on the road for an hour, Leigh felt completely at ease. Her aunt and uncle seemed easygoing and good-humored. They didn't talk down to her. They treated her like an adult, a friend.

'Are you getting hungry?' Mike asked.

'I'm okay,' Leigh said.

'Thought I heard your stomach growl.'

'Not mine.'

'Well, I'm pretty sure there's a McDonald's around the next bend.'

Leigh doubted it. They were traveling along a two-lane road deep in the woods. The Big Bass Bait & Tackle Shop was the last business establishment Leigh had seen. That had been ten minutes ago.

Mike steered around the bend. 'Guess I was wrong. I remember I was wrong once before.'

'You can remember that far back?' Jenny asked. 'Admirable.'

'You'd better break out the provisions, Tink.'

Jenny turned around. Kneeling, she reached down behind the seat. She handed back three cold cans of Hamms to Leigh.

Mike started to sing the Hamms beer commercial about lakes and sunset breezes. Leigh pictured a cartoon bear playing a log like a tom-tom.

'We thought you might appreciate an authentic native snack,' Jenny said, twisting around and sitting down again. She had a box of Ritz crackers in one hand, a pottery crock in the other.

The crock contained smoked cheddar, which she spread on crackers while Leigh broke open the beers with a can opener from the glove compartment.

'Now, we know we're corrupting you here,' Mike said, 'but we rely on your good judgment to keep your folks ignorant about this.'

'Mum's the word,' Leigh promised.

'Don't tell your mum, either,' Jenny warned.

The beer was cold and good. Maybe it was her hunger, but Leigh thought she had never eaten cheese and crackers half as delicious as these. She drank, ate crackers, passed some from Jenny to Mike, and later took over the cheese-spreading chores when Jenny knelt on the seat again to get three more cans of beer.

Leigh already felt light-headed, a little numb behind her cheekbones. So she watched herself, being careful to hold her giddiness in check and pronounce her words correctly when she talked. It wouldn't do at all for them to think that the beer was getting to her. During the second beer, the numbness spread to her cheeks. The cheese and crackers tasted better all the time.

'I've about had it,' Jenny finally said.

'More for the rest of us,' said Mike, clamping his beer can between his legs and taking another cheese-mounded cracker from Leigh.

Soon, the knife was coming out of the pottery crock with no more than a thread of cheese along its edge.

'Better swoop up the rest of it with your finger,' Mike advised.

'That would be gross,' Leigh said.

'You're among friends.'

So she cleaned out the remaining cheese, licking it off her finger.

When her beer was finished, Leigh folded her hands on her lap, sighed, and settled down in the seat. 'That really hit the spot,' she mumbled. Soon, her eyes drifted shut.

When she woke up, the car was passing a lake. A boy standing in

The Lake

a motor boat was handing a tackle box to a man reaching down from the dock.

'We're not there yet,' Mike said.

'A couple more hours,' Jenny told her.

'You guys must really live far out.'

'Far from the madding crowd,' Mike said.

Later, they stopped for gas at a place called Jody's with two pumps in front and neon beer signs in the windows. A thin, red-haired man in bib overalls stared down at them from a rocker on the porch. 'Mary Jo,' he called in a flat voice.

The door swung open. A girl wandered out and squinted toward the car as if she couldn't quite puzzle out where it might have come from. 'Don't just stand there collecting dust.'

With a shrug, she trotted down the porch steps. She didn't look older than twelve. Leigh took an immediate dislike to the man – sitting on his butt and ordering the kid to do the work.

'Help you?' she asked at Mike's window.

'Fill her up with ethyl.'

The girl went around to the rear. 'I don't know about you guys,' Mike said, 'but I'm going to make a pit stop while I've got the chance.'

The man watched them in silence as they left the car and climbed the porch stairs. Leigh was glad to get inside, away from him.

'A real charmer,' Jenny whispered.

'His kid's no prize, either,' Mike said.

They walked past a deserted lunch counter. At the far end were two doors, one marked, 'Pointers,' the other 'Setters'.

'Well, I'll be dog-gone,' Mike said. He smirked and opened the Pointers door.

Jenny motioned for Leigh to go first. Inside the rest room, Leigh bolted the door. The window was open. She looked through the screen to make sure that the man wasn't skulking around. Behind the building was a jumble of weeds, then the forest.

The toilet seat looked clean, but she didn't sit on it. She braced herself above it until she was done. After washing her hands, she held on to a paper towel as she unbolted and opened the door. She didn't want to touch anything in this place.

Jenny entered. Mike was already at the other end of the lunch counter, wandering among shelves at the other side. Leigh went to join him. This part of the room had groceries, souvenirs and sporting goods. 'Something for everyone,' Mike said.

The man came through the door and stared at them. Leigh stepped closer to Mike.

'Help you?'

'Just looking around, thanks.'

'Gas comes to eight-fifty,' he said, and stepped behind the small counter next to the door.

Leigh went to a wire book-rack as Mike headed over to pay him. The paperbacks were mostly westerns and mysteries. Some had bent covers and white lines down the spines as if they'd already been read.

'Where you folks headed?' she heard the man ask.

'Up to Lake Wahconda.'

Leigh wished that Mike hadn't told him. Then she felt foolish. What was she afraid of? Did she think the creep would pay them a visit?

After paying the man, Mike wandered over to a wall map near the door.

What was taking Jenny so long?

Leigh returned her gaze to the book carousel. The man stayed behind the counter. He seemed to be watching her, but she forced herself not to look at him. She would not look. Her stare slipped sideways. He was staring at her, all right. Not at her eyes, though.

At the peace button?

She wished that she had left it in her purse.

Hearing quiet footsteps, she turned her head. Jenny was striding between the lunch counter and the tables. 'All set?'

With a nod, Mike opened the door.

'Don't be strangers,' the man said, a smile on his flushed face.

Leigh hurried to catch up. With Jenny now on the porch and Mike outside holding the door, Leigh was alone as she passed the man.

'Bye, now,' he said.

She looked at him as he stepped back from the counter. She tried to smile, and thought for an instant that he was missing an arm. Why

The Lake

hadn't she noticed that before? She started to feel sorry for him. Then she realized that he wasn't an amputee, at all. His right arm, from the elbow down, was inside his bib overalls. The bulge of faded denim made by his arm angled down to his crotch. There, the jutting fabric stirred with the motions of his hand.

Leigh rushed outside and dodged just in time to avoid a collision with Mary Jo. 'Sorry,' she muttered.

The girl narrowed her eyes, stepped past her, and went through the doorway.

'Are you all right?' Mike asked.

'Yeah, fine.'

'You look a little shaky.'

She shrugged.

Before climbing into the car, Leigh glanced over her shoulder. No one came out of Jody's. She didn't look again. Safe between her aunt and uncle, she gazed at the dashboard. The car bumped over ruts, then moved along the smooth pavement of the road and soon rounded a bend.

She felt frightened, violated.

When Mike turned his head slightly to check the rear-view mirror, Leigh twisted around and looked back. A pickup truck was close behind them. Reflections on its windshield prevented her from seeing inside. The pickup swung into the other lane, gaining speed. Her stomach tightened. As the truck pulled alongside their car, a young woman nodded a greeting through the passenger window. Leigh glimpsed the driver, a heavy-set man in sunglasses, wearing a baseball cap with its bill tipped up. She settled back into her seat as the pickup sped by. A safe distance ahead, it eased back into the northbound lane.

'Something wrong?' Jenny asked.

'Just that guy back where we got the gas. He gave me the creeps.'

'You and me both,' Jenny said. 'Not that he did anything in particular to deserve it.'

Oh no? Leigh thought.

'Too much isolation,' Mike explained. 'It has a way of warping the mind.'

'He was warped, all right,' Leigh muttered.

'I feel sorry for his daughter,' Jenny said.

'Who?' Mike asked. 'Mary Jo? What makes you think she's his daughter? She and her folks stopped by for gas last summer. Ol' Jody bashed their heads and planted 'em out by the woodpile, kept the girl.'

'That's not very funny, Mike.'

'I guess not. You've got to admit, though, some pretty weird goings-on happen around this neck of the woods.' He glanced at Leigh. 'There was a fellow a few years ago, Ed Gein . . .'

'Don't get into that,' Jenny warned.

'Well, I don't want to frighten you, Leigh.'

'Then don't,' Jenny told him.

'But I want you to keep your eyes open while you're staying with us. Just because you're not in the big city, don't let your guard down. We've got our share of weirdos.'

Mike was Dad's brother, all right. This lecture had a very familiar ring to it.

'Mike is right about that,' Jenny said. 'We've never run into any problems, ourselves, but . . .'

'I wouldn't exactly say that.'

'Nothing serious. But you do want to be careful, especially if you go around anywhere by yourself.'

'I will be,' Leigh assured them.

Gazing at the tree-shadowed road ahead, her mind traveled back to Jody's. The guy there had wanted her to see what he was doing. That was why he'd spoken to her as she was leaving, so she would look at him, see his overalls sticking out like a teepee. His hand in there. Moving around. Rubbing himself. While he stared at her.

Mike's story took hold.

She finished in the bathroom and opened the door, and stumbled over Mike's body. Jenny was sprawled atop the lunch counter, screaming as the man plunged a hunting knife into her belly again and again. He stopped. He turned to Leigh. His face was splattered and dripping blood.

'Now you're all mine, sweet thing.'

Licking blood off his lips, he stepped toward her. The knife in his left hand carved slow circles in the air. His right hand tugged his zipper down, reached

The Lake

inside, and freed his huge, engorged penis. He slid his hand up and down, slicking his shaft with blood.

I'd bite it off for him, Leigh thought.

No, I'd make a break for it.

She pictured herself whirling around and locking herself inside the bathroom.

He kicked at the door. Her only escape was through the window. A tight squeeze, but maybe . . . She boosted herself up. Started squirming out. And saw the girl, Mary Jo, standing in the weeds below with an ax in her hands. 'Oh no, you don't,' the girl said and grinned. 'We got her cornered, Pa!' she yelled.

Leigh's heart was thudding. Her mouth was dry. How in hell would she get out of this?

Don't worry, she told herself. It didn't happen and it won't. He's a goddamn pervert, but we're out of there. We're all in one piece.

If he had tried something, Mike would've fixed him.

Unless he took Mike by surprise.

Don't get started again.

Why did Mike have to tell him where we're going?

He *isn't* going to come.

He could leave Mary Jo behind to pump gas, run the grill and look after the shop. Take a gun and knife out to his pickup truck.

'You goin' after that gal?' Mary Jo asked.

'Prime stuff, weren't she?'

'Well, bring some back for me, Pa. You know how I like gizzards.'

Good Christ, Leigh thought. I must be going nuts, thinking up this kind of garbage. 'Hey,' she said, 'maybe we ought to sing something.'

'Great idea,' Jenny said.

'Do you know "Waltzing Matilda"?' Mike asked.

'Just the refrain.'

'Well, you're with a couple of teachers.'

'Yep,' Jenny said. 'We'll teach you the words.'

'Singing's dry business,' Mike told her. 'Better break out some brews.'

463

Chapter Twelve

Her experience at Jody's stayed in Leigh's mind like a spider huddled in a ceiling corner – a black speck, always there and vaguely disturbing, but not much of a threat. So long as it didn't start to travel.

During the first few days at Lake Wahconda, Leigh watched for the man. She went nowhere by herself. She knew he would not show up. But he might.

Even if he didn't, Leigh had no guarantee that someone with a similar warp might not be lurking in the woods.

The western side of Lake Wahconda was fairly well populated: a vacation camp with a lodge and a dozen small cabins near the south shore, and a chain of eight or ten cabins and A-frames, with a good deal of forest between them, extending up to the north shore. The nearest island had a large stone house on it. The rest of the islands were uninhabited.

It was as if civilization had captured the western shore and the single island, then ventured no farther. Except by boat. Out fishing with Mike and Jenny, Leigh sometimes saw rickety docks, ancient rowboats, cabins and shacks hidden among the trees. She occasionally heard wood being chopped, a distant crack of gunfire. People lived along these shores. A few, anyway. But Leigh didn't spot any of them; she didn't want to.

As the specter of the man from Jody's diminished, Leigh began to take the canoe out by herself. She enjoyed the peaceful solitude, the feel of her working muscles, the challenge of making the canoe glide over the water. But there was something more – a sense of anticipation. Alone on the lake, paddling the length of its western shore, she

The Lake

felt as if something mysterious and wonderful might happen at any moment.

The feeling was vague and without definition, at first. On the fifth day of her visit, however, that changed.

They had gone out fishing in the Chris-Craft early that morning until almost noon, so Leigh missed her morning canoe trip. After lunch, Jenny drove into town for supplies. Mike stayed at the cabin to watch a double-header on television. Leigh, invited to go into town with Jenny, had declined. She felt restless and eager. She wanted to be on the lake.

'I think I'll take the canoe out for a while,' she told Mike.

'Fine,' he said, looking up from the television. 'Have fun.'

Outside, she made her way quickly down the path to the shore. The outboard was moored at the dock, the canoe beached where she had left it yesterday. She tossed her rolled towel into the canoe, then lifted the bow and pushed. The aluminum hull scraped over the sand, then slipped easily onto the calm surface of the lake. Leigh hopped in. She scurried in a crouch to the stern. There she knelt on a flotation cushion, picked up the paddle, and swept the canoe past the dock. Her sense of impending adventure was stronger than ever. It gave her flutters in the stomach.

Fifty yards out, she turned the canoe southward. The sun blazed down on her.

Soon her blouse was clinging to her back and she felt sweat trickling down her sides.

On her morning trips, she was always perfectly comfortable in her blouse and cut-off jeans. But she had anticipated the afternoon heat, so she was prepared for it.

Resting the paddle across the gunnels, she looked over the glinting water at the shore. She was across from Carson's Camp. She saw people on the diving raft, a few swimming, others sunning themselves on the pier. The sounds of laughing, yelling kids and a distant, scolding mother came over the water to her. All the kids she had seen there during the past few days were young. Too young. The oldest boy she'd spotted seemed no older than twelve or thirteen.

Which did not necessarily mean that a guy closer to Leigh's age wasn't among them.

And maybe watching.

Her fingers trembled as she opened the buttons of her blouse. She pulled the damp blouse off, dropped it across her knees, and struggled out of her cut-off jeans.

She was wearing her white bikini, not the one-piece bathing suit that Mom had bought her at Macy's. The sun felt hot on her bare skin, but there was a mild breeze that felt very good.

She took a deep, shaky breath, bent forward, and slipped a squeeze bottle of suntan oil out of her rolled towel. She forced herself not to look toward shore as she spread the oil over her shoulders and arms, over her chest and the exposed tops of her breasts.

She felt her nipples harden, a tremor low in her abdomen and moving, liquid heat.

Suddenly she understood.

Those restless feelings. That sense of expectation.

What she was expecting was to meet a *guy* while she was out here alone in the canoe.

A guy on vacation, most likely staying at Carson's Camp. Someone lean and tanned and handsome to spend her time with. Someone who would fall for her. The lake and woods were so romantic, especially at night. She needed a boyfriend, a lover, to make it all perfect.

So where *are* you? she wondered, looking toward shore.

How come you're not swimming out to meet me?

Here, where I performed this nifty striptease for your benefit.

You've got to be there. Right? So where are you?

She saw only kids, and a few older guys who no doubt had wives and kids in tow. She didn't want an older guy. That would be scary. And wrong. She wanted someone her own age, or close to it.

Leigh picked up the paddle, dipped its blade into the water, and sent the canoe sliding forward.

Maybe *he* was watching her right now, wondering about her, wanting to meet her.

She couldn't expect a total stranger to come swimming out like Tarzan, or something. Though that, she supposed, was exactly the type of adventure that she'd been anticipating all along, even if she hadn't realized it until now.

The Lake

More likely, he would arrange an 'accidental' meeting. Position himself out here in a boat, tomorrow, pretending to fish while he waited for her to come along.

Dream on, she thought. This is Boondocks U.S.A. and the chances of running into Dustin Hoffman out here are about zip.

Dustin Hoffman isn't such a . . . Jim Morrison, *he*'d be more like it. Since you're dreaming, dream big.

She smiled and shook her head at the irony of it. Hey Mom, hey Dad, get a load of your revolutionary kid paddling around a lake with visions of Jim Morrison dancing in her head.

Nearing the southern shore, she turned the canoe around and started back. How come I've suddenly got boys on the brain? she wondered. It wasn't that way at all, back in Marin. She hadn't gone regularly with a guy since Steve when she'd been a sophomore, and that hadn't been any great romance.

She would still have been a virgin if it hadn't been for that time when she'd got high with Larry Bills last November. They'd shared a joint in his station wagon after leaving the Charles Van Damm. She hardly even liked Larry Bills. But that night, she was feeling lonely and horny, and the grass made her *very* horny, and it just happened. It wasn't too bad, either. But she'd made up her mind, after that, not to get it on with anyone unless she really liked him. A lot. She found plenty of guys she liked, and scads of them who obviously wanted to make it with her, some calling her uptight when she refused, but she'd found no one special enough. Which had suited her fine. The need just wasn't there.

So why is it *here*? she wondered. How come I'm suddenly hot and bothered, and scouting the shores for a handsome prince?

The fresh air. The heat. The woods. The lake. The balmy nights. The moonlight on the water. It's this *place*. Must be.

I'd better get myself under control, is what I'd better do.

Blinking sweat out of her eyes, Leigh stopped paddling. As the canoe glided along, turning slowly with the current, she scooped up water with her hands and splashed her face. It felt icy on her heated skin. She flung water onto her shoulders, squirming as it streamed down her back and chest.

She was across from Carson's Camp. Of course.

Anybody watching?

Where are you, pal?

She arched her back, stretched her tightening muscles, then lifted the paddle and continued along her way.

She didn't turn in at Mike and Jenny's place. Instead, she continued northward past the neighboring homes. A woman in a red halter waved at her from a pier. She waved back. A motorboat carrying a couple of middle-aged fishermen crossed her path. She waved at them, too, and wished she had her blouse on. Her canoe bobbed as the wake washed beneath it.

After passing the boathouse that marked the end of the populated western shore, she did put on her blouse. With a feeling of disappointment, she headed home.

That evening, after supper, she took a walk along the dirt road behind the cabin. It led through the woods along the rear of Carson's Camp. A family with three small kids was having a barbecue beside one of the cabins. The smoke and grilling hamburgers smelled wonderful. Leigh walked by, smiling at the wife who looked up from setting a picnic table.

Leigh felt good, but a little jittery. She had bathed and shampooed her hair before supper. She wore the orange blouse from Macy's and her legs looked sleek and tawny between the white of her new shorts and the white of her socks. Her skin glowed with the heat of a mild sunburn.

She had considered using make-up, but her reflection in the bathroom mirror had convinced her to leave it alone. A couple of dabs of cologne, and she'd been ready.

Ready for her big night out.

Ready to venture to the source.

If this fails, she thought as she strolled past another cabin, I'm out of luck. Well, maybe not. Most people probably only spent a week or two at Carson's Camp before heading home. Then new vacationers would arrive. She could take some consolation in the steady turnover.

Leaving the dirt road, she took a footpath toward the lodge. The trees opened up. She gazed out at the lake. Though she was in shadow,

The Lake

the early evening sun still fell on the water, and trees on the nearest island looked dusted with gold. A few boats were out, people fishing in the calm. The peaceful beauty of it all made Leigh stop. She stood there, saddened, wanting somehow to be part of it, not just a spectator.

Well, she thought, go for it.

She turned away, walked the final distance to the lodge, and opened one of its heavy doors. The lobby was deserted except for a lone boy in a wicker chair. He glanced at Leigh, then returned his gaze to the television. She followed the sounds of conversation and clinking silverware to the dining room entryway.

Only about half the tables were occupied, mostly those near the windows, the ones with the best view of the lake. Leigh's gaze wandered from group to group, starting with the closest table and moving down the room until she had seen everyone.

Maybe she'd missed him.

She had missed no one.

So damn much for summer romance.

Lower lip clamped between her teeth, she turned away and hurried outside.

It was too much to hope for. She was being silly.

But it hurt.

Hell, who wants to get involved anyway? If you did meet a guy, it'd all be over in about three weeks and you'd probably never see him again. Who needs that?

The next day, she met Charlie.

Chapter Thirteen

Quiet knocking aroused Leigh from her sleep. She raised her head as Jenny called through the door. 'Time to rise and shine, if you want to go after the big ones.'

'I don't know,' Leigh told her. 'I didn't sleep very well.'

'That's fine if you'd rather catch some extra zees. If you change your mind, though, we won't be leaving for fifteen or twenty minutes. Either way's fine.'

'Thanks,' Leigh said, and lowered her face into the pillow.

She felt bad about lying to Jenny. She'd slept perfectly well. She just didn't want to go out with them. Not this morning. She didn't want to do anything.

I should go along, she thought. What's wrong with me? It'll be great out on the boat. I don't really want to stay behind. Once they've gone, I'll probably wish I was with them.

You'd better get a move on, then.

What for? I'm not going.

She rolled onto her back. The window was open, the gauzy curtains billowing inward and flapping. The breeze brought a mild scent that reminded her of Christmas trees. From the feel of it, she guessed that the sun hadn't been out for long. Drawing the sheet aside, she felt the soft breath stir over her nightgown and bare skin.

She heard quiet voices beyond her door. Through the open window came birdsong, the soft sounds of leaves rustling in the breeze, the sputtery hum of a motorboat like a powered lawn mower far away. After a while, she heard the screen door of the porch slap shut. Climbing from the bed, she stepped to the window. Mike and Jenny, loaded with

The Lake

fishing gear, were heading down the wooded slope. She watched them walk onto the pier. Mike stepped into the Chris-Craft and set down his gear. Jenny handed her rod and tackle box to him, then untied the mooring lines while Mike started the twin engines. Jenny hopped aboard. Mike, standing in the cockpit, backed the boat around the arm of the L-shaped pier. The pitch of the engines rose. The bow tipped upward, and the boat headed out, churning a frothy wake.

Leigh stood at the window long after the boat was out of sight. She wasn't sure what to do with herself. She should have gone with them.

Her gaze lingered on the lounge chairs and table at the end of the pier. A couple of evenings she had sat out there with Mike and Jenny after supper. It had been pleasant then. It would be nice now, while the sun was still low.

At the bureau, she took off her nightgown and opened the drawer where she kept her white bikini. In a corner of the drawer was her necklace, the leather thong with its sea-thing ornament. Her good-luck necklace.

Leigh could use some good luck.

She knotted the rawhide thong behind her neck. The bonelike ornament felt smooth and cool between her breasts. She hadn't worn it since the day of her arrival.

The man at Jody's.

So what makes you think it's a good-luck charm?

The jet didn't crash, did it?

The guy didn't grab me.

Don't start thinking about him.

His overalls sticking out, his hand inside.

Mary Jo. Maybe he closed up as soon as we left, and . . . No. She's only a kid, probably his daughter. In spite of what Mike said.

Stop this.

She put on her bikini.

The girl had walked right in. She must have seen what that guy was doing.

Leigh's stomach hurt. 'There is a house – in New Orleans,' she started to sing. She picked up her sunglasses and a paperback, and left the room, still singing to block out the thoughts.

She smelled coffee. She spent a few minutes in the bathroom. With her hair in a ponytail, she pulled her beach towel down from its rod, rolled up her suntan oil in it and went into the kitchen. She poured herself a mug of coffee.

Then she walked down the slope to the pier.

The boat was out of sight, either hidden from view by an island or in one of the many coves around the borders of the lake. The painted slats of the pier felt cool under her bare feet. They creaked as she walked out. The warm breeze felt wonderful on her skin. She set her coffee mug, book and suntan oil on the wicker table, then spread her towel over one of the lounge chairs.

Turning, she scanned the shore. To the right, three piers up, someone was swimming with slow, ballet-like strokes. It had to be a woman. Far beyond the swimmer, a motorboat was chugging out, trailed by wisps of bluish smoke. She guessed that the two men were the same who had passed her yesterday afternoon. To the left, a kid was sitting at the end of the nearest pier, fishing with a cane pole. Beyond him, at Carson's Camp, a family was loading one of the dozen motorboats available to the guests.

At the pier's end, a boy and girl, side by side, dove at the same instant. Leigh heard their splashes. They raced out to the diving raft that floated on metal drums about thirty yards beyond the pier. Leigh waited to see who won. The girl did. 'Thatta way,' she whispered.

Then she straddled the lounge chair, sat down, and leaned back. Drinking coffee in this position, she realized, would be a neat trick. So she sat up straight and crossed her legs. She picked up the mug. Steam still drifted off the coffee. The breeze caught it and twisted it away. She took a sip. The coffee tasted rich and good.

The swimming woman had gone far out and was now turning back toward shore. The motorboat with the two fishermen was moving past the point of the nearest island. Far off, near the northern shore, was a rowboat – someone getting his or her morning exercise. Leigh couldn't tell, at this distance, whether the rower was male or female.

Nearby, a motor sputtered to life. She didn't bother turning to look. It had to be from the boat of the family at Carson's Camp.

The Lake

She took another drink, set the mug on the table, and reached for the plastic bottle of suntan oil. Before touching it, however, she stopped. The stuff was messy. It would cling to her hands, no matter how hard she might try rubbing it off, and end up on the pages of her book. So she left the oil alone and picked up the paperback.

It was *Boys and Girls Together*, a book she'd bought at the City Lights bookstore. William Goldman was the author. She'd bought two books by him that day because she remembered how she'd loved his first one, *The Temple of Gold*.

Boys and girls together.

Don't you wish.

At least you'll be able to read about it.

A fly settled on her leg. She waved it away, and noticed some hair curling out from the edge of her bikini briefs. Real cute, she thought. She fingered it out of sight, and decided that she had better give herself a trim the next time she was in the bathroom. Or shave it off entirely.

What if you have to go in for a physical before it grows back?

You already had your annual checkup.

What if you got in an accident?

Just explain that you didn't want it sticking out when . . . Explain? What's the doctor going to do, tell on you?

She took another drink of coffee.

The rowboat was closer now. The person at the oars didn't seem to be wearing a shirt. Probably a guy, she thought.

Finishing the coffee, Leigh set the mug aside. She uncrossed her legs, stretched them out, and leaned back. Through her sunglasses, the cloudless sky was a deep blue-green. A mallard flapped by. She opened her book, raised it high enough to block out the sun, and began to read.

Soon she was caught up in the story. She was *in* the story, living it with the characters, though part of her mind was aware of herself enjoying the book, aware of how good she felt with the soft cushion beneath her and the sun hot on her skin, the mild breeze roaming across her body. She turned the pages. Her arms, muscles still aching from all the canoeing over the past few days, grew heavy from holding the book high enough to shade her eyes.

Maybe go back up to the cabin and get a hat. Get a refill of coffee, while you're at it.

Wait till the end of the chapter.

She kept on reading.

'Baskets!'

The voice made her heart lurch. She lowered the book.

The rowboat was straight ahead, no more than sixty feet off the pier. It was loaded with baskets, some the size of clothes hampers, others that looked like picnic baskets, fishing creels, bread baskets. The young man in the center seat held the boat broadside, barely moving its oars.

'Selling them?' Leigh asked.

'Sure am.'

He wore a black hat with a high, rounded crown, a wide brim and a red feather on each side of its headband. The feathers stuck up like horns.

'Handmade,' he said. 'Can't buy no better.'

Leigh sat up straight and took off her sunglasses to see him more clearly. His face, shaded by the hat brim, was lean and handsome. He had a slight cleft in his chin. His bare torso was slim and muscled, his sleek skin glossy with sweat. He wore jeans so old and faded that they were almost white. Their knees were in shreds.

'I can show 'em to you,' he said.

Leigh nodded. 'Yeah, okay.'

'I'll beach her.'

She watched him turn the bow. He leaned far forward to start rowing. His back muscles rippled, gleaming. His jeans were low. She glanced at the shadowy crevice between his buttocks and wondered if he wore underpants.

Come off it, she warned herself.

Her heart continued to pound fast as she watched him bring the boat closer. Her mouth was parched. Standing up, she put her book and sunglasses on the table. She plucked the sweaty seat of her bikini briefs away from her skin. Looked down at herself. Fine. Nothing showing that shouldn't be.

With glances over his shoulder, the young man guided the boat

The Lake

around the end of the pier. He headed for the beach area where Leigh kept the canoe.

She forced her eyes away from him as she walked down the pier. She didn't hurry. She strolled along, head up, back arched, keeping her belly muscles tight though she knew she was too slim to bother with that.

For God's sake, she thought, calm down.

He's gorgeous.

He's a local.

So what?

So plenty. Maybe.

Stepping from the pier onto the sand, Leigh watched the young man ship the oars. As the boat glided silently toward the beach, he hopped out. He grabbed a gunnel and waded, towing the boat beside him. He dragged it onto the sand. Let go. Straightened up. Turned to face Leigh.

She tried not to let it show. Her shock.

He had three nipples.

She looked quickly to his face and walked closer. 'Let's see what you've got,' she said. Her voice trembled a bit.

'Got real fine baskets,' he told her. 'All shapes and sizes. Homemade.' Turning away, he lifted out one of the large ones. He set it down in front of her. It held several smaller baskets. Reaching inside, he took out two of them.

It wasn't a nipple. Thank God. It was a red heart-shaped tattoo above and slightly to the right of his left nipple. Scrawled inside the heart design, in small, flowing red letters, was the word 'Mom'.

Leigh took a deep breath. 'Did you make these baskets yourself?' she asked, feeling her shock subside.

'I just sell 'em,' he said. 'Mom makes 'em.'

'They look very nice.'

He handed her one. 'Can't get something this fine in no store. My family's been making 'em going back a hundred years. Maybe longer.'

The basket in her hands was long and narrow, just the right size for a loaf of sourdough. It was woven of reedlike wooden strips, a deep brown instead of the straw color she was used to seeing. The top edge was neatly rimmed with heavier strips fastened into place by tiny nails. She didn't know much about baskets, but this one did look a lot nicer than the ones her parents had at home. It would make a nice gift for Mom. 'What does something like this cost?'

'Twelve dollars.'

Not exactly cheap.

She had to buy a basket from him, though. At least one.

'Look at the others before you make up your mind. The smaller ones, they don't cost as much.' Bending over the boat, he lifted out one with a hooped handle. It looked like an Easter-egg basket. 'Something like this, it's good for candy or nuts.' He nodded toward a picnic basket near the stern. It had double handles and the kind of lid that flapped up from hinges in the center. 'That's the most popular, that picnic basket there. It goes for twenty-five.'

It was identical to one owned by Mike and Jenny.

'Have you sold baskets to these people here?' she asked, nodding toward the cabin.

'Sure, I sold 'em some. There's not much of anybody on the lake I haven't sold some to.'

He looked into Leigh's eyes.

She felt a low, pleasant tremor.

'You a relation?' he asked.

'I'm their niece. My name's Leigh.'

'You were waterskiing Monday.'

She nodded.

'I saw you.'

A blush warmed her face. 'I hope you didn't see me fall down.'

'You had on a white swimming suit.' He looked at what she was wearing. 'Not this one, but it was white like this one. There was more to it.'

'Oh.'

'This one here's better.'

'Thanks.' She swallowed hard. 'About these baskets. I'd like to buy this one.'

'I'm Charlie. Charlie Payne. That's P-a-y-n-e, not like a hurt.'

'Nice to meet you, Charlie.'

The Lake

'You said your name was Leigh. What's your last name?'

'West. Like the direction.'

He nodded. He smiled. He had extremely white teeth.

'My money's up in the cabin. Why don't you come along and get out of the sun?'

He nodded again.

Leigh turned away and started walking. She glanced back. He was following, but staying a distance behind her as if wary of getting too close. 'Do you live on the lake?' she asked.

'Over at the other side.'

The eastern shore, where the only homes were those creepy-looking shacks.

And not many of them. Leigh had suspected that Charlie came from there. Still, having it confirmed made him seem even more alien. He was from a different world, a place that seemed both mysterious and somewhat sinister.

She didn't feel threatened, though. Nervous, excited, but not threatened.

She climbed the shaded path, the breeze cool on her damp skin. Though she didn't look back again, she was certain that Charlie must be studying her. The feel of the fabric taut across her moving buttocks kept her aware that she was nearly naked.

Maybe he was getting turned on.

Or maybe his people didn't dress this way and he found it offensive.

No, he'd said that he liked the bikini.

At the top of the slope, she followed an offshoot of the path to the cabin. Charlie's footfalls stayed behind her. She climbed the wooden stairs, opened the screen door of the porch, and held it wide.

Charlie stopped.

'You coming?'

'I better wait here.'

She thought of her parents' strict rule about not having boys in the house while they weren't home. Well, this wasn't their house. Mike and Jenny had imposed no such restriction.

'It's okay,' she said. 'Nobody's home.'

'Mom, she don't want me going in folks' places.'

'What she doesn't know won't hurt her.'

His eyes narrowed.

He doesn't trust me, Leigh thought, annoyed. 'Suit yourself.' She turned away.

'Guess I can wait on the porch,' Charlie said.

She held the door open for him, and watched him approach. His torso had brown, curly hair starting at his navel and spreading downward like a triangle to the belt of his low-cut jeans. Leigh stayed in the doorway while he climbed the stairs. He turned sideways to avoid touching her as he stepped by.

He looked around the porch.

Leigh gestured toward the swing suspended by chains from the ceiling. Obediently, he went over to it and sat down. The chains groaned and creaked quietly.

'Back in a second.'

Leigh carried the basket into her bedroom and tossed it onto the bed. With trembling fingers, she opened her shoulder bag and found her billfold. She took out a ten and two ones. Then she hurried into the kitchen. The lower shelves of the refrigerator were loaded with cans of soda and beer. She hesitated, then folded the bills, tucked them under the elastic at her hip, and took out two cans of beer.

She had swung the refrigerator door shut and started out of the kitchen before she changed her mind. Mike and Jenny might not approve of her serving beer to Charlie. On top of that, she didn't want Charlie getting the wrong idea. So she put the beer away and took out cans of black-cherry soda instead.

She opened them and carried them out to the porch. Charlie's hat was on his lap. His brown hair was plastered to the top of his head and stuck out, unkempt and shaggy, around the ears.

'Would you like a cold drink before you go?' she asked.

'Don't want to put you out none.'

'You'd better take one,' she said. 'They're already open and I can't drink them both.' She handed one of the cans to him.

'Thank you.'

He was sitting near the middle of the swing, an arm draped over

The Lake

its back. Leigh considered asking him to move over, but that seemed a bit too pushy. Besides, if she joined him on the swing, it would make looking at him awkward. So she stepped away and leaned sideways, shoulder against the door frame.

'Your mother makes the baskets, and you sell them to people around the lake?'

He took a drink and nodded.

'Are there enough people around to make it worthwhile?'

'Don't need much.' His gaze flicked downward, then back up to Leigh's face. 'There's four lakes. Did you know there's four of 'em?'

'No.'

'Wahconda, Circle, Goon and Willow. There's channels. You can get from one to the other. I sell on all of 'em. There's places like Carson's where you've got folks coming and going all summer. That's where I sell the most.

'New folks all the time, and they like Mom's baskets. They got money, too, a lot of 'em. Made sixty-five dollars off just one lady a couple weeks back.'

While he talked, his eyes kept straying down Leigh's body. Then he would look elsewhere fast as if he feared being caught.

'It sounds lucrative,' she said.

Charlie lowered his gaze to the top of his soda can. 'That lady didn't want just baskets.'

'What else did she want?'

'Well, she liquored me up.'

Leigh was suddenly very glad that she'd decided against the beers.

'Then she went grabbing at me, but I made her quit. Mom, she give me a good switching.'

'How did your mother find out?'

He shrugged. 'Smelled the liquor on me. I told her I made the lady quit, but she hided me anyhow. It didn't count I sold five baskets. See, I went in her place and got a snoutful and put myself in the path of temptation.' He didn't sound resentful against his mother; more as if he had strayed and deserved the punishment. 'She'd likely switch me,' he added, 'if she found out I was here.'

'Well, I hope you're not planning to tell her.'

'I don't guess I will,' he said, and looked up at Leigh with wary eyes.

'Don't worry, I won't liquor you up and grab you.'

The red of a blush showed through his tan.

'Your mother sounds pretty strict.' Sounds like a regular bitch, Leigh thought.

'She just don't want me doing wrong.'

'Does she let you date?'

Charlie looked confused.

'You know, go around with girls.'

He shook his head, looked back down at his can of soda and took a drink.

'You mean you never had a girlfriend?'

'Just never mind,' he muttered.

'Okay. Sorry.' She sipped her black-cherry soda. As she tilted the can, a cold drop fell to her breast. It trickled down. She saw Charlie look up in time to watch her brush it away. 'What about your father?' she asked.

'He run off with a tramp. I was just a kid. I don't remember him at all.'

'That's rough,' Leigh said.

'He was no good.'

'Maybe your mother's afraid *you*'ll run off with a tramp.'

'Not me.'

'That would explain why she doesn't like you seeing girls.'

'You shouldn't talk that way about her.'

'I'm sure she's a fine person.'

'That's right.'

'I just think maybe you're missing out on a lot, that's all. Most guys your age – what are you, nineteen or twenty?'

'Eighteen,' he said.

'Okay, eighteen. Guys your age, that's about *all* they ever think about, is girls. Don't you feel like you might be missing out on something?'

'I know what you're up to.'

'I'm not up to anything,' she protested.

The Lake

'Oh no? How come you keep talking about me and girls?'

'I'm just curious, that's all.'

'You want me to do things to you.' There was a challenge in his eyes. Leigh felt caught. She wanted to snap out a denial. But Charlie wouldn't believe her anyway. He knew what he knew.

'It's crossed my mind,' she admitted. 'Don't get any ideas, though. I'm not about to let you try anything with me. It's not that I don't like you. I'm glad we met, and I think you and I could be friends if we got to know each other better. The thing is, I've already got a boyfriend. He's back in California, but I'm not the kind of person to fool around behind his back. So we could be friends, you and I, but it would have to be strictly hands-off.'

'Well, how come you brought me up here, then?'

'I came up to get the money, remember?' She pressed on, confident now that he seemed to be buying her story. 'Just because you had one bad experience, Charlie, you shouldn't jump to conclusions. Everyone isn't like that woman who tried to grab you. And you shouldn't go putting all the blame on her, either. If you were looking at her the same way you've been looking at me, it's no wonder she got ideas.'

Charlie's eyes widened. His mouth fell open.

'She probably thought you were asking for it.'

'I didn't look at her that way.'

'Well, you've sure been looking at *me* that way.'

'She weren't near as—' He stopped himself, and scowled down at his soda can.

'Near as what, Charlie?' Leigh asked in a soft voice.

'You know.'

'Mean and ugly?'

He shook his head.

'Fat and stinky?'

He smiled, fought it away, and raised his gaze to her.

'She weren't near as pretty,' he said.

'Probably not near as naked, either.'

The smile broke out again. This time, it stayed. His eyes still had a nervous look. 'Not to start out with, anyhow.'

'Oh?'

'But what she had weren't something I much wanted to see. It put me off my feed for a week.'

Leigh laughed.

Charlie laughed a little himself, shaking his head. 'I seen better-looking tits on a road apple. And she had a hind-end . . .' He stopped again. His face was suddenly solemn. 'I beg your pardon,' he said.

'You don't have to beg *my* pardon.'

'I gotta go now.' He gulped down the rest of his soda, put on his strange hat, and stood up. 'Thank you for the drink.'

Leigh nudged herself away from the door frame and stood up straight as he came toward her. 'I'm glad you came up here, Charlie. It's been nice talking with you.' He gave the empty can to her, pulling his hand away quickly as if afraid of being touched. Leigh set both cans down on a wicker table. She caught the screen door as it swung shut. 'Hold up, okay? I'm going back down.'

He waited for Leigh to join him.

'So you'll be selling baskets the rest of the day?' she asked as they started down the slope.

'Yeah. I'll make a stop at Carson's, and then head on away.'

'Do you go to all the lakes in one day?'

'I guess I'll just get over to Circle today. It's a full day trip, making Goon and Willow.'

'So they're on tomorrow's agenda? How would you like a helper?'

He shook his head.

'I've never been to those other lakes.'

'You can't come.'

They reached the sand, and Charlie took long quick strides as if wanting to leave her behind. Leigh quickened her pace. 'What are you scared of?'

'I ain't scared.'

'You just don't want me with you. That's real nice. It really makes me feel good.'

At the boat, he faced her. 'It's nothing against you.'

'Oh, sure.'

'It just wouldn't be right.'

'What would be wrong with it? Oh.' Nodding, she pointed at the

The Lake

heart tattoo on his chest. 'Your mother wouldn't approve,' she said softly. Her fingertip touched the tattoo. Charlie flinched, but didn't move away. 'I wouldn't want to get you in trouble with your mother.'

She put her open hand on his chest, feeling his smooth skin, his quick heartbeat. Sliding it down over the firm slab of his pectoral, she felt his nipple stiff under her palm. 'Maybe you'll come around again sometime,' she said, and took her hand away. She was trembling. 'Maybe I'll buy another basket.'

'I gotta get going.'

Leigh stood on the warm sand until Charlie had pushed off his boat. Then she walked onto the pier and watched him row past.

She raised a hand in farewell.

Charlie looked at her as he worked the oars, but he said nothing.

Chapter Fourteen

Charlie's boat was beached at Carson's Camp. Leigh had watched him unload baskets and carry them up the slope.

She could go over there.

But she didn't want to spook him.

God knew, she had already pushed matters as far as she dared. She'd probably scared him away for good.

Looking back on it, she was shocked by the way she had acted, the way she had felt. What was wrong with her? Never in her life had she come so close to throwing herself at a man.

It might be best, she told herself, if I *don't* ever see him again.

Forget about him.

She turned her lounge chair to face Carson's Camp. Lying back, she rubbed herself with suntan oil but in her imagination it was Charlie's hands spreading the slick fluid over her skin.

After a while, Charlie returned to the boat. He loaded some baskets inside, took out two of the picnic baskets, and hurried back up the slope. Later, he returned empty-handed.

Leigh was glad he'd made some sales.

He pushed off his boat.

She thought of the canoe.

Follow him.

No.

Just leave him alone. Forget about him.

All day, she thought about him. That night, in bed, she stared at

The Lake

the ceiling and wondered about tomorrow. She knew where he would be: at Goon and Willow. She had found out from Mike where the channel was. She could intercept Charlie, if she dared. She trembled, thinking about it.

I won't go over there, she told herself.

You want to bet?

She pictured him gleaming in the sunlight, strong and sleek, the jeans low on his hips.

Fancy meeting you here, Charlie.

He would know, of course, that it was not an accident.

Get out of here and leave me alone.

No, he wouldn't say that. He would sneak glances at her body. He wanted her, but he was scared.

Stop this, Leigh thought.

Restless, she threw her sheet aside. The breeze from the window cooled her damp nightgown. It smelled wonderful. It felt wonderful. Sitting up, she looked toward the moonlit window. She heard birds and crickets chirping in the night.

Why not go outside and enjoy it? she thought. You're not going to fall asleep anyway.

She stood up slowly, listening to the quiet squeak of the bedsprings, and crept to her door. Her heart thudded wildly as she eased the door open.

What are you jumpy for? You don't have to *sneak* out. Mike and Jenny wouldn't care.

It's not them, she realized. It's this. It's going out alone, at this hour, in your nightgown.

She wasn't afraid, she was excited.

It's no big deal.

Then how come you're shaking like a leaf?

Except for creamy moonlight from the windows, the cabin was dark. She rubbed the goose bumps on her arms, then walked silently to the front door. She inched it open and squeezed through the gap, her breath snagging as the edge of the door rubbed her stiff right nipple. Trembling, she pulled the door shut.

The porch floor was cool and smooth under her bare feet. The screen door groaned, but the noise didn't worry her. She stepped down the wooden stairs.

You're out. You made it.

When her feet touched the ground, she stopped. She took a deep breath. A lightning bug drifted by, glowing and fading. Closing her eyes, she let herself feel the breeze. It stirred her hair, blew softly against her face, stroked her arms and legs, moved the nightgown against her skin. Its touch was subtle and erotic.

Her legs felt weak as she walked down the steep path to the lake. At the pier, she looked both ways. She saw no one along the shore. Water lapped and sloshed quietly around the pilings. To the right, the moon made a silver path over the lake.

She walked to the end of the pier. The breeze was stronger here. It fluttered her nightgown and slipped beneath it – lover's hands, gentle, exploring with tentative, intimate caresses.

Leigh wanted to take the nightgown off, to stand naked in the moonlight and feel the breeze all over her.

Not here, at the end of the pier. Someone might be watching.

From over the water came a quiet groan.

It didn't sound human.

Metallic, almost like an oarlock.

The sound startled Leigh out of her dreamy languor. She stiffened. Her eyes searched the darkness.

The boat was a vague blur on the lake's black surface. In the center sat an upright shape. She couldn't believe that she hadn't noticed it at once; the boat was directly ahead, no more than fifty feet beyond the end of the pier.

It was going nowhere.

Charlie?

She almost spoke his name, but stopped herself. What if it wasn't Charlie?

It might be anyone.

The man from Jody's.

She felt her skin prickle.

Don't be silly.

It might be someone night-fishing.

The Lake

She couldn't see a pole.

It *is* Charlie. It *has* to be.

This is too weird, she thought. Spooky weird.

What's he doing here?

'Charlie?' she asked. She didn't raise her voice. In the silence, it wasn't necessary. She knew that the name would carry out to him.

The oarlocks groaned, more loudly this time. She heard the soft swoosh of the blades raising out of the water. The dim silhouette leaned forward and back, beginning to row. The boat turned.

He's coming for me.

Oh, dear God.

Leigh's heart felt as if it might smash through her rib cage.

This isn't happening. It's a dream. A very weird dream. You're going to wake up any second.

She knew she was not dreaming.

She locked her knees to keep herself upright.

Calm down, she thought. You wanted something like this. Well, it's happening.

She was a little frightened, but excited. She couldn't stop trembling.

Then she realized that the boat wasn't moving closer. It was heading away.

Charlie had lost his nerve.

He'd been drawn here, late at night when she would be sleeping, only to stare at the cabin, to . . . what, fantasize?

Calling out to him would do no good.

Leigh dove, leaping from the edge of the pier and stretching out, hitting the water and slicing down beneath its surface. The first shock of cold made her flinch. Then the rush of water felt good. She arched upward and broke the surface. Taking a breath, she blinked her eyes clear and spotted the distant shape of the boat. She swam for it.

She knew that Charlie must have seen her dive. Rowing away, he would be facing her. He had to see. But would he stop or row all the harder, hoping to get away?

Leigh was a strong, swift swimmer. In a canoe, Charlie would have been able to leave her behind, but rowboats were heavy and ungainly.

She was sure that she could catch up with him, no matter how hard he might row.

She kicked steadily, darting out one arm then the other with smooth, easy strokes, turning her head for a breath on every sixth stroke.

He probably thinks I'm crazy, she thought.

I *must* be crazy.

I could've taken the canoe.

This is better.

A corner of Leigh's mind, which seemed to be observing her from a distance, was admiring her nerve. And was a little amused. You've really gone and done it.

She raised her head.

The boat was broadside to her, not far ahead. So Charlie was no longer trying to get away.

Good for him.

He wasn't wearing his odd feathered hat.

She lowered her face into the water and kept on swimming.

What if it's *not* Charlie?

She considered taking another look. That wouldn't solve anything, though. Too dark.

It better be him.

What if it's not?

She went tight and cold inside.

She told herself not to worry. It had to be Charlie.

But she was very close to the boat, getting closer with every stroke. She saw herself grab the gunnel and pull herself up. A face above her. A stranger's face. A woman's. Charlie's mother. Her hand clutched Leigh's wrist. *Now I gotcha!*

It was a crazy thought, but she couldn't get rid of it. She stopped. Treading water, she wiped her eyes.

The boat was two yards away.

The man in its center had Charlie's shape, but the face, a dim blur, could have belonged to anyone.

'Charlie?' she asked.

'Might as well grab an oar,' he said. The hushed voice was Charlie's. He didn't sound overjoyed.

The Lake

Leigh kicked closer, caught hold of the slippery oar blade and pulled herself along its shaft. Then she clutched the gunnel with both hands. 'Thanks for stopping.'

'What am I gonna do, let you drown?'

'I wouldn't have drowned.'

'Well, you gonna climb in, or what?'

'I haven't decided.' She thought about her nightgown. Wet, it would be transparent. 'What were you doing out here, Charlie?'

'Nothing.'

The boat was empty except for an anchor on the deck near the bow. 'Not selling baskets, I see.'

'I just come out for some fresh air. Too hot in the cabin.'

'You rowed all the way over here for some fresh air?'

'Think I come by to spy on you?'

'Something like that.'

'Well, you're full of it.'

'It's all right, Charlie. I don't mind. I was thinking about you, too. That's why I couldn't sleep and came down to the lake. I missed you. I was afraid we wouldn't see each other again.'

'How come you were thinking about me and not that boyfriend of yours?'

'There isn't any boyfriend. I just made him up. Comin' aboard,' she said.

Charlie scooted away to balance the boat, and Leigh thrust herself up. Bracing herself on stiff arms, she waited for the boat to stop its wild rocking. Then she swung a leg over the side and tumbled in. She landed on her back, grunting with the impact. Her knees were in the air, parted, so she quickly rolled to her side.

'Hurt yourself?' Charlie asked.

'I'll live.' She ran a hand down her rump and leg. The clinging fabric didn't end until just above her knee. She sat up, then scuttled backwards to the edge of the stern seat. She boosted herself onto it. 'Graceful entrance, huh?'

Charlie moved to the center of his seat and caught the handle of the oar that he'd left dangling. He lowered both handles to his thighs. The oars jutted out like strange, uptilted wings.

Shivering with cold and excitement, Leigh looked down at herself. As she'd expected, the nightgown was glued to her skin and she could see right through it. She folded her arms tightly across her breasts. She hunched over. 'You wouldn't have a towel?'

'You can have my shirt,' he said.

'Thanks.'

He shipped the oars, swinging them toward Leigh and inward, resting their paddles on the sides of her seat. Then he took off his shirt and tossed it to her.

Leigh draped his shirt across the seat beside her. 'Shut your eyes,' she said.

'What for?'

'Because I'd like you to.'

'Okay.'

'They shut?'

He nodded.

Leigh couldn't see whether they were really shut. Half expecting him to peek, half wanting him to, she raised herself off the seat and peeled the nightgown over her head.

She wadded it into a tight clump and wrung it out into the lake. She set it aside and lowered her gaze. Her skin looked dusky where she was tanned. Her breasts were pale, her jutting nipples almost black in the darkness. Taking a deep, tremulous breath, she picked up Charlie's shirt and put it on. It clung to her damp skin, but took away the cold. She fastened the two lower buttons, and arranged the hanging front to cover her lap.

Even with the shirt on, she felt naked. It was the painted plank seat, wet and slick against her buttocks.

'Okay,' she said. 'You can open your eyes.' Charlie nodded.

'You didn't peek, did you?'

'No.' He fidgeted a bit. 'You asked me not to.'

'Well, good. Thanks for the shirt. It feels good. I was freezing. Are you cold without it?'

'No. I'm not wet.'

'How long have you been out here?'

He shrugged a bare shoulder. 'Not real long.'

The Lake

'Does your mother know?'

'She was sleeping.'

'What if she wakes up and finds you gone?'

'Well, I guess she'll whale on me pretty good when I get back.'

'But you came anyway.'

'I didn't . . . I just got in the boat and ended up here. I didn't mean to. It just sort of happened.'

'I'm glad.'

'You weren't supposed to know.'

'Take me someplace, Charlie.'

He rubbed his mouth with the back of his hand. 'I oughtta take you back to your pier.'

'You won't, will you?'

Shaking his head, he raised the oars over the sides and lowered them into the water. He held one oar motionless under the surface and stroked with the other until the bow swung around to the opposite direction. Then he rowed northward. The boat swept along, oarlocks squeaking, blades making quiet slurps as they came out. They left straight trails of droplets on the surface until they dipped in again. They stroked back smoothly, silently.

Leigh watched Charlie. He sat with his back arched, legs stretched out, his bare heels planted against the ribs along the inside of the hull. Leaning forward with his arms stiff, he slipped the paddles in. Then he eased back, drawing them through the water, coming forward again as they broke the surface, letting the boat glide as he brought the oar handles toward his belly in a graceful circular motion before extending his arms again and bending far forward to start over.

'You're very good at this,' Leigh said.

'Thank you.'

She stretched out her legs until her feet touched Charlie's. He kept rowing. He didn't try to move his feet away.

'It's beautiful out here at night,' she said. 'So peaceful. Have you always lived here?'

'Yeah.'

'It must be nice.'

'Sure. It's okay.'

'Do you have any brothers or sisters?'

'No.'

'Neither do I.'

'I had a twin but it was born dead.'

'I'm sorry.'

'Well, it don't bother me. I never knew it, so it weren't like a loved one going toes-up on you.' He rowed a few strokes in silence. 'Would've been queer, having a brother around that looked the same as me.'

'I know some twins. They pretend to be each other. They've put over some good ones.'

'It's in the lake.'

'What?' Leigh asked, uncertain what Charlie meant.

'My old man, he took it out on the lake and tossed it in with an anchor. Guess it's still down there.'

Leigh frowned, trying to make sense of what Charlie had said. Suddenly, she realized that 'it' was his stillborn twin. Charlie's father had weighted the body with an anchor and left it in the lake.

She'd been *swimming* in the lake . . .

There wouldn't be much of it left by now, she told herself. That was, what, eighteen years ago?

A dead baby down there.

Its bones, anyway.

The lake's dark water with its silver-moon trail didn't look quite as tranquil and beautiful as it had a few minutes ago.

'Funny to think about it down there,' Charlie said.

Hilarious.

'You know how sometimes a fish'll jump and you look real quick but you don't see it? There's just the ripples moving around? Well, when I was a kid and that used to happen, I'd think it was iitî coming up.'

'Jesus,' Leigh muttered.

'Didn't scare me. I just kept looking quick, hoping I'd get a peek at it. I was mostly curious, is all. One time, I jumped in.' He shook his head. Leigh saw the white of his teeth. Was he smiling? 'Had it in mind I might dive down and grab the body, get a good look at it.'

Leigh didn't want to hear any more. 'How far's the high school?' she asked.

The Lake

'Oh, twenty miles.'

'How do you get there? Do they have a bus?'

'I never gone.'

'You never went to school?' She wasn't very surprised.

'What do I need school for? Mom teaches me all I need to know.'

'Your mom's a teacher?'

'She was, a long time ago.'

'Well, you'd meet people.'

'Don't have much use for 'em.'

'You'd meet girls.'

'You gonna start on me about girls again?'

'Not if you don't want me to.'

'Well, I don't see no point. You're a girl. You're here. What's the point talking about girls I don't even know?'

'None, I guess.'

'I never seen one, anyhow, as pretty as you.'

'Oh, I bet you have.'

'Nope. And I see plenty of 'em, too, going around the lakes hawking the baskets. None of 'em are as nice, either. Mostly, they act funny like they're scared of me.'

'Why would they be scared?'

For a few moments, he didn't answer. He drew back the oars and leaned forward again. ''Cause I'm not the same as them, I guess. Is that why? You're scared of me, too, so I guess you must know how come.'

'I am not.'

'Sure. Only difference is, you don't let it stop you.'

'If I were afraid of you, I wouldn't be out here in your boat in the middle of the night.'

'That so?'

'Yes, that's so. I'm no idiot.'

'You're scared, but you're not scared off. Maybe you got a streak of daredevil in you.'

'I've sure got a streak of *some*thing, Charlie. And you're the one who gave it to me.' She drew in her feet. 'Move over,' she said. Staying low, she made her way to the center seat, raised the oar handle out of her way, and sat down beside him. 'Let's make this baby fly,' she said, and started to row.

Leigh matched Charlie's movements, leaning forward as he did, dipping in her paddle and drawing it back, feeling her body against his – his arm and hip and leg.

He speeded up, and so did she.

The boat skimmed along, faster and faster toward its destination, a destination known only to Charlie.

Chapter Fifteen

With a *shoosh* of hull against sand, the boat skidded to a stop. Leigh and Charlie swung their oars in, resting them on the stern seat.

'Well,' Charlie said, 'here we are.'

Leigh nodded, a little breathless from the rowing.

'You like it?'

'Just fine,' she said. Except for its opening – not much wider than their boat – the inlet was surrounded by high trees. It looked totally isolated. It was a far better place than Leigh had hoped for. She smiled at Charlie. 'In fact, it's terrific.' Peering over her shoulder, she saw that they had landed on a dim stretch of sand. 'It's even got a beach,' she whispered.

'That's 'cause it used to have a house. Still does, only no one lives there.' He got up from his seat and stepped to the bow. There he lifted the anchor and flung it. The concrete block hit the sand with a quiet thud.

'I'll be right with you,' Leigh said, still in a whisper. This place *made* her whisper. She went to the stern. Bending over, she felt the shirttail slide up, felt the soft breeze on her buttocks, wondered if Charlie was watching.

Her nightgown was a damp wad. She shook it open and spread it on the seat to help it dry, then walked the length of the boat and hopped down. The sand felt soft and warm under her bare feet. She moved closer to Charlie. She was breathing hard now, but not so much from the rowing.

Just beyond the small patch of beach, the trees began. Leigh saw a few lightning bugs drifting among them. Her gaze wandered up the wooded slope. The dwelling was barely visible among the trees: squared-off corners of darkness, a cabin or shack.

'You sure nobody lives there?'

'Want to go up and find out?'

'Not especially.'

She stared at Charlie. She wished there was more light so she could see his face. His deep-set eyes were lost in shadow, his lips a blur. For a terrible instant, he was a stranger. Then she touched his face, and he was Charlie again. Her trembling fingers wandered down his cheeks, his jaw. As they settled on his shoulders, Leigh stepped against him, drew him closer, and kissed his mouth.

His lips felt rigid. She slid her tongue along them, and they parted slightly. The tip of his tongue met hers. She flicked at it, then sucked it into her mouth. Moaning, Charlie put his arms around her. He squeezed her tightly and opened his mouth wide, lips pressing, tongue filling her mouth.

Leigh squirmed, caressing his smooth back from shoulder to waist, then clutching him closer. He was tight against her, chest hard against her breasts, flat belly pushing against hers as they breathed, the button of his jeans digging into her skin.

Charlie's hands felt enormous on her back. But they didn't move. They stayed still, just below her shoulder blades. Leigh wanted them moving, exploring. She wanted them under the shirt, on her skin.

It's all right, she told herself. He's new at this. He's never been with a girl before, doesn't know what to do, or knows but is frightened.

She slid a hand down Charlie's back, and pushed her fingers under the waistband of his jeans. He didn't have underwear on. His buttocks were smooth, firm mounds.

'How about if we . . . take a swim?' he asked.

'Great.' Leigh pulled her hand out. 'I didn't bring my swimsuit. Neither did you.'

'That's okay,' Charlie said.

'What will I wear?'

'You can wear my shirt if you want.'

The Lake

'I don't want to get it wet for you.'

'I don't mind,' he said. He let go of Leigh. She eased away from him. She put her hands on his sides. 'Do you want to help me with the buttons?'

He unfastened the two buttons, spread the shirt open, and stared at her. Leigh closed her eyes. She felt the shirt slip off her shoulders, its sleeves glide down her arms. She stood in front of Charlie, naked, trembling, waiting for his touch.

'I sure wish it was light out,' he said in a husky voice, 'so I could see you better.'

'There's always Braille,' Leigh whispered. Charlie just stood there. Opening her eyes, she reached for the button of his jeans.

He pushed her hands away. 'Go on and get in the lake,' he told her. He didn't sound annoyed, just nervous.

'You don't have to be shy,' Leigh said.

'I'll be right in.'

'Okay.' Turning away, Leigh walked down the sand. The water washed over her feet. She remembered its chill when she dove from the pier. It didn't seem that way now. It felt as warm as the night air.

'Now, don't look,' Charlie said.

'Okay, bashful.' The water rose around Leigh with mild caresses. She caught her breath when it lapped the place where her thighs met. Then she leaned in, lifted her feet, and glided forward. When she sought the bottom again, the water was neck high. She let her arms drift to the surface. She stared out at the line of trees ahead, the narrow moonlit mouth of the inlet.

Soft splashing sounds came from behind. She waited for Charlie's arms to encircle her, his hands to find her breasts. She waited for the feel of his body against her back.

He swam past her, only his head above the surface, then turned to face her six feet away. 'This sure feels good,' he said. 'Nothing like a night swim.'

'Come here, Charlie Payne.'

He laughed softly. 'Betcha can't catch me.'

Leigh didn't feel like playing games. 'What are you scared of?'

'Not it! You're it!' His head turned away and he started to swim.

'Damn it, Charlie.'

'You ca-an't catch me,' he chanted over his shoulder.

'Don't think so, huh?' Muttering 'Shit,' she lunged forward, dropped beneath the surface and swam underwater. She passed through a chilly current. She went deeper. Her lungs hurt, but she kept going.

She pictured Charlie treading water. His long legs. His penis.

She should be almost directly below him.

The water stirred against her. She heard the muffled sounds of splashes. He was making a getaway.

Seems like he's *always* trying to get away.

Leigh surfaced, gasping, her face splashed by Charlie's kicks. She darted out a hand. Grabbed one of his ankles, pulled. 'Gotcha!' Tugging the ankle, she reached higher and clutched his leg. She expected to find skin. Instead, there was denim. 'Hey!' She hooked fingers into a rear pocket and yanked. Charlie slipped backward. He twisted around, freeing himself.

'What's the big idea?' Leigh demanded.

'Huh?'

'You've got your jeans on.'

'So?'

'Well . . . for one thing . . . what makes you think they'll be dry by morning?'

'Guess they won't be.'

'You gonna tell your mother . . . how they got wet?'

Charlie didn't answer. Obviously he hadn't thought about that. Leigh eased herself backward until her feet found the rocky bottom. Charlie moved closer. He stood, the surface of the water just lower than his shoulders. 'It takes a long time for jeans to dry,' she said. 'If you give them to me right now I'll wring them out for you and hang them up. Maybe the breeze . . .'

'I wouldn't have nothing on.'

'That'd make two of us.'

'You think they'll dry out in time if they're hung out?'

'Maybe.'

'All right, but . . .' He didn't finish. His shoulders moved slightly, then he ducked beneath the surface. His movements under the water

The Lake

sent currents brushing against Leigh. He was below for a long time. His head finally popped up with a burst of water. He thrust the jeans toward Leigh.

'Don't go away,' she said, taking them and wading for shore.

That little ploy sure did the trick, she thought. She still felt a little annoyed that he'd kept his jeans on in the first place. It was cheating. It was also pretty damned peculiar. How many guys, in his place, would've stayed in their pants with a naked girl waiting in the water? Zip, that was how many.

So what's new? He's been peculiar from the start.

Never been with a girl.

His mother's got him so screwed up . . . Well, this time it backfired on her. If Charlie wasn't so frightened that the wet pants would give him away, he might've never taken them off.

Leigh waded out and stood on the beach, her back to the inlet. The breeze made her shiver. She gritted her teeth at the feel of cold droplets trickling down her skin. As quickly as possible, she twisted each leg of the jeans, wringing them with all her strength. When she shook them open, the fabric was still wet but no longer dripping.

To reach the nearest trees, she had to leave the beach. Twigs hurt her feet. Undergrowth snagged her ankles. She looked up at the dark shape of the cabin, wondering if it really was deserted.

What if somebody . . . ?

Don't start.

He might be hiding among the trees, watching. A hand inside his overalls . . .

Don't worry, Charlie's here.

Here? Out in the water.

Would he come and help if someone rushed out?

A quiet, crackling sound came from further up the slope. Leigh stopped. A tree was only a few steps ahead. Her eyes studied the dark woods, but nothing seemed to move. She wanted to glance back and see how far away Charlie was, but she didn't dare. If she looked away, even for a moment . . .

What the hell am I doing here?

You're trying to hang up Charlie's jeans.

What am I doing *here*? My God. I swam out to this guy's boat in the middle of the night and now I'm standing here bare-ass like some kind of maniac. I must be crazy. I should be back at the cabin asleep. I should be home in Marin, asleep. Jesus H. Christ on a rubber crutch, what am I *doing* here?

Trying to get laid by Charlie, that's what.

Which he's afraid to do because his mother wouldn't like it.

And even if he was eager, you're nuts to be going for it this way. You don't even know him. He's definitely a little weird.

Forgetting about the threat from the woods that had so unnerved her a few moments ago, Leigh stepped close to the tree. She reached up and draped Charlie's jeans over its lowest branch.

She turned away and started back. Charlie was still in the lake. He looked as if he'd been cut off at the neck.

Leigh's nightgown was a pale shape spread over the stern seat of the rowboat. She walked toward it.

She pictured herself putting it on.

Game's over, Charlie, take me home.

He wouldn't come out of the water without his jeans.

You could go back for them.

You could leave him here and walk back to the cabin. Just follow the shoreline, then make your way up to the dirt road.

Standing by the boat, she stared down at her nightgown.

Do it, she thought.

She bent over and picked up her nightgown. The breeze caught it, lifting and rippling its weightless fabric.

'What are you doing?' Charlie asked.

I don't know, Leigh thought. God, I haven't the slightest.

She pressed the nightgown to her front and held it there, covering herself.

You're really going to call it quits?

It never should have gone this far. I was out of my mind.

She heard quiet sloshing sounds. 'Leigh?' Charlie was wading closer, the black surface of the water dropping.

'What're you doing?' he asked again.

'I think I'm ready to leave,' she said.

The Lake

You *think*?

'What for? Don't you like it here?'

'It's awfully late,' she said.

Late. How lame.

Charlie stopped. He was bare to the waist. Just another step or two, Charlie. 'What's wrong?' he asked.

'Nothing.'

'You mad at me?'

'No. It isn't you.'

'You're mad at me 'cause I left my pants on.'

'No, I'm not.'

'Well, they're off now.'

'It doesn't matter,' Leigh said.

She stared at the dark surface in front of him. Of course it doesn't matter, she told herself. Oh sure.

'I should've took 'em off,' he said. 'I knew I was s'posed to. I was just too yellow, that's all. I'm awfully sorry. I wanted to, that's for sure.'

'Charlie, we shouldn't be like this.'

'I guess not. But I don't want us to leave, though.' He waded out. He walked up the beach, hands crossed to cover his groin. 'Cold,' he whispered.

Leigh draped her nightgown over the boat seat and went to him.

You were going to leave, she reminded herself. What are you doing?

Her heart thudded. Her mouth was dry. She met Charlie and put her arms around him. His wet skin felt cold. His arms went around her back. His open mouth found hers, and his tongue pushed in. She squirmed against him, moaning with the feel of his penis pressing thick and hard against her belly.

Where their bodies met, the chill went away. But the skin of his back was still wet and cold. Her hands moved down to his buttocks. Charlie, following her lead, moved his hands down to her rump. They felt big and warm.

Soon, Leigh took her mouth away. Kissing the side of his neck, she reached behind and took his wrists. She eased away from him. She lifted his hands to her breasts, and trembled at their touch. His hands were callused but gentle. Leigh closed her eyes. She clung to his hips as he caressed her. His hands glided over her breasts, enclosed them, held them tenderly, tightened and squeezed, roamed them, exploring, then squeezed again.

'Kiss,' Leigh muttered.

He crouched. She held his shoulders, and he kissed her left nipple. His tongue thrust. Leigh moaned as he sucked the nipple into his mouth, tongue swirling and probing.

Fingers in his wet hair, she urged his head closer. Her breast felt engulfed.

He rubbed her thighs. His mouth went to her other breast and his hands moved higher as he licked the nipple. Higher until his thumbs stroked the creases of her groin.

Leigh's grip tightened on his hair. Charlie made sucking noises, tugging at her nipple. His hands swept over her hips, around her buttocks, the backs of her legs, then up again, curling in and pressing. With a gasp, Leigh locked her knees to keep her legs from buckling. Her breast was drawn deep into his mouth. One of his hands went away and came to the front. Its edge pressed her vagina. She shuddered as it sawed back and forth, rubbing, opening her, sliding between her folds, slick and hot. His thumb rose into her.

'*Charlie,*' she gasped.

His mouth pulled away from her breast, leaving it wet and tingling. 'Does it hurt?'

'Hurt? No. Dear God.' She hugged his head between her breasts. His thumb pushed and circled. His hand pressed hard, part of it rubbing her clitoris. She squirmed on it.

Then she released his head and squatted. Charlie sank to his knees, his thumb still inside her. He curled his other hand behind her neck to hold her steady. She reached between his legs. His penis felt huge. Her fingers enclosed it, slid down its length. She gently squeezed his scrotum, glided her palm up the underside of his shaft, then let herself fall backward onto the sand.

Charlie loomed over her, kneeling between her bent legs, holding himself up with stiff arms. Leigh stroked his sides. 'In me,' she whispered. 'I want you in me.'

'You sure?'

The Lake

'My God.'

'I mean . . . you won't get a baby?'

'It's okay.' Probably, she thought. She had already counted. Her period was due in four days.

Charlie pressed down, his hips forcing her thighs even farther apart. She dug her heels into the sand, lifting herself to meet him.

His penis rubbed her. It moved slowly, spreading her, barely inside, sliding along her slit. Then it began to ease in. Leigh thrust up. The penis filled her.

Charlie's tongue pushed into her mouth. She sucked it. His tongue was in her, his penis was in her. She possessed both, and they possessed her. She writhed. His tongue thrust and retreated, matching the strokes of his penis. She gasped through her nose. She heard wet sounds and Charlie moaning. She dug her heels into his buttocks. He rammed deeper, and suddenly went rigid. Leigh sucked his tongue hard. Her insides quaked with the feel of him all the way in, jerking and throbbing and pumping a flood.

She cried out into his mouth.

Chapter Sixteen

A gentle rapping woke Leigh up. She raised her head off the pillow and groaned.

'We're going out for the big ones,' Jenny called through the door. 'Want to come along?'

'Okay,' Leigh said. 'Time for me to shower first?'

'No problem.'

Fishing was about the last thing she wanted to do, but she had made up her mind, in the early-morning hours, to go with them today. If she missed two days in a row, they might suspect that something was amiss.

Something was amiss, all right. Every muscle in her body ached when she pushed herself up. Her insides felt battered.

Moaning, Leigh limped to the chair by the window. Her nightgown was draped over it. She lifted the gown and inspected it. It was dry, but dirty. She wadded it up and made her way to the dresser. She hid it at the bottom of a drawer. She could do her own laundry later, and take care of it. Nobody would be the wiser.

In the mirror, her hair was a straggly mess. She combed out the worst of the snags and brushed it. Sand sprinkled her shoulders.

Back at the bed, she brushed sand and bits of leaves and other debris off the pillow and bottom sheet. She found a small, stiff place on the sheet. She guessed it was dried semen. Checking herself, she found some flaked in her pubic hair, and a patch of it on her inner thigh that felt tight and looked like skin peeling from a sunburn. She left it there and made the bed.

The Lake

She took her robe from the closet, put it on, and went to the door.

Mike, in the kitchen, was pouring coffee into a thermos. 'And how are you this fine morning?' he asked.

'Great,' Leigh said. 'A little stiff from canoeing yesterday.' She tried her best not to limp on her way to the bathroom.

Inside, she hung her robe on the doorknob. She looked at herself in the full-length mirror. Her breasts were a little red. Otherwise, none of the damage showed. Turning around, she looked over her shoulders. Her back was all right except for a few faint red marks on her buttocks where she had lost the scabs from her scrapes at the anti-war demo.

The cop dragging her.

That seemed like years ago.

It seemed like it had happened to someone else.

She made the water as hot as she could stand, and stepped under the shower. The spray beat down on her. It felt wonderful. Sighing, she stretched her sore muscles. Then she slicked herself with soap. She scrubbed between her legs to make sure she got all the semen off.

Probably more inside, she thought.

There must've been a gallon last night.

Four times.

Three, not counting the mouth.

No wonder I ache.

Even her cheeks felt sore.

What a night.

The memories of it rushed through her mind, triggering fresh desire.

She couldn't wait to see him again.

She began to shampoo her hair.

Before parting, they had agreed to meet at three o'clock where the channel from Wahconda entered Goon Lake. He said he knew of a secret place to take her, a place where no one could see them even in daylight. It sounded terrific. She hoped that she wasn't too sore to enjoy it.

Leigh's mind was full of Charlie as she finished her shower, dried, and returned to her room. She wondered what time he would be leaving in his boat to take the baskets over to Goon and Willow. Maybe she would see him. The possibility made her heart race. She parted her hair in the middle, brushed bangs down over her forehead, and gave herself a ponytail. She wanted to wear her good white shorts, but decided to save them for the rendezvous. She put on her cutoffs instead, and a faded blue T-shirt.

Heading down to the pier with Mike and Jenny, she thought she had never felt quite so fine. In spite of her aches. The morning air was sweet with the scent of pine. The breeze caressed her. The calm blue lake shimmered with sunlight.

'You're looking pretty chipper this morning,' Jenny said.

It showed? 'Guess it's the fresh air,' she said, and stepped down into the boat.

When the gear was aboard, Mike steered the boat out around the pier. Then he asked if Leigh would like to take the controls. 'Sure,' she told him, and stepped to the helm. 'Where to?'

'Anywhere you want.'

Opening the throttle, she swung the boat northward. She watched the shore. Soon, she saw the opening of the inlet where Charlie had taken her. When the boat was directly across from it, she glimpsed the beach.

She felt the sand against her back, Charlie pounding into her.

A few more hours . . .

In the sunlight, they would be able to see each other.

Near the north shore, she turned the boat to the east. The foreboding she used to feel along this side of the lake had gone. Approaching an old dock with broken planks dangling toward the water, she scanned the woods until she spotted a shack hidden among the trees. Was this Charlie's place? Probably not. She suspected that he lived farther down, maybe even along the eastern shore.

'Where we going?' Mike asked, appearing at her side.

'How about between those two islands?' she suggested, pointing at the patches of woods far ahead.

'Looks good to me,' Mike told her.

Yesterday morning, Charlie had said that he'd seen her water-skiing. Well, she'd been skiing over much of the lake, but the nearest she'd

The Lake

got to the eastern shore was when she'd circled those two islands. Maybe that had been when Charlie spotted her.

Let's not be too obvious about this, she thought as she neared the islands. You don't want to wind up on his doorstep.

The islands were about a hundred yards apart. As the boat entered the area between them, Leigh cut the engines. 'If I were a fish,' she told Mike and Jenny, 'this is just the place I'd hang out.'

Mike dropped anchor.

Jenny opened the picnic basket – one of Charlie's baskets. She poured coffee into mugs, then handed out egg-salad sandwiches wrapped in cellophane. It was their custom to eat before baiting the hooks.

Leigh's cheek muscles ached as she chewed, reminding her again of last night – her lips tight around Charlie, her mouth full, the slick smooth hardness of him, her sucking. She'd been on top, Charlie's head between her legs, his tongue . . . Her mouth was too dry for the sandwich. She struggled to swallow, and washed the food down with coffee.

Stop the daydreaming, she warned herself. Save it for later when you're not with Mike and Jenny.

She joined in the conversation. Soon she was calm enough to finish her sandwich.

They baited their hooks.

The current had swept the boat sideways. Leigh dropped her line over the port side so that she could face the east while she fished. The wooded islands acted as blinders, blocking much of the lake's shoreline. She could see no pier or dwelling along the visible stretch of shore. Just thick forest, curtains of green drooping toward the water, roots here and there reaching down from the banks. She wondered if Charlie's place was nearby, maybe on the other side of one of the islands.

If so, there was a chance that she might see him when he rowed out with his baskets.

The white top of her float rode the small waves, rising and falling. She watched it. She watched the lake.

Her thoughts returned to last night. She let the images play through her mind, the feelings come back. It was almost like being with him again.

She *would* be with him again, this afternoon. They would go to his secret place.

I'll take along the suntan oil, she thought.

Charlie would spread it over her naked body, then she would rub it on him. She pictured their skin gleaming with oil. She felt them squirming together, all slippery.

In just a few more hours.

She watched her float. She watched the lake.

There was no sign of Charlie.

Maybe he'd started early and was already on one of the other lakes. Of course. He would've wanted to finish his selling rounds as fast as possible so that he could be ready to meet her.

At three o'clock.

She wondered if she could stand to wait that long.

At two-thirty, Leigh left the cabin after telling Mike and Jenny that she planned to 'go exploring' in the canoe.

They said to have fun.

Her heart thudded hard as she made her way down to the shore. She felt tight and trembly inside. She wore her fresh shorts, just as she had planned, and a red sleeveless blouse. She carried a towel. Rolled inside the towel was the plastic bottle of suntan oil.

She pushed the canoe into the water, wading out for a few steps before climbing aboard. She took out the suntan oil, then knelt on the towel and paddled away.

Though Leigh wanted bright sunlight for the rendezvous, there were high clouds shadowing the lake.

If the sun's not out, she thought, we won't glisten.

There wasn't even a cool breeze to compensate for the sun's loss. The air was still and muggy.

Leigh's blouse clung to her back. It was tucked into her shorts, and it pulled at her shoulders each time she leaned forward.

After passing Carson's Camp, she swung the bow eastward. She blinked sweat out of her eyes.

Awfully muggy.

Resting the paddle across the gunnels, she looked around. The

The Lake

nearest other boat was so far off that the people aboard looked vague and featureless. She tugged her blouse out of the waistband of her shorts and lifted the front to wipe her face. She wished she could take it right off, but she was wearing nothing beneath it.

Guys are so lucky, she thought. They can take off their shirts in weather like this.

She unbuttoned her blouse, lifted it around her lower ribs, and tied the front.

A lot better.

She picked up the paddle and dug it into the water. The canoe started forward again. Soon it was shooting over the calm surface.

Leigh kept a close watch on the southern shore. At last, she spotted a field of lily pads with a narrow path of open water down the middle. This had to be the channel to Goon Lake. She swung the canoe's prow toward it.

The canoe glided in, a bit to the left of the open water. The lily pads rustled like paper against the hull. Setting down the paddle, she let the canoe drift. She was out of breath, drenched with sweat. She pulled the towel out from under her knees and wiped her face with it. She wiped the back of her neck, and felt glad she was wearing the ponytail: it kept the hair off her neck. Still gasping for breath, she plucked open the knot to let her blouse fall open. She rubbed her dripping sides and belly and chest.

As soon as the towel was gone, her skin felt damp again.

It was the heavy, hot, humid, suffocating air.

Air that smelled faintly of rain.

She wished that it *would* rain.

Fat chance.

Leigh paddled farther into the channel. Ahead, there was no sign of Goon Lake. She looked behind her. Wahconda was out of sight.

Dragonflies hovered over the carpet of pads. She saw a green frog hop and splash. The motionless air seemed silent, but she realized that it was noisy with buzzes, chitters, water plops, bird squawks and chirrups. No human sounds; that was what made it seem like silence.

Leigh took her blouse right off. She leaned over the side with it, the canoe tipping slightly, the aluminum gunnel pushing hot against her breast. Then she plunged her blouse into the water. She lifted it out. It dripped on her thighs. She sighed deeply as she pressed the wet, cool fabric to her face. She dunked it again, shook it open, and swept it against her torso. It plastered her from shoulder to waist.

She peeled it down, soaked it one more time, then struggled into it and tied the front again.

It had felt good while it lasted.

It hadn't lasted long.

She needed to be *in* the water. Swimming. With Charlie.

Soon now.

Slowly, she paddled forward.

The channel curved one way, then the other. From the air, it must look like stacked S's. Or a snake, she thought. This was probably a good place for water snakes, though she hadn't noticed any so far.

She kept dipping the paddle in, drawing it back slowly, trying not to exert herself as she guided the canoe along the twisting channel.

Finally, she came out at the other end. She laid the paddle across the gunnels. As she folded the towel and sat on it, her gaze swept Goon Lake. It was much smaller than Wahconda, maybe half the size. Like Wahconda, most of the piers and dwellings were along the western shore. She saw a skier being towed behind a motorboat, and three other boats off in the distance with people fishing from them. She didn't see Charlie.

Maybe he'd hit a delay.

Maybe he was doing a brisk business in baskets and didn't want to cut it short.

There were several small islands. One of them could be blocking Charlie from her view.

She waited.

He was nowhere in sight. Maybe he was still over on Willow Lake.

Leigh considered heading over to Willow, but she had no idea where the channel might be. She supposed she could find it. If she tried, however, there was some chance she might miss Charlie. He could end up waiting here while she was busy searching for him.

This is where we planned to meet, she told herself. I'd better stay put.

The Lake

The canoe kept drifting back into the lily pads. After paddling it free a few times, she decided to simplify matters by landing. She headed to the right and brought the canoe up against the trunk of a fallen tree. Clamping her towel under one arm, she scurried in a crouch to the bow and picked up the mooring rope. She tied its end to one of the dead, leafless branches. Then she climbed onto the trunk, made her way carefully back toward its cluster of roots, and hopped to the ground.

At a shaded place close to shore, she toweled away her sweat once again, then spread the towel on the ground and sat on it.

From here she had a full view of the lake.

She still did not see Charlie.

What could be keeping him?

He'll be along. He's only a little bit late.

Probably half an hour late already, and no sign of him in the distance.

Does he have a watch? Leigh had never seen him with one.

I should have brought a book.

She was sitting cross-legged. The ground felt very hard. After a while, her rump and legs began to go numb and tingly. She leaned back, bracing herself on her elbows and stretching out her legs. She kept her head up to watch the lake. That felt a lot better, at first. But soon the strain of her already stiff neck and shoulder muscles became painful. She wanted to lie down.

If you do that, you'll fall asleep.

She had napped for a couple of hours after lunch, but that hadn't been enough to make up for last night.

If she fell asleep now, she might miss Charlie. He could show up, not see her or the canoe, and figure that she had either stayed away or given up on waiting.

Moaning with aches and weariness, Leigh got to her feet. She climbed onto the tree, walked along its wide trunk past the place where the canoe was tied, and sat down. The water felt smooth and cool around her feet.

The skier had gone. One of the boats was moving slowly near an island, its motor a faint hum. She spotted a rowboat!

Her heart quickened.

511

It's about time, she thought.

She gazed at the rowboat. Slowly it drew closer, then turned as if heading for one of the piers. A cloud moved briefly out of the sun's way. The rowboat caught sunlight and glinted.

It was aluminum.

Charlie's boat was wood, painted green.

It's not him.

Leigh's disappointment came out in a long sigh.

'Where the hell is he?' she muttered.

He'll be here, she told herself.

Maybe he chickened out.

Or he had to change plans. Maybe his mother wanted him to postpone today's trip for some reason.

Am *I* in the right place? How do I know for sure this is Goon Lake? Maybe this is Circle, where Charlie went yesterday, and he's waiting for me at the channel into Goon and wondering where *I* am.

Mike told me yesterday where to find the channel to Goon.

Maybe Mike was wrong.

Something went wrong, that's for sure.

Trickles slid down her cheeks. She felt like crying, but these weren't tears. She rubbed her face with the backs of her hands. The backs of her hands were wet too, and only smeared the sweat on her face.

Couldn't there at least be a breeze?

Where is Charlie?

I'm not giving up. I'll wait here till Hell freezes over.

Fat chance of *anything* freezing over.

A tickling drop of sweat slid down her neck and between her breasts. She wiped it away.

And remembered her sea-thing necklace.

She didn't have it on.

Maybe that's the problem, she thought. Should've worn my good-luck charm.

I didn't wear it last night, though, and I had plenty of luck without it.

The necklace has nothing to do with luck.

Still, she wished that she was wearing it.

The Lake

Even if you're not superstitious, always a good idea to keep the bases covered.

From now on, I'll wear it.

Leigh kicked her feet, making the cool water splash her legs.

The hell with the necklace, I should've worn my bikini.

She'd thought she wouldn't need it. She'd planned on skinny-dipping at Charlie's secret place, expecting it to be an inlet similar to the one last night, or maybe a stream or pond.

Here, nobody was nearby. But there was no real privacy. She couldn't go in naked.

With a shrug, she pushed herself off the trunk. She dropped into the waist-deep water with barely a splash, took a few steps along the slippery rock bottom until she was clear of the trees, then lifted her feet. The coolness engulfed her. It felt wonderful. She glided beneath the surface until she needed air, then came up. She rolled onto her back. Floating, she closed her blouse over her breasts. Then she shut her eyes.

Buoyed up, it felt like she was lying spread-eagled on a cool, liquid mattress. She had to hold her back arched to keep from sinking, but otherwise no effort was needed. The water turned her slowly, toyed with her limp arms and legs.

I should've done this a long time ago, she thought.

She felt fine and relaxed and drowsy.

Like this, I could wait all afternoon for Charlie.

He'll be along . . .

. . . pretty soon.

A nose full of water startled Leigh awake. Spluttering, she slapped the surface and kicked. A few quick strokes took her close enough to shore so that she could stand. She coughed and blew her nose. Then she was all right except for a burning sensation behind her eyes.

Wonderful, she thought. Drown, why don't you?

Wiping her eyes, she turned around and scanned the lake.

No Charlie.

It must be four o'clock by now.

He's not coming.

Goddamn it.

She waded ashore and flopped face down on her towel.
Come on, Charlie.
Where are you, Charlie?
Goddamn it to hell, anyway.
Shit!
Leigh began to sob.

Chapter Seventeen

Leigh rolled over, sat up and knuckled the tears from her eyes. Like a kid at school. Despite her frustration at Charlie's absence, the idea struck her as a little amusing. Tears welled up again, but she thought better of it. Wouldn't do for Charlie to catch her like this; eyes all red and puffy from crying.

If Charlie deigned to put in an appearance this side of tomorrow.

Fine. Put it down to experience, Leigh. World's *full* of gals who've been let down – *are* being let down at this very moment, she told herself. But she could *swear* Charlie had been serious last night. Serious enough to come out to look for her, anyhow.

Not today, though.

Must have had second thoughts.

Maybe his mom hided him when she saw his wet pants and he's stayed home.

Who gives a shit, anyway . . .

She wasn't a gal to hang around after some guy who couldn't stand up to his own mother.

She must be a tough old bitch.

Not like *her* mom.

Leigh imagined her own mom, and Dad – if they could see her now. Waiting around for this guy who sells *baskets* for a living, how would *they* react? 'Don't tell me,' she muttered. 'They'd be all self-righteousness and pursed lips. Accusing eyes. Mom's would be red with weeping.'

'Pull yourself together, young lady,' Dad would say, with a pleading glance at mom, like, 'We got ourselves a situation here, Helen. She's *your* daughter, too, y'know. Tell me, what *are* we going to do with her?' Mom would just shake her head, wring her hands, stem back more despairing tears.

'What are Mike and Jenny *doing*?' she'd blurt. 'Allowing her out on her lonesome like this? Leigh's so vulnerable just now. What with that showdown with the police and everything. Your brother should have had more sense than to encourage her to meet up with this – this *basket-seller*!'

'*My* brother. That's rich! My brother indeed! I don't recall *you* putting forward any of *your* family to help out with your errant daughter . . .'

'You mean *our* errant daughter!'

God, what a mess!

For the millionth time (it seemed like the millionth), Leigh lifted her head and scanned the lake. She was weary with waiting. Charlie had either forgotten or was being held captive by that witch-bitch mother of his.

'That's it,' she muttered. 'Mom found out, locked her precious boy in the closet and swallowed the key. Jeez. What kind of fool *am* I? Driven to the point of suicide by some kid who can't even stand up to his own *mother*?'

Some kid who's gagging for sex but doesn't even know it yet. Wouldn't know a pussy if it jumped up and bit him. 'No,' she told herself. 'That's not true.' She remembered Charlie last night; the state he was in (the state they were *both* in) and knew that no way was that true.

Time to haul ass and head for home, honey. Quit being a prize idiot and just get gone.

She looked at her wristwatch. 5:57. Mike and Jenny would be getting worried. More than that. They'd most likely be hairless by now. Wondering if they should call Mom and Dad.

Or the cops . . .

No, they wouldn't do that. Not Mike and Jenny. They were okay guys. Sensible. Level-headed. Teachers, for God's sake. Through her

The Lake

tears, Leigh was sorry for what they must be feeling right now. They'd be thinking they had let her parents down.

Let *her* down.

Jesus.

At least she owed them the courtesy of an appearance before they called the police department.

She climbed to her feet. Her back and legs were wrecked; she felt like she'd done a fifty-mile route march.

Aaaghh . . .

She limped over to the canoe. Clambered into it. Sat down and eased the paddle off the gunnel. It was *so* muggy and hot. She unbuttoned her blouse. Her *almost* new blouse, the one she'd worn only twice before. She liked it too, knew that the colour red looked good against her fair hair and sun-bronzed skin.

But it wasn't looking so new, or so good, now.

Hanging off her shoulders like a limp rag.

She dragged it together and tied the ends in a knot. Under the thin fabric, she felt the weight of her breasts as she leaned forward, preparing to skim the paddle through the water. She scanned the dark pines and the shining lake, spread out before her . . . and saw Charlie up ahead, powering his rowboat toward the shore with strong, well-muscled arms; his back against the sun, his front in shadow.

Like last night, he wasn't wearing his hat.

Leigh could see his gleaming white teeth.

Because he was *smiling*, for chrissake.

The smile did it for her.

Goddamn you, Charlie. I don't *believe* this. All bright-eyed and bushy-tailed and I've just spent an entire *afternoon* waiting for you. Shit, Charlie. How *could* you?

He steered the boat around, easing its hull onto the sand. All so laid-back . . . and, goddamn it, he looked so . . . unconcerned. He lifted the anchor and let it drop into the water.

Then, effortlessly, like an athlete, he leapt from the rowboat and came toward her. Gleaming muscles, slender hips – and jeans bulging in all the right places. He sure looks mighty pleased with himself, she thought, angrily.

'Charlie, you useless piece a' shit. Where *have* you been?'

'Mom told me to take more baskets out on Wahconda. There's a whole new buncha vacationers over at Carson's Camp, and . . .' He stopped, saw her angry face and dropped his gaze.

He looked trapped, uncomfortable.

'Charlie,' she persisted. 'You *knew* we arranged to meet today. At three o'clock, we both agreed. It's now turned six. What *is* the matter – can't you tell the time?'

His face reddened, his mouth trembling slightly.

Alarmed, Leigh thought that he was going to burst into tears.

Oh, my God.

Don't *do* this to me, Charlie.

I want a goddamn lover, not a crybaby.

Take me in your arms. Sweep me off my feet.

Do *something*. But don't just *stand* there like an idiot.

He looked confused – innocent, like a child; melting her anger like a snowball in the sun. More than anything else in the whole world, she wanted to hold him close. Gather him to her breast; caress him with gentle hands.

And for him to *ram* himself inside her.

Now.

He could have committed murder for all she cared.

Maybe had.

Maybe his mom lay bleeding to death right now, a stained hunting knife tossed to one side. The lifeblood pumping out of her.

All because she wouldn't let him go to the evil bitch who lusted for her precious Charlie's sex.

Give it to me, Charlie. Here. Now. In front of anybody who cares to watch. Just *give* it to me.

Leigh opened her blouse, letting it fall from her shoulders as she moved toward him.

His eyes widened. Then he smiled, shyly, fixing his gaze on her naked breasts. They were heavy and swinging as she walked toward him.

He held out his arms and, with a moan, she pulled him to her. Wrapped an arm around his neck and pressed her open mouth onto

The Lake

his. Their tongues met. Her free hand struggled to undo the top button of his jeans.

They're so *tight*.

It's a wonder he isn't raped every time he goes out, she marveled, peeling down the zipper. Easing her fingers in between his legs, she found the hot, pulsating bulge lying there. Waiting for her. With both hands, she reached in further; cupped his scrotum and penis, and drew them out. He moaned, squirming in her grasp.

'*In* me, Charlie,' she breathed.

'The house. Come into the house,' he whispered hoarsely.

'Why not here? Anyway, *what* house?'

'My secret place. It's private. Come with me.'

She pouted. Annoyed at the interruption; her body aching with need. If he's gonna play games again, it's finito. I'm outta here.

Still pouting, Leigh followed him up the limb-strewn beach to a house set back in the pines. Watching out for him across the lake, she hadn't noticed it before. He led her across the rickety porch, to the stoop and through the half-open door.

'You been here before?' she asked, warily.

'Yeah. Lotsa times,' he told her. 'Not with nobody else, though. I come here alone. So's I can think.'

'Whose place is it?'

'B'longed to some rich New Yorker guy, back in the thirties, Mom said. Shot his wife, buried her out back in the woods. Guy hanged himself from that there balcony – y'see, up there?'

'How did they know he'd shot and buried his wife?'

'Left a note on the kitchen table. Confessin' all. Said he'd caught his wife in bed with Jed Johnson, local Ranger hereabouts. Nobody'd live in the place after that. It was left to go to rack 'n' ruin. Y'can still see bloodstains on the kitchen floor,' Charlie explained with enthusiasm, as if proud to impart this piece of local lore.

The house was dark inside; it smelled earthy and damp. Leigh wrinkled her nose as she caught the moldy odor of decaying wood – *or was it dried blood?*

Shivering, she wished she'd picked up her blouse from off the beach.

It had been wet, anyhow.

Might have dried off by now, though.

A sharp shiver brought goose bumps to her naked flesh. Hunching her shoulders up to her ears, she wrapped her arms around her breasts.

Charlie led the way up the stairs.

'Mind that one – and the next. These old stairs are real unsafe. Don't want you breaking a leg, now.'

'God, Charlie. Do we *have* to do this? I mean, this place could put a person off it, y'know . . .'

She flung out an arm to balance herself, clutching at the balustrade. It was tacky with damp and mold. She dragged back her hand, checking her fingers.

'Yuck. This is *gross*. Charlie, you're doing this on purpose. Tell me you don't want to make love to me, and I'll go. Just fade out of your life for ever . . . I don't *need* all this.'

Tears of disappointment welled in her eyes.

Disappointment? Try *terminal frustration*! He's playing games with me – just like last night. Who the hell does he think he is . . .

'Charlie?'

They reached the landing. A mezzanine arrangement with several doors branching off into various rooms on the right. Must have been quite a house, once upon a time, she thought miserably.

'*Charlie . . .!*'

He turned, sweeping her into his arms – easily, as if she were a child – and carried her into one of the rooms. By its size it'd probably been the master bedroom. A tick mattress lay in the center of the floor.

Jagged, broken windows overlooked the pine-fringed lake. It was a mighty fine view, Leigh had to admit.

Any other time . . .

Empty beer cans, food wrappers and other junk was piled in the corners of the room. Squatters, campers . . .

Even murderers . . . She pictured the New Yorker guy, rope in hand, taking one last look at the lake below . . .

Charlie put her down, then went over to an old-fashioned dresser. He opened a drawer, took out a folded sheet and an Indian blanket.

The Lake

Leigh perked up.

Looks like this could be a regular routine.

She felt let down. Cheap, tawdry. She'd *hoped* she'd been his first. Looked like he'd been lying through his teeth when he told her he'd never had a girlfriend.

Guys. What is it with them?

Wondering what he'd come up with next, she watched, hands on hips, eyebrows raised.

'Uh-huh,' she murmured, eyeing the bedcovers and wondering who'd used them before she came along. 'Very handy.'

'I snuck these in last night, after you'd gone.' He looked as if he expected her to pat him on the head and say, 'Gee, thanks Charlie.'

She didn't.

He spread out the sheet on the mattress. Then he put the blanket on top.

At least they're clean.

If they'd been dirty, I'd've been out of here, Leigh told herself. Then she felt guilty immediately. Charlie had done all of this for *her*. She was sure of it.

He was smiling eagerly. Folding down the bedcovers, he motioned for her to get in.

Still, she was cynical.

'The romance is killing me, buster . . . Can't wait for dessert.'

Cocking his head to one side, he tried to understand her words. Her mood. He hadn't seen her like this before. His stare shifted to his feet.

'I . . . I thought you'd like my secret place . . .' he said, quietly; disappointed that she seemed displeased.

Leigh let out a small 'Aahh' of guilt. She couldn't *bear* to see him hurt. Innocently, his gaze questioned hers. Like a small boy who'd brought his mom a special gift, only to be told that she didn't want it.

She relented; couldn't take his discomfort any longer.

'Okay, Charlie. I give in. This sure is some place you got here.'

Moving over to the makeshift bed she clambered in, hugged her knees and smiled up at him.

Charlie looked happier already. It dawned on her that, in his own special way, maybe Charlie was in love with her.

She opened her arms and he came to her.

They lay there for a while, he stroking her breasts, her belly, her thighs and legs. Doing it carefully, like she was a piece of precious china.

Lying by her side, propped up on an elbow, head in his hand, he looked at her. She smiled deep into his eyes.

His arm dropped down.

They lay together, their bodies touching. The pain, the hard ache between her legs, began again. He caressed her back, gently. Kissed her lips, her eyelids, her cheeks.

Then tenderly, and with infinite feeling, her lips again.

She sensed the *different* kind of passion.

Not the wham bam, thank ya, ma'am stuff that'd happened yesterday. This was wonderfully titillating foreplay to the main event.

Leigh responded, gently at first, then with impatience and a growing need. She moved on top, straddling him, her lips opening on his, finding his tongue, sucking, sucking and pulling it into her mouth. Drawing it into her throat.

Wishing it was *him* that she had in her mouth.

Like last night.

She left his mouth. Sliding down, she trailed her tongue over his slick, muscular chest.

Charlie's body tasted good; it was hairy and salty with sweat.

She licked harder now, her breath coming in short, hard gasps. Her tongue traveled past his navel and through the dark curly hairs spreading across his hard belly.

Down to his huge erection.

She grasped it and took it in her mouth until he came, writhing, moaning, spurting into her. Sobbing and gagging, she swallowed his come.

Gasping, tears running down her face, she lay with her head between his legs, panting, breathless. Pulling her up against his chest, he massaged the backs of her thighs with firm, smooth strokes.

The Lake

His mouth found hers again and he took her tongue and sucked at it, hard. Shifting slightly, his pubic hairs rubbed against her belly. Then, with a strength she wasn't expecting, he shoved a hand inside her.

Aaaaghhh . . .

She cried out. In shock. In pain.

With a catlike movement Charlie was on top, thrusting himself deep into her center. Pounding into her, gouging, shaking her body to the core. She rose to meet him; raw, hurting, pressing herself against him, raking herself up and down his shaft till she could take no more.

He came into her again. And again. Still gasping, crying a little, she lay back on the tousled, sweat-soaked sheet. Charlie lay on his side, looking down at her hungrily.

Panting. Wanting more.

Playing with her dark, softening nipples.

She felt the hard ache rise again . . .

'Charlie,' she breathed, closing her eyes, lifting her arms to hold him.

But Charlie leapt up, grabbed his shirt and thrust his arms into it. Fumbling with the buttons, he gave up trying and dragged on his jeans.

Hopping from one leg to the other, he looked almost comical.

Except it wasn't funny.

Leigh was in shock.

Crying out in disbelief: 'Charlie?'

Astounded.

Bereft.

'Where are you *going*? You can't leave me now . . . not like this . . .'

'I gotta I gotta . . .' he stammered desperately. 'I promised Mom I'd be home for supper. She thinks I'm out collecting wood for tomorrow . . . I gotta go . . . I just gotta . . .'

He looked around wildly.

Torn. Willing himself to be somewhere else.

Night shadows had gathered. She couldn't make out his features.

Couldn't see if he was disappointed.

What had gone wrong?

Had she been too forward?

Whatever. Looked like she'd frightened him off . . .

And now he was leaving her.

But he *couldn't*.

Not when we've had it so good together.

Nothing, *no one*, is gonna keep us apart!

She sprang up and grabbed him; he wrenched away from her urgent, shaking hands that were grasping his shirt, holding on to him.

'Mom'll be looking for me. She's expecting me . . .'

They fell to the floor, struggling, fighting. He rolled away from her.

Pushed himself up.

Unable to believe what was happening, she reached out to hold him.

He fell back, away from her, shoving an elbow hard on the floorboards. With a rending, splitting sound the rotten floor gave under his weight.

He plummeted to the ground below.

She stared at the black space where the floor, *where Charlie* had been.

Hearing his low, hurt grunt as he hit the bottom.

The dull crack that was a thud and a *splish!* all at the same time.

Like a ripe melon bursting open.

Terrified, Leigh scrambled to her feet.

'*Charlie oh my God Charlie Charlie!* Wait, I'm coming, I'm coming.'

Naked, she bounded across the landing and took the stairs two, three at a time.

Ouch.

Shit!

She caught her toe in a split board and stumbled.

Flinging out her arms, she clawed at the balustrade, almost falling headlong.

No need to search for Charlie.

His legs were splayed at weird angles where he lay in the room facing her.

The Lake

'Charlie. I'm here. Don't move . . .'
Then Leigh's heart stood still.
She was terribly afraid.
More afraid than she'd ever been in all of her eighteen years.
Her stomach turned to ice.
But she went forward, through the doorway.
To get to Charlie.
Lying there.
So still.

She was in an old-fashioned kitchen. Dark with shadows. Shuttered windows. Narrow rays of the setting sun carving through dust motes rising from where he'd fallen. He sprawled in an awkward nest of wood and flaking bits of plaster.

She stared at Charlie.

'*Oh, God. NO! NO NO NO-OOO!!!*'

Forced herself to look at what had been his head.

Clumps of brown hair clinging to slivers of scalp, scattered in a mess of brain and shattered skull.

Slimed with matter, the base of the stove poked through the red mush of Charlie's face. An eye, a bloodshot globe attached to bloody strings, escaped from its socket.

Leigh stared. The eye slipped a little.

Showing the brown iris.

It knows I'm watching it. It's smiling Charlie's smile at me . . .

Leigh heaved, swayed, doubled over and slid to her knees on the dusty clay floor.

Breath burst from her lungs in great, ragged gasps.

Hot, chunky vomit rose in her throat.

This, this . . . wasn't . . . *couldn't be* Charlie.

Charlie's beautiful, strong – and he loves me. I know that. *He loves me . . .*

Taking one last look at Charlie, flaked with dust and plaster like a discarded tailor's dummy, she fled down the passageway, out onto the stoop, and stumbled down the steps.

Whimpering.

Fighting back vomit.
Sobbing, muttering as she ran.
Straight into the small, rigid figure of a woman.
Charlie's mother.
Thin, birdlike.
Open-mouthed.
Shocked. Staring at Leigh's naked body with horrified, accusing eyes, bright as polished stones in the fading light.

The woman rushed past her. Into the house. Leigh hurried on, toward the canoe, her feet cut and bleeding as she fled over stones and fallen branches.

The scream, coming from the house, pierced the evening quiet, rending the air like a knife through silk.

Pure. Vibrant. Agonized.

An animal caught in a trap. Then . . .

'Whore! Lilith! Poisonous bitch! Filthy murderess!'

Under a glowering sky, Leigh pushed her canoe into the lake and climbed in. Grasping the paddle, she worked it hard, bending forward and back; dipping, skimming through the dark water. As she traveled, crisp white wavelets lifted around the bow, telling her that the wind had changed direction.

She shivered, feeling its chill on her tear-streaked face, on her cold, trembling body.

Paddling hard, her uneven breaths coming in raw, hurting gasps, she left Goon Lake behind.

The screams of Edith Payne followed her like arrows from hell.

Chapter Eighteen

'Hey. Earthling. Anybody home?'

Jenny eyed Leigh across the breakfast table. She didn't like what she saw. Yesterday Leigh had been bright and breezy. Today it looked like her personal piece of sky had just caved in.

'Sorry, Jenny. I . . . I didn't sleep too well last night.'

'Didn't hear you come in.' A pause. 'We waited supper, just in case. Then, when you didn't show, we ate your share and decided to turn in.' Jenny paused again, not wanting to appear heavy – after all, Leigh *was* on vacation. She decided on the concerned-aunt routine, hoping that it wouldn't come over too strong.

'Didn't you know that Mike and I would worry if you stayed out late? 'Specially nights . . . What happened, Leigh – or is it a state secret?' Beneath her determined smile, Jenny was worried.

If this is what life with a teen is all about, Mike and I sure missed out on all the excitement.

They'd regretted not having kids, though visiting Jack and Helen on the West Coast once in a while made up for it to some degree. That, and teaching kids at high school, helped them both understand what went on in those young minds.

Leigh hung her head. Put her fork down and pushed away her untouched eggs. Her lip trembled. She scraped back her chair and rushed from the table.

Jenny followed her to the guest bedroom. She spotted Mike coming out of the bathroom and put a discreet finger to her lips. With raised brows, Mike carried on rubbing his damp hair and went on his way.

Kids, eh?

Jenny sat on the bed and drew the sobbing girl to her. 'Come on now, tell Aunt Jenny,' she said gently, cradling Leigh's head against her shoulder.

Leigh let everything go, crying as if her heart would break. Eventually, the great, gulping sobs trailed off into silence. She seemed to be wondering where to begin her story, as if the plain, unadulterated truth was just too *awful* to say out loud.

'It's bad, Jenny. It's real bad . . .' Leigh broke down again, heaving and sobbing into her aunt's soft, accommodating bosom. A cold shiver touched Jenny's spine. This *was* bad. She knew she wasn't going to like what Leigh was about to tell her.

Had the girl been raped? Oh, my God. What do we tell Jack and Helen?

'Take your time and tell me all about it, baby,' she said in a soothing voice. 'Tell your Auntie Jenny.'

Leigh's parents listened in horror over the phone to Mike's story. 'Not that we wouldn't like her to stay with us a while longer,' he'd explained in a calm but concerned voice. 'It's just that I – we – think that Leigh needs her parents at a time like this . . . And, of course, there is the matter of her being questioned . . .'

Mike met Jack and Helen at General Mitchell International. They'd brought a change of clothes in their carry-ons, expecting only to stay overnight before taking Leigh home.

The journey to Wahconda was not a good one. Along the way, there was a wearing mix of tearful accusations from Helen interrupted by irate remonstrations from Jack – punctuated by Mike's patient explanations. Fielding their outbursts wasn't easy, and Mike wished like hell that Jenny had come along as referee.

He sighed. He'd expected the drive to be a nightmare. It was – and more besides.

They arrived at Wahconda in the early hours, fatigued and more than ready for the fragrant coffee but not, for the aggrieved parents, the cheese sandwiches and apple pie that Jenny placed before them.

The Lake

Still, preparing the snack beforehand, Jenny hadn't reckoned on them doing much eating in any case.

She was right.

Jack and Helen demanded to see their daughter, who'd taken sedatives prescribed by Doc Barton and was asleep, pale and barely breathing, when her parents arrived.

'Not a good time to wake her, Helen. The poor dear has been through a lot these last twenty-four hours. Best let her rest while she can.' Jenny looked anxiously at her sister-in-law. The last thing they all needed was one of Helen's tantrums.

'You're right, of course,' Jack said, placing an arm around Helen and steering her back into the hallway. 'Come along, dear. Let's get us some rest. Plenty to discuss tomorrow.'

'You're not kidding,' retorted Helen, glaring at him through red-rimmed eyes. 'Leigh had better have a real good reason for going off on her lonesome like that.' She darted an accusing glance at Jenny. Clearly, right now, she was blaming her in-laws for the mess they were in.

Daylight found them drinking coffee round the kitchen table again. Still tired, but determined to see this thing through like sensible people.

'At least,' Jack said, 'Leigh's alive. That's a blessing in itself.'

Leigh, pale and dazed from her drugged sleep, joined them in the kitchen. Smiling wanly at Mom and Dad, she avoided their questioning looks and gratefully hugged the mug of steaming coffee that Jenny placed before her.

'Good morning, young lady,' Dad began.

Leigh groaned inwardly.

This I can do without.

After . . . Charlie . . .

Tears welled and fell down her face. Mom rose and took her daughter in her arms. They both had a darn good cry. Then Mom told her: 'We love you so much, sweetie. How could this *awful* thing be happening to us . . . ?'

'Now, Helen,' Dad put in. 'All we can do is get our little girl through this unfortunate incident. We have to be strong, for her sake.'

'Agreed,' Mike murmured. 'At this stage, recriminations are redundant. Leigh needs all the help we can give her.'

Jenny nodded, smiling bravely. 'That's right,' she said. 'We must pull together, whatever happens.'

'Now, perhaps you'll be kind enough to tell us in your own words what happened back there, the day before yesterday . . .' Dad noticed Mike's raised brows, realizing that maybe a confrontational attitude wasn't going to work with his little girl. Not this time.

'It's okay, Dad. I'll tell you as best I can . . . I appreciate that you need to know the facts before the cops get here.'

Mom and Dad exchanged glances. This was their errant offspring. Chastened and acting grown-up, for a change.

They listened in stunned silence to Leigh's halting account of her brief affair with Charlie. Afterwards, Mom stifled tears, her cheeks getting redder all the time. She fiddled nervously with the gold cross hanging on a chain around her neck. Dad looked shocked and embarrassed by turns. For the first time in living memory, he had nothing to say to his daughter.

Leigh sank into a bewildered daze, reliving the nightmare of Charlie's death – the way he'd looked – over and over again. It was the most horrendous thing she'd ever experienced; something she'd never, ever, forget even if she lived to be a hundred years old. Tears streamed down her face and she just couldn't face her parents' wounded expressions.

Just as if it had happened to *them*.

But they had every right to be horrified.

And so, she told herself, had Charlie's mom – *she* had more right to hate Leigh than anyone.

Losing her son that way.

Mom got upset and Mike called the doc who said it was okay if Mom used a couple of Leigh's sedatives. No problem. They were just your average sleeping pill, he told them. Nothing too strong. But let her take them only till the initial shock passes over, you understand.

Dad was grimly stoical. Patient. At least there were no more black looks. Leigh couldn't bear it when he looked at her as if she were some kind of stranger and called her 'young lady' instead of Leigh.

The Lake

Meanwhile, he spoke urgently with Mike in low tones while Jenny went around making more coffee, filling in the awkward gaps and trying to keep tension at bay.

By the time officers Fallon and Henty dropped by to get the story, Leigh had taken to her bed again.

Apologizing for the trouble, they waited for Leigh to emerge – meanwhile, Fallon confided that Edith Payne had made wild accusations against the young lady who had been . . . ahem . . . *with* her son at the time of his death.

'Not that we're paying any attention to all that.'

Fallon didn't think that now was a good time to quote the words Charlie's mom had *really* screamed at them. Like: 'Find the whore who murdered my son. Or I will.'

No, sirree. Instead, he gave the girl's mom a reassuring smile, telling her that he himself had an eighteen-year-old daughter and so was no stranger to the workings of a young girl's mind . . .

Leigh's mom stopped him short with a sour look.

The officers questioned Leigh for half an hour or so and at the end of it all went so far as to say that what they had here was a case of Accidental Death. Not, in their opinion, Murder One.

Relieved that this part was over, Leigh returned to her room.

'Thank ya kindly, ma'am.' Henty smiled, nodding briefly at Jenny as she came around with yet more coffee. Fallon turned to Leigh's mom and dad. 'We've known for some time that old house out on Goon was a death trap,' he admitted. 'But,' he went on, 'the place is in probate and we can't do a dern thing about it. However, in the light of . . . er . . . recent events, we'll try for a court order to take the place down. Demolish it. Clear the site. Leave things as they are,' he added, 'and more kids could get hurt.'

'She's asking about the funeral,' Mom said, flatly.

'Funeral?' Glancing at his partner, Henty decided to lay it on the line.

He did. Confiding that this particular funeral wouldn't be such a good thing for a young girl to experience.

'Not as if it'll be your regular funeral,' he said, sending Leigh's dad a level look, in a man-to-man sort of way. 'We're talking personal tragedy here. Big time. Lotta raw feelings on the loose, that kinda thing. Old Ma Payne's a weird piece a' work. No telling what might happen, under the circumstances.

'Yessir. Best take the young lady on home . . .'

'And so,' the preacher said, 'as the coffin sinks slowly into the ground, we bid a fond farewell . . .'

Leigh's heart lurched.

Coming here is not the smartest thing I've ever done, she told herself, with a shudder.

Charlie's mother approached. She walked around the end of the grave, slowly. Standing apart from the small group of mourners, Leigh held her breath, watching the small, upright figure dressed in black.

She'd known where to come.

She'd heard Mike tell Dad that Charlie's funeral would be at the Seventh Day Adventist Church.

Here, on Wahconda.

It services the lake people hereabouts, he'd said.

Keeping her eye on the mother, Leigh shivered some more. No sun reached this desolate plot hidden in the pines, just north of Carson's Camp, and she wished she'd worn something warmer.

I shouldn't be here at all, she chastised herself. But God knows, I had to come. *Needed* to be at Charlie's funeral. I owe him that much. If I hadn't gone with him to the old house everything would've been okay . . . Charlie's death was all my fault . . .

Stay back.

No, don't point at me. Oh, my God!

Her heart raced. She took a step backward as the mother approached . . .

The following day, Leigh and her parents said their goodbyes to Mike and Jenny and flew back to the West Coast. In the days that followed, Leigh waited anxiously for her period.

It didn't happen that month.

Nor the next.

Tests showed that she was pregnant.

Chapter Nineteen

Sunday, June 29, 1986

'Mom.'

'Uh-uh?'

'Michael J. Fox just called to ask me for a date. That okay with you?'

'Er . . . what was that?'

'Mom. You haven't been listening to a *word* I'm saying. I could sprout wings and fly away and you wouldn't even notice. What's up? Your man Mace playin' on your mind?'

'Sorry, hon. Sure, I got things on my mind. What with this guy and his ìunfinished businessî, and everything . . .'

'Okay. So this guy and his unfinished business. We keep on our guard 'n' call Macie baby if we get spooked – what else can we do? Detective Harrison seems like a pretty smart cookie to me. He'll catch that weirdo before we even know it.'

Deana put her arm around Leigh's waist. Feels like I'm a regular grown-up, she thought. What goes around comes around, I guess. I'm glad Mom was there for me over what happened to Allan – now it's *me* comforting Mom.

She liked the warm feeling this gave her. How it should be. Anyways, Mom knows what I'm going through. She's been there. History repeating itself.

Except *I*'m not pregnant.

I don't think.

Nah.

Didn't get the chance back there in the woods.

Thanks to that madman.

She caught Leigh's sigh and frowned a little. 'C'mon, Mom. Tell Deana. What gives?'

'What gives? Isn't all this enough, young lady? Madman on the loose. Nelson sounding off back at the restaurant. Mace playing this whole thing down – but heaven knows, I can tell that he's worried. God, Deana. How can you be so *blasé* about it all?'

'Sorry, Mom. I really am. If Allan and I had gone to the movies like we said, all of this wouldn't be happening.' Deana's eyes filled, and Leigh softened.

'Baby, don't you worry. We'll get through all this. I promise . . .' She stroked Deana's cheek and forced a bright smile. 'Everything's gonna be okay. Promise.'

'Sorry to be such a kid about everything.' Deana was apologetic. God knows Mom didn't need all this. 'You should be back at the restaurant. I'll be okay here. Honest. I'm not likely to go wandering off anywhere. Not until everything's cleared up. What's Nelson griping about, anyway?' As far as she could gather, Mom left Nelson to do what he did best: create memorable meals.

Hmmm . . . Pretty cool name for a restaurant.

Memorable Meals.

'Nelson? Oh, the usual. Having one of his sulks again. Wants to come out from behind the scenes occasionally. Be somebody. Meet the clientele. But, frankly, I'm afraid that his appearance might put them off.'

'Yeah. With his eye patch and big hook nose, he ain't no Paul Newman and that's for sure!'

'Hey. There's the door. Probably Mace with some good news . . .'

'I bet,' Deana agreed.

We should be so lucky.

Leigh made for the front door. Deana followed. Saw Mom peek through the small round spy-hole – and drop the door chain. It chittered and clattered, swinging to and fro.

Then . . .

Mom was opening the door.

The Lake

Reeling back, gasping oh my God . . .
Tripping over the doormat.
My nightmare – all over again.
Nelson.
In his chef's hat; clutching a meat cleaver.
Holding it high.
He's gonna hack Mom.
Then me.
In broad daylight.
And there's no one around to help – to call the cops.

The hedges between the houses were high. Bad news for nosy neighbors; terrific for intruders. 'Keeps us nice and private, honey,' Leigh had told her when they'd bought the place. 'We've cameras and gravel all around to deter intruders. Anyway – one phone call, and the cops'd be here in no time at all.'

Yeah. Neat plan. But somehow, Deana didn't think it was gonna work today . . .

Nelson changed his mind.

He dropped the cleaver. It crashed to the floor, the clatter echoing through the hallway.

His arm shot out. He grabbed Mom by the throat . . .

Squeeeezed it tight.

Mom spluttered; a strangled half-scream burst from her lips. It died. Next came this awful gurgling sound.

Deana gasped, her heart pounding. This *can't* be for real.

It can't . . .

It can. It is. It's my nightmare come true . . .

You better believe it.

He'll kill Mom.

Then he'll kill me . . .

Nelson with a cleaver. Outside my window. Threatening me. Mace was right. It's me he wants. Oh my God, this isn't a dream.

'I'm coming to getcha . . .'

'STAY AWAY FROM HER!' Deana yelled.

Nelson lost it.

Drawing back a bony fist, he slugged Deana on the chin. Hard.
She heard the crack.
Felt the *blinding* pain.
Saw shooting stars.
And slipped into deep black space . . .

Before she went down, Deana saw Nelson's black patch and one fierce protruding blue eye, gleaming hatred, straining from his thin, hollow face.

His mouth was a gaping black hole. Spittle swung from his grizzled chin, trailing and dripping down his chef's tunic.

Paul Newman he ain't.

Dazed, Deana clamped a hand to her jaw; wincing with pain. She watched Mom wrench away from Nelson, get to her feet, turn and make for the phone.

Nelson's big hand reached out; clawed at Mom's shoulder.

Sending her down again.

Leigh crumpled to her knees, hitting the tile floor with a sickening thud. She rolled away from Nelson, then leaned up on an elbow, shaking her head. Moving in slow motion.

Still stunned and not quite with it.

'Mom!' Deana screamed. 'Get up, he's gonna kill youuuu!'

Grunting like an enraged pig, Nelson snatched up the cleaver. Raised it above his head.

Deana screamed: 'NO-OOOO!'

Leigh stared. Like a rabbit caught in the thrall of a snake. Watching Nelson's arms slice down . . .

'*FREEZE!*'

Mace.
And Mattie.
In the doorway.
Behind Nelson.
Guns pressed into his back.

Nelson's hand opened, letting the cleaver drop again. It clattered and clunked on the foyer tiles.

He sprang forward, leaping over Leigh and knocking Deana to one

The Lake

side, lurching down the hallway toward the back of the house; panting, pushing, shoving furniture behind him as he went.

Mattie raced after him, head down, dodging Mace's flying bullets. *Shit!*

The kitchen door slammed in her face. She felt her nose crack. Shit shit *SHIT!*

She kicked open the door, cursing as the outside door swung to and fro.

Nelson was gone.

'You *bastard*,' she spat. 'So you got away. *This* time!'

Mace dropped down on one knee. 'Leigh. Leigh. You okay?'

'Uh-uh. Thank God you came – just in time. Guess you saved our lives. You okay, Deana?

'*Deana!*'

Leigh crawled over to Deana, stretched out on the floor, an ugly red bruise already staining her lower jaw.

Breathlessly, Mattie returned to the others, stabbing out the connection code on her cellphone, cursing to herself as she did it. 'Fuckin' bastard got away. How the *hell* he did it beats me. He just disappeared. Obviously knows the territory.'

At the other end, Mill Valley PD picked up, getting an earful of Mattie's dialogue.

'Yeah.' She was terse. 'You heard me right. Man with a cleaver, attacked woman and daughter. 104, Del Mar on Mark Terrace. Lost the suspect but we have the weapon. Try putting out an all-points – he's on foot. Maybe. Could be the killer of the Powers boy in the Mount Tam vicinity, the other night. Yeah. We have two injured people here. Call an ambulance.'

Deana groaned. Mace guided Leigh to the living room and settled her on the sofa. Mattie was already busy in the kitchen, wringing out a cold compress to put on Deana's jaw.

Mace strode back to the hallway. Nudging the cleaver with the toe of his shoe, he called out: 'Know who this guy is, Ms West?'

'Do I. His name is Nelson Willington and he's head chef at the Bayview.'

Mace and Mattie, both in the living room now, exchanged glances.

'What did ya do, Leigh?' Mattie asked. 'Cut his pay in half?'

'You could say that. I fired him a coupla days ago.'

Nursing her jaw, Deana perked up. So that was why Mom was so . . . so preoccupied with Nelson.

'You *fired* him?'

Mace, too, was all ears. 'How come?'

'He wanted a piece of the action. A partnership in the business. Said if it weren't for his cuisine I wouldn't be where I am today. One of the best restaurants in Tiburon etc, etc.'

'*The* best restaurant in Tiburon,' Mattie put in.

'Thanks.' Leigh gave her a wry smile.

Mattie brought out a plastic sack from her shoulder bag. Shook it open. Put on protective gloves, went to the hallway and picked up the meat cleaver.

It looked like a nasty piece of work. Honed to a fine sharpness, Mattie guessed that it'd slice through bone just as easily as through butter.

Gingerly, she put a forefinger to the blade.

'Ouch,' she murmured, slipping the cleaver into the sack.

'Careful, Mattie. Don't want you losing any fingers out there,' Mace said lightly.

'Butt out, Charlie. Do either of you ladies recognize this thing?' Mattie carried the cleaver into the living room. It had an intricate dragon design on the handle, winding its way up to the blade.

Before Leigh could answer, Deana said, 'Yes. There are two in the kitchen at the Bayview.'

'Sure are,' Leigh agreed. 'Nelson uses them for cutting up sides of beef.'

Sirens began to wail. Lights flashed in the driveway. Mattie went to the front door.

'Over here, guys,' she called out.

'Maybe I don't need hospital treatment,' Leigh said. 'I'm okay. But how about you, Deana? You look as if you might have a fractured jaw – best we have it checked out.'

The Lake

'You *both* need checking out, Leigh,' Mace put in. 'Mattie, go along with the ladies. I'll hang around here a while longer.'

Deana pouted. Hospital didn't seem like a smart move right now. Especially as the action seemed to be hotting up a little. She flinched as a stab of pain shot through her skull.

'Okay. Okay,' she muttered. 'I'm going. Macie baby's right. As usual.'
'Deana.'

'Sorry, Mom,' she said thickly. Her jaw throbbed. It felt like she was talking through cotton-wool lips. 'We'll miss all the fun, though.'

'What fun, Deana? You want that creep to sneak back in, wait till you're in bed, then zap?' Mace slapped the palms of his hands together with a loud crack.

Deana winced. Leigh shot him a cool glance.

'Right, folks. We're ready to roll!' Mattie called out. Sensing the tension, she looked sharply at Mace. 'You okay, alone here?' she asked.

'Sure. Stopped worrying about bogeymen twenty years back.'

'Yeah, I bet.' Mattie tossed him a tight smile over her shoulder. She followed the two women to the ambulance. The tip of her nose, where it'd collided with the kitchen door, hurt like hell.

'Don't worry your heads none about Mace,' she told Leigh and Deana. 'Our mad axman catches up with Mace, he'll wish he'd never bothered.'

Picturing Mace's well-built muscular five-eleven against Nelson's thin, gangling frame, Leigh almost felt sorry for the chef.

At the hospital, Leigh and Deana were treated for shock. Leigh had bruising to the neck and shoulder and contusions to her elbows but not much else. Deana had severe bruising to her lower jaw. Thankfully, no fractures. They were issued with painkillers and allowed to go home.

Mattie called around early next day.

'Hi, guys. How ya doin'?' She followed Leigh into the living room, waving away the offer of a seat. She got straight to the point.

'As you know, we have the meat cleaver from the scene. Now I'd like you to show me where Nelson keeps his. The ones you say he uses.' She shrugged. 'Could be there are two, three or even more in circulation. We need to narrow the field as much as possible.'

Deana asked, 'Thought you weren't officially on this case. As in, no longer working with Mace?'

'Right,' Mattie replied. 'I'm here by special request.'

'Special request?'

'Uh-huh. Mace put in a request for me to work on this case with him. So that I could look after you lucky ladies – and, well, here I am, folks. Personal bodyguard at your service.'

Deana looked at Mattie.

'That was good of Mace, being so concerned about us.'

'Yeah. Seems like he has a special interest in the Powers case.'

Leigh appeared nonchalant, but her heart skipped a beat. It *was* good of Mace to go to all this trouble.

Appointing Mattie as their bodyguard – no prizes for guessing who'd come out on top if she and Nelson happened to meet up.

Mattie drove them to the Bayview. She was an expert driver, Leigh noticed. Comes with playing cops and robbers for a living, she guessed, as they slid to a halt in the Bayview's private parking lot.

Leigh's pride and joy was a smartly painted, double-fronted restaurant on Main Street, looking out onto the harbour. Brass-framed menus in the doorway offered a wide choice of ethnic and traditional dishes.

Bay-caught fish were a house specialty.

Leigh led the way through the dark interior, then on through to the kitchen. The aroma of fresh bread hung on the air – Leigh prided herself on her bread rolls, ciabattas and French sticks, freshly baked on the premises.

She shivered.

The place felt strange without Nelson.

No lanky figure leaping about, mixing, grinding, creating his famous dishes; his one good eye rolling round in its socket like a billiard ball.

Instead, Nelson was on the run. With his cleaver.

They looked around the kitchen. Leigh went to the metal stand where Nelson hung his array of choppers, knives and other kitchen implements.

Both cleavers were missing. Looked like Mattie had Exhibit A, the one Nelson had dropped when he'd fled – then he'd sneaked back into

The Lake

the restaurant to pick up Exhibit B. So now Nelson, plus cleaver number two, were out there, seeking vengeance.

The women exchanged glances.

'We need to nail Nelson pronto,' Mattie said, briefly.

Leigh met Deana's gaze. 'I'd say that was the understatement of the year.'

Chapter Twenty

Brrring . . . Brrring . . .

Leigh's fingers felt around the nightstand, then stretched out to reach the telephone. Her grazed elbow twinged. She made a face, squinting at the red numbers on the clock.

11:22.

Christ. Who *is* this?

At this hour?

She fumbled around some more and clicked on the bedside lamp.

Something's happened, she thought. *They caught Nelson. They've—*

'Yes?'

'Hi, Leigh. Mace here. Called to see if you're okay.'

'Uhh . . . I was asleep, if that's what you mean . . .'

'Sorry. Just thought you looked a little wrecked earlier.'

'Well, thanks a lot, Mace. You woke me up to tell me *that*?'

'No, it's just that I don't want you worrying yourself over that maniac. Is all.'

'Cheers for that, but I'm – we're – okay. Truly. Right now, I need some rest. Took one of those bazookas an hour ago and I'm sleepy as a kitty-cat.'

'Yeah. Sure. Sorry for the intrusion. You phone me if you have any problems. Or need to talk. Y'hear me, now?'

'Sure, Mace. Sure. G'night.'

Smiling, she put the phone down.

What a jerk! But quite a *nice* jerk . . .

The Lake

She smiled, snapped off the light, turned over and closed her eyes. And opened them again.

God, much as I like the guy, I wish he hadn't called.

'Cause now I'm really awake.

She sighed.

Take another sleeper.

No, don't.

Doc said only three a day. I've taken three already.

She twisted up on an elbow, and gasped a little.

Ouch! That hurts.

Making a face, Leigh punched and plumped up her pillow. Then sank back into it.

Mmmm . . . That's better.

Gradually, her lids drooped and her breathing evened out.

Brrinng . . . Brrinng . . .

GOD! MACE! What *now*? I'll swing for that guy. Doesn't he *ever* give up?

'Mace?' she yelled into the phone.

'Ms West.'

Her heart leapt into her mouth. Pounding, hard.

Racing like a traction engine.

'Nelson.' A breathless pause. 'What d'you want?'

'You shouldn't have done it, y'know . . .'

Mustn't let him think I'm scared.

'Done what? Whatever did I do to you that wasn't completely justified? Tell me that!'

She was sitting up now. Shaking. Rocking with terror, her free arm hugging her knees. Almost screaming into the phone.

Deana burst through the door.

'*Mom!*'

Leigh shook her head.

Put a finger to her lips.

Shush, Deana. Quiet!

She pointed to the extension phone in her hand. Then stabbed a forefinger at the open door.

Deana frowned.

Leigh rolled up her eyes.

She mouthed, '*Deana. Pick up the other phone!*'

Deana raced out of the room.

'I was the best thing you had, lady,' Nelson whimpered. He seemed lost, uncertain, and Leigh relaxed a little. She could handle a pathetic Nelson. 'An' you didn't know it,' he went on. 'You didn't *'preciate* me. Called me an oddball and then *FIRED* me.' His pace picked up a little. 'ME! The finest chef in the whole of the Bay. I coulda cooked at 'Frisco's finest, and you know it!'

Let him talk. I can deal with that okay.

Maybe.

'Nelson, calm down.'

Leigh heard a faint click as Deana lifted the phone in the hallway.

'Whass that?' Nelson was suspicious. Twitchy. His tone upped a couple of octaves.

'Just the line, Nelson. I should get it fixed. Been playing up on me for a week or so now.'

'Sure. You do that. Where's that kid a' yours?'

'Deana? Oh, she's spending the night with a friend . . .'

'*You lie!*' he shrieked. 'The light was on in her room a half-hour ago. Don't you lie to me, Leigh West. Or you'll *both* regret it.'

His voice dropped. He spoke slowly, spelling it out: 'You'll *both* wish you hadn't. Geddit?'

'Nelson, *please*. Why would I lie to you?' Leigh knew that she was pleading and hated herself for it.

But she'd best play it his way.

Plead. Beg, if she had to. She smiled grimly.

He'd like that.

Christ. He'd been creeping around the house?

Where the hell was Mace?

On the phone. Asking me if I was okay. Jesus, Mace. You shoulda been out there, protecting us!

No. That's not fair. Mace has to go off duty some time. Not his fault.

'You still there, Leigh?' The voice was low. Derisive. Mocking. Like

The Lake

he knew that he had her in the palm of his hand. Running scared.

Her heart started to pound again.

She was panicking; couldn't control the way her breath came out, all huffy and shallow.

She turned away from the phone, hoping he couldn't hear her quick, uneven breathing.

Please, God. Don't let him hear me.

For a split second, she paused, steadying herself.

'Yeah. Sure. I'm still here, Nelson.'

'Y'know, you said some pretty hurtful things back there, Leigh. An' all I ever wanted was *recognition* for my work. I deserved better. I know I'm not much to look at, but I'm an *artiste* in my own right. My creations *made* the Bayview the place it is . . . And my Beef Willington's a masterpiece.' He choked out a sob. 'Everybody says so . . .'

Leigh calmed down a little. Nelson wasn't angry, spiteful or threatening anymore. Just downright pitiful.

'You *knew* my worth,' he went on. 'You knew how *good* I was . . .'

Leigh listened to his pathetic whining. Not quite sure how to handle it now. Thinking that this entire conversation could go horribly wrong; change into something bad . . .

Mustn't offend him, she thought.

Play him like a fish.

Placate him.

Let him spit it out. Whatever it was he had to say.

'All I wanted was to hit back at you.' His voice wavered. Leigh was finding it difficult to hear him now.

'. . . An' make you worry like crazy. So the way I figured, I should follow your girl and scare the *shit* outta her . . .'

His sobs were noisy, heaving gulps, vibrating over the line.

Leigh moved the phone away from her ear. Listening from that distance, Nelson's voice made thin, tinny sounds; ineffectual squawks coming from a long way off.

He was crying, too.

'Nelson. Don't take on so.'

She heard Deana's gasp of horror.

Jesus. Quiet, hon. There's my girl . . .

'I didn't mean that boyfriend of hers should get killed. I didn't want for that terrible accident to happen. I was so riled up, I couldn't help myself. I'm sorry . . .'

Listening to him groveling, Leigh grew more sure of herself. 'Nelson,' she said. 'What you did was really bad. You killed that young man. You deprived him of a fine future. But, if you're as sorry as you say you are, all you have to do is give yourself up. You'll have a fair trial, Nelson. Believe me.'

Sure. All things considered.

A fair trial.

The guy's a maniac. Not a pervert.

Not an obsessive killer at all.

What he needs is a straitjacket. Not the chair.

Her thoughts flew back to Deana.

Hope she has the sense to call Mace on my cellphone . . .

'Nelson, where are you? I mean, are you close by?'

Hope to God he's not outside the house.

Could be.

She heard a wet, gasping sob.

'Christ, Nelson. Where are you?'

Deana, use my phone, for God's sake.

Call Mace.

'Just wanted to get it off my chest . . . how all of this happened. So you know it was *your* fault. You coulda told me you didn't want me for a partner. Not just *fired* me . . .' The whining tapered off. Then, 'Coulda lived with *not* bein' a partner.'

A long pause.

'I been feelin' real tuckered out lately. I worry about my work an' all . . .' Nelson sounded beat now. 'Anyways. I won't be botherin' you no more, Ms West. You'll be fuckin' rid of me for good! But I hope you'll remember as long as you've breath left in your body that *you* brought it on your own fuckin' self . . .'

'NELSON! What d'you mean, I'll be rid of you . . .?'

Silence. Then: 'Ah'm goin' away, Ms West. For ever. You'll not hear from me again.'

'Nelson.'

The Lake

Say something. Anything. Just keep him talking.
'Was it you who returned my necklace? You took it, didn't you? From the restaurant?'
Nelson wasn't listening.

The phone fell from his grasp. It dangled, swinging to and fro on its connection cord. Fascinated by the pendulum-like movements, he watched it for a moment, his toothless mouth making a small black 'o'.

Somewhere deep inside his mashed-up brain a smile began. A grimace of triumph that tried but didn't quite make it to his tear-streaked face.

He'd told her, all right.

He'd told that high-handed bitch what for.

Spittle swung from Nelson's chin. Snot dribbled into his mouth. His tongue came up and licked it away. The stuff tasted good and sweet.

Lurching away from the pay phone, he crossed the sidewalk and teetered along the edge, his arms outstretched for balance.

Cars came at him from nowhere.

Like bats out of hell.

Squinting in the glaring headlight beams, his face lifted to meet the cool night breeze.

It felt all right.

Clean.

He was a boy again. Out on one of them lakes beyond Point Reyes Station. Fishing with his pa. Taking in great gulps of fresh, clean air. Hearing the squawk of Pa's oars in the oarlocks, the slap of wood on water, making ripples and waves dance around their smart new rowboat.

And the fish he brought home.

Yessirree Bob! Ma sure knew how to cook her boy's fish.

Tender as a baby's smile, they fell to pieces soon as look at 'em.

Fog shrouded the far end of the Golden Gate Bridge.

Nelson grinned and walked toward it.

Chapter Twenty-one

'He's gone, baby.' Leigh shrugged into her toweling robe. She drew the belt tight around her. Giving a long sigh of relief, grateful that the ordeal with Nelson was over.

He'd sounded weak. Beaten.

Not a threat anymore.

Please, God.

She looked up as Deana appeared in the doorway, wrapped in her robe, hugging it around herself. 'Wow,' she breathed. 'That was something else. Nelson sure flipped this time . . .'

Hope to Christ he's gone for good . . .

She gave a small yelp, and clamped a hand to her jaw. 'Ouch. This really hurts, Mom.'

'I know, honey. Just take it easy, now.'

Leigh knew that it had been a shock for Deana to hear her shouting into the phone like that.

Poor kid. She doesn't need it. Not after Allan . . .

All because of my upset with Nelson.

Guilt merged with a growing sense of urgency.

'We gotta call Mace. Tell him Nelson—'

'Been there. Done that.'

'You have?' Leigh felt relieved. And proud. Of *course* Deana would call Mace. She was a smart kid. Her daughter.

Leigh relaxed – then jumped as the doorbell rang.

It sounded extra loud.

The Lake

And strident.

This time of night.

'That's Mace, now.'

'You sure about this, Mom? Could be Nelson coming back to finish what he left off . . . Remember last time you answered the door?'

Leigh hurried into the hallway. 'Mace?' she called through the door.

'Leigh. It's me. Mace. Open up.'

Leigh almost fell into his arms as he stepped into the foyer.

Deana made a face.

Mom, she cringed. D'you *have* to do that? Get all swoony like some dopey kid in high school?

'It was Nelson . . .' Leigh said.

'Gathered that from Deana's call. Smart move there, kiddo.'

Deana glared grumpily at Mace. She was in no mood to be patronized. Digging her hands into her robe pockets, she snatched another look at him. He wore a white T-shirt, tight black jeans and a black leather biker jacket.

Apart from his weapon bulging out of his hip holster he wasn't looking much like a policeman tonight. She stared a while longer.

Mmmm . . . Sexy, or what?

Oh yeah?

That'd be wonderful. Making a fool of myself with Mom's boyfriend. Pardon me, Mom's not-quite-but-soon-to-be boyfriend.

How can I be such a *shit*, anyway? Allan's only just . . . Her eyes watered.

But Mace sure looked attractive. Tanned complexion, sun-streaked hair. A regular California surfer look.

The Beach Boys.

Yuck.

Not quite as over the hill as the Beach Boys.

Mace's maybe thirty-six – going on thirty-eight?

Same age as Mom?

He *is* sexy, though . . . in a tough, roughneck kinda way. A body like that, he must work out pretty much every day.

Mace's gaze held hers briefly.

A tight smile flicked across his face before he returned his attention to Leigh.

'Could be that we're getting closer,' he said. 'Not often perps get to call their victims and apologize for their misdeeds.'

'No, I guess not,' Leigh said. 'Coffee?'

'Thought you'd never ask.' Mace grinned.

'Sugar?' Leigh asked as the coffee started to perk.

'No,' Mace said. 'Gotta keep in shape, y'know.'

'Mmm, some shape,' Deana murmured.

So soon after Allan . . . What kind of schmuck am I?

Forgive me, Allan. Please.

Leigh shot her a warning look.

Deana threw a quick glance in Mace's direction. Had he heard her last remark? Watching him settle back into the sofa, she decided that there was no way of telling if he had.

She *hoped* he hadn't heard.

If he had, it'd be too embarrassing for words.

Anyway, where's Mattie tonight?

Or is this a *personal* visit?

Mace accepted his coffee from Leigh. No cream. No sugar. Deana pictured his abs. Taut. Toned. A regular Rocky. A regular *blond* Rocky.

Suddenly, Mace was all cop. 'Now, ladies,' he said. 'Tell me again what happened when Nelson called.'

There's your answer, Deana. He's here on business . . .

Deana and Leigh pieced together the conversation as best they could. Finally, Leigh said, 'And I just *know* he took my lucky necklace. Must have been a coupla weeks ago. I was real upset about it at first – thought I'd lost it for good. Then I remembered I'd left it at the restaurant. Nelson didn't admit it, but I somehow *knew* he'd taken it, just to spook me.'

'And now he's disappeared.' Mace's tone was brisk. He was more interested in Nelson's future plans than in Leigh's sea-thing necklace.

'Yeah. He *did* sound pretty downbeat.' Leigh hesitated as another possibility struck her. 'D'you think he's going to *kill* himself?'

'Maybe. Sounds like he confessed – or apologized, whichever way you look at it. Had a fit of the guilts and aimed to pull the plug. You

The Lake

said he maybe left the phone hanging. Didn't terminate the call?'

'No "maybe" about it,' Leigh told him. 'Nelson said he'd seen the light in Deana's bedroom half an hour before his call. My guess is, he was lying; that he hadn't been here at all. He wouldn't have had the time to be outside our house and then make the phone call from the Golden Gate Bridge at the time he did.'

'The Golden Gate?'

'Yes. I held on to the phone for a while and heard traffic zooming by. Non-stop and a lot of it, I'd say.

'And I could swear there was a foghorn in the distance.'

Chapter Twenty-two

'Mace is quite a guy, don't you think?'

'Deana!'

'No worries, Mom. *I* don't want him. Believe me, after . . . you know . . . I need some space for a while. 'Sides, he's too old for me!'

'Just remember, my darling daughter, that Mace is here to do a job of work. As in nailing Allan's killer.'

Leigh had had a special meal brought in from the restaurant. We both deserve a break, she'd decided. These last few days have been a nightmare.

Beef Willington may have been off the menu, but Carl, her new, hastily appointed chef at the Bayview, had produced a wonderful dinner of marinated swordfish topped with spicy mango-and-tomato salsa.

Squishy chocolate dessert followed.

Deana's favorite.

'Here's to us! One door closes; another opens,' Leigh proclaimed with a wry smile. She took a sip of cool sparkling Californian wine. 'Mmmm. This is good. And Carl's doing great, too.'

'Yeah. Good riddance to you-know-who.'

'Well, not exactly, honey. Nelson *did* have his moments. And he'd made a name for himself. In Tiburon, at least. Apparently his previous experience came from working with some fancy Italian supremo at a top joint in New York. So he told me.'

'Pity he didn't stay there.'

The Lake

'Mmmm . . .' Leigh was more relaxed than she'd felt since Mom and Dad had departed after the family get-together.

Only it hadn't turned out to be a *proper* family get-together.

All that awkward stuff with Mom . . . and Deana and Allan leaving so soon after dinner . . .

Thank *God*, Mom and Dad had gone off to Boulder to be with Aunt Abby. Before everything happened.

Leigh glanced fondly at Deana. So young to have gone through such an awful experience. But, apart from her bruised jaw and a faraway look in her eyes now and then, Deana seemed to be holding up.

As funerals went, Allan's had been pretty tense and grim. Understandably, she reckoned. Mary Powers, a single mother, so it turned out, was pale, tearful and near to collapse. Luckily there'd been a sister, Allan's Aunt Beth, to support her and help her through the ceremony.

Both women had been distant with Leigh and Deana, darting just brief looks of recognition at the outset.

Nothing more.

Unlike Leigh's own nightmares over Charlie's funeral . . .

Charlie.

After eighteen years, memories of his death still lingered.

Maybe there is a curse on us, after all . . .

Leigh dismissed her gloomy thoughts and looked over at Deana. She gave a contented sigh. It was good, sitting here in the candlelight, chatting, eating nice food.

Despite the cloud of Allan's death still hanging over us . . .

Not wanting to spoil tonight for either of them, Leigh made a determined effort to lighten up, recalling another event.

One that had happened only that day.

A vivid reminder of the past.

Cherry.

'Cherry. Cherry Dornay!'

The red-haired girl looked up.

'Leigh West. As I live and breathe.'

'How're things, Cherry? And—' Leigh paused. 'How's Ben?'

'Oh, Ben's okay. Never married, of course.'

There was an awkward silence. The red-haired girl moved on, hastily. 'And you? I recall you were set on owning your own restaurant, all those years ago.'

'Yeah. I was. And I did.'

'Huh? You mean . . . all *this* is *yours?*'

Leigh gave a pleased smile, and Cherry said 'Wow!'

They chatted.

About this and that.

The old days.

How things had changed. Cherry taught art now, and was living in the San Fernando Valley. Ben was in I.T. – and still in San Diego.

They laughed a lot, reminiscing together. Yet Leigh still felt an awkwardness, a barrier that time had placed between them. She smiled at Cherry, remembering the 1970s. San Diego. Lazy days on Mission Beach; meeting up with the crowd at Pepe's Place on J Street. That trip to Tijuana when Ben had lost his precious guitar . . .

So *much* had happened since then.

A lot of water had gone under quite a few bridges.

She thought of Ben. Strong, gentle; fair curly hair, worn shoulder-length, hippie style. And the beard. Don't forget the beard!

Yeah. Ben had been quite a guy.

Leigh and Cherry exchanged telephone numbers.

Promising to keep in touch.

Maybe.

'Mom. The door. I'll get it.'

Deana left the table and went into the hallway.

'Wait, honey. Don't open up yet.'

Deana looked through the spy-hole.

Mace.

Does the guy never give up?

'Well?' Leigh asked.

'It's Mace.' Deana pouted. Ordinarily, she would have been a little excited. Tonight she was disappointed. She'd had Leigh all to herself – and they'd been sharing some rare intimate moments.

The Lake

Precious mom-and-daughter time.

Till around thirty seconds ago.

Screw Mace.

Had he been laid off or what?

Leigh opened the door.

'Why, Mace!' Her head lifted. She laughed, raking a hand through her hair. 'This *is* a surprise.'

'Yeah,' Deana muttered. 'Fancy seeing you here.'

Stepping inside, Mace threw her a wide grin, not missing a beat.

He fished around in his pocket and came up with a palmful of sunflower seeds. He tossed them into his mouth. Watching Deana all the time, his jaws worked around the seeds.

Deana frowned back.

Who does he think he is?

Still grinning, his lips peeled back, showing her his rows of straight white teeth.

But his eyes stayed cool. Alert.

He turned to Leigh.

'Dropped by to say we backed your hunch that Nelson maybe *was* in the vicinity of the Golden Gate last night. We have a coupla police launches patrolling the area – in the unlikely event they find his body.'

Mace and Leigh sauntered off into the living room.

Deana followed. Suddenly feeling left out.

Looked like Mom and Mace were already an item.

Christ!

Okay. Maybe Mom *does* need a boyfriend.

But *Mace?*

She pictured Mom and Mace making mad passionate love. His mouth on hers. Running his hands over her naked body . . . Mom panting a little, pushing him into her . . .

Deana squirmed at the thought.

'Oh, I'm sorry,' Mace said, eyeing the table. 'Were you two having dinner? I'll be on my way. Have to catch up with Mattie, anyhow. This time of night and she's *still* at the depot. Spends more time on her computer these days than she ever did when we were out on the streets.'

'Thought you and she were history. Like, you're no longer partners?'

'Right. Mattie got a little bored in the car all day. Cramped her style, she said. Got herself an office job instead.' Mace huffed out a harsh little laugh.

Looking at him, Deana got the feeling there was probably more to Mace and Mattie than met the eye.

Maybe they *had* been an item, both on and off duty.

'Deana,' Leigh put in. 'How about some coffee?'

Trying to get rid of me, Mom? Okay, but please don't make a fool of yourself. I'm not jealous. Just don't want you getting hurt . . .

'This is my first day back at the restaurant,' Leigh was telling Mace.

'That so? Sure you're up to it?'

'Yeah. Got to make a start sometime. Besides, what else can I do to solve the mystery of Nelson's disappearance? It's up to you guys now.'

She changed the subject.

'Seems like the new chef is shaping up real good. Thank heavens.' Leigh gestured toward the remains of their meal – and the wine. 'Oh, I'm sorry, Mace. Would you have preferred a glass of wine rather than coffee? I do apologize. But, naturally, I thought you were still on duty . . .'

'I'm not, as it happens. But coffee's fine. Just mighty pleased to see you and Deana are coping so well. Under the circumstances.'

'Well, we've felt better, I can assure you. But, we're getting there. We'll be okay when you find Nelson. He seemed like a man at his wits' end – so maybe he won't be much of a threat to us anymore.'

'Can't be too sure about that, Leigh.' Mace met her gaze candidly. For a moment her heart warmed. He was being very thoughtful. And she was grateful for that.

Briefly, she considered the yawning gap in her life. The space that she hoped a partner would fill one day.

Admit it, Leigh, she told herself. A man in your life could be a lotta fun.

Yeah. In my dreams!

The Lake

There *had* been guys.

After Charlie.

A handful. Maybe even more. But her life had always been too busy for a full-on relationship.

Because there'd been Deana. Not counting the restaurant. Plus the hard work that went with all of that.

The late nights. Early mornings.

There'd been no time, no place for a permanent man in her life.

Looking back, there'd only been one who'd even remotely fitted the bill. He'd have married her like a shot if she hadn't been so goddamned intent on her career.

Ben.

What a fool I've been.

He'd have made the perfect partner.

Meeting Cherry today had brought all those memories flooding back . . .

'Something on your mind?' Mace placed a warm hand over her cool one.

She started. 'Sorry. I . . . met someone today. Someone from the old days. Triggered off a few memories, I guess. A blast from the past, you might say.'

Leigh smiled into Mace's eyes. They were dark; she hadn't noticed *how* dark before. Looking into them now, she saw warmth and concern – and behind that, a raunchy twinkle.

He likes me, she told herself.

Mace likes me.

A squirm of excitement stirred between her thighs. It had been far too long . . .

'Come and get it!' Deana bustled in with the coffee pot, cream and sugar on a serving tray. She paused, sensing the atmosphere.

Seems like I'm interrupting a special moment here.

Good.

'Uh-huhh.' Clearing a space on the table in front of them, she plonked the tray on it.

'I feel a date with my TV coming on. According to TVS, *Sleepy Hollow*'s showing after the news. So it's coffee for two, I'm afraid, folks.'

'Oh, *that*'s a shame.' Mace almost sounded sorry. 'Well, don't wait up. I'll stay and chat with Mom a while longer.'

Deana threw Leigh a questioning glance.

Is this *really* what you want?

Leigh's face stayed bland.

'Okay, honey. Try to get some rest, now. I won't be long.'

With a thoughtful face, Leigh watched Deana go.

'Hey. The kid'll get over it. Kids do. It's been a real bad experience for her – for you both – but she's a survivor. She'll be okay.'

'Think so, Mace?' Leigh seemed unsure. She concentrated on pouring the coffee. Black for Mace; white, no sugar for herself.

'Right on. Few weeks from now and it never happened.'

She still wore a worried frown, and he took her hand in his.

'Nice place you got here, Leigh. Great view of the Bay. I'd sure like to take some shots. All that perspective, sweeping down to the Gate. Wonderful vantage point – best I've seen.'

'Shots?'

He laughed. 'Not *those* kinda shots. Shots as in photographs.'

'Oh, you take pictures. Professionally?'

'Nah. Just a hobby. But I like to think, once in a while, that they'll be good enough for exhibition. Had one or two in an LA gallery last year. Got some okay reviews.'

'Nice going, Mace. And, sure. Feel free. You're welcome to take shots from my window anytime!'

They exchanged glances and smiled.

Sharing the joke.

They lapsed into silence. It was one of those rare, comfortable moments when Leigh felt at peace with the world.

It was a good feeling.

'Mace?'

'Uh-huh?'

'This is great. Y'know that?'

'Mmmm . . . Yeah. Suits me, too.'

'Do you . . . have anyone? I mean, anyone special?'

'Me? Nope. Girl I met at college was the last *special* one that I recall.

The Lake

Wanda Baker, her name was. Yeah. She *was* something special. Till she got herself carved up, that is.'

'Mace! What*ever* happened?' She glanced at his face. It looked dark. Closed. She shivered a little, then said, 'There's no need to tell me if you don't want to.'

'That's okay. I don't have a problem with that. Not anymore.'

He leaned forward, studying his Nike sneakers, arms resting on his knees, hands hanging slack between his thighs.

'She was the prettiest little thing,' he said eventually. 'Blonde. Five-two and a bit, and neat with it. Y'know? Her dad died when she was a year old. Her mom committed suicide, so she was brought up by an old aunt.

'Wanda was an old-fashioned kinda girl. Quiet. Kept herself to herself.' He eased back into the sofa. Staring through the glass wall into the night.

'Oh, Mace. What a terrible story. And for her to get murdered . . .'

'You move on, Leigh. Have to. Otherwise you break. Anyway,' he said, looking deep into her eyes, 'you said you met someone from *your* past. Tell me about it.'

'How about a Courvoisier?' Leigh asked him.

'Long story, huh?'

'No. That time of night, is all.'

'Sure. Like I said, I'm not on duty. A drink'd be fine.'

Leigh stepped over to the bar and decanted cognac into two balloon glasses. She handed one to Mace, took the other and sat sideways on the sofa, facing him.

'It was eighteen years ago. I was pregnant with Deana. Mom and Dad sent me to an aunt in San Diego . . .' She caught the question in his eyes. 'I was eighteen and single,' she explained. 'I needed somewhere to have my baby.'

Mace frowned.

'I had my baby. Made a life for myself. Oh, I was capable, all right. Knew it all. Rebellious. Anti-everything, so Dad said. Practically a member of the Great Unwashed . . .' She grimaced at the thought. 'I went on marches, though. Did demos.'

Mace grinned. 'You were a hippie?'

'Looking back, I suppose you could say that. But it wasn't all flowers in the hair – peace, man and all that jazz. Sure, I did demos. Got involved with the cops.

'Anyway, that was here in Tiburon. Before I got myself pregnant. After that . . .' Leigh paused. 'When I went to San Diego, I met a young art student, Cherry Dornay. She was a great kid. Free as the wind, happy and a real pleasure to be around, I guess.

'She had a brother, Ben. Now *he* was a real hippie. Long hair, beard, wild shirts, Jesus sandals. Into the Beatles. The works.'

She broke off, embarrassed. She felt awkward. Guilty, divulging this piece of her personal past to a comparative stranger. She hadn't even told *Deana* about her friendship with Cherry and Ben.

Mace was smiling at her. She relaxed again. The mood was just right: warm, friendly, with more than a hint of sexual awareness – which she knew they both were feeling. Her heartbeats quickened, bringing a flush to her cheeks.

'Sounds like you really enjoyed life back then,' he said.

'Yeah, I guess I did.'

'And you met this girl again today?'

'Right. It was a . . . wonderful surprise. We had a lot of catching-up to do.'

'You never kept in touch?'

'No.' Leigh gave a wistful smile. 'I guess I was too busy. Too busy making plans. Set my heart on having my own restaurant. Not easy, with a baby. But I managed; Mom and Dad helped me financially. Kept us both clothed and fed . . .'

'You didn't go back there? Home, I mean.'

'Not straight away. I was proud. Wanted to prove myself. Wanted to *redeem* myself, I guess. Show Mom and Dad I could be a success. Show them I'd grown up and could look after my daughter okay.'

'You've sure done all of that, Leigh. You've got a great kid who's going to college in the fall, and a successful restaurant. Your folks must be real proud of you.'

Leigh saw a shadow cross his face.

Maybe not. Trick of the light, she guessed.

Sighing, she glanced at her wristwatch.

The Lake

Almost midnight. Deana's probably asleep by now.

'I can take a hint. Time I was somewhere else. Thanks for the drink. And for your company,' he whispered. 'My treat next time. You choose the place – and we'll make a date.'

'I'd like that, Mace.'

'You would?' He smiled eagerly.

'Yes, I would. Very much.'

He bent his head and kissed her lightly on the cheek.

'Night, Leigh. Take care, now.'

Her heart raced again.

She saw him to the door, then watched the taillights of his black Trans Am snake away into the night.

Chapter Twenty-three

Deana lay in bed.
 Listening to Mace go.
 She heard Mom's voice. Light. Laughing a little. Then Mace's, low and intimate.
 Looks like he got Mom on the hop.
 Bastard!
 It was one of those nights again: hot and muggy.
 I sure could use a shower.
 Deana shoved the sheet down with her feet and lay still.
 Feeling the sweat go cold on her body.
 She lifted her nightgown away from her breasts and blew down inside the bodice. It made her feel hotter.
 'Phewww!'
 A night like this when I had my dream . . .
 That was no *dream*. It was the real thing.
 Nelson and his hatchet.
 Sorry. Meat cleaver.
 What's the difference?
 Either way, you end up the same – a chopped-up body.
 Could've been *my* chopped-up body.
 Oh, God. Let them find him soon.
 Mom thinks he threw himself off the Bridge.
 Hope so.
 Then we'd all be safe.

The Lake

But he *was* out of his tree.
Anyone could see that.
Those wild eyes. Mistake. *That* wild eye. Slobbering mouth.
Uhhh. Yuck!
She swung her legs out of bed and stood up.
The breeze whispering through the open window felt good. Lifting her nightgown over her head, she let it drop to the floor – changed her mind, picked it up, wadded it and tossed it in the hamper.
She looked down at her body, pale and slick with sweat. Her full, firm breasts, flat belly and long, muscular legs.
Gleaming in the darkness.
No full moon tonight.
Not like the night Nelson paid me a visit.
Nelson. Fucking maniac.
If it weren't for him, Allan'd still be here . . .
She opened the nightstand drawer, pulled out Allan's gym shorts and buried her nose in them.
She took a deep, deep sniff.
And couldn't believe it.
Allan's smell was gone.
So soon.
How could a person's *smell* disappear like that? It was like it had died with him.
Bit by bit, piece by piece, Allan was going away.
Leaving her behind.
This is how it's gonna be. I'll forget what he looks like next. Except I have that photograph of him I took at Stinson Beach a couple of weeks back.
The one where he looked like a young Robert Redford. Tousled blond hair, broad smile, gorgeous teeth, eyes crinkled up against the sun.
He was wearing those tight shiny swim trunks . . .
Oh, God, Allan, I'll never forget you. Never. I promise!

Knowing that Allan was gone for ever hit Deana hard.
Again.

Tears stood in her eyes, then coursed down her cheeks. She wiped them away with the shorts.

She sighed, fighting back a sob. Gently, she folded the shorts and replaced them in the nightstand drawer.

Allan's smell might have disappeared, but she would always have his shorts to remind her of the good times they'd had.

Could *still* be having – if it weren't for that sick fuck Nelson.

Loud, hurting sobs broke through, bursting from her throat.

She threw herself on the bed and lay weeping into her pillow, drawing up her knees till they touched her chin. She rocked and sobbed, her tears drenching the pillow; hopelessness sweeping over her like a tidal wave.

Allan was gone.

For ever.

I'll never forget you, darling . . .

The tears gradually subsided. She felt calmer now and turned over on her back.

Staring at the ceiling.

Watching the shadows from her tree spread across it like giant fingers.

If I could find Nelson, I'd kill him. That's what I'd do. If I saw him tonight and killed him, nobody would know.

I could slit his goddamn throat. Stab him to death. Then hide the body.

Roll it away into someone's garden.

Or into the stand of redwoods, back of the house.

Nobody'd ever think of looking there.

She leaned over Nelson's body, watching the blood streaming from the wound in his gut, pouring from his mouth. Sobbing and choking at the same time, he pleaded with her to stop, get help.

He hadn't meant to do it.

Oh no?

He was *sorry* – he hadn't wanted to *kill* anyone . . .

She laughed at him, scornfully, kicked the knife into the bushes and strolled back into the house . . .

* * *

The Lake

Deana sat back on the bed, planning her next move.

Knife. That's what I need; a knife.

Her mind flew to the kitchen.

Mom's vegetable knife.

It was lethal. Short, strong, with a pointed blade. You could lose a finger and not even notice.

I could handle it, though.

Deana pictured Mom holding the knife.

Chopping carrots.

Quickly, expertly, like a machine; the root falling away in cross sections from the knife like small orange counters.

Yes, Mom's vegetable knife could kill Nelson okay.

No problem.

Deana swung herself off the bed, shivering with excitement. The idea of killing Nelson was scary, but it was turning her on.

It would be *so* easy.

And she'd get away with it.

Nobody'd suspect her.

If they did, well, she was a girl, wasn't she – still distraught at the death of her lover.

They'd say she didn't know what she was doing.

Maybe they'd think a young girl like her wouldn't have the courage, the strength to kill a grown man . . .

Nelson won't be hanging around, though, waiting to be killed.

Not if he has any sense.

Or would he?

Maybe he *has* got this fatal attraction to Mom and me.

Maybe he won't be able to stay away.

She crept to the door.

Listening out for Mom.

Seems like she's already in bed. Having cleared away the supper things, got into her nightgown, cleaned her teeth . . .

Probably went to sleep thinking of Mace.

Yuck.

The silence was everywhere, except for the rustling tree outside her window.

Reminding her of Nelson; the way he'd scared the daylights out of her . . .

I'll scare the butt-ugly bastard shitless. If and when I find him.

Deana dressed quickly, her resolve to find Nelson growing by the second. She pulled on a black long-sleeved sweatshirt and matching tights.

Bundled her thick hair into a knot.

Dragged a black knit cap over her head, safely anchoring the hair in place.

No black sneakers, though.

Damn!

Then, 'Yes!'

Brilliant!

A brain wave . . .

She picked out black knee-length wool socks from her drawer and pulled them over her white Nike running shoes.

I look like a cat burglar!

Cary Grant in *To Catch a Thief*.

Slipping quietly into the kitchen for the knife, she *felt* like Cary Grant in *To Catch a Thief*.

Holding her breath, she stood still, listening.

No sign of Mom stirring.

Tiptoeing over to the cutlery drawer, Deana pulled it open, carefully.

It rattled slightly. Drawing in a quick breath, she held still for a moment. Then took out the vegetable knife and ran her fingers lightly over the steel blade.

Wow!

It was *really* sharp.

She closed the drawer, freezing as it rattled, louder this time, on its way back into the dresser.

A gurgling sound belched behind her. She caught her breath again – and let it out with a gasp.

Phew . . .

Water in the pipes.

I think.

The Lake

I hope . . .

Through her soft sweatshirt, she fingered the door key on its chain, lying in the deep cleft between her breasts.

Might need this in a hurry if things go wrong.

Like I'm standing over Nelson's bleeding body . . . and someone sees me holding the knife dripping with blood . . . and I have to run like crazy to make it home before they call the cops.

Must be an idiot to think that Nelson'd be hanging around.

Waiting to get stabbed to death.

But you never know.

I got this feeling that I could be in luck tonight.

One way or another.

Anyway. I'm out there for a run, aren't I?

Not aiming to kill anybody.

I'm taking the knife along in case Nelson happens by.

Then I promise you, Allan, I'll kill the bastard.

Deana slipped out the front door, holding the knife blade forward. She ran lightly up the driveway.

The knife felt awkward at first. Then she got used to it, gripping it tightly and pumping it in and out as she ran.

The socks were great. Like this, she could run on in silence. No one would hear her muffled steps.

Blending in with the shadows, she felt like one of them herself. Part of the scenery.

Black clothes make perfect night camouflage, she told herself.

Wearing black made her feel a lot safer.

But it was still spooky out here.

Scary.

And it was hot. Her head was sweating already.

I'll take off my cap in a minute . . .

She paused to work out her strategy.

She'd reached the end of the drive. Now, which way – up or down?

If Nelson's around, which way is *he* likely to go?

Might be coming up to the house.

Got himself another car, maybe? The cops have his old one.

Something rustled in the juniper bushes to Deana's left.

She stiffened, not daring to breathe, flattening herself against the shrubs by the gatepost.

Yeoowwww . . .

A cat streaked out in front of her. She gasped. Then, feeling relieved, she laughed a little. Fuckin' cat!

Okay.

Start running.

Downhill?

Best go uphill; it'd make for an easier journey on the way home.

After I've annihilated Nelson.

She turned and jogged upbank, gently.

Looking around her.

Is someone watching?

Wondering what the hell that girl is doing out at one a.m.?

Asking for trouble . . .

A thrill buzzed in the pit of her stomach.

It *was* spooky.

But it was exciting, too.

She could meet *any*body.

Or any*thing*.

Dressed in black, the odds were that no one could see her anyway.

On the other hand, there could be some guy out there, thinking about what he'd do to her if he caught her . . .

She hastened her step.

Maybe she should turn around?

Go back home . . .

Not yet.

I'm not *that* scared.

Keep on truckin', Deana . . .

And eyes front, all the way.

It'd be a dumb move to look around, enjoy the scenery as she ran along.

Yeah.

Asking for trouble for sure, that way.

Mostly, it'd make her feel scared, worrying about *who* or *what* could be out there.

The Lake

I should worry. I have a knife.
Mom's vegetable knife.
Don't make me laugh.
Some karate kid comes along and kicks the knife outta my hand.
Then what?
Then you get jumped, raped – or worse – you dope.
Murdered.
Raped *and* murdered.
You're an idiot, Deana West. What *are* you doing out here, anyway?
Mom'd have a fit.
If she knew.
She'll never know.
I'll be home in ten minutes. Fifteen and I'm tucked up in bed. No one any the wiser.
'Hey.'
A shout.
Ringing out in the night. Echoing, loudly.
Deana gasped, melting into the shadows of a redwood spreading out from a driveway.
Her grip tightened on the knife.
She stood poised, ready for action.
'Hey. You want to look where you're going.'
A German shepherd dog sprang up out of nowhere.
Knocking her to the ground.
Pounding the breath, the *life*, out of her.
Curling into a tight ball, Deana shielded her face with her arms; feeling the dog's weight as its heavy front paws pinned her down.
She kept still.
Do that, and the dog won't eat me.
At least I *hope* it won't.
You never can tell with dogs . . .
She moved position and the knife skittered away, its spinning blade glinting in the darkness.
Mom's vegetable knife.
How quaint.
'Here, boy. Saber. Heel!'

Deana peeked though her fingers. The voice didn't *sound* like it belonged to a rapist.

Or a murderer.

It sounded strong. Ordinary. Youngish.

The dog backed off, its long tongue lolling over some seriously pointed teeth. The dog fixed its gaze on its master, like it was waiting for the next command.

Deana blushed in the darkness.

It's only a *dog*, for chrissake! Just a big stupid mutt.

The mutt turned its attention to her curled-up legs. Snuffling around some, giving her a steam-clean with its big slobbery nose.

Yuck. The *beast*!

Deana scrambled to her knees. Stood up, then bent down quickly to pick up the knife.

In the shadowy darkness, the blade flashed embarrassingly bright.

'What's this?' The guy grabbed her hand, twisting it backwards. Her grip loosened and the knife clattered back down to the sidewalk.

He yanked her wrist again, making her yelp with pain.

'What d'you think you're doing?' he demanded.

She regained her balance, drew back a leg and aimed a kick at his crotch.

He danced back. Just in time.

Then, holding up both hands in mock surrender, he laughed.

'Hey. You're looking at friend here. Not foe!'

'What the hell you doing with that dog? It could kill a person, jumping out at them like that!'

Deana scowled at the dog. It was hauled in on a short lead now, sitting quietly by its master's feet, tongue lolling out of mean-looking jaws . . . Hot breath clouding the night air.

'Sorry. I'm Warren Hastings. This is Saber, my trusty sidekick.' Warren held out a hand. 'You must have been really scared.'

Deana ignored the hand.

'You aren't kidding. That's a *monster* you've got there.' She was still fighting back tears of relief.

'That's no monster. That's my mutt. Let me tell you, there's a kitty-cat lurking beneath that rugged exterior. Right, boy?'

The Lake

'Some kitty-cat. He scared me half to death, I'll have you know.'

Warren smiled.

'You dropped your knife. Make a habit of carrying a knife? Make a habit of midnight runs, come to that?'

'A girl's gotta stay safe. Never know who she might meet up with. And yes. I like to run at night. Got a problem with that?'

'Nope. But why not run during daylight hours? Safer that way, so they tell me.'

'What's it to you? What were *you* doing out here, anyway?'

He laughed; a warm, infectious sound. 'Why don't I offer you a mug of cocoa? To make up for my marauding mutt.'

'Thanks, but no, thanks.'

'I make a mean mug of cocoa, when I've a mind.'

Warren tilted his head to one side. His smile was infectious, too. Deana found herself relenting and grinned back at him.

Steady on. Mustn't let him think I'm easy meat.

'How do I know—'

'That I'm not a rapist? Or a serial killer? That the problem?'

'About the size of it.'

'Look. That's my house, there. The one with two redwoods in front. Moved in just a coupla days ago.

'Here's the deal. I make us some cocoa and you fill me in on the neighborhood. Might even run to a cookie or two . . . ?' He smiled, showing nice white teeth.

'*Your* house? You live there alone?'

'Not alone. There's my sister, too. She's called Sheena. You'd like her.'

'I really oughta go. Mom'll be worried . . .'

'Does Mom know you're out?'

Nice one, Warren. You sure know how to press the right buttons.

'Sure she does. She doesn't mind me running at night.'

'With a knife?'

'Just let me pass. I gotta get on home.'

'As you wish. Take a raincheck on the cocoa, though. Finest on the West Coast. Got Best Frothy Choccy Drink Award last year . . .'

'Goodnight, Warren.'

'Let me walk you home. Saber'll defend us from would-be rapists.'
Don't keep using that word. Makes me scared.
'No, thanks. Only a block to go and I'm there.'
'Suit yourself.'
'Yeah. Goodnight.'
'Goodnight, oh nameless lady in black. We shall meet again, maybe.'

Deana turned and ran swiftly downhill, her sock-covered feet beating a muffled rhythm on the sidewalk. By the time she got to her driveway she was breathing hard.

Running lightly down the slope, she reached the stoop, steadied herself against the doorpost and felt for the key. It nestled hard and warm between her breasts.

She hauled it up, lifted the chain over her head and felt hair.

Shit, I left my cap on the sidewalk!
After the trusty Saber jumped me.

Carefully, she slid the key into the lock.

She cringed slightly. Sometimes the lock made a loud metallic scraping noise.

But not tonight.

Thank God.
Wouldn't do to meet up with Mom.

Deana snuck into her bedroom.

She closed the door and leaned back against it, breathing a deep sigh of relief.

Her legs were shaking. Her heart still pounded.

Must be the excitement of her nocturnal adventure, she guessed. Not the exercise; she'd had too much practice for that to be a problem.

Warren.

She gave a wry smile.

Looks like I made a new friend.

Allan's image flashed before her.

I went out there to kill Nelson, Allan. To kill your murderer – I got waylaid, though. But we'll get him, soon.

She flooded her mind with thoughts of Allan till, suddenly, he was there.

She tilted her head and sniffed, catching a whiff of his scent. It eddied all around her.

The Lake

Then it was filling the room.
Allan's here!
His hands cupped her breasts; his upturned thumbs stroked her nipples.

Shuddering with ecstasy, she remembered how he liked doing that. How he loved the feel of her skin. Warm, silky, so *ultra sexy*, he'd told her.

For a long time Deana stared at the window, at the soft billowing drapes and the flickering shadow of the tree . . . Thinking about Allan.

Slowly she undressed, piling her sweats back into the drawer.

Throwing herself onto the bed, she stared at the ceiling for a long, long time, feeling hot salt tears stream down her cheeks.

Allan would always be special to her.

She'd never forget him.

How could she?

'Even when I'm old,' she whispered. 'I'll *always* remember you, Allan . . . and cherish the memories of the good times we've shared.'

Yeah. The good times.

Before the horror of *that* night took them all away.

Before Nelson . . .

No. She'd never, ever forget Allan.

Some adventure she'd had tonight, though.

Warren was quite a guy.

Bet he *did* make a mean cocoa.

She smiled . . .

He had a nice voice. Warm and friendly.

Good teeth, too.

Hadn't seen much more in the dark.

Maybe, soon . . .

The mutt would have to go, though.

Deana sighed.

Didn't get to kill Nelson.

Fuck Nelson. I'll hack him to death some other time.

With Mom's vegetable knife . . .

Oh no!

It was on the sidewalk. With her cap.

Chapter Twenty-four

Oh God. This gets worse. I've gotta go out there and get the knife. Can't go back now, though. Warren'll be asleep. And his dog. Fat chance I have of sneaking into his house to see if Mom's vegetable knife's in there, with Saber around.

Maybe it's still on the sidewalk. Maybe someone kicked it into the bushes.

No way. An urgent little voice told Deana that the knife was now in Warren's house. She stared at the curtains, billowing inward. Felt the soft breeze. Sniffed at the air, thinking she'd caught a whiff of Allan's scent, again.

Stop it.

Now!

She let her eyelids droop. Wriggled her shoulders. Relaxed her body right down to her toes. Breathed deep. In, out, in, out . . .

But her special relaxation technique wasn't working tonight. She couldn't get the knife out of her mind.

Mom's gonna miss her knife. She uses it almost every day.
  She's gonna think that someone stole it . . .
  No way would she think she'd *lost* it . . .
  She always puts it back in the drawer.
  Hope *Warren* did *find it*.
  Probably took it indoors, intending to return it later.
  The knife *and* my cap.

The Lake

Doesn't really matter about the cap.
Idiot. Warren doesn't know where I live.
Didn't give him the chance to *ask* where I lived.
Didn't want to tell him, either. He could've been a rapist.
Nah.
Not with a dog that size. Rapists creep about on their lonesome.
Preying on girls.
Dog like that, a would-be rapist wouldn't have a victim to rape. They'd be dead with fright, or halfway down the street.
Only one thing for it. Wait till Mom goes to bed tonight, then sneak out.
Again.
If I'm lucky I'll catch Warren walking his dog.
Then I'll ask him if he saw the knife, and did he happen to pick it up? And if so, please can I have it back?
Make it easy on yourself, Deana. Buy a new one.
Can't do that.
Mom'd notice the difference.
She'd wonder why she's suddenly got a new knife in place of the old one.
Phweww . . .
What a tangled web . . .
Only one thing for it.
Gotta go out there and find Warren.
Sample his cocoa.
Maybe. Whatever. Just get the knife back.

Chapter Twenty-five

Nelson shivered.

It was dark and getting colder all the time.

Blinded by the glare of headlight beams, he couldn't make out where he was walking.

His pirate patch was long gone – his sewed-up eye looked like it had been sucked back into his skull. Hot tears welled up in his good one.

He was exhausted; his head throbbed with a muzzy ache. The tears made everything blurred and hazy. He lifted a hand to dash them away.

Christ, this is one mean mother of a headache . . .

He'd lost his floppy chef cap, and his tunic was all dirty from when he'd last fallen.

Clutching the cleaver, he held it, blade up, like a rifle on his shoulder. Just *having* it there gave him a warm, safe feeling.

'Anybody messes with me 'n' I'll use it,' he muttered to himself. 'Bank on it, you fuckpigs out there; I'll hack ya t'pieces, jes' like a cut a' meat.'

Nelson stumbled off the sidewalk. Into the path of an old Ford truck. Brakes slammed on. The truck screeched to a halt. Then, with a crashing of gears, it swerved around him, almost knocking him off his feet.

Through a hazy blur, he caught the driver's face, bloated, maniacal; mouthing profanities. The nearside window dropped down. The man shook a meaty fist at Nelson.

The Lake

'What *are* you, punk – a fuckin' loony, or WHAT? You wanna die? Do us all a favor, lemme help ya do it!'

The driver's big face shoved itself through the window. A wad of phlegm shot out like a bullet, landing on Nelson's tunic.

Noisy blasts and honks peppered the air.

Sobbing, Nelson hurled himself back onto the sidewalk. The hatchet escaped his grasp and clattered to the ground. He scrabbled around on his knees, his hands circling the gritty path. Then, with a cry of relief, he caught the blade, fingered it carefully and felt his way down till he found the haft.

Cradling it lovingly to his chest, he rocked back and forth, his face turned skyward.

'Thank you, Lord,' he sobbed huskily. 'I found my cleaver. The only thing left . . . from Nelson's *magnificent* goddamn career . . . His dear old cleaver . . .'

Nelson rocked a while longer, crying like a baby, then wiped his eye on the sleeve of his tunic.

That's better.

His good eye was clear now.

'Thank you, thank you . . .' He wagged his head up and down. The Lord was on his side, he knew it.

Raising his arms in triumph, he hoisted the cleaver high, its blade shining in the glare of the streetlamps.

A siren wailed behind him.

He jerked around.

Cops!

Pressing into the shadows, he became one of them.

Bastard cops!

After him.

The shadows suddenly gave way to an embankment. He scrambled upright, and tentatively put one foot over the edge. Then the other . . .

Soon he was slipping and sliding down over rough grass. Clutching at weeds, stretching out his arms, hanging on to the cleaver; trying not to tumble headlong into the awful darkness below.

Crying out, his feet caught in tangled roots and bushes. He lurched forward, slipped again, lost his footing, fell backward and landed smack on his butt. He slipped down some more and panicked. No way could he stop.

He plummeted down.

Still clutching the cleaver.

'Yo . . . What have we here?'

Grabbing at the weeds with his free hand, Nelson shoved his heels into the turf. He shuddered to a halt and went quiet. His heart lurched. He gripped the hatchet tighter.

Whoever's out there, he thought, will think maybe I'm a drunk. Or a dopehead . . . If I'm lucky, they'll leave me be. If'n I'm not lucky . . .

A throaty chuckle rumbled in the darkness.

A hand grabbed his ankle. Yanked him further, *much* further down the slope.

Into a deeper, darker place.

The smell was awful. Rank. Like bad meat.

He scrabbled and clawed at weeds and tufts of grass, frantically trying to halt his progress . . .

The hand pulled harder.

Someone sniggered.

'S'matter, boy? Don't ya want to join us down here? My, aren't *you* the party pooper? *We* want ya to join us.' The voice rose a notch. 'Don't we, guys? Always a hearty welcome for new blood around here . . .'

Nelson sobbed. His heart lurched again; this time it bounced around his chest like a big chunk of rock.

'*Please* . . . let . . . me . . . GO!'

Another yank and he was on the move again.

Undergrowth tore at his face, burning the flesh in raw, hurting patches.

He struggled like a mad thing, rolling from side to side; wrestling to free himself from the vicelike grip.

The hand held firm.

It dragged him across more rough ground. Garbage; jagged cans,

The Lake

glass, sharp objects, scraped and cut into him as he bumped and jolted along.

Still gripping his hatchet.

Can't let it go . . . Gotta use it to hack my way outta here . . .

Suddenly the hand let go. Nelson broke free, rolling over and over . . . and over. Into a stinking ditch; into water that was thick, cold and slimy.

Acrid odors hit his nostrils.

Oil and . . .

Sump oil, seems like . . . but what else?

He scrambled out of the ditch, his shoes filled with slime, the bottom half of his pants clinging to his legs.

He heard uneven, panting breaths coming from behind; feet pounding steadily through the undergrowth; sounds of kicking, cans and other stuff being scattered out of the way.

More gasps and pants . . . They, whoever they were, were catching up. Hands clawed at his tunic. Sour breath warmed his neck.

'Fuck! Geddoff me, ya fuckin' bastard, he's mine – arrghhh . . .'

The whiny voice cut off short; growls of *others* joined in, arguing like a pack of starving hounds.

Christ Jesus! How many of 'em are there?

The pursuing trolls or whatever they were came to a ragged halt. Whispering, sniggering.

Listening out for me, most likely.

'C'mere!'

The voice came up close. Right behind him.

Terrified, Nelson held his breath; hugging the cleaver tight to his chest.

Can't breathe – dear God . . . I can't – breathe . . .

His heart rocked, lurched; fluttering around like a big wounded bird.

A goddamn angina attack!

Cold beads of sweat broke out on his forehead.

Rolled down. Dripped through his brows.

Itching, irritating. Falling into his good eye.

Stinging like salt.

Then—

'Hey. Quit that, you *filthy* fuckin' pervert, you.'

A woman's voice. Sharp. Imperative.

Sounding scared. Very scared.

A male voice now.

Gruff, threatening.

'You fuckin' whore, you'll do as you're told. Paid you good money, didn't I? On the nose. *Before* I got the goods. Do it my way or—'

'Or what . . .?

Smack. A brittle crack. A piercing squeal, reminding Nelson of pigs in abattoirs. Stun guns rammed up their asses.

Nelson's breathing began to settle down. He kept quiet in the murky dark; his knees, his entire body shaking like he'd got the ague.

What the hell's going on?

'Gotcha, my pretty. Come to Poppa, there's a good li'l gal.'

Nelson knew the voice: low, throaty, *phlegmy*. It belonged to the hand that had dragged him down here. Its owner was breathing hard.

Wanting.

The woman shrieked again.

Nelson caught the sound of wrestling bodies, grunting, gasping. Muffled screams, then—

'No, no, *PLEASE, please, somebody . . . HELLLPPP!!*'

More grunting, then rapid scrabbling sounds.

Someone panting and gasping, footsteps pounding along; running away into the fuckin' darkness . . . scrambling up the grass bank, sounded like.

Nelson pictured it: this desperate guy reaching up, grasping. Losing his grip. Slipping back and down into the stinking cesspit . . .

The woman's sobs grew fainter. They were fading away now, into whimpering little gasps.

Nelson doubled up. He started to heave at the soft, gurgling, *bubbling* sounds that came next.

There was more grunting and . . . slurping. Then disgusting wet noises: growling, and a low humming, like animals feeding.

More slurps.

The Lake

Vomit shot from Nelson's mouth. Gasping, struggling for breath, he clamped a hand to his lips and ran.

He stumbled, running in awkward leaps and bounds; breathless, nauseous, his heart pounding like a mad thing.

Gotta get outta here, afore they—

Tears streamed down his face, into his gasping mouth.

His face was all shiny, runny with sweat and tears and snot.

Nelson lurched on. Stumbling over more rough terrain, dim obstacles, jagged stumps; up another rise, then . . .

Thank you, God!

He heaved himself onto the sidewalk. Panting hard, his lungs raw, hurting, pain erupting through his body – but *hallelujah*, he was back on a street!

Looking over his shoulder, he spotted the pay phone he'd used earlier. He raced towards it.

His legs wobbling like jelly. His arms pumping, his breath making hissy, whistling sounds. Then—

Ahhh, NO!!

He pulled up short, crying out in despair, making small, whiny noises.

'My cleaver . . . I left it. Back there . . .'

He gulped as a knotty hand hooked his throat.

Slipping sideways, he whirled around and wrestled free. Then, bounding forward, he turned for a moment – and caught sight of his assailant.

Jesus Christ!

A huge, bearded giant; filthy rags flying out behind.

Head down, almost *touching* him.

As the streams of inbound traffic flowed off the Bridge, haloes of light shot blinding beams into Nelson's face. Grimacing, his arm flew up to shield his eye.

His breath came in great heaving gasps.

Panic gripped him. His lungs were packing up . . .

The towering troll was on him . . .

Arms outstretched.

'No, you don't, buddy boy . . . The party's *just* about to take off.'

Strong, grimy hands snatched at Nelson's tunic.

Dragging it up, twisting it tight under his chin.

Nelson's head jerked back and sideways.

He felt his feet leave the ground. Found himself staring into blood-shot eyes. At long filthy dreads matted up in a foul tangle with the troll's greasy straggly beard.

An old-time hippie gone bad.

And MAD.

Mad for flesh.

His.

Anybody's.

The derelict leered, his wet lips pulling away from dark broken stumps of teeth. Globs of blood dripped from his beard.

Unspeakable fumes gusted into Nelson's face. Transfixed like a frightened deer, his good eye swiveled and opened wide. Air hissed from his sagging lungs.

Uhhh . . .

The troll gave him a final violent shake, then slammed Nelson hard against the railings.

Chapter Twenty-six

Deana lay under her bedsheet. Wearing black sweatclothes. And her sneakers, with the wool socks pulled up over them.

Ready to venture forth on another midnight run.

To find Warren, get the knife back and, she hoped, return it to its rightful place.

But Mom wasn't even in bed yet.

She was moving around in the kitchen, clearing dishes, running water, washing them off. Deana heard the quiet click of a cupboard door.

Mom: not wanting to wake her.

Doing her stuff and trying to keep quiet about it.

For my sake.

Hope she doesn't decide to peek in through my bedroom door, to see if I'm fast asleep.

Good thing I'm not wearing my cap . . .

Mom was in the bathroom now, humming quietly to herself.

Thinking about Mace?

You bet.

At last Mom's bedroom door closed.

Then opened again.

Mom wants me to know that she's around; if I should wake in the night.

Deana smiled.

Mom was so thoughtful.

* * *

Wonder what Warren's doing now?

Probably getting ready for his nightly stroll.

With Saber, his trusty canine friend.

Maybe I should take along some pepper to throw in the mutt's face if he attacks me.

Oh yeah.

That'd *really* impress Warren.

He'd *hate* me for it.

Oh well, scrub the pepper. Have to trust Warren to drag Saber off me. *If* he decides to go for my throat, or something . . .

Deana twisted her head sideways. She looked at the clock on the nightstand.

00:12.

Tomorrow already.

She held her breath, keeping quiet and still.

No sound from Mom's room.

Okay. Let's move it.

She swung off the bed.

Twisted up her hair and pulled another knit cap, a navy one this time, over it. This cap had NY embroidered in white on the front. She grinned a little; she always felt like a ghetto kid when she wore this one.

Looking down at her feet, her sneakers covered with the thick wool socks, she decided that she looked more like a yeti.

All she needed now was a weapon.

In case Nelson was lurking out there.

Maybe the pepper'd be a good idea.

Nah.

Nelson wasn't around last night.

Probably won't be around tonight, either.

Mom thinks he's snuffed it. Maybe his body's out there at this very moment, floating in the Bay, bobbing around in the cold, dark water, being chawed by fish. Sharks, even – their deadly teeth tearing off his arms and legs. Chomping on his stringy innards.

She shivered, thinking about it.

That is *really* gross.

The Lake

Nelson was a weird guy, but he didn't deserve a death like that.
Deana crept out into the hallway.
She stopped a while, and waited.
Bet Mom's asleep by now.
Dreaming about Mace.
Yeah. I can see it now.
Mace and Mom. Like Bogart and Bergman in *Casablanca*. Staring into each other's eyes across some crowded bar . . .
Play it again, Sam.
Ugghhh.
Gruesome.
She felt for her door key, caught inside her sweatshirt.
It was safe and sound.
Good.
Nothing like spending the night huddled on the stoop; Mom opening the door and saying, 'Good morning, honey. Your own bed not comfortable enough for you?'

Now for one of Deana's famous midnight runs.
'Gotta find Warren's house first,' she murmured. 'I reckon it's about a block away. Up the hill. Good thing I'm fit. All this running, and tennis with Mom, keeps me in good shape.'
At the end of the driveway she looked up, then down Del Mar. She felt a buzz of excitement; the thought of being alone in the darkness brought goose bumps scurrying up her body.
Yeah. It sure is scary.
Everybody's asleep. Except me. I'm awake and ready for anything.
Almost.
She couldn't see anyone around.
Staring up the street some more, her excitement took a downturn.
Del Mar. Dimly lit by too few streetlamps, making long stretches of street almost totally black. The trees were giant shadows; the houses, dark formidable places.
She suddenly felt very scared.
'*Nightmare on Del Mar*,' she muttered. 'It'd make an awesome movie. Maybe I should write me a film script someday.'

Humming a little, she began to mark time on the spot. Shoulders back, knees pumping up and down.

Up down, up down, up down . . .

Usually this exercise focused her on the run ahead.

Thank God tonight was no exception.

Feeling loose-limbed and relaxed, she began running up the incline toward Warren's house.

A shadow stepped out in front of her.

Deana gulped, stopped and danced back into the shadows.

The shadow came toward her.

At her.

She held her breath. Moving sideways. Backwards. Any way but forward.

Every move she made, the thing blocked her path.

Weaving, dodging, dancing in front of her, stopping her from moving on.

She fought back panic, her heart hammering in her throat.

Then there was this shrunken death's-head swaying before her. Its eyes gleaming at her from deep, dark sockets, its wrinkled mouth drawn into a tight black 'o'.

Backlit by a streetlamp, wisps of hair stood out around its head like a silver halo.

Maybe it just crept out from some crypt or other . . .

Nah. It's not the living dead.

It's solid flesh and blood . . .

A bent, skinny old woman!

The hag grunted, then pulled up short in front of Deana. She was clinging on to an untidy bundle in her arms. The bundle twisted and jerked, then out jumped a small dog. It raced across the street and disappeared down a tree-lined drive.

'*Shit!*' the hag shrieked. '*Now* look what you've done! Harry! Harry! Come to Mommy . . . Haaarrryyy!'

A small white head with pointed ears appeared at the driveway opening.

Harry.

Thank God.

The Lake

Deana, not believing what she was doing, called out, 'Come on, Harry . . . Come here, there's a good dog!'

The tiny head darted back, then disappeared into the shadows again.

'Fuck!' The crone stepped forward, her fierce, raddled face glowering at Deana. She raised a skinny, clawed hand and whacked it across the girl's cheek.

'*Ouuchh – you bitch!*'

Deana's neck twisted up and sideways. The crack was like gunfire inside her head. Staggering back, she clamped a hand to her face.

Damn!

The punch had landed *exactly* where Nelson had slugged her. Pain shot through her jaw again.

'Sonofabitch,' she cursed through clenched teeth.

Let her find her own fuckin' dog.

Huh. Harry – what kind of a name was *that* for a dog, anyhow?

Head down, still nursing her cheek, Deana hurried past the old woman. Breaking into a run, she slammed smack into someone else hurrying toward her.

Dazed by the impact, Deana shook her head. She heard excited barks. Then loud wuffing noises, echoing up and down the street.

Saber.

Thank *God*.

She didn't think she'd ever been *this* grateful to hear a barking dog.

'What the—?' Warren held on to her, tight. 'It's the midnight runner, if I'm not mistaken. What brings you out here again?'

'Warren. Am *I* glad to see you . . .' Deana broke off with a grim laugh. 'My God. What an *experience*. I can't *believe* it!'

They fell quiet for a moment, listening to the hag's shrill voice, still calling: 'Harrryyyy. Come to Mommy, darling . . . !'

Deana looked at Warren. Their gazes met and they grinned at each other. It was a nice friendly moment.

Then, with a yelp of pain, Deana clamped a hand to her jaw.

Warren frowned. 'You all right?' he asked. 'I could drive you to an emergency room. There's one a coupla miles from here . . .'

Deana shook her head.

'No? Okay. Then sit here on the wall awhile. Get your breath back.' He led her to a low brick wall. She lowered herself down, carefully, and leaned back into the bushes.

'It's great to see you, Warren. And the mutt. Believe me – things got a bit nightmarish back there for a while.'

A large wet nose examined her knees. Saber made loud snuffling sounds. Deana smiled. Pushing the dog away, Warren said, 'Saber. Sit. Sit, boy!'

Saber sat.

Warren dropped down by Deana's side, wrapped an arm around her and pulled her gently to him. Feeling safe and comfortable, she sighed and snuggled into the crook of his shoulder.

Saber squatted, bright-eyed, watching. Steamy breath plumed from his mouth like puffs of gray smoke.

'How about that cocoa?' Warren said at last.

'Sounds like a swell idea.'

'Sure? What if I'm a mad rapist?'

She drew back and faced him. 'I'll take my chances that you're not.'

'Good. Nice to know I can be trusted.'

'Didn't say that. Just meant that I'm willing to take my chances. Personally, I don't *think* you are. Anyway, even if you were, I can look after myself.'

'Yep, I guess you could. You sure *look* like you'd hold your own in an emergency.'

Is he joking, or what?

Maybe not.

Anyway – now's a good time to ask about Mom's knife . . .

And try out his cocoa.

'Follow me,' he said.

Deana tagged along behind, while Warren led the way up the driveway. She smiled. It'd been *his* wall they'd been sitting on. And, like he said, there were two redwoods in front.

Saber trotted by Warren's side.

Without quite knowing why, Deana glanced back through a gap in the redwoods. She could just about see the street.

A car was nosing its way past the driveway.

The Lake

She caught her breath.
It was long and black, with tail fins. No lights.
The glare from the streetlight hit the vehicle's windows. They were black, too.
She shuddered.
It's going real slow . . . like a funeral car.
The car passed out of sight and she hurried to catch up with Warren.
Warren was at the front stoop, reaching into his pocket. Bringing out a key, he slid it into the lock.
The door opened inward on a dark hallway.

Chapter Twenty-seven

Here we go, Deana thought.

Straight into the lion's den.

The vestibule had a warm smell. A faint aroma of food hung on the air.

Pot roast – last night's dinner, she guessed.

Warren took her arm, leading her along the hall and through an entryway at the end.

He clicked on the light. It flooded a small compact area that obviously served as both kitchen and breakfast bar.

He gestured toward a pinewood chair. She sat down and scooted it along the tile floor to the table. It made a loud scraping noise. She wondered if she'd disturbed anyone.

Warren took a stool at the bar. Looking at her quizzically, he made the first move.

'Let me guess. You've come for your knife, right? I have it here. *And* your cap. Although I see you've found another one. Must need quite a wardrobe; going out, losing your things like that . . .'

'Okay, Warren. I confess. I *did* come back for my knife. It's Mom's and she'll go ballistic if she finds out it's missing . . .'

'Looks remarkably like a vegetable knife to me . . .'

'So what? *Any* kinda knife is a good idea for someone out running at night.'

'Sure,' he said seriously. 'But maybe it's *not* such a wonderful idea. Midnight running, I mean. Especially for a young girl . . .'

The Lake

'I'm eighteen. I can look after myself.'

'Eighteen?' He looked impressed. 'All of eighteen?'

'Look. Hand me my knife, please, and I'll be on my way.'

'Knife *and* cap. You ought to thank me.'

Uh-huh. Here it comes.

I have to thank him.

Serves me right for being so dumb.

For walking into his trap like a complete moron.

'Oh yeah? Thanks, but no, thanks.'

'I meant by accepting my offer of cocoa. Nothing more.'

Warren seemed a little offended that she'd read something more into his words.

'Okay,' Deana replied, relenting slightly. 'But we'll have to make it snappy. I might be missed.' As an afterthought, she added: 'Mom's well in with a guy from Mill Valley PD.'

'Really? In that case, a quick swig of my special brew and you must be on your way. I'll escort you, if you like. In case you meet up with Harry and Mommy Dearest again.'

'Whatever.' Deana was intrigued by his easy, light-hearted manner. He sure didn't *look* threatening. She glanced at Saber, lying, head on paws, under the sink unit. His bright eyes fixed on hers.

Watching every move.

Good one to have on the home team, Deana decided.

The cocoa was great. The best she'd tasted so far.

'What's your recipe?' she asked.

'My secret.' Warren smiled.

'Well, it's tasty, I'll give you that.'

He gave a smug smile, looking pompously complacent.

Then he winked at her.

'Told you I got awards for it. Anyway, how about you? At high school?'

'Going to Berkeley in the fall.'

'Mmmm . . . A little past that stage, myself. Though I confess, I *do* recall it with some affection.'

'Oh.' Deana looked at him. He didn't exactly *look* like he was past it.

'What do you do, then?'

'I have a bookstore. In San Anselmo. I put out searches for rare and out-of-print books. Request a book, any book, and I'll get it for you . . . Eureka.'

'Uhhh?'

'Eureka Bookstore. As in striking gold? Remember the old '49ers?'

'Sure, sure. Got it.'

'Neat, huh?' Warren sounded childishly pleased, explaining the name of his place to her this way.

'Cute,' she replied. 'Anyway, you look too young to be mixed up with old books.'

'I'm twenty-two, if that helps.' He smiled brightly.

'Really?'

'Yes, really. Quite ancient, aren't I? As for the bookstore, my parents left me a small sum after they died, and as I've always loved books, I decided to make them my life's work. *Voilà*, I bought myself a bookstore.'

'You mentioned your sister . . .'

'Yes. Sheena. She's out right now. Should be back around five-thirty. Home with the dawn chorus, usually.'

'Stays out late, your sister?'

'Mmmm. You could say that. She works at a club. In San Jose. Hangs around in case of trouble.'

'That so? She keeps fit, then?'

'Oh, sure. Used to coach for a college baseball team. Gave it up. Too much like hard work, she said.'

'Must be quite a gal.'

'She sure is.'

'Younger than you?'

'No. Quite a bit older.'

Deana began to feel uneasy. She was thinking about the car she'd seen earlier.

The black *funeral* car.

She shivered.

Okay, it was interesting enough, all this personal stuff; but she really oughta be getting on home now. If it weren't for thinking about that

The Lake

goddamn car, *and* worrying about Mom's knife, she told herself, she could have stayed all night, no problem.

Chatting about whatever came into their heads.

Perhaps even more *personal* stuff.

She had the feeling that Warren would make a good listener. Maybe she *should* hang around a little longer . . .

Except Sheena might object and throw me out.

If I stayed till five-thirty. Which I won't.

'I gotta go.'

'Of course,' Warren said. He rose and pulled open a drawer by the sink unit.

'Here's your knife.' He handed it to her, handle first. 'Oh, and your cap. Saber found it and brought it to me. You may have to launder it,' he added.

Fishing around in a lower cupboard, he picked out the cap and passed it over.

Deana sniffed it, wrinkled her nose and smiled.

'Get your drift. About laundering it, I mean . . .'

'I'll see you home . . .'

'It's okay. Really . . .'

'I'd *like* to see you home,' he interrupted, cutting her short. 'I'd worry that you might meet up with a real live rapist – or worse, Mommy Dearest again.'

'Okay. *If* you can keep up with me. I like to run.'

'Lead on, Macduff.'

Warren held open the kitchen door for her, then looked back at the dog.

'Saber. Stay.'

'Don't think we'll need his services again tonight,' he said, adding, with a wink, 'Any rough stuff and we'll deal with it ourselves. Okay?'

'Sure. Let's ride.'

They left Saber glowering from his den under the sink, his eyes accusing them both. Shifting around on his butt, the mutt was obviously dying to follow.

Once outside, Warren grabbed Deana's hand. They set off down the dark driveway, matching stride for stride till they reached the gate.

No sign of the black car.
Thank God.

Out on Del Mar, Deana filled her lungs with the warm night air.

The darkness seemed friendlier somehow, the shadows less threatening than they had been earlier.

Maybe the chat with Warren, *and* his yummy cocoa, had done the trick.

It helped a lot that the car had gone.

Idiot. Probably nothing sinister about it.
Just some kid, nosing around. Not really a threat.

She hoped they *didn't* meet up with the skinny hag and her pet pooch.

Saber should be here, she thought. Any trouble, maybe he'd eat Harry, just for me . . .

It was good jogging downhill with Warren, their feet slapping the sidewalk.

At least, Warren's feet slapped.

In the thick wool socks, Deana's were quiet and muffled.

And he was right when he'd said he was no stranger to running. Gets plenty of practice too, Deana thought, struggling to keep up with him.

No sign of Mommy Dearest and the faithful Harry.
Probably tucked up in bed and asleep by now.

They ran on till they reached Deana's driveway. She huffed to a halt. Warren, too.

Waiting a moment till they got their breath back, Warren said, 'Well, my lady in black – here you are. Safely delivered to your door. Care to come jogging with me again sometime? Or maybe we could do something a little more formal? Like the movies. Or dinner . . .'

Quaint.
The movies or dinner . . .

Either way, though, Deana thought, feeling a strange new surge of excitement, would suit me fine.

She thought of Allan and immediately felt guilty.

'Yes?'

'Sure,' she replied nonchalantly. 'I'll let you know. Maybe we'll meet

The Lake

up when I'm out running sometime – then we could arrange a date.'

She lifted a hand in salute. Warren stood awhile, watching her run down the driveway.

He turned, walked away and was soon jogging again. Getting easily into his stride; legs pumping hard, muscles straining to keep up the punishing pace.

Between harsh, measured gasps of breath, an amused smile played on his face.

Chapter Twenty-eight

Sheena left the club early.

Pacey hadn't been any too pleased, but when she told him, 'Either I go an' I come back again tomorrow night, or I go an' don't come back at all,' he'd shrugged and said, 'Family crisis? Sure. We all have one a' those from time ta time. *I* should know, believe me. Okay. Do it, Sheena. But don't make a habit of this. I can't afford for you not to be here.'

He was damn right, too. The other guys working the door at Pacey's Place couldn't handle it the way she could. She was proud of her physique. A powerful five-ten, and stacked with it. Down to all those workouts. She gave a tight smile. Her karate was pretty impressive, too.

Tonight, Sheena had had one of her 'insights'.

They didn't come often, but when they did she knew better than to ignore them. They'd been with her for as long as she could remember, but tonight's had been the strongest so far.

She was uneasy about Warren.

Swinging her Chrysler coupe into Del Mar, the feeling of unease mounted. She eyed the low black job up ahead. It was coasting along like it was looking for someplace. Sheena put her foot down; the engine roared and she released the pressure slightly. The street was like a goddamn morgue. So *quiet*. Nobody around. But hey, Warren liked it, and it was within easy reach of 'Eureka' . . .

The Lake

Sheena cruised up the hill till she saw the two redwoods. Home. Home? She didn't think so.

The car in front was still doing around twenty-five, thirty. Slightly annoyed, Sheena slowed down. She continued with her train of thought.

Guess I have this monkey on my back – have to keep on the move. She gave a wry smile. No place like home, isn't that what they say? *What* home, I ask myself . . .

'Hey, buddy. Get a move on, why don't ya?'

She removed a piece of gum from its wrapper and wadded it into her mouth. The fingers of her free hand tapped the wheel impatiently.

Suddenly, the black job revved and disappeared up the street.

Nearly there now.

Sheena's breath quickened.

She felt strangely alert.

Like she was homing in on a target of some kind. She was reading all the signs. Super-aware.

This is *it*.

Her stare pierced the darkness. Instinctively, she drove past her driveway and stopped in a dark, shadowy place a couple more yards on. All her senses were taut, oddly *acute*; a part of her brain told her she needed a workout. One of those hard, punishing jobs when all she focused on was the pain of her hurting lungs and straining muscles.

It was a strange yet familiar feeling – more a *compulsion*, really. She always felt this way when she had one of her 'insights'.

Yeah. I need a workout.
But that'll come later.
After that, sleep.

Same routine every time.

She heard voices.

Peered into her rear-view mirror.

It was Warren and some kid. The kid's face showed up ghost-white against her black clothes.

They were jogging out of the driveway. Laughing quietly. Looking into each other's faces. Sharing a joke.

Surprised, Sheena's brows raised a little.

Nice work, bro.

What happened to the 'one man and his dog' routine?

The joggers rounded left and set off down Del Mar.

Sweat glistened on Sheena's forehead.

Her hands clenched the wheel.

Something was wrong.

Chapter Twenty-nine

Deana went to the kitchen in search of coffee. It was eight a.m.; just six hours since she'd left Warren's place. All she needed was a mug of hot coffee and maybe, just maybe, she'd crawl back to bed . . .

The flowers were standing in the sink.

'Wow, Mom. Who sent those? Don't tell me. Your new friend, tah-dah: Detective Mace Harrison!'

'Right first time, hon,' Leigh said. 'They're from Mace. Aren't they just beautiful?'

Deana stared at the bunch of flowers. Exotic pink orchids mixed with sprays of white freesias. Still encased in their cellophane wrapper and tied with a pink satin bow.

Some bouquet.

Puzzled, she looked at Leigh.

'I had no idea that things had gotten so far. So soon.'

Leigh smiled dreamily. 'You better believe it, hon. Mace and I are getting along *very* well. He's *so* kind and thoughtful. It's been ages since anyone gave me flowers like these.'

Leigh disappeared into the utility room, busying around finding a vase large enough to hold the flowers. Moments later, she reappeared with a tall, elegant one, decorated with a blue and white Chinese design.

Removing the bow and cellophane, she began arranging the blooms to her liking. She hummed a tune to herself.

Deana couldn't remember seeing her mother this happy – so bright-eyed and her cheeks all flushed like a teenager in love.

Warning bells rang.

Mom's got it bad.

Worse than bad. Deana had this sinking feeling that Mom was more than 'getting along very well' with Mace.

Leigh stepped back to admire her display and caught Deana's expression. A worried frown clouded her face.

'Deana, honey. Smile, please. Be happy for me.'

'Sure thing, Mom. I'm thrilled for you. Really.'

Choked, Deana turned away. She went to her bedroom and closed the door.

So Mace had been here again last night.

Jeez. What an asshole. Bringing flowers like that. He probably stayed the night.

A thought occurred.

If he *was* here overnight, did he hear me come in this morning?

Count on it.

Mace is a cop. A real pro. And they say cops on a case never sleep. Right?

And from what Mattie had said, Mace was pretty much joined at the hip to his job.

Maybe he heard me come in this morning and decided not to tell Mom. Like, he's saving the news to blackmail me later . . .

I should tell Mom about Warren.

Before Mace does . . .

She'd be real worried, knowing about my midnight trysts.

She'd worry herself sick . . .

God. That's the *last* thing she needs, what with Nelson still on the loose, and everything.

After I'd promised I wouldn't leave the house I wander off without her knowing.

I'll *have* to tell her about Warren.

Before Mace gets there first.

She'd never forgive me if that happened.

Her mind in a turmoil, Deana returned to the kitchen.

Leigh was still lingering over the flowers.

Deana cleared her throat.

'Mom. I have something to tell you.'

'Oh? What is it, honey?'

Mom looks so radiant. So happy.

I *can't* spoil it for her.

'Mom,' she began. Hating herself. Knowing she was about to chicken out of telling the truth. 'I'm really happy for you. If this is what you want, I hope it works out for you and Mace.'

Christ.

I'm such a *liar*.

A deceitful, scheming bitch lying her way out of a seriously tricky situation.

I *could* say I met Warren accidentally. That might take her mind off Mace for a while.

She pictured what would happen when she told Mom about Warren.

'And where did you meet him, honey? We both agreed you should stay in the house; not go out, unless I was with you . . . Yes, I know it's hard, Deana . . . Oh. You met him when you were out running . . .'

A pregnant pause.

Then, '*AT NIGHT*?'

Yeah.

Can you just imagine it?

Finito. No more midnight runs.

Door key confiscated.

Chained to the bed – till Mace nails Nelson . . .

Yeah. *Great*.

Like sometime, never – that's when Mace'll nail Nelson. Just so he can hang around Mom some more. *If* Nelson's still around to nail, that is.

'Mom. Was Mace here last night?'

'I told you he was, dear.'

'Yeah, I know he *visited* last night, Mom. Like late. But when did he *leave*? Did he spend the night here?'

Leigh blushed.

Deana cringed. She hated embarrassing her mom like this.

'Okay, Deana. Yes. He called me after you'd gone to bed. And we talked . . . In the end, as we had so much to discuss, I asked him to come on over.'

'*Mom!*'

Her hunch had been right, then.

Mace *had* been in the house when she came back from seeing Warren.

Could be they were both awake when I arrived home.

In the early hours.

Two twenty-five, to be precise.

Christ!

So Mace could've heard me come in!

But Mom hadn't?

If she had, she'd have asked me about it, first thing this morning.

'Where did he get the flowers from?' Deana demanded, borrowing time, not quite knowing what to say next. 'That time of night?'

'Woke up old Fess Winters, the florist on Main Street? Told him he wanted the biggest bunch of the most expensive flowers he'd got. And here they are. Mace is *so* romantic, isn't he?'

Yeah. A pretty impulsive guy.

Bet Old Man Winters thought so, too.

Nice going, Mace.

No wonder Mom looks so dreamy, so starry-eyed this morning.

Orchids for the lady.

I think I'm gonna throw up.

Chapter Thirty

When Leigh left for the restaurant, Deana leafed through the telephone directory for the Eureka Bookstore's number.

She came up with zilch.

Should have asked Warren for his card.

Would've made things a whole lot easier.

Well, I didn't, did I?

Good thing, too.

I can see it now . . .

Phone up this guy you hardly know, tell him the detective from Mill Valley PD stayed with Mom last night. Remember, the one I told you about? Yeah, that one.

And he'd say, 'Okay? So what business is this of mine? Moms have a right to private lives, too, y'know.'

Deana replaced the phone book in its alcove.

Wandering aimlessly into the living room, she stared through the glass wall at the panorama below.

The day spread out before her, like an empty rain-washed sky.

What shall I do?

Read a book?

What book?

Watch daytime TV?

Yawn.

What about . . . ?

She rushed to the hallway. Grabbed the phone book and looked up 'Hastings'.

Dummy!

New to Del Mar a couple of days ago, Warren's name wouldn't be listed yet.

Three blocks away. That would probably make it in the three hundred and sixties . . .

And under the name of the last occupant.

She'd *never* work it out that way.

Shit.

Maybe she'd enough to occupy her mind, thinking about Mace calling Mom, telling her I was out last night . . .

Leigh, darling. Did you know your daughter was *out* there on Del Mar. Seeing some *guy*?

He'd just love that . . .

As she went to her bedroom, Deana pictured Warren's kitchen. Cosy. Friendly. Smelling of pot roast . . .

And Saber, harboring dark thoughts beneath the kitchen sink.

Some dog, that.

Dangerous.

At least he rescued my cap for me.

Cap.

She'd tossed it, and her black sweats, into the hamper. They sure could do with a wash, after all that excitement.

Probably stink like hell.

'That's what I'll do while Mom's out,' she decided. 'Wash my black things. Get them dried and put away before she sees them.'

Deana opened the hamper. Dragged out her sweats.

Her knitted cap fell to the floor.

So did Warren's card.

Showing his business address *and* a scribbled phone number on the reverse.

His home number!

'Eureka!'

Must have put it inside her cap before he handed it to her. When he scrabbled about in the cupboard under the kitchen sink.

Smart guy.

Now what?

Call the number, dummy. Even if he's not home, his sister will be . . .

The Lake

A squirm of excitement stirred between Deana's legs.

Maybe this wasn't going to be such a boring day, after all.

Do it, Deana. Go for it.

She sat on the bed, dialing out the number on her extension line.

Brrinngg . . . Brrinngg . . .

'Yeah. The Hastings residence . . .'

The woman's voice was deep, brisk. Businesslike.

For someone who didn't get home till five-thirty a.m., this sure was some together lady . . .

'Er . . . May I speak with Warren, please?'

'Who's asking.' A statement. Not a question.

'A friend. Just say the midnight runner. He'll know who it is.'

Deana heard the phone slap down onto a hard surface.

Silence. Then, in the background, 'Hey, bro. Gal here says she's the midnight runner.'

Deana blushed.

My God.

Sounds like I'm some kind of weirdo.

Giving out code names over the phone.

Silence.

More conversation in the background. Garbled now. Further away.

Then Warren's voice, slightly breathless.

'Hi. You just caught me . . . To what do I owe the pleasure? So soon, too.'

Deana heard the smile behind his words.

She felt foolish; not *quite* knowing why she'd rung.

Of course she knew.

She'd rung for the hell of it, hadn't she?

No, not that.

What she'd really rung Warren for was to talk about Mace.

Come to think of it, what *could* she say about Mace, without being a traitor to Mom?

'Hello? Are you there?'

'Sure . . . Hi, Warren,' she said, weakly. 'Sorry to bother you. Tell me I'm a nuisance.'

'No, I won't. What is it, my midnight lady? Hey. What's your name, anyway? Can't keep coming over all Shakespearean. It's enough to take the edge off any budding friendship.'

'Deana. Deana West.'

'Deana. Mmm. Nice name. So . . . Deana. How can I help?'

He sounded calm, sensible. Understanding.

She snuffled, feeling hot tears well up.

'Why don't I come over there? Cheer you up a little?'

'That'd be great, Warren, if you could. What about Eureka? Shouldn't you be there by now?'

'There's nothing spoiling back at the store. A quick call and my trusty assistant will open up. She has a key.'

She?

Deana suddenly felt too tired, too exhausted to talk or even *think* anymore. The events of the last few days, never mind Mace being in the house last night, were just about all she could handle at the moment.

'I'd like that, Warren,' she said, quietly.

Chapter Thirty-one

Friday, July 4

Lisa Bonetti was eighteen years of age. She had long dark hair and a tall, athletic build. She played tennis, enjoyed swimming, and was a hotshot at archery.

Due to go to UCSC in the fall, Lisa was the apple, as they say, of her father's eye.

At 15:01 she was on her way to Kathy's Diner on Main Street to meet her friend Margy for coffee and donuts. She'd missed out on lunch, so she was looking forward to a couple of Kathy's fresh apple donuts. She had no idea that she was being followed.

The black car cruised by a couple of times, then drew up alongside as she hurried along the sidewalk.

'Miss!'

The black window slid down and an elbow, then a man's face appeared. The man looked both serious and concerned. He glanced up, nodding briefly.

'Lisa Bonetti? I'm Detective Joe Napier, San Jose PD.' The man flashed police ID at her and returned it to the inside pocket of his leather jacket.

He leaned across the passenger seat and swung open the farside door.

'Ms Bonetti, your father's in Cedar Heights. Had a near-fatal heart attack around two this afternoon. News came through as I was going off my shift. Chief asked me to drive you over to see him.'

The girl paled. She frowned slightly.

'But there must be some mistake . . . I mean, my father was okay this morning when I left him. He took his pills as usual and walked down the driveway to wave me off . . . I've been watching the parades – didn't think to call and check . . . Uh, who phoned your office to say he was ill . . .?'

Lisa's face was ashen now. Clearly, news of her father's attack had come as a bad shock. The man in the car smiled, then said gently, 'Lady name of Lydia Ashmont, your next-door neighbor, I believe, phoned us to say, pass on the message to his daughter Lisa that Tony's in hospital. Right? You *are* Lisa Bonetti? And your father *is* Tony Bonetti?'

'Sure. Take me to him. And *please* hurry.'

Lisa stepped into the car, leaned forward and placed her purse by her feet. She fastened her seat belt, settled back and turned to look at the driver.

'How long will it take?'

Smiling, he said, 'Not long, Ms Bonetti. Not long.' He touched the remote button and the driver's window slid up with a neat whirring sound.

He reached into the glove compartment on his side of the car and produced a hypodermic syringe.

Turning to face the girl, he smiled into her eyes – and emptied the syringe into her arm.

She gave a small gasp and slumped back in her seat.

Anyone seeing her would have said she was asleep.

Roughly, the driver lifted her head; making sure that she was out for the count. He felt around in his jacket pocket, brought out a few sunflower seeds and palmed them into his mouth.

Taking a brief look in the rear-view mirror, he released the handbrake and eased away from the kerb.

Chewing on the seeds, the man glanced at the clock on the dash. 15:05.

His lips curved in a smile.

Whole thing'd taken around three minutes.

Lisa Bonetti's naked corpse was found two days later in a remote,

The Lake

seldom-used spot on the Marin Headlands. The body had been carved open from the throat to the pubic bone. The vaginal cavity contained the victim's severed tongue, heart and other internal organs.

Tony Bonetti was heartbroken at the discovery of his daughter's remains. In his grief, he took his old service revolver, gripped the muzzle between his teeth and blew his head clean off.

Chapter Thirty-two

Monday, July 7

'So Nelson's dead.'

Leigh gripped the phone, feeling startled yet vastly relieved. She heard her voice shaking.

What Mace had to say was good yet bad news. He chose his words carefully.

'We have a body, Leigh. But it hasn't been officially identified yet. Nelson have any family?'

'None that I know of. Parents died in a fire when Nelson was ten or so, I believe. He never spoke of brothers or sisters. Something of a loner, I gathered.'

'We need someone to identify him, Leigh. Feel up to it?'

Oh, my God, she thought. *I'm not sure . . . I need time to think about this . . .*

Avoiding his question, she asked, 'Where'd you find him, Mace?'

'Buncha kids spotted something out on the Headlands. Washed up on the beach. Thought it was a mess of old rags at first. Turns out it was a body. Been in the water five, six days by our reckoning.'

Five or six days. What's left to identify?

'Okay,' Leigh gave a deep sigh. The last person she wanted to see was Nelson. Especially a *dead* Nelson. 'If it has to be done, I'll do it.'

''Preciate it if you would, Leigh. But I warn you. He's not a pretty sight.'

I bet.

The Lake

'Pick you up in, oh, twenty minutes?'
'Sure.'

Stepping out into the hallway, Leigh went through to Deana's room. Deana was lying in bed, awake. Leigh went over and sat on the bed. Stroking her daughter's hair, she said, 'Nelson's gone, honey. He won't bother us any more.'

'He's dead?'

'That's right. They found him washed up on a beach over on the Headlands. Must've jumped off the Bridge.'

'My *God*.'

'I have to go identify him. Mace's due to pick me up shortly. You be okay?'

'Sure. I don't envy you, Mom. Identifying a corpse. Especially one that's been in the water so long.'

'Somebody's got to do it. No one else around who knows him . . . Staff back at the Bayview, maybe; but when all's said and done, as his employer it's probably down to me.'

'Sure. Okay. Oh, Mom . . .'

'Yes?'

'In an *awful* kinda way, everything's turned out for the best, hasn't it?'

'Sure it has, honey. Thank God it's all over now.'

Chapter Thirty-three

Leigh looked at the lights sweeping down to the Bay, twinkling like stars in the darkness.

She smiled, and said softly, 'What a wonderful view. Know something, Mace? I'm one lucky gal . . .'

Mace grinned. 'Sure you are, Leigh. The luckiest. Fabulous house. Great restaurant. Looks. Style. Smart kid – and me.'

Facing her in the tub, he traced swirls through the bubbles on her left breast. Fascinated, he watched her nipple emerge as he teased the foam with his forefinger.

His other hand caressed her thigh.

She lifted her head and took a deep breath. The night air was balmy on her wet skin.

She met his gaze, and smiled.

Bathing together in the hot tub had been an idea she'd played around with all day.

Well, at least from lunchtime.

After identifying Nelson this morning, hot tubs, not to mention fun and games with Mace, had been a million miles from Leigh's mind.

Later she'd reneged on that.

Why *not* chill out in the redwood tub?

With Mace . . .

Could help to clear my mind of Nelson.

The *remains* of Nelson, she corrected herself.

The Lake

On the way over to the morgue, Mace had told her to think objectively. 'Is a corpse we got here,' he'd said. 'Not a human being. All you gotta do is identify some itty-bitty thing: a signet ring, clothing, anything on the body you recognize as belonging to Nelson.'

One look at the gray, sodden, *eaten* face with holes for eyes, the chewed, ragged hands, and Leigh had gagged; found herself folding to her knees. Mace caught her, and held her tight. She leaned into him, gratefully.

Fighting back the vomit burning her throat, her gaze returned to the sheet-covered body. The chewed stringy arms lay outside the sheet.

She saw a gold ring – Nelson always wore one on the forefinger of his right hand.

Except now it clung perilously to a flimsy gray stump that *used* to be the forefinger of the corpse's right hand. Dumbly, she nodded. As far as she could see, this was Nelson, all right.

Mace took her home and poured out a brandy. He stood by while she drank it down.

Surprisingly, Leigh wasn't feeling as wrecked as she'd expected. At least seeing Nelson's remains meant that she and Deana could put him and his sick little games behind them now. Reluctant to leave her alone, Mace asked, 'Sure you're gonna be okay?'

'Yeah. No worries,' she answered with a brave smile. Seeing his concern, she added, 'Really, Mace. I'll be okay.'

'You make sure you rest, now. I'll drop by later. Check you out.'

As good as his word, Mace arrived after dinner – complete with a bottle of Dom Perignon champagne.

Deana pouted when she saw him, and stomped off to her room.

Shit.

Screw Mace.

It would have been nice to spend just *one* evening alone with Mom!

She switched on her TV, channel-hopped for a while, then decided on a rerun of *Friday the 13th*.

She'd seen it before.

But tonight – especially tonight – *Friday the 13th* suited her mood precisely.

Chapter Thirty-four

Leigh planned the hot tub, intending it to be a nice, relaxing thing for them both to do. And if they moved on to *other* things – then so be it.

She figured either way would be great.

But the end result wasn't working out quite as she'd planned. For one thing, Mace was still wearing his white T-shirt. *And* his undershorts.

Leigh reminded herself that it was *she* who'd pulled Mace into the tub. Fully clothed. And, strangely, it seemed like he was in no rush to remove his duds.

Except for his jeans. He'd tugged at them, under water; struggled around, then tossed them onto the decking.

She grinned.

Good thing he'd left his leather jacket and gun holster in the living room.

She turned up the bubbles.

Mace was ready to play.

But, suddenly, she wasn't.

What is it with me?

Why don't I want to join in the fun?

Admit it, Leigh. You can't get Nelson out of your mind.

Okay. He's gone. But she *still* couldn't shake off the feeling that she was partly responsible for his death.

She shuddered.

The Lake

It'd been so *horrible*, identifying his body, this morning . . .
Thank *God* that was all over now.

Catching Leigh's faraway look, Mace frowned. Christ, he thought impatiently, is she *still* thinking about Nelson?

Or was something else playing on her mind?

Right now, Mace had something on *his* mind.

And it sure wasn't Nelson.

'Leigh. You know how I feel about you . . .'

'Don't spoil it, Mace. Let's just enjoy ourselves for now. Save the serious stuff for later, huh? It's been an emotional time all round and I think we're both feeling the pressure. Let's just relax . . .'

She slid down into the bubbles till only her head and the tops of her shoulders were visible. She felt Mace's thighs moving in the water, touching hers.

Steam rose and puffed around them. She fought to stay awake, but her eyelids were dropping. As the bubbles massaged her body, her limbs began to feel heavy.

Her eyes closed all the way.

Mace slipped down too. Tangling his legs with hers.

Under the water his hand reached out . . .

Leigh jerked, went taut, pressing her legs together. Waves swelled up over her chin. She swallowed a couple of mouthfuls, and for a moment her face was submerged.

She swooshed to the surface, shaking her head, running fingers through her wet hair. Struggling around on the seat, her pale skin gleamed in the darkness.

'Mace,' she snapped. 'Quit foolin' around!'

'Ssshhh!' Mace put a finger to his lips. 'You'll wake Deana. Do that, and she might want to join us!'

'*MACE!*'

Still feeling on edge, Leigh rose from the tub. The turbulent water swished and swirled around her. The cool air chilled her body. She shivered and folded her arms tight across her breasts.

Mace leaned back, admiring her slick form glowing in the darkness above him. He whistled softly. She looked like Botticelli's Venus rising from the foam.

'Mmmm. Ms West. D'you know you have *the* most desirable body? Stay as you are . . . I'll go get my camera.'

She gave an abrupt laugh and Mace stood up, water sluicing his body. He stepped out of the tub.

'Hurry,' she said tersely. She felt impatient, but managed to smile *and* shudder with cold at the same time.

'Can't wait, huh?'

Mace held out his arms. Leigh climbed out of the tub, hesitated a moment, then snuggled into them. Clinging together, they shivered a little in the night air.

Murmuring into her smooth wet hair, he said, 'Forget the shots, baby. They can wait. Let's go get us a drink.'

Pressing into his body, she felt his erection growing, pushing, probing her pubic hair. She leaned up toward him, her open mouth closing on his.

Slipping her hand inside his wet shorts, she found his shaft and curled her fingers around it. Sliding her hand up and down, she felt him growing stronger all the time. Her mood changed. The yearning *ache* returned.

Taking his hard-on with both hands, she pulled it to her, jabbing it against her opening.

Gasping with longing, she tightened her legs around him, her vulva throbbing painfully.

'I want you in me, Mace. In me, *now*. For God's sake, *Mace* . . .'

'No,' he said, holding her hair, pulling her head back and up to meet his face. 'No, my angel. Down here, first.'

Drawing back, she let go of his erection.

Her heart sank.

Smiling, he lowered his gaze, looking at his shaft, pushing her down till she was on her knees in front of him. 'Some head first, honey,' he said huskily. 'Just to get things moving.'

Disappointment sliced through her like a knife.

She *wanted* him.

The Lake

In her.

Not this way.

She wanted him to ram *deep* – like he'd done last night.

She grabbed at him; disappointed, impatient. Holding his shaft with both hands. Feeling it jerk in her grasp.

God, she was *desperate.*

She *needed* him.

But if this is what it takes, she thought, then so be it . . .

She took him in her mouth, sucking, swirling her tongue around his bulk, feeling the ridges, the tight silky skin.

Then gagging, as he thrust himself deeper and deeper into her, holding her head hard against him.

She broke away, choking, gasping, looking up at him, her eyes bright, wide with shock.

'Mace,' she whispered thickly. 'That was *too* much. I nearly choked on you there.'

'You loved it, Leigh. You know you loved it.'

'No, Mace. It *was* too much. Just hold me, will you . . .' She broke off, her lips trembling, hot tears falling down her cheeks. His bittersweet *taste* strong in her mouth.

She'd ached for him, *wanted* him inside her. She'd do almost anything but, Christ, that . . . that hadn't been the most sensitive way of making love, not tonight.

Leigh choked back a sob. How *could* he treat her like this? After *all* she'd been through today . . .

Shivering, she struggled to her feet, brought up her arms, wrapped them tight around her body. She swayed slightly, still hugging herself.

God. The disappointment. The tension.

It was all *too* much.

She felt cold. Utterly exhausted.

A smile played around Mace's lips. Raising his eyebrows, he held out his arms. 'Come to Mace, then. There, there . . . don't take *on* so. Thought you were a gal who'd appreciate some rough and tumble – but seems I was wrong. Sorry about that, Leigh.'

His eyes glinted in the darkness and the smile, vaguely mocking a moment ago, suddenly softened to one of concern.

Leigh's arms fell to her sides. She relaxed, moved in against him, feeling his warmth, his strong, hard body . . .

'Come now, honey,' he murmured. 'How about opening that bottle of champagne I brought us? A coupla drinks and we'll start over. Huh?'

'Sure.' She smiled up at him. They walked through the patio door, and entered the dark living room. Maybe she *had* been a fool, she told herself. Making a stupid fuss over nothing.

Just that I'm feeling *vulnerable* tonight.

'I'll go get us some towels,' she said quietly.

Moving away from him, she turned on the lamp on the coffee table and went to the bathroom.

Feet planted firmly apart, hands on hips, Mace watched Leigh go. Her buttocks swaying, her long shapely legs moving leisurely, she looked like a catwalk mannequin.

Hell, he thought, she'd give most movie stars a run for their money. She had glamor. Something he liked in a woman.

She returned to the living room, wearing a soft bulky robe, the sash tied tight around her waist. Mace thought how young and vulnerable she looked.

Too young to have an eighteen-year-old daughter . . .

She carried a couple of towels under her arm. Tossing one over, she said, 'Here, don't want you catching your death. Take off those wet things, too. I'll dry them for you.'

He caught the towel. He wrapped it around his waist.

Leigh began rubbing her hair with the second towel.

'*Very* sexy,' he murmured, watching her through half-closed eyes as he made for the bathroom.

She quit rubbing and shook her head. Her golden hair fluffed out like a halo. Her legs were shaky. She was still feeling a little awkward about her earlier outburst.

Time to relax, she told herself.

She went to the kitchen, reappearing moments later with the champagne in an ice bucket. Ice chinked around as she placed it on the coffee table.

The Lake

Mace emerged from the bathroom, holding his wet T-shirt and shorts. He wore a white towel robe; one that Leigh's dad used on the rare occasions when he and Mom stayed over.

Mace's tanned body showed up in sharp contrast to the white robe. Eyeing him with reluctant admiration, Leigh felt a flicker of excitement. For a long time, their stares met. Then, smiling, she dropped her gaze. Took his wet clothes and stepped into the kitchen.

Arranging them in the dryer, she tried to convince herself that they could still enjoy the remains of the night.

Chapter Thirty-five

'Let the orgy commence!'

Leigh winced as Mace grabbed the champagne. Catching her expression, he gave a wry smile, tore off the foil top and twisted up the wire.

The cork flew out with a loud pop.

They giggled, searching around for it on their hands and knees, their earlier tension all but gone.

'Over here,' he called. 'Under the TV table.'

He paused, looking at the photographs placed either side of the TV. Family shots: memorable Kodak moments showing Leigh and Deana laughing into the camera, arms around each other. Two older people – Leigh's parents, he guessed.

And Deana standing alone. In a white bikini. On a seashore . . .

'I want to keep it,' Leigh was saying. 'Call me old-fashioned, but I think it's kinda romantic to save corks from champagne bottles. Write dates on them, names, that kinda thing. Folks do it all the time in the restaurant . . .'

'Women!'

He laughed, tossing the cork to her.

'That's what I love about you, Leigh West. You're all woman. Beneath that cool exterior, I swear there's a soft, sensual seductress just crying to be let out.'

Mace poured the fizz into two flutes, already set by the ice bucket. Waiting till the bubbles settled, before filling up the glasses.

The Lake

'Here's to . . . to what?' His eyes twinkled. He paused, brows lifted enquiringly.

'To the future, Mace. A future without Nelson.'

'To us, Leigh.' He looked into her eyes.

Leigh flinched slightly at the intensity in Mace's gaze.

Relax, she told herself. *It's party time. Go with the flow. Let it all happen.*

She smiled at him. 'To us,' she said, chinking her glass against his. Then, 'Mace . . .'

'Uh-huh?'

'Mace, about what happened back there. I'm sorry.'

'*You*'re sorry? My fault, Leigh. Shouldn't have pressured you like that. A guy gets a little carried away sometimes. So let's say no more about it. I'm sorry. Didn't spoil our night, I hope?'

'No, of course not.' Leigh gave a hesitant smile, wishing that were true.

It's been too long between men, she reasoned. *I've almost forgotten how it was with them.*

Her mind slipped back.

To Charlie. Her introduction to oral sex. Comparing Mace's macho display with Charlie's tender, boyish passion.

So long ago now.

Christ. Eighteen years, and she still remembered . . .

Her face had been sore for days afterwards.

Before that, Larry Bills – her first-ever lover.

Ugghh.

She cringed inwardly, embarrassed at the memory.

After Larry, there'd been Tad Bronski, then Jake Hartmann from high school. Nice guys, both of them. Each respected her – and Jake had been deadly serious about their relationship. That was, until his folks hauled him off to Canada when his dad changed jobs.

Her mind lingered on Charlie again. He'd been a pretty hot lover – *on those two occasions* . . .

When he'd stopped being so goddamn shy, and scared of his mother. He'd been kinda *innocent*. A victim, somehow.

You could say that again.
A lamb to the slaughter...
Yet, from the first, she'd detected something *different* about Charlie. A kind of Quality X. Something of the unknown about him. Something ever so slightly *sinister*.
And of course. His witch-bitch of a mother.
Edith Payne.
Leigh shuddered, not wanting to start that over again.
Yeah. *All* her boyfriends had had their moments.
Except Larry Bills. He was a one-off and didn't count. Boy, was that the *mother* of all mistakes...
And, of course, Ben.
Ben was a pussy cat. So kind and thoughtful; he'd never do *anything* to hurt her.
Now there was Mace.
She smiled to herself. Mace was all man.
And, she had to admit, that's what did it for her.
His taut, powerful body. His *attitude*.
And his control.
Always his tight control.
Me Tarzan. You Jane.
That's Mace, all right.
He'd been an absolute rock for her over Nelson.
Kind. At first neither suggestive nor sexy. She'd felt safe just having him around the place – and God knew, she'd been grateful for that.
She hadn't exactly rebuffed him, either. She'd *encouraged* him, if anything.
She'd called *him* the other night. Practically begging him to keep her company in the long dark hours.
No prizes for guessing they'd end up in bed.
She, tearful; he offering his special brand of comfort...
So what happened tonight?
Where had it all gone wrong?

Mace took Leigh's hand in his.
'Hey,' he laughed. 'Don't go quiet on me, Leigh. I came armed

The Lake

with champagne, hoping to bring a little joy into your life.'

He toyed with his glass, swilling around the remains of his drink. Knowing that something still bugged her.

'Leigh. I *care* about you. You do know that, don't you?'

'It *had* crossed my mind, Mace. You spending more time here than in your own apartment, an' all!'

'Any objection to that?'

'Mace. You *know* I don't object. You're beginning to mean a lot to me, too. I, we – Deana and me – would have been lost without your help, your advice and . . . concern. It's real good to know you're there for us.'

'Is *that* all? I'd hoped there was something more . . .'

Her robe slipped off her shoulder. Her mouth opened slightly as she gave him a puzzled smile.

'Of course there's more, Mace. *Much* more. And you know it. It's just that tonight . . .'

Suddenly he was in front of her, hunkering down, looking anxiously into her face. 'I'd hoped there was, Leigh.'

He dropped to his knees, resting his head on her lap. Feeling his warmth against her, she stroked his hair, still damp and tousled from the hot tub.

They stayed this way for a while: quiet, content, just being together.

Then he was sitting on the sofa beside her. She leaned against him, feeling relaxed and a little sleepy.

'Time to go,' he whispered, his breath warm against her neck.

'Go? So soon?'

'Time to go to bed. For me to make love to you till . . . sunup, at least. I love you, Leigh West. And tonight, I'm gonna show you just how much . . .'

Mace left before six next morning; leaving Leigh in bed, drowsy, clinging, not wanting him to go.

'Gotta ride, Leigh. Things to do, places to go.'

He kissed her warm, open mouth. It tasted sweet as honey, making him want more.

He lingered over her, kissing her neck, caressing her shoulders. His hands slid down to her breasts, feeling her nipples tense and stiffen. Tracing swirls around them with his forefingers, he tweaked them slightly. She squirmed a little, sighed and curled into his arms.

Finally, he whispered, 'Call ya later, Leigh. 'Bye.'

Quietly, he let himself out of the house.

Not wanting to wake Deana.

Dipping into his jacket pocket, he hooked out a palmful of seeds. Flipping them into his mouth, he chewed them for a while.

His lips curved in a slow smile.

Thinking about Deana sneaking in at two-thirty a.m.

Still munching, his face broke out in a grin.

Suddenly, he didn't give a monkey's shit about waking Deana. He hoped he had. He quite liked the idea of her lying there, listening . . .

Hearing him leave her mother's bed.

Chapter Thirty-six

Leigh was leaving for the restaurant when the phone rang. It was Mattie.

'Hi, what's up?'

'I'm coming over, Leigh. Be there in five, six minutes?'

'Sure. See ya.'

What did Mattie want so early? I know she's supposed to be our personal bodyguard – but hasn't she *heard* that Nelson's dead?

From the tone of her voice, Mattie had sounded subdued. Upset, even. Leigh frowned. What on earth was wrong?

Was it anything to do with *her*?

Perhaps Mattie needed a shoulder to cry on.

Leigh didn't have to wait long to find out.

'Coffee?'

'Sure. As it comes. The blacker the better.'

Leigh set two mugs on the kitchen table. More informal here than in the living room, she decided. If Mattie had something on her mind, she'd probably prefer to discuss it in the intimacy of the kitchen.

Leigh poured coffee, passed Mattie hers and sat facing her over the table.

Leigh added sugar to her own coffee, while Mattie worked around to the real reason for her visit. For a while she stirred her coffee, concentrating on the swirling black liquid.

'Not keeping you, am I?' Mattie asked, glancing up.

'Not a bit of it. The gang's all there, back at the Bayview. Beavering away, I hope.' Leigh smiled at her.

Mattie said, 'Heard the news about Nelson. So, you identified him?'

Leigh sighed and nodded. 'Yeah. All of that. Not a pleasant experience, I might say.'

'Yeah. I seen bodies that've been in the water for a while. Good thing you even *recognized* Nelson. Fish tend to mess things up.'

Leigh shuddered. 'Don't, Mattie. It was bad enough as it was . . .'

'Mace told you about Nelson?'

'Yes, he did. He's been very supportive.'

'I'll bet.'

Leigh started at the cynicism in Mattie's tone.

'Meaning?'

'Meaning that Mace can be a *very* supportive person.'

Leigh didn't care for the way she said that.

'You got something on your mind? If you have, spit it out. I'm all ears.'

Mattie hesitated for a moment, then said, 'Lemme tell you a story, Leigh.'

'Go on.'

Mattie paused again, deciding where to begin.

'Five years ago, when I first came to Mill Valley PD, I was a raw, hurt young girl. Naive, if you like. From a li'l hick town near Lodgepole, sequoia country . . .

'I'd met up with some guy there who *did* things to gals. To get his wicked way.'

She huffed out a short, cynical laugh.

Then, with a meaningful look at Leigh, she said, 'Know what I'm sayin'? On the other hand, Leigh, maybe you wouldn't *wanna* know what I'm sayin'. Even if you *did*, I'm not about to tell ya what that guy got up to.

'This I *will* say. What happened back in that small hick town made me want to get outta there, smoke out all the pervs, the rapists – the *psychos* lurking in every goddamn corner of this big, beautiful country of ours . . . and give 'em hell. Or at least what the fuck they deserved – as far as the law allowed, that is.

The Lake

'I joined Mill Valley Police Department. Became a crack shot; did martial arts. One of the guys, they called me.

'Met Mace. Worked with him. He 'peared to be an okay guy, all right. Looked after me. Gave me back my confidence in human nature, I guess. Rounded me off.' Mattie's mouth curved in a mirthless grin. 'I was a pretty messed-up gal in those days . . .'

Leigh frowned. 'Mattie. I'm sorry. Really sorry. You must have been badly hurt . . . But what has this—'

'Got to do with Mace?'

'Right.'

'Well, I'll tell ya, Leigh. I got to know Mace pretty well, bein' his partner. He was my *shadow*. Christ. We didn't even have to *speak* to know what we were both thinking.' Mattie dropped her voice and looked away. 'Yeah. We were that close.'

Leigh sipped her coffee without even tasting it.

What *had* Mattie come to say?

Something about Mace?

If it was, she had a sinking feeling that she didn't want to hear it.

'I know you're seeing a lot of Mace. And I don't blame you. Or him. You're a wonderful lady, Leigh. Money. Nice home. Great restaurant. A daughter who's a credit to you . . .'

'Cut the bullshit, Mattie. Let's just get to where you're at.'

'I mean, Leigh, the guy back there in Yellow Bend ain't the only one who likes to hear a gal scream.'

Mattie left soon after delivering her parting shot, leaving Leigh to make sense of the conversation as best she could.

Mattie'd spilled the beans, all right, Leigh thought. Leaving me with *plenty* to think about. Jesus. Most of what she'd said was beginning to make a lot of sense.

Carefully, Leigh picked through Mattie's words; going over her sketchy innuendos. And she didn't mind admitting that it hurt like hell. For chrissake, Mattie couldn't mean Mace was a *psycho*. Could she?

Shuddering, Leigh dismissed the thought.

Sure. Mace had a macho streak.

Most men have, she told herself.

But he isn't a *sadist*, as Mattie had implied. Mace was kind, civilized and . . . normal.

Wasn't he?

Sure he was. Look how he brought me flowers, champagne. Was always around to protect us from Nelson.

But, she told herself, *I* was the one who encouraged him.

He didn't jump me.

I was the seducer; he, the seduced . . .

Leigh hesitated. She held her breath, last night's little drama fixed firmly in her mind.

Some head first, honey. Just to get things moving . . .

A cold shudder ran through her body.

A lot of guys like their head, she reasoned.

It's all part of the foreplay.

But she'd reacted in such a goddamn *crazy* way. Like a dumb kid crying 'rape'.

On the other hand, if what Mattie implied was true, that whole darn episode could be a taste of things to come . . .

Chapter Thirty-seven

'Hi, Mom. Thought I heard voices.'

'That's right, honey. Mattie dropped by. To see how we're doin'. Just checking.' Leigh gave Deana a bright smile. 'Want some coffee? It's still hot. Or will be, once I've perked it up a little.'

Leigh switched on the percolator. Still thinking about Mattie. What *was* it with her? She fancy Mace herself, or something?

Way she went on, she all but hated him.

I've heard there's a fine line between love and hate.

Could be she's just plain jealous . . .

'Hey, Mom. The coffee's perked. Pour mine while I get dressed, will you?'

'What did your last one die of, young lady?'

'The usual. Lack of breath, I guess.' Deana left the room, smiling. Mom was the best. Always so cool and nice about everything.

She felt a stab of guilt.

She didn't *like* having secrets from Mom. It felt like betraying a friend.

Slipping into blue jeans and yellow T-shirt, Deana decided that the time was ripe to introduce Mom to Warren.

She'd like him. He was so sensible and grown-up.

And he had his own business.

That ought to impress her.

Deana returned to the kitchen, her ponytail swinging jauntily. Mom was at the sink, rinsing out the two used coffee mugs. Deana picked up her fresh one from the table.

Wisps of aromatic steam met her nostrils.

She felt better already.

I gotta tell Mom about Warren.

How shall I play it?

Dummy. Why not tell it like it is?

Just go for it, Deana.

'Mom.'

'Yes, dear?'

'There's someone I'd like you to meet. Guy called Warren Hastings. Lives on Del Mar with his sister. And his dog Saber.'

Leigh turned to face Deana.

Deana had met someone so soon?

'And how did you meet this . . . Warren, honey?'

Deana grimaced slightly. The next bit wasn't gonna be *quite* so simple.

'He owns a bookstore, Mom. In San Anselmo.'

Yeah. San Anselmo. Where Allan and I were supposed to have gone to the movies that night.

'I ordered a book by phone one day . . .'

She cringed.

More lies. My God. I can't believe I'm doing this. What am I – the original daughter from hell?

'But how romantic, honey. You should have told me. And is he *nice*, this Warren?'

'Yes, he's real nice, Mom. You'd like him.'

'So, when do I get to meet . . . Warren?'

'I'll give him a call today. We can arrange something.'

'Dinner would be fine. Just let me know. I'll get something sent over from the restaurant.'

Leigh's mind slid back to the night when Deana had brought Allan to dinner. When he'd met Mom and Dad – was it only a fortnight ago?

My God.

The Lake

What can *happen* in two weeks!

Your world turned upside down; a boy dead; your daughter devastated by it all.

Although she *appears* to be getting over it . . .

And Nelson . . . Thank *God*, Mom and Dad hadn't been around to see it all happen.

She hated herself for even thinking this way, but it was a blessing that Mom and Dad had had to make that emergency dash to Colorado. And if it didn't seem so *awful* on Aunt Abby, she hoped that Mom and Dad would stay there a while longer . . .

Deana smiled at Leigh.

'Good thing Gran and Pops are in Boulder. They would've made things ten times worse. Pops shouting, Gran crying and everything . . .'

Leigh nodded. 'Got to agree, honey. They been here, Mom and Dad could've made things a whole lot worse!'

'You gonna tell them about Allan and Nelson and everything?'

'Uh-huh. But not yet awhile, honey. Just let's see how things go.'

Chapter Thirty-eight

It was dark on Del Mar tonight. Really dark.
A gentle wind disturbed the trees.
Scudding clouds hid the moon and stars from view.
Apart from the rustling leaves it was quiet, too.
Deathly quiet.
Only Deana's breath sounded harsh and loud as she hurried toward Warren's house.
She hadn't called him as she'd told Mom she would. Instead, she'd decided to slip out again. Meet up with Warren as he walked Saber.
I'm the midnight runner again.
A thrill of excitement brought goose bumps to her skin. The hair on the back of her neck rose and prickled.
It was scary out here on the street.
In the dead of night.
It might be scary but the thrill of running alone through the night was worth every second.
Anyway, with Nelson gone, there wasn't too much to be scared of.
Except Mommy Dearest and her dog.
Maybe a rapist or two.
And the black car.
Don't forget the black car . . .
But she was a fast runner.
She could hide in shadows, dart down alleyways, or tackle anyone who looked like they were going to attack her.

The Lake

Mom still didn't know about her midnight runs.

Warren did, though.

And Mace.

Fuck Mace.

Somehow, though, she didn't think that he'd inform on her.

He'd keep it all to himself.

It was their little secret.

She shuddered.

She *hated* keeping things from Mom.

And she *loathed* the idea of being in league with Mace. The mere thought of it made her flesh crawl.

Anyway, she had too many midnight runs under her belt to start explaining things to Mom now.

Besides, I get a real kick out of it . . .

Could be I'm *addicted* to midnight running.

Can a person become addicted to running at night?

I guess so . . .

Nearly there now. I can see the two redwoods; their branches reaching out onto the street.

Where's Warren?

Not here yet.

Deana felt a twinge of disappointment. It had been *so* romantic, thinking they'd meet up again this way.

And he'd be really surprised, and pleased, that she'd shown up again.

Tonight, when she saw him, she intended to invite him to dinner. She felt a squirm of excitement at the prospect of him coming to her home. Again.

This time, she wanted to show off a little.

'Cause Mom really knows how to throw a dinner party.

She'd look elegant, chatting to Warren. Charming him, but not *too* much, with her intelligent conversation.

She knows about books, too . . .

Deana ran on, her mind turning to her wardrobe. Mentally going through all her clothes; deciding what she'd wear, the night of the party.

A really big decision.

Maybe her new black dress with the low square neck? She knew it showed off her breasts and her small waist to perfection.

Well, maybe not *that*, not yet. Don't want to scare him off.

Black's way too formal, anyway. Because we'll go somewhere *after* the meal.

Don't bank on it, Deana.

Mom'd be suspicious. A new boyfriend *and* bunking off together already.

Like I did with Allan. The night Gran and Pops came to dinner . . .

Allan.

Deana West, you are a *shit*.

Allan dead only ten, eleven days and you're out on some midnight tryst? Meeting up with a guy you've seen only three times before . . . And don't forget. He already came to the house, the other day . . .

Mom doesn't know about that. She'd be real upset to know that I've had Warren over and not told her about it. Not that anything *happened*. Didn't get to discuss Mace, like I'd planned. We just talked about books and everything. Warren told me about his store, and promised to get me a copy of *Get Shorty* by Elmore Leonard.

And now you're drooling on about going out with him *after* the wonderful dinner Mom is gonna put on – 'specially for the benefit of her darling daughter.

The darling daughter who *lies* through her teeth.

What a *bitch* I am . . . Soon as I introduce Warren to Mom, there'll be no more lies. Promise.

Chapter Thirty-nine

Christ, it's even darker up here.

Deana put a spurt on.

The wind had gotten worse. It shook the trees, whipping the leaves around in a frenzy.

Deana shivered but kept up her pace.

It was a night when almost *anything* could happen.

She ran on, her mind full of Warren. Picturing his face when she invited him to dinner. Hoping he'd say yes – after all, he *did* say he'd like a date.

Dinner or the movies, he'd said.

Remember?

How could I forget!!

What a hoot, she'd thought at the time.

But admit it, Deana. You were secretly thrilled at the idea of going out with Warren.

Sure. He *is* kinda sexy, and a date could be a lotta fun. Then Mom suggested dinner . . .

So here she was, running up Del Mar.

Risking God knows what . . .

Her heart skipped a beat. She began thinking of the funeral car and how spooky it'd looked, crawling along outside Warren's house, its windows all black and shiny . . .

She gave a grim smile.

Probably just some jerk, cruising around . . .

She ran on.

Then, mixed in with the keening wind, she caught a faint whimper. Like a small animal was lost or something.

A hand clawed at her ankle.

Her mouth went dry.

She gasped.

Her knees sagged, and she fell – onto a lumpy kind of hump.

The hand slid away.

'Who . . .? What the *hell* . . .?'

Shit! She'd landed on a sack of household garbage.

'Goddamn stupid thing to do; put your garbage out on the sidewalk,' she muttered.

'Git offa me . . .'

Deana started at the weak, whiny voice.

She scrambled to her feet.

'My *God*! . . . Oh, it's you!'

Mommy Dearest.

Lying in a heap on the sidewalk.

Clutching Harry, wrapped in a blanket.

The blanket fell open and Harry rolled out, his legs in the air. His eyes jerked around. His mouth hung open, panting, his small red tongue lolling against needle-fine teeth.

Harry was in a bad way.

'Help us, please!' Mommy Dearest pleaded. 'Had one a' my derned attacks agin.'

The hag shook her head, her wispy hair floating in the wind. She looked a little confused.

'Never shoulda come out t'night,' she muttered.

'Here, let me help,' Deana told her. 'Lean on my arm, I'll take you home. Where d'you live?'

'Back there a ways, dear.' The hag gestured behind her, pointing somewhere up the steep hill.

'Well, hold on to me.' Deana helped Mommy Dearest to her feet. 'How about Harry? He looks sick, too. Want me to hold him as well?'

'Don't y'let him fall now, will ya?'

'Course not.'

The Lake

The hag clung to Deana's arm. Deana held Harry tight, rolled in his blanket. Leaning into the wind, they made it up the hill a little way. The hag drew to a halt outside a fancy iron double gate.

Deana stared through the railings.

The driveway was pitch dark.

A cold shiver ran down her spine.

Could be *anything* down there . . .

Mommy Dearest lifted the latch, the gate creaked open and Deana helped her inside. The hag kicked the gate shut with a resounding clash.

Deana did a double take.

That sure was some kick! Mommy Dearest musta perked up a little.

Still clutching Deana's arm, the hag limped her way down the drive. Deana held on to Harry. He was jerking around in his blanket, making loud, snuffling noises.

Her heart hammered. Blood pounded in her ears.

Hope to God he doesn't die on me, 'cause I really gotta go – don't wanta miss Warren . . .

They halted outside a huge front door. Dry straggly growth matted around the two columns at either side.

'Jeez,' Deana breathed. 'What a *place*!'

The house was tall, dark and deathly quiet. It looked like something out of a horror movie. She pictured Lurch from *The Munsters* opening up the door . . . and Gomez hovering in the spooky hallway, grinning around his cigar, rubbing his hands together . . .

She squinted at a faded wood sign above the door.

She could just make out the words: 'The Flora Dawes Rest Home for Distressed Gentlefolk.'

Deana grimaced.

This is so spooky.

Time I was gone.

Her heart beat faster.

Gotta catch up with Warren, before it's too late.

Desperately, she wished that he and Saber were with her now.

At her side, Mommy Dearest let out a gasp. She was clutching her chest.

Deana's heart sank.

'Maybe I should just see you inside,' she said quickly. 'Then hurry on home. Promised Mom I'd be back by ten-thirty . . .'

With a loud groan, the door swung open. Mommy's hand gripped Deana's arm. She dragged her forward into the shadowy hallway.

Gray light sliced the gloom. Darkness fell as the door clanged shut. The noise echoed eerily through the house and Deana's heart stood still. Panic set in. A dank, musty smell met her nostrils. She'd smelt something like it in a thrift store in Sausalito – a mix of old clothes, cooking, bodies, dusty books and other junk . . .

As she became accustomed to the gloom, Deana saw dozens of bright eyes staring at her. It seemed like an army of dwarfs had gathered in the lobby to greet them. The dwarfs were curious. Impatient, craning their necks to get a better view.

Jesus H. Christ!

She held on to Harry and stared closer.

These aren't dwarfs . . . they're little old women!

Like one of the living dead, a wizened hag stepped forward. She reached out a scrawny blue-veined hand . . .

Deana reeled back. Into the arms of Mommy Dearest.

No sign of 'one of her derned attacks' now . . .

Like bands of steel, Mommy's arms grabbed Deana.

Harry yelped, leapt out of his blanket and scooted into the shadows.

Struggling, panicking, Deana twisted around, trying to free herself. The hag held on tight.

'No, you don't!' Her voice was high and strong.

It had an insane ring to it.

The hairs on the back of Deana's neck crawled.

Goose bumps rose on her body.

My God, the woman's a fucking lunatic. She's raving mad!

Christ! How did I get into all this? I shoulda left her to die out there . . . Hell, I do one good turn and look where it gets me!

A horrible thought crossed her mind.

Nobody knows I'm here.

I'm trapped, with all these . . . loonies!

The Lake

'Say something, girl!' a witch with an eye patch and long white hair demanded. Deana backed away.

Mommy Dearest shoved her forward.

'Best I could do,' she told the hags. 'Not too many young 'uns out on Del Mar t'night!'

'What d'ya think of Mr President?' called out a shaky voice from the back. 'Ya reckon he's on to them delinquents throwing bombs inta classrooms yet?'

A raucous voice shouted: 'Whassyername, honey?'

'Aw, give it a rest, Clarabel,' somebody said. 'Can't ya see the kid's scared? Reckon we oughta bring her inter the back, give her a cuppa coffee 'n' a slice a' pie . . .'

A low mumbling filled the hallway. Punctuated by hissy, whispering sounds. A shriek of laughter rang out.

The hags looked at Deana, waiting for her to speak. They were like gaunt gray vultures. Restless. Needy. Hungry, like they hadn't seen young flesh in a long time.

Deana froze at the thought.

They came for me in a pack – I guess they could tear me to pieces.
Oh my God!

Her eyes narrowed. She gritted her teeth.

Just let them try!

The hags shifted forward.

The white-haired one taunted her.

'Don't ya like it here, dearie? Ain't fixin' to leave us, are ya?'

Deana saw red. She screamed, 'Bank on it, you fuckin' old witch. I'm outta here . . .'

She whirled around, but Mommy Dearest grabbed her arm. 'Mind ya manners, young 'un,' she snarled, 'Pay more respect to ya elders!'

Deana shook herself free. She glared at the hag.

What's the bitch got against me? I did my Girl Scout thing. Helped her when she was in trouble.

I coulda left her there to die.

Wish I had now . . .

Boy, does this place suck . . .

If the old sow's brought me here to entertain her gang of trolls she's gonna be mighty disappointed. Show's over, folks. I'm outta here before I get eaten alive!

A scrawny hag in a long, cotton frock limped forward. Stretching out a knobbly finger, she touched Deana's arm. 'Don't go, dearie,' she said. 'Talk to us. We won't hurt ya none. Promise. We jest wanna see some young blood, is all. Haven't set eyes on a youngster like you in a long, long time . . . Tell me – seen any good movies lately?'

The old woman's eyes held a pleading look. She smiled, her face creasing into a network of wrinkles.

Deana gasped.

My God, I gotta get outta here!

She turned, made for the door, but with vicelike fingers Mommy grabbed her again.

She was *incredibly* strong.

A hag at the back of the crowd elbowed her way to the front. She stroked Deana's free arm, then plucked at her sweatshirt sleeve.

'Nice top you got there, young 'un. Hey, Martha. Come an' take a peek at this sweater. Sure ain't Nieman Marcus but it's better'n the one you're wearin'!'

Martha toddled over, her head shaking with every step. 'Why, yes,' she said in a trembly voice. 'You're right there, Betty-Lou. Think I'll have me this one. Jest my color, too.'

Betty-Lou shrieked with laughter. 'Black? You aimin' to wear it to ya funeral, Martha?'

Deana gasped. They'd take my *sweater*?

The *bitches*!

And there'd been a moment back there when I felt *sorry* for them!

Betty-Lou snatched at her sleeve.

She tore it down.

Exposing Deana's bare shoulder.

Mommy Dearest hung on to her other arm.

There were whistles. Hoots of laughter. Hands tugged at the flapping black cloth. Deana's left breast suddenly burst free.

She panicked, tearing herself away from Mommy's iron grip. 'Lemme GO!' she yelled. 'HELP!!!'

The Lake

'Whassamatter, dearie? Don't ya *like* it here?'

The hags hadn't enjoyed themselves so much in ages. Betty-Lou couldn't stop cackling.

'Remember that time in Vegas, Martha? The night the lights went out at The Sands . . .'

Tearing herself free, kicking, shoving, knocking Mommy out of the way, Deana charged for the door.

With a triumphant yelp, she reached it, flung it open and raced out into the night.

'Y'ain't bein' very friendly,' Mommy Dearest croaked after her. 'Gals here only want a li'l ol' chat. They get lonesome sometimes . . .'

'Hey. You like Tyrone Power?' yelled the raucous one. Her voice got carried away on the wind but Deana still caught the words. 'He's my favorite, y'know. Did ya see *The Mark of Zorro*? Well, did ya?'

'Dear *God*,' Deana muttered as she ran. 'What a *madhouse*. They plan to eat me alive or talk me to death – they'll have to catch me first!'

Way behind, she heard the inmates pile out of the house. They sounded bewildered. Confused. Gabbling to each other in high, tetchy voices. Going quiet as they hit the cool night air . . .

Deana didn't stop till she was outside the gates. Only then did she draw to a halt, panting hard, trying to steady her breath.

Wow. I'm outta there.

Goddamn bitch!

Luring me in . . .

She grimaced.

Resident fuckin' entertainer at the Zimmer City Rest Home?

Oh yeah?

Eat shit and die, you crazy old bitch!

Deana started to run downhill.

Toward Warren's house.

Chapter Forty

A low growl brought her skidding to a halt.

Her heart lurched.

Saber.

And Warren, holding Saber's lead; being yanked along as the dog rushed forward to greet her.

'Why, if it's not the midnight runner! Good to see you, Deana.'

'Great to see you, too, Warren. And Saber – how ya doin', big boy?' She smoothed Saber's forehead. He got excited, danced back, then bounded forward, nudging his wet nose into her hand.

'Sure looks like he's glad to see you again.'

'Yeah.'

Warren's gaze was curious.

He looked at her torn sweater, at the left side of her bra gleaming white in the lamplight.

He took off his fraternity warm-up and draped it around her shoulders.

'What *happened* to you back there?'

Deana gave a cracked sort of laugh. '*Happened?* Tell you what happened, Warren. Nearly finished up as entertainer of the year, that's what happened.'

He frowned.

Laughing shakily, she held on to his arm.

'Remind me to tell you about it sometime.'

He guided her to his place, his arm around her waist. She liked the

The Lake

way it felt. His arms around her. His jacket around her. Making her feel warm and safe.

Most of all, *safe*.

Saber trotted by Warren's side, eyes eager and bright, his ears held high.

Guess he *is* glad to see me, Deana thought. Could have done with him when I visited the old folks' home. He'd have come in real handy . . .

'Anyway, Warren,' she said, quietly, pushing the vision of distressed gentlefolk out of her mind. 'Are you *really* glad to see me?'

He stared at her quizzically, a broad smile spreading across his features. 'Yes,' he said simply. 'I'm very glad to see you again.'

'Came to ask if you'd like to have dinner with Mom and me sometime.' Adding, 'Mom would really like to meet you.'

'Think I'd pass the grade?'

'What's up, Warren? Running scared? You *did* say you'd like to see me again. And I said I might be out one night and that we could arrange something?'

He scratched his head. 'Yep. I believe I do recall something along those lines . . .'

'Warren – are you coming to dinner at my house, or what?'

'It'll be my pleasure, Deana. But why not use the phone? Would've been easier than running up here in the dark . . . getting . . .'

Mauled by Mommy Dearest's buncha geriatric weirdos? You're not kidding . . .

''Cause I like running. Especially at night. Developed quite a taste for it, as it happens.'

'Does your mom know you're out?'

'Get to the point, why don't you? Matter of fact she doesn't. It's just that it seems so *exciting* for us to meet in secret like this.'

'Mmmm,' he said, his eyes twinkling. 'Guess I feel a hot chocolate coming on. How 'bout you?'

'You bet.'

Chapter Forty-one

Sitting in Warren's kitchen, nursing a mug of his yummy chocolate drink, Deana relaxed. It felt good to be here in Warren's home – especially in his friendly, slightly untidy kitchen.

Saber retired to his den under the sink. He lay there, checking out Deana's movements. Then, snuffling into his paws for a while, he closed his eyes.

But his ears stayed alert.

Like sentinels on guard.

Good old Saber. Some dog, that. Deana smiled.

Then frowned slightly.

If only I knew what to tell Warren.

How *much* to tell him.

Or how *little*.

And not only about tonight, either.

She thought about Mace.

Warren deserves to be put in the picture.

What picture?

Dammit. There's so *much* to say . . .

Oh God. If only things weren't so *complicated*.

'Anybody home?' Warren watched her, his eyebrows raised.

'Sure. Can you keep a secret?'

'Try me.'

'Well, you're right, Warren. Mom doesn't know I'm out tonight. She doesn't know about the other nights, either. Jesus. She'd go hairless if she *did* know.'

It was a start, anyway . . .

The Lake

'I see. Go on.'

'Something happened to us. To Mom and me. Two weeks ago. I can't explain it yet. But, trust me, it's been a horrible experience. People died. Violently. It's been bad, Warren.'

He hugged his chocolate, stared into its creamy depths. Giving her time to choose her words.

'Mom's been concerned for my safety – and I for hers, come to that. We've both been in danger.' Deana stopped, then carried on, more cheerfully this time. 'But in the end it turned out okay. Thing is, I don't want Mom worried about me going out at night. She's been through such a lot.

'I told her I met you when I phoned your store for a book.'

Warren looked up, sharply.

Deana smiled.

'So, Warren, I'd be really grateful if you'd keep our . . . night-time assignations to yourself. Oh, also your visit to the house.'

'I see. Had an idea there was more. I have a nose for mysteries.' He tapped the side of his nose with a forefinger. '*Murder She Wrote* was a favorite show of mine.

'Okay,' he continued, choosing his words carefully. 'I'll go along with that. But let me tell you here and now, I don't like unsolved mysteries. And I don't go for subterfuge, either. Especially where mother and daughter are concerned. So, least said, soonest mended, huh? Give you time to sort things out with Mom.'

Deana nodded. For a moment there, she'd been about to confide in him.

Give him the *works*.

Tell him her feelings about Mace.

But now was *not* the time to mention Mace.

Later. Maybe.

Pity.

She'd have dearly liked to discuss Mace with Warren.

But maybe later. *Much later*.

Get too heavy and Warren might cry off.

'So.' Warren smiled at her encouragingly. 'I'm invited to dinner, am I?'

'Sure are.'

'Best bib and tucker?'

'Mmmm . . . Not necessarily. Smart casual, I think. Mom's kinda casual herself.'

'Ah.'

'So how about evening after tomorrow? You doing anything that night?'

'Er . . . let me see.' Warren took his time. Humming a little. Studying the ceiling, as if checking out the evening after tomorrow. He looked at his wristwatch. It showed 00.14.

'Let's get this straight. It's already tomorrow, so does that make our date tomorrow evening or the one after that?'

They burst out laughing. Deana felt relieved. She'd been feeling quite tense, talking about the stuff that she and Mom had gone through these last few days.

She was glad to relax a little.

'Tell you what, Deana. Ask your mom which night is okay, and give me a call – at the store or at home. Phone's on answer when we're out at work.'

'I'll do that.' She felt good and warm inside. Things were so *easy* with Warren.

'Anything else I should know? Subjects to avoid – current political situation, weather in Florida, stuff like that?' He threw her a warm smile. Then, turning serious, he added, 'Given that you've both gone through a sensitive time just lately.'

His gaze held hers. It was as if he were telling her not to worry. Things'd turn out okay. That he'd be there for her.

'Nope. Just talk books and sport, like swimming and tennis – Mom loves those. And movies; seventies stuff. Oh, and food. Compliment her on the food.'

'Your mom likes to cook?'

'Sort of. She owns the Bayview restaurant in Tiburon.'

Chapter Forty-two

Sheena studied the redwoods out back.

Not really seeing them, because her mind was elsewhere. She'd gone way back; saw her ten-year-old self in class. Big for her age, awkward, alone. Writing wasn't her strong point, but here she was, struggling with an essay on the life of a fuckin' sperm whale. She looked at her spidery joined-up writing, all blotchy with ink.

Then, behind her, the fuckin' teacher said in that cold, icy voice of hers, 'Sheena Hastings. I do declare, the standard of your work gets worse. See me after class!'

All eyes turned toward her. Nadine Hassler, sitting in the row behind, sniggered. Titters rose in waves from the rest of the class.

Her head jerked back.

Nadine. Tugging at Sheena's long dark braids.

She remembered how her eyes had watered up, how *ashamed* she'd felt . . . She'd never been much good at writing.

Christ. She'd *hated* her childhood. And school most of all. Who fuckin' said schooldays were the happiest days of your life?

Whatever goddamn motherfucker it was, they wanted to come up with one more thing like that and then go blow their fuckin' brains out.

But all of that was a long time ago. Those lousy schooldays; her lousy *childhood*, period. Only thing kept her going was beating the hell outta them kids on the sports field. Yeah. She was the greatest at sport, in those days.

THE BEST.

Was then, is now.

Pumping iron in the gym: judo, karate, kick boxing, you name it. She'd done it all – and better than most men, too. She knew all about the pain barrier. Going through it, stretching her muscles to the max. Almost passing out. She'd been there. Done that.

And when she figured her body could take no more – there were plenty of other ways to feel pain . . .

Oh yeah, *other ways*.

Sheena's lips curved in a triumphant smile.

In the early days, only one other person understood her. *Really* knew what made her tick.

Kat Tod, her partner.

Kat knew about pain; she'd had a cartload of it herself. Bad childhood. Bad marriage at sixteen years of age.

All of them *painful* experiences.

Kat'd gotten herself killed last October. Memory of it still hurt Sheena. It'd been a bad business. S&M, the cops called it. Okay. That's what *they* called it. But she knew that Kat had been following her own path of redemption.

Redemption?

Self-destruction, more like.

Yeah.

Ended up a mess a' bloody ribbons in some shitty back alley . . .

Jesus. What a gal. She'd gotten mixed up with a real bad crowd. Rented herself out. An' paid for it in full, that one last time . . .

Sheena turned away from the window. Contemplating her 'insight'. Her gift for premonition, whatever. She hated it, yet loved it, all at the same time.

It was *part* of her.

What she *was*.

Love it or loathe it, that gift was an important part of Sheena Hastings. Life as a kid hadn't been a whole lotta fun, but she sure knew that her special talent – and her sporting prowess – set her way above the rest.

The Lake

In the bad times, she held on to this.

Mom and Dad had tut-tutted her claims that she 'knew about things before they happened'. They'd chastised her. Called in the local priest. Encouraged her interest in sport.

Finally, there'd been the psychiatrist.

He'd prescribed Valium. Why, for God's sake? She was happy the way she was. Only person who understood that was Warren. They trained together. They talked together. She was a few years older, but she hung around with him most of the time.

Warren *understood* her. Like now. He *knew* she was happy at Pacey's Place. Among her own kind. Problem people. Misfits. Weirdos. They got together, understood each other. No questions asked.

Now there was this 'midnight runner'. Who in hell was she? Whoever, whatever she turned out to be, she was involved with Warren.

Without knowing why but trusting her instincts, Sheena felt a squirm of apprehension.

Chapter Forty-three

It was Thursday evening. Night of the get-together with Mom and Warren.

Mom wasn't home yet.

Warren wasn't due for a couple of hours.

In her bedroom, Deana stripped to her bra and panties.

'Hope everything works out okay,' she murmured to herself. 'Shouldn't be a problem. Two nice people. Civilized guys who know the score. They'll get along fine.'

She peered into the dresser mirror. Inspecting herself. Practicing how she'd look. A dry run for later.

She went over to her bed. Laid out were two outfits; her final *final* selection. A maroon cotton pantsuit – a blue jersey crossover blouse and a short denim skirt.

Smart casual, she'd told Warren.

No way was the black dress an option. Far too formal for a muggy evening.

It's gotta be the crossover blouse and the denim skirt, she decided. The blouse would be great, if—

If what?

If Warren wanted a closer inspection?

Deana hugged herself.

I know he likes me.

She could tell by the way his eyes swept over her in an approving but not suggestive way. Maybe he'd guessed that she wasn't

The Lake

interested in sex at the moment. Understood it was too soon . . .

Her relationship with Warren would grow gradually and at her own pace, she decided.

She swung around. Looked into her dresser mirror again, posing, admiring her body. She eased up her breasts till the tops bulged out from her bra. She posed, hand on hip, drawing in her midriff so that her waist looked really small and neat.

Her flimsy panties stretched across her hipbones. She sure was glad she'd kept up with those abdominal workouts. They'd been a bore, but they made one helluva difference to her figure.

'Not bad!' she told the mirror. 'Warren's eyes are gonna stand out on stalks when he sees me tonight . . .'

Thick black hair tumbled around her shoulders.

Full, firm breasts brimmed out of their bra cups. Her nipples *almost* showing . . .

What would Warren think if he saw me now?

Deana imagined his eyes watching her, himself longing to touch her, take her in his arms – but then, *not* wanting to; not after the bad experiences she'd hinted at.

What if Warren wanted to . . . wanted to see *more* of me? Anything's possible – especially if I kinda give him the go-ahead. Maybe I should go over myself with the LadyShave. Just in case.

She ogled her reflection in the mirror.

Then teased each breast out of its bra cup, pushing them up, just a little more, till she could see the dark pink areolae of her nipples.

That's better!

She literally flowed out of her underwear now.

Almost *too* much . . .

Tossing a seductive smile at her reflection, she slowly stroked her breasts, her waist, her hips. She pushed her panties down ever so slightly, revealing her taut flat belly – and a few dark curly wisps of pubic hair.

Deana groaned, hating the wiry growth peeking out of her panties.

She paused.

What was that?

A movement. A step, disturbing the quiet beyond the open door of her room . . .

Is anyone there?
Can't be Mom . . .
She's still at the restaurant.
I'm alone in the house.
Warren?
Nah. He hasn't got a key.
And Nelson's dead.
Isn't he?
Then who else . . .?
Catching a ragged breath, her heart leapt into her throat.
She frowned. Peered into the mirror.
A familiar figure filled the doorway.
It moved toward her.
Slowly.
Mace!
His eyes dark. Intense.
Staring at her.
His mouth hung slack, open a little. She caught a glimpse of white, even teeth.
Horrified, Deana whirled around. Her arms flew up, crushing her breasts.
Mace.
How did he get *in*?
He stood in front of her.
His hands reaching out . . .

Chapter Forty-four

'Stay away from me, you creep!'

Terrified, Deana backed away.

MACE!

The bastard – what's he doing here?

Mace's arms dropped to his sides. His shoulders hunched slightly. 'Deana. Ssshh,' he whispered. 'I'm sorry . . . Didn't mean to scare you . . .'

'Oh, no? What d'you take me for – a *moron* or something? What're ya doing in my room? In my *house*, come to that?'

'Take it easy, will ya? I said I'm sorry. What more—' His eyes looked dark, wild.

'What *more* do I want? I'll tell ya what more. I want you *outta* my room and outta my LIFE. Outta *my* life and Mom's, too.'

Deana snatched up her robe, struggled into it, wrapped it around her body, holding it tight closed.

'You're a fuckin' creep. You know that?'

Mace backed away, hands lifted, palms up.

He looked dazed. But his eyes still looked wild.

And his mouth still gaped open like he was in a trance. His brow and upper lip were shiny with sweat.

God, he looks so weird. What's up with him?

Seems like he's having a tough time with his words, too. He was stumbling around, trying to find the right ones.

Not much like the Mace she'd known up to now.

Where'd his control gone? One thing about Mace. He was always so *in control*. Of himself and situations.

It was weird, the way he was now.

'Er . . . look, Deana,' he said, thickly. 'I'm going. Right? I wasn't here, right? No . . . no need to tell Leigh . . . I'll tell her myself. Later . . .'

'You *bastard*. You come in here spying on me, and now you tell me to keep my mouth *shut*?'

'About the size of it, Deana. Keep your mouth shut – and so will I.'

Suddenly he was getting more lucid by the minute.

The old Mace.

The one she *hated* so much.

Deana held her breath. Tried to calm down. Wouldn't do to get him riled up. Way he'd looked a few moments ago, he might just *turn* on her . . .

But she had to know exactly what he meant.

'Whaddya mean – and so will you?'

'We both have our little secrets, honey. Don't we? Like you sneaking back into the house around two-thirty a.m. You tell your Mom about that, did ya? Or your visits to that house with the two redwoods in front?'

She picked up her hairbrush from the dresser, and Mace backed off.

'Okay. Okay. I'm going. Sorry for coming on to you like that. It's just . . .'

He faltered. Looking bewildered again.

'It's just *what*?' prompted Deana.

Don't think I'm gonna be able to handle him like this. God, Mom, where are you, for chrissake?

This was a different Mace, all right.

An *iffy* Mace.

'Nothin'. Nothin' at all,' he muttered.

His voice was low. She could scarcely hear it. Like he was talking to himself.

He turned and made for the door.

The Lake

Then stopped dead.

They'd both heard the same thing. The muffled sound of an engine; a car pulling up outside.

The sound of a door slamming shut.

Mom.

Thank *God*.

Mace turned. Put a finger to his lips.

As he looked across at her, he was back to normal. All business. Fierce. Intense. In control.

The old Mace.

'Ssshh. I'm warning you, Deana.'

The finger sliced across his throat.

Deana held still.

She watched him go.

What if Mom found her like this, half-dressed – with Mace hurrying down the hallway? She's gonna think something fishy's going on.

Shit. This had to happen tonight, of all nights!

The night Warren was coming to dinner.

The night when she'd *prayed* everything'd go according to plan.

What the fuck was up with Mace, anyway?

He hadn't *looked* as if he were about to rape her.

He'd just *stared* in that awful *creepy* sort of way.

Okay. He knew about my sneaking in at two-thirty. But how did he know I'd visited a house with two redwoods in front?

Did he know about Warren?

The thought that he might made shivers run up and down Deana's spine.

How much does the bastard *really* know?

She heard voices.

Mom saying, 'Hello, Mace. Didn't expect to see you today . . .'

'Courtesy call, Leigh. See how you both are, an' all.'

'My, this is a real treat. So soon after . . .' Mom's voice softened into a murmur.

Silence. More murmurs . . .

Kissing.

How *could* she?

But of course she doesn't know yet.

About Mace's surprise visit to her darling daughter.

And I can't *tell* you about it, Mom.

Can't *warn* you about Mace.

Christ, Mom. He's *real* bad news, and I can't tell you. *Because he's blackmailing me!*

Deana felt like throwing up. Mace could sneak in, spy on her, scare the shit outta her, and then cosy up to Mom like he meant it.

Christ, what a *crud*!

Deana was angry. And scared. She'd seen a whole different Mace back there. And it was not a pretty sight.

It sure was *spooky*, the way he'd *gaped* at her.

Not exactly like he wanted to rape her, either.

More like he'd never seen a woman half-naked before.

Which is a load of bullshit.

She knew that.

Mace must've had *scores* of women.

Guys like him take women, use 'em and throw 'em away . . .

God. *Mom!*

Coming this way.

Deana straightened her robe, flung her hair over her shoulder, and busied herself putting the pantsuit back in the wardrobe.

'Hi there, honey!'

Mom put her head around the door.

'Hi yourself, Mom. Just deciding what to wear tonight.'

'Yeah, I bet. Take you all afternoon?'

'Something like that.'

'Good of Mace to call around, although he *did* know I was working all day. Had a lot of catching up to do: ordering, consulting with Carlo . . . All of that. Carlo's doing a good job. Not like Nelson, of course, but— You okay, honey?'

'Sure, Mom. Just want to make a good impression tonight, is all. What d'ya think about my *final* choice?'

She held up the soft jersey top and denim skirt.

'You look great in all your things, dear. I'm sure Warren will think

The Lake

so, too.' Leigh looked at her wristwatch. 'Must fly, darling. I'll leave you to it . . . Must go have a shower; smarten *myself* up a little, too.'

Leigh stepped into the hallway.

As ever, Deana thought, watching her go, Mom looks wonderful.

She paused. Waiting for Mom to say something about Mace.

Like, how'd he get in?

Or did *you* let him in?

Dressed, or should we say *un*dressed, like that?

Or maybe Mace has his own key?

Mom wouldn't have given him a house key so soon in their relationship.

Would she?

Mom and Mace had been an item for just over a week . . . That's all. She *wouldn't* give him his own key.

But she *is* pretty well struck on him.

Mom poked her head back around the door.

'Mace been here long?'

Here it comes.

Darling daughter does the dirty on Mom.

Again.

'Five, ten minutes is all.'

'Good thing you were around to let him in.'

'Yeah.'

Bullseye. The sixty-four-thousand-dollar question answered in one go.

Mace hasn't got a key.

Not yet.

'If I'm in the shower when Tony calls with the food and wine, will you see to him, darling?'

'Sure, Mom. Leave it with me. Mace gone?'

'Duty calls, he said. Asked him to join us, but he said he'd gotta ride.'

Gotta ride!

Huh. I'll bet.

Deana frowned.

Just what was Mace up to? He'd sure started to act strange. Not his usual self.

Showing a side that she and Mom hadn't seen yet.

Don't *want* to see it anymore, either.

Obviously Mom thinks he's okay.

And she wouldn't tolerate a *weirdo*.

Would she?

She'd gone along with Nelson. And *he*'d been a weirdo.

But his meals were something else. That's what he was there for – to cook good meals. Mom couldn't *really* complain about him.

Look what happened when she did . . .

What would have happened if she hadn't?

Christ! This is leading nowhere fast.

Gotta get ready.

At this rate Warren'll be here before I'm dressed.

She listened to Mom splashing in the shower.

Humming to herself.

Happy.

Not knowing how spooky Mace could be.

What'd happen if I told her about him sneaking up on me? How do you *tell* your mom that her boyfriend's a peeping Tom? That he gets off staring at your half-naked daughter?

Come to think about it: how the hell *did* he sneak up on me?

Mom hadn't given him a key.

So how'd he do it?

Get in through the window?

What window? All their windows were intruder-proof. They opened only so far. And no farther.

He could have stolen a key.

The spare one that Mom left under the magnolia bush by the front stoop?

Maybe he was simply being what he was. *A good cop.*

He'd made an impression of the key under the bush and had another one made, Deana murmured to herself.

Intruders do that all the time.

She'd read about how they did it.

Lesson One. Don't leave your house key under the magnolia bush.

Wonderful.

The Lake

Mace going around with a key to *our* house!
Deana's mouth went dry. Her heart leapt to her throat.
Mace can enter our home whenever he feels like it!
Whenever he wants to scare the pants offa me.
Our home isn't safe anymore.
Deana dressed carefully. She brushed her hair and put on her make-up. But her heart wasn't in it.
All she could think about was Mace.
Creeping into her room again.
When Mom was out and she was all alone.

Chapter Forty-five

Deana was setting place mats on the dinner table when the doorbell rang. It echoed through the hallway.

She froze.

It has to be Warren – but how can I be sure?
Could be Mace!

Nah. Mace wouldn't return so soon after spying on me. Would he? That's just the kinda awful thing he *would* do.

She heard Mom go to the door.

Open it.

Mom was talking. Her tone bright and friendly.

A low voice alternated with Mom's higher tones, indicating that an animated conversation was taking place.

Whoever it was, he was standing in the hallway.

She heard Warren's voice and huffed a sigh of relief. She raced through the living room and into the hallway.

'Hi, Warren. You two already met, I see!'

Mom was shaking Warren's hand. She looked flushed and bright-eyed – as she always did with guests. That was the nice thing about Mom. She knew how to make people feel at home.

'Hi there, Deana. Your sister was just making me welcome.'

He winked at Deana.

Mom laughed, flushed some more and went off into the kitchen.

They were alone.

Warren eyed Deana approvingly. 'My,' he said. 'You look stunning

The Lake

tonight.' His voice dropped to a conspiratorial whisper. 'You should wear blue more often. Much more becoming than black.'

Deana grinned. She put a finger to her lips. 'Don't you dare . . .'

Warren smiled and crossed his heart.

'Mum's the word,' he mouthed.

Deana led him to the living room. She motioned for him to sit on the sofa.

'Dinner isn't quite ready yet,' she said. 'Care for a drink?'

'Whatever you're having would be great.'

Warren looked around, taking stock of the room.

As if he hadn't seen it before.

'Fabulous view you have over there.' He nodded in the direction of the glass wall.

'That's what everyone says. White wine?'

'Sounds good to me,' Warren said, smiling at her.

Deana went to the kitchen, and returned with two glasses of Chablis on a serving tray.

He's a handsome guy, she thought, watching him take his glass. In a clean-cut kind of way. Dark slicked hair, gray suit, white shirt. A club tie of some sort.

Underneath all that, she sensed his taut, well-honed body. A squirm of excitement stirred between her legs.

Wondering how he'd look, bare-ass naked.

'So you own a bookstore, Warren?' Mom said over dinner.

'That I do. For my sins.' Mom looked at him enquiringly. He laughed. 'Sorry – a figure of speech! I love my work, Ms West . . .'

'Leigh, please,' Mom said, smiling. 'Makes life a lot simpler.'

'Leigh. Nice name, if I may say so.'

Deana glared at him.

Warren smiled back, sending her a sly wink at the same time.

I *know* he's just being friendly, Deana thought. And Mom does have this effect on people. I should be used to it by now.

But she *did* feel a little on edge.

It's that asshole Mace, she decided.

Suddenly appearing like that.

661

Scaring the pants offa me.
Well, not quite.
But he sure had me spooked there for a while.
What had *really* spooked her, though, was the way that Mace had looked.
Zoned out.
Unsure.
As if he'd been *really* sorry about going into her room like that.
She stole a glance at Mom who looked happy enough. Perhaps she hasn't ever seen Mace as I saw him this afternoon.
Maybe I should let it stay that way . . .
Deana wanted to forget, but found that she couldn't. Mace coming at her like that was something that worried her a lot.
Warren and Mom were talking books. How Mom liked historical novels and biographies; she'd been searching for something on Bob Dylan. Warren said he'd look out for this really good one he'd heard about.

'Wonderful meal, Leigh,' Warren said, wiping his lips on his napkin.
'Thanks, Warren. Glad you enjoyed it. Duck à l'orange prepared this way is a Bayview special. Goes down well with the clientele.'
'Mom,' Deana put in. 'Would you mind awfully if Warren and I went for a drive somewhere?'
Leigh's face paled slightly.
Watching her, Deana almost changed her mind about going for a drive with Warren.
She's remembering the night of the family party. When Allan and I left her to it with Gran and Pops.
'Mom. We'll be back in an hour or so – won't we, Warren?'
'Er, yes, of course. Would you mind, Leigh? I always hate to eat and run. But perhaps you'd both do me the honor of dining at my place sometime soon?'
Leigh smiled at Deana. 'Sure,' she said. 'That would be wonderful, wouldn't it, darling?'
'Yes, Mom. It would.'

* * *

The Lake

After Deana and Warren had left, Leigh cleared away the dishes, piling them up, intending to wash them later. She took a bottle of Chablis from the fridge and poured herself a glassful.

Strolling back to the living room, Leigh's mind was full of her daughter and Warren. Mmmm. She liked Warren. He seemed mature, and sensible; probably a safe date was what Deana needed right now. After all our problems, she could do with some relaxation . . .

Leigh switched on the TV.

Maybe I should call Mace . . .

Or maybe I should take some time out by myself. Relax. Chill out.

Like an irritating insect, the tub scenario still lurked in a corner of her mind.

Afterwards, though, Mace had made up for it.

They really *were* good for each other.

She was sure of that.

Her gaze followed the figures on the flickering screen, not really seeing what was there. She came to, focusing on David Letterman interviewing some celeb from *Cheers* . . .

Leigh made a face. Reflecting that she must be the only person on the planet who wasn't into *Cheers* . . .

There *must* be something else worth looking at . . .

She played around with the remote, finally settling on an old Steve McQueen movie. Smiling to herself, she remembered she'd had this humongous crush on Steve McQueen after watching *The Great Escape*.

Steve on his motorbike . . .

Ultra *sexy*.

Taking another sip of Chablis, she watched the screen some more. Not really understanding, now, why she'd been so over the moon about dear old Steve.

Her eyes strayed to the framed photographs on the TV table.

Something odd there . . .

One was missing.

The picture of Deana wearing her first bikini.

Showing off. Posing on a rock, her dark hair blowing in the breeze, the sea rolling in behind her.

Leigh remembered that day down at Point Reyes Beach. The first time she'd realized that Deana had suddenly become a woman . . .

The same day Deana had reminded Leigh of Charlie.

There'd been something about her daughter's smile. That small cleft in her chin. The way she stood there. At one with the elements.

Nature girl, Leigh had called her.

Now the photograph was gone.

Perhaps Deana gave it to Warren as a keepsake.

I'll ask her later.

Leigh felt a twinge of regret.

That photo had been a good one of Deana.

One of her favorites . . .

Chapter Forty-six

'Where to? Anywhere special in mind?'

'You choose. I'm in your hands.'

'Okay. Hold tight. Just close your eyes and relax!'

Deana pushed back into the seat, snuggling against the soft upholstery. Nice car, she thought dreamily. A two-seater Porsche coupe.

A tangy whiff of leather hit her nostrils.

She felt a little shaky. Slightly out of her depth.

It was the first time that she and Warren had been together like this. Up close and *really* together. Sure, she'd been to his house. Drunk his scrummy cocoa. Become best buddies with his dog. A gal can't get much closer, she told herself, smiling slowly.

She stole a glance at Warren's profile. Straight nose, firm chin. Lit up now by the headlights of a passing car. He looks kinda sexy in that white shirt, she thought, the way it shows up against his tan.

The night was warm and sticky and Warren had discarded his suit jacket, loosened his tie and rolled up his sleeves. His forearms were strong, matted with dark hair and well muscled. She watched his hands, holding the wheel loosely. Imagining how they'd feel wandering over her naked body . . .

Stop that!

Still, she couldn't help thinking about it. A picture leapt into her mind. Warren, running his hands over her shoulders, holding her breasts, squeezing her nipples. His mouth opening against hers . . .

A thought struck her. She frowned. Who knows, Warren might decide that he was too old for her, smile kindly and say, 'Goodbye, eighteen-year-old ex-high-school-kid Deana. Go find somebody your own age . . .'

Warren felt her gaze, and smiled. His eyes flashed as he turned to look at her.

'Will I do?'

'Do?'

'Yeah. You've been staring at me for the last coupla miles . . .'

'Sorry. Just thinking that you look kinda sexy. In the dark. With that intense expression on your face, you seem so intelligent and . . . mature, somehow.'

'I hope by that you don't mean that I'm too decrepit for a young gal like you?'

'On the contrary, I feel *safe* around you. Felt it that very first time you invited me to your house. You have this, I don't know – *gravitas*, I guess you'd call it.'

'Wow! Sounds heavy.'

They'd dropped down to a crawl, climbing along a rutted road. For the first time she looked out the window.

Her breath quickened. She shivered. Almost panicked.

Goose bumps scurried up her body.

'Warren . . .'

'Uh-huh?'

'Where are we going?'

'I thought we'd maybe go over to Stinson Beach. Take a stroll in the moonlight . . .'

Deana's face turned ghostly pale.

'Why, Deana, what is it?'

They'd arrived at a clearing now.

The clearing. The parking area for the outdoor theater . . .

The Porsche purred to a halt.

'Warren!' she wailed. 'How could you *do* this to me?'

'Do what, Deana? For God's sake, what d'you mean?'

Dismayed, he looked at her. She'd drawn up into a small tight ball, her hands held clenched to her face.

'You brought me *here*, Warren. How did you *know*? Why did you bring me *here*?'

The Lake

Tears coursed down her cheeks.

Then he got it.

Whatever had happened to Deana a short while ago had happened here, in this clearing.

He pulled her gently to him, making soothing noises as if she were a child waking scared from a nightmare. She shook, sobbed and cried, all at the same time; her face was wet and shiny with tears.

He waited till she'd calmed down a little.

'Take me back, Warren,' she said, quietly. '*Please*. Take me away from this place!'

'Sure, honey. Just don't *cry* any more. You're safe with me.'

Deana snuffled, and Warren produced a tissue from the glove compartment. She took it gratefully, and dabbed at her face. 'I must look a real freak,' she said, sobbing again.

'You look wonderful, Deana. You always do.'

'Thanks, Warren,' she said, still sniffing loudly. A pause, then: 'I think I owe you an explanation.'

'Not necessarily. But I can guess. Something to do with what happened to you – and your Mom?'

She nodded, her lips still trembling.

'No need to explain. Don't want you upsetting yourself anymore. I'm just sorry I chose this place, is all.'

'Not your fault. *I* said that you should choose. Didn't say anything about *not* going anywhere near Mount Tam. So don't blame yourself. You weren't to know. But can we go home now, please?'

'Sure,' Warren said, turning the key in the ignition, still looking at her anxiously. 'Sure you're okay now?' Deana nodded, snuggled back into her seat again, and stared out into the night. Remembering Allan.

How he'd leaned in to open the car door for her, and how there hadn't been a cat in hell's chance of him escaping.

Then the old Pontiac, whooshing by, lifting him off his feet.

Allan. Allan . . .

Another sob shook her body. Vivid pictures flashed through her mind. She saw herself running away from Allan.

Saving her own skin . . .

He could've been *alive*.

Maybe I could've *saved* him.

Don't think about it anymore . . .

She gasped.

Something . . .

Someone was back there, in the bushes. The car moved on past. Warren maneuvered it slowly, carefully over the ruts.

But Deana could still see it . . . the white face, with dark holes for eyes. No, not dark holes. It, whatever, *whoever* it was, had an eye. It'd looked at her. Its mouth gaping wide . . . Its scrawny hands parting the bushes . . .

Then it faded into the dark beyond.

She turned around. Stared hard.

Saw nothing.

She frowned.

The face had been a lot like Nelson's. Thin, white. Eerie. Positively *ghoulish* in the dark shadows.

It *can't* be Nelson, she told herself.

Nelson's dead.

Mom identified the body.

Her breath evened out. Her mind had been playing tricks again. Coming here hadn't been one of Warren's greatest ideas.

Glancing across at him, she met his gaze. He smiled gently. 'Okay now?'

'Okay,' she said, quietly.

She was still shaking, though.

Thinking about Nelson.

But a *dead* Nelson, she reminded herself. Hope I can sleep tonight. Hope I don't see him again. Walking past my window, waving his hatchet.

Bullshit, Deana.

Pull yourself together.

Nelson's dead.

This is two weeks on. We're safe now. Mom's okay. She's got Mace 'n' I've got Warren to keep me company. I hope. Unless I've scared him off by tonight's little performance.

'*And as we lie there*,' Allan's voice whispered in her head, '*our naked bodies sweaty and tangled . . .*'

The Lake

Oh, my God.

Stop it.

Allan's dead. *Gone*. Please, God, don't let me go over *that* again . . .

She looked at Warren, felt the bumps and jolts as the car sped downhill, bouncing over the ruts. He met her gaze, smiled and said, 'You've got me now, Deana. I'll take care of you.'

Chapter Forty-seven

'Leigh, tell me about your pregnancy. The early days, when you were getting by all alone . . .'

There was enough of a pause for Leigh to look up, puzzled.

'Go on,' she said quietly.

'Sorry, Leigh. Does my asking questions upset you? I'm just interested in *you*, is all. I want to know *everything* that ever happened to you. That make sense?' Mace tilted his head, smiling quizzically.

Leigh returned the smile. 'Sure it does, Mace. But I already told you all there is to know about my misbegotten youth. I was a bit wild. Got pregnant. Those days folks took it a little more seriously than they do now. I was sent away and – well, you know the rest.'

Leigh shrugged, then smiled. It was an end to the matter as far as she was concerned. 'Why don't I get us another bottle of wine from the fridge?' She left the sofa and made for the kitchen.

Reaching for clean glasses and setting them on the serving tray, Leigh began to feel good and warm inside. She was glad that she'd changed her mind and called Mace when Deana and Warren had left after dinner.

She'd wanted to relax. What better way to do it than with Mace by her side?

Ten o'clock.

Another hour or so and Deana'll be back. Must remember to ask her about the missing photograph. Not tonight, though. Leave that until tomorrow.

The Lake

Bring her home safely, Warren, she thought, shivering . . .
Please, God, don't let it be like last time . . .
She looked up, saw Mace standing in the doorway.
'Hey,' he said, coming forward. 'Let me open that for you.'
'Thanks. Nice to have a man around. To open things, and . . .'
'And what else, may I ask?'
'Oh, to open things and just *be* around the house, I guess.'
They took their wine through to the living room. Settled into the sofa, while Leigh told him, 'Anyway, if you must know, there's not much more to my story. I got knocked up. Wasn't the first. Won't be the last. Girls do it all the time. I wasn't in love with the father, so there was no question of him being involved . . . He died, anyway.'
Mace stayed silent. He took her glass and set it down on the coffee table.
Then he moved in against her. Her hand slid up his thigh . . . she felt his hard-on, bulking up, growing big inside his jeans.
'Perhaps we should take the wine into the bedroom,' he whispered. 'Relax a little, take in some TV, and . . .' He bent down, his mouth finding hers, his tongue edging in, hard, searching.
She flinched away slightly.
'Sorry, Leigh. Only if you want to, of course.'
'Mace, you *know* I want to. I'm just worried about Deana. She went out after dinner. With Warren, her new boyfriend. They should be back soon. She said maybe an hour or so.'
He eased away from her, searching her face. 'Hey. She shouldn't worry you this way. Y'know? Maybe I should have a word—'
'No, please don't,' Leigh cut in with a short laugh. 'Warren's okay. Really. He's mature and very sensible. Deana's perfectly safe with him.'
'She still shouldn't do this. Not so soon after Nelson an' all.'
'Really, Mace. Everything'll be fine. Honestly. I feel it right here.' Leigh touched her chest over her heart. The silk robe she'd changed into earlier gaped open, showing the soft curve of her left breast.
Mace grinned. 'Do that again and I warn you, I won't be responsible for my actions!'
'That's my Mace. Mmmm. You're *so* masterful at times.'
She stood up, took his hand and pulled him toward the bedroom.

'What about the wine?'

'What wine?' she said, smiling slyly. 'We'll enjoy that later!'

Leigh went ahead of Mace into the dark bedroom, her robe sliding to the floor.

He picked it up and tossed it over the bedrail. 'Come here, you crazy woman.' He grabbed her by the waist and flung her on the bed. She reached out to switch on the bedside lamp, but his hand closed over hers.

'No,' he murmured. 'We don't need light. We got hands. We got touch. Ve-erry sexy, so they tell me . . . and a guaranteed turn-on!'

'Okay. Okay. Just *give* it to me, Mace. Hard and long.'

'Am I hearing this right? You saying ìGive it to me.î Any way. Anyhow?'

'Sure. Why not? Just *do* it, Mace.' With trembling fingers, Leigh began struggling with his jeans. Unzipping them, pulling them down. She reached out, felt his coarse curly hair, shuddered, and curled her hands around his shaft. Sighing and moaning a little, she breathed, 'My God, Mace. *Give* it to me.'

She was panting now.

Pulling him to her.

Wanting him.

However he wanted it . . . She shrugged down under him, feeling his weight straddling her, leaning over, his hair falling forward. She grabbed his penis with both hands. Close up, it was huge. Engorged. She rammed it into her mouth. Hard.

Mace pulled away . . . 'No,' he said softly. 'Not that way. The way *you* want it.'

She gave in and straightened out. He lay on top, covering her face with kisses, tracing his tongue gently over her mouth, her neck, then slipping down to her breasts.

He cradled them in his hands, caressing them. He went down again. Taking small quick licks, his tongue playing around her nipples, feeling them go rigid. She wriggled beneath him, pressing onto his shaft, feeling the moist warmth rising . . . He went in deeper and deeper . . . She rose to meet him.

The Lake

Moaning, panting, Leigh rammed herself onto him. He responded, pressing deep, shafting her with long, hurting strokes. He came quickly, flooding her in hot, releasing bursts. Finally he pulled away. Moving off her. Falling back on the bed, breathing hard, his body slick with sweat.

She lay there, staring into the darkness, still panting softly. At last, her breathing evened out. She felt full, satisfied. Complete.

A clicking sound came from the hallway.

They tensed, holding their breath.

A light clatter of heels on the clay tiles.

Deana.

Home.

Leigh breathed a sigh of relief.

Mace turned his head, smiling in the gloom.

A gray light crept in from the window, playing across the bed. Trembling shadows from the trees outside shifted around, touching the walls, the ceiling.

'Deana's home,' she whispered, finding his hand.

He took hers in his and squeezed it. 'Okay. I give in,' he whispered back.

She turned on her side, facing him, curving in to his body. Feeling the sweat, slick and warm on their skin.

Mmmm, she thought, smiling softly, everything is just so *perfect*! Her eyelids began to droop. She felt spent, happy, relaxed.

Mace dropped a kiss on her shoulder, then lay back on the pillow, watching the shadows shift on the ceiling.

Soon, their breathing became a steady rhythmic sound. Still holding hands, though more loosely now, they slept.

Leigh jerked awake. For a moment, remembering the thrill of how they'd made love. And that Deana was home. Asleep by now, she guessed, lifting her head from the pillow.

02:55.

God, it's so *hot*. A shower would be nice. Drenched with sweat, the bedsheet clung to her like a live thing. Plucking it away from her skin, she felt the night air chill her body. Pushing down the sheet, carefully so as not to wake Mace, she let it lie a moment, crumpled, damp and cool across her thighs.

She glanced down at her body, gleaming pale in the darkness.

Do it, Leigh. Go get yourself a shower . . .

Holding her breath, she worked her feet, slowly, pushing down the bedsheet some more. Turned to look at Mace. Still sleeping. She pictured him on her, his come pumping deep inside her.

A tremor of excitement flickered in her groin.

She felt so tender there. And sore.

His warm semen still seeped between her legs. He's some *hunk*, she thought dreamily; that blond hair, those dark eyes. And his body . . . Tight abs. Well-muscled arms. His just *being* there made her want him all over again.

Her glance swept down Mace's body, his chest rising and falling as he slept. It was the first time she'd taken a real good look at him while he was naked.

But something was wrong.

In the moonlight she could make out the thick black hair covering his arms, chest and belly and clustering between his legs. She looked at his penis, lying pale and shrunk now, in a *mass* of pubic hair. Her glance switched to his face. Clean-shaven, as ever.

A chill began in her stomach.

This was a *different* Mace.

A stranger.

He stirred, feeling the air chill his skin. His muscles tightened; he hugged his arms around himself. Then his eyes opened. He lifted his head. Looked down at himself.

Uncovered.

Naked.

With a growl, he leapt up.

'What in *hell* are you doing?' he demanded. Leigh drew back, startled at his tone. Terrified by the sudden anger. His mouth opened and his eyes flashed dangerously.

Suddenly he was on top of her.

His fist coming down . . .

The Lake

Smashing her face . . .

Knocking her into the pillow. Then more blows, to her throat, breasts, stomach . . .

Leigh heard herself gasping, weak little sounds . . . He still straddled her, laying into her body again and again, pummeling hard.

She threw her hands around her head. Trying to stifle her screams . . . Then, rolling into a ball, she turned away from under him and slid off the bed.

Standing, trembling, shivering, terrified, her arms hugging her body.

Mace sat up. Staring at her. Breathing hard. Suddenly, the fight left him and he drooped forward, shaking his head.

'Leigh, I'm so sorry,' he murmured. '*Please* believe me. You woke me – I was having a helluva nightmare. Leigh, you *have* to forgive me.'

'A *nightmare?*' Leigh backed away. She grabbed her robe from the bedrail. The silk clung to her damp skin. Struggling into it, she dragged it around her body.

Remembering Mattie's words.

'*The guy in Yellow Bend ain't the only one who likes to hear a gal scream . . .*'

'You'd better leave, Mace,' she said, her voice quiet and shaky. 'I think we both need some space. Time to think things through.'

He grabbed the bedsheet and held it up to his chin. But she turned away, not wanting to look at him anymore. Not wanting to see him, or remember him this way. Angry. Violent. Punching her. Beating the daylights out of her.

She heard him searching around for his things. She switched on the light and walked into the bathroom. Hoping that Deana hadn't heard her cries. Heard him laying into her.

Please, God, she hadn't heard that.

Chapter Forty-eight

'Mattie. We need to talk.'
 'We do?'
 'Yeah. Time to spill the beans, Mattie.'
 'About friend Mace?'
 'Right. Maybe there's something else I should know?'
 A pause.
 Then Mattie said, 'I'll be right over.'

Mattie was off duty, and the way she looked when she arrived at the house took Leigh off guard. Red blouse tied at the waist and denim cutoffs. She strode into the hallway, her long tanned legs taking her straight to the kitchen. She looked like a high-school kid on her way to the beach.
 'What's the matter, Leigh. Got a problem?'
 Leigh followed, then busied herself making coffee. It was eight in the morning and she hadn't fixed breakfast yet. Deana was still in bed.
 'Yeah. You could say that. Take a seat.' Leigh motioned to the bench by the kitchen table. 'The other day you implied that Mace had ìanother sideî to him. Maybe a black side. An *iffy* side. Care to tell me more about that?'
 Mattie took the mug of hot black coffee that Leigh placed in front of her.
 'Where shall I begin?' She spoke slowly, giving a tight smile. 'Guess the beginning's about the best place.'

The Lake

Mattie looked up, peering into Leigh's face.

'Well, shitski, honey! Where'd you get *that*?' She gestured toward the bruise already showing purple on Leigh's cheek.

With a self-conscious gesture, Leigh's hand went to her face. 'Does it look *so* bad?' she asked anxiously.

'Bad enough,' Mattie replied, shaking her head.

Leigh gave an embarrassed grin. 'Maybe I should put on some more make-up. I'll do that before Deana shows. Don't particularly want her to see me in this state. As it is, she can't stand the sight of Mace . . .'

'Look,' Mattie said briskly. 'Mace is good at his work. You might say too good. He wants somebody, he goes out there and nails 'em. Yeah, he's well respected back at the department. But beneath all that there's a certain something that says potential rogue cop – know what I'm sayin'?'

Leigh gave a short, harsh laugh. 'I get the picture,' she said. 'Have you *seen* Mace flare up? Go stark, staring crazy?'

Mattie took a swig of coffee, then looked Leigh in the eye. 'A coupla times. One day he put a guy in jug; the guy calls out for a lawyer. Unfortunately, he caught Mace going off shift. Mace goes straight in there and slugs the guy out cold. Guy lying there, still out cold and Mace starts kicking him. Couldn't stop. I had to drag him off. It wasn't easy. Then Mace turns on me. I get a bruised jaw for my trouble. He apologizes, says he doesn't know what came over him.'

Mattie shrugged her shoulders.

'Next time, he slugs a girl in a club. Broke her jaw, turns out. Anyway, he shows his ID, tells *el patron* the girl's makin' a nuisance of herself. Girl's fired on the spot. Mace walks free. No hassle. No problem.'

Leigh listened in silence, then said, 'Uh-huh, seems like our Mace is bad news. Like he's two separate people. Never taken me to his apartment . . . I did wonder why. Maybe he's got somethin' to hide. Know what? I'd sure be interested to know what makes him tick . . .'

Mattie swung her leather shoulder bag around to her front. She lifted the flap, dove into it and came up with a key. Waving it in front of Leigh's eyes she said, 'How about we have ourselves a little adventure?'

'You mean *that*'s Mace's house key?'

'Sure is. I happen to know that he's out on a case right now. Should take him all day . . .' Mattie's stare challenged her.

'Why not?' Leigh said.

Mace's apartment was in darkness.

Leigh suppressed a shiver. What *had* Mace got against good honest daylight? What *was* he, Count Dracula or something?

The apartment was very neat. *Too* neat for a bachelor pad, she thought. No magazines. Straight lines of paperbacks in a cheap wooden bookcase. No mess, no beer cans, no evidence of take-outs.

Nothing.

She frowned. It was unnatural.

Place is like a damn funeral parlor. Especially with the blinds all drawn like this.

She shuddered. There was something about the neatness of it all that spooked her.

Mattie glanced around. Leigh smiled. Good ol' Mattie. Casing the joint. Once a cop, always a cop . . . Bet nothing escapes her notice.

Leigh was right.

'Place hasn't been slept in these last coupla nights.'

'How can you tell?' Leigh felt guilty. Of course Mace hadn't spent the night at home for a while. He'd been with her, hadn't he? Well, last night, anyhow.

'Desk calendar says July 8,' Mattie said. 'It's now July 11.' She went through to the small kitchen area and opened the fridge door. 'The milk's past its sell-by date.'

Leigh's eyebrows went up. 'Looks like Mace isn't the only good cop around here,' she remarked drily.

'Hey. How about this?' Mattie, at an open drawer of Mace's computer desk, was waving some photos.

Leigh perked up. Photographs, especially one missing from her place, held a particular significance for her right now.

She looked at the photos fanned in Mattie's hand. Mainly art shots, nicely lit ones of people, places, water, rivers, the sea, rocks and some amazing skies. Most in mono; some in full color.

'Our Mace hopes to make the big time one day,' Mattie explained. 'He's got an award somewhere. Told me about it once. The Smith-Griffon Award for Best Seascape or something, I remember.'

Mattie returned the photographs to the drawer and opened another one. She came up with bundles of letters and bills.

Leigh began to feel uneasy.

Suppose Mace walked in.

At this very moment.

She imagined footsteps hurrying down the corridor outside. A key scraping in the lock.

The door opening . . .

'Mattie. We really oughta go now. I don't feel good about this whole thing.'

'*You* don't feel good, huh? Come on over and look at these. Then tell me you don't feel so good.'

Mattie's tone was serious. Leigh's heart skipped a beat.

Mattie sank into a soft leather sofa, holding a large scrapbook on her knee. Leigh went over. Turning pale as she stared at the pages Mattie was flicking through.

Bodies.

Dead bodies.

Carved.

Placed in awkward, artificial *artistic* positions.

Bodies of girls. Twisted. Writhing in their final death throes. Bloody. Naked . . .

Page after page of photographs.

Mono press shots. The blood all black and glistening.

A few in startling full color.

Head shots, showing the final agonies.

Face pleading. Mouths wide. Screaming for the man with the knife to stop. *PLEASE . . . STOP . . .*

Leigh gagged as vomit lurched in her throat. She felt herself fold at the knees. She collapsed on the sofa.

'Wowww . . .' breathed Mattie. 'We gotta get outta here . . . But wait a minute, there's something else. A letter . . .'

Leigh looked over Mattie's shoulder at the bunch of creased handwritten pages she was holding.

And read the words...

'I, Edith Payne, hereby...'

My *God* – not *Charlie's* mother...

Quietly, the door opened.

Chapter Forty-nine

'Why, ladies, this *is* a pleasant surprise,' Mace said. 'You wanna read my private stuff?' He snatched the crumpled pages from Mattie. 'Here,' he said, thrusting them at Leigh. 'Take a look, sweetheart. Ring any bells?'

'Mace, I'm sorry . . .'

'Oh, don't be sorry, honey. I don't mind you sneaking in here. Poking through my private things . . .'

'Wasn't Leigh's fault, Mace,' Mattie broke in calmly. '*I* had your key. *I* decided to pay you a visit. Don't blame Leigh. She came along for the ride.'

'Came along for the ride, huh?' A corner of Mace's mouth lifted. But he wasn't amused. His eyes were cold, dark as bottomless pits. Whatever it was he felt, he was holding it in. Keeping everything under control.

As usual.

'So, Leigh. Thought you'd nose around, did you? Time you knew, anyway. Time you finally paid the price. After – what is it now? Eighteen, nineteen years?'

'What do you mean, Mace?' Her heart lurched. Damn right she knew what he meant. Was he Charlie's avenging angel?

Mace relaxed a little; easing into the game, getting conversational. 'Read it,' he said. 'And watch it all make sense, baby. Just a little reminder of that wonderful summer, all those years ago.'

Slowly, Leigh took the letter from him.

'Go on, sweetheart. Read it. Put some coffee on, Mattie. We could be here for some time.'

Mattie stayed where she was. Alert. Ready to pounce.

Mace sat himself down, legs astride a chair. Grinning. Watching Leigh. Enjoying her discomfort.

'Hey, baby. Don't mind me. Settle back in that easy chair, why don't ya? Just want to see your pretty li'l face when you read what Deana's grandmama has to say!'

Mattie glanced at Leigh. Her expression said, *You okay?*

Leigh nodded briefly.

She sat on the edge of Mace's armchair. Lips trembling, she looked at the yellowed pages. Ma Payne had a good hand. Legible. Of the old-fashioned copperplate school. Charlie had said she'd been a teacher . . .

Leigh drew a deep breath. Quickly, her eyes scanned the pages. Scarcely believing what she read:

I, Edith Payne, hereby state the True Facts regarding my Three Children and the Terrible Events that took place after their Birth.

On December 15, in the year of Our Lord 1949, I gave birth to three babies: Jess, Charlie and Tania. Their father was my husband Charlie Payne. My, but they were three fine healthy babies! Beautiful as ever three babies could be. My Gifts from Heaven, I called them.

Firstly, I should state that I came to Lake Wahconda as a teacher. I taught the children of the lake people hereabouts. It was here that I met and married Charlie Payne, a man of native Indian descent, and of little means and education. I tried to teach him to write, but he didn't take kindly to this and soon gave up trying. He was a man content in his traditional ways.

Charlie said little when the three babies came along, but from the start he seemed fearful of our little girl. All the babies had a good head of dark hair, but Tania had more than the boys. Charlie insisted that she was a child of ill omen, mumbling some tale that a female child covered in black hair was a bringer of bad fortune. When he was liquored up, he spoke of this old

The Lake

legend, telling that a woman mating with a wolf at Full Moon would give birth to such a child.

Charlie Payne was a simple man. He stood by his beliefs and nothing I said could change his mind. Tania must die, he vowed, to save us all from misfortune. He was set on this path. I begged him not to kill our daughter, but he was deaf to my pleas.

I knew he would soon kill Tania, so I stole Mary-Ann Baker's baby while she was at the lake washing clothes. The child was barely a week old. I dressed her in Tania's shawl, and placed her in Tania's cradle. I hid my own daughter in the woods. Charlie Payne took Mary-Ann's baby, hacked off her head and sank her weighted body into the lake.

This was a terrible thing to witness and in my distress I told him that he'd killed the wrong baby – that this one was not ours. He demanded to know where I'd hidden Tania. Distraught, I told him that I'd concealed her in the woods. He went to find her. I hurried to the woodshed, took the ax and followed him. In his drunken state he tripped and fell in the undergrowth. I hacked him as he lay screaming for mercy. I just hacked and hacked till he was dead.

After the disappearance of her newborn, Mary-Ann Baker drowned herself in the lake. Folks still say they hear her ghost moaning in the night as she searches for her little one.

Teaching class and making baskets brought little enough money to support my children. People hereabouts were next to dirt poor themselves. So I gave away two of my little ones. I gave Jess to my friend Ellie Burke and her husband Tom, in Duluth. I believed Ellie would give him a good home and look after him well, as she herself had not been blessed with children. I gave my daughter to a family of travelers. They seemed good, honest folk who vowed that they would care for her.

I kept my baby Charlie. I loved him with all my heart and, as best I could, kept him away from all that is bad and wicked in this world.

When my boy Charlie was almost grown, he took up with a no-good whoring slut. A vacationer she was, out for any innocent young boy she could lay her hands on. She seduced and then murdered him and walked free of this terrible crime. Accidental Death, they called it. But I know different.

I pray that someday God will repay this Jezebel in full for her wickedness. May her slate NEVER be cleansed of the terrible wrong she did my Charlie and me.

Let it be known that this statement is for the eyes of my son Jess Payne only. Tania is long gone. Wherever she is, I hope that she is happy.

May God forgive me. All I want now is to Rest in Peace.

[Signed: Edith Mary Payne.]

Chapter Fifty

Stunned, Leigh let the pages flutter to the floor. She heard Charlie's voice telling her 'it' was in the lake. But hadn't he mentioned a *brother*? Maybe that'd been his own conclusion.

If he'd been told that he had a twin, he might've naturally thought that 'it' had been a brother. And it looked like Ma Payne hadn't been in any goddamn rush to explain otherwise.

And who was Jess? Where did *he* fit in?

Mattie shot a quick glance in her direction. It said, *Leigh. We gotta get outta here. Fast.*

Agreed.

But first, we waltz our way past *Mace*?

Are you kidding?

'Where's that coffee, Mattie? We sure could do with a shot here.'

Mace watched Leigh's face. Saw her bewildered, agonized frown. Saw how the past had leapt alive for her, prodding and poking her in all the most vulnerable places. He was enjoying the prospect.

Time she learned the truth about her in-laws, he thought, smiling softly. The *real* truth about the genes her precious daughter inherited.

All that *Payne* blood running through Deana's veins.

His lips curved. His eyes glittered – black, sloelike.

Leigh got it, all right. No problem. The truth came at her thick and fast. She raised her head. Saw the smear of sweat gathering on Mace's upper lip.

He's getting off on this, she told herself. He's enjoying every minute of it.

She knew it now. Jess was *Mace*.

Charlie's brother. Deana's uncle.

Oh my God, I don't believe this. Please let it be some terrible mistake . . .

She thought about the insanity in the Payne family. Edith Payne, screaming at her, eyes dark and wild. Seems like Charlie's pa was mad, too. Liquored up, and on another planet. A killer. Of a tiny baby. A baby hacked in such a horrible way. *And Mace*. Hard. Cruel. Raging when she'd uncovered him last night. Seen his black body hair.

Must've bleached the hair on his head to appear blond to the outside world. Trying to hide, *eradicate* all trace of the familial black growth.

And Deana.

Oh my God, my darling daughter. Her thick black hair. The *body* hair she was always complaining about. From her father's side. From the Payne side.

She pictured Deana, her own dark-haired daughter – the vision merging with Edith Payne's Tania. But, she told herself gratefully, Deana had no manic streaks, no strange ways; nothing to say she'd inherited the 'bad' Payne blood.

Thank God, Deana had West genes, too.

I was a bit of a rebel though, Leigh reminded herself, recalling the hippie days, the demos, her anti-everything buttons pinned all over her clothes . . . A teenage rebel she'd definitely been.

But Deana hadn't caused her *that* much trouble. Had she?

'Coffee. Black. And plenty of it!' Mattie brought in three steaming mugs on a tray.

'Gee, thanks, Mattie.' Mace grinned. 'Just what we need. A shot of good ol' caffeine to get us all rarin' to go. What say you, Leigh darlin'?'

'Coffee. Sure,' Leigh said uncertainly. What a *nightmare*. How do we get out of here in one piece . . .?

'Y'always did make great coffee,' Mace went on. 'Am I right, Mattie?'

'Okay, Mace. Quit the bullshit. Whatever it is you and Leigh have going here, I'm outta this place. You comin', Leigh?'

The Lake

'That's where you're wrong. You an' Leigh ain't goin' anywhere.' Mace reached behind his back. Fingering his holster.

'Mace. You're making one big mistake.'

'Come now, Mattie. You know better than to go against ol' Mace. You *know* who's boss around here.'

'Quit playin' around, Mace. I put one call through and the cops'll be buzzin' around here like flies an' you know it.'

'Think so?'

'Know so. Just stay cool and let us pass.'

'You were breakin' and enterin', Mattie. And you, Leigh. Wouldn't have thought it of you. So ladylike an' all.'

'Mattie. Meet Mace, Deana's uncle. Surprised, huh?' Leigh gave a mirthless laugh. She was playing for time. Trying to catch him off guard. What then? She'd no idea.

Go with the flow. Take our chances, I guess . . .

'Thought there was something more to our friend than he made out,' Mattie put in, looking at Leigh. She turned to Mace. 'Let us pass, Mace. You want to continue your illustrious career at the department? Let us by and we won't say a word.'

'Mmmm. Not bad, Mattie. Not bad at all. Taught you well, didn't I? Tricky situation and you turn the tables with a slick remark. Won't work this time, Mattie baby. You're talking to the master. I got me two perps here. On a breakin' and enterin' charge. I got me a result.'

Leigh's mind worked overtime. She was sure that Mace planned to finish what Charlie Senior had been unable to do.

She remembered Mace's theory about Nelson. He might come back. Finish where he left off, he'd said.

Charlie Payne Senior didn't get to kill his black-haired baby girl. So now Mace wants to do it for him. No Tania around? So what about Deana, Charlie Junior's black-haired daughter?

Oh my God. *Deana*.

I gotta get on home. Protect her. Send her away. Like Ma Payne sent Tania away.

Well, not *quite* the same.

Talk to Mace, she decided. Persuade him to let us go. But don't let him know I'm on to his little game.

She turned to Mattie.

'Mattie, why don't you clear away the coffee things? Mace and I need to talk.'

A brief glance at Leigh, and Mattie took the hint.

'Well now, Leigh. Thought we'd finished talking for good last night. Nothing much left to say.' He tilted his head, watching her, his eyes half-closed, skimming her body with his stare, undressing her as she stood in front of him. Like he'd done so many times before. How she'd *enjoyed* him doing that.

Leigh blushed slightly, annoyed with herself for the predictable reaction. 'Mace,' she whispered. 'I'm so sorry for the way I behaved last night . . .' She took a step forward. Playing for time. Looking guileless, innocent.

She smiled at him. That special, intimate smile she often gave him. Except it wasn't working today.

He was tense, alert. Listening. But not to Leigh.

He whirled around. Grabbed Mattie's hand, the one holding the gun. He twisted it up. The gun pointed skyward.

'Yo! Gotcha, Mattie baby. Can't cheat ol' Mace. Should know that by now!'

'Oh no?' Mattie's left leg shot out in a karate kick to the groin. He dropped her arm, danced back and came up with a sideways chop to her neck. Mattie gasped, whirled away, but lost her gun. Leigh sprang forward, snatched it up, and jabbed it against Mace's head.

Mattie dove into her back pocket, opened a pair of cuffs and snapped them around Mace's wrists. Grabbing the gun from Leigh, she swiped the butt across his head.

A short 'Uhhhh . . .' burst from his lips as he folded to the floor. He collapsed in a heap.

Mattie grabbed Leigh's arm and they both made for the door. They heard Mace groan, turned and saw him shake his head. They didn't wait; they bolted, disappeared down the hallway and raced out into the street.

Driving back to Del Mar, Mattie said, 'So what is it with you and Mace? Care to tell me?'

The Lake

Leigh hesitated, then said, 'It's a long story, Mattie.'
God, my life's one procession of 'long stories' . . .
She took a deep breath. 'Here goes. When I was eighteen, I went to visit an aunt and uncle in Milwaukee. Out in Lake Country . . .' She told her tale, briefly and to the point, ending with Charlie's death and how she'd found herself pregnant.

There was a long silence.

Then: 'Wow,' Mattie said. She whistled softly. 'That's one helluva tale . . .' She paused. 'So now Mace has this thing about dark-haired girls . . .'

Looking at each other, the same thought occurred to each of them.

'But all the time,' Mattie went on, 'Mace is really searching for Tania. Meanwhile, he can't find her, so *any* dark-haired girl will do . . .'

In her mind, Leigh saw the gruesome pictures in Mace's scrapbook. 'Don't, Mattie, please,' she whispered. 'I don't want to think about it . . .'

'Leigh. We gotta get to Deana. Fast.'

'Oh my God,' Leigh breathed, her eyes filling up. Her mind raced, considering the awful possibilities if Mace got there first. She felt trapped. Helpless. This was one helluva nightmare, all right.

If Deana was a target.

Maybe she wasn't.

Maybe Tania'd show up.

Like that's gonna happen . . .

Mattie changed gear, making a right into Del Mar. Driving up towards Leigh's house, she wondered how she was going to deal with this one. They had no positive proof that Mace was involved in murder. Without such evidence she knew the department would never believe her. So he saves gruesome pictures. Could be the scrapbook's something he picked up someplace.

No accounting for taste.

She'd have it out with Mace . . . Oh yeah? She grimaced. She could see it now. Mace saying, 'Gee, thanks, Mattie, that was some clout you threw back there . . . Guess I owe you one for that . . .'

For a moment, she saw herself lying at his feet, her lifeblood spilling out, soaking the carpet . . . Maybe dead.

Hell, no. It wouldn't be like that.

She was sure that Mace was no killer. He had a temper. And a weird taste in pictures. But they were buddies, weren't they? They could always talk things through. She'd suggest that he take time off, she'd cover for him . . . She'd wheedle the truth out of him. What he intended to do . . .

'Mattie.'

'Uh-huh?'

'Why d'you call people Charlie?'

Mattie gave a hoot of laughter. 'I guess that holds a little resonance for you right now. Yes?'

'You could say that.'

'Well, it's like this. Remember little ol' Yellow Bend? Like I told you, where I came from?'

Leigh nodded.

''S far as I remember, seemed like everybody was called Charlie in that goddamn town. So, talk to a person whose name you didn't know – I reckoned if you called 'em Charlie, you'd be right on the nose!'

'Makes sense. I *think*.'

'So you thought I knew about *your* Charlie, did ya?'

'It's possible that Mace could've told you!'

'Huh!' Mattie snorted. Then, 'Okay, Charlie. You're home.' Showing her even white teeth in a broad smile, she turned into the driveway. The battered Ford rumbled to a halt at the front stoop. Leigh got out of the car, closed the door, turned and leaned in through the open window.

'Thanks a lot, Mattie. Looks like between us we brought matters to a head. Mace-wise, that is. You gonna be okay?'

'Sure.' Mattie grinned. 'Leave Mace to me. I can handle him. Just watch out for that daughter of yours.'

Leigh wondered if Mattie *could* handle Mace. After all, things *had* taken a turn for the worse – he could get nasty. She hesitated, then asked a question that she'd thought about for a long time. 'Mattie. Have you and Mace ever . . .'

The Lake

'Nope.' Mattie smiled back. 'Wasn't that kinda relationship. Tried it on a coupla times, but he wasn't having any. At the time I guessed he must've been "funny" that way. Y'know? As in gay? Turned out I was wrong. He fell for you all right, Leigh!'

'You think so?'

'I know so. 'Bye. Take extra care, you and Deana. I'll keep you posted.'

It was late afternoon. Time for a shower, Leigh decided. Then I'll prepare supper. Wonder what Deana had for lunch?

She eased the key into the lock. The door swung open.

'Deana,' she called.

No reply.

Her heart racing a little, Leigh bit her lip.

No worries, she thought.

Maybe Deana went over to Warren's place.

Chapter Fifty-one

The sun was going from the front of the house.
Fingers of shadow spread across the hallway.
Leigh held her breath. A twinge of dread plucked at her stomach.
She listened.
Heard a slight flutter . . .
Probably a bird outside . . .
Then . . .
Light footfalls scurried behind her.
A hand clawed out, roughly, catching her hair, cupping her mouth.
Cutting off her cry of 'HELPPP . . .'
Struggling wildly, she broke free. Twisting away, she swung around.
And gasped, her heart lurching, the color draining from her face.
Her legs trembled.
She felt herself swaying.
It can't be.
It was . . .
Nelson.

Chapter Fifty-two

'I'd best be getting on home. Mom'll be worried. I called to say I'd be back by ten.'

Warren glanced at his watch. Ten-fifteen.

'I'll drive you,' he said, adding, 'I'd be happier that way.'

'Okay. Thanks.'

They stepped into the darkness. It was cooler now. And quiet. Except for the breeze stirring the leaves around them. Deana thought about the funeral car, and shivered.

Inside the Porsche, she said, 'Mom worries about me these days. Since . . . *it* all happened. I guess I should really be home, keeping her company.'

'Y'know, that's what I love about you, Deana. You're so nice to your mom.'

'Oh yeah? How about all that poetic stuff? Skin like milk, eyes like deep pools, etc, etc.'

'Oh, so you want Dark Lady of the Sonnets?'

'Mmmm, Shakespeare. Now you're talking – although I'll have you know, Warren Hastings, *my* reputation is whiter than white. Compared to the Dark Lady's, that is!'

An excited tingle began in Deana's stomach. Warren hadn't mentioned the word 'love' before. Allan had, when they talked about the *Friday the 13th* movie, the night he got killed. 'I love the way you squeal and cover your eyes . . . and peek through your fingers,' he'd said.

But when Warren said 'love' in that quiet, sincere way, the word took on a whole new meaning. He said it as if he really meant it.

Stealing a glance at him, her excitement mounted. She hardly dared breathe. He slid the key in the ignition and started the car. Reaching the end of the driveway, he made a right and slowed down. He brought the Porsche to a halt.

Turning to her, he said, softly, 'Y'know, I *do* care about you, Deana. I care a lot.'

He's gonna kiss me, I know it . . .

She swallowed hard, and whispered, 'And I like you, Warren. You've been great this last week.' Then, as an afterthought, 'And Mom likes you, too.'

She cringed inside, and made a face.

And Mom likes you, too!

What a *dork*! As sweet nothings go, Deana West, that sure takes the biscuit!

She gave a wry grin.

'Great,' he said, winking at her. 'A guy always likes to know he has parental approval!'

She grew embarrassed. 'Why d'you always make a joke of everything?'

'Nerves. When things get serious, I resort to humor. Which, I might add, doesn't mean I'm any the less serious about you – *if* you get my meaning?'

'Sure I do, Warren. That's why I like you. You're so . . .'

'Mature?'

'Well, yeah, that's the word – now you're joking again!'

Their gazes met. Deana caught a ragged breath. Her heart pounded. Deliciously aware of Warren's proximity, she reached over and gave his knee a tentative squeeze. Looking deep into her eyes, he began tracing a fingertip down her cheek.

She shivered, pressing her thighs together, feeling the sharp tingly buzz between them.

He stopped stroking, pulled her forward and kissed her softly on the lips.

Her breath quickened and she leaned into him, her breasts crushing against his chest. Her nipples stiffened. Her heart raced.

The Lake

It was like they'd been searching for each other all their lives.

This is so fantastic, Deana thought. *I don't want it to stop. Ever.*

Good thing I'm wearing my wrapover . . . and left off my bra . . .

His hand slipped inside her blouse; it felt warm against her breasts. Massaging them gently, feeling their weight, running his fingertips over her nipples.

Her lips found his again; she was gasping, *wanting* him so much. He came away, found her breasts and freed them from her soft jersey top. She pushed a nipple into his mouth. He nuzzled hungrily. Her eyes closed . . .

Then snapped open.

A rap on the windshield, Deana's side of the car, caught them off guard.

They heard a high, simpering giggle.

Deana bolted upright, taut, alert. Dragging her top across her breasts, she pulled away from Warren.

Who the hell?

Mommy Dearest . . .

In a trilby hat, set at a rakish angle. Wearing a dark, tailored jacket, a floppy handkerchief flowing from its breast pocket. Her hands in shabby white gloves poked through the open side window.

With a gasp, Deana drew back.

'Christ!' Warren muttered, staring at the apparition. 'What's *she* doing here?'

The hag's eyes narrowed.

They looked *different* tonight. Ringed with smudgy mascara, they reminded Deana of black hairy spiders. 'My God,' she breathed. 'Nightmare City made flesh . . .'

Better say something.

Anything.

Like what?

Howdy. How're the old folks back home?

She managed, 'Where's Harry?'

The whiskery chin jiggled at them.

'Harry died. Little runt went tits-up on me. Weren't nothin' I could do.'

'Oh. Sorry to hear that. You must miss him.'

Jesus *Christ*! What am I, stupid? Sitting here talking to this *maniac*?

Mommy Dearest batted her lashes in a grotesque wink.

'Caught ya at a bad time, did I, dearie?'

Deana exploded. 'Y'know I could report you for abduction? Serve you right, too. And y'know the cops could get you for keeping those old broads locked away like that? They almost *ate* me alive back there . . . How come the authorities let you run a home, anyhow? You should be locked away yourself!'

Mommy's head came forward, her eyes glaring. They leveled with Deana's. The hat slipped, tilting to one side. She looked weird, scary – like she was about to tear open the car door and drag Deana away.

Back to her abominable brood . . .

Deana shrank back into her seat.

Warren touched the remote. The window whirred up.

Grinning like an animated zombie, the hag from hell pressed her skinny nose to the glass. Quickly, Warren turned the key, revved the engine. The car leapt forward. A little way down the street, he peered into the rear-view mirror.

The hag was gone.

'So, Harry popped his clogs.'

''Bout the size of it. Smart move. Wherever he is, he's gotta be in a better place than in that weirdo's freaky rest home!'

Warren shot Deana a quizzical glance. He guessed all this had something to do with her experience the night she'd invited him to dinner. He decided not to ask.

She gave him a weak smile. 'Wearing that stupid hat, she looked like that gay English guy, Quentin Crisp . . . God, what a *hoot*!'

'You're not kidding!'

'Well, that's Mommy Dearest,' she said faintly, 'Or should I say *Daddy* Dearest? What a *freak*! No idea she was a transvestite.' Remembering the hag's strong, scrawny arms tight around her, Deana murmured, 'What do you reckon? Is it a "she" – or a "he"?'

Warren gave a thin smile. 'Who cares? Let's just make sure we avoid her in future.'

'Agreed. Apart from that, she *did* interrupt something rather special. Don't you think?'

'Mmmm. You're right there. We started . . .'

'Started what, Warren?'

'We started something I'd rather like to finish later. How 'bout you?'

'Yeah,' she said softly. 'Me, too.'

Deana went quiet for a moment. Then tears welled up. Slowly, they fell down her cheeks.

Warren stopped the car.

'What is it, Deana? Not something *I* did, I hope?'

'No. Nothing like that. What we did was all so . . . wonderful. It's just that everything seems to be *happening*. One thing after another. Especially tonight, coming face to face with that freaky old witch again. And then there's Mace . . . I don't know, I'm so *scared* of him. And of what he's doing to Mom.'

She almost said, 'And how he came to my room . . .' but stopped herself, reluctant to spoil things by discussing Mace.

Warren drew her to him and kissed the tip of her nose.

Looking into his eyes, she said quietly, 'You're all right, Warren. Y'know that?'

'You, too,' he replied. 'And don't forget, whatever happens, I'll always be here for you.'

Leigh met Deana at the door.

'What's up, Mom? You look as if you've seen a ghost.'

'I just did, honey. Nelson.'

Deana's jaw dropped. She stopped in her tracks.

Oh, my God. Not Nelson!

What the hell *is* happening to us?

Chapter Fifty-three

'He's sick, Deana. He wanted money.'

'Where is he?'

'He left. He was just a pathetic human being. I guess I must have identified the wrong body. It was real hard to tell. I called Mattie.'

'You called Mattie? Not *Mace*?'

'No, honey. Not Mace.'

Something in Leigh's tone made Deana hesitate. There was a tension in it that she didn't like. If there's a problem with Mace, she thought, I need to know about it. 'Mom. About Mace—' she stammered.

'How's Warren?' Leigh interrupted, a little too quickly. Deana closed her lips. Maybe now wasn't the time to say anything about Mace.

'He's okay.' She pictured Mommy Dearest and her band of trolls, tucked away in the twilight zone. Best keep *them* under wraps, too. Mom doesn't look like she can take any more shocks.

Deana led Leigh to the living room. 'Guess you could use a drink,' she said, going over to the bar and decanting a cognac into a balloon glass. 'Anyway,' she said, rapidly changing the subject. 'How're things at the restaurant?'

'Er . . . I didn't go today, hon.'

'No?'

'No. Something came up.'

'Oh? Like what?'

The Lake

'Deana, better grab yourself a drink, too. There's something I should tell you.'

Brriinngg . . . Brriinngg . . .

Leigh's heart lurched.

'The phone, Mom . . .' Deana reminded her, gently. 'Shall I get it?'

'No, dear. It's probably for me.'

It was.

Mattie.

'We got Nelson, Leigh. He's in a bad way. Something terminal, I guess. But he'll be looked after, where he's going. Don't you worry about him. Thing is, looks like he's still harboring some kinda grudge. Swears he's gonna get you – when he comes out. Which he won't, of course. Come out, I mean.'

'Thanks for that, Mattie,' Leigh said. She gave an uneasy laugh. 'Makes me feel a whole lot better. I don't think.'

'Nelson's going no place, Leigh. Trust me – and you can take that to the bank. He's behind locked doors. So, no chance he'll bother you or Deana ever again.' Mattie hesitated, then asked, 'You okay? Musta been quite a shock . . .'

'Yeah. *Right*.' A pause. 'And Mace?'

'He's gone, Leigh. Vacated his apartment. Skedaddled. Vamoosed.'

'Oh my God . . .'

'Keep your doors locked, Leigh.' Mattie spoke quietly. Leigh, catching the urgency in her voice, felt a little faint. Mattie was asking, 'Has he got a key to your place?'

Leigh's heart missed a beat.

'Yes . . . No. I don't know. I never gave him one. But he knows where I keep a spare.'

Mattie's silence spoke volumes.

'Maybe you should have a minder,' she said. 'I'll get somebody over there. Whoever it is, I'll bring them over myself, so when I call you'll know it's okay.'

'Right.' Leigh shivered, bringing a hand to her throat. 'This is getting worse, Mattie.'

'It will do. Until we nail Mace. And doing that won't be easy. He's one slippery customer.'

'You're not kidding,' Leigh murmured. Then said, 'Okay, Mattie. See you soon.'

'That Mattie?'

Leigh nodded. Hugging herself, leaning against the door frame, going over the conversation. Deana studied her, frowned, and said, 'Mom, you look awful.'

Leigh managed a bright smile. 'Gee, thanks, honey. That's all I need to know.'

'Here, take a sip of this.' Deana handed the glass of cognac to her mother. 'You look as if you need it.'

'Thanks.' Leigh took a swig and winced. 'How people can *drink* this stuff, I'll never know.'

'Mom. You had something to tell me . . . What is it?'

Leigh sighed. She wasn't feeling up to repeating the whole thing over again.

'It's a long story, honey.'

Here we go again.

Here lies Leigh West.
Hers was a mighty long story . . .

She sighed and felt sick, going over what had happened today. But Deana *has* to know. Best get it over with now . . .

Easing into the sofa, Leigh took a sip of cognac and shuddered. At the other end, Deana faced her, her legs drawn up, chin resting on her knees. Her glass lay untouched on the table.

An uneasy silence hung on the air.

'Honey,' Leigh began in a quiet voice. 'You've always wanted to know more about Charlie, your father. Well, today I learned the truth of the matter – straight from the horse's mouth. Or, to put it another way, straight from the pen of Edith Payne, Charlie's mother.'

The Lake

Wide-eyed, Deana stared at Leigh. 'And?'

'When I was your age, I was a bit of a rebel. Mom and Dad packed me off to Aunt Jenny and Uncle Mike's in Milwaukee. It was there that I met your father . . .'

Leigh's hand reached out to touch Deana's. She gave a hesitant smile.

At last the tale came tumbling out. All of it. No holds barred. Leigh hoped to God that Deana could deal with it. She watched her daughter's face, afraid that she'd see disgust, bewilderment, even contempt. Afraid things between them might never be the same again.

But what Leigh saw was Deana growing up before her eyes. She'd been listening intently, a small frown creasing her brow as she absorbed the details.

'And you never *once* suspected that Mace was Charlie's *brother*?'

'Never. Not in a million years would I think such a thing could be true. Until . . .'

'Until what?'

'Until I saw Mace's body last night.' Leigh felt a little awkward talking to Deana like this, but as she'd gotten this far she felt that she had to carry on. 'You know, like he's a blond? Well, he had *black* hair. Pubic hair and stuff. He was a different person. He has a tan, but with the black hair, his bronzed body looked so *natural* . . . Like he was born with it – nothing to do with the sun.'

She paused. Realizing that Deana would spot the link.

She did.

Black hair. Black *body* hair. Like her own. Deana grimaced. The awful truth was beginning to hit her.

'And I'm *related* to that *creep*?'

Gently, Leigh said, 'That's right. He's your uncle, Deana.'

'Oh my God!!!'

The doorbell rang. Shattering the silence.

Their hearts raced.

Leigh rushed to the hallway.

Mattie was on the stoop.

'I'm alone, Leigh. Decided to go it alone. I know Mace's mind better than anyone.' Quickly, she stepped inside the hallway. 'We put out an all-points,' she explained. A moment's pause, then she asked quietly, 'Does Deana know?'

Leigh nodded.

'How's she taking it?'

'Well, I think. Probably hasn't hit her yet. When it does, there'll be repercussions – bound to be. But at the moment, she's okay. It's quite a story for her to deal with, Mattie.'

'Yeah, a pretty tough one to swallow, I agree. But she'll pull through. She's a sensible gal for her age. Best she knows what we're up against; that way she'll be aware of what *might* happen.'

'The devil you know, etc.'

Mattie frowned. 'Something like that,' she said quietly.

They went into the living room.

'Hi, Mattie.'

'Hi yourself, Deana.'

'Deana, huh? Sure that's not *Charlie*?'

'No, honey. No more Charlies. Enough of them around as it is, huh?'

Leigh broke in. 'Hey. It's been a busy day – and night. How about a nightcap before we turn in?'

'Sounds good to me. Thing is, I don't reckon I'll be doing much sleeping . . .'

'Me neither,' Deana put in.

Leigh went over to the sound system. She put on some Sinatra. Sexy ol' Frank. 'My Way' was her favorite. A good one to relax to at the end of a hard day.

They chatted and laughed. Trying to chill out. Trying to ignore what had happened earlier. But, beneath it all, their minds were on Mace. Wondering where he was.

What he was doing.

Finally blocking him out of her mind, Deana switched over to Warren. Thinking about how they had almost made love.

Yeah. Almost.

Then she pictured Mommy Dearest – and her band of old broads.

The Lake

Forget her, she told herself. *She's history . . .*

Deana's thoughts slipped back to Warren.

Wishing he was here. Promising herself she'd tell him the whole story; just as Mom had told it to her.

A terrifying thought crossed her mind.

Warren could be in danger himself . . . Mace *knows* about him. Knows where he lives, too.

He might threaten Warren.

Harm him, even.

Oh, God – that couldn't really happen, could it?

'Mom,' Deana said, hurriedly. 'What about Warren? Mace knows about him being my boyfriend and everything.' She turned to Mattie. 'Do you think he's in any danger?'

'Warren?'

'Yeah. I met him recently. He's a nice guy. Has a dog called Saber. And a sister called Sheena. She's a bouncer at a night club in San Jose.'

Mattie looked interested. 'Perhaps we should warn this . . . Warren? Got his number?'

'Yeah.'

'Best give him a call, Deana.'

'Okay.'

Deana went to the hallway. She dialed Warren's number.

Two short rings. Then: 'The Hastings residence. How may I—?'

'Warren?'

'Hi, Deana. How ya doin'?'

Her heart warmed. He sounded so calm and *sensible*.

'Warren. Sorry to call so late. But we, er . . . might have ourselves a situation here. Mom's boyfriend, pardon me, *former* boyfriend Mace – from Mill Valley PD?' Deana rolled up her eyes and made a face. Come on, Warren. You *must* remember . . .

'Yes?'

'Well, I can't explain now but he's on the run. Gone ape-shit. And he *knows* about you. We thought he might try to contact you . . .'

'Really?'

Deana got worried. If only she didn't have to involve him like this.

Worst-case scenario: it could mean goodbye to Warren. And they hadn't even made love yet. Not *properly*, anyhow.

'Deana. Are you and Leigh okay?'

She breathed a sigh of relief. He didn't *sound* as if he was about to disappear out of her life for ever.

'Sure. We have a police officer here.' Turning, she looked through the doorway and smiled in Mattie's direction. 'She's keeping guard over us.'

'Deana. I'm coming over.'

'You sure? What about Sheena?'

'She's not due in until five-thirty.'

'Yeah. You said . . .'

Putting a hand over the mouthpiece, she told Mattie, 'Warren's coming over. Okay?'

'The more the merrier!'

Deana spoke into the phone.

'Sure, Warren,' she said. 'But be careful. Bring your car down the driveway. We'll be waiting for you.'

'Right. Be there in about fifteen minutes?'

'Sure. Oh, Warren?'

'Deana?'

'What about Saber?'

'I'll leave him here. Intruders come a-callin', they might change their minds and go home.'

Deana giggled. 'Sure. Let Saber guard Sheena. Or should that be the other way around?'

She could picture Warren smiling at the other end of the phone.

'Intruder breaks in here, Deana, it'd be a question of who gets him first – Sheena or Saber!'

Chapter Fifty-four

The phone rang out.

It seemed louder than usual.

Mattie motioned to the women to stay seated. 'I'll get it,' she said quietly.

Alert now, Leigh and Deana heard Mattie pick up the phone. 'Yes?' she said. Next time she spoke, she sounded angry.

Mattie listened intently, feeling her blood pressure rise. 'But I'm on police surveillance here. Tell the Chief to go fu—'

'This *IS* the Chief, Blaylock.' The voice thundered in her ear. She jerked the receiver away from her head. 'An' I'm ordering you to git the hell outta there. Just git that tight little ass a' yours over here, pronto. DO YOU COPY?'

'But these people are in dang—'

'Those *people* can have alternative surveillance. I'll assign another officer to the job. I'll have one over there right away, Mattie. Something just showed up here. We need you and your goddamn womanly instincts t'help us out. Got me?'

'Okay. Okay,' Mattie said wearily. There was no stopping the Chief when he was in a lousy mood. 'I'll be right over.'

'Sorry, guys. Gotta go. Chief's in an uproar back there. Sounds like something big with a capital B's just broken out. Another murder, I guess. He's sending over an officer pronto. So I'm gonna have to say goodnight.

'Doors and windows have been double-checked, but no harm done if you check again. Do *not* open doors – or windows – to *anyone*. Right? I'll give the guy a code word. What d'ya suggest?'

Deana perked up. 'How 'bout "Eureka"?'

Mattie shrugged. 'Eureka it is. I'll call ya soon as I'm through with World War Three goin' on back at the ranch.'

Mattie left. After she'd gone, Leigh and Deana didn't have much to say to each other. In the semi-darkness, the living room suddenly seemed scary. Shadows, trembling in the flickering light from the TV, became potential intruders. And even with the sound turned low they felt that *Psycho* was a bad choice of movie to watch tonight. But they let it roll on, neither of them feeling inclined to switch channels.

11:28.

No Warren.

And no replacement bodyguard, either.

The phone rang. Shattering the stillness. Smashing into their thoughts.

Leigh looked across at Deana.

'Mattie said she'd call. That must be her now.' She got up, straightened her back, and went into the hallway.

Deana heard her say, 'Can't *you* deal with it, Tony?'

Leigh's grip on the phone tightened. She was stunned.

Tonight of all nights. There *had* to be a major problem at the Bayview.

'I'm a waiter, Ms West. Not a bouncer,' Tony reminded her.

'Call the cops, then.'

'They're coming out just as soon as they can. Thought you needed to know that. Before you get here.'

'But Tony – can't *you* deal with it?' Leigh persisted, wearily. Her hand brushed her forehead. She felt sick.

'They want *you*, Ms West. They specifically said for you to be here. Christ! All hell's breakin' loose . . . My God – you better get over here fast!'

The Lake

Leigh sighed. She didn't want to leave Deana alone. But it looked like she had no choice.

'Honey, there's a fight at the restaurant. Apparently the place is being trashed as we speak. Police are on their way over. I gotta go, honey. I hate to leave you here alone, but . . .'

'I'll be okay, Mom. I'll stay *glued* to my seat. Anyway, Warren's on his way over. So is the replacement officer.' Deana gave a weak smile. 'I'm gonna be OKAY. Really. Jeez. Sorry about the restaurant. Tonight of all nights. Hope it isn't *too* bad.'

'Thanks, honey. Knew you'd be sensible about this. Call me the minute Warren shows up – don't open the door to anyone else. Except the officer, of course. And don't forget the password.'

'I won't, Mom. Take care. See ya later.'

Leigh started the car, unable to shake off her misgivings. She hated leaving Deana like this. But the Bayview – how come it was being *trashed*?

Who would *do* this?

Not something her usual clientele would get up to . . .

At the top of the driveway, she made a left and turned down into the street. Be glad when this whole thing's over, she thought. Can anything *else* go wrong tonight?

Good thing I didn't mention Mace's scrapbook to Deana. God. She would have been so *scared* . . .

Deana snuggled into her armchair.

Thinking, where's Warren? Said he'd be here in fifteen minutes. It's way past that now . . .

She switched over. *Psycho* had been a real bad choice. She channel-hopped and found a low-budget sci-fi movie. She stared at the screen. So far, all the action seemed to be happening in a spaceship, with some crazy alien crew leaping around in tight suits.

Boring . . .

She switched off the TV.

Everywhere was spooky quiet.

The shadows, shifting around in the semi-darkness, grew scarier by the minute.

Seemed like the house had taken on a life of its own. The trees outside rustled and sighed. The moving shadows they made crouched like animals ready to pounce.

A low rumble jolted her upright. Huhhh. Goddamn water cistern again!

She slumped down, huffing a sigh of relief.

But – what was *that*?

A faint click . . .

Her mouth went dry.

Her heart raced. Her breath came out in short, harsh bursts.

Then silence again . . .

It was *so* eerie.

Even the trees weren't rustling.

Deana relaxed, switched on the TV.

Psycho was still on.

It'd reached the part where Norman Bates was talking to his dead mother in the attic.

The movie was almost finished . . .

What then?

Warren should be here by now . . .

The doorbell's gonna ring any minute.

Maybe I should call. Something could've gone wrong . . .

She heard movement, a faint rustle behind her.

She stiffened. Froze. Her mouth dried up again.

'Hey, sugar. How 'bout a cuppa coffee for your Uncle Mace?'

His voice was soft, warm, familiar.

Deana jerked around.

'You,' she gasped.

'Who else, darlin'?'

Mace grinned, friendly-like. He opened his arms, palms held out. As if to say, *Hey. Here I am!* Like the night in her room. The night Warren came to dinner.

Mace. The bastard!

She'd handled him then. But she wasn't too sure she could do it now.

The Lake

Knowing what she did.

Remembering what Mom had told her.

Her legs felt shaky. Her breath jerked out in quick shallow gulps. Trembling, trying to play it cool, she steadied herself.

'Coffee? Sure. Take a seat, Mace. I'll go see to it right away.'

She got up, made a move to the kitchen, thinking, if I'm quick I could use the extension in there. Call Mom, the police, Mattie. Warren. *Anybody*.

Mace watched her go, chewing on seeds, a loose smile playing on his lips.

Deana clattered around in the kitchen. Fixing coffee. Setting mugs on a tray. An eye on the phone all the time.

Do it now do it now.

What if he's watching?

Fuck that.

Just do it.

He moved forward, catlike. Grabbing her hand. Twisting it behind her back. Holding it there. Tight.

She was hurting, but no way would she let him see it.

He pulled her close, their bodies touching.

She winced, catching a whiff of mulchy breath.

Goddamn seeds . . .

He grinned.

Clamped his free hand over her mouth.

Kept it there.

Deana struggled, trying to come up for air. Beneath his hand, she forced open her mouth, trying to say, 'Warren'll be here any minute.'

Only it came out like some weird mumbo-jumbo.

Mace frog-marched Deana into the living room. Flung her face down onto the sofa. Rammed a knee hard into her spine. Grabbing a handful of hair, he jerked her up and back, and wound a black silk scarf tight around her head. It cut into her eyes, across the bridge of her nose.

Leaving only a slight airway.

She panicked. Struggled. Barely able to breathe.

Pausing, he stepped back, watching her mumbling, kicking, gasping for air. Then, dragging a coil of twine from his jacket pocket, he began to wind it around her arms.

Her blue top slipped from her shoulders.

Mace gaped at her for a moment, seeing the rise of her soft round breasts, a glimpse of dark nipples, feeling himself rise, pulse, and grow hard.

Deana looked so . . . good and sweet. Scared. Vulnerable.

He smiled tersely.

Later, he promised himself.

Plenty of time . . .

He spoke softly. 'Take it easy, sweetheart. You should know better than to fight with Uncle Mace.'

Deana lay quiet. Wondering what in hell Mace planned to do next. Straining hard to hear his movements. Trying to guess what was happening.

A blanket dropped over her head. She struggled, feeling the twine bite into her arms, sweat break out and stream down her body. She gagged against the coarse, prickly cloth as he bound it around her.

More twine. Then he was hoisting her onto his shoulder.

Bumping along, she felt his muscles, flexed and hard, beneath her, the jolts and sickening thuds to her stomach and breasts . . . Heard the click of his cowboy boots on the tiled hallway . . . Felt a draft of air on her legs and feet. Her mules had gotten lost in the struggle.

They were outside now, the cool night air flowing fresh around them.

She felt herself falling as he swung her down, setting her upright on the gravel.

OUCH!! Shit!!!

Jagged stones jabbed the soles of her feet . . .

Deana heard the click of the trunk opening. Felt herself lifted and tossed into it. *Rammed* inside it. Mace was tucking in the blanket. The sharp edges of a toolbox or something jabbed her chest.

She gave a sharp gasp of pain.

The lid slammed down, cutting off whatever fresh air there'd been.

The Lake

She found herself inhaling coarse, prickly fibers. They caught in her throat. She began coughing.

Christ, I'm gonna choke to death . . .

Suddenly, she was panicking, spluttering.

She swallowed hard.

Again. And again.

Soon, her throat muscles were under control . . .

Thank God!

But it's so hot . . .

I'm gonna suffocate in here. I'm gonna DIE. Nobody'll find me till it's too late . . .

Deana felt vibrating throbs as the engine turned over. Heard it slip into gear, move up the driveway. Mace made a left, she slid a little, her foot tensing against metal . . . Jesus, she thought, *I'm suffocating . . .*

Panic welled up again.

Don't scream . . .

If I do, I could start choking all over again.

Her hands strained against the twine.

No way would it give . . . Desperate, gulping sobs rose in her throat.

She began to gag, choke . . .

Streams of sweat drenched her body.

Lie still. Save what air there is . . . He can't drive all night. He has to stop. Please, God, make it soon!

They were bumping over rough ground.

Jolting over ruts and rocks. Deana's body shook, jolting up and down.

Nauseous waves swept up from her stomach . . .

The scarf bit into her face.

Sweat, slick and hot, oozed from every pore.

My God. WHERE ARE WE?

Don't tell me. Mount Tam. I know it – sense it. Goddamn fuckin' place. I HATE it. I get outta here, I'll NEVER, EVER come back to this freakin' place again . . .

More jolting. More ruts.

The car pulled to a halt.

Deana's heart lurched.

What now? Is this where I get it? Right where Allan got his?

The trunk lid swung up.

Thank God.

Cool air streamed in.

Mace was pushing her, then rolling her forward. Feeling around for something. A weapon?

Christ! He's gonna kill me!

He picked her up.

Hoisted her back onto his shoulder.

She was bouncing and flopping around again, like a sack of laundry.

Mace stopped.

He was fiddling with a door lock, stepping over a stoop, his boots stamping across a wooden floor. Then she went flying through the air. Landing on a springy mattress. She heard, *felt* the harsh metallic squeak of bedsprings . . .

He was loosening her bonds now. Peeling off the blanket.

Thank God, thank God.

Now I can *breathe*.

Get this thing off so I can see, maybe I can talk him out of killing me.

The scarf stayed put.

So did the twine around her wrists.

Oh, the goddamn *heat*!

Her skin felt slick. Slimy.

Uggh . . .

If only I could *see*!

In her mind, though, she *could* see the headlines:

GIRL CAPTURED BY MANIAC UNCLE!

Lost for weeks out in the wilderness, the eighteen-year-old's emaciated body was found by hikers, today. Looked like she'd starved to death. Slowly.

The Lake

Or maybe hacked to death. Quickly . . .

What's it to be, folks?

'Gonna leave ya now, sugar. Uncle Mace has gotta ride. Places to go. Things to do.'

Deana felt his lips on her forehead.

And his kiss.

Light, soft.

She caught the odor of his sour breath.

'Back soon, honey,' he whispered.

She heard the *click, click* of boots as he walked away. A door slammed to, a key turned in the lock.

The car engine revved, then raced. It moved away. She listened till the sound faded.

She was alone.

Hey, come back! Don't leave me like this!

Save your breath, Deana.

Maybe he won't be too long . . .

She waited.

And waited.

S'pose he never comes back. S'pose he just leaves me here to rot . . .

It was almost light when Mace returned.

Chapter Fifty-five

'Deana! Deana! Leigh! Open up!'

Warren thumped the door so hard that he thought he'd bust his knuckles.

'Christ, where *are* you, Deana?'

It's like Sheena said . . . They've gone . . .

What had Deana meant by 'Mom's boyfriend's on the run . . . Gone ape-shit.' And why did she emphasize 'he *knows* about you'?

Sounded like anything could've happened . . .

Probably had.

They could both be dead.

'Oh my God. Not that . . .'

Sheena had arrived home early. A couple of minutes later and Warren would have hit the road, driving over to Deana's.

'Warren, maybe I won't be goin' back to Pacey's no more,' Sheena said quietly. 'He kinda objects when I leave him in the lurch.'

She seemed preoccupied. He knew that look.

Only too well.

His mouth went dry.

'Sheena! For chrissake, tell me what's up. What was so important you left the club early?'

She said she was scared. Had had one of her feelings . . .

Warren saw beads of sweat on her upper lip. He'd never seen her this tense before.

The Lake

'You're not gonna like it, Warren, but this gal o' yours. She's in deep trouble. I feel she's in a place that's small – and dark. Yeah. It's real dark in there and she . . .'

Sheena hesitated, knowing what this was doing to Warren.

His face went white. 'For God's *sake*, Sheena, she *what*?'

'Call the cops, Warren. Let them deal with it. It's none a' your business. Don't want you getting yourself killed on account of some gal you only just met!'

But Warren was already . . . out the door.

'Deana, if you're in there, open up. PLEASE!'

Twin headlight beams swooped down the driveway. Warren squinted, bringing up a hand to shield his eyes.

Leigh's car screeched to a halt. The nearside door swung open and she jumped out.

'Warren!'

'Leigh! You're safe . . .'

'Yeah. But what about Deana?'

'What d'ya mean, Leigh?' His heart lurched, and sank like a stone. He *was* too late. He'd known it all along.

He stood aside while Leigh prodded the key into the lock. The door fell open. They rushed inside.

The hallway was dark.

They ran to the living room. Trembling light from the TV threw uneasy shadows into the darkness. A talk-show host laughed, holding a mike close to a grinning member of the audience . . .

'Deana! Deana, darling! You there?'

Leigh darted into each room, calling, her heart sinking, her legs all shaky.

When she returned to the living room, her shoulders were hunched. She looked drawn, defeated. Exhausted.

Oh my God, thought Warren. *Sheena's right. I shoulda called the cops.*

Leigh caught his concern. 'Did you only just *get* here?' she demanded, her face hostile.

'Yeah, Leigh, I'm sorry. I got held up . . .'

'My God, Warren. You got held *up*? Don't you *see*? Mace arranged all this, so he could take her . . .'

'What happened? And where were *you*, Leigh?'

Leigh broke down, sobbing. There'd been no fight at the Bayview. All had been quiet when she'd got there. Just another civilized night. Customers enjoying their meals, paying their checks, saying their goodnights. No 'all hell breakin' loose' as Tony had said . . . Tony? It hadn't been Tony who'd phoned her. It'd been a hoax caller. And she'd bet her bottom dollar it'd been Mace who'd done the calling . . .

The phone rang.

Leigh sprang forward, grabbed it. 'Yes?' Her voice was terse.

Mattie.

'Thank *God* you're okay, Leigh. Have to report there was no emergency back here. Musta been a hoax call. Chief signed off early. Went home to his wife. She'd gotten sick. Nobody here's aware of any emergency. Don't ask me why . . . Leigh? You and Deana okay?'

Leigh met Warren's stare. Hot, frightened tears began to well up.

'Deana's gone, Mattie. She's not here.'

A moment's silence, then: 'It's Mace. Y'know that, Leigh, don't ya?' Mattie's voice rose. 'Goddamn fuckin' asshole Mace. The shit fooled us all.'

Chapter Fifty-six

Almost sun-up.

Mace eyed his wristwatch. 'Maybe a half-hour till it gets light,' he muttered.

Gotta move it. Though I should worry, he told himself, I got nothin' but time. He set his holdall down on the stoop and pushed the key in the door's lock.

He grinned. This was a real good place for his 'other activities'. Nobody, but nobody'd come this way in weeks.

The air was cool and clear, the dew still heavy on the rough grass humps along the track. He scanned the terrain. Mountains on one side: well wooded with dark impenetrable pines. The cabin, hidden in rocky territory, was almost impossible to access. He'd used the dirt path, betting not many others would attempt it – wouldn't want to. You could wreck a vehicle driving over the rough tracks hereabouts.

He glanced over to his right. Into the wide misty space beyond. Before that, though, came a steep drop to the valley below. In the growing light, he heard the distant sound of roaring water. The river. He'd done some white-water rafting down there a coupla years back. When he first discovered the cabin . . .

Yessir. One lonesome place. But, like the professional he was, he always covered his tracks so nobody'd ever discover his 'other activities'. He'd been fortunate to find such an isolated spot.

He went inside the cabin.

'Hi, honey. I'm home!' he sang out.

Silence . . .

Then a muffled sob from the bed.

'Well now, Deana darlin', how ya doin'?'

Mace set down his holdall and went over to Deana. Humming a little to himself, he untied and peeled off the silk scarf. He released her wrists from the twine.

Deana gasped, scrunching up her eyes, peering into the half-light.

Saw Mace standing over her.

Giving her one of his twisted smiles.

'PLEASE, MACE. TAKE ME HOME!' she blurted.

'Why, sure enough y'*are* home, sugar.'

'Where *am* I?'

She rubbed at her wrists. Wincing as she went over the burn marks. Her hands still felt dead.

'You're tucked away nice 'n' safe where nobody can find ya, honey.'

Deana looked around at the cabin. A tin bucket stood in the corner. *Coulda done with that hours ago*, she thought, aware of the dark patch, now cold and uncomfortable, between her legs. She saw packs of bottled water, an open cardboard box, a rickety chair – and Mace's holdall, directly in front of her.

Shuffling till her back was against the wall, she took in the gray tick mattress. Old brown stains made big patchy patterns across it.

Blood?

There were more stains than mattress, it looked like.

She stifled a gulp of fear.

'Mace, what are you going to do to me?' she asked, despising the tremor in her voice.

'Haven't decided yet, sugar. But take my advice, don't you worry your pretty li'l head about it.' He walked over to the cardboard box, took out a wrapped bread roll and handed it to her. 'Here. You must be hungry. Some time since you last ate, huh?'

She took the roll, peeled off the wrapper, opened up the top layer and peered inside.

'Won't hurt you none.' He watched her closely, an amused grin on

The Lake

his face. 'Can't guarantee it'll be Bayview quality, but it's as good as you're gonna get.'

He picked up a bottle of water, twisted off the top and passed the bottle to her. 'There,' he said. 'Salami on rye and a swig a' water and you'll be fightin' fit in no time at all. Mmmm . . . Looks good.' He nodded at the sandwich. 'Don't mind if I have one a' those myself.'

Helping himself to a roll and fresh water, Mace sat facing Deana, astride the chair. He broke off a wad of bread and shoved it into his mouth. 'Guess you must be wonderin' why you're here,' he said, chewing around on the food. 'Why I'm taking such a special interest in my pretty li'l niece.'

'You could say that,' Deana said slowly, not taking her stare off his face. How could she *ever* have fancied him? He looked like an over-the-hill biker with his leather jacket, bleached hair and crumbs falling down his front.

Scrub over-the-hill biker.

Mace is one hundred per cent cop, Deana, an' don't you forget it. A cop gone bad – and mad . . .

Her heart began to hammer.

Mace chewed on his food, smiling at her like he knew something that she didn't.

Deana didn't like the way he did that. She shivered.

'Tell ya a little story?'

'If you must.'

'Gotta keep y'entertained, honey. Can't have ya gettin' bored, now, can we?'

She made a face. He smiled.

'I tell you a tale, then I take your photograph. Deal?'

He offered a hand and she took it, warily.

She didn't much like the sound of 'photographs' but at least it didn't seem like he was going to kill her yet.

Mace got up and stood looking through the cabin's murky window. 'Guess your mom told you about Edith Payne's letter?'

'Er, sure, she told me about it . . .'

'I'll go one better, sweetheart. I'll tell ya *my* version!'

Turning on his heel, he faced her. Looking into her eyes, saying nothing. Just staring like she was a stranger he'd never seen before.

Then giving her that twisted smile again.

Deana glanced away, feeling nervous, uncomfortable. Why the hell didn't he sit down and get on with his story?

As if he'd read her thoughts, he sat himself back astride the chair. He began talking.

'How d'ya think it feels to know that your own mother killed your pa then gave you to somebody who couldn't care less whether you lived or died?'

His eyes glowed at her, burning with a hate that she didn't understand.

Shrinking from his gaze, she said slowly, 'Don't know how that'd feel exactly, but . . . I guess it'd be awful . . .'

'You don't know how that'd feel exactly.' Mace's voice rose a couple of octaves, mimicking her words.

Curling his mouth in disgust, he resumed his tale.

'Well, I'll tell ya, Deana. It feels bad. Real bad. It makes you hate a person so much you wanta make 'em suffer – the way you suffered. All those years.'

Deana stayed quiet.

'My pa didn't have a chance. He was sick. And drunk. No wonder, with Edith Payne for a wife. My pa believed he was right. And I guess he was . . . No girl should be like my sister Tania. Dark and . . . covered in hair . . .' He slumped forward over the chair. His face creased up. He looked beat.

Deana's mouth stayed shut.

Maybe he's gonna cry.

Then I can hit him with something and escape . . .

Casually, she looked around. Saw nothing she could use as a weapon. Except the chair . . . and he was sitting on that.

'I searched for my sister, y'know. Didn't track her down, though. But not once have I given up hope. She's out there. Somewhere.' His voice rose. 'Causin' grief and makin' things bad for somebody else, I guess. Yeah. I KNOW she's still out there – somewhere . . .'

'So, what do you intend doing when you find her, Mace? Or should that be Jess?'

The Lake

Right on, smart-ass! That should get you killed okay. You wanna die? Carry on this way and you'll get your wish . . .

Lifting his head, Mace's eyes leveled with hers. They seemed oddly vacant, yet they glittered with a wild, dangerous look.

Deana shuddered.

Christ, I got him riled again. What am I, a fuckin' moron?

His mouth quirked in a humorless twist.

'Well, now. Ain't *you* the funny girl? Just call me Uncle Mace, honey. That'll be fine by me.'

'Sorry, Mace. Didn't mean to upset you,' she said in a small voice.

'You didn't upset me none. Me, I'm just your nice, friendly ol' Uncle Mace.'

'You joined the police so's you could find Tania? What did you do before that?'

He grinned. 'Smart kid, ain't ya? Oh, I bummed around 'Frisco, working bars – pumpin' iron. Knew all the gyms in the Bay area. Boxed a little; this 'n' that. Then Mom got sick. She was an old lady by then. I went back to Wahconda but she was dead already. Only inheritance she left was the cabin I was born in – and that letter . . .'

Deana almost felt sorry for him. He sure was a mixed-up guy. Yeah. Sick. Dangerous. But sad, too.

Suddenly, Mace was on his feet, staring out the window again. His hands went up to his hips, his jacket lifted and she caught the bulge of his hip holster.

'Mace?' she ventured, quietly. 'Why don't you let me go home? Keeping me here isn't gonna do you any good. People'll be looking for me. They find me and—'

'Find you? What makes you think anybody's gonna *find* ya, sweetheart?'

'Well, they'll search for me. Probably trace me to here . . .'

'No way. *Nobody* saw you go. *Nobody*'ll find you here. Reason I use this place is because nobody ever comes up here. 'Cept me.'

Then he was standing over her. His legs apart. Grinning. Stroking her hair. Smoothing the dark strands resting on her shoulders. Over and over again.

She winced.

Too scared to move.

Her eyes leveled with his crotch.

Saw him pulse inside his pants.

God, no. He's gonna rape me. Please, God, NO!

He grabbed her head and pressed it to him. His hard-on rose some more. She felt it throb against her face.

Breaking away, Deana squirmed back across the mattress, edging off it, landing on her knees.

She scrambled to her feet.

'Just let me go, Mace. Before we both do something we'll regret.' Her gaze wandered to the chair. One quick smash and it'd be in pieces.

I could use one of the legs to hit him with.

Kill him, if I have to.

Oh yeah? You an' whose army?

His stare mocked her. 'Don't do anything stupid, Deana. Remember, I could break yer pretty li'l neck, just like that.'

He swiped the air with a swift karate chop.

She blinked. Picturing his hand coming down, whistling toward her.

Watch it, Deana.

Maybe I'll get him while he's asleep . . .

If he falls asleep . . .

She shivered, suddenly getting the feeling that he was reading her mind.

Instead, he looked confused, bewildered. Shaking his head. Heaving a sorrowful sigh.

'I'm gonna have to put y'away, Deana. Y'know that?'

'Put me *away*? What d'you mean, put me away?'

'Put you someplace where you'll come to no harm. Where you'll be safe. Come to Uncle Mace, li'l girl.'

Mace beckoned, smiling. Like he was offering candy to a baby.

Deana glared back. Not moving.

'C'mon, sugar. Uncle Mace might turn nasty if Deana doesn't come when she's called.' His voice had a sing-song lilt to it.

'So, what are you gonna do, Mace?'

'Something I shoulda done right from the start.' He picked up the

The Lake

twine from where it had fallen earlier. She watched him advance slowly, winding it around his hands.

She backed away, stumbling against the cabin wall, her arms shooting out, spread-eagled against the wood slats.

'C'mon now, Deana. There's a good girl.'

Fascinated, she watched him twist the twine around his fingers. Her hand rose to her neck.

'No, Mace. Please don't,' she panted. 'DON'T DO IT, MACE!'

She lost it . . . somehow got caught up in a swirling black cloud.

Screams rang out, shattering the deathly quiet . . .

Vaguely, Deana wondered who it was, crying out like that.

The screams died.

Then she heard sobs . . . tiny, whimpering sounds.

Chapter Fifty-seven

'Just calm down now, honey. Uncle Mace ain't gonna hurt ya. Yet.'
Mace stood over Deana, busying himself with the twine. Wrapping it neatly, tightly, around her legs. The way he went about it, she could tell he'd done it before.

Probably many times.

She struggled, trying to kick out at him, but all she managed was to make futile little scuffles with her feet . . .

Goddamn bastard's hobbled me – like a horse!

Tears of frustration streamed down her cheeks.

Mace's mouth curved in a bright smile.

'Now, now, darlin'. No struggling. A gal could get hurt that way.'

He slapped her face. Her head jerked up and sideways, then flopped. Her hair swung around her shoulders. Giving a little cry, she gasped, ready to give him an earful of abuse.

Thinking better of it, she clamped her lips tight.

No use goading him. I could wind up dead . . .

Gonna wind up dead *anyhow* . . .

'Hey, sugar,' he whispered. 'Didn't y'care for that?'

No reply.

Catching the defiance in her eyes, Mace whacked her again. With the back of his hand.

Seems like Uncle Mace is having himself a rare old time.
Stay with it, Deana.

The Lake

He wants you to crack. Break up. Plead for mercy. Okay. Like he'll wait for ever. No way is the bastard gonna see I'm scared . . .

He studied her face; saw the tears, her clenched jaw. The defiance still there.

His smirk broke out again.

'That's a good li'l gal. Uncle Mace don't like gals who get flighty . . .'

Deana wriggled her feet.

The twine sliced into her calves and ankles.

She pulled a face. Struggling only worsened the pain.

Mace is one sick fuck, she fumed inwardly, *but he sure knows how to tie a person up.*

In desperation, she stared at her legs: pale, puffy, criss-crossed with twine. 'Dear God, Mace,' she gasped. 'This *hurts* – I'm gonna get gangrene if you don't untie me.'

Suddenly, the full realization of what Mace *could* do hammered home. The damage . . . the *pain* he could inflict.

She began to shake.

'Scared, honey?'

Her lips stayed shut. She shot him a sour look.

'No reply, huh? Maybe you'd care for another crack?'

The next one rocked her jaw.

Harder this time.

Starting up afresh the pain where Nelson had slugged her.

'Uuugghh . . .' Deana gasped, shaking her head. She felt a gush of blood spurt and rise inside her mouth, but her top teeth seemed to be embedded in her lower lip. She eased them free. Blood flowed out and down her chin.

Do this one more time, the fucker's gonna break my neck.

Cringing with pain, her hand flew to her jaw. Her lips felt slick and rubbery. She scowled, clenched her teeth and muttered, 'Up yours, shit-face.'

Mace's eyebrows lifted slightly.

'Let's pretend I didn't hear that, sugar . . .'

She glared at him. But he seemed distant, as if his mind was on other things. It was.

Tilting his head, he looked at her, admiring his handiwork. The swollen eyes, bruised mouth, cut lips, the trickle of blood sliding down her chin . . .

Then, reaching forward, Mace slipped Deana's blouse off one shoulder.

Not satisfied with that, he pulled it down some more, until her breast peeked out.

Deana cringed. Went taut. Goose bumps squirmed all over her body.

Gently, Mace fingered her breast, tracing swirls around it, touching up the hard dark nipple.

Her stomach crawled. She pulled away from him, scarcely breathing.

His stare held hers for a moment.

Daring her to move . . .

She lurched forward, thinking about screaming, throwing herself at him, clawing at his face, blinding him with her nails . . .

Then he was moving away, stepping back like an artist assessing his masterpiece.

Deana gave up. She went still.

Now for the final touch . . .

That long black hair.

Mace's hands came at Deana, reaching out, holding the dark shiny strands between his fingers . . . savouring the silky feel. Then he fussed around, arranging it over her shoulders.

'Mmmm-huh!' He seemed pleased with the effect. Humming under his breath he took a little time poking around in the holdall. He brought out the Nikon and several unopened reels of film.

No need for Polaroids today. The light's okay.

Everything should go according to plan.

He was about to create another Mace Harrison masterpiece. A surge of satisfaction, *anticipation*, welled up inside him. It felt good and warm.

Lifting his eyes skyward, he gave a cynical smile.

'This one's for you, Daddy,' he whispered.

Chapter Fifty-eight

Mace bunched his lips in a fake kiss.

'Smile for the birdie, sweetheart,' he murmured, putting the camera's viewfinder to his eye. Moving back slightly, he extended the lens and adjusted it, twisting it round between finger and thumb.

He wanted *all* of Deana in the frame. First off, standing against the cabin wall. It'd be the perfect foil for her pale, bruised body. Plus the fact that there'd be no giveaway clues . . .

Just Deana and the shitty ol' pinewood wall.

Deana; tears coursing down her cheeks, jaw hanging loose, bloodied lips all swollen . . . eyes dark, frightened, pleading . . .

He aimed to cover every angle.

Left side . . .

'Stay still, sugar.'

Front.

Then the right side . . .

'I'm comin' in now . . .'

He zoomed in. Getting one or two head shots in close-up.

Engrossed in his work, Mace clicked away for fifteen minutes or so. Changing the film when necessary.

That done, he replaced the camera in the holdall.

Deana blurted out a gasp of relief. She slid down the wall, feeling the floor cold and damp beneath her buttocks. She felt wrecked. Salt tears welled, spilling down her cheeks, stinging her cut lips.

Eyes on him the whole time.

Watching him warily, like a mouse in the thrall of a cat.

Mace beamed, showing his straight white teeth. 'How 'bout breakfast?' he said, zipping up the holdall. 'I'm starvin'!'

Over at the food box, Mace brought out a sandwich. 'Here,' he said, peeling down the wrapper. 'Take a bite.'

Deana couldn't stop the rush of blood rising to her head.

'Get some therapy, Mace,' she spat through thick, puffy lips. 'Think I'm gonna do *exactly* what you want? Go fuck yourself. You're a goddamn sicko and you know it! When they find me you're gonna pay for what you've done!'

Mace shrugged his shoulders, sat himself astride the chair and bit off a chunk of bread. He began to eat, grinning around his food, crumbs flying from his mouth.

He pointed the sandwich at her.

'You don't wanna eat, then don't eat. And I ain't gonna kill you. Yet. Things to do first. But you'll regret not eatin', sugar. Could be *days* 'fore I decide to . . .' He left the sentence unfinished.

Deana trembled, holding on to her voice, keeping it low and level; trying to form the words without showing how much he'd hurt her. It wasn't easy.

'Before you decide to do what?'

'You'll see, sugar. You'll see!'

Done with his sandwich, Mace bent down and picked up the blanket. Opening it out, he threw it over her head, held it tight over her shoulders.

Deana spluttered, screamed.

Kept on screaming and struggling.

Pulling her close, calming her down, Mace was amused. He huffed out a short laugh. 'Might as well stop that, honey. There's no one around to ride to your rescue – least of all that prick of a boyfriend a' yours. Whassisname? Warren? Huh! Warren *cocksucker* Beatty?'

Mace was in jovial mood; he chuckled to himself, like he'd just made the joke of the year. Still holding Deana tight.

Then, snatching away the blanket, he grabbed at her top and gripped it tight, twisting it around till she almost choked.

The Lake

He wasn't laughing now. Instead, he had that wild animal look again. Baring his teeth, he lifted her off the floor, slammed her against the wall and held her there.

A mirthless grin twisted his mouth.

He let go. She slumped forward. Then, quickly, he began winding the blanket around her.

Holding her up with one hand.

Unbuckling his belt with the other.

Snapping it like a bullwhip, looping the belt around her, trapping her arms.

Drawing it tight.

Buckling it up.

Still holding her upright.

Deana wasn't screaming now – she'd almost stopped breathing.

Can't breathe . . . and scream at the same time.

Gotta breathe.

Short, shallow huffs.

Panic welled. Her head hurt.

Sweat oozed, slick and hot, from every pore.

My God. He really, really means to kill me!

I'm gonna die and no one'll ever know . . .

Hoisting her onto his shoulder again, Mace shifted around, his bulk kneading her guts as he balanced her weight. Her head swung low and her blood throbbed and pounded, hard.

He stepped forward, catching her head against the door frame as he went out. Smashing it sideways with a sickening thud.

Deana felt blinding, flashing pain. Her head spun . . .

A rush of vomit surged in her throat . . .

Mace was outside now. His breath coming quick and heavy as he traveled over rough terrain . . . undergrowth, bushes, snagging his boots. With each step, each lurching jolt, his shoulder humped into Deana's belly, pummeling her aching gut. She gasped, heaved, not knowing how much more she could take . . .

Through the blanket, the sun scorched her back. Nausea rose again in her craw. She retched, forcing it back down.

Then she hit dirt, feeling hard knobbly humps beneath her buttocks. She rolled over, steadied herself . . . and came to rest on her back.

Listening to Mace stomp away.

Seconds later, a door opened.

Mace returned. Hoisted her onto his shoulder again.

A sudden draft caught at her legs. Earlier, jolting along on his back, it'd been hot.

Now . . . it's icy cold . . .

Where am I? Where's he taking me?

Deana started to cry.

Wishing that Warren was here.

If – when Warren finds me, he'll get even with Mace. Pound his brains out. Tear him apart. Kill him with his bare hands. Then he'll take me home.

Dank, earthy odors stole through the blanket, curling into her nostrils. It was cold here . . . wherever it was . . . Damp and so *cold*.

A sunless place.

Oh my God!!

She plummeted down. Hit something that gave under her weight; it felt soft, but not springy.

Like a mattress on a hard dirt floor.

She heard Mace's breath, huffing out in short sharp grunts. Felt him pulling at her middle, picking at the belt, loosening it. Unwinding the twine from her legs . . . Pulling the blanket from her face.

Christ, the *stench* . . . Bad, rancid dirt beneath her, water slick on the walls . . . She focused her eyes but it was so *dark*, she couldn't quite see where she was.

Uhhh . . . It's so COLD!

Like the grave . . .

Shuddering, whimpering, she dragged the blanket to her. Fierce, fiery, *tingly* pain seared her legs as the blood came pumping back.

Tears spilled down her cheeks.

'Let me go, Mace. PLEASE,' she blurted. 'I've done nothing to hurt you. I kept quiet about you coming into my room like that. Mom doesn't know a thing . . . when I get outta here, I promise I'll never tell . . .'

'No sweat, sugar. Uncle Mace *knows* you won't tell.' His voice

The Lake

dropped a notch. It went quiet, calm, confiding.

'Best listen up, kiddo. You won't tell, 'cause – you're – going – NOPLACE. Geddit?'

His eyes glittered, shining in the dark.

Deana stayed quiet.

A chill crawled up her spine. The numbness, the tingling, the pain in her legs were nothing to the fear that she felt now.

Her heart hammered.

Goddamn maniac! He's gonna kill me! I'm gonna die here and nobody's gonna find me . . .

In her mind she pictured Mace carving, gouging all her intimate, secret places – then tearing her apart . . . slurping on her flesh with fiendish glee, sucking his lips, his bloodied fingers . . .

Her hands flew to her face.

Feeling grateful relief that he'd done with her.

For the moment.

She heard him stomp away.

Then she was crying, with hard, hurting sobs.

Peeking through her fingers.

Catching a slice of daylight as he went out the door.

The door slammed.

A scattering of debris hit the floor.

A key rattled home.

With a harsh scraping sound, it turned in the lock.

Chapter Fifty-nine

The thing came closer . . .
  Moving quietly with animal stealth.
  She heard its raspy breathing.
  Felt its foul breath as it hung over her bed . . .
  From out of nowhere a cloth fluttered down.
  Covering her face.
  Clinging so tight that it felt like a second skin.
  A surge of panic set her screaming, tearing at it.
  All the while the thing watched.
  She saw the huge veined wings spread out behind it . . . Ropes of matted hair. Small darting eyes. Spiky teeth. Curved, clawed hands reaching down.
  Her screams turned to whimpers and died. She lay rigid with fear. Sweat, like globs of blood, oozed down her body. She opened her mouth to cry for help, but no sound came. She tried again, straining, willing her voice to work. Her jaws ached, her throat was like sandpaper, dry and parched.
  As she twisted and turned, the hands gripped her neck, tighter and tighter . . . until . . . she was falling . . . into deep dark space . . .

Leigh struggled awake, tearing the bedsheets from her slick, damp body, clutching at her neck, looking around for that eerie nightmare creature . . .
  The curtains billowed softly. Cool air played on her sweat-soaked skin . . .
  Still not convinced that she was alone, she stared anxiously into the

The Lake

shadows, seeing familiar things – her wardrobe, dresser, wicker chair, hamper . . . pictures on the wall . . .

She sighed. Her breath evened out. Everything's okay, she told herself.

Then: *No, it's not* . . .

Panting again, she peered into all the gray creepy spaces; into the shadows where *anything* could hide . . .

She trod the bedsheet down with her feet.

Feeling her nightgown up around her neck, cutting across her throat, almost strangling her. This hadn't happened since that last nightmare, when Edith Payne had grabbed her, shrieked at her by Charlie's graveside . . .

Charlie's funeral.

Now it could be Deana's . . .

NO NO NO!!!

STOP THAT. RIGHT NOW!!!!

Deana's safe.

I know it I know it. I'd know in my heart if she was d— Can't say it. *WON'T SAY IT* . . .*!*

The realization that Deana was gone engulfed her once more. This was the second terrible night of drugged, blacked-out sleep. Sleep broken by hideous phantoms. Ghosts invading the night like demented harpies.

Leigh's heart sank. Mattie had said that she'd call the minute she had news . . . when any clue, no matter how small, showed up. There'd been nothing.

Zero.

Zip.

She knew that the cops were on the case, and with Mattie on their tails they'd stick at it . . . But there'd been no sign of Mace. No sign of Deana.

Leigh swung her legs off the bed. The night air began to chill her skin. She shivered, feeling worn, unutterably weary; waiting for news. Mattie had insisted, you're more use at home than out there, looking for Deana. She may call . . . You gotta be ready . . .

She'd waited. But there'd been no calls from Deana. Just anxious ones from Warren. Reassuring ones from Mattie.

There were two cops in the house. Guarding her. Watching out for intruders. Checking in with the office now and then for updates on the case.

None so far.

In her heart, she knew that Mace had what he wanted.

Deana.

A surrogate Tania.

Oh God, Deana, don't rile him.

Use your intelligence. Spy your chance . . .

Spy your chance?

With a rogue cop, a trained killer, a *maniac* like Mace for company?

Dear God, please help my baby girl.

Leigh got to her feet. She swayed, put a hand to her forehead, fell back and flopped on the bed.

Reaching for the glass of water on the nightstand, she saw the small brown container of sleeping pills . . . Her hand strayed forward, but she snatched it back.

I gotta stay awake.

Deana may call.

Don't want to sleep anyhow . . . not with these nightmares . . .

Pulling on a robe, she went to the hallway, feeling ice-cool tiles beneath her bare feet. She padded into the living room. Dawn had broken – its pale gray light made eerie moving patterns on the carpet.

She looked around . . .

Caught her breath . . .

Something was wrong.

The place was quiet.

Too damn quiet . . .

Okay, Officers Halliwell and Bodine were probably catching a few zees. One in the den; the other in the kitchen, where she'd left them . . .

But somehow it wasn't the peaceful quiet of people asleep. This was more an overall deathly hush. Like the world was holding its breath. Waiting for . . . what? Armageddon?

The Lake

Impatiently, she shook her head and huffed out a long, low breath. Don't be a fool, she told herself. You're hyped up. Worried out of your skull about Deana.

And fearful that—

Something isn't quite right . . .

Leigh screamed.

Loud and long.

Even as she screamed, she remembered Edith Payne, shrieking like a wounded animal when she discovered Charlie's broken body, all those years ago . . .

'Oh no, oh NO!!!' Leigh sobbed out frightened little cries, her hands crushed to her chest. Her knees folded and hit the carpet with a sickening jolt.

She scrabbled over to the TV.

Grabbed at the photographs fanned out on the floor.

Horrified at what she saw . . .

Terrified.

DEANA!!! Oh NO!

A dozen or so black and white shots.

Deana, her face all bruised, lips cut and swollen. Eyes puffy, almost closed. Hair arranged neatly across her naked shoulders . . . curling around her breasts.

Oh, my God . . . Deana!

Leigh snatched up a print; pressed it to her mouth, sobbing, her tears making smudges, carving lines down the bromide. She stopped. Looked at the others.

Picking them up, slowly, one by one. Her stomach twisting, her tormented eyes seeing the damage that Mace had done . . .

Oh, my God . . .

Must tell Mattie. There may be some sort of *clue* hidden in the photographs. Somehow. Some*where*.

Mattie would find *something*.

She knew Mace like no one else did.

Leigh stumbled to her feet, clasping the photos to her breast. Something else caught her eye.

Another photograph. One she knew well. Deana at Point Reyes

Beach. In her new white bikini. Laughing at the camera.

Fuckin' bastard Mace.

He'd had it all along.

Deana *hadn't* given it to Warren . . .

The goddamn evil beast! What a fool I've been – harboring a psycho like that!

Guilt welled up.

If she hadn't rowed with Nelson.

If she hadn't taken up with Mace.

If she hadn't gone to Aunt Jenny's in the first place.

Grow up, Leigh. This isn't your fault.

But maybe you should have listened to Deana. She'd never liked Mace anyway.

Now Deana was held captive by Mace.

And her dork of a mother never even *guessed* that he—

Leigh hurried into the hallway. To rouse her bodyguards. Tell them that Mace had sneaked in . . .

Could still be here . . .

Her blood ran cold.

The house was eerily quiet.

Huh!

Some bodyguards . . . Allowing an intruder to sneak past them . . . Come to that, they should be around; they must've heard me walking about.

Leigh quickly discovered why the two cops were silent. They lay sprawled in pools of blood. Congealing loops of it sliding from gaping slits in their throats.

'Mattie! *Mattie!*' Leigh cried into the phone, willing her to pick up. She didn't. Hurriedly, Leigh yelled at the answerphone. 'Mattie. Please come over as soon as you can. Something's happened here. Something serious. I want you here. NOW!'

Christ! No Mattie. Just a conversation with her answerphone . . . A great start to the day – all alone in the house with those awful images of Deana playing on her mind – not to mention two stiffs for company.

Warren! He'll know what to do . . .

The Lake

Letting the prints drift to the floor, Leigh went through her little black book with trembling fingers.

She found Warren's number. Dialed it.

Knees shaky, heart in her mouth, she prayed for Warren to speak to her.

'The Hastings residence.' A woman's voice.

Sheena.

'This is Leigh West. I must speak with Warren.'

'You got it, sister.' Sheena's response was instant. Like she'd been waiting for Leigh's call.

A moment's silence, then, 'Leigh. Warren here. What is it?' His voice rose. 'Deana?'

'Warren, please come over. Someone's been here. An intruder. It *has* to be Mace. And . . . the two officers . . .'

'Yes?'

'They're dead, Warren. They've been murdered.'

'Christ.' Warren's voice was terse. 'I'm coming over, Leigh. You called the cops?'

'I phoned Mattie. She's not in. Left a message for her.'

'Mill Valley PD?'

'No. I'll do it now . . .'

'Stay right there, Leigh. I'll phone the cops from here, and I'll be over in a coupla minutes. Don't touch a thing.'

'He left photographs, Warren,' Leigh went on, sobbing.

'The *bastard*! . . . I'll be right over, Leigh . . .'

Sheena turned to Warren. 'I'm coming too. I need to know what's going on.'

'Best stay put, Sheena. Might just complicate matters you being over at Leigh's house.'

Leigh gave a heavy sigh and shivered. She felt chilled to the bone.

Pulling her robe around her, she found the belt and tied it tight. Thank God for Warren, she thought. Deana was right. He's such a sensible, capable guy . . .

She glanced toward the front door, wanting, *willing* him to be there.

To tell her everything was going to be okay. He'd find Deana . . . Bring her home . . .

She looked at the prints scattered at her feet. She bent to pick them up.

A hand slipped around her waist.

She gasped, jumped.

Froze.

Chapter Sixty

The hand around Leigh's waist tightened.

Another clasped her arm.

They brought her up.

Pulled her round.

Lips closed on hers. Gently . . .

Mace.

'Why hello, sweet thing,' he said softly. 'How ya been?'

'YOU! You BASTARD!! What're you doing here? And where's Deana? Tell me where you've hidden her. TELL ME!!' Shaking off Mace's hands, Leigh grabbed his biker jacket, jerking him close. 'Just tell me what you've done with my daughter. You'll *never* get away with it. TELL ME – WHERE IS SHE?'

'Hey, steady on there. And let go a' me. Can't tell you where li'l Deana *is*, but I *do* know she's alive and well . . .' He thought about it, blew out breath slowly and shook his head. 'Y'could say she's several country miles from bein' all *right*. But she's okay. At the moment,' he added, grinning.

'Where? Just tell me *where* she is, Mace!'

He backed off into the shadows, his eyes glittering in the half-light. Suddenly, out of nowhere, he had a knife in his hand.

His eyes narrowed.

Pointing the blade at Leigh, he whispered, 'That's for me to know – and our little friend Warren to find out.'

'Warren? Why Warren? All of Mill Valley PD is looking for Deana

. . . never mind Mattie . . .' She looked at him uncertainly . . . Where *is* Mattie? she wondered.

Her heart froze.

She *must*'ve picked up my message by now . . .

'Really?' Raising his eyebrows, Mace gave her a chilling smile. 'Wouldn't count on that if I were you!'

He turned. Disappeared into the kitchen.

She heard the back door open, then click shut.

Stunned, she wondered what Mace had meant.

I wouldn't count on that if I were you . . .

Surely, he hadn't . . .

Chapter Sixty-one

The doorbell rang. She leapt. Her stomach clenched . . .

Who . . .?

She looked around, half-expecting Mace to appear . . .

'Leigh, Leigh! It's Warren. Open up!'

Sobbing with relief, she ran to the door, slipped the chain from the catch, and opened it.

She stood there, swaying, tears making silver trails down her cheeks. For the second time in the last half-hour, she felt her knees folding.

Warren lunged forward. Grabbed her waist. Kicking the door shut behind him, he guided her to the living room, and helped her onto the sofa.

It was almost daylight, but not yet light enough to see clearly. Flashing a brief smile at Leigh, murmuring 'A little illumination wouldn't go amiss,' he turned on the TV lamp. Its warm yellow glow lit their part of the room.

He asked gently, 'Feeling better now?'

'Warren,' Leigh said in a small voice. 'I can't tell you how relieved I am to see you. Did you call the cops?'

'Yeah. They should be here any minute now . . .'

'I didn't want to get you involved like this . . .'

'I *am* involved, Leigh. Try not to worry – we're gonna get her back in no time . . .'

'I'm not so sure, Warren. You may change your mind about that.

Take a look at these . . .' Leigh jerked her head at the photographs she had spread on the table. Tears welled up again.

Warren's face darkened as he scanned the pictures. 'My GOD!' he breathed, his voice rising. 'He left THESE? How could he *do* this – to her . . . then take pictures . . . and bring them here . . . The guy's psycho, a sadistic fuckin' maniac!' His voice broke off.

'You're telling me. I couldn't sleep . . . came into this room – and found these here on the floor. As well as one he'd stolen earlier. I called Mattie. She wasn't around . . . so I left a message on her answerphone. And I found the two officers . . . God, it was just too awful.'

'You need a drink.' He went over to the bar.

They heard thumping on the door.

'Police, Ms West. Open up!'

Warren left the bar. 'I'll get it. You stay here.'

Leigh nodded dumbly.

She heard Warren open the door and introduce himself. Then men's voices. One said, 'Where are they?'

Leigh got up. She met the cops coming down the hall.

'They . . . they're . . .' She cleared her throat. 'One's in the kitchen – the other's in the den . . . Through here, officer. And you are?'

'I'm Officer Craig and this is Officer Bronson, ma'am.'

They showed their IDs and disappeared into the kitchen.

'You okay?' Warren asked, following Leigh to the living room.

'I'm so worried . . . and there's something I didn't mention, Warren. Mace was here. He was in the house when I called you. He implied that something might have happened to Mattie. Hope to Christ it hasn't.'

She looked at him anxiously.

'Maybe he got to her. Like he got to those cops out there . . .'

Warren's jaw tightened.

The phone rang.

Leigh hurried into the hallway. She picked it up.

It was Mattie.

Leigh gasped a sigh of relief.

'Got your message, Leigh. What happened? It sounded serious.'

The Lake

'It was. *Is*. Halliwell and Bodine were murdered. Mace got to them, Mattie.'

There was a gasp of shock from down the line.

'The cops are here now,' Leigh continued. 'So is Warren. Any news of Deana?'

She closed her eyes tight. Please God let there be news. *Good* news.

"Fraid not, Leigh. I'm comin' over a.s.a.p. Tell you what I know. We can compare notes . . .'

Leigh put the phone down. Hoping Mattie had something constructive to say. Like she'd got a plan, had an idea – anything that'd save Deana from Mace.

By the time Mattie showed, the bodies had been taken away. More officers were poking around. Checking doors, windows. Taking prints.

Mattie noticed the photos scattered on the coffee table.

'Just run it by me, Leigh,' she said quietly. 'What happened?'

Leigh repeated everything that she'd told the officers.

Including the fact that Mace had still been in the house when she'd called Mattie.

'It's been a terrible experience for you, Leigh,' Mattie said.

Leigh remained silent, then said, 'Mace implied that something might have happened to you, Mattie.'

'Well, it hasn't. Don't intend that it should, either. As for the photographs, Leigh . . .' She let out a deep sigh. 'What can I say – that it's Mace up to his old tricks again? Yeah,' she said, shaking her head, her lips tight, remembering the scrapbook that they'd found at his apartment. 'We sure gotta find that badass in one helluva hurry.'

Diving into her shoulder bag, Mattie picked out a folded plastic bag and protective gloves. She drew the gloves on, easing them over her fingers.

Glancing at the photographs, she separated them with her fingertips. Staying silent for a while. An icy chill creeping through her body. This looked like the business. She hoped they weren't too late.

Slowly, she gathered the prints together.

Shook open the bag, slid them inside.

'I'll get these over to the lab. Have Forensic check them out. Could be, apart from Mace's dabs, some little thing – fibers, soil deposits – that might give us a lead. We're gonna catch him, Leigh . . .'

Leigh choked back a sob. 'That's my daughter out there, Mattie. Sure – we're gonna catch him, but when? I can't just wait here! God, Mattie.' Her voice rose. 'I can't just do *nothing*!'

'What *can* you do, Leigh? We got trained people out there. We know what he's up to – given his family history an' all. He's tracking down his sister . . . Meanwhile, he's . . . Christ, we're talking serial ki—' She broke off, embarrassed. 'Sorry, Leigh – shouldn't have said that. Anyhow, we brought Ava Sorensson in on the job. Maybe she'll come up with something.'

'Ava Sorensson?'

'Yeah. She's a criminal psychologist. Best in the business. If she can't crack Mace, nobody can.'

'Well, if she can help . . .' Leigh murmured, doubtfully. Then she noticed Warren staring at her. 'Mattie, it's time Warren knew the story behind all this.' She gave him a hesitant smile.

'It might help,' he put in wryly.

'Sure,' Mattie said. 'That figures. Let it roll, Leigh.'

Warren settled back and listened.

Chapter Sixty-two

Deep in thought, Warren left for home, leaving Leigh with Mattie and a team of cops. Wishing they'd move their asses, get out there, comb the countryside or whatever it was they were supposed to do. But just find Deana.

He prayed that she was still alive . . .

Christ, she'd better be. If I knew where the hell to look, I'd find the bastard myself . . . Warren sat at the dining table, head down, scanning a map of the West Coast, hoping some divine hand would guide him to where Deana was hidden . . .

He wasn't having much luck.

Frowning, he traced a finger around the Bay area, up to Mill Valley, then to San Rafael, then down again to the Santa Cruz Mountains . . . Sighing impatiently. Knowing that he hadn't a hope in hell of finding Deana this way . . .

'I know where your girl is, Warren . . . At least, I think I do.'

His head came up. He threw Sheena a sharp glance.

Standing there, her back to the picture window, she looked pale and disoriented.

'Well?' he asked tersely. 'Tell me. Right now, Deana's probably being beaten up, abused – Christ only knows what else the bastard's doing to her. She's in real danger, Sheena, so whatever you think you know, let's have it before it's too late.'

'Y'ain't gonna like it, bro.' Sheena's pallor made him wonder what the hell she'd 'seen'. Usually, he didn't set much store by her 'feelings', but right now any lead was better than none – and by the way Sheena looked, she might, just might, have hit on a clue.

'She's in a dark place . . . could be underground. Whatever, wherever, she's in a dark, enclosed space. And,' she added quietly, 'she hasn't long to go. She knows it, too.'

Warren leapt up and raced to the window. He grabbed Sheena's shoulder.

'Can you tell me where this . . . dark place is? Can you see any landmarks – *anything*?'

She shook him off. Going quiet again, before resuming her story. 'I keep getting these deep, desperate *fear* feelings. It's dark, and I can't see . . . I just know she's in danger. Someone's aiming to kill her. But not before he's . . . *done* things to her . . .'

'Christ – anything else?'

'She's in the wilderness, Warren. Metaphorically, and physically . . . D'ya know what I mean?'

'Jesus, sis. We've gotta tell Mattie about this!'

'She's a cop?'

'Sure. She knows the sicko who's doing all this stuff to Deana. In fact, Deana's mom just told me the whole story. Sounded far-fetched, but it's all kinda linked in with Deana's disappearance.'

'A story, huh?' Sheena frowned. 'A ìfar-fetchedî story . . . You better tell me about it . . .'

'So, Ma Payne got rid of her kids? 'Cept Charlie. Jess turned into Mace and now Mace wants to kill Deana, because he can't find his sister Tania – meanwhile, any black-haired gal, but especially Deana, will do. And Jess, a.k.a. Mace, can't forgive Mom for killing Pa – and for giving him, Jess, away like that . . . Am I right?'

'That's about it, sis. This guy Mace is one fucked-up psycho. He carves women up. Leigh said she and Mattie found a scrapbook at his apartment, with pictures and press cuttings of his gruesome deeds . . . God only knows what he's doing to Deana right now. At this very moment . . .' He faltered. 'Maybe you can figure it out, Sheena. I certainly can't!'

Warren paced up and down. Working things out. He'd go find

The Lake

Deana himself. But first, he'd got to decide which route to take.

Saber sat, ears pricked, watching from the doorway.

Sheena's gaze leveled with Warren's. Sending him a cool glance, she said, 'I know how this Mace character feels, Warren.'

'You WHAT? What the hell are you saying, Sheena? You can *understand* why this sicko is doing the things he does?'

'No, not that, bro. All I'm sayin' is, I *understand* this Mace character hatin' his mom for givin' him away. Remember, Warren, I've been in the same position myself. I was adopted, too.' She turned and stared out the window, her anger showing. He could tell that by the way she squared her shoulders, held her back ramrod straight.

Sure, he knew she'd been adopted. They both had. Just that he'd never felt the need to discuss it with her before. Far as he was concerned, Sheena was his big sister. Had been for as long as he could remember. And they'd both been treated equally by Mom and Dad – that had been their way.

Sheena turned from the window, her face harsh with concern. 'Understandin' the *feelings* of this guy – it's the only thing that strikes me right now, bro. I'm sorry, believe me. And sure, if you think it'll help, I'll talk to this Mattie woman.'

Chapter Sixty-three

The door opened.

Deana flinched, twisting away from the blast of light.

She stumbled, tripped. Fell backwards onto the mattress.

'That pleased to see me, huh?'

'Mace. I need water. *Please* let me have some water . . .'

'Hey. That's nice. I like to hear my li'l girl saying pretty please.'

'Screw you, Mace . . .'

'Now, now. Don't you go blottin' your copybook. Say sorry, Deana – or do I have to smack your butt?' Mace put down his holdall and swaggered slowly toward her. A vague gray light snaked in through the dirt-streaked window; lifting the gloom slightly, filtering across the grimy mattress. Deana crouched back in the shadows, hands clasping her drawn-up knees. Hugging them tight to her chest.

Mace bent down. He peered at her, smiling, his teeth a white slash against the dark of his face.

'Saw your mom today.'

Deana's eyes widened. Her breath quickened.

'Wanna know how your mother *is*, sweetheart?'

She choked back a sob.

'How is my mother, Mace?'

'Frightened, sugar. Your mom's one very frightened lady.'

Tears welled up. Hearing him say 'mom' like that made her want to cry.

Mom, oh, Mom . . . You gotta come an' get me. Please!

The Lake

Despair and a searing desolation swept over her. She broke down, blurting shuddering sobs into her hands.

'Come, come. Here, I got you somethin'.'

She glared at him with red swollen eyes.

He held up a film-wrapped sandwich. Shook it in her face. 'C'mon. Eat. Don't want y'dyin' on me now. Eat – like a good girl.'

'I want water. Gimme some water, Mace!'

'You'll get your water when you've had this.'

She reached out, grabbed the sandwich, peeled the film from the bread, and stuffed one end into her mouth. She started chewing, then choking, her throat was so dry.

'Hold it!' He held up his hand. 'Now wouldn't that make a pretty picture for your ever-lovin' mom to see? Her little girl eating up her food?

'Stay like that, sweetheart. Don't ya move now.' He rummaged inside the holdall, bringing up the Nikon.

Lifting it to his eye.

Playing around with the lens.

Adjusting the flash.

Squinting into the viewfinder, firing off a few shots.

Done with that, Mace straightened his back. A wide smile lit his face. 'Y'take a good photo, sugar, I'll say that for ya. Your mom's gonna be real pleased to see these.'

'Where d'you get off, Mace? If y'think Mom's gonna break down before your eyes, you better think again. She's one tough lady and don't you forget it.'

'Mmm-huh. Know what? Y'could be right, honey. But let me tell you one thing . . . You're bad blood. Y'know that? Only one thing to do with bad blood an' that's git rid.' He dropped the Nikon into the holdall and zippered it shut.

Deana shuddered. The bread stuck in her gullet. She began to choke again.

Careful now. Don't rile him anymore . . .

'Yeah, you're bad blood, sweetheart,' Mace went on in a calm, conversational tone. 'Pa wanted you dead, Mom saved you and then hacked him, *killed* him, for doin' what he *knew* was right. After that, y'could say most of us Paynes came to a bad end. Pa murdered. Me farmed out to those God-fearin' folk in Duluth . . . Charlie dead after fornicatin' with that whorin' slut. An' you . . .' His eyes accused her. His face was a dark, wild mask. Spittle hung from the side of his mouth.

Terrified, still coughing, Deana edged back into her corner.

Change the subject. Attract his attention. Anything – just make him stop this crazy stuff . . . It's driving me nuts . . .

'Mace. I want some water, please. I *need* water.' She coughed some more.

'Water? WATER? I ain't got no water.'

Mace shook his head, trying to clear it, shut out the memory of his mother's face, the superstitious fears . . . The dark, desperate feelings of anger.

He'd avenge Pa's murder, all right.

Rid his soul of Tania.

He glared at Deana. His eyes taking in her long dark hair. Her white shoulders. Remembering how she'd looked half-naked, that day in her room. How her breasts heaved and wrestled, tumbling out of that too-tight bra of hers.

Tania . . .

Taunting him.

Laughing at him.

Bawling at him to go away.

You BASTARD, she'd screamed.

Yeah. Tania has ta go . . . She brought a curse on us Paynes . . . Pa shoulda killed her right at the start . . .

'Mace . . . What're you gonna do?'

Stupid damnfool question, but Deana had to keep him talking. Keep his mind on the straight and narrow. Keep it from wandering. She'd seen this film – what was it called? She couldn't remember now, but the girl in it kept talking to this crazy guy to stop him from throwing her over the cliff. She'd talked and talked till the cops came and took the crazy guy away.

In her mind, she pictured this happening to her.

The Lake

Mace'd have his hands around her throat, squeezing the life outta her . . . Then she'd start talking. Maybe arguing. For hours on end. Mace'd give up, go away and then Warren and Mattie and a gang of cops'd show up and take her home . . .

As if . . .

Her blood ran cold.

'Do?' Mace asked, surprised. 'Why, go a-callin' on that whorin' slut, sugar. After I've rid me of sister Tania . . .'

Reaching down into the holdall, he drew out a hunting knife.

Drawing it from its sheath, he held it up to the window. Then, smiling softly, he wiped it on the seat of his pants.

Chapter Sixty-four

Saturday, July 19

The girl up ahead caught his attention.

She was stacked – tall, athletic-looking with long dark hair caught up in bunches that bounced jauntily against her candy-pink sweatshirt. A tennis racquet swung in her hands. He eyed her long, shapely legs as she swung down the sidewalk.

Her feet, in white socks and sneakers, almost danced in her hurry.

A glimpse of tight white shorts peeking out from beneath the sweatshirt got him going. He felt himself rise, go hard.

'All *right*,' he murmured to himself, a loose smile playing around his lips. 'The kid's a honey; a real live dancin' queen. Most likely hot for it, too.'

Already wreckin' lives, spreading her filthy evil all over town . . .

His gaze fixed on the swinging bunches. Long and black, they curled a little at the ends.

Thinking ahead to her tennis date, smiling to herself a little, the girl didn't see the black Tornado cruise by, nor the driver slouched in the dark interior, wearing reflective shades, his left arm hanging out the window.

The car slid to a halt some twenty yards ahead of the girl. Through his rear-view mirror, the man watched her swing toward him.

Drawing level with the parked car, she looked in the open passenger-side window. Saw the man at the wheel. Wearing a black leather biker jacket and one of those funky sports wristwatches that did everything 'cept play 'The Star-Spangled Banner'.

The Lake

He was chewing, his jaw working around with a steady rhythmic movement.

Later, in one of his three rented Bay area apartments, Mace surveyed his work. Dipping his head from side to side, appraising his latest victim, assessing the need for a little more embellishment.

He grinned, his white teeth glistening in the soft light from the bedside lamp.

One less evil bitch, he told himself.

In the small cramped space that the realty office had euphemistically described as a living room, the blinds were drawn. And not only against the glare of the midday sun.

Mace eased the knife from the slit in her throat. It came away with a sharp sucking sound. Fresh blood welled, pumping over the girl's shoulders. Matting the long strands of her hair. Making a pool on the pillow behind her.

She groaned, moved slightly. Her legs made small jerky tremors. Bubbles gurgled gently from the mouth-shaped slit. Her fingers twitched, then lay still.

Her eyelids fluttered gently, then opened.

The eyes staring up at him were blank, glazed.

Dead already.

Mace hefted the knife like a dagger. He raised his arm, visualizing the long clean slit he would carve from throat to pubic bone.

His hand came down, slicing the firm white flesh, the blade juddering slightly as it hit the breastbone. Like a jacket unzipped, the torso sagged open.

More blood seeped from the 'mouth'; trickling onto the pillow . . . till the dark hair floated in a small black lake.

Mace paused. Then hacked some more. Edging up the skin with the tip of his blade, flapping it open, peering at the hot steamy coils within.

He could *smell* her evil.

Warm, mulchy, sour.

Sniffing, breathing it in, he grinned, then flicked the skin back again. Kneading it into place with quick, practiced fingers. Patting the breasts, hanging loose, lolling sideways, away from the incision.

He fondled them, squeezing the soft dark nipples.

Frowning.

They'd been so *taut*, so *ready*, a half-hour ago. When she'd squirmed beneath him, strong and agile. Yeah. She'd given him a hard time, all right, but he'd made it, ramming her, spurting his come into her moist warmth.

How she'd bucked, squirmed, screamed out.

Shoulda given her a double shot . . .

Not 'liquid ecstasy', though.

This time he'd used his trusty hunting knife. 'Yessir,' he muttered, panting a little, remembering. It'd been a real pleasure, slicing that smooth white throat.

He'd shut her mouth, once and for all.

And he'd made another. One guaranteed to stay open, no matter what . . .

He liked that.

A harsh laugh blurted from his lips.

Never did catch her name . . .

Probably something like Debbie, Jennifer or Susan.

Typical middle-class product.

He took a wild guess . . .

Wealthy daddy. House in Pacific Heights. Tennis and the beach all summer. UCSC in the fall. All set for a big exciting career in Daddy's LA office.

Maybe . . .

Not any more, though.

With that black hair . . . she'd've always been evil . . . Doin' bad things the resta her life . . .

He'd done the world a favor.

He'd gotten rid of one more Tania.

Hate twisted his face. His teeth clenched.

He turned away. Busying himself with his holdall, throwing in the almost empty phial of GHB, the syringe . . .

He brought out the Nikon and began taking shots. Full-on. Sideways. Then zooming in for a close-up of that gaping 'mouth'.

The Lake

It'd be a real change from the others in his scrapbook, he told himself.

A medical shot. *Like a do-it-yourself tracheotomy guide in a textbook.*

He gave a short laugh.

His bloodied fingers stained the camera.

Streaks of blood smeared his face.

Tugging the knife from the body, he threw it into the holdall. The Nikon followed, clattering against his spare service revolver, more phials of GHB, the pack of unused syringes.

Then, picking up opposite corners of the bedsheet he pulled them across the body and knotted the ends; top left to bottom right. Top right to bottom left. A slim hand, slack and bloodied, slid out through a gap. He shoved it back inside the bedsheet.

Hoisting the bundle off the bed, he paused for a moment. Figuring out the means of disposal. He could stash it in the wardrobe. Leave it in an underpass. Or wait till dark, put it in the car trunk, and toss it over a cliff someplace . . .

Slumped in an armchair, a can of beer in one hand, the TV turned low, Mace waited till dark.

Chapter Sixty-five

Sheena stared at her reflection in the dresser mirror.

She looked pale, shaken; felt chilled to the bone.

She'd been stroking her hair with an ebony-backed brush. Now it lay where it had fallen, in her lap.

Slowly, she set the brush on the crystal tray in front of her. The tray held combs, bobby pins and a couple of hair bands.

Her eyes went to a small wooden doll, hand-carved, dark with years of handling. The doll stood propped against the mirror.

She was seeing a brightly painted wagon. A woman, passing the doll to a small girl perched up front. The child was maybe two, three years of age. A man and woman sat either side of her. The shackled horse stamped and snorted, anxious to be gone.

Sheena sniffed. She smelled the horse's breath, grassy, steamy, hot. Felt the child's wonder, excitement at sitting up so high, at the horse shifting around. All the time wary of those strange people wrapped in furs by her side . . .

The thin-faced woman in the long gray dress wore an apron tied at the waist. She was saying, 'Here, child. Don't you forget this, now. It'll keep ya company in the long nights ahead . . .'

Sheena began to shake. Her breath hissed out low and shallow . . . Sweat beaded her forehead, her upper lip. She felt its flush warm her armpits, then spread hot and slick down her body.

She went over the scene, again. Recalling each detail. Figuring out its purpose, its meaning.

The Lake

Knowing full well . . .
She was that child.
The doll was hers.
The thin-faced woman, her ma.
Edith Payne.

Her mind was picking up on something else.
A different scene this time.
The cold, dark place where Deana was.
Familiar territory . . .
Wild. Isolated. High in the mountains.
Along a rough dirt path.
One of many such paths.
Water thrashed and rumbled below.
She reached out, touching the girl on a mattress . . .
In that cold, dark place . . .
She *was* the girl on the mattress.
Feeling confused, in pain, desperate, knowing that she couldn't hold out much longer . . .
I'm gonna die and nobody'll ever know . . .

Sheena leapt up.
Raced into the living room.
'Hey, bro!' she called out. 'Make it snappy. We'd best take the Chevy.'
Warren looked up, his face pale.
'You've "seen" Deana? Where is she, sis?'
'I know the area, Warren. She's a few miles from here. Somewhere in the mountains. In Santa Cruz country . . .'

Chapter Sixty-six

'You comin' with me?'

'I'm not sure, Mattie. There could be news of Deana . . . Do I *have* to be there?'

'Shitski, Leigh. You *gotta* be there!'

Mattie drove Leigh to the Bayview.

They were quiet, their faces tense, serious.

Thinking about Deana.

And the upcoming meeting with Ava Sorensson.

Hoping she'd come up with some clues for them to work on. *Any* clue – however small – would be welcome. So they'd know where to start.

The cops had gone through Mace's Tiburon apartment with a fine-tooth comb. Apart from his dabs, some photographic equipment and the goddamn scrapbook, the place was clean.

He's still out there, though.

Leigh shuddered.

And Deana . . . tortured, abused . . . Christ knows what by now . . .

She stifled a sob.

Please, God, she's still alive.

Life just couldn't get worse.

Like a survivor clinging to a shipwreck, Leigh clung to the knowledge that Deana was strong, athletic. She was also feisty, resourceful, intelligent. Leigh gave a wry smile. She'd just described herself at that age.

Yeah, she acknowledged. *Deana's tough. But would she be a match for Mace?*

Leigh gave up trying to banish the scary scenarios playing in her mind. She felt shot to pieces. Her head throbbed. She hadn't slept again last night. Nor, it felt like, for nights before that. Not since the day Deana disappeared.

Mattie swung into the Bayview parking lot. The old Ford shuddered to a halt. They climbed out and made their way to the front door on Main Street.

Ava Sorensson was seated at a window table overlooking the harbor. Outlined against the daylight, her profile was lean, clear-cut. She wore her fair hair smoothed back from her brow.

Now forty years of age, Ava had gone to law school, gained a master's degree in criminal psychology and then had set up a lucrative practice in Boston. The black pinstripe pantsuit and black-framed eyeglasses added to the crisp DA-in-waiting look.

Turning, she met Leigh's gaze.

Nodding to Mattie, she rose from the table and held out a hand to Leigh. 'Ava Sorensson. I guess Mattie's filled you in as to why I'm here, Ms West?' Her mouth curved in a friendly smile. Leigh's eyes focused on the bright red lips and straight white teeth. As well as being the best in her field, Ava Sorensson was also a looker.

Leigh returned the smile and sank into a wicker chair at the table. 'It's Leigh, by the way. May I call you Ava?'

'Of course.' The psychologist settled back into her chair.

Mattie made a grab for the menu. 'Let's eat,' she said. 'Then we get down to business.'

Ava dipped down and rummaged in her briefcase. She hauled out a sheaf of papers.

'So,' she said, looking over her eyeglasses, first at Leigh, and then Mattie. 'We have a rogue cop on the loose. A rogue cop with an unusual history. An ethnic, superstitious father, who was also a drunk and a child-killer.

'Way I see it, our subject, given away as a child, swears vengeance on the mother who slew his father. The mother who later farmed him out to strangers.

'He's also seeking the sister his father set out to kill.'

Ava took a sip of coffee, glanced at Mattie and said, 'We also have a sequence of abductions of dark-haired young women. Long and short is, we have a serial killer here – any update on where he might be?'

'You mean, you have no *idea*?' Leigh burst in.

Diners began to sit up and take notice.

Leigh lowered her voice.

'You're the expert,' she said tersely. 'We thought that you'd point us in the right direction. You've done profiling Mace, now *you* tell *us* where he's likely to be. My daughter's out there . . . and Christ knows what he's done – *is doing* with her . . .'

'That's understood, Leigh.' Sorensson sounded sympathetic. She must have experienced the wrath of anguished family members in the past. 'I'll do my best,' she said gently. 'Having studied this guy's history, I found it . . . quite interesting.' She paused, then said, 'His crimes are symbology-based.'

Mattie raised her brows.

Ava continued. 'Let me explain. Psychopaths often identify with an aggressive role model – in this case, Payne Senior. It's my guess that had he lived, he would undoubtedly have abused both Mace and his siblings.'

'So where's this going, Ava?' Leigh asked, her voice beginning to rise again.

Mattie laid a restraining hand on her arm.

'As we know,' Ava continued, 'Payne Senior was murdered by his wife Edith, and Jess a.k.a. Mace now appears to identify with the *myth* that is his father. He puts himself in his father's place. *Assumes* the persona. *Is* Payne Senior.

'At the same time, he hates his mother for killing his father, never mind for her rejection of himself by passing him on to the family in Duluth. Because of these issues, plus the superstition surrounding his dark-haired sister, Mace sees women as evil, untrustworthy people.'

Ava paused, giving Leigh a moment to assess her words before continuing. 'All Mace's pathological maternal hatred, plus the desire to avenge his father's murder, is now directed toward his "evil" sister Tania.

'In the absence of the real Tania, Mace is systematically working his way through a series of dark-haired women. With each killing, he's avenging Payne Senior's death and, in effect, carrying out his father's plan to murder his sister . . .'

Ava's gaze leveled with Leigh's. 'I'm sure you understand, Leigh. We're dealing with a dangerous psychopath. A man with a mission. We desperately need to bring him in . . .' She bit her lip. 'Like many psychopaths, Mace Harrison is an intelligent man. John Gacy, Ted Bundy and others disguised themselves as law-enforcement officers in order to gain access to their victims. And very convincing they were, too. Mace Harrison doesn't need to *act* that part. He already is, pardon me, *was* a well-respected cop, who did his job in exemplary fashion.'

Mattie's face was taut. 'Damn right,' she muttered. 'That sick fuck was the cleverest sonofabitch I ever did meet!'

Leigh felt faint. Her head began to swim.

'Please, Ava,' she whispered. 'Tell me where you think Mace is – and where he's hidden Deana!'

Sorensson placed a warm hand over Leigh's icy one. She smiled gently, and said, 'I'm afraid I can't tell you where your daughter is, Leigh. But I think I know where Mace is headed. It's my guess he'll return to his roots, his old stomping ground . . . Go back to where it all began.'

'You mean . . . the lake? Lake Wahconda?'

Ava nodded.

Shaking, and on the verge of tears, Leigh looked at Mattie.

Then she was staring past Mattie's shoulder, at two people entering the restaurant.

A red-haired girl.

And a big guy with a beard.

She blinked and swallowed, hard.

After all these years . . .

Cherry Dornay and her brother Ben.

Chapter Sixty-seven

Deana lifted her head.

Her face was a vague blur in the darkness.

Her stomach clenched; she stared at the door.

The crashing, splintering sounds got louder.

Oh, my God! Who is it? What's happening?

Nursing her head, she bit her lip, making her mouth bleed all over again. The blood tasted warm, salty . . . she felt it slide down her chin.

Then the door burst open, shattering the dark with a blast of light.

Outlined against the sun, a figure stood in the opening.

'Deana? *Deana!*'

A man's voice.

She was *almost* sure it was Warren – coming to take her home.

What if it's not?

She crouched back in the shadows, her eyes fixed on the man. He moved forward, peering into the darkness.

It could be Mace . . .

Said he'd come back. Use his knife on her. Cleanse her sins away. Rid her of her bad blood . . .

The man got closer.

She cringed. Still not making out who it was . . .

Maybe a figment of my imagination – been having some really weird dreams lately.

A pause.

Yeah . . . That's it. I've gone stark staring crazy!

Her hands shot up, covering her face, her fingers making a narrow 'V'.

The Lake

She squinted through it, breathing hard.

I might be in an insane asylum right now . . .

Cringing back, she saw someone else behind the man . . . A tall woman with long black hair. Dressed in black. Denim cutoffs. Iron Maiden T-shirt . . . Deana's eyes focused on the woman's long, well-muscled legs.

'Deana! It's me, Warren,' the man said gently. He was standing over her now. Then lowering himself, kneeling . . . reaching out.

Deana screamed.

'Don't touch me. *Please* don't touch me . . .'

Her screams trailed off into faint whimpers. She pressed blood-streaked hands to her mouth and her eyes were desperate, pleading.

'Warren? Is it *really* you?'

She peered at him through narrowed eyes.

'I guess they do things like this to mad people,' she said slowly. 'Fuck about with their brains . . . Like get their hopes up, then—'

A cold wet nose snuffled at her knees.

'Down, Saber. Sit!'

Warren – *and Saber*.

Oh, thank you, God, thank you, God!

Warren's voice came low, urgent. 'Gotta get you outta here, Deana. Fast. Can you walk?'

Dumbly, she shook her head.

'No? Then I'll carry you . . .'

He bent down, lifted her in his arms.

She flinched as he held her, her body hurting all over . . . Still not believing that Warren was here. That he'd found her. Just when she'd given up hope that he ever would . . .

The woman's voice hissed out.

'Gotta hurry, Warren. I can hear an engine . . .'

'Open the car door, Sheena. I'll be right over.'

Saber loped ahead with the woman.

Picking up speed, Warren ran the last few yards over dry, sparse grass; roots and scrub snagging his boots, cold mountain air rasping at his lungs.

Frowning anxiously, willing him on, Sheena stood by the open door of a Chevy. The vehicle on the other side of the ridge was getting closer. They heard its engine chugging, whining, the tires skidding over rough dirt road.

Hunching herself into the driver's seat, Sheena revved up the Chevy, eager to be gone. Looking back anxiously as Warren laid Deana across the back seat, pulling a blanket over her.

He climbed up front beside Sheena.

Saber, panting out hot steamy canine gasps, leapt in and curled around his feet.

Warren slammed the door shut.

Sheena, her white-knuckled hands clenching the wheel, stepped on the gas, swung the Chevy round, the tires squealing and racing as they hit ruts and rocks.

Then she let it ride, manhandling the wheel with strong capable hands.

The black customized Commando mounted the hill. It headed toward them.

Through the dust-covered windshield, they saw Mace, his teeth bared, snarling. He was picking up speed.

Sheena drove at him hard and fast. Aiming to go straight through the Jeep or knock it off the mountain path. Mace hesitated slightly, then rammed the gas pedal to the floor.

Sheena yelled, 'Hold tight!'

She went for Mace.

The Jeep swerved to the left, then skidded to a halt, showers of dust belching up behind. The left-hand door swung open. Mace slid out. Jerking his revolver out of its holster.

Scurrying crablike, darting behind rocks and bushes, he dropped on one knee, both hands gripping the gun. He got Sheena in his sights.

Aiming to take her out, he pulled back the trigger . . .

Warren ducked. Sheena drove. Smashing into the blacked-out Jeep. They watched it teeter, then topple over the ridge with a rattle of dirt and stones. Shots rang out. Whining by. Missing them by only a fraction.

The Lake

Quickly, Sheena zigzagged the Chevy out of range. Hanging on to the wheel, speeding, slipping, sliding down the trail in a shower of dust and stones.

Warren straightened up.

He peered through the rear-view mirror.

Mace was gone.

Chapter Sixty-eight

'Leigh, we got Deana.'

'Christ, Warren! You've GOT her?'

'That's right, Leigh. Is Mattie there?'

'She sure is.' Mattie snatched the phone from Leigh's hand and yelled into it. 'I should tan your butt, Warren Hastings. Why the hell didn't you *tell* me about this before you went chasing off? You coulda wrecked this case, y'know that? Coulda got Deana killed . . .'

'Sorry, Mattie. There just wasn't time. We had to go. Anyway, we're coming in now. And Deana's alive, okay? She's had a rough time, but s'far as I can see, her injuries look kinda . . . superficial. Can't say for sure, though . . . She's a little bewildered. Got an injured jaw. Black eyes. Otherwise okay.'

Wrapped in blankets, Deana lay on the sofa, Leigh by her side, holding and stroking her hand.

'How did you find me?' Deana asked Warren. Her words came out thick and slurred. She was weak as a kitten, couldn't stop shaking, not yet believing that the nightmare was over.

Warren's eyebrows went up. He looked across at Sheena, standing silent by the glass wall, staring out at the view. 'Over to you, sis,' he called out, grinning.

She turned nonchalantly, lifted a shoulder and tilted her head. 'Yeah. Right . . .' she said, looking at Deana. 'I'll tell y'about it sometime. Just say I wander around those parts myself, now and again. When I

The Lake

need to think, get my head straight, know what I mean? I just take out the old Chevy and have me a little campin' trip up there in the mountains.'

'Yeah, but . . . that . . . that place I was in, it was so well hidden . . . It couldn't have been easy.'

'Let's just say my woman's intuition played a part – it led me to where you were.'

Leigh broke in. 'And I'm sure glad it did. I can't *begin* to thank you both . . .' She paused, still stroking Deana's hand, throwing Sheena a grateful smile.

Looking over at Mattie she said, 'So, what do we do now, Mattie? Take Ava's advice and fly out to Wisconsin? How about back-up?'

'Don't you worry about that, Leigh. FBI, local troopers, you name it, every fucker with a badge is about to descend on lake country as we speak. I'm shippin' out later today.'

'And I'm coming with you,' Leigh said.

Mattie looked doubtful.

Warren met her stare.

Quietly, he said, 'I think Sheena should go along too.'

There was a pause while Mattie did a double take.

'You do? Why?'

'Apart from being pretty useful when it comes to one-to-one combat –' he winked across at Sheena '– she has a . . . vested interest.'

Mattie's eyes narrowed.

'Whaddyamean? A *vested interest*?'

'I'm Tania,' Sheena said. 'Mace's sister.'

Chapter Sixty-nine

The lake looked pretty much the way Leigh remembered it.

The same clear, bright air. Inlets, sandy coves, sunbathers stretched out like fish to dry. Dark stands of pine to the south. Water lapping gently around the pilings. The sputter of motorboats – canoes, one or two rowboats . . .

Charlie's was green, she remembered.

Could I forget . . .

And loaded with baskets.

The sound of vacationers laughing, shouting to each other from the smartly painted piers, floated across the water. Bringing up an arm, shielding her eyes from the sun, Leigh saw them, the size of ants from her side of the lake.

A motorboat with a water-skier in tow zipped by on a crest of white foam . . .

Leigh smiled softly, remembering how it had been eighteen years ago. After the accident, Uncle Mike and Aunt Jenny moved camp. Away from Wahconda. They'd sold the cabin and had summered in Colorado from then on.

In the early eighties, they'd retired to Florida.

Carson's Camp was under new management. All modernized and spruced up with a change of name – Lakeside Holiday Homes. In place of the old log cabins were smart new ones in varnished pinewood, with porches, loungers and barbecues out front.

The Lake

Over to her right, Leigh could see the new cabins, shiny yellow in the sunlight. She saw a twist of smoke, caught a scent of grilled burgers hanging on the air. Nothing really changes, she thought, smiling.

Squinting into the sun, her eyes scanned the lake.

They picked out a green rowboat.

Her heart lurched. For a moment, she felt the same tense excitement of eighteen years ago. When she'd spotted Charlie out there. Charlie, bare-chested. Wearing his funny hat, with its high rounded crown, wide brim, red feathers tucked in the headband . . .

Charlie.

Waiting offshore.

Silent.

Unmoving.

Paddles resting in the oarlocks as he watched her showing off, posing in her white bikini . . .

She fingered her sea-thing, nestling in the cleft between her breasts. It felt so *right* to wear it again, here at Wahconda. The place where once she'd truly believed it was her good-luck charm. Despite the way that things had turned out. This trip, she'd slipped it around her neck, figuring it deserved another chance . . .

'Penny for them?'

Mattie was smiling at her.

'Mulling over a coupla things,' Leigh said. 'As you do. But that was then. Right now we got business to attend to.'

Mattie didn't miss a beat.

'Nothin' like old times for bringin' on a case of the jitters, eh?'

'Tell me about it,' Leigh said.

Mattie studied the far end of the lake. 'So those people back there at the Bayview – the gal, that your friend Cherry Dornay?'

Leigh nodded.

'Mmmm . . . Nice hair. And the guy?'

'Ben. Cherry's brother. A good friend from way back when I was in San Diego having Deana. Yeah, he was a very good friend . . .'

She sighed.

Thinking about Ben.

Her knight in shining armor, she'd called him.

A bunch of kids strolled by. Wearing swimsuits, towels hanging around their necks. Laughing and joking on their way to the lake.

Leigh watched them pass.

Her lips curved in a grin. 'Ben was a great guy. The best. But I walked, Mattie. Eighteen years ago – and again yesterday, back at the Bayview . . .'

'You have a lot on your mind right now, Leigh. And I get the feeling your Ben'd understand just why you walked out the door – when you've a chance to tell him, that is. D'ya think you might get it together again some day?'

'Maybe. In my own time. When I'm good and ready.'

They'd made reservations at the Lakeside. At the height of the summer season they'd been lucky to get two cabins – a double and a single. Sheena and Mattie chose the double. Leigh took the single.

They ate burgers and fries in the bright, airy restaurant. Red check cloths on the tables. Red check curtains at the windows. Mostly, this time of day, the place would be humming with activity; right now it was deserted, except for a young couple sitting quietly in the corner drinking coffee, a map spread out in front of them.

Sheena was uneasy, on edge. She played with her food. Finally, pushing her plate aside, she said she needed a run. Promised she'd be back in half an hour.

Mattie watched Leigh's face. She was looking strained, pale. The tension of the last few hours was beginning to take its toll. Mattie hoped that Leigh would be up to it when they came eye-to-eye with Mace.

If they came eye to eye with Mace.

Hope to God we do. Maybe we're on a wild-goose chase.

Sorensson could've goofed.

Mace could be back there, on Del Mar.

Stalking Warren.

Watching Deana.

Deana had pleaded to join Leigh and the others, but the doc had advised a 24-hour hospital check-up. That done, Warren was to look after her at his place. Mattie had arranged for a round-the-clock watch on them both.

* * *

The Lake

Leigh assured Deana that she'd be back in a couple of days. She hated going, but felt she needed to be on the spot, to help Mattie catch Mace.

For the umpteenth time, she satisfied herself that Deana was in safe hands.

Until a small voice in her head whispered: *Oh, yeah? Just how safe is safe?*

Leigh felt cold and sick inside.

Nothing fazed Mace, she knew that.

If Deana or Warren were to be found, Mace'd do it . . .

Shit, Leigh. Pull yourself together – they'll be okay. Go out there; do your thing. As in help Mattie nail Mace.

Between the three of them, she had every confidence they would.

Sheena alone was a one-woman army . . .

Mattie was also a pretty tough cookie.

And Ava assured us that Mace'd be here.

Ava could be wrong, the voice piped up again.

No way, Leigh told herself. He *is* out here. Regressing. Reliving his childhood days. Thinking about God knows what.

She recalled Sorensson's face, pale, intense. 'Be convinced, Leigh,' she'd said. 'Harrison's moved on. The West Coast's behind him now. He's out there in lake country . . .'

'We get some sleep, then plan a course of action,' Mattie told them before Sheena left to go running. 'We're on a covert operation – and it's a team effort. Leigh, if you think of anything, let us know. Such as likely places where Mace could be – and Sheena, you're welcome to come up with your ideas. Any ìfeelingsî you may have . . .'

They parted.

With severe misgivings, Leigh went to her cabin. She turned on the shower and undressed. Calming down a little as she stepped under the shower, soaping herself, feeling the warm water sluice her body. It felt good and, for a short while, relaxing.

Toweling herself dry, she put on her only change of clothing – a loose navy sweatshirt and pants.

But lying on the bed her former unease returned.

She tossed around, staring at the ceiling, all the while experiencing bad memories; then fears about meeting up with Mace and escalating concerns about Deana whirled through her mind.

Leigh sighed.

One thing was for sure.

With all this going on in her head, she didn't feel much like sleeping . . .

Chapter Seventy

A hand curved slowly around her neck.

'It can be like this again, Leigh,' he told her.

So tenderly, she almost believed him . . .

Wanted to believe him.

His eyes glittered down at her.

His mouth hung open.

Her heart hammered. She drew back, her hands flying to her face.

'I loved you,' he whispered. 'Things just got a little mixed up, is all . . .'

Her eyes snapped open.

Chapter Seventy-one

'MACE!'

'I'm here, sugar. And y'came all this way to say hello? I'm touched, darlin'. I truly am.'

The late-afternoon sun dipped behind the trees, but it was still hot. The cabin was deep in shadow. Shafts of light from the open window pierced the semi-gloom.

A light breeze from the lake bellied the curtains.

Leigh gasped. How the hell had he gotten to her? The door was locked . . . and the windows?

Shit!

Like a fool, she hadn't checked the windows.

Her stare darted back to Mace.

A different Mace now.

Plaid shirt. Combat pants – your average guy taking a well-earned summer break. A little fishing. A few beers . . . It figured, all right. Dressed like that, he'd pass unnoticed in a crowd.

His hair was darker, longer; the blond surfer streaks were gone.

He was a stranger.

A dangerous, unpredictable intruder.

Her blood chilled at the thought.

He swayed a little. A hunting knife hung loosely in his right hand.

'You shouldn't've come, Leigh. Nosin' around. Disturbin' a man payin' his respects to the place of his birth . . .'

His voice was flat, toneless.

The Lake

Slowly, Leigh edged up the bed, flinching as her back caught the slatted rail behind. She pulled away from him.

Scarcely daring to breathe.

Sweat, slick and hot, flowed down her sides.

Mace leaned in, his knife making circles near her face. His eyes were deep pits. Grape-black. Glinting into hers.

Hypnotizing her.

Tearing her gaze from his, she thought, *I've gotta break the silence – keep him talking* . . .

'You did some awful bad things to Deana, Mace. Why did you do it?'

'She was a whorin' little slut, that's why. She deserved to die.' He spoke slowly, his voice slurring slightly. 'She's out of the way now. Yessir, where she is, little bitch won't be causin' no more grief.'

'Deana's still alive, Mace . . .'

'Wrong, Leigh. I killed her. She had to die . . .'

He's killed her! THE BASTARD'S KILLED HER . . . OH NO!

She shot upright, her heart racing.

Reaching out her left hand, edging it sideways toward the water glass on the nightstand, she extended a finger. Nudging the glass a little; cringing as it crashed to the floor.

In the silence it sounded like a bomb going off.

Mace came in with his fist.

Mashing her jaw.

Whipping, *cracking* her head sideways.

Making a low 'Uuggghhh . . .' sound she slumped back on the pillow.

Out cold.

Wrestling Leigh onto his shoulder, Mace went through the kitchen bar to the front door. Unlocking it with one hand, closing it behind him, he hurried out back.

Chapter Seventy-two

The cabins were behind Mace now.

Still running, he turned, snatching a look over his shoulder. Through the trees, he saw the cabins recede into the distance.

All clear.

He stumbled on through another deserted copse, stepping over branches, loping through rough grass.

Soon the grass gave way to pebbles.

Okay so far . . .

Out of the trees now, the late-afternoon sun's slanting rays caught him off guard. Squinting into the light, he shook his head, trying to clear the noise, the clutter, the nonsense inside it.

He made his way to a secluded inlet.

Reached the rowboat.

Lowering Leigh into it, he pushed the boat forward.

It slid quietly across the sand and slipped neatly into the sparkling water.

Leigh groaned.

Leaning over, Mace slapped her face. Her eyes opened, stared at him groggily for a moment, then closed again.

She was out okay.

He stepped into the boat, settled down, eased the paddles from the oarlocks, and stroked out across the lake.

Chapter Seventy-three

'He's got her, Sheena. I heard a crash, went to investigate and she'd gone. It could only be Mace. Do you see anything out there?'

Sheena, two-way radio pressed to her ear, listened intently.

'I'm approaching the lake now, Mattie . . . Can't see anything this end . . .' Her voice was hurried, breathy, as she jogged over uneven scrub and pebbles.

Drawing to a halt, she scanned the water. 'There's a guy in a rowboat. Dark hair, plaid shirt . . . Stroking like hell . . . He's looking over his shoulder . . .'

She paused, then said quickly, 'Mattie. It's Mace. Travelin' south. Heading for the pines out there.'

'You sure about that?'

'Sure as I'll ever be. The guy's in an awful hurry. Hey, didn't Charlie have a hideout around here – like the place he died in? And yeah. There's something in the boat, Mattie. Like a pile of clothing or—'

'Sheena, keep an eye on that boat. I'll pull rank, requisition a launch. Rowboat. Inflatable. Whatever.'

Sheena kicked off her sneakers and waded into the lake till she was breast deep. Then, lifting her arms, she struck out after the rowboat.

Chapter Seventy-four

Slowly, Leigh opened her eyes, trying to focus on the room. Everything blurred around her.

Her eyelids closed again.

Gingerly, she felt her jaw. It moved around freely – a little too freely for her liking. Pain shot through her face, stars exploded like fireworks in her head.

Her eyes opened. They darted to Mace.

'Recognize where y'are, darlin'? Recall this li'l ol' place, do ya?'

Leigh went cold. She began to shake.

She was lying on a palliasse of some sort. It was lumpy, hard, with no give to it – like it was filled with straw or something.

She closed her eyes again. Shutting him out. *Smelling* the place . . . The damp, earthy, *moldy* odor . . .

Her eyes snapped open.

THIS WAS IT!

THE HOUSE WHERE CHARLIE DIED . . .

The nightmare began again.

Screams echoed round and round in her head, like those other screams all those years ago.

Edith Payne's screams. When she'd discovered her son Charlie, lying broken and bleeding. His head caved in . . .

'Never did take the old place down,' Mace was saying. 'Left it here to rot. Gotta tread careful now . . . Could fall down one a' these biiiig

The Lake

holes . . .' He grinned at her, standing on the edge of one, jumping up and down, testing the old boards, judging how much they could take.

Leigh shuddered, feeling them shake, vibrate; hearing debris crumble and fall into the void below . . .

Mace gave a hollow laugh.

'All comes floodin' back now, darlin'? Day you killed my brother Charlie?'

His fist came at her again. Smashing her head back to the mattress. He stood there, grinning and chewing, hearing her groans, her soft cries.

Then he was down, grabbing the neck of her sweatshirt; twisting it round his hand, bringing her up close till her face touched his.

Leigh's stomach lurched with fear and loathing.

Mace's grip tightened.

Chapter Seventy-five

'STOP! Police! I got ya covered, Mace!'

Mattie.

Right behind him.

Both hands gripping her gun.

Shoving it into his back.

His hands went up.

Carefully, still keeping him covered, Mattie reached for her belt. Unhitched the cuffs. Snapping one open, she moved forward to slip it onto Mace's wrist . . .

Then Sheena appeared. Wet from her swim.

'Save it, honey,' she told Mattie, not taking her stare off Mace. 'He's mine.'

Droplets pooled round her naked feet. She glowered at the back of his head.

Mace stiffened, his hands dropping a little, poised for action.

Sheena was ready.

'Back off, Mace,' she snarled. 'Or should that be Jess?'

Mace froze.

Then his shoulders and hands relaxed.

He swiveled around and stared, a bemused smile tilting his lips. Taking in the long black hair, sleek and wet, dripping over her shoulders. The tawny skin gleaming in the shadows . . .

She was like a warrior queen, risen from the sea. Dressed in black; Apache-style band around her head, 'Guns 'n' Roses' T-shirt clinging to her body. Her breasts and nipples standing proud beneath.

The Lake

His stare played around her breasts, then dropped to the tight leather shorts showing a couple of inches below her top.

'Seen enough, punk?'

Mace didn't reply. His gaze still traveled over her. It was hungry. Taking in the shiny, well-muscled arms. The long shapely legs, planted firmly apart.

A slow smile curved his lips. 'Sister Tania,' he said quietly. 'We meet at last.'

Her gaze leveled with his. Daring him to move.

'Time to turn in ya stripes, Mace,' she said, softly.

Slowly, her hand reached back, easing up her T-shirt, feeling for the knife in its holster. It rested warm and hard against her damp leather shorts.

'C'mon now, sis. This is your brother here. Don't wanta harm your own kin now, do ya?'

Suddenly, his arm went up and Sheena was staring down the muzzle of a 9-millimeter Sig. Sidestepping neatly, she brought up her knife. Whirled it through the air. It landed, quivering, in Mace's bicep.

Blood spurted a little, then slowly, steadily, pumped down his arm.

His face darkened. He made a grab at the wound. The Sig hit the floor with a clunk and Sheena lunged forward, forcing his arm back and down.

Mace snarled. She snatched back her knife.

'My move, punk,' she said, smiling briefly and wiping the blade across his shirt front. She leapt back, crouching, weaving from side to side, tracing circles in the air with her blade.

Spying his chance, avoiding the knife, Mace bounded forward, throwing a sideways kick at her face. He missed.

Then aimed a karate chop to her throat.

Sheena danced away, still crouching, knife in hand, arms outstretched, still weaving from side to side.

Mace saw red.

'I'll get ya, bitch!' he spat out, his eyes bulging.

He aimed his stiffened hand and missed again, his arm slicing through thin air.

* * *

Mattie closed in, cuffs at the ready, edging her way around the hole in the floor, while Sheena went for Mace with her knife. Looking wildly from one to the other, he tripped and lost his footing.

Leigh gasped, 'Oh, my God!'

The hole. The same one that Charlie had gone through.

They watched Mace fall in a cloud of dust and splinters, his legs swinging around in the deep black void, his hands scrabbling, grasping at the soft rotted wood.

They heard him whimper, then gasp out 'Help me, help me . . . help . . .'

Fascinated, they watched the wood crumble and break away in chunks as he grabbed it. Then he dropped, screaming, into the dark below.

A final blood-curdling shriek and a dull squishy thud told them when Mace hit the deck.

Dust motes danced from the gaping hole, caught in a shaft of the dying sun.

They stared at each other in silence.

Later, as the police launch carried them back across the lake, Leigh slipped the sea-thing necklace over her head. Some lucky necklace – a curse, more like.

She hurled it high into the air and watched it fall with a splash into the moonlit water.

Chapter Seventy-six

'Mom!'

'Yes, honey. We're back.'

Leigh didn't want to believe her ears.

'Er . . . how was Boulder?' she asked faintly. 'And Aunt Abby, of course.'

Drinking black coffee in the living room, Deana and Mattie pricked up their ears.

'Fine, dear. Boulder's hot and Abby's taking her beta blockers. But I have to tell you, honey, it's *wonderful* to be home again!'

'Sure, Mom. Dad okay?'

Jack West broke in. 'I'm fine – and how's that granddaughter of ours? She been behaving herself?'

'Sure, Dad. Deana's okay and she's right here. Want a word?'

Leigh caught Deana's eye, jiggled the phone at her, and mouthed, 'It's Pops. You wanta say hello?' Deana nodded, made a face at Mattie and walked over to Leigh. She took the phone.

'Hi, Pops. How ya doin'? Aunt Abby better?'

'She sure is, darlin'. But, like your gran says, we're real glad to be home. So, what's my favorite granddaughter been doing all summer?'

'Well, er . . . oh, just messin' around.'

'Just messin' around, huh? When your gran and I are unpacked and showered, we'll be right over, then we can have a nice long chat. So don't go rushing off, young lady. Like you did at my birthday dinner!'

'Okay, Pops. I'll be here . . .'

The doorbell jangled.

Mattie raised her eyebrows. Deana and Leigh exchanged glances. Leigh's heart sank. How could she *ever* explain to Mom and Dad all that had happened since they went away to Boulder?

With a resigned sigh, Leigh went down the hallway and opened the door.

'Oh . . . hi, guys!' Her voice picked up a notch when she saw Warren, Sheena and Saber on the stoop. Warren was holding a couple of books.

'It's so *good* to see you both again!' Leigh said in a relieved voice. Warren stepped inside, Sheena followed. Saber trotted behind.

When they were all in the living room, Warren told Deana, 'I brought the books you asked for. Maybe now you'll get a chance to read them.'

Deana winked at him. 'Nice timing, Warren,' she said. 'Gran and Pops are back from Boulder and they're due here any minute.'

They arrived a half-hour later.

Deana made for the kitchen to heat up the coffee. Warren followed.

After the introductions, Mom lowered herself down on the sofa. Shooting a fearful look at Mattie and Sheena – Mattie in her MVPD sweatshirt, denim cutoffs and gun holster, and Sheena, Amazon-like: long flowing hair, tight black tee, leather shorts and studded belt.

Leigh glanced at Mom's face – red and mottled as she stared first at the women, then at Saber, tucked in tight by Sheena's bare legs.

Leigh rushed over to the bar and poured out liberal measures of Jack Daniel's into two glasses. She handed them to her parents.

There was an awkward silence.

Leigh's bruised face glowed as she met Mom's glance.

'Now, young lady.' Dad, glass in one hand, massaging the back of Mom's neck with the other, threw a meaningful look at his daughter. 'I think you have some explaining to do . . .'

Christ *Jesus*, Leigh groaned inwardly. It's Wahconda and Charlie all over again.

Not quite.

It's Wahconda and Charlie, *eighteen years on*.

What goes around comes around . . .

The Lake

Clear as crystal, the words of the song popped into her head, making her smile. She felt a million years old. Very wise, and somehow philosophical about all that had happened this summer.

Sitting cross-legged at the far end of the sofa, she smiled at Mom, took a deep breath, and said: 'Remember Nelson? He of Beef Willington fame?'

Taking a sip of brandy, Mom nodded slowly . . .

In the kitchen, Deana gave Warren a cheeky grin. 'Looks like we got ourselves a situation out there!' She paused, head tilted to one side, then said, 'So, lover boy, you came over to deliver our books?'

'Right.'

'That sure is one *lousy* excuse! Admit it, Warren Hastings, you just couldn't keep away!'

They smiled broadly as their gazes met.

Suddenly they weren't laughing anymore. They were deadly serious.

'God, Deana. It's been a helluva long time.' Warren's voice was low, breathy. 'Too long.' He held out his arms. 'Wanta finish off our . . . unfinished business?'

'Mmmm. Don't I just . . .'

Deana snuggled into him, pressing close, her arms tight around him. Their lips met. His searching, impatient; hers puffy, bruised and hurting like hell. She pressed into him some more, feeling him stir and rise against her belly. Moaning, she felt the teasing ache between her thighs.

Damn right, she thought. It's been a long, long time . . .

Too long . . .

She trembled as Warren's hand stole inside her blouse, shivering as he reached for her naked breast. He held it, squeezed it a little, his thumb stroking her taut nipple beneath the filmy cloth of the blouse.

She moaned, squirming, wanting more – but, drawing away abruptly, she whispered, 'Later, Warren. Soon as Gran and Pops are gone, we can . . .'

'Promise?'

'Mmmmm,' she sighed, a surge of joy welling up inside her.

'I'll hold you to that,' he said, kissing the tip of her nose.

She smiled softly as her arms tightened around him . . .

Afterword
or
How Things Turned Out

by Deana Hastings

Everybody has a dream. Well, pretty much everybody I knew at Berkeley had one. Something to pin your hopes on, y'know? Mine was to write the great American novel. Oh, yeah? I know, I know . . . but seriously, that's why I read American Lit. And considering the stuff we'd been through that summer, I figured I'd enough material to write several novels. So that's what I do.

Write novels, I mean.

Couldn't have done it without Warren, though. Had his support all the way – once we decided to 'finish what we started' the night we saw the last of Mommy Dearest.

We married soon after I graduated, and our first joint project was to co-author a non-fiction work, *Lore & Legend of Native America* – which later, would you believe, became a smash-hit TV series!

Since then, as well as running *Eureka*, Warren's written a couple more books. Pretty serious stuff: *Shakespeare & the Dark Lady*, based on his theory that she was actually an illegitimate daughter of King Henry VIII of England.

Next up was *The Secret Side of Edgar Allan Poe*.

That went down really well in the UK. We were *so* thrilled when it hit third place in *The Times* non-fiction bestseller list. We're keeping our fingers crossed for upcoming film rights, too – maybe starring Michael J. Fox? He's still my favorite actor, by the way.

Our second joint project, and most successful to date, were our triplets – yeah, *triplets*, how about that?

Spooky, eh?

We named them Jack, Warren Junior and Helen. And get a loada this. At birth, Helen had a head of *thick, black hair*. The nurses swore they'd never seen anything like it before!

Jeez. I'm trying not to dwell too much on that. For now, she's simply our darling little daughter . . .

Anyhow, six months after the Mace ordeal, Mom met up with her old pal, Ben Dornay. They married a couple of weeks later. Ben Junior came along ten months after that.

Then Mom opened three more restaurants on the Coast – phew, that woman is truly amazing – she has *so* much energy! Ben Senior realized *his* dream, too (everybody has one, right?), and founded the successful animation studio Megatron. The man is pure genius!

Right now, they're enjoying the good life in Beverly Hills and, in the best movie tradition, are living happy ever after. Mom and Ben make a perfect couple. I've never seen Mom look so content – and that's fine by me. She sure deserves it!

As for Mattie and Sheena – well, they got together shortly after the Mace affair and now live in San Diego. Mattie's gotten her own personal security company, hiring herself and her team of bodyguards out to some pretty important people: Hollywood stars, government officials, heads of state . . .

Sheena opened up Movers & Shakers, a club in West LA, a 24-hour hangout for gays and other kindred spirits. The club attracts major celebs – incognito, of course – and I'm told it's a huge success. As a legacy from her Pacey days, Sheena often stands on the door. Keeping her hand in, she calls it.

And yeah, Sheena and I get along fine – after all, we *do* have something in common, apart from Payne blood. Like diehard sport! When she drops by our place in Mill Valley, she gives me kick-boxing lessons – and I take her out on my 'midnight runs'. With Warren, of course. He worries about the weird characters sneaking around at night. *Men!*

Oh, and Saber comes, too – except when his hips play up. Then he stays home and takes it easy. He's just reached his tenth birthday – and I'm told that's pretty good for a German shepherd dog!